White Roses

By
Judith Yonkers

thankyou for hosting my 1st book signing ever! Judi

2 MOON Press

MARSHALL - MICHIGAN
800PUBLISHING.COM

In January, 2000, and idea for a book sprang to mind. Little did I know that twelve years later, it would finally be published, and that it would inspire nearly a dozen more, all sequels to White Roses, one picking up right where the last one left off. My family and friends have read them, and it's time to share with anyone else who would like to dive head first into Gabe's world.

I'd like to thank my family and friends, being my husband Kevin, my sons James and Jordan, and my parents for their continued support. Also, endless amounts of thanks to my sisters, Jane, Jill, Jen, and Katie. Thank you to Vic, who has helped more than she'll ever know in so many ways, and Tiffany, one of Gabe's favorite fans. Finally, thank you to Gabe and Kyle, who are an endless amount of entertainment for me, and the best imaginary friends a gal could ever have.

~Prologue~

Christmas Eve, 1995

Although the past month at work had not been a busy one, it had been emotionally devastating for Annie Benton, who worked as a nurse on the pediatric floor at Brighton Memorial Hospital.

The facility was a large one, built with an eye toward the future of the rapidly growing community of Waterston, Michigan. It contained a Level I trauma center, a Level III neonatal intensive care unit, an advanced oncology ward, and the only Children's hospital within the tri-county area. If anyone was ill, injured, or in pre-term labor, Brighton was the place to be. But no matter how advanced the technology or how skilled the staff, not everyone could be saved.

One of Annie's long-time patients and good friend had just passed away.

Annie sat in a darkened corner of the empty cafeteria, hoping that it would remain deserted for a while; she was in no mood for company right now. Well, except maybe… Oh, she couldn't even *think* his name; the pain was just too great. At least Eric, after years of suffering, was finally at peace.

She looked down at the rosebud in her hand, which he had given her just before he died, and twirled the stem in her fingers, watching the flower spin… back and forth, back and forth. The white petals blurred with each rotation. Just like her life… indistinct and with no definition. Like the rosebud in her hand, all her hopes and dreams met a sudden demise, cut down before they could fully bloom.

Her thoughts turned back to the young man upstairs who was waiting for the morgue cart to come and collect his cooling body. She was going to miss the boy who'd been almost like a son to her. Miss him terribly. His passing seemed to close a door, in a way; a door to a life full of hope and dreams that were no more. She'd never felt so alone.

Annie stopped twirling the rose between her fingers and looked at her watch. Ten past midnight… It was Christmas. Peace on Earth and Goodwill to All Men.

Rather hard to capture the spirit, considering the sadness of the last hour.

A sliver of light flashed as the cafeteria door opened, and she looked up to see who had entered.

A tall man wearing a leather jacket, jeans, and a battered Stetson walked slowly to a table on the opposite side of the room. He looked neither to the right nor to the left until he sat, and then stared straight ahead for a full minute before dropping his head on his arms, which were resting on the table.

1

Annie watched as the cowboy began to cry, his shoulders shaking violently with silent sobs.

"Oh God," she whispered to herself, "not tonight of all nights…"

She stood, wanting to go to him, but hesitated. She had to though, no matter what she was feeling. He needed her and she would never let him down again, no matter what she was feeling.

Annie stood next to the cowboy and placed the white rose in front of him. He looked up at her, his intense, dark blue eyes bright with tears.

"Buy you a cup of coffee?" she asked him.

~Part One~

Ships in the Night

Late autumn, 1990

Chapter One

Annie's hands were trembling when she hung up the phone. She had a mere two hours to pack, rearrange her work schedule, and get to the airport in time to make her flight. She prayed she wouldn't be too late.

The garbled, confusing phone call she had just received from her mother had shaken her to her core. The details were sketchy and confusing, yet Annie had managed to decipher that her father had been taken to the hospital following a heart attack, and her mother had been left alone in the apartment for two days. Bob and Colleen were never apart if it could be helped, and Annie had to wonder what had separated her parents, especially at a critical time like this.

"Come on, Marti, please hurry," she muttered, throwing her clothes into a suitcase and slamming it shut. "I'm running out of time."

The crunch of gravel in the driveway drew her attention and she raced for the front door of her home. Her parents' home actually; they'd let her stay after they retired to Arizona.

"Annie!" Marti cried, flinging open the car door. "Your dad… Have you heard anything new?"

"No… I don't even know which hospital he's in. I tried calling Mom back but there was no answer. I'm worried sick!"

"I can imagine. Here, let me get that." Marti tossed her friend's luggage into the trunk of her car, and soon they were speeding to the airport.

"Call me as soon as you can, Annie. I'll be praying…"

"Thank you so much, Marti, and I will."

The women gave each other a hug. Annie went to board her plane with minutes to spare.

The flight to Arizona seemed to take forever and Annie was too nervous to do anything but think…

Her father couldn't die…

Even though Bob and Colleen lived far away, they were the only family Annie had left in the world. Well, there was her sister Amanda, but she lived in England, and the only time Annie heard from her was when a short note was stuck into a Christmas card.

Oh yeah, there was her ex-husband Richie, but he didn't count. Annie had married him two weeks after they graduated from high school and divorced him eight months later. He was such a loser. A good-looking loser, but still a loser. He partied while she worked and went to school full time. He called her boring. She called him irresponsible. He called his old girlfriends. She called a lawyer. He kept the apartment. She moved back into her childhood home with her parents and never looked back. She concentrated on her studies and was hired by Brighton Memorial Hospital the same day she passed her state board exams.

Her father couldn't die…

…Not when they had finally grown close again.

Annie's childhood had been a lonely one. Amanda was fifteen years older and off on her own by the time Annie was even old enough to realize she had a sister. There were no other children her age in the neighborhood and the few friends she had at school lived too far away to play with on a daily basis. Bob and Colleen didn't care for animals, meaning no pets, so Annie pretty much had only herself for company… except for those wonderful days when she got to spend time with her grandmother Rosalind Charles.

Gramma Rose…

Annie smiled at the memory of her beloved grandmother. The two of them used to spend hours together in the gardens her grandfather had planted before he passed away. She loved to listen to the tales of days gone by. Rosalind was a superb storyteller and Annie could almost see the wonderful parties and dances that her grandparents had attended. Handsome young gentlemen and beautiful young ladies, all waltzing around a grand ballroom… Annie thought it would have been a great time to have been young and in love, just like her grandparents.

Grampa Charles was considerably older than his bride. Gramma never told Annie exactly how she met her husband but talked frequently of the fun and romantic times they shared, especially in the garden.

Grandpa started the gardens during their first year of marriage, beginning with two rose bushes and adding to it each spring. His pride and joy were the magnificent white roses in the center of the garden. Late in the summer, on their wedding anniversary, he would pick his best roses and present them to his wife. He would always say it wasn't much, but Gramma knew how much time and effort he had put into growing the flowers; to her it symbolized dedication, commitment and love – and now he was giving it to her. They would have a romantic picnic by a lake and then watch the sunset. After dark, beneath a star-studded sky, they would dance to music only they could hear. For fifty years they celebrated their anniversary this way, and when they could no longer make the long trip to the lake they celebrated in the gardens.

After Grampa died, Gramma couldn't bear to go into the gardens. For two years she ignored them as best she could until late one summer, as she sat alone on the porch swing and as she looked at the stars overhead, a breeze brought the faint scent of roses. For a brief moment her beloved husband was beside her again, handing her the anniversary bouquet. The next morning Rosalind donned some old clothes and went to work restoring the gardens to their former glory. Instead of the pain of loss and sorrow, the flowers brought back precious memories of a perfect love.

That was the most romantic story young Annie had ever heard, and she wanted to find a love just like the one Gramma had – that is if she ever decided to have a boyfriend. At ten years of age, boys rated a distant second behind horses as far as something Annie wanted to be around all the time. Except that one boy...

One summer as Annie was arriving at Gramma's, another car was pulling out of the long driveway. Annie caught a glimpse of an older woman driving and two heads of black hair in the back seat. As the cars passed each other, a pair of intense, dark blue eyes met hers and she wished the car would return so she could meet the boy. Was that his brother with him? From what she could see, they looked identical.

Gramma didn't supply much information when Annie asked about them; all she found out was that they were the grandchildren of Rosalind's friend, they lived out west, and they visited every summer. Annie found herself thinking of that boy quite often until...

Gramma passed away when Annie was thirteen. The death devastated her, and she withdrew into herself. The one person she had been closest to and let herself truly love was gone, resulting in unbearable pain Annie never wanted to be hurt like that again. A wall of armor went up, protecting her fragile emotions. She vowed it would forever remain.

Her parents decided to sell Gramma's house even though Annie begged them not to.

"Who will take care of the gardens?" she cried.

"Annie," her father said, "that's the least of our problems right now. Rosalind hadn't paid taxes on that property for nearly ten years, and we just can't afford to take on a burden like that!"

"But it's just a little house," she argued. "It can't be that much..."

"Small house on a lot of property, Annie. If I were working, we might be able to swing it. But until the plant opens back up, I'm sorry, honey, the house must go."

Annie accepted it only because she had no choice, but felt her parents didn't try hard enough to find another solution.

The family spent the weekend after the funeral organizing Gramma's belongings. Annie was told that she may keep anything she wanted as mementoes, but the rest of the estate would be auctioned off.

She couldn't decide what she wanted. Her happiest moments with Gramma were spent in the gardens, and Annie couldn't keep them. She wandered through the house, looking for that one special item that might keep those memories alive. As she explored the rooms, her depression deepened. She could find nothing she wanted to keep other than a small black porcelain horse – which she only took because she loved horses, and this particular horse she had admired at Gramma's friend's house years ago. Fighting tears and needing to be alone, she crept up to the small bedroom her mother had occupied as a child, and the one Annie used on those special nights when she slept over with Gramma.

She flopped into the desk chair and kicked at the wall in frustration. She nearly screamed in shock when she heard a loud thunk come from inside the closet.

After picking up her horse, which she had dropped in her alarm, she ignored the tingle that ran up her arm at the contact with the miniature equine, and then she slowly opened the closet door.

"H… hello?" she stuttered, peeking into the tiny room. Feeling silly in her trepidation, she flipped on the closet light. She glanced around, but could not find the source of the noise.

Weird.

With a shrug of her shoulders, she backed out, only to catch her shoulder on a low shelf just to her left.

She wanted to swear at the pain, sure she'd have a heck of a bruise in a few hours, but Annie never said bad words.

Never.

She sure wanted to. Instead she merely stuck her tongue out at the stupid shelf, an infantile gesture at best.

It was then that she saw them. Dozens of leather-bound books were stacked along the wall, all bearing the initials R.D.C., and dating from the early nineteen hundreds until just a few years ago.

RDC… Rosalind Delaney-Charles? Were these journals? Her journals?

More excited than she'd ever been. Annie snatched a book from that hurtful-hopefully-helpful shelf. Slowly opening the burgundy leather cover, she was delighted to see her grandmother's elegant handwriting covering the pages.

This was it. This is what she wanted to keep.

She ran downstairs for some boxes, her ebony steed still in her hand. She raced back up to pack her treasures, even though she wanted to sit and read, but her father was calling for her to hurry.

"Darn it," she muttered, gently placing the books in the boxes.

After she finished, she picked up her little horse and looked into its soft brown eyes.

"I'm leaving you here to guard these… Hmm, what would be a good name for you?" she mused, studying the animal.

Of course it didn't answer, but she did feel that odd tingle again. She switched the statue to her other hand and wiggled her fingers, nearly dropping it again as lightning flashed and thunder crashed outside, illuminating the room for just a moment in a vivid blue light.

"Weird," Annie muttered, shaking her head, but no big deal. She was often experiencing odd little happenings and strange "feelings." She didn't even give it a second thought anymore.

"Annie! Let's go!" Bob called up the stairs.

"Quick… A name…"

She stared hard at her new guardian.

"Angel," she said with a nod. "Angel, guard these until I can get them again. They mean more to me than anything!"

She kissed the cold, hard nose of the beast and placed him gently in the box. She ran down to tell her father that she had found her mementos. He said he'd see to it that she got them, and then hustled her out to the car before the storm unleashed its promised fury.

Annie declined to attend the auction, the very thought of Gramma's cherished belongings ending up in the hands of strangers…it made her want to vomit. They would never understand what that vase meant to Rosalind, the bottom of its silver elegance engraved with "Forever Summer, all my love on our 25th, or the white rose bud dried and flattened between two pieces of glass. It just plain made her sick.

Had Annie been there, she could have prevented the journals and their new "guardian" from being auctioned off along with lot of miscellaneous books. That little oversight of her father's strained the parent-child relationship to the point of breaking. The journals were never found and Annie blamed her father for not caring. She would never understand how her parents could sell all that was so important to her mother's mother. Were they that unfeeling? Likewise, her parents couldn't understand why their daughter was so upset by the whole affair. Sure, they loved Gramma Rose, but the woman was gone and the Benton's finances were in dire straits at the time. They had no choice.

Annie finished high school, and was married, mainly to escape her unhappy home. Her elderly parents retired and decided to do all of the traveling they had missed during the leaner years. Within a year, her marriage to Richie fell apart, so Bob and Colleen invited her to live with them. She accepted.

Her resentment towards her parents faded over the years, and once again the trio shared a happy family relationship.

Her father couldn't die…

Annie said a short prayer that she'd arrive in time to tell him she loved him, and to apologize for all those lost years of her childhood. She sighed, wiped away a tear, and stared out of the jet's tiny window as the landscape below her went by in a blur.

Chapter Two

"Dude, I can't believe you're flying all the way to Arizona for a stupid package that would cost maybe twenty bucks to ship."

"In case you hadn't noticed, you're flying with me, Kyle. I could have left your ass home and saved me a few hundred. This package is very important; I don't want it handled by some incompetent moron making minimum wage and sporting maximum apathy. It's just too goddamn important."

"You gonna tell me what's in it? Dude, you're not into drugs again, are ya? Oh God, Gabe… no…"

"Of course not, Kyle! That's just too absurd… I was never into them in a quantity basis… merely quality…"

"Stupid. Just plain stupid. Okay, so if it's not drugs, what is it?"

"Kyle, it's still too painful to discuss, but I can tell you it's some of Steve's belongings. Apparently he left something behind in a motel. I uh, I was contacted about it last month. It took them nearly a year to track me down. Anyway, I just now managed to get up the nerve to go see what it is."

"Whoa, dude… I'm so sorry. Does Dee know?"

"Some. I told her I was picking something up, but I didn't tell her whose it was. She's still hurting, Kyle."

"Aren't we all?"

Gabe nodded and looked out of his window in the business class section of the 747 that was winging them to Phoenix. It was all he could do not to bawl like a baby, the death of his brother still a painful, too-fresh memory enveloping him.

Steve…

Steve. Gabe sighed and reluctantly opened his mind just enough to let a few of those memories escape. Steve… his nearly identical twin brother and best friend for twenty-nine years. He was until the gentle Evans twin was brutally murdered last year. He was killed he was rescuing dozens of horses from a stable fire. He was bashed over the head with a shovel and left to burn.

Steve and Gabe were as close as any brothers could be – best friends actually, and had enjoyed a near perfect childhood growing up in Bittersweet, Montana, and east of the Crazy Mountains. Although their parents weren't wealthy, the boys lacked for nothing. There was always plenty of food, good clothes, and endless amounts of love from Al and Marie, their mom and pop. The twins, being the little cowboys, were given ponies on their eighth birthday and horses on the Christmas of their tenth year because they had outgrown their smaller mounts. The boys became proficient horsemen and blew away their competition in team roping.They shared numerous adventures and saved each other's lives from just as many mishaps. As they grew older, Steve became more involved with horses than ever, learning all he could about them and gaining quite a reputation in the equine world. Gabe still loved to ride, but at the age of sixteen, discovered a new passion in women. Women were drawn to his cockiness and massive ego, his exceptional build and good looks, and he gladly took what they offered. However, Gabe, being the complex creature that he was, needed more.

He always knew he had talent as a singer – just like Steve and Pop, and even Uncle Tony before he disappeared, Steve also found his writing skills rivaled his wonderful voice. He considered pursuing music as a career, and took guitar and piano lessons.

Steve's only dream was to be a cowboy and follow the rodeo circuit. He spent his free time perfecting his roping skills.

Tragedy struck in the summer of 'seventy-five, when the boys were fifteen. Steve's beloved horse, Duke, was found dead in a far pasture. It appeared the horse had been poisoned but had no evidence to prove it.

Steve was devastated, and Gabe offered to let him have his horse, Buck, until... Well for just as long as Steve wanted him.

Steve was touched by his spoiled brother's generosity, although no other horse could ever compare with Duke.

Or so he thought.

The following spring, Al took Steve to a horse auction as a late birthday present. After looking at nearly every horse, Steve was disappointed. He'd narrowed his choices down to four animals, but feared the prices they would fetch would be more money that Pop had.As the two Evans sat on the top rail of the corral, Steve hinted to his father about his chosen horses. He was hoping Pop would give him a little input – either for or against. Al didn't say much and Steve was ready to give up. He sure didn't want to strap Pop's wallet, and he knew darn well Al would spend too much if he thought it would make his son happy.

Steve sighed and was ready to leave when he felt a sharp pain in his backside. He spun around ready to chew out the animal that had nipped him, and came face to face with a large black yearling colt. He had found his horse. Or should he say it had found him...?

Either way, the pair bonded immediately and shared a rare relationship between man and horse. Gabe was sure that Steve and Whizbang could understand each other's thoughts.

The years went by and the boys remained close as they pursued their separate goals. Until Danni came along, that is.

Danielle Young... Tall and slim with dark green eyes and strawberry-blond hair that hung down her back to the top of her jeans...

Steve had her and Gabe wanted her. He wanted her badly. Hell, hadn't he been seeing green eyes and red hair in his dreams for forever? He was damn sure that Danni was meant for him, but loved and respected his brother too much to try for the lady himself.

All his good intentions were tossed aside and blown away by a brisk

December wind when the trio took a ski trip together. Steve was slightly injured in a fall and decided to sit out the last run or two. As Danni and Gabe rode the ski lift, they shared a very hot kiss and then they skied off to continue the little affair before Steve saw them. . Nothing happened after another kiss, because Gabe came to his senses, but not before it was too late. Steve had seen them and suspected the worst. His heart was broken even though he pretended as if nothing were wrong. Although full of subconscious resentment, he still loved Danni as much as ever and loved Gabe even more.On the night of their high school graduation, Steve proposed to Danni.She broke up with him realizing that it was Gabe she had loved all along. Although her feelings for Steve were deep, they were that only of a very dear friend.

Steve was once again devastated, got drunk and passed out. Danni had no ride home from the party then, and Gabe felling guilty as hell and piled Danni and his friends into his Pop's truck and hauled them home. He tried, anyway.

Halfway to Danni's he swerved to avoid an animal in the road, flipped the truck and threw everyone out. He was arrested for driving under the influence and possession of marijuana, and spent the summer behind bars.

After he was released, he was more than stunned to find out that Danni and Steve were still friends, and that she still loved Gabe. He worked through his guilt – a little anyway, after Steve gave them his "blessing," and let himself love Danni too.

They spent their first year at college sharing a small apartment together while Steve lived in a dorm on campus. Steve was always available with a shoulder for Danni to cry on after Gabe hurt her yet again. Not that he meant to, but the messed up Evans twin found himself sinking deeper and deeper into depression, and sought escape through alcohol and drugs. He'd take off for hours and sometimes days at a time, never telling Danni he was leaving or where he'd been after he returned. She thought he was having an affair; and he thought she was insane to even think such a thing. He may have had some problems, but he'd always been loyal to her.

Their relationship ended before the end of the school year. Danni moved back to Helena, the Evans twins went back to Bittersweet.

Gabe let his memories fast-forward a few years, past when he met Kyle and those wonderful, horrible years when they became superstars. Past all those years of drug abuse and groupies, making millions and trying desperately to be happy as he searched for his dream…

Gabe realized he'd hit rock bottom when he found himself totally caught in the grip of cocaine. When Steve tried to help him, Gabe had punched him. That was the turning point, and he quit touring with his band. He, Kyle, and Kyle's growing family moved to Michigan and opened a recording studio. Meanwhile, Steve and his horse Whizbang had been riding with the rodeo circuit, making a name for themselves as they climbed the ladder to success. Steve wrote weekly letters to his brother and Gabe managed to fire one off every few months. He would have written more, but his life was stagnant at that point and he didn't have a whole lot to say. Besides, he had recently purchased a decrepit old mansion and was deeply involved in its restoration… and he finally felt somewhat happy with his life.

Towards the end of October in '89, Gabe received a letter from his brother that would change all of their lives forever. Steve was getting married. Gabe was extremely skeptical regarding the matter, being far too cynical about women during that time, and unable to understand how anyone would put up with his twin's nomadic lifestyle. Not that Steve wasn't quite the catch from a female's viewpoint… never that. The gentle Evans had even more attractive qualities than Gabe! Tall, dark, handsome, witty, intelligent, athletic… Gabe had all of those, but Steve went beyond with his serene presence and love and respect for all. Still, his choice in a mate stupefied Gabe.

For Deirdre Burnside, it was love at first sight when Steve rescued her from a charging bull at a rodeo she had attended with her actor friends. Likewise, when Steve saw his "Juliet" all decked out in her costume from the play she was in that afternoon, it was like a dream come true. The couple had dinner together that evening and was inseparable from then on. They traveled together, falling more in love every day, and by the end of the summer she found that she was with child. Steve was thrilled and proposed to her right away. He wrote to Gabe telling him the most wonderful news, and asked that his brother be best man in the wedding. Mmhmm… Gabe wrote back that he would, but had reservations as to the wisdom of Steven's decision.

Life seemed perfect for the young couple until Deirdre decided that her fiancé should give up his cowboy ways and get a proper career. She insisted that he sell Whiz, and use the money to buy them a home. Steve was horrified! Sell his best friend and partner for the last thirteen years? Never! They fought, Steve left for a few hours, and Deirdre headed for the next town over to teach him a lesson, all of this happening only days before the wedding.

As Steve sat at the stable where Whiz was being boarded in the interim, tipping back a few beers and wondering just what the hell had happened between him and his ladylove, a fire broke out in the barn. He dropped his beer and went to save his horse, and then continued with the rescue efforts with the other horses until he was dropped by a lunatic and his deadly shovel. The killer ran into the fire and committed suicide. Steve lived only long enough to realize his horse had come back into the burning barn to save him. Whiz stood over his fallen partner, protecting him from falling bits of burning timber, until help arrived… although too late for man and beast. As Steve's body was being hauled from the conflagration, a huge beam fell on Whiz just as the horse was leaving the barn.

Al arrived about then, being told that his son was playing hero, and was forced to witness as medical personnel pulled a sheet over Steve's lifeless face. The shock and stress were too much for the man. He collapsed.

Gabe was only an hour behind, driving like a maniac from the Billings airport, as waves of unknown dread washed over him. He was met at the ruined barn by an old school chum-turned-cop, and told of the double tragedy. He felt as if his life had ended right then and there.

Marie had been picked up at home, and together they headed for Silver Creek General Hospital where Al was recovering from a heart attack. Funeral arrangements were made for Steve, while Whiz was cremated and his remains placed in an urn. The whole town turned out for the service of the popular duo.

Deirdre returned to Bittersweet on the day of her wedding ready to apologize to her love and get married, only to find that she became a widow before she was a bride. The shock sent her over the edge, and Gabe found her at Silver Creek. He was filled with hate for her, blaming her for the death of his brother. He tolerated her presence at the funeral because Danni, and Kyle's wife Jenna, asked him to be tolerant of her. No one was more surprised than he when he asked her to go back to Michigan with him and live in his huge house. Steve had loved her, and for that reason alone Gabe would do his best to protect her and the child she was carrying.

That was a year ago, and since then Gabe and Deirdre found that they loved each other very much. He married her weeks before the twins – yes, twins - were born, and so far had an almost perfect marriage. Almost… Although they loved each other deeply, Deirdre was not in love with him nor he with her. She would always and forever love Steve, and Gabe was still searching for his green-eyed dream. He had been anyway. After he said "I do" to Dee, his dream was tucked away on a dusty shelf in his mind, only to be pulled out and savored in his rare moments of loneliness and self-pity.

"Gabe."

"Hmm…"

"I said, we're gonna be landing soon. I'm gonna go take a pee first."

"Yeah, whatever, Kyle…"

"Dude, I know you're hurtin', but…"

"Kyle, leave me the hell alone, okay? I… I just want a few more minutes to myself before I have to… to face whatever it is waiting for me there."

"'Nuff said. Back in a few."

Gabe nodded and continued to stare out the window, lost in his thoughts.

A year ago… a year and two days to be exact, but it seemed like yesterday that he was identifying his brother's soot-covered body. Aw God… why? Why the hell did Steve have to be the one and not him? Steve never hurt a soul, and it seemed all Gabe ever did was hurt those he loved. Even Deirdre. Well, he wasn't all that sure he hurt her, but he never should have done what he did. She did cry afterward… but it was her idea in the first place! Christ, what a mess.

Gabe shook off his regrets from two nights ago, and finished off his drink. With any luck he could get one more down before they quit serving…

He knew it was wrong, but she looked so beautiful, so sad, there in the moonlight. She asked him if he ever felt lonely… "Of course!" he answered. "Have you ever felt lonely for a woman?" she wanted to know. He nodded, and picked her up into his arms. He laid her on the bed, kissing her with a passion that surprised and overwhelmed them both…

"Mr. Evans?"

"Yes?"

"Another drink before we land?"

"Uh, yes please. Same thing… Chivas. Neat."

The flight attendant gave him a smile and walked away.

He should have stopped at the kiss, but she wanted him as much as he wanted her. Maybe not so much wanted – hell, he'd never been physically attracted to her, but more like needed. They needed each other. Steve had been on both of their minds all day, and by the time the sun sank in the west, they were both fighting tears.

He had found her crying softly, and had joined her in his grief. Minutes later they were making love. Married all these months and making love for the first time. Now he regretted every single second of it. Deirdre regretted it too, and they looked at each other after it was over, silently vowing never to come together that way again. The love they shared was enough. It didn't need, or even want, the physical side.

Gabe spent the night in the park across from his home, alternately hating what he'd gotten himself into and yet loving it just the same. He loved Dee, he loved his nephews – now sons, James and Jeremy, and he had nothing at all to complain about. This was his life. He could do nothing but make the best of it. Still, it was all he could do to face his wife after their misguided coupling, and now he was running away. Granted, it was only for a day or two, but he was still running. Always seemed to be running…

"Dude… Man, I'll never get over how goddamn small them bathrooms are," Kyle sighed, dropping into the seat next to Gabe.

"It's not like you are planning on doing gymnastics in there, Kyle, just a quick bodily function…"

"But my knees hit the door when I sit!"

"Spare me the details. God, I'm not looking forward to this…"

"What, the details? I can write them down for later…"

"Kyle… just shut up. I'm not looking forward to… well, you know."

"Yeah, I know. Just tryin' to cheer you up, buddy."

"I know, and I thank you. I sure as hell hope our car is ready. I don't feel like waiting around any longer than I have to while they empty a goddamn ashtray or something."

"So get a dirty one."

"I will."

"You do that."

"I plan to."

"Can I write 'wash me' on the outside if it's dirty?"

"The car? Hell, I don't care, just not until I'm done with it."

"Spoilsport."

"Put your seatbelt on, Kyle; we're about to land."

14

"I can read, pal. Put yours on too."

Gabe slammed back the drink just handed to him and settled in as they set down.

"Gabe, wait up! God, you in a race or something?"

"No, just anxious to get his fucking ordeal over with. Um… Kyle, that isn't my bag."

"It's not? But I thought…"

"Your first mistake… thinking. Although they *are* similar… But take it back to the claims area so that the poor soul frantically looking for it will cease to do so."

"So if this isn't yours…"

"Did I not just say so? Mine is black with gold accents… these are silver, Kyle."

"Huh. Yeah, guess you're right…"

"As always."

Gabe turned to the lovely lady at the Avis counter and favored her with his famous lop-sided grin. "Geoffrey Evans… Is my car ready?"

"Of course, Mr. Evans. It's the navy Taurus in lot number 4."

She smiled back and handed him the keys, then sighed. *Such a beautiful man…*

Gabe signed the papers and went out to the parking lot to wait for his buddy, and the correct luggage.

"I'm sorry; miss, but we have no more vehicles available. If you can wait until tomorrow…"

"But I can't! My father… Oh jeez… My father is very ill and I have to get to him as soon as possible!"

"I'm sorry, Miss…"

"Benton. Are you sure? I'm desperate…"

"If only you'd called ahead…"

"I barely had the time to get on my plane! Oh God…"

Annie staggered over to a bench near the Avis counter and dropped her head into her hands. She could call a taxi to take her to her mother's apartment, but it was all the way on the other side of town and would cost a fortune. In her haste to leave she had left her cash sitting on the dining room table. Did taxis take credit cards? She did have those, fortunately, and her ATM card. Too bad there wasn't a money machine in sight. Bad enough her luggage didn't follow her off the jet.

"Dude… Man, I felt so bad in there!"

"Why's that, Kyle?"

"Some lady's ol' man is sick and she needs a car… and we got the last one. Lost her luggage too."

"Sucks to be her then, eh, Kyle?"

"That was cold, man…"

"I'm sorry, but I can't be rescuing the world. I have a lot on my mind right now and the last thing I need is to be a super hero to some poor old lady…"

"She was hardly old, dude…"

"Even worse then. I'd be recognized and I'd never get rid of her…"

"Hell, I wouldn't even try! She was hot, man!"

"God, Kyle… I'm sick of women – period. I have Dee and Jen… and occasionally Danni if I want female chatter, and leave it at that. Now get your ass in the car so we can go."

"Whatever you say, pal. I still think we could have at least *seen* if there was anything we could do…"

"Kyle… Shit. Okay, where is she?" Gabe shut down the Ford and looked at his buddy.

"Right inside. You didn't see her sitting on the bench?"

"There was no one there when I was there…"

"Huh. Must have missed her then."

"Brilliant deduction…"

"Fuck you. You really gonna help her?"

"Yes, I'll do what I can, if for no other reason than to avoid…"

"Cool!" Kyle sprinted for the door.

"So, where is this mythical damsel in distress, Kyle?" "She was right here, not two minutes ago!"

The men scanned the terminal, but found no one looking as if they needed assistance.

"Must be she found another Sir Galahad, Kyle. Let's go."

Kyle gave one last look around and shrugged a shoulder. Well, he tried…

"Wish we could have found her…"

"It might have been more helpful had you given me a description, Kyle. I had no idea who to look for."

"Uh… yeah, I guess so. But I thought…"

"A dangerous undertaking for you, Kyle… thinking."

"Kiss my ass. Just for that I'm going to tell you now. All I really saw was her hair, but God… what hair! All red and gold and brown…"

Gabe slammed on the brakes and stared at his friend.

"What did you say?"

"Huh?"

"Her hair! What did you say about her hair?"

"Uh… red and gold and…"

Gabe pulled out into traffic, did a U-turn, and raced back to the airport.

"Man, are you nuts?" Kyle screamed, watching his life flash before his eyes. "What the hell are you doing?"

"It could be *her*, Kyle! Oh God, I hope we're not too late…"

"Who her? Jesus, Gabe, talk sense!"

"*Her,* Kyle! The woman I've been seeing in my dreams…"

"Dude… Uh, aren't you forgetting something?"

"I used my turn signal…"

"Not that, you asshole… You're married! M-A-R-R-I-E-D! And married to the best woman on earth! Next to Jen of course… What the hell are you doing looking at other women already? And for that matter…"

By that time Gabe had pulled over and stopped, his hopes were dashed once again. It wasn't her, and even if it was, Kyle was right. He was a married man now, no matter that it was a marriage in name only, and he had no call to be looking… wishing… hoping.

"…And for that matter…"

"Kyle, just shut up. Just shut up and leave me to my…" *Misery…*

Annie only spent a moment or two on the bench, wanting to burst into tears in her frustration but needing to get to her mother. No time for self-pity…

She went into the gift shop and found a money machine, and then called a taxi. On the way back through the lobby, she happened to see her suitcase sitting next to the conveyer, and ran to collect it.. Thank God…Things were beginning to look up just a bit for her.

"Sign right here, Mr. Evans."

Gabe's hand was trembling as he put pen to paper, and then picked up the package from the desk clerk. Whatever was in it had belonged to Steve…

"Gabe?"

"Gabe!"

"Huh? Oh… yeah…"

"Are you gonna stare at that thing all day or what?"

"N… No. Let's go, Kyle…"

"Want me to drive?"

"Could you?"

"*De nada.* You'd get us killed anyway… out in left field again. Dude, if it bothers you that much, why…"

"Because I had to, Kyle. Steve didn't leave a whole lot behind, so every tangible thing we have from him… of him, is precious. I… I just hope this is something…"

"So open it and find out."

"Right now?"

"Sure, why not? The contents won't change before we get to our hotel, ya know."

"I know, but what if it's something… I don't know… personal?"

"Well then if it is he'll get pissed off, come down from Heaven, and kick your ass!"

"I'd give anything for that to happen," Gabe sighed. "But I'll wait. I uh… I want to do this in private."

"Understandable. Which hotel?"

"No, the Warlock hotel," Gabe quipped, making a sorry stab at humor. He needed all he could get about now.

"Bite me."

"Holiday Inn."

"We're there, dude…"

Annie shoved a handful of bills at the cabbie and raced up to her mother's door.

"Hey lady, where you want these?" he called, dropping her bags on the pavement.

She just waved a hand at him and beat frantically on the front door of the apartment.

The driver was just going to dump the luggage and run, but got a good look and the cash in his hand. Had a change of heart, and carried them to the front porch.

"Thanks," Annie told him absently, and called again for her mother. "Mom, open the door! It's Annie!"

She thought she heard movement from the other side, and stopped to listen.

Silence.

Was Colleen even there? Maybe she'd gone to the hospital after all, and hopefully left a note saying which one.

Annie stepped into the bushes so that she could peek into the window…

"Mom!" she screamed, seeing the older woman slumped in a chair. She picked up her suitcase and smashed the large pane of glass, careful not to get cut as she hauled herself over the windowsill.

"Mom, wake up! Oh God… what happened?"

Colleen was awake but disoriented and the left side of her face had a noticeable droop. A stroke? Annie checked the muscle tone of leg and arm on the same side, horrified to find the limbs limp and unresponsive. She was lucky Colleen had even been able to use the phone at all.

Annie picked up the phone to call 911, but hit the re-dial button by accident. "Darn it," she muttered, and raised her thumb to disconnect.

She stopped immediately when a pleasant voice answered, "Southwest Ambulance Service, may I help you?"

"Uh… Uh, yes! I hope so anyway… First of all I need an ambulance to six-oh-six Mayfair, apartment C. The patient, my mother, is a sixty-eight year old with a possible stroke. Left-sided paralysis. Please hurry!"

"We're dispatching. May I have your name please?"

"In a minute. First, could you tell me if you picked up a man at this address within the last few days? Possible heart attack? I can't find my father…"

"One moment, ma'am…"

"Come on…" Annie muttered, alternately keeping a close eye on her mother and watching the street for emergency vehicles.

"Your father, you say?"

"Yes, Robert Benton. I'm Annie Benton."

"October twenty-eighth at sixteen-forty we transported him to Canyon Mercy, but I'm afraid that's all I can tell you."

"It's just what I needed to know. And thank you."

Sirens screeched in the distance and Annie disconnected the call, and prayed even harder.

"Annie luv, our connection is horrid! Perhaps you could ring me later…?"

"Amanda, no. It's Mom and Dad… You have got to come home right away!"

"I am home…"

"I mean here."

"I'm afraid that's impossible, Annie dear. My schedule is hopelessly full, and…"

"But they're dying! Amanda, please…"

"Oh for God's sake… So melodramatic! Annie…"

"Amanda, listen! Dad had a heart attack, it doesn't look good, and Mom had a stroke. Please, please come home!"

"Dear God! Why didn't you say so in the first place?"

She tried…

"I'll arrange for a flight immediately. Oh, Annie…"

"Amanda?"

Nothing but a dial tone.

Well crap.

✦ ✦ ✦

Gabe set the package on the bed, staring at it as he sipped a pint of scotch that was still in the brown paper bag from the EZ Mart. Kyle had given him one of those damn disapproving looks when he bought it, but Gabe needed a little fortification since Dee wasn't there to lean on

At least Kyle had the decency to take a walk for an hour or so. Gabe told him to go across the street to the hospital, and amuse himself by laughing and pointing at any doctor who left the men's room trailing toilet paper from any and all articles of clothing.

Kyle laughed, and went to change into the appropriate attire.

"Oh God… Kyle, must you?" Gabe groaned when he saw what was written on his buddy's tee shirt.

"Dude, you bought it for me…"

"And I should be shot for it. Remind me to dispose of that entire line of clothing when we get back home. And remind me to kick myself in the ass for encouraging you to take that goddamn Latin class with me way back when…"

"Too much remindin'. Later, gator…" Kyle looked down at his shirt and laughed again, reading it out loud. "*Cave, vomiturus sum!*"

"Look out, I'm going to barf," Gabe translated, and shoved his buddy out the door. He sighed and sat down on the bed.

So, this was it…

Now or never…

Do or die…

Christ, why did he have to think "die"?

Gabe picked up the package, closed his eyes, and tore the wrapping from the box.

No demons jumped out at him, no wailing wraiths could be heard, there was no smell of decomposition, and all he really experienced was a hint of a tingle when his fingers met cardboard.

Just where in God's name did all of those morbid thoughts come from? He took a deep breath and dumped the precious contents on the bed.

Oh God… A virtual treasure trove! There were several cassettes of Gabe's demo tapes that he had sent to Stevie years ago, and a few magazines sporting pictures of Gabe and Kyle and their band SD. A photo album held articles of Steve and his roping career, small and not too wordy, but there nonetheless. Two gold belt buckles won in calf roping and bronco riding were wrapped in tissue paper, and a picture of Deirdre, dressed as Juliet and seated high on Whizbang as she smiled lovingly down at Steve, was nestled in a velvet lined box. Under it all was Steve's battered, much-read copy of "Romeo and Juliet."

Gabe was damn glad that he was already sitting down. Jesus, these were Steve's most prized possessions! How in the hell did they manage to get left here of all places? Gabe didn't even remember Steve competing within a hundred miles of the place during the last year.

Too fucking weird.

He took a last look at everything and placed them gently back into the box. Deirdre would definitely want these, no matter how much it hurt. Steve's sons should have some memories too, even if it *was* decided that he would always be "Uncle Steve" and Gabe would be "Papa."

He finished off his booze in three long pulls, hating like hell to be drinking again. In a sudden fit of pain and anger, he chucked the empty pint to smash against the wall.

Life sucked.

He wished he had a goddamn cigarette.

✦ ✦ ✦

"Mom? It's Annie."

"Nee…" came the slurred reply.

"Oh, Mom…" Annie's eyes welled with tears as she bent to hug the frail woman.

"I… I saw Dad," she sniffed. "He… he's critical but stable. He's awake, Mom, would you like to see him?"

Colleen nodded, the tears running unchecked down her twisted face.

A nurse assisted Annie in placing her mother into a wheelchair, and the Benton's headed for the coronary care unit.

Colleen's eyes widened in fear when she saw the… the thing that was supposed to be her husband.

"I know it's scary, Mom, but he needs all of this," Annie explained. She took Colleen's hand as she talked her through all the equipment.

"The scariest-looking thing is the breathing machine – the ventilator. He needs more oxygen than normal, and help breathing it in…"

Colleen nodded her understanding.

"All of the tubes, the IV lines, are for nutrition and medication. He needs so many… Antibiotics, blood thinners, medicine to keep his blood pressure stable…"

Again Colleen nodded.

"The monitor over the bed shows heart rate and respirations…"

Annie trailed off and flinched when three premature contractions blipped together on the screen. *Oh God…*

He went back into sinus rhythm and Annie let out the breath she didn't even realize she was holding.

"The other lines you see up there are monitoring the pressure inside his heart, and how much oxygen is in his blood…"

Annie glanced at the vent to see just how much O2 he needed. Sixty percent as opposed to the twenty-one of room air, and his pulse ox was only at eighty-three percent. Not good… not good at all. She wasn't all that familiar with cardiology, but numbers were numbers and she didn't at all like the looks of these.

Bob's hand flickered in a twitch, and then was raised.

Colleen leaned forward in her chair in an effort to be near him.

Annie wheeled her mother over so that her parents could share together what little time was left to them.

"I'm worried about him, Jenna. He's drinkin' again. The room smelled like cigarette smoke when I got back too."

"At least it isn't dope, Kyle" she sighed.

Gabe had been doing so well about staying clean ever since they made the move to Michigan. He'd quit smoking, rarely drank more than a few beers at a time, and totally gave up his dope, coke, and speed altogether.

After he married Deirdre he was even better, and when the twins were born Gabe Evans had reached near perfection as the man any woman would want. Only her longtime, deep love for Kyle kept Jen from having a fantasy or two about the magnificent Evans.

"I know, Jen, but…"

"Is he drunk?"

"No… just mean and moody. All he said was for me to fuck off."

"Ooh! He is out of sorts! Just what did it *this* time?"

"Oh, he picked up a package of Steve's things… I think it threw him for a loop. He's got that look in his eye. You remember the one he used to get after he had that dream?"

"The nightmare? Oh no…"

"No, that other one, Jen. Green eyes…"

"That's just as bad. Poor Deirdre… having to live with… with the ghost of someone who doesn't even exist, if he *is* thinking about her again.

"Her who? Hell, he doesn't even know if there *is* such a person. Just a fantasy…"

"As long as that's all it is. Kyle, when are you coming home? I miss you, lover."

"Aw God… me too, Jen. I'll be home tomorrow. How're the kids? I miss them too."

"Will is staring into the mirror to see if he has whiskers yet…"

"Jesus, Jen, he's only ten years old!"

"So he'll stare for a few more years. Oh, and he's perfected the song that you taught him on the guitar. Been playing the damn thing all day… Kyle, why did you have to choose "Wipe Out"?"

"Good exercise for his little fingers. How's my princess?"

"Hannah is just fine. She made head cheerleader for the fourth grade basketball team."

"As well she should. They *have* a basketball team?"

"Intramural…"

"And cheerleaders…?"

"Unofficial."

"As long as she's happy. Uh… how's Emily?"

"Happily bouncing… no, wait. Happily kicking a ball against Sarah's playpen. Oh Lord… Sarah has her stuffed bunny in the 'I'll protect you from the ogre, honey' hold. She's so cute…"

"All my children are no less than perfect, Jen. And my latest? How's our baby…?"

"Kicking the crap out of me. I can't wait until he's born! This is the last one, lover…"

"Anything you say, Jen…"

"Say you love me, Kyle…"

"I love you, Jen…"

"Kyle! I need the phone!"

"Gotta go… he bellows."

"Give him a hug and a kiss for me, Kyle."

"Don't bet on it. Uh, tell the kids I'll be home in time for trick-or-treating. Costumes ready?"

"And waiting."

"Cool. God, I love Halloween! It's my favorite holiday."

"Every holiday is your favorite, Kyle…"

"Kyle! I'm waiting…"

"Fuck you, Gabe. Bye, Jen…"

She laughed and hung up, and went to rescue Sarah and her bunny from the evil soccer ball of Em the ogre…

"Geoffrey!"

"Hello, Deirdre. All's well there, I hope?"

"It couldn't be better! The boys are happy and healthy, I feel wonderful, and the weather is beautiful…"

"That's nice, Dee…"

"Geoffrey, what is it, dear?"

"Hmm? Oh, nothing…"

"Geoffrey, I know you all too well. What is it?"

Gabe took a deep sigh and wondered just how much he should tell her over the phone. What the hell…

"It… it's Steve, Dee. I came out there to pick up some of the things that he uh, left behind."

"Oh… oh my! Oh, Geoffrey! Oh… I'm scared to ask, but… I must know. Was our picture there? The one of Whizbang, Steven, and me?"

"Uh, yeah! How…?"

"I remember that it, along with a small chest of items, came up missing while we were in Arizona. He thought we'd been robbed and he was devastated. None of those things had any material value, but to him they were priceless. I wonder how on earth they ever got to… Geoffrey, where were they?"

"A hotel in Phoenix."

"You don't say… Geoffrey, we were never in Phoenix!"

"I didn't think so, and I'm just as baffled as you. But we have them now, Deirdre, and we can thank God for that. I uh, I should get going. Give the boys a kiss for me."

"I will, Geoffrey."

"I… I love you, Dee."

"I love you too, Geoffrey."

He didn't hear her though, as he had already disconnected. Goddamn green eyes were dancing through his brain again.

Chapter Three

"Oh God... Amanda! I'm so glad you're here!"

"Annie... Mum and Dad; how are they?"

"Dad... Amanda, Dad passed away last night. His heart just gave out..."

"Dear God... Annie, I tried to get here sooner..."

"I know, and I told him you were on your way. He said to tell you he loves you, and... and..." Annie broke down, crying too hard to continue.

Amanda put an arm around her little sister and led her into the ladies' room.

"Dry your tears, luv," she said, handing her a wad of paper towel.

"Thanks, Amanda," Annie sniffed.

"Are you better?"

Annie nodded. "I'm sorry, but... Uh, I guess we should go see Mom."

"How is she handling all of this? She and Dad were inseparable..."

"Surprisingly, quite well. They were together when he... when it happened. I was just about to take her back to her room, since she got to visit him for only ten minutes at a time, but she insisted that she stay. She refused to leave even though her strength was nearly gone. I kind of had a feeling something was up... it was weird. Anyway, they sat there and held hands, and he just kind of faded away..."

"Didn't the doctors try and save him? Good God, what the hell do we pay them for?"

"Amanda, it was time. He had massive damage done... Barely any of his heart tissue was still viable. He – we - were lucky he lasted this long. I think he was waiting for you..."

"Is that some snide remark about my lengthy absence...?"
"Not at all! You're his daughter and he loves you! I think he wanted to see you one last time before... Oh jeez, let's just go see Mom...." But deep down Annie felt that Amanda could have come home for a visit at least once over that last twenty years.

"Oh, Annie, she looks terrible! So old..."

"What did you expect, Amanda? Jeez, you haven't seen her since she was the age you are now! She has been ill for several days..."

"Are you ever going to tell me what happened?"

"I planned to, but we haven't had the time. C'mon, let's go get a coffee."

"As close as I could make out what Mom was saying, she had a spell or something on the twenty-eighth and passed out. Dad called an ambulance, and then had a heart attack as he was lifting her to the bed. She had recovered enough by the time the medics got there to let them in. They saw Dad, took him, and left her all alone. She had several more 'mini strokes' over the next day, and it was all she could do to call me! The last one she had, the bad one, happened right after she called me "Dear God…""I know. Amanda, what are we going to do? She can't live alone anymore and she refuses to move back home with me. I can't quit my job and move out here…"

"I certainly hope you don't expect me to take her!"

"Uh, no! I hadn't even thought of that! I just don't know what to do… And then on top of that I have to arrange the funeral…"

"I suppose I could help with that. Did you happen to know if Dad left anything regarding his wishes?"

"Not really. Mom mentioned cremation and a memorial service at the retirement village's community room."

"That sounds simple enough."

"It is, but I uh… Amanda, I think Mom will go soon too."

"Why do you say that? God, you were just all in a twit about what to do with her!"

"I… I don't know! I just had this weird picture in my head of… of two urns surrounded by flowers…"

"You've always been a strange one, luv. Now let's go back upstairs and talk to Mum. As hard as this is, she should have a say in what we do with Dad."

"I agree…" Annie sighed, and finished her coffee.

Colleen wouldn't discuss the memorial service, telling her daughters to wait a day or two before they made arrangements. She did agree to her husband's cremation, but told her girls that they could talk about unpleasant things later, as she just wanted a pleasant visit with them for now.

Annie was amazed at how her mother's speech had cleared up over the last few days. Her paralysis was still there, but it was as if the right side of her mouth compensated for the dead left side she was quite easy to understand. It was a blessing for which Annie would be forever grateful.The three Benton women talked for hours, reliving childhoods, sighing over lost dreams, and just getting to know one another all over again. Colleen fell asleep, and the girls went out for dinner.

"Annie, why is it you never married?"

"I did! Well, for a few months anyway…"

"Like that was a marriage? More like a sleep over…"

"That's for sure… The slumber party from hell," Annie laughed. "Amanda, how could I have been so stupid as to marry that… that loser? I never even really loved him!"

"I have no idea, Annie. Haven't you met anyone since? Dear God… it's been ten years! Aren't you lonely?"

"I suppose. I don't know… I work so much overtime that I really don't have time to think about it!"

"All work and no play? Annie…"

"I play once in a while…"

Amanda grinned, waiting for the juicy details. "Do tell!"

"Not like *that*! Jeez... I... uh, there hasn't been anyone like that since Richie, and with him it was only once or twice..."

"A week?"

"Ever. I... I just couldn't do it. I guess I don't blame him for cheating on me."

"That prick."

"It wasn't his fault. We just weren't meant to be, Amanda. I don't know that I'll ever find anyone..."

"Do you at least look? You do date, don't you?"

"Date?"

"Date. You know, go out with a man... dinner and drinks... get to know..."

"Yeah, I have..."

"Dear Lord... In this century? Annie, what do you do for *fun?*"

"I read a lot. Go to the movies once in a while..."

"Yawn. When was the last time you got out to socialize? Hmm?"

"With a man or..."

"With anyone!"

"I uh, I did go on a double date with Marti and two of her friends. It was okay."

"And this was when?"

"Two months ago?"

"Oh God..." Amanda groaned.

"Well, I'm sorry. I like being alone! I don't have to answer to anyone, I can do what I want when I want, and... and..."

"And what? You don't even *do* anything! You live in Mum and Dad's huge house, using every spare minute you have to keep it tidy. Don't argue, Annie; I know you better than you think I do. You have the biggest heart in the world – would do anything for anyone, and yet not a soul knows it because you hide. Or work, as the case may be. You're a beautiful young woman. Why is it that you aren't married or even involved?"

"I... I don't know..."

"Well I think I do. You have been locked in that hard little shell of yours ever since Gramma died..."

"How would you know? You weren't even around then, Amanda! How would anyone know?"

"Because I'm a very perceptive woman and I know *people...* and I did keep in close touch with Mum over the years. She was so worried about you, Annie. And I am right, am I not? You're afraid to love, aren't you, sis. You don't want to be hurt ever again..."

Annie swallowed hard and nodded slowly. Amanda was so very right. It was so much easier to pretend to be happy all by herself than to take a chance at falling in love, only to be rejected or hurt or lose that love. Even though she never really loved Richie, it still hurt her beyond belief when he cheated on her.

She would never take that chance again. No way…

"That's what I thought," Amanda sighed, leaning back into her chair. "Annie luv, when you get home I want you to look inside yourself and ask what you really want. The life you have now or something more? You weren't meant to spend the rest of your days all alone… no family, few friends… It just isn't right. I know, we'll talk to Mum about selling that house, at least you'll be free of that burden, and then you can get a nice little flat somewhere, do *something* with that hair of yours, and find your knight in shining armor," Amanda laughed.

Annie smiled when her sister flipped a lock of her red curls into her face. Yeah, her hair was something else…

"I'd rather have a cowboy," she giggled.

"A what?" Amanda asked, not quite sure she heard correctly.

"Oh nothing… it's stupid."

"A… a cowboy? Dear God, Annie, you still aren't *horse crazy*, are you?"

"No! I mean, I still love them and all, but… Amanda, did you see that movie… the one Ashton DeLaCroix did?"

"Ash… Oh! Oh God yes! It was all the rage! Ooh… he's… Annie, is *that* the cowboy you want? Oh my God!" Amanda laughed.

"No! Of course not… but you have to admit, he does look great in a pair of jeans!"

"Mmhmm…"

"But he uh… well, if I was looking for someone, that's what I'd be looking for. Tall, black hair, that cute smile…"

"He's all man, luv. To tell you the truth, I'm not at all sure they even actually exist! My Bernie… well, he used to be something, but over the years… Lost his hair and gained a paunch. I still love him though."

"I should hope so! Oh jeez…" Annie moaned, glancing overhead to where some numbers were flashing on a paging system.

"What is it?"

"They're paging a 'zero' code to Mom's floor. Someone is dying…" Annie jumped up and ran out before Amanda could ask another question.

"I'm sorry, Miss Benton, but she was gone before we could do anything…"

Annie nodded. "I understand… I don't know that she would have wanted to go on anyway. Not without Dad." She turned to look at her mother one last time.

Colleen was at peace, and in death her twisted face had evened out again. The girls kissed their mother goodbye and left the room.

✦ ✦ ✦

"Gabe buddy! Miss me?"

"Only about as much as razor blades in my Halloween apples. Did you score big on your candy scavenge last night?"

"Dude, we kicked ass! I even made sure Sarah got her fair share of the loot."

"As in you let her have some, or just made sure everyone contributed to her goody bag?"

"Goody bag. She's just a baby, Gabe…"

"I'm aware of that, Kyle."

"You're looking better. Um… Did Dee handle what was in that box okay?"

"Actually, she was quite thrilled about it. There were a few tears, but we uh… we got through it okay. She loved that frame I picked out, by the way."

"The one for the pic of her and Steve and Whiz?"

"That would be it. And that's what brought the tears…"

"A frame? Why?"

"I… uh, never mind."

Gabe could hardly tell his buddy the truth about the marriage, and that he wanted to honor Steve and Deirdre and their endless love in the best way he knew how. That was to frame that precious picture and present it to her. She understood completely. Odd that he and Dee didn't have to talk to communicate; they could merely look at each other and know what was being thought. It was such a tragedy that their marriage couldn't be the real thing.

"Kyle, what are your plans for the day?"

"Work, home, Jen… Why?"

"I… I think I'll take the rest of the day off. Go for a ride…"

"Dude, you're not doin' it again, are you? Gabe…"

"Doing what? Jesus, Kyle, it's a beautiful day out and I'd like to enjoy it."

"Doin' that runnin' thing. God, I thought for sure you would in Arizona… Seein' that redhead and all…"

"What redhead?"

"Shit… should'a kept my mouth shut…"

"What. Redhead. Kyle?" Gabe grabbed his buddy's shirt and pulled him closer.

Kyle knew it was futile to evade the issue, and sighed. "The same <u>one</u> <u>that</u> was at the airport. I saw her at the hospital pushin' some old lady in a wheelchair. Then again that night at the hotel when I went out for beer… She was goin' into a room two doors down. I thought for sure you seen her when you tossed me the car keys…"

"Goddammit, man, why didn't you tell me! I… Aw God…"

"Why the hell should I? You got no right to be lookin', pal…"

"Forget it, Kyle. You're right. I'm sorry. Now if you'll excuse me, I need some air…"

Gabe grabbed his jacket and left his office, and went for a very, very long ride in his truck. Arizona was tempting, but he stayed within the borders of Michigan.

Chapter Four

"God, this house hasn't changed a bit in twenty years, Annie. Don't you even care about redecorating?"

"Why? First of all, it isn't mine to decorate, and secondly, who would care? Marti is the only one that ever comes over, and she cares less for wallpaper and paint than I do."

"Well, no matter now. Let's just sell it as is and call it good. What time do we meet with the lawyer?"

"Two-thirty. What time does your plane leave?"

"Eight."

"Oh, yeah. Amanda, I'm sure Mom and Dad left everything to the both of us… Why don't you pick out what you want right now? It will save time later."

"What about you? Isn't there anything here you'd like?"

"A few things, but I doubt we'd care about the same things, Amanda. We lived different lives in different times…"

"Annie, that was… was nearly profound!" Amanda laughed.

"Kiss my butt, sis…" Annie laughed back, she so very glad to have this new, close relationship with her older sister. All those years wasted, not having each other…

"Then you really don't mind if I choose first?"

"Not at all. Um… The only thing I'd really like for myself is that cameo ring Gramma left to Mom. It's…"

"Special, I know. And it's yours, Annie."

"Thanks, Amanda. Well, shall we?"

"Rather morbid, but I suppose…"

"I know. But they would want us to."

The sisters spent several hours looking for the memories they wanted to keep, but came up with very little when all was said and done. Amanda had a few of the older photo albums, most of Colleen's jewelry, and a silver platter that was only used on Thanksgiving. She told Annie that she was welcome to the rest.

Annie clutched the heirloom cameo in her hand and wanted nothing else. Well, the rest of the photo albums, but that was it.

The girls agreed to donate the clothing and furniture to the homeless shelter, sell the house, and split the money. That's if they were left the house in the will, and they'd find that out soon enough.

"So that's it, ladies. Everything they had is to be divided equally between the two of you. Er… is that something you will need assistance with?"

"No thank you, Mr. Howe, we uh, we pretty much have it figured out already," Annie murmured.

"Splendid! I love it when these readings don't end in a brawl," Howe laughed.

"We could if it would amuse you," Amanda flirted, liking this young lawyer very much. He wasn't nearly as stuffy as his father, who had handled Annie's divorce and a few legal matters for the Benton family over the years.

"Not necessary, Amanda. Annie, could I have a word with you in private?"

Amanda raised an eyebrow. Oh? Was he looking at Sis now…?

"Sure, Mr. Howe. Uh, excuse us, Amanda?"

"Far be it from me to intrude," she said dryly, and strolled from the office.

"What is it, Mr. Howe?" Annie asked when the door clicked shut behind her sister.

"Call me Tyler."

"Tyler…" Annie smiled.

He smiled back. "A few things. First of all, how are you doing? You seem so in control…"

"I'm fine. I… I wasn't all that close with my parents. I loved them, but they… they were gone more often than not… traveling…"

"Mmhmm. They were good friends of my parents, you know."

"I know. I still remember having dinner at your house."

"God, that was a long time ago. You were just a little kid!"

"So were you!"

"No… I've got a few years on you. But I must say you grew up to be a beautiful woman…"

"Th… thank you, Tyler," she said, blushing.

"Back to business, Annie. We can socialize later… I hope."

She gave him a surprised look.

"Annie, there was a little more to the will than what I told you and your sister about. Bob and Colleen wanted you to be told this privately, and whether or not you inform your sister… well, that's up to you."

"I don't understand. Everything they owned was mentioned…"

"Not everything. They owned some more property in the northern part of the county. I guess it's quite extensive. Anyway, I have a key to a safe deposit box for you. It contains the deed to the land and a letter from your parents. I think everything will be explained when you read it."

"Property? I… oh jeez! North…?"

"Yes. Around Hidden Lake, I believe. Do you know where that is?"

"Of course I do! My grandmother's house was near there."

"Well, here's the key. If you hurry you can make it to the bank before it closes and have all your questions answered."

"I… uh, thank you, Tyler."

He held out the key, dropped it into her open palm, and closed his hand around hers.

"Annie, this may be a terribly inappropriate time to ask, but uh… would you like to have dinner with me tonight?"

"Tonight?" she gulped, glancing down to where his hand dwarfed hers.

"I was hoping…" Somewhat embarrassed at his boldness, he pulled away.

"Oh gosh… I'm sorry, but I can't. Amanda's plane leaves at eight…" Annie was relieved, and yet curiously disappointed with the loss of contact.

"I understand. Perhaps later this week?"

"I… Yes, I think I'd like that, Tyler," she answered. Why not? Her sister had been right about her not having a life, and Tyler was very nice… and quite handsome!

"Wonderful! I'll give you a call. I have your number," he said with a wink.

Annie blushed again and picked up her coat.

"Thank you for everything, Tyler."

"My pleasure. My condolences on your parents' passing. If I can do anything…"

Annie nodded and went to find Amanda.

"Well?" Amanda said, just this side of catty.

"Well what?"

"What was so private back there?"

"Uh… Nothing really. Mom and Dad left me something else, but I'm not sure what it is."

"How can you not know?"

"It's a key to a safe deposit box, and Tyler said there was some property involved. That's all I know for sure."

"*Tyler?* Rather chummy all the sudden, Annie…"

"He told me to call him that, Amanda. We did know each other as children…"

"I remember. Lord, he certainly grew up well, didn't he? I wouldn't mind…"

"Amanda! You're married!"

"Only at home, luv. Not that it matters any more… I'm leaving soon. Are you taking me to dinner?"

"Sure! Any place in particular?"

"Some place fun! You *do* know some place fun, don't you?"

"I uh… not really. I'll call Marti and see what she suggests. She knows all the best places in the lower half of the state!"

"Maybe I'll have her take me out then," Amanda chuckled.

"I can ask…"

"I was joking, Annie. God! Oh! Here's something to cheer you up! I saw that cowboy of yours…"

"What?"

"Well, not *Ashton*, but… Oh Lord, this one was even better! And he looked familiar but just can't place it… No matter. Annie, he was tall and dark, had eyes to die for, and I'm sure he's a romantic soul as well. He was carrying a dozen roses for some lucky lady…"

"Taken," Annie sighed, and then laughed. "And I think you're making this up, Amanda."

"Think what you will, but I saw him! Boots, hat, leather jacket and all! He even drove a pick-up truck, luv."

"Mmhmm. Well, let's get home. I'll call Marti and we'll go have some fun."

"So, Annie-bananie, glad to have your sis gone? Lord, she's a trip!"

"Marti! You're so bad! I'm going to miss her if you want to know the truth. We got pretty close over the last few days. I'm glad she came; it would have been very difficult to go through this alone."

"I'll bet. So you already had the funeral and everything?"

"Just a memorial service is all. They were cremated, and the next day we had a little service in the community room of the retirement home. It was very nice."

"Sounds… well, not fun…"

"No, it wasn't fun. But all of their friends were there, and the flowers… Marti, I have never seen so many flowers in one room! All kinds, and hundreds of them! Oh! You should have seen this one bouquet… Fifty white roses in a huge, mother-of-pearl vase."

"Fifty? Did you stand there and count them or something?"

"Well, yeah! It was incredible! The flowers were bigger than my fist! Funny though, there wasn't a card or anything telling who they were from. Nobody there knew either, and when I called the local florists to find out, not one of them even has that many white roses in stock let alone to make a delivery that large. Weird."

"Weird?"

"So weird that I brought some home with me. We donated the rest of the arrangements, but these were so… so interesting, and beautiful, that I had to bring some home."

"And you still have them? It's been what, a week?"

"Yes. C'mon, I'll show you."

"Oh my God," Marti gasped, circling the table where the vase of flowers reigned. "They're beautiful! And not even wilting yet!"

"I know. Must be some new strain. Uh, Marti?"

"Yeah?"

"Touch one."

"Touch? Not smell?"

"Well that too, but… Anyway, go ahead."

Marti shrugged a shoulder and pulled a bloom from the bunch.

"Yeah? What now?" she asked, inhaling the scent of rose.

"You don't… feel anything?"

"No, why? Are the thorns extra sharp or something?"

"No… Never mind."

"Tell me, Annie. What's up?"

"I don't know..."

"Yes you do."

"It's stupid."

"Big deal. And remember who you're talking to, Annie. I'm the queen of 'anything goes'!"

"True. Okay... Marti, every time I touch those flowers I get this... this tingle or something. It's like a very mild electric current running from my fingers to my... my heart."

"Maybe you have an electric eel on your father's side..."

"Marti! I'm serious! You don't feel it?"

"No, and I think you work too much. Take a vacation, Annie. I know, let's go to the Caribbean. A cruise! Let's go on a cruise!"

"Down, girl. And I couldn't right now even if I wanted to. I have to take care of this house, and find a new place to live, and..."

"Let me know when you're ready to play, Annie. Well, I should get going. It's my last night of freedom before I have to work again, and I'm still rarin' to go. When do you work next?"

"Monday, and I'm on for six straight. It's going to be one, long week."

"Assuming you survive. Well, g'nite, Annie. Sweet dreams!"

"Bye, Marti. Same to you."

Annie sat at the table and stared at the vase of white roses. Very strange... She hadn't seen flowers like this since she'd been in Gramma's garden fifteen years ago.

Very strange...

✦ ✦ ✦

"Geoffrey, you shouldn't have," Deirdre sighed, admiring the dozen, blood-red roses he had handed her.

"I do a lot of things I shouldn't do, Dee, and yet I continue."

"Well I'm glad you did this. They're beautiful! Any special reason...?"

"Do I need a reason to do anything?"

"You? Not that I'm aware of, you rogue. Geoffrey, are you still fretting over... over Steven's things? Something has you down."

"I don't know. Maybe. Probably just 'that time of the month'," he said with a small laugh.

"Well if that's the case, go buy your own chocolate and leave mine be. Or better yet, why don't you and Kyle go out for a while. You hardly ever spend time with him anymore."

"I know, but we have our own families now, Dee. His seems to be forever expanding, but..."

"Then come spend time with yours, Geoffrey. The twins are growing so fast, and I'd hate for you to miss anything."

Gabe nodded and took her into his arms.

"Thank you, Deirdre," he whispered, kissing her forehead.

"For what, Geoffrey? I should be thanking you! If not for you I'd be penniless and homeless, dragging my poor, fatherless children through the streets as I begged for a crust of bread…"

"Aw God," Gabe burst out laughing. "Dee, you're priceless! You'd hardly be homeless, although I don't even want to think of my nephews growing up in… in Los Angeles of all places! But your parents would have taken you in and made sure you had no less than the best. After all, they did release your trust fund to you, correct?"

"Correct. I was forgiven for running off with the worthless drifter cowboy after I married the wealthy celebrity. I almost hate them for being so shallow, Geoffrey."

"Never hate your parents, Dee. Family is just too precious to throw away…"

"I could never hate them. That would involve emotion, and there was very little emotion in our home. Cold, proper, distant… It's difficult to believe that two wonderful actors such as my parents couldn't even dredge up a little 'acting' and act like they cared for their children. Oh, I had the best of everything, but never got what I really wanted."

"And that was…?"

"Love, Geoffrey, love. I found it with Steven… and… and now…"

Gabe hugged her to him again when she began to cry.

"Dee, hush. You found that perfect love… and as trite as it sounds, it's better to have loved and lost than never to have loved at all. Or so I hear. I've not yet had the pleasure."

Deirdre looked up into his intense blue eyes, wishing she could help him find that most wonderful love. If not with her, then with his green-eyed dream. Oh, she knew all about his fantasy love. Geoffrey had shared every single bit of his life with her, from the most glorious moments of his incredible success to the dark, shameful secrets of his drug addiction and sleeping with any woman he desired. She held him in the night when he woke from his horrid nightmares, screaming in fear and drenching the bed linen in sweat. She listened to his hopes, his fears, and his dreams. All of his dreams…

Likewise, there was very little Geoffrey didn't know about her, from her cold childhood to the real reason she left home, escaping from her stepbrother and his thoughts of incest.

"You're right, Geoffrey, I have known that kind of love. I hope that someday you will too."

"No… won't happen, Dee. Not now, not ever."

"Why not? I've told you time and time again that I'd let you go if you ever found her!"

"I won't do that, Dee. I promised you forever, and you're stuck with me

34

forever. I won't have my… my nephews raised in a broken home, especially when it's totally unnecessary to be broken in the first place. I love you, Deirdre, and this is the path I've chosen of my own free will."

"Geoffrey, I love you too. And the babies… They're your *sons*, Geoffrey. You are the only father they will ever know."

"I wish to God they were my sons, Dee."

"They are! You were there through nearly my entire pregnancy, and you were holding my hand as they were delivered. It was in your arms that Jeremy, and then James were placed, and it's you they see every single morning and then again when you tuck them into bed. They love you every bit as much as you love them, Geoffrey. You *are* their father!"

His eyes pricked with tears and he pressed his lips into her pale blonde hair. She was right, but also so very wrong. She'd never understand how he wanted his own children, not his brother's. Of course he loved the twins as if they were his own and his love for them grew every day, but to have his own son or daughter… The product of his seed with the woman he loved. Never. It would never happen now.

Gabe shoved that dream to the back of his dusty mental shelf, right next to green eyes. He picked up his wife and swung her around, and then planted a kiss on her delicate cheek.

"Deirdre, I'm starving. What's for dinner?"

"Reservations, Geoffrey. It's Friday, remember?"

"Huh? Oh yeah… Pizza night at T.J.'s! Should we just have them deliver and spend our evening watching James and Jeremy drool as they cut new teeth?"

"I'd love that, Geoffrey. Are you feeling better yet?"

"Much, my dear. I've told you before that you saved me, Dee. You just did again."

"Because I love you, Geoffrey. You're such a good man…"

She ran a hand along his jaw and under his chin. He looked so much like Steven. Why couldn't she love him like Steven? He deserved to be loved… needed a wife in every way, and not just someone who shared his last name.

Gabe looked down into her cornflower-blue eyes and thought about kissing her. Really, really kissing her. God, he needed someone and not just to talk to either. But not Deirdre, never again. Too bad he took his marriage vows so goddamn serious, because it sure would be easy to head out and look for some companionship to jump into bed with once the family was tucked in to theirs. Yeah right. Instead he'd jump into some running shoes and do about ten miles. Again. Fifteen if the weather held. And everyone wondered why he was in such great shape…

Chapter Five

Annie's long workweek turned out to be four longer than the expected six days. An early-arriving influenza virus hit Waterston, keeping medical staff home with the illness as Brighton Memorial filled up with the sick.

Annie bounced from Pediatrics to the Neonatal ICU, filling in where ever a warm, skilled body was needed. She didn't mind all that much; her mind was occupied at work, and then too tired to think about her loneliness when she was home.

Tyler called daily, leaving his dinner invitation and asking her to please call him back. Although she felt horribly rude about it, Annie never picked up the phone. Too much work, too little sleep, and trying to get the house ready to sell left no time for a social life. Jeez, she hadn't even made it to the bank yet to check on her mysterious inheritance. It was driving her crazy.

"Got plans for your nights off, Annie-bananie?"

"Only to sleep for a week. Too bad I only have three days to squeeze it in, Marti."

"You're nuts, you know that don't you?"

"Look who's talking. You're the one wore the turkey feathers into work last night."

"So?"

"On your butt? Jeez..." Annie laughed.

"Well there's nuts and there's nuts. I'm fun nuts..."

"And I'm boring nuts?"

"You said it, girlfriend, not me."

"Jeez... I am boring. Maybe a new hairstyle? I know, I'll get a cut and color, and use that as a start in my personality makeover, Marti. Should I go blonde or brown...?"

"No! Annie, I swear to God if you so much as change a single strand of that hair I'll kill you!"

"Huh? Why? Jeez, it's a mess! I can barely get a comb through it, and it can never decide what color it wants to be! Some days it's red, some days gold..."

"Don't touch it, Annie, it's your trademark. Can't change a trademark."

"Amanda thought I should."

"That bleach-blonde fake? I'm sorry to say that about your sister, but..."

"I know, but she means well. Okay, so what do you suggest to get me out of my rut?"

"Hmm... Is that lawyer still after you?"

"He's called."

"So call him back. Have him take you some place really nice... I know, The Reef!"

"Oh no... That place is way too much. Marti, I heard that they don't even have prices on the menus!"

"Big deal. He's got money, and you can really judge a man in that environment…"

"I don't know…"

"If you don't call him I will, Annie. Get out and relax…"

"But I don't have anything to wear! Jeans, but…"

"So we'll go shopping tonight. With all the money you made in overtime, we can really *shop*!"

"What about my hair?"

"I know just what to do with it. Now get home, get some sleep – call the lawyer first, and then meet me at the mall at five."

"I don't know…"

"Ooh! Annie!!"

"Okay, okay… The mall at five."

"Call the lawyer first…"

"His name is Tyler Howe, and I will."

"You'd better!"

Annie smiled at her friend and went to her car.

"Mr. Howe? Tyler? It's Annie Benton…"

"Annie! I about gave up on you! You haven't been down with this nasty flu, have you?"

"In a way. I've been filling in for people at work who are down with it. I'm sorry I didn't call you back sooner…"

"As long as you called. I hope this call is to say 'yes you'll have dinner with me'."

"I… uh, yes…"

"Wonderful! Uh, when are you free?"

"T… tomorrow?"

"How about Friday?"

"Friday's fine…"

"Great! Did you have any place special that you'd like to go to, Annie?"

"No… Any place is fine."

"Then we'll do it right. The Reef at eight… Is that all right with you?"

"The… The Reef?" *Oh jeez, what were the odds of that?*

"Not all right? We could go…"

"No! I mean, that's fine, Tyler. But don't you need to make reservations weeks in advance?"

"Usually yes, but I was dining there with a client and his wife anyway – strictly social though, and now I can show up, proud to have you on my arm. Uh, I hope that doesn't offend…"

"Not at all, Tyler." *Oh goody… Dinner with some stuffy old rich couple… Oh well.*

"And after dinner we can go somewhere for a drink, just the two of us. I promise to remain a gentleman, Miss Benton."

"I would expect nothing less from you, Mr. Howe," Annie laughed. "Friday at eight?"

"I'll pick you up at seven-thirty. Until then…"

"Good bye, Tyler."

"Bye, Annie."

She hung up the phone and practically floated to bed. Wow… Dinner at the most exclusive restaurant in town, and with a rich, handsome man to boot! Things were definitely looking up. Too bad power, money, and looks meant nothing to her if love wasn't involved. She knew there would be nothing more than a casual friendship with Tyler. He just wasn't the one.

Just before Annie drifted off, a pair of intense, dark blue eyes flashed in her mind. She smiled at the familiar, yet far too infrequent vision, and went to sleep.

"Deirdre, the boys will be fine with Jen; it's not like she's never taken care of a baby before!"

"I know, Geoffrey, but I just hate leaving them…"

"It's only for a few hours; dinner and then home. Wouldn't you like to go out for a while?"

"Yes, but…"

"They'll be fine. Besides, you deserve a night out. You work so hard around here taking care of all of us… Quite frankly, I don't know how you do it. God, just keeping up with all of *my* messes is a full-time job!"

"Oh, you're not that bad, Geoffrey. You've finally managed to throw your clothes in the direction of the hamper," Deirdre laughed.

"An accomplishment to be proud of," he answered dryly. "I'll never figure out why I can't pick up after myself. I never could. My poor mother!"

"You have more important matters to tend to than socks on the floor or an ice cream dish left on the table, Geoffrey."

"No excuse. How about if I hire someone to help you out, Dee?"

"Absolutely not. It's an unnecessary expense." "What? I can afford it…"

She raised an eyebrow at him.

"Well I can!"

"Geoffrey, it's not necessary. I love what I do around here. At the risk of admitting to eavesdropping, I happened to hear your distressing conversation with your accountant the other day."

"You did? Aw God…"

"Geoffrey, you're welcome to my money…"

"Absolutely not! I'm not broke yet. That money is yours; I refuse to touch it."

"That's silly…"

"Call it what you will, but I won't touch it. We decided to use it for the twins' future."

"Not all of it, Geoffrey. I still have quite a bit in my account."

"And it's going to stay there, Deirdre. I still have a few million left…

provided another company I've invested in doesn't close its doors. But enough of this sorry conversation. Do you want to go out Friday or not?"

"I'm assuming it's not T.J.'s?"

"Far from it. This reminds me… Your wardrobe is sadly lacking, love. Why don't you go shopping today? I'll watch the boys."

"What about the studio, Geoffrey? I thought you had an important meeting today."

"Not anymore, Dee. That was Ray on the phone earlier, telling me they cancelled. We lost another client."

"Oh, Geoffrey… I'm so sorry! That's three this week, isn't it?"

"Four, but who's counting? I just can't understand it either! Sure we're a relatively new company with an even newer record label, but we do a damn good job producing. I don't know… It's hard to compete with the big guys. I need to expand into video, but the funds just aren't there."

"What about a loan?"

"No way. I've never so much as borrowed a dime in my life and I'm not about to start now. I'll lay off some staff, talk to Kyle, and spend more of my time hustling up some new business instead of sitting back and assuming it will come to us. I've let it go for far too long. Steve's been gone for well over a year and… and it's time I let go and get on with my life, Dee."

"Geoffrey…"

"Are you going shopping or not? You'll need something elegant… expensive."

"Just where did you plan on going?"

"The Reef. You've heard of it, right?"

"Of course! That's where we're going? Oh my…"

"Mmhmm. Tyler Howe – you remember Ty? He's the one who set up the trust fund for James and Jeremy…"

Deirdre nodded.

"Anyway, Ty and I have been friends ever since I moved here. We run together once in a while, and used to get together once a month for drinks and poker. We made plans weeks ago for dinner, but at first it was just the two of us. I thought it was time you got out, and he said he might bring a date too."

"Might?"

"He's been after some nurse for a few weeks now, but all she ever does is work. So… If she can get time off, he's got a date. If not…"

"The poor man! Shame on her for keeping him up in the air like that! He's quite a catch, Geoffrey…"

"Oh? Are you interested?"

"Don't be silly. I have everything I need right here, Geoffrey dear."

"Not everything, Dee," he sighed.

She gave him a hug and a kiss. "Everything, Geoffrey."

He wished it were true.

Chapter Six

"Annie-bananie, if he doesn't propose to you the second he sees you, he's insane! I can hardly believe it's you!" Marti sighed, adding just a hint more blush to her friend's already glowing cheeks.

Annie stood up and finally dared to take a look at herself in the mirror."

"Oh my…" she whispered, staring at the stranger staring back at her.

Marti was indeed a miracle worker. She had chosen a long, wool-blend dress in a shade of deep, forest green, and topped it off with a matching jacket – at Annie's insistence, saying that a little too much shoulder and cleavage were visible in just the dress. Marti pooh-poohed her and hauled her off to the jeweler's. There she picked out a gold necklace with an emerald pendant, saying that it matched Annie's eyes exactly.

"Marti, I can't afford emeralds!" Annie cried when her friend wanted to look at some matching earrings.

"They're fake, Annie, but they're still gorgeous!"

Annie had to agree, and now seeing the package all together… Wow!

Her hair, which she had wanted to cut, looked incredible. Marti had piled it high on her head, letting a few tendrils escape here and there to frame her face. A little eye shadow, mascara, and lipstick… and Annie felt almost pretty for the first time in her life.

"You look fantastic, Annie; just one thing missing."

"Huh? What? Are my shoes wrong?"

"No, your wardrobe is perfect. I was talking about a smile, hon. Think you can dredge one up?"

"A… a smile? I don't know… I'm so nervous!"

"Oh for God's sake, Cinderella! You're going out to dinner with some guy you've known for years!"

"But Marti, it's a date! And to the Reef!"

"You'll fit right in, and if you don't have every guy there drooling over you, it's only because they're gay. And then you just might change their mind!"

"Marti!"

"Well, it's true. You wouldn't believe how jealous I am of you, Annie."

"You're kidding. Why? Because of Tyler?"

"No… Well, not too much, but… Annie, look at yourself."

"Yeah, and…"

"Lord… If you can't see it, never mind. Well, I'm gonna scoot before lover boy gets here. I'll be at Bouncer's Bar if you get bored later. Maybe I'll find someone," she sighed.

"Thanks for everything, Marti. I'll call you tomorrow and let you know how it went."

"You'd better," she said, making a few adjustments to her friend's already perfect hair. "You look beautiful, Annie. Have a good time."

Annie walked Marti to the door, wondering how she could possibly be jealous. Jeez, Marti was a perfect size six, could easily be a swimsuit model, had beautiful large, blue eyes, and silky brunette hair. Her outlook on life was forever optimistic, and she lived for fun.

Annie, on the other hand…

She looked back into the mirror. Short, almost stocky, hips a little too wide and her breasts almost a little too full. Her thick mass of multi-colored curls seemed to have a will of their own, already escaping from the pins holding them captive. And her face… True, her eyes were striking and she been told quite often that she has a sweet smile, but beautiful? No way.

Oh well. It was just a silly date… at a very expensive restaurant.

Oh God, what if she used the wrong fork or requested the wrong wine with her dinner? Was it red with beef and white with fish? Oh Lord… what if she wanted a beer instead? Did they even serve such a common beverage there?

A beer… now that sounded wonderful. A nice, cold beer and a big bowl of popcorn… flannel 'jammies' and an old movie. She was so tempted to call and cancel until a knock on the door interrupted her from her cozy little fantasy.

Darn it.

"Annie Benton, is that you?" Tyler gasped, truly in awe of the vision before him.

"I'm not sure, Tyler. I sure don't feel like me. Jeans or scrubs are more my style."

"Whoo! I'm glad Evans went and got himself a wife or I wouldn't stand a snowball's chance in hell with you tonight! I'm still half tempted to take you someplace else so he doesn't see you and divorce his wife on the spot," Tyler joked.

"Evans?"

"My client. He can be a little… overbearing, so don't let him get too you. He's much tamer when his wife is around though, so he might not be so bad. His wife's a dear. She's from England, and still has a bit of that charming accent. She might seem a little hoity-toity at first, but she's very sweet. A true lady. And young! Just turned twenty-one…"

Annie nodded blankly, not hearing much of what he said in her fear at meeting some overbearing old man and his hoity-toity child bride.

"Are you ready?"

"Mmhmm. Let me get my purse."

Tyler very much enjoyed watching her walk away, and liked it even better when she came back towards him. God, what a dress! He almost hated helping her into her jacket.

"Another glass of wine, Annie?"

"I'd better not until after we eat."

"True... I just can't understand why he's late! He's a stickler for punctuality."

"Maybe he got a flat tire or something and is waiting for road service."

"That's a laugh. More likely he saw someone with a flat and stopped to change it for them. But don't tell him I said that," Tyler laughed. "He seems to think he has this 'bad boy-tough guy' reputation, when in reality he'd give you the shirt off his back."

"Overbearing yet generous. I can't wait to meet him. So who is this enigma, Tyler?"

"You're going to just die when I tell you. Actually, he's quite famous! Was anyway... he dropped out of the spotlight a few years ago. His name is Ga..."

"Excuse me, Mr. Howe?"

Tyler turned to look at the waiter.

"Yes?"

"You have a phone call, sir."

"Thank you. Excuse me, Annie."

She smiled and hoped it was "Mr. Celebrity" calling to tell them he couldn't make it. She was nervous enough with all the high-class people dining around her. At least she hadn't knocked her water glass over yet.

"Gabe? What the hell are you doing out here? Go sit, and I'll be right with you; I have to take a call."

"I'm the call, Ty. I'm sorry I'm late, but Deirdre wasn't feeling well. She insisted I come anyway and now that I'm here... Well, I think I should go home. I'm afraid she's got that goddamn flu bug and shouldn't be by herself. My apologies."

"That's okay, man. You get on home and take care of her."

Gabe nodded and shook his friend's hand. "Hey, Ty, did you ever hook up with that nurse?" he grinned.

"Oh God yes! Do you want to meet her? It will only take a minute."

"Another time, Ty. Deirdre..."

"Sure, Gabe. Well, have a good night."

"You too..." Gabe trailed off when a bouquet of flowers on the sideboard in the lobby captured his eye. He plucked a white rose from it and handed it to Tyler.

"Give this to her along with my apologies, Ty," he grinned. "Later, man."

Tyler smiled back and nodded, and returned to Annie.

"I'm sorry, Annie, but he couldn't make it after all. That was him in the lobby. He said to give you this along with his apology..." He handed her the flower.

Annie took it, smiling at the thoughtfulness of the mystery guest, but nearly dropped it as soon it hit her fingers. *Oh jeez...*

"Annie?"

"I... I'm all right. Just a thorn..." But it wasn't a thorn at all. The instant she touched the stem, she felt an incredible sensation shoot up her arm and nearly explode in her heart. She felt just a little bit dizzy, and there was a flash of a… a face? No, just eyes… Intense, dark blue eyes.

"Are you sure? You look a little pale."

"Just hungry, Tyler. May we order now?"

"Uh… sure." He picked up his menu and wondered why she just sat there staring at that stupid rose. Tyler was very glad that Evans hadn't joined them after all.

"Geoffrey, that was a short dinner."

"I didn't go, Deirdre; I couldn't leave you here alone."

"As much as I'd like to argue and send you back to The Reef, I just don't feel well enough, Geoffrey dear. And thank you."

"Can I get you anything, Dee?"

"Some tea, perhaps?"

Gabe nodded and went to the kitchen, regretting like hell that he didn't meet Ty's date. But why? Why did he feel like he'd just missed out on the most important thing in his life?

He filled the kettle, put it on the stove, and grabbed one of Dee's delicate cups from the cupboard.

What was with that goddamn rose? He couldn't have cared less that he missed dinner with Tyler, felt like he was coming down with the flu himself, but to apologize to someone he'd never met? Probably wouldn't have met if not for Ty's hasty date?

Nuts.

Just fucking nuts.

Gabe pulled out the box of tea bags, staring at the green writing and the red rose…

Green eyes and a white rose…

Hot tea on a cold autumn night…

Autumn hair and a rose of white…

He felt like crap, but in a few minutes he'd be sitting on sofa with his wife…

His wife, but not his life…

"Geoffrey dear?"

"Yeah?"

"The kettle is whistling… Are you alright in there?"

"Yeah, I'll be right out."

"Annie, I had a wonderful time. I… I'd like to take you out again."

"I had a good time too, Tyler."

"And…?"

"And?"

"Can we go out again?"

"I... Sure, why not?"

"You don't sound too sure. No spark, huh?"

"Spark?"

"Between us. On your part anyway..."

"I'm sorry, Tyler. I've had a heck of a long week, and I'm a little more tired than I thought."

"I understand," he sighed.

She wasn't getting away all that easily. If nothing else, he was going to at least get a kiss goodnight.

Tyler walked her to her door, and gently turned her around to face him. "Annie, I really did enjoy our time together tonight. Thank you." He lifted her chin and gave her lips a soft kiss. *Oh God... Spark quickly escalated to flame, and then to an all-out explosion!* Tyler moaned a little and pulled her closer... kissed her harder.

Annie tolerated it for just that long, and broke it off. *He wasn't the one...*

Tyler knew it. Goddammit and he was already halfway in love with her. But he wouldn't force the issue, and dropped a light kiss onto her forehead. "Goodnight, Annie," he said with a sad smile.

"Goodnight, Tyler," she answered, "and thank you again."

She escaped into her house and ran straight to the bedroom. She dumped her purse on the bed and picked up the slightly crushed rose she had been thinking about all night. The tingle enveloped her again, and tears formed in her eyes. What was it about that stupid flower that made her so sad?

So lost...

So alone.

~Part Two~
Discoveries

Chapter Seven

Annie woke up the morning following her date feeling groggy and grumpy, very unlike her, and thought the best way to clear her head would be a ride in the country. She'd drive up to Hidden Lake; she hadn't been there since… jeez, since Gramma died! Too bad she hadn't had the time to check out the safe deposit box and find out exactly where her acre or two was.

Just in case - by some miracle – the bank was open, she stuck the key in her pocket and went out of her way a bit to check.

Oh jeez, she couldn't believe it! Mr. Hilliard, the bank manager, was just locking the front door. Why he was there on a Saturday morning in the first place she'd never know, but it wouldn't hurt to ask if she could have ten minutes of his time. He'd always been very nice…

"Good morning, Mr. Hilliard!"

"Good morning, Annie! You're up early today… not quite noon, is it?"

"I had last night off. Are you working today?"

"No, just taking care of a special request for a friend. May I help you with something?"

"I hope so. Can you spare a few minutes?"

"Anything for you, Annie my dear."

"I was wondering when you would come in for this. Rather coincidental that you happened to drive by at just the right time. Let's go into my office and I'll get my keys.

Annie followed him in, and was immediately struck by the faint, lingering scent of a very nice, very masculine, very sexy cologne. Woodsy-spicy… Oh jeez… it made her head spin! She inhaled deeply, wondering where it came from.

Hilliard noticed, and smiled.

"Quite distinctive, isn't it?"

"Hmm? Oh…" She could feel herself blushing.

"My friend was in here not five minutes ago. He always leaves a little bit of himself behind. I'm sorry if it's too strong."

"No! Not strong at all… Very nice, actually. I can't place it though."

"Don't even try. It's something his wife had made special just for him."

"Wife," Annie murmured. *Figures…*

"Ah, here we go! Are you ready?"

Annie pulled out her key and gave him a nervous smile.

"I'll give you a few minutes alone, Annie. Come back to my office when you've finished. Oh, and feel free to take as much time as you need."

"Thank you, Mr. Hilliard. I won't be long.

She hesitated before opening the box, a little nervous at what she might find. Why the heck was that cologne still lingering in her mind? Not that she minded. Oh. to meet the man it belonged to…

Back on track, Annie girl…

The lid was removed, revealing a manila envelope with her name on it, and a thick stack of paperwork inside.

Annie pulled them out and found the deed to the property, a map, another envelope containing dozens of what looked like bonds and a note from her parents.

Oh God…

"Dearest Annie," she read, "We know how heartbroken you were when your grandmother died and we were forced to sell her house. It was not a decision easily made, but our financial situation at that time was grim, with no relief in sight. Unfortunately, Rosalind had neglected to pay her property taxes for several years before her death, and it was either sell the house or lose it to the state.

Now for the good news. We sold the house on a land contract, with the down payment taking care of the tax problem. The buyer failed to keep up the payments and the house was turned back over to us. Several months later it was struck by lightning in a storm, and burned. We used the insurance money on future taxes and to purchase more of the surrounding property.

Knowing how much you loved the place, we planned to give it to you as a wedding present. But quite frankly, we didn't care for your ex-husband and didn't want him getting his hands on it. So for all these years the property has been there waiting for you.

As stated before, we purchased additional acreage, including the lake to the southwest of where the house stood. It is quite a sizable piece of real estate. We felt certain that this would mean more to you than anything else we could leave you.

Take care, dearest daughter, we love you so."

Annie didn't even try to fight back the tears as she read of her inheritance. Her parents had known her better than she had thought. They *did* understand!

The lake property? Wow…

She quickly scanned the deed, not quite believing how the modest little estate of her grandparents had grown over the years. It now totaled thousands of acres, including rolling meadow, woods, and the lake. Pretty much the whole west side of Hidden Lake Road for five miles!

Annie was familiar with the area out there, and it was the nearest thing to Paradise that she could imagine. She wondered how much it had changed. After fifteen years, she wondered if she could still find the gardens.

"Mr. Hilliard? I… I'm finished."

"Pleasantly surprised, were you? He asked, smiling.

"Oh yeah! Gosh, I can't believe it!"

"I can well imagine. You're quite a wealthy young lady now, my dear."

"Oh no… I don't plan to sell. That property means so much to me…"

"Sell? Oh no, I was referring to the bonds…"

"Bonds?"

"Yes. Quite a number of them, purchased right here. They are in there, aren't they?"

"Oh gosh, the envelope! I'd forgotten all about it!"

Annie dug around in the larger package, looking for the smaller one, and handed it to Hilliard when she found it.

"I didn't really look inside," she murmured.

"Then you'd better sit while I do," he grinned.

Her eyes grew large as he totaled them up.

"…One hundred thousand…"

"One… one hundred? Oh God…"

"Would you like me to check again, Annie?"

"Uh… no! I mean, I just can't believe it! Where on earth did they ever get the money?"

"When your father returned to work after that prolonged lay-off, he came to me and asked how he could protect his finances so that he'd never have the fear of being nearly penniless again. We did some research, made some incredibly lucky investments, and rolled those profits into some even better ones. Bob never touched a penny of that money except to reinvest in anything long term, low risk, and high yield, hence this little cache of savings bonds. He did it all for you, Annie."

"Oh my…"

All this time she had thought him a little on the cheap side, pinching pennies for years and then using their savings to travel on. Not that she begrudged them that, but… she still felt awful.

"Annie, don't. Enjoy it! Take a vacation; buy something silly and expensive… Your parents would want you to."

"I… I have to let it sink in first, Mr. Hilliard. Oh jeez, I think I'd better put it back in the box though. I'd sure hate to lose it!"

"Wise decision, Annie. May I take an heiress to lunch?"

"Huh? I uh… thank you, but no. I have plans…"

"Heading out to look at your new kingdom?" he grinned.

She blushed and nodded.

"You couldn't have picked a better day for it. My goodness, can you believe this weather? I think it might hit close to sixty degrees today."

"Feels like spring, that's for sure. Well, I should be going. Mr. Hilliard, thank you so much for taking time to… to let me…"

"No thanks necessary, Annie. If anyone deserves thanks, it should be Evans. Crazy fool… Wakes up at four in the morning with an idea, calls me at seven, and then bribes me with breakfast turned business. If it hadn't been for him, it would be Monday before you could use your key there, and you'd be looking at your new land under a foot of snow. That's what they're predicting…"

"I know. Well, thanks again."

They shook hands, and Annie headed for the car.

Just where the heck did she hear that name before? *Evans…*

Annie turned down Hidden Lake Road, hoping her memory wouldn't fail her as far as where Gramma's house had been.

She overshot the overgrown driveway by a half mile before she realized none of that particular area was even vaguely familiar, and turned her car around.

There it was, weed-choked and forlorn. She pulled into it as far as she could, sadder than sad at how this once beautiful yard was nothing but a veritable forest now.

She sighed, grabbed her tote bag, and went to see if any of the gardens remained.

Annie's hopes of possibly building a new house where the old one had been were soon dashed as she wandered around the perimeter of the crumbling foundation, and looked at the trees that had taken root in what was once the kitchen and living room. Jeez, most of them were over fifteen feet tall. So much for building there…

What of the gardens? She steeled herself at what she might find, and fought her way through the miniature jungle.

A broken piece of garden gate poked up through the thick, dead foliage, and Annie was relieved to know she was on the right track; for a moment she had feared she was lost. She stepped over it and moved deeper into the brush.

"Oh wow," she murmured, finding the marble table and matching stone benches where she and Gramma had spent many pleasant hours chatting. Although covered in fallen branches and dead leaves, the furniture was in surprisingly good condition. Annie brushed the debris from a bench and sat down to look around.

Nothing remained of the beautiful gardens.

"I'm so sorry, Gramma," she whispered, "All the love and energy you put into this place and it's all gone."

Annie leaned back against the table and closed her eyes, raising her face to the sun. She felt its heat and smiled a little; it had been way too long since she'd been able to enjoy the outdoors. A breeze caressed her face and a familiar scent brought her to her feet.

It can't be…

She looked around again. To her left, through the trees, she noticed what appeared to be a clearing. She moved towards it. The aroma became stronger.

Roses.

She pushed past a thick clump of brush and couldn't believe what she saw. In the center of the clearing were several magnificent rose bushes full of white blooms.

"How on earth could they have survived all these years?" she said aloud, amazed that they were still blooming this late into the fall, even if there hadn't been a hard frost yet.

Annie circled the bushes, which were easily four feet high and just as big around. The flowers were larger than her fist.

"My God..." she whispered in awe.

She leaned closer to inspect the eerie discovery. The plants had been carefully pruned to promote lush growth; the soil beneath them had been mulched, and appeared to have been recently watered.

Annie reached out to touch a flower and felt an odd, yet strangely familiar tingling in her fingertips. She withdrew her hand and closed her eyes as an image came to mind. It was of a man she had never seen before, at least not that she could place, but he seemed so familiar. He had black hair, intense, deep blue eyes, and very white but not quite perfect teeth behind a lop-sided grin. He was wearing faded jeans and an old leather jacket, scuffed boots and a Stetson. His hand rose in the air as if reaching for her, and then he was gone.

"Holy crap!"

Annie's eyes flew open and she sank to the ground, stunned.

"What the heck was that?" she murmured. Jeez, she was pretty used to the flash of eyes that shot through her sleep-deprived mind every now and then, but this was so... so vivid! She could almost swear he was actually there!

She closed her eyes again, hoping, yet not really wanting, to recapture the image.

Nothing...

Her eyes opened again, and from her lower vantage point she could see where someone had cut flowers from the rose bushes. It looked like dozens had been harvested... all around the same time. The bushes were large enough to provide such a bounty, but that's not where Annie's thoughts were headed. This was where the roses from the memorial service for her parents had come from.

But how?

Who?

Why?

Despite the heat of the sun beating down on her she felt a chill, and yet there was an odd sense of comfort too... like someone was watching over her. She thought that perhaps the spirit of her grandmother filled the clearing, but the more she thought about it, the more the presence seemed... masculine.

This was getting too weird. Annie wasn't one to believe in the supernatural, but she couldn't discount it either since several odd things had happened to her over the years for which she could find no explanation.

Okay, Annie, perhaps now would be a good time to check out the rest of the property...

She rose to her feet, staring at the roses, and felt compelled to touch them again... But didn't quite dare.

She backed away from the flowers.

Get a grip, Annie. They're not going to jump out and bite you in the butt if you turn around…

Yet she didn't, continuing to stare towards the flowers as she left. It was only when she reached the relative safety of the trees did she take her eyes from the giant white blooms and race for her car.

Annie drove down the road until she came to a very high hill, and stopped at the top. Before her lay fields of winter wheat on the right, and a rolling meadow leading to a lake on her left.

Hidden Lake, and it belonged to her.

Oh God, it was beautiful!

She put her car into gear and looked for a place to park so that she could explore.

At the bottom of the hill was a deer trail leading into the meadow and to the lake, and Annie followed it to the water's edge.

The lake was unbelievably clear. She could see pebbles at the bottom about ten feet from shore, where she estimated the depth to be about six feet. After that there was a drop off, with only the tops of aquatic plants visible. She smiled when a bass swam by, patrolling his territory. Too bad it was too chilly for her to jump in.

Mmm… What a glorious day it turned out to be. Annie kicked back against a nearby tree and surveyed this little bit of paradise.

It was like something out of a nature magazine. The meadow sloped gently to the small beach of the narrow, very deep, crescent-shaped lake. High hills surrounded the water on the entire east side and an occasional outcropping of rock could be seen through the thick trees. The deep blue of the cloudless sky reflected on the lake, and Annie's heart soared when a deer stepped from the brush across the water and bent down for a drink.

Perfect…

She turned her attention to the sloping meadow where a flat area interrupted the hill halfway up. Oh jeez, what a great place to build her home. She couldn't wait to get started on it.

Annie pulled a bottle of water from her tote bag and took a few sips, and then decided to do a little more exploring. The thought of what was around the corner of the beach intrigued her; a hike it was. She left the shoreline and entered the trees.

The walk was easy if one stayed near the water's edge, but to go deeper into the woods would require a bit of physical exertion given the steepness of the hills.

Annie came to another deer path leading from the lake and into the trees. She looked up the trail and felt an overwhelming curiosity to see what lay at the top of the hill. She took a deep breath and began her ascent.

It wasn't as difficult a climb as she had thought it would be. The trail wound through the trees, which offered a handhold to pull herself up, and five minutes later she had reached the top of the hill.

Annie pulled out her water bottle and nearly finished it off in several unladylike swallows as she turned to face the lake.

Unbelievable!

She could see darn near forever. Apparently this was the highest hill on the lake, and Annie could see over the treetops on the far side to the countryside beyond. What a great place to watch the sunset…

She also noticed that the trees in the area had been cleared and trimmed to provide the panoramic view. It appeared that even the grass, when it had been growing during the summer, had been trimmed.

Oh Lord… not another mystery clearing… One a day was plenty enough.

Annie tipped back her water bottle to catch the remaining sip, and something caught her eye. At first the object appeared to be a large, flat rock, but she felt the hair rise on the back of her neck when she moved closer to it. The rock was actually a marble bench, and one looking much like the ones in Gramma's garden.

Okay… cue the Twilight Zone music. Doot doot doo doo…

She wanted to turn and run back down the hill but couldn't get her legs to move. At least she didn't smell roses… yet. Annie realized that she didn't actually feel scared, but couldn't really describe how she felt. Confusion, intrigue, and a curious sense of anticipation were some of the words that ran through her mind.

She finally willed her legs to move over to the bench, and stared down at it. It was identical to the ones in the garden, right down to the intricate carvings on the legs. Her fingers reached out to trace the design, and once again she felt a tingle.

Her vision faded and the image of the black-haired cowboy formed in her mind's eye.

Apprehension, excitement, longing…

"Quite a piece of work, don't you think?"

Annie whirled around at the sound of a most pleasant male voice.

"Wha…?" She nearly screamed, but checked herself. As her vision cleared, she was very aware that she was looking at a flesh and blood model of the image she had just seen.

Almost, but not quite.

"The bench. Quite some craftsmanship… The carvings?"

"Uh… yes…"

Annie stared at the stranger. She thought she should be frightened, being all alone in the woods with him, but she couldn't dredge up even a drop of fear. Weird…

"Oh God… I'm sorry! You didn't know I was here, did you? I thought you had seen me already; you looked right at me." The man approached her with his hand outstretched. "I'm Michael. Michael Anthony."

His bright, serene smile reached his clear blue eyes.

Annie trusted him immediately.

"Annie. Annie Benton."

She accepted his handshake, the grip firm, confident, and gentle.

"I looked right at you? Where were you?" she asked him.

"I was on the other side of the clearing where the trail picks up. I was pretty surprised to see someone else up here, so I just stopped right where I was. You looked right at me," Michael explained.

He nodded towards the area he was referring to, and could see that the deep shade of a pine tree hid the entrance to the trail, a reasonable excuse for her not to have seen him.

Annie followed his gaze.

"Nope, didn't see you. So, have you been here before?"

"Yep. I come up here whenever I'm in town, so to speak. This place is at the end of nowhere, but I've been comin' up here since I was a kid. Back then it was to explore... have an adventure. Now it's to... to meditate," he told her.

"So you much know this area pretty well?"

"Every square inch."

"And maybe some of the history?"

"Depends on what you mean by history. I haven't found any dinosaur bones, but I did come across an arrowhead or two."

"No, that's not what I meant. Actually, I'm curious about the marble bench, and who cleared and maintains this area. It's almost like a park," Annie said as she walked to the bench and sat down.

Michael sat beside her.

"Ah," he said, tipping back his battered Stetson and giving her a smile. "Are you in the mood for a love story?"

"I'll bite..."

"Okay. Now this story is third hand. My grandmother told it to me many years ago, and me bein' a hopeless romantic... Well anyway, I was with her one day when I was a kid... oh, about twelve or thirteen or so, and I found this area while on one of my forbidden adventures. Grams was visiting her best friend at the time... Anyway, ten minutes of tea and female chatter was enough to try the patience of any young man so I took off. Ended up here. I told her about it later, although at the expense of possible punishment for wandering too far. She told me that her friend's husband had proposed to her on this very spot, and on their first anniversary brought her back up. He set up a picnic... flowers, candles, the works... And every year after that they would come her for their anniversary. There used to be a table up here, but he had it brought back down to the house after they were too old to make the trip, and they continued the tradition there. I guess he was some kind of gardener... Grew all kinds of flowers."

Annie stared at him, her eyes blurred by tears.

"What... Was the story that bad," Michael joked, wiping away a salty drop that escaped down her cheek. "Bored to tears, were you?"

"No, it was a great story. It's just that I think you were describing my grandparents. I never met my grandfather, but Gramma talked about him quite a bit. And he was a magnificent gardener... The table and the benches that match this one are still in Gramma's garden, or what's left of it."

"Well what do you know..." Michael took Annie's hands into his, and brought them to his lips for a soft kiss.

"Happy tears or sad tears?" he asked, wiping away another trickle of emotion from her beautiful face.

"A little of both, I guess. I... I miss my grandmother. She died when I was thirteen... We were very close."

"Mmhmm. Mine passed when I was a little older. It was the first time in my life I had to deal with death. Didn't much care for it... Didn't much like it the second time either," Michael sighed.

Annie could only nod her agreement, thinking of her parents.

"Well Miss Benton, I hate to cut this short, but the sun will be settin' soon and it gets dark pretty fast up here. May I escort you to uh... Just how did you get here?"

"I drove. To the meadow, anyway... My car is parked on the road. And no thanks, I can get back by myself."

"Perhaps we'll meet again." Michael said, giving her his serene smile.

"I hope so. Uh, I mean... Well, since this is my property I intend on spending a lot of time at the lake. I... I hope to build my home there soon," she said, blushing again.

"I'll look forward to it."

"Oh, do you happen to know who maintained this area so well? They've done a great job of preserving the natural state of the land, yet allow for this great view!"

"Yours truly," Michael confessed.

"But why? From what I gathered, you live out of town."

"Honestly? I'm not too sure. It's a beautiful spot to unwind in, and I've never forgotten the story Grams told me. Just uh...preserving a bit of the past maybe?"

Annie remained silent, thinking.

"Do you want me to stop? I mean, I don't want to be trespassin' or anything."

"No, go ahead. I like the way it looks, and I'm sure my grandparents would have approved. Far be it from me to take this little slice of Heaven away from you," she laughed.

"Yeah... It's about as close to Heaven as I've been able to get so far," he mumbled. "And don't worry, Annie, I won't ever intrude on your privacy unless I'm invited."

He gave her hand a squeeze.

She returned the gesture.

"Michael, you have a standing invitation."

He stood and gave her a bow, swinging his hat low before him.

"Until we meet again, Miss Benton…"

She blinked, and he was gone.

"Geoffrey, where have you been? I thought you'd be home hours ago."

"I'm sorry, Deirdre, but I… I needed to think, and I took a long drive. I should have called…"

"What's troubling you, Geoffrey dear? The studio…?"

"Partially. I… I met with Hilliard for a pre-approval in case I… oh God, in case I need a loan."

"Oh, Geoffrey…"

"Just a precaution, Dee. I had some other business to talk with him about too, and then my curse of a brain kicked into overdrive and I needed to get away for a few."

"Well, I won't pry, Geoffrey. You'll tell me if you feel I should know. Are you ready for dinner?"

"Huh? Oh, yeah… Smells good. Are the boys awake?"

"Just. I was on my way upstairs for diaper changes when you came in."

"I'll do it, Dee. You go relax for a minute, and I'll bring them down when they're no longer smelly," he told her. Even managed to dredge up a lop-sided grin, not that it would fool her. She knew him too goddamn well.

Deirdre stood on her tiptoes so that she could plant a kiss on his chin, and then went into the kitchen.

Gabe ran up the stairs two at a time, eager to see his… his sons.

His sons… Now five months old and cuter than any babies he'd ever seen in his life. He pulled them from their cribs and gave them each a hug and a kiss before he started the diaper changes, and then afterward sat in the rocking chair. With a twin in each arm, he sang them a fun little song.

The babies cooed and giggled, and patted Papa's hands for more when the tune was over.

"Not now, gentleman," Gabe laughed. "Your mother has dinner practically on the table. Speaking of your mother, you didn't spill the beans about her Christmas gift, did you?"

Jeremy blew spit bubbles; James merely drooled.

"Good. We leave the first week of December and will arrive back home on January fifth. You'll love Montana, munchkins, and you'll finally get to meet your grandparents. Kyle won't be very happy about me being gone so long, but he'll just have to deal with it.

"Kyle… Guys, he's in trouble again. He doesn't know I know, but I found out… And I cannot for the life of me understand how he manages to spend so damn much money! His credit cards are maxed out again, he's all but overdrawn on his checking account, his savings… who the hell knows, and yet he continues to spend as if the money will never end! Well, it's ended. The studio has been in the red for months now… just as we saw black, and our album sales had dropped off to non-existent. God, I've been paying everyone's wages – including Kyle and Jen's, out of my own pocket, and I just don't know what the hell to do! That's why I saw Hilliard this morning. I transferred thirty grand to Kyle's account – again. He's so dense when it comes to money he won't even notice. I've also arranged it so that your most wonderful mother *won't* be using her money to help me out. And don't fret, young ones, your trust funds are more than safe. But Christ, I can't have Dee using her money to bail my ass out. I have a horrible feeling she'll need that someday, and I want it to be available to her.

"Maybe Kyle and I should tour again… do a few concerts for some quick cash. We're still in demand you know… Not everyone has forgotten your Papa was a huge star. Christ, I blew that too. Had to quit before I killed myself with drugs… And now… now that your daddy isn't here to save my ass from myself, I don't know if I dare get back into it. The touring that is, not the drugs. I have to do something though… Maybe I should hire someone to manage our money for us instead of trying to do it all myself. I really screwed up in the last quarter's taxes… Christ, misplace on little decimal point and bam! The IRS comes down on you like…"

"Geoffrey, dinner!"

"Be right there, Dee."

The twins squirmed to the floor when they heard their mother's voice, and attempted to crawl to the door.

"Aw God," Gabe laughed, watching as the boys as they rocked back and forth on pudgy hands and knees. "I get the message. No more of Papa's whining gloom and doom…"

He picked up his children, kissed them, and then put on his little happy face before he went downstairs – even if it wouldn't fool Deirdre a bit.

✦ ✦ ✦

"Gabe buddy! Miss me?"

"Only about as much as inserting my hand into the cold, dead flesh of the Thanksgiving turkey's rectum to remove the package of giblets. What's up?"

"Christ, thanks for that visual! Just wanted to know if you wanna go out for a beer. It's been forever…"

"I know, and I'm sorry. And yes I do… I need to talk to you."

"Uh oh… That don't sound good, man."

"Yes and no. Where would you like to go?"

"I dunno… Bouncer's?"

"Too 'trendy'. How about Olde Country Brew Pub. We can sample each and every one of their home brews…"

"Jesus, Gabe, they make ten kinds of beer there!"

"Then we'll sample each one twice. My treat."

"Oh God, you do have bad news!"

"Not bad, Kyle… And I'll meet you there in an hour."

"Uh… yeah. Later, dude."

"Two beers, eight to go, man," Kyle sighed, reaching for his third. "And you still haven't dumped on me…"

"I wanted you happy first. Are you happy, Kyle?"

"I'm *always* happy, Gabe! You ever see me not happy?"

"Once or twice."

"Fuck you. You're the moody one…"

"Won't deny that, but anyway… Kyle, I'm going to be gone for a while…"

"Aw God… Gabe, no! You can't leave Dee and the kids!"

"No, Kyle, they're coming with me. We're spending the holidays with my parents."

"Oh. Well that's cool I guess. God, they haven't even seen James and Jer yet, have they"

"Only in the weekly pictures I mail to them. They need to get to know Deirdre too. Their last meeting wasn't too… warm I guess I could say. God, they wouldn't even speak to her at Steve's funeral."

"Pretty cold, man…"

"Although, I was beyond rude to her, too. God, Steve loved her over all other women, and for that fact alone I should have treated her with a little more respect. And Kyle, she's so… so…"

"Perfect?"

"Exactly, and I'm sure that once Mom and Pop get to know her, they'll love her as much as I do."

"And me."

"Oh?"

"Well, you know…"

"Kyle, you're blushing!" Gabe laughed, and smacked his buddy upside the head. "I'm telling Jen you have the hots for my wife!"

"I do not!"

"Do too."

"Do not."

"Do too… And lust away, buddy! Although she wouldn't have any more to do with you than she does with… Oh, never mind."

"Dude, I never thought of her that way! God! That just ain't right, man…"

"How so? She is beautiful, Kyle…"

"Too beautiful. Jen is too, but in a different way. I don't know… Deirdre reminds me of the Madonna or something… Holy… Look and love but don't think dirty thoughts," Kyle said quietly, and with just a hint of reverence.

"Mmm. I guess it's fitting that Saint Steve would hook up with Saint Deirdre then… Subject change. Back to the original, actually. Kyle, I'm leaving the first of December and won't be back until after the first of the year. I'm shutting down the studio during that time and…"

"But Gabe! What about Christmas? They can't go without a paycheck that long!"

"They won't miss so much as a nickel, Kyle, and I'm throwing in some bonuses."

"We can do that? I thought we were in the red again."

"I will be doing it, not SD Productions. *My* dime, Kyle."

"Then I wanna help too. We can split… fifty-fifty."

"Good enough. Pay me when I get back."

"Remind me…"

"I will." *As if…* It would be Gabe's own cash he was being repaid with anyway.

"Gabe, do you have to be gone for so long?"

"I do, Kyle. Ever since I left home I've been going back for the holidays, and I should carry on the tradition. God, it's going to be so hard without Steve, but I think the best present I could give my parents is their grandchildren. They look so much like him…"

"You too. They look just like you, buddy…"

Gabe nodded and excused himself to go to the restroom. Wouldn't do for Kyle to see him break down, and he was on the verge of it.

Kyle was glad his friend left for a minute. He missed Steve as much as Gabe did, and didn't want tough ol' Evans to see the tears in his eye

Chapter Eight

Annie looked around her new apartment and smiled. It was small, but she didn't have all that much anyway.

"This furniture sucks, Annie! Why did you move in this dump anyway? God, who knows what's living in this sofa?" Marti groaned, kicking the piece of furniture in question. She looked to see if any vermin would scatter after having their home disturbed.

"It's clean! I'll buy all my own things after my cabin is built. I moved in here because it's cheap and temporary."

"Cheap? You're rich, Annie!"

"Hardly. Most of that money is for my retirement. I don't want to have to worry…"

"That's years away. You should have married that lawyer and retired early."

"I don't think so. Tyler's nice, but not the one for me."

"Can I have him then?" Marti laughed.

"Go for it."

"I will when you're finished with him. Annie, why are you still dating him if you know there's no future?"

"Because he's fun. We're friends and talk about everything… and we both need this in our life right now even if it never goes any further. He's fully aware of how I feel about him, so don't think I'm leading him on…"

"As if you were capable of subterfuge…"

Annie gave her a little smile and blushed.

"He's fun… Annie, are you *sleeping* with him?"

"Not *that* kind of fun! Jeez…"

"He's no good in bed?"

"I wouldn't know. And before you ask, he's only kissed me a few times."

"You need a life, girlfriend…"

"I have one!"

"Yeah right. Work and sleep and a date every now and then…"

"But I'm happy, Marti."

"Are you?"

"Let's toast my new apartment," Annie answered, evading the issue.

Marti didn't push it, and grabbed two beers from the grocery bag by the door.

"Well, what are your Christmas plans, Annie?"

"I'm working. I don't have any family, so I might as well."

"Didn't Tyler invite you over? You spent Thanksgiving there…"

"He did, but I declined. I don't know… I just wasn't comfortable being the only non-family member in that mob. There were at least twenty people there.

Maybe if we were more than friends, but…"

"How about that Michael guy you met? Have you seen him anymore?"

"No. Jeez, with all the snow we've had, I don't dare hike up there on the off chance he'd even be there. I doubt I'll ever see him again."

"But you'd like to, right?"

"Mmhmm…" *Very, very much…*

"Well, let's decorate that branch you call a Christmas tree, and then I have to get home. My sister and I are heading for Midland to spend another dysfunctional week with the folks…"

"Oh come on. You're parents are great!"

"I know… but we're all pretty wacky. The neighbors think we're nuts."

"You are. Hand me those lights," Annie laughed, although she felt like crying. If only her parents were still around.

"Deirdre, don't cry! She didn't mean anything…"

"She… she hates me, Geoffrey! She still blames me for… for Steven's death. Oh God…"

Gabe sighed and wrapped his arms around his wife. Yeah, she was right, goddammit. Even after nearly a month, Marie was still cool towards Deirdre. That crack at dinner about the *proper* way to raise twins… God! He couldn't believe his wonderful mother could be such a… a bitch! He'd chalk it up to her missing Steve too much, but one more condescending or derogatory remark to Dee, and he was going to go off on her. Pop had better not say a word if it happened, either.

At least Al welcomed his new daughter-in-law with open arms, and both of the elder Evans' were thrilled to meet their much-anticipated grandchildren. If only Mom and Dee could hit it off…

"Geoffrey, what can I do to change her mind about me? Dear Lord, she still thinks I'm one of those… those cheap Hollywood actress wannabe types. Hinting that I starve myself to keep thin, and dye my hair… Oh Geoffrey…"

"Dee, she's just… well, she's spent pretty much her whole life in a small town, and only knows what she sees on television and reads in scandal rags. She's warm and loving and bright, but tends to stereotype when she shouldn't. God knows I hope she'll come around, but if she doesn't you'll still have me. Not that I'm any prize, but… but I do love you, Deirdre Evans, and nothing will ever change that." He emphasized his words with a tender kiss to her forehead. *God, why couldn't he really, truly love her?*

"Thank you, Geoffrey. Oh, I don't know what I'd do without you…"

"You won't ever have to find out. Um… a tip regarding mom… Family is the most important thing in the world to her, so just continue being the loving mother you already are to the twins. She can't fault you on that."

"She tried…"

"Unfounded innuendos. Those boys are the luckiest babies in the world to have you for a mother, Deirdre."

"Once again, thank you, Geoffrey."

"Now dry your tears, put on your little happy face, and get out there."

Gabe gently wiped away the moisture on her cheeks with his thumbs, and gave her a quick hug.

"Geoffrey dear?"

"Yes, Deirdre, love?"

"She… she knows we haven't been sleeping together. She asked me today what kind of wife drives her husband out of the bedroom… won't share a bed with him."

"Like it's any of her goddamn… Oh, sorry. Like it's any of her business. How'd she find out?"

"I think she caught you spending your nights in that apartment over the garage. It's so cold and drafty up there… The heater isn't even working!"

"I'm fine, Deirdre. It's not so bad."

"Geoffrey, there are two beds in your room… It's not like we're sharing a bed. Maybe if you spent the whole night in there she might change her mind about me a little."

"I think I can make the sacrifice. Aw God… I didn't even think! Deirdre, has if been difficult for you to stay in Steve's and my old room? All those pictures and everything…"

"Difficult, but I'm so glad I am, Geoffrey. He told me so much about his childhood, and now I get to see it."

"God, I miss him."

"So do I. But Geoffrey, could… could you stay with me?"

"I will. But separate beds, Dee…"

She smiled, and went to try and win over her mother-in-law one more time.

Annie sat in her lonely little apartment, sipping on her third beer since Marti left. Here it was, two days before Christmas, and life just sucked. No family, and her only real friend gone for the next week.

Some life, Annie…

She about jumped out of her skin when someone knocked on the door. *Marti…?* It had to be. No one else knew where she'd moved to, and she'd only been there for less than a day!

"Just a minute, Marti," she called out, setting her beer down.

She didn't even bother to check the peephole to see who was out there, but flung the door open wide.

"Merry Christmas, Miss Benton!"

"Michael? Oh my God…"

"Am I interruptin' anything? I'm sorry... It's late..."

"No! I mean, come on in! Oh jeez, I can't believe you're here! How'd you find me? I just moved in today, and you don't even know where I lived before!"

"A little angel told me," Michael grinned. "Merry Christmas..." He handed her a small package.

"Oh jeez... I don't know what to say. I don't... I didn't..."

"Annie, you're babblin'. Invite me in, hand me a beer, and open your gift," he laughed.

For an entire second she pondered the wisdom of inviting this virtual stranger into her home, but only for a second.

"Come in, Michael."

"Cozy place you have here."

"Meaning small, and it suits me just fine. All I have is Miller Lite..."

"I've had worse. It's cold, isn't it?"

"I hope so. I stuck them out on the balcony; my refrigerator is on vacation, I think."

"Perfect. Now open your gift."

Michael popped open the brew handed to him and took a long, satisfying swallow. It had been a long time since he'd enjoyed a cold beer. Way, way too long.

Annie looked at the package in her hands, totally confused. How on earth did he ever find her? Showing up just in the nick of time...

"It won't open itself, Annie."

She smiled and tore into the festive wrapping.

"Oh Michael, it's beautiful! Would this happen to be the little angel that told you where I live?" she asked, holding up the small, crystal prism complete with wings and a halo.

"I'll never tell."

"I love these," Annie sighed.

She held it to the light and gave it a quick spin. Colors flashed from the facets, shooting a rainbow around the room.

"Me too. I saw that and thought of you."

"Now really, how did you find me?"

"You wouldn't believe me if I told you, and to tell you something believable would be a lie. I never lie, Annie."

"Then I won't force you into a sin. Gosh, it's good to see you! I just can't believe it!"

"It's good to see you again too. So... What's new in your life?"

"Oh jeez... For you, everything! You don't know a thing about me, Michael."

"You'd be surprised."

"Well do tell..."

"Mmm... not now. But I do know that you needed some company tonight, so here I am. Correct?"

"Right on the money, Michael. So… Tell me about you. Jeez, it feels like I've known you forever… Now that sounds strange… but I do! And yet I know only your name…"

"Then I'll tell you a little more. I'm twenty-nine and holdin', was born and raised out west, hence my clothes here…"

Annie laughed. Yeah, he was a cowboy all right!

"I have a brother who lives in town, and I suffered through two years of college before I chucked it all and made a livin' chasin' cows."

"Oh wow… So you really are a cowboy?"

"All my life, ma'am," he drawled.

"And you have a… a horse?"

"Sure do, but uh… I don't do much ridin' lately. Not like I used to anyway. Injury…"

"Oh, I'm sorry. I love to ride, but I hardly ever do. A few hours at a riding stable a couple of times a year is all. What's your horse like?"

"Aw God," Michael laughed. "He's a big black cuss with a mind of his own. Lucky for me he usually agrees with what I want. There's been a few times…"

"I'd love to meet him… but uh, he probably lives out of town too?"

"Yep, although sometimes he travels with me."

"Are you here to spend the holidays with your brother?"

"Nope. I thought about it, but it seems he's on vacation. Came to see you if you want to know the truth."

"You… you did?" *Oh wow…*

"I did, Annie. Hope you don't mind…"

"Of course not! Um… don't you have other family though?"

"My parents and my brother and his family are all."

"No wife? Girlfriend?"

"Never been married, and… and my fiancé ended up marryin' someone else. Can't blame her though. He's a heck of a guy and I'm happy for her."

"That's kind of sad. Well, it looks like we're in the same boat, Michael. Um, do you have plans for Christmas?"

"Not yet. You?"

"No… Oh wait. Jeez, I have to work."

"All day?"

"All night. I work from seven to seven."

"Long night. How about tomorrow?"

"Nope. Day off."

"Want some company?"

"I… I was going to the midnight service at church…"

"Want some company?"

"Seriously?"

"I never lie, Annie."

"I'd love it. Um, does it matter which church?"

"Annie, God is God and he doesn't much care where you are when you talk to him. Million-dollar cathedral or a chapel of pine trees… It doesn't matter."

"I've often thought that, but others… It's all for show…"

"Mmhmm. Annie, I think we're gonna be good friends. What do you think?"

"I think you're right, Michael. And you never lie, do you?" she laughed.

"Never."

"Hungry?"

"Starvin'."

"Preference?"

"Can you cook?"

"Apparently… Do I look undernourished?"

"You look perfect."

"You're lying…"

"You're blushin'."

"You're horrible!"

"And you're stallin'. What's on the menu?"

"Oh jeez… Michael, I don't have any food in the house!"

"Phone hooked up?"

"Yes…"

"T.J.'s pizza?"

"Perfect."

"I like you, Annie Benton…"

"I like you too, Michael Anthony…"

She thought for a moment that he was going to kiss her, almost wanted him to, but after running a calloused finger under her jaw he leaned back into the sofa and picked up the phone.

She was just as relieved as she was disappointed.

"Geoffrey, please don't leave me alone with her!"

"You won't be alone; Dee; Pop and the twins will be here too. Besides, the ride is too long for the boys… not to mention the roads are crap."

"Must you go?"

"Yes, Deirdre. I haven't seen her in over a year, and she did ask me to come. I'll be home in plenty of time for midnight service."

"Well then, tell Danni I said hello."

"I will."

"Be careful driving, Geoffrey. I worry about you…"

"I'll be fine. But I'd better get going. It's a long way…"

Gabe kissed his parents, kissed and hugged his boys, and held Deirdre in his arms for a little longer than he usually did.

"You'll be fine, love," he whispered, and then kissed her good-bye.

"I'll never understand what he sees in that Danielle," Marie sighed, watching her son leave to pay a visit to his ex-lover. She glanced at Deirdre and said, "But there's no accountin' for taste."

"Marie…" Al growled, and hauled his wife into the living room.

Deirdre fled to Steven's childhood bedroom and collapsed into tears.

"Gabe Evans, you big creep! Get in here… It's freezing!"

Danni grabbed his jacket and yanked him into her home. Cal stood not far behind her, smiling gently.

"Hi, Gabe, how are you?"

"Fine, Cal, and you?"

"Not bad. How was the drive?"

"Shit from one end to the other, but I persevered. Where's Benny? I brought him a present."

"He's out sledding with his friends, Gabe," Danni answered. "He should be back any time."

"I hope so. I only have an hour or so, and I'd hate to miss him."

"He wants to see you too. Come on in and sit down. Can I get you something to drink?"

"Anything is fine, Danni."

"Uh… I have to make a phone call, Gabe. If you'll excuse me?"

"Sure, Cal."

Cal made his way out of the room after kissing Danni's forehead.

"He thought we should have a few minutes alone, Gabe."

"I figured that out, Danni. I'm not a fucking idiot, you know."

"And he knew we'd be fighting before we got three sentences out."

"He's so perceptive, ya bitch," Gabe grinned. "How've you been, Danni? You look great!"

"Fine, and you're just as magnificent as ever…"

"A compliment from you? Why Danni… I'm touched! C'mere and give me a kiss."

"In your dreams, creep."

But she did anyway.

"Mmm… You not only look great, you feel great too," Gabe murmured, holding her close. "Why was it we broke up again?"

"Oh for God's sake, Gabe!" Danni cried, shoving him away. "You know damn well why!"

"Oh yeah… Because I was such an asshole. Oh well… it worked out for the best," he grinned. "Cal's a great guy, and you've never been happier."

"Right on both counts, Gabe. And for you too… How is Deirdre?"

"Trying to overcome Mom's prejudices at the moment. Otherwise she's fine."

"Are… are you happy, Gabe? You look a little down…"

"I'm as happy as I can possibly be, Danni. Deirdre is a perfect wife…"

"But she's not the one, is she?"

"Of course she is! A man couldn't ask for better! She's beautiful, bright, loving, a great mother…"

"Gabe, you can't lie to me and you sure as hell can't lie to yourself. You're still looking for her, aren't you?"

"*Who* her, Danni?" he sighed in exasperation.

"You know… The reason you could never truly love me. God, you used to say her name in your sleep every night. I hated her and I didn't know if she even existed!"

"Danni, drop it. It was just some stupid fantasy that I… that I've outgrown. I'm happily married, not to mention a father by default, and…"

"Can't lie to yourself, Gabe. Oh! Ben's home; come and say 'hi'."

"Ben, you remember Mr. Evans?" Danni smiled softly as her son came in from the other room.

"I sure do!"

"Hey, Benny… and none of that 'Mr. Evans' crap. Call me Gabe. God, you're getting huge! How old are you now?"

"Ten, sir."

"And polite! Must take after your father's side of the family. Your mom's never been that nice to me," Gabe teased. *Whoever the hell the kid's ol' man was…*

He knew for a fact it wasn't Danni's first husband, and she refused to say any more than that. Gabe would still bet his last buck that it was Steve, though. Christ, the kid looked just like him! Stevie always denied it, but often said he wished Ben was indeed his son.

"I brought you a present, Benny. Do you like music?"

"Yes sir!"

"Great. Then annoy the hell out of your mother with this…" Gabe pulled a large box from where he'd stashed it behind a chair, and handed it to Ben.

"Wow…" Ben sighed, his intense blue eyes shining. "That's for me?"

"Yep, and every time you play it, remind your mom where it came from," Gabe laughed. "It will give her one more thing to hate about me."

"Oh gosh… a… a guitar! Look Mom, Dad… Mr. Evans gave me a guitar!"

"Gabe, you shouldn't have," Danni moaned.

"Aw, it was nothing…"

"No, really. You shouldn't have! He'll drive me nuts!" Danni laughed.

"And that's my present for you, Danni dear…"

"Creep."

"Bitch."

"Uh, Gabe? The boy…?"

"Oh, sorry, Cal, but your wife brings out the best in me."

"If that's the best I'd hate to see the worst."

"It's ugly, Cal…"

"Danni?"

"Yes, Gabe?"

He blew her a kiss and subtly pointed to his ass.

She scratched an imaginary itch on her nose with her middle finger.

Gabe and Danni burst into laughter.

Cal sighed and shook his head.

Ben ran off to his room with his new guitar.

"I did get you actual gifts though," Gabe told them when the laughter died down.

"Oh Gabe, you shouldn't have…"

"If I had a nickel for every time I heard that… But anyway… Cal, you are the man who has everything, so I got you nothing. No, wait. Here…"

"A… a pen? Uh, thanks, Gabe…" Cal looked at the inexpensive pen he was handed. It was obviously used.

"You're welcome, Cal. It's not just an ordinary Papermate. No, this one is suitable for signing all those pesky little court documents, mighty district attorney that you are now, and if a judge pisses you off, just press the little hearts on the clip and it fires a laser…"

"Gabe…"

"And you can use it to sign traveler's checks. Which brings me to Danni's present… Danni, why did Mickey divorce Minnie?"

"Huh? I don't know…"

"Because she was *fuckin'* goofy!"

"Oh God… That was so stupid! Go home, Gabe…"

"And Kyle loves that joke… But anyway, here. You can ask Mickey yourself."

"Oh… oh Gabe! Tickets to Disneyworld?"

"Ever been there?"

"Uh, no!"

"Me neither. Send me a postcard. There are flight vouchers in there too, to be used at your convenience. "

"Gabe, that's way too much…"

"She's right, Gabe…"

"Not really. I won it all in a poker game."

"You're so full of shit…"

"Watch it, Danni; you bring out the best in me…"

She went to him and gave him a hug.

"You creep," she whispered.

"Love you too, ya bitch," he whispered back.

He turned to Cal and shook his hand.

"I should be going… nasty drive through the mountains."

"Gabe, thank you," Danni said, releasing him. "Um… we have a gift for you too."

"You do? It won't explode, will it?"

"Not until you're at least fifty miles away."

"I'm so relieved…"

"Uh huh. But anyway, I kind of hesitated to give it to you, you'll see why when you open it, but when I found it in the attic… Oh Gabe, I hope I did the right thing!"

"Danni, you could do no wrong," he said, giving her that special grin she had always loved.

Gabe took the gift and unwrapped it.

"Oh… oh God," he murmured, running a finger over the glass of the picture. "Steve…"

"It was the last picture taken of the two of you together… two years ago at Christmas. He sent it to me, and I had it enlarged and framed. Do… do you like it, Gabe?"

He could barely get the words out, and continued to stare at his twin and himself as they stood in front of the Holiday tree, arms slung over each other shoulders. That was the year they did the video of themselves and the choir singing carols.

"Danni… Oh God, thank you! This means more to me than… Oh God… Steve…"

Cal turned away so that he wouldn't have to witness the tears in Gabe's eyes.

Danni gave her ex a comforting hug. "Gabe, I'm sorry if I upset you."

"No… not at all, Danni. It's just not having him around on the holidays… goddamn hard. And I have to go…"

He stumbled out to Pop's truck, clutching his precious picture, and managed to make it home safely… Although he didn't remember any of the drive back to Bittersweet.

JJJ

It crossed Annie's mind as she drove Michael to the midnight service that he was in the same clothes he'd been wearing the last two times she had seen him, and it wasn't all that appropriate for church. He still looked every bit a cowboy… But he did manage to knock some of that dark dust off of his hat. The poor guy probably didn't have much money either if he wasn't working… No matter. He was easily the nicest man she'd ever met, and was falling deeper in love with him with every passing moment she spent in his company.

Falling in love, yes, but she had no romantic feelings for him, just couldn't imagine living her life without him in it.

He opened her door for her and escorted her into the church, smiling broadly and nodding a "hello" to everyone they passed.

Annie smiled and nodded too, even though she only knew a few of the parishioners. She didn't attend services regularly due to her heavy work schedule, and didn't feel it all that necessary to show up every week just to prove she believed.

"This is a beautiful church, Annie," Michael whispered as they took a seat near the back of the nave.

"Small, but nice. It's non-denominational… I just can't seem to pick a religion…"

"It doesn't matter in the long run, Annie. As long as you live a good life, obey the 'Golden Rule' and give of yourself without expectin' anything back… That's what's important."

"You sound so sure."

"I am."

She believed him.

The service was the predictable Christmas one, with Bible passages read by children and carols sung by the choir, but to Annie it was the most beautiful one she had ever attended. She thought that her happiness, that feeling of peace and serenity she felt, had a lot to do with the man at her side. He silently mouthed ever bit of scripture, and she was even more intrigued with him and this surprising bit of knowledge he was unknowingly displaying.

Just who was he?

Where did he come from?

Why did he choose her of all people to befriend?

It didn't matter. He was there for her when she needed someone most.

They stopped at an all-night diner on the way home.

"My treat," Annie told him, thinking he was probably strapped for cash.

"It makes me less of a gentleman, but I'll let you buy, Annie. Call it a Christmas present from you." Michael hated to let her, but he *was* a bit short on funds. Pretty much non-existent, actually. He wished he could hit his brother up for a loan, didn't dare ask though.

Not wanting to have her spend too much, he ordered pumpkin pie and coffee. Annie ordered the same.

"I didn't know you could sing, Michael," she said, drawing a shapeless design in her whipped cream with her fork.

"Yep. My whole family is gifted that way. I guess I could have made a career out it with my brother, but it just wasn't my callin'."

"Well you should have. Jeez, you nearly brought tears to my eyes when you sang Silent Night. It was beautiful, and so emotional! Even the people around us stopped singing just so they could listen to you."

"Aw… I wouldn't go that far."

"Well it's true. What other secrets do you have, Michael?"

"Too many to go into, hon, but I'm harmless," he answered with a grin.

"Ever going to fill me in?" she teased.

"Eventually… when the time is right. You gonna play with your food or eat it?"

"Huh?" It was then she noticed that she hadn't taken a single bite.

Michael took a dab of whipped cream from his pie and touched it to the end of her nose, and burst out laughing when she crossed her eyes to look down at the mess.

"Michael!"

"Aw God... My brother used to make that same face to make me laugh," Michael chuckled. "I sure do miss him."

"When will he be back? Does he even know you're in town?"

Annie cleaned her nose off with her napkin.

"He doesn't know, and I think he'll be back in a week or so. Not sure if I'll still be around though."

"You're leaving?" Annie cried. "Oh no..."

"'Fraid so. I don't have much say about when and where I end up."

"Job related?"

"You could say that."

"Who do you work for, Michael?"

"Can't tell you, Annie; one of my secrets," he said with a smile.

"Why not? Oh jeez... are you a *spy* or something?"

"Mmm... no, but I've been entrusted with keepin' an eye on people."

"I don't think I should ask any more..."

"Good, 'cuz I can't lie and I can't tell you the truth either."

"Then I'll save you the worry. Well, we should be going."

"Mmhmm. And thanks again for the treat, Annie."

The drive back to the apartment was pretty quiet. Annie didn't want Michael to leave, but to invite him in so late at night... well, he might take it wrong and expect something she wasn't willing to give. Then again, he didn't seem attracted to her that way any more than she was to him.

He walked her to her door and whispered, "Merry Christmas," and gave her a soft kiss on her forehead.

"Same to you, Michael," she whispered back, and let herself in.

She went straight to the window, which overlooked the parking lot, and watched him walk to his car. Or so she thought. He reached the end and turned onto the street. Oh jeez... he was *walking* in this weather?

Annie threw open the window and called out to him.

He hesitated, took two steps, and then turned back around to look up at her.

She waved him back; she could at least drive him to wherever he was staying.

"What is it, Annie?" he asked when he saw her waiting for him at the door.

"You're walking? Why didn't you say something earlier? I could have dropped you off."

"My uh... ride didn't show up."

"Let me get my coat, I can take you..."

"Annie... Aw God, I don't have any place to go..."

"You don't? Oh yeah... your brother's gone and you were going to stay with him, right?"

Michael just smiled, neither agreeing nor disagreeing.

"You... you can stay here if you'd like," Annie said quietly. *Oh jeez, did she just invite him to spend the night?*

"I couldn't; wouldn't be proper, Annie."

"Who cares? You need a place to sleep, and I think the sofa would work. I have extra blankets..."

"You sure?"

"Don't argue, and get in here."

He smiled again and obeyed.

"This was always my favorite part of Christmas," Michael murmured.

He and Annie were sitting close together on the sofa, sharing a warm, soft blanket and sipping hot chocolate. The room was dark except for the twinkling lights on Annie's tree, and the wind howled outside, driving the heavy snow into the window.

"Yep..." Michael continued, "After my brother and parents went to bed, I'd sneak back out and just look at the tree. It was always so pretty... I really missed it after I left home."

"You never had a tree after that?"

"Nope. Was on the road most of the time. I did go home for Christmas though. Last year was the first time I couldn't make it back. Couldn't this year either, so you lettin' me stay tonight means a lot to me, Annie. Thank you."

He set his mug aside and put his arm around her.

"No one should have to be alone on Christmas, Michael."

She let her head rest against his shoulder, and then melted against him.

"You've been alone too long, Annie. I hope to change that."

She couldn't imagine what he meant by that remark and said nothing, but did let herself savor the warmth and strength surrounding him.

Christmas morning found them still on the sofa, snuggled up under the blanket, and sound asleep in each other's arms. What Annie didn't know was that her new friend left for a few hours after she had drifted off in slumber.

Gabe took his time driving back from Helena to his parents' house, careful not to slide off the slippery roads, but more to have some time to himself; the picture Danni had given him had really gotten to him.

He had just enough time for a quick change of clothes, and then loaded his family into Mom's car while his parents got into Pop's truck.

"Oh, Al," Marie sighed, finding the picture of her sons, which had been left behind in Gabe's haste to get ready.

"Ree... Where'd you get that?"

"It was on the seat here. Gabe must have left it for us. Remember that night?" she sighed, running her finger over Steve's smiling face.

"Two years ago tonight, Ree. Lord, what a night it was, too. Gabe ordered all new robes for the choir, and then he and Steve led them in carols. Videotaped the whole thing for us too."

"I just can't bear to watch it though. I miss him so much."

"Me too, Ree, but at least he left us some grandchildren. James and Jer are the spittin' image of him."

"Oh dear… Al, this isn't for us. There's a card here from that Danielle…"

"Well, Gabe was in a hurry, or maybe he didn't want Deirdre seein' it."

"Deirdre…" Marie said in disgust. "How she could go from one brother to another like that… it just isn't right."

"But she loves him, Ree. Anyone with eyes in their head can see it, and he loves her too."

"Then why don't they share a bed?"

"None of our business, Ree."

"I think it was for his money… she married him for his money and for a home for the babies."

"None of our business, Ree."

"Hmm."

Marie looked back down at the photo of her sons, identical except for their smiles. She wondered if like Danielle, Deirdre was just replacing one brother for another.

"Dee, I'm sorry I was so late, but the roads were awful."

"You got back safely, and that's all I care about, Geoffrey."

"Did you and Mom get it together yet?"

"She hasn't said a word to me all day."

"I can't understand what's wrong with her," Gabe sighed.

"How is Danielle doing?"

"Changing the subject, eh, Dee? And she's fine. She sends her love."

"I remember her from Steven's funeral. She was so very nice to me…"

"She and Jen were the only ones. I sure didn't have any use for you… Oh! She uh, sent along a present. She said it was for me, but I think it would mean just as much to you. God, I left it in the truck…"

"Then you can show it to me when we get to church. What is it, anyway?"

"A picture of Steve and me… two years ago," was all Gabe said, and the remainder of the trip was silent.

"Gabe Evans! Gosh it's good to see you again! I heard you were back… I was hoping for a visit before tonight though."

"Father Harmon, it's good to see you too."

The men shook hands, and then Gabe pulled Deirdre up next to him, a smiling baby in each of her arms. Gabe took Jeremy from her and kissed him.

"Harm, I'd like you to meet my wife Deirdre, and my sons James and

Jeremy."

"Deirdre... I'm very pleased to meet you, and so glad that you could make it tonight."

"Thank you, Father Harmon..."

"So Gabe, will you be singing tonight? My gosh, the congregation still talks about when you and Steve... Oh dear, I'm sorry."

"That's okay. Life goes on... And I'd be glad to, Harm. Just the last song though."

"Wonderful! Well, it's time..."

Father Harmon Grossman changed his sermon just a bit, still telling the story of the Christmas miracle, but adding a word or two about family, and to never waste a single, precious moment in discord with them. Loved ones could be taken away all too quickly...

Gabe's hand closed around Deirdre's when he heard those words, and he brought it to his lips for a kiss. She was probably thinking about Steve, just like he was.

Deirdre was so touched by the gesture that tears sprang to her eyes. She knew what Geoffrey was thinking, and wanting to comfort her. She covered his hand with her own.

Marie didn't miss a minute of it, and thought that just maybe Deirdre truly did love Gabe. It was too dark in the church for her to be puttin' on an act for the folks around her to notice, so why would she bother with emotions like that if they weren't real?

"...And finally, we have something special for you tonight," Harmon told his flock. "Nearly every year for the past twenty-five, the Evans brothers have ended our Christmas Eve mass by singing Silent Night. And as you know, we lost Steve a little over a year ago. Even though he no longer walks this earth, his warm, serene spirit lives on in all of us. He was truly a wonderful person, always giving of himself and full of love for his fellow man. I'm sure if he could, he'd join his brother in the final song tonight... but for now, this is the best we can do."

Harmon pulled out a poster-sized photo from behind the pulpit and set it in front of the stand.

Gabe nearly choked when he saw that it was the same one Danni had given him. Aw God...

Deirdre fought to keep a sob from escaping, but was unsuccessful. Gabe hugged her, and then placed her hand into his mother's. She was crying just as hard as Deirdre was. They could get through this together.

"Now Gabe, if you please?" Harmon waved the surviving Evans twin to the front.

Gabe sat down at the piano, never taking his eyes from the over-sized picture of him and his brother. God, Steve's eyes seemed to follow him.

He played the introduction, and then his most-wonderful voice filled the church. Filled the ears of the parishioners… filled their hearts.

Marie's hand closed on Deirdre's, and she turned to smile at her daughter-in-law.

Al's arm went around his wife, thanking God that she had finally gotten over her little snob attack.

James and Jeremy giggled and cooed in their infant seats as they listened to Papa sing to them again.

Everyone else in the church enjoyed Gabe just as much as ever, but wondered when Father Harmon had installed the special lighting.

A faint blue glow surrounded Gabe as he sang… just like the one shining on the picture of him and Steve.

Chapter Nine

Spring, 1991

"Any word on when your house will be done, Annie?"

"The builder said next week. Oh Marti, I'm so excited!"

"I'll bet! Are you going to throw a big house-warming party? I'll help you plan it…"

"I don't think so. Maybe this fall, but the place is just too muddy out there and… and I don't have… Well, not yet," Annie sighed.

"Annie, he'll be back. Didn't he say you'd see him again?"

"He did, but I haven't heard from him since January, and here it is April! Not one word…"

"Maybe his job is keeping him too busy. Anyway, I sure wish I could have met him. He sounds wonderful…"

"Michael is the nicest, the sweetest, the… Marti, he's so perfect. Why is it that I… I don't…"

"You don't what? Love him?"

"I do! But like a brother or something. Anyway, I miss the heck out of him."

"A brother…? Annie, are you sure you 'like' men?"

"Huh? What do you mean…? Marti! Of course I do!"

"I wonder. Richie didn't last very long, and then not much of anything until Tyler… who didn't interest you. And now you have a veritable god of a man after you, and you love him like a brother? What's up?"

"A… a god? Oh jeez…"

"Well that's how you described him. Tall, handsome, muscles on his muscles, that hair and those eyes… Mmm…"

"I didn't say that!"

"Well maybe not in those exact words, but…"

"Your imagination is in full control again, Marti, and the day shift is here; time for report."

"Finally! I'm so tired!"

"Me too. See ya tonight."

"Later, Annie-bananie."

✦ ✦ ✦

"Geoffrey, get Jeremy! He's heading for the stairs again!" Deirdre yelled, trying to diaper a squirming James.

Gabe dropped his razor and flew out of the bathroom, shaving cream still dripping from his face. He grabbed his son just as the baby was backing down the first step.

"Jeremy," he sighed, picking him up and hugging him, "don't you know how dangerous it is to go down there by yourself?"

Jeremy giggled and slapped his hands on his papa's face, sending a spray of white foam everywhere.

"Aw God… Now I have to change my shirt," Gabe moaned. And he'd be late for his goddamn meeting…

He wiped the stinging suds from his eyes and dropped his naughty child into the playpen.

"Deirdre, why didn't you stick him in here in the first place? I don't have the time to be chasing…"

"I did, Geoffrey! He piled up his stuffed animals and crawled right out!"

"Lord… And who ever heard of a ten-month old walking already? Shouldn't they just be crawling at this age?" Gabe asked, unbuttoning his shirt. He yanked it off and wadded it into a ball, and then chucked it at the clothes hamper.

He shoots, he scores!

Deirdre looked up and tried not to stare at her husband's bare chest. She rarely ever saw him unclothed, and oh what a view…

"Dee?"

"Oh! Uh, well, they have Evans blood, Geoffrey, so they can't help but be extremely intelligent… not to mention advanced for their age," she laughed.

"I guess, but I'm about ready to put a leash on both of them. And in the meantime…" Gabe yanked the toys from the playpen and tossed them aside.

"Just try to get out now, you little beast," he told Jer, running his fingers through the boy's black curls. God, he loved his kids.

Jeremy snatched a little of the foam from Papa's face and smeared it on his own. He wanted to be just like Papa…

Gabe tossed a blankie over the baby's head and went to finish his morning shave.

"Dee, I might be late tonight. We're auditioning some new talent and I'm not sure how long it will take."

"That's fine, Geoffrey. Should I hold dinner for you?"

"No, I'll grab something on my way home. Have a good day, love."

"You too, Geoffrey dear."

She accepted a quick kiss to her cheek, and shut the front door behind him. Now to start her own busy day… the twins and the housework, and then a charity luncheon. Back home to make phone calls, soliciting donations for the homeless shelter, and then back to the boys. She was very glad that Geoffrey had convinced her to let a girl come in a few times a week to care for the twins and give her a little break.

She sighed and went to Geoffrey's office, and sat on his worn leather sofa. The picture of Steven and Geoffrey hung on the wall to her right, and she looked at it through tear-bright eyes.

"I miss you so much, Steven," she whispered. "Why did you ever have to leave me?"

Of course he didn't answer, just looked back at her with his bright blue eyes and serene smile.

✦ ✦ ✦

"Gabe buddy! Miss me?"

"Only about as much as an overly-full diaper pail. You're late, Kyle."

"So are you, Gabe. I pulled in right behind you."

"I had a little mishap just before I left; had to change my clothes."

"Oh? Did you get Dee's credit card bill and shit your pants?"

"Kyle… that is just so… God! And she hardly spends a dime."

"Wish Jen was like that. She's always bitchin' about money."

"Only because you spend far too much. Kyle, until the company is back on its feet you are really going to have to watch your budget."

"That's Jen's job…"

"Yours too. I can't keep helping… Oh, never mind."

"Helpin' what, dude?"

"I said never mind. And tuck in that goddamn tee shirt! Couldn't you have dressed a little nicer? Christ, we need to look somewhat respectable if we want to make a good impression…"

"Hey, we're just tryin' to get a loan, dude, not date 'em!"

"We should at least look like we have the ambition to attempt to pay them back should they see their way clear to give us said loan, Kyle."

"Whatever. You want coffee?"

"I'd rather have a beer, but I'll suffer…"

"Mr. Evans?"

"Yes, Lynn?"

"They're waiting for you in the conference room."

"Thanks, Lynn. Well, Kyle, are you full of bullshit today?"

"Today and every day, *mon ami*! Shall we go dazzle them?"

"Or baffle them…"

"Goddammit!" Gabe roared, chucking his shot glass against the wall.

Kyle dodged the predictable, inevitable shards of glass that bounced off the already damaged paneling. *Shrapnel happens…*

"Dude…?"

"We didn't get the loan, Kyle."

"We didn't? Why the hell not?"

"Because it seems we're a poor risk. After two years we've barely made a dime, and the fortune we made as SD the band is long gone. We're fucked."

"Aw God… Isn't there anything we can do?"

"Yeah, but I don't want to. Christ, I can't believe they turned me down! Me!"

"What about Hilliard? Didn't you talk to him a few months ago?"

"Yeah, but he retired at the first of the year, and his replacement is some tight-ass who acts like the money is coming out of his own pockets. These guys today were out last chance, buddy."

"But you have a back-up plan, right? Gabe, I need a paycheck! Five kids and that huge house, and…"

"You'll be paid, Kyle."

"So what's your plan?"

"First of all, we have to lay off staff again. Jen will need to pick up some freebie hours dong Ray's job…"

"Dude, you're firing Ray? He's the office manager!"

"I don't have a fucking choice! As a matter of fact, all administrative staff will be let go, as well as most of the production people. You and I and Jen can pick up the slack… not that anyone of us had been overworked lately…"

"Damn. Okay, what else?"

"I'm using some of my money to get us through the next few months. And… you and I are going to do a few shows… maybe if the music-hungry public is reminded of SD, they'll buy a few albums."

"Do… do some shows? Aw God! Gabe, that's great! Seriously? You and me on stage again…?"

"Yeah… God, I hate to do that…"

"Why? It's not like we're gonna tour… Are we gonna tour?"

"No, just local gigs. No money in it, but I'm going for the exposure. I hope to God it works."

"Have you called any of the guys yet? Mick or Wolff or Dave…"

"No, and I don't plan to. As I said, there's no money in this right now, and I can't pull them from paying jobs to haul my ass out of the fire. It's up to us, Kyle."

"Are you sure? They'd come back in a second if we toured again…"

"No tours! I… I just can't. Not now…"

"I uh… I'll call Jen and let her know, Gabe."

"You do that, Kyle, and shut my door on your way out."

What a fucking mess this all was. SD Productions was nearly bankrupt, Kyle still had no idea on how to save a buck – and Gabe was still stupidly funding his buddy's bad habits, his own bank balance had dipped to a million and a half, Deirdre was getting on his nerves – although he had no idea why because she was as perfect as ever, and Gabe's frustration level was reaching critical mass.

Oh, to just go out and tie on a good drunk and fall into bed with some warm, willing female who didn't even care to know his name as long as he could satisfy her. That was one thing he'd always been successful at…

He just couldn't do it. He was married, had children, and too well known in this town to step over the line.

Goddammit.

Didn't mean he couldn't take a road trip though.

Forget it, Gabe. You couldn't cheat on Dee…

Wouldn't actually be cheating… wasn't like they had a real marriage… So go for it!

He'd feel too guilty.

Guilt… what a wasted emotion.

But he'd feel it regardless.

What ever happened to "Bad Boy Gabe"?

He died… right after he got married.

Gabe slammed a fist on his desk, grabbed his hat, and headed for the gym. An hour or two of strenuous exercise should wear him out. After that, maybe a long drive in the country…

Annie hauled the first box from the bed of her new truck and carried it up the steps of her new home.

Home…

Her very first, very own home. It was perfect.

She pulled a hammock from the box and hung it from hooks at the end of the long, covered porch, and sat down.

Just perfect…

Annie let her gaze wander from the deep blue lake to the left of the cabin, and the new pole barn nestled against the high hill. Five acres of pasture had been fenced in, anxiously waiting for the day when a horse or two would be out there grazing.

She could hardly wait.

Behind the cabin were acres and acres of rolling meadow, leading to a large woods that ran for miles to the west.

To the east was the road, and beyond that were fields of corn, soybeans, and winter wheat. On the northeast end of the lake was a swampy area, thick with cattails and invisible yet vocal bullfrogs.

It all added up to privacy, peace and tranquility… her little slice of Heaven.

Annie sighed contentedly, wiped the sweat from her brow, and began the strenuous task of unloading the rest of her belongings. Not that there was all that much… maybe twenty boxes of clothes, dishes, linens and bedding, books, a dozen or so CD's, and a couple of bags of groceries, but it was hot and muggy and just plain miserable out.

Once all was on the porch, Annie opened the front door of her new home to begin the unpacking. She stepped inside and looked around… at all that empty space. Oh God, she didn't have any furniture!

How on earth could she have possibly overlooked something so important? Easy enough… Her other place had been furnished, as well as her parents' home, and it just never occurred to her… She smacked a hand upside her head and called herself every synonym of stupid that she could think of.

Darn it, and where to go on a Sunday afternoon? The whole town, large as it was, pretty much shut down on Sundays, and to go to Battle Creek or Grand Rapids... well, she just wasn't up to the drive. Nor could she unload it by herself had she purchased any larger items.

She couldn't go back to her apartment either.

A motel?

Hardly... not looking forward to spending her first night in her new home like she was.

Well, it was warm enough out; she could grab some blankets and sleep in the hammock.

In the meantime, it was time to move in.

It didn't take her all that long to unpack and put most everything away, and when she was done she flattened out the cardboard boxes, piled them up, and sat down on her only "chair."

Ooh... and it was getting hotter by the minute too. Sweltering and muggy... Annie wiped the sweat from her brow and went outside. The weather had definitely taken a turn, and the promise of a spring thunderstorm was heavy in the air. Well just great... she wouldn't be sleeping in the hammock after all.

She went back inside and opened a beer.

Ah... much better. And now to think about what furniture to purchase. Annie started at the top, in the loft that ran over the two large bedrooms and bathroom. She'd need a desk and a filing cabinet, a few lamps, and maybe she'd just break down and buy a computer while she was at it. Heck, Mr. Hilliard told her to splurge, right?

Right.

The bedrooms were next. She'd need beds of course... A king size for her and a queen for the guest room. Night tables and dressers... and the fifteen by fifteen foot rooms would still look nearly empty. But after she hung some window treatments over the large bay windows it might "cozy" it up a bit. Even her walk-in closet looked barren with her meager wardrobe hanging in it.

Back into the main cabin area...

The kitchen, dining room, and great room were all one, separated by an "island" of cupboards between the kitchen and dining area. Add a table to the shopping list.

The great room would need a sofa and a few chairs, not that she needed all of that, but it looked so darn bare! The only thing in there at that point was a cast iron woodstove in the corner... and the nearly empty bookshelves of course. Oh jeez, she'd need some pictures to decorate the walls, and maybe an entertainment center too. A really nice system and perhaps a television. Annie almost regretted donating *all* of her things, but then again, the once-modern furniture of the seventies would have looked horribly out of place in the country theme of the cabin.

She went into the bathroom last, her one extravagance in the building of her home. She didn't need to purchase anything for that, but she just like to look at it. Gosh, she'd really splurged with that room. And why not? Her favorite way to relax was to fill the tub, go a little heavy on the bubble bath, and sink into it with a drink and a good book.

It would be all that much better now. The entire back wall of the bathroom was translucent glass block – almost like being outside but with privacy. The over-sized, gloss-black Jacuzzi was surrounded by a ledge of gray slate, and sat on a raised platform. Annie couldn't wait to add some plants and dozens of candles, and relax in the lavender-scented swirling warmth. Not tonight though – just too darn hot out, and she'd settle for a tepid shower in the glass stall in the opposite corner.

She finished her beer and peeled off her damp clothes, grabbed a towel, and turned on the tap. And waited.

Aw jeez… the water wasn't working. She ran down to the half-basement to check and see if it was turned on at the source. Yep, no problem there. Must be in the electrical, and that's why the pump wasn't working. She was out of luck until tomorrow.

Now what? She needed a shower in the worst way, and she'd need water for the toilet too, not to mention for washing dishes and such.

Annie kicked a frustrated foot at the shower door and stomped back into the empty great room. What the heck else could possibly go wrong? No furniture, no water, no place to sleep… Dammit.

She yanked another beer from the fridge, wrapped her towel around her, and went out to sit on the porch steps.

The sun was still high in the sky, and the temperature and humidity were climbing… just like her frustration. A flock of sparrows flew overhead and landed near the barn. Annie watched them, envying their freedom from material needs.

The birds hopped around on the ground… right under the hand pump Annie had had the foresight to install. Oh yeah… she had water! It would be a chore hauling it up in the few pots and pans she had, but it would work in a pinch. No shower though… although there was that beautiful lake out there.

Yep, time for a swim. She trotted back into the cabin and picked through her yet-to-be-put-away clothes, looking for her suit. Sure… like it would be there. Add the missing swimwear to her list of crappy luck.

Dammit.

And she was just angry enough now to go over her two-beer limit and open a third.

Still wrapped in her towel, she went back outside and looked at the lake.

The sun reflected on the glittering water, teasing and looking so refreshing… and she was so hot.

She stared at the lake.

The lake stared back.

Sweat trickled down her back and between her breasts.

A pair of geese landed on the water, sending up a rainbow spray.

The beer buzzed in Annie's brain.

The lake called to her.

It was time for a swim…

Feeling positively wicked, she ran down to the beach and stood ankle deep in the water, laughing a little drunkenly at the sin she was about to commit. Here she was, nearly thirty years old, and was about to skinny dip for the first time.

Annie gave a quick glance around to see if anyone was watching, and laughed again at *that* silly idea. Hers was the only home on the ten-mile stretch of road, and she'd yet to see another car pass by.

She took a deep breath and dropped her towel. She swam to the middle of the chilly lake and flipped over to float on her back, closing her eyes as the sun beat down. Her hair floated about her in a red-gold cloud, and the nip in the water put a pink flush on her pale skin. She felt refreshed, just a little lazy, and positively decadent for the first time in her entire life.

From the marble bench, high on the hill in the clearing, a pair of blue eyes watched Annie swim. She wasn't close enough for him to see her features, but the fact that she was nude was obvious. A rough hand ran trembling fingers through thick, black hair, and he felt shamed for having intruded on this woman's private moment. He had actually thought about joining her even though he had no right to think such things. But God, he wanted her…

Gabe arrived home well after midnight, losing his way in the sudden thunderstorm that he should have seen coming but was too wrapped up in his thoughts to notice. Green eyes and autumn hair had been on his mind again…

Deirdre was going to be pissed that he hadn't called to tell her he'd be so late. Well, not exactly pissed, but she give him that loving "you've been a naughty boy, Geoffrey" look, and then kiss him goodnight. Sometimes he felt as if he were James and Jeremy's sibling instead of their Papa when Dee looked at him like that.

He let himself into his mansion and went immediately to his office for a drink. Christ, he heated to be starting that shit again, but his life was beginning to fall apart. His business was heading down the crapper, he was trapped in a sham of a marriage, and he still missed the hell out of his brother. Oh yeah… can't forget he'd nearly succumbed to the temptation of a very willing female, and extricated himself from *that* situation before it got out of hand. God, what a mess…

"Geoffrey?"

"In here, Dee."

"You're home."

"Obviously."

"I wish you would have called; I was worried."

"I'm a big boy, Deirdre; I can take care of myself."

"You needn't be short with me, Geoffrey…"

"I'm sorry, love. My day wasn't… wasn't what I had hoped," he sighed.

She went to him and wrapped her arms around him. Poor Geoffrey… He'd sacrificed so much to provide for her and the twins.

"I'm sorry," he repeated, and held her close. God, he really did love her and shouldn't have snapped.

"Let's go to bed, Geoffrey…"

He stiffened at her words. *Together?* Christ, he was just lonely enough to contemplate it, and after his close call tonight… Whew! He shoved the thought away. Of course she didn't mean together; just how stupid was that? Merely his own lustful thinking.

Gabe ran a rough hand through his thick, black hair, and escorted his wife to *her* room, and locked *his* door behind him.

Refreshed from her swim, Annie was in a much better mood as she fixed a light dinner. She sat on her porch and ate her ham and cheese omelet, watching the clouds roll in. Lightening flashed, thunder crashed, and the kitten yowled in fear.

Kitten?

Oh jeez…

Annie set her plate aside and ran down the steps, looking for a little lost feline.

"Here kitty," she called out, not really all that sure she heard anything at all.

Huh. Nothing. And it was beginning to sprinkle so she went back to the shelter of the porch and the remainder of her meal.

She was just about ready to bite into a chunk of ham when she heard it again, only this time it was more of a regular "meow." She set her fork down and listened.

Sure enough, it was coming from under the porch.

Once more, Annie went to investigate.

Annie went down on her knees, trying to coax the kitten from its hiding place. Amber eyes stared at her from under the steps. She held her hand out, palm up, and wiggled her fingers a bit.

That was all the kitten had been waiting for: an invitation. With more arrogance than the small body could hold, the kitten strolled over to Annie and sat exactly three feet away, just out of arm's reach.

The female would have to prove her worth and come to the feline… Through half-closed lids, the amber eyes challenged her to make the next move.

Annie sat back on her heels. This was indeed a different animal! He seemed so... intelligent. *A kitten?* And his eyes... they were so unusual, almost as if they held the wisdom of the ages.

She leaned forward to touch him.

He didn't move a muscle, just continued to observe, so she picked him up and stroked his head.

Much to Annie's pleasure, the kitten began to purr.

Much to the kitten's embarrassment, he began to purr.

"No, this will not do," thought the young feline, but it was too late. *"Alas, might as well enjoy it..."*

He leaned into Annie Rose's hand for more attention.

She stood, cuddling her new pet close to her. He was so very thin and she wondered when he had last eaten. Well, he wouldn't have to wait much longer.

Annie ran through the now heavier rain, grabbed her plate, and went into the cabin. She set the kitty on the floor, the remains of her dinner on the counter, and wondered what to feed him.

What did cats like besides Little Friskies?

As she looked in her sparsely stocked refrigerator, pondering the question, the kitten walked to below where her plate was and meowed. He stood on his hind feet, batting a paw at the ham and eggs.

Annie turned and laughed at the comical scene. Yes, this kitty was indeed different! She scooped a kitten-size portion onto a saucer and set it on the floor, and then sat herself next to the cat to finish her own meal.

The little puss finished eating before Annie did. He looked at her, at her plate, and then back to her. She plucked a piece of ham from her dish and tossed it to him. A lightning-fast paw shot out and slammed the meat to the floor before a hooked claw flipped it into his mouth. It reminded Annie of a volleyball player slamming the ball over the net.

"That was some spike, cat," she laughed.

The kitten licked his paw clean and surveyed Annie Rose through half-closed eyes.

Yes, she would do quite nicely; he would remain with her.

He stood and stretched, and then wandered around looking for a place to nap. Annie followed, curious as to his plan. She laughed again when he jumped into a box of her underclothes and winked at her.

He groomed his pumpkin-orange fur from head to tail, and then curled up into a kitten ball to sleep.

Yes, this would do nicely...

Now if only Annie could find someplace just as comfortable.

The cardboard wasn't the best bed, but it wasn't as hard as the floor she decided after tossing and turning for nearly ten minutes. Wouldn't be very much sleep going on tonight though. Maybe if she read her most boring book it would have her comatose in an hour or two.

Annie sighed and flipped on a light. She wrapped a blanket around herself, the storm had cooled the air considerably, and all she was wearing was an over-sized tee shirt and panties.

Halfway to the bookshelves she was startled by a knock on the door. Oh God… did she dare answer it? Moot point since it wasn't locked. It was probably Marti anyway, a bottle of champagne in her hand and ready to toast Annie's new abode. She grinned and ran to welcome her friend.

"Marti!" she cried, flinging the door open wide.

Not Marti, but Michael.

"M… Michael?" she stuttered, staring in shocked wonder.

"Didn't change my name… Must be," he smiled. He fought hard to keep his eyes from traveling down her half-dressed figure. *Aw God…*

"Michael! What are you doing here? Oh jeez… Come in!" She stood aside to let him pass.

"I saw your light on; thought I'd stop in and say 'hi'."

"You did?" And hadn't she just turned it on? And what the heck was he doing all the way out here at this time of night?

"I did. And I suppose you're wonderin' what I'm doin' here…"

"Uh, yeah. I mean I'm glad to see you, but…"

"Annie, I have a confession to make. I've been beddin' down in your barn for a few days…"

"You have? Why?"

"I uh… needed someplace…"

"What about your brother?"

"I can't stay there. Can't tell you why just yet, but…"

"Oh gosh… In my barn?" *Oh God… had he seen her swimming earlier?* Annie blushed a deep, deep shade of red.

"Only at night, Annie. I uh… I have things to do during the day."

"Oh. Uh, how long have you been out there?"

"A few hours…"

Maybe he hadn't seen her. He sure didn't act like he had…

"And you've been sleeping out there?"

"Yep. Pretty comfortable actually."

"I don't know how…"

"I've got a bedroll, and I used to camp with my brother a lot. I'm used to it."

"Well, it's not much better in here," Annie laughed nervously. She crossed her arms in front of her, realizing that she wasn't dressed for company.

Oh jeez…

Michael looked around the room and grinned.

"Who's your decorator?" he quipped.

Annie stuck her tongue out at him and went for her blanket. Decently covered, she returned to where he stood just inside the kitchen door.

"The barn?" she asked.

"The barn," he nodded.

"I… I have an extra room… can't call it a bedroom yet, no beds, but you're welcome to stay…"

"It would only be for a day or two…"

"You're welcome here for as long as you need it, Michael. I… I missed you."

"I missed you too, Annie."

"Are you hungry? Have you eaten…?"

He shook his head and gave her a pathetic smile.

"Not hungry or haven't eaten?"

"Haven't eaten…"

"I don't have much yet, but I can do a mean omelet."

"Sounds good, but don't go to any trouble."

"Michael, it's no trouble at all. Now go pull up a… box, and I'll have it ready in a few."

"Thanks, Annie."

"But first I'm going to go change; rather chilly in here…"

Michael walked to the thermostat and gave it a slight twist. Seconds later the furnace kicked on, sending that nasty, "first heat" smell throughout the cabin.

"Well, at least *that* works," Annie sighed, wrinkling her nose.

"Oh? What's not workin'?"

"The water pump. I had to haul water from the barn."

"Want me to check it out?"

"Could you?"

"Gotta earn my keep somehow…"

"The basement door is right under the stairs to the left. I checked, but I don't know much about those things…"

"You need a man around, Annie, "Michael winked, and went to see if he could help.

"Lord, do I ever," Annie mumbled, and went to put some clothes on.

Michael was back upstairs before she had quite finished dressing, and she was zipping up her jeans as she rushed out of her bedroom. They bumped into each other as they were exiting their respective doors.

He grabbed her to keep her from falling.

She overcompensated for her backwards direction, and fell into his arms.

He looked down at her, staring into the emerald depths of her eyes.

She gazed into his bright, deep blue eyes, and shivered when another pair of intense, deep blue ones flashed through her mind.

"Annie?"

"I… I'm okay. Did you figure it out?" she whispered, unable to take her eyes from his face. It was so familiar… *Him but not him.*

"I figured it out a long time ago, Annie…"

"Huh?"

"Uh… the water. Just a circuit breaker that didn't get flipped on. It should work now."

"Then you've earned your dinner. Milk or orange juice?"

"Juice, unless you have an extra beer."

"Help yourself."

He realized that he was still holding her and let her go.

She hurried into the kitchen to prepare his meal.

"Annie, this is wonderful."

"It's just eggs…"

"Prepared with a master hand. You'll make someone a great wife someday."

"I'm not holding my breath…"

"Why not? Tyler not workin' out for you?"

"I never anticipated that he would, Michael. We're just friends."

"His loss. Any other prospects?"

"Not outside my dreams, no."

"Oh? Got someone all picked out and waitin' to meet him?" Michael asked.

Ooh… that hit too close to home.

Annie blushed and looked away.

"So what's he like, Annie?"

"Michael…"

"Like me? I'm honored!" he laughed.

"Stop! I don't want to talk about it…"

"Not even to me? Your best friend?"

He was? Yeah, he was. She barely knew him, and yet she'd known him forever. And felt she could tell him anything…

"Do you promise not to laugh ?" she asked.

"Promise."

"Okay, as a matter of fact I do. Have someone in mind, that is."

"And?"

"And… Michael, I've been seeing his eyes in my head for a while now. Oh jeez, and then last fall I… I had a vision. It was so real! Not just the eyes, but… but all of him…"

"And?"

"He… he was tall – about your height, and had coal-black hair and deep blue eyes, and a… a dimple right under his lower… lip…" She trailed off, staring at almost the same man she was describing.

Him but not him…

"Any other distinctive features?" Michael grinned.

"He… he wore jeans and a leather jacket, and a… a hat rather like yours…"

"Maybe it's my evil twin, Annie."

"Michael, this is serious! You said you wouldn't…"

"Aw, I'm sorry. I just like the way your eyes flash that green fire when you're ticked. Forgive me?"

She gave him a sidelong glance.

"You're forgiven," Annie sighed.

"Thank God. I didn't relish sleepin' in the barn again."

"Don't push it, cowboy…"

"Annie, please don't call me that. And don't ask why either."

She nodded. The word felt wrong as soon as it passed her lips. He wasn't *her* cowboy.

"Hey, what's this?" Michael said, watching the kitten stroll over to where he was sitting. "Where've you been, you little flea hotel?"

The kitten sat a few feet away from the man and snorted in disgust. *Flea hotel indeed…*

"You know him?" Annie gasped.

"Yep. Kept me company last night, but hated it. Imagine a cat not likin' a barn."

The kitten flipped his tail in annoyance. He'd come out for a midnight snack and received nothing but insults. He was half tempted to ignore the piece of ham Michael Anthony was holding out to him.

"I wonder where he came from." Annie mused.

"Probably dumped off. Did you name him yet?"

Michael gave up offering the meat, and tossed it to the temperamental kitten.

A lightning-fast paw shot out and slammed the morsel to the floor.

"Spike," Annie said. "His name is Spike."

Spike didn't mind the odd name bestowed upon him, since a human could not pronounce his true name anyway. He consumed his treat, and then washed his face with a silky paw.

"Annie, thanks again for puttin' me up."

"Or putting up with you?"

"Touché. I do appreciate it though."

"What are friends for? I just wish the accommodations were a little better."

"I've been in worse. Goodnight, Annie."

"Goodnight, Michael."

They stood in the center of the short hall, each waiting for the other to make a move. Make *the* move.

He knew it wouldn't be right, far, far too many reasons that it wouldn't be right. He gave her his serene smile and backed into the guestroom.

Him but not him…

Annie let out a sigh of relief, and curled up on her crude cardboard bed. Sleep was a long time coming, but oh, the dreams she had…

Chapter Ten

"He's *living* with you? God, Annie, how long has this been going on?"

"Around two months now, Marti. Ever since the night I moved in, actually."

"Oh… oh God. I don't believe it! You're *living* with a man? And just why haven't I seen him when I've been over?"

"For one, you're hardly ever over…"

"True…" Marti nodded.

"And secondly, he's not always around. At least during the day anyway… mostly at night. But he helps out so much; I don't know what I would do without him, Marti."

"Ooh… girlfriend! Annie, I never would have taken you for the type. Little Virgin Annie…"

"Huh? Oh jeez… No, Marti! It's not like that at all! We're just friends and he's using the guestroom. I hardly ever…"

"Mmhmm. Annie's got a boy toy…"

"Marti!"

"Does your cat know?" Marti laughed. Oh, this was too much fun, and Annie-bananie was turning as red as a beet with all the teasing.

"Spike likes him very much, if you want to know the truth. Jeez, and there's nothing *not* to like about Michael."

"But you're *not* sleeping with him…?"

"Of course not! It… it would be like sleeping with my brother or something…"

"Now that's just sick. Here you have Mr. Perfect right where you want him and no sex? Annie…"

Annie shook her head.

"You've never even thought about it?" Marti asked.

"N…no, not really…"

"So you have!"

"Marti, it wouldn't be right. He… he's not the one. Him but not him."

"I give up trying to figure you out, Annie. So when do I get to meet him?"

"I don't know. He's a very private person… And please, please don't tell anyone about him!"

"Your secret's safe, but I still want to meet him."

"I'll ask, but don't expect anything. He really is very private…"

"Mysterious… Sneaky! I'll bet he has a wife somewhere… No, then he'd be with her at night. Unless she works nights like we do…"

"Marti, he's just a nice guy who's down on his luck and staying with me until his nasty brother will let him live with him."

"Nasty brother? He's got a brother?"

"Mmhmm. Michael talks about him quite a bit...their childhood and all the fun they had, but never says anything about the last few years. It sounds like they used to be quite close too, and yet he never even tries to visit... I can't understand how anyone could shut Michael out like that."

"Hence the 'nasty' brother?"

"Yeah, that's my opinion. Michael never says a bad word about anyone."

"Neither do you. He's got you whipped, Annie..."

"Break's over, Marti."

"You're still no fun, Annie-bananie..."

"And yet you hang out with me."

"Yeah. Go figure."

The women smiled at each other and went their separate ways.

"Kyle, congratulations! Another son..."

"I know, Gabe! Kicks ass, don't it?"

"He's a big one too!"

"Nine pounds even. Christ, I don't know how Jen does it!"

"Grows large babies?"

"No, gets them out! Gabe, you wouldn't believe..."

"Kyle, enough!" Gabe moaned, raising his hands for silence. "There are just some things I'd rather not know."

"Wanna see him?"

"I thought you'd never ask. Lead on, McDuffy-dad!"

Kyle grinned and brought his best buddy to Jenna's room.

"Jen, he's beautiful," Gabe sighed, taking the whimpering infant into his arms. He kissed the baby and sang softly to him, just like he'd done with all of Kyle's children.

"Thank you, Gabe," Jenna groaned, repositioning her tired self to find a comfort zone she could tolerate. Her pain meds had long since worn off.

Gabe finished his lullaby and handed the infant back to his mommy.

"Beautiful," he murmured, and gave Jen a tender kiss on her forehead.

Jen knew that comment was meant for her and not her latest child. She smiled up at her hero.

"Pick a name yet?" Gabe asked.

"Picked one the day she told me she was pregnant, Gabe."

"And what would that be, Kyle?"

"Jack. Steven Jack, but we'll call him Jack."

"After my brother?"

"You got a brother named Jack?"

"No, you ass! Steve..."

"Yeah, we did. You don't mind, do you?"

"Not at all, Kyle. He'd be honored..."

✦ ✦ ✦

Michael pounded in the last nail and gave his handiwork a shake to check its sturdiness. Yep, mighty fine chicken coop if he did say so himself. Annie planned on pickin' up her chicks on the way home from work that morning, and she'd be surprised as heck to find out that he was finished already.

He took care of his tools, and then sat on the top rail of the fence by the barn for a short break.

Yep, life was pretty good lately. Wasn't the one he would have chosen for himself, but it could have been a whole lot worse. He sure missed the hell out of his fiancé though, and still checked on her every now and then, unknown to her of course. Michael was grateful to see that she was content with her husband and children, and that there was a lot of love in their home. She kept busy to keep her mind off the void in her life – Michael, and she knew that if there was any way they could have remained together, they would have.

But fate had other plans…

He jumped down from his perch and called to Dog, Annie's latest pet, and the pair went to the cabin for breakfast.

Spike growled a warning when the boisterous puppy ran too close to him on the way to the kitchen. *Obnoxious canine anyway…*

Dog didn't take the threat seriously, and gave the half-grown cat a drolly lick before they both headed in for their meal. Dog was served on the floor, and Spike on the dining room table. Annie always joked that she was probably breaking some rule for feeding an animal at the table, but who cared? And he did act practically human at times.

Spike flipped his tail at the canine and casually began his breakfast.

Dog… A month after the arrival of Spike, Annie had been on her way home from work when she had first seen the pup sitting in the center of the road. It was foggy that morning, fortunately, and she had been driving slower than usual and saw the animal in time to avoid hitting it. She stopped the truck, and the pup stood and walked towards her. When Annie jumped down from the cab, the dog trotted over.

It was obviously neglected, covered with matted fur, and alive with fleas. Annie was reluctant to even touch it, but the pup had other ideas. He rose on his hind legs and plopped muddy paws on her white scrub pants.

Oh jeez… just what she needed. She grabbed the dog by the scruff of the neck and raised him to eye level. Bright gold eyes looked into hers, and his tongue flicked out in an attempt to lick her.

Annie smiled.

Now what to do? She didn't want the filthy thing in her new truck, and yet was afraid that if she put him in the back he would jump out. She couldn't just leave him there. Annie glanced around, not even sure of what she was looking for as the fleas began to migrate up her arm. The mere thought of the vermin made her itch all over. She dropped the pup in the pick-up's bed and began brushing fleas and mud from her hand. Lord, what a mess...

The pup sat down and barked once, almost as if he were laughing at her. Well, maybe he'd stay put during the ride home; she was only about two miles from the cabin.

He never budged an inch.

Annie took the dog straight to the bathroom for a thorough scrubbing. Lacking a flea shampoo, she soaked the furry critter for an extra-long time, hoping to at least drown the blood-sucking bugs inhabiting his body. Spike had watched the spectacle of the squirming puppy bath from the relative safety of the counter next to the sink. *Filthy canine...*

Cleaned and brushed, the puppy was quite handsome. His fuzzy coat was a honey-gold color, and his muzzle and fox-like ears were edged in black. His big feet and long legs indicated that he would be a large dog when full grown.

Annie made an appointment with the local vet for a check-up and shots, but by that time she had been up for nearly twenty hours and was ready to collapse. Of course it was one of those days when Michael was nowhere to be found...

She took the pup outside and he immediately ran down to the edge of the lake. Annie groaned, picturing him finding a dead fish to roll on or a nice bit of muck to wade through. She was just about ready to slam the door on the whole mess, when she saw the pup circle an area next to the woods. He quickly relieved himself and came tearing back up the hill. He sat next to her feet and lifted a paw in the air, looking for approval.

"Who do you think you are?" Annie laughed, "Lassie?"

A wagging tail was her answer.

She took him inside and fed him, borrowing food from a disgusted Spike, and then went to bed after setting her alarm for three o'clock.

Puppy breath and a cold nose woke her at two-thirty. Annie hauled herself out of her warm bed and let the dog outside. He repeated his run to the lake, and never left her side for the rest of the day.

The vet guessed the dog's age to be around twelve weeks, and possibly a Chow-Collie-German Shepherd mix. He admitted to being unsure of what breed contributed to the pup's potential size.

Annie had a heck of a time coming up with a name for her new pet. Nothing seemed to suit him, and by default, he remained "Dog." On several frustrating occasions when he came home smelling of skunk, he was elevated to "Damn Dog." Spike was amused... a dog didn't deserve a proper name anyway.

...Filthy canine.

Michael poured himself a cup of coffee and sat down to wait for Annie. He didn't relish tellin' her his news, but he had no choice. He had to leave.

"Leaving?" Annie choked. "Leaving? But why? Michael, you can't!"

"Sorry, Annie, but I have to. I uh... got another temporary assignment."

"Oh. So you have your job back?"

"Never lost it, Annie. I've been working…"

"I wondered where you'd disappear to for days at a time…"

He nodded. "It doesn't pay all that much. Practically nothing actually, but I love it. Um… you figure out how much I owe you for rent and I'll pay you as soon as I can."

"Rent?"

"Rent. Heck, I've been stayin' here for weeks… I owe you, Annie."

"Oh no. You've more than paid your way with all the work you do around here, Michael. Jeez!"

"It wasn't all that much…"

"Oh yes it was! Gosh, you moved all the furniture in, split a ton of wood for the winter, do all the cooking when I have to work, plowed up all that dirt for my garden… planted half the vegetables and keep them weeded, built that nice tack room in the barn, taught me to milk that silly nanny goat *after* you delivered her kids, and then went and built that coop! Not all that much? Michael, I don't know what I would have done without you!"

"I told you that you needed a man around the house," he said with his serene smile.

"And you're leaving…"

"I'll be back, Annie. I'm not sure when, but we'll see each other again."

"When… when are you going?"

"Tomorrow."

"Where?"

"Can't tell you that, Annie."

"Big surprise," she said, just a little bitter. "You've been with me all this time and I still don't know much more about you than I did the day we met. Why are you so secretive?"

"Not much about me that you need to know right now, Annie. Not much you'd want to know."

"But I do! I want to know everything about you… What you were like as a child, your cowboy days… why you and your fiancé aren't together anymore; I know you still love her… And your brother; why don't you ever go see him? I want to know your hopes and dreams… I want to know *you*!"

"Annie…"

"And why do you have to leave?" she cried, tears beginning to stream down her face. "I *need* you, Michael! I… I love you…"

"Annie," he sighed, taking her into his arms, "I love you too, but I have to go. And as far as needing me… You only think you do, and I… there's others that need me more right now. Please try to understand."

She sniffed and nodded. "I'll try…"

"Well, you'd better get to bed, Annie. Sleep late and I'll have our dinner ready when you get up."

"No. This is your last night here and I think it should be special. Let's go out."

"Not a good idea, Annie…"

"Why not? We've never gone out, and I want to do this as a… a thank you. We can go someplace really nice, and…"

"I can't."

"Why the heck not?"

"You've seen my wardrobe, hon; I don't exactly have the duds for a night on the town."

"Big deal. We can go shopping."

"Nope. Annie, if you want to know the truth, I don't want to take the chance of runnin' into my brother… or his friends. It's not a good time right now…"

"Probably wouldn't do me any good to ask why…"

"I'd tell you if I could."

She sighed and walked to the window, and looked at her truck in the driveway. It just occurred to her that Michael never had any form of transportation, and she lived miles and miles from anywhere. She turned around with a new question on her lips.

"Don't even ask, Annie."

She shut her mouth.

"And if it means all that much to you, you can take me out to dinner, but not in Waterston. Maybe one of those little towns south of here…"

"We could do that," she said, attempting to smile, even though her heart was breaking.

"But no place fancy, okay?"

"No place fancy, but no place with a drive-thru either," she said, moving back into his arms. "Michael, I'm going to miss you so much."

He held her tight and buried his lips in her autumn hair.

"I'm going to miss you too, Annie. God, I'm going to miss you…"

Gabe sat in his office at the studio, reviewing his dismal financial situation. He never got his much-needed loan to expand and upgrade, but his recording business wasn't quite so bleak any more. He'd managed to sign on a few new bands, quite popular in the area and with the promise of some decent record sales.

He and Kyle had chucked the idea of doing some shows to promote SD, figuring that they'd look too "has been" and really turn the buying public away. Gabe had long since lost the desire to perform anyway. Didn't care to play, sing, or even write any more.

His financial situation at home was no better, but no worse, and he was almost content with that.

Home… The twins were now a year old and hell on wheels, wearing both Deirdre and him down as they tried to keep up with the mischievous toddlers. Deirdre was still heavy into her charity work, and was also doing a little acting in the community theater. She tried to convince Gabe that he'd be fantastic on stage, but he turned her down. Oh, he knew he could do it, had done it in college many times, and then again in his music videos with SD, but he couldn't dredge up even the smallest bit of enthusiasm. Hell, he was downright apathetic about pretty much everything, and spent most of his time staring off into space. He loved his wife and children more than ever, but he still felt lacking. If only he could find *her*…

Yeah right. And then what?

Chet, the African Gray parrot that lived in his office, squawked, and Gabe turned around to glare at him. Kyle had given him the bird for Christmas right after they moved to Michigan, and the foul fowl had been annoying and entertaining him with dirty little ditties ever since.

"You were saying…?" Gabe snarled, handing the bird a bit of dried fruit he kept in the drawer for just that purpose.

Chet took his treat in a claw and nibbled on it, staring at the man he loved to harass.

"Well…?"

"Sooner than you think," the bird squawked, and turned his back on Gabe.

"Sooner? What the hell did Kyle teach you now?"

But Chet wouldn't answer.

Gabe chucked a chunk of apple at him and headed for his truck. He needed some air…

"How about here?" Annie asked, slowing down in front of a popular bar. It wasn't all that busy yet, and Michael would fit right in with his "wardrobe."

Michael looked around, checking to see if he recognized any of the vehicles in the parking lot. Nope…

"Looks fine, Annie. The food good?"

"According to Marti it is."

"Then let's go."

She parked the truck, and they went inside and found a quiet booth in the corner.

Annie was thrilled that they were finally out together, and would hopefully have a good time. Sure, she cherished their quiet evenings together in the cabin, doing nothing but talking or watching old movies, but she'd gotten a little taste of a social life dating Tyler and she found she enjoyed it very much. She wanted Michael to have that same pleasure.

Michael left his hat on and pulled low over his eyes, and checked out every single person who walked through the door. He'd made sure to pick a table close to the back door too. God, he was nervous, and hoped this wasn't all a big mistake. If it hadn't meant so much to Annie, he sure as heck wouldn't have left the cabin. Just never knew who might see him and recognize him…

Annie noticed his nervousness when he wouldn't make eye contact with the very nice waitress who took their drink order. She chose not to say anything to him.

"Well, what looks good?" Annie asked, scanning the menu.

"Pretty much everything. Artichoke dip?"

"Very tasty. Want some?"

"What the heck is an artichoke?"

"You're kidding…"

"No I'm not. Well, I *know* what one is, but can't say that I've ever thought about eatin' one."

"Really? They're very good. Gaining popularity around here too…"

"Not something you'd ever see on the menu where I come from," he laughed.

"Which is…"

"Out west, Annie."

"That narrows it down. Just tell me the state and I won't ask any more."

"Promise?"

"Promise."

"Montana. I'm from Montana. Born and raised there."

"Really? I went there once. I spent a week in Billings when I was seventeen. It was the only vacation I ever took… I love it out there."

He already knew that, he'd even seen her there, but encouraged her to talk about it. If she were talking, he wouldn't have to.

"The only vacation?"

"Mmhmm. It was on spring break, and I stayed with a friend who'd moved out there the year before to go to college. We were kind of close before that…"

"And did you have a good time?"

"Pretty much. We did some sight-seeing, went horseback riding, and almost went on a double date."

"Almost?"

"Mmhmm. She was dating some guy named Steve. I never met him, but she thought he was the best. Anyway, we were all supposed to go out. They'd hooked me up with Steve's brother but he backed out at the last minute or something. I didn't really mind though. He was a few years older than me and kind of on the wild side."

Michael smiled and nodded. *Yep…*

"But I had a good time out there."

"Do you still keep in contact with her?"

"We send a letter every once in a while. She's a veterinarian now with a thriving practice in Denver. Kinda sad though…"

"What, her thriving practice?"

"No… silly! No… That Steve guy she was dating? He died. It tore her up. They hadn't seen each other for years, but she kept track of him."

"She did?" Michael asked, somewhat surprised.

"Mmhmm. He was a rodeo star or something like that. I wasn't even aware they *had* rodeo stars…"

"I wouldn't call them stars, but a few are well known on the circuit. Hard life," Michael said, shaking his head.

"You sound like you've been there."

"And done that. The artichoke dip is pretty good, you say?"

"Go ahead, change the subject," Annie laughed. "And yes it is… for an appetizer. Now what would you like for dinner?"

She had a Blackened Chicken Caesar Salad and he ordered a medium-rare steak with all the fixin's. They talked and laughed and ate, and had a great time until the door opened near the end of their meal and Michael looked as if he'd seen a ghost. Annie couldn't see who had put that look of apprehension on her friend's face, but when he asked if they could leave before dessert, she didn't argue. Didn't ask questions, just paid the bill and left out the back door.

Gabe drove until dusk, heading in a vaguely southerly direction. Didn't much care where he ended up, just felt the need to drive until he ran out of road. Ended up stopping at a busy little tavern with a reputation for great food, and wandered inside. He didn't look around, just wandered to the bar and ordered a beer. Ordered one more, drank it, and left, never even speaking to a soul except the bartender.

The trip back home was depressing as hell, and all Gabe could think about was his brother… and them goddamn green eyes and autumn hair that had been haunting him forever.

After he was back in his home, he played with his sons for a while, mumbled an apology to his wife for being late again, and then went to bed with a headache – and a heartache. Why couldn't he be happy…?

Annie and Michael took one last walk together, wading in the shallow warmth of the lake's edge and watching the full moon rise above the trees.

"You really miss her, don't you?" Annie asked quietly, lacing her fingers into his.

"Yep. How'd you know?"

"Your face. I don't know much about you, Michael Anthony, but I know that look of a lost love. You had it just now."

"I was thinking about her… She was the best thing that ever happened to me, Annie. God, I never thought it was possible to love anyone as much as I love her."

"Love… You said 'love' and not 'loved'. There's no chance that you could ever get back together?"

"Not in this lifetime, Annie. Perhaps in the next," he answered with a sad smile.

"I'm so sorry. But Michael, if you know you'll never be with her again, shouldn't you move on? There's bound to be someone out there…"

"Annie, I can't."

"Sure you can! You can learn to love again… I… I did."

"You don't understand. I can't. And I can't tell you…"

"You know you can tell me anything…"

"Not this. But I can tell you I've loved three women in my life. The first loved my brother more than me, the second I lost forever… and the third… the third I'm not really allowed to love."

"Not allowed?"

"That didn't come out right. I mean I can, but… Oh God, it's just too complicated to explain."

"These women… well, the third actually, is… is she the reason… Oh jeez, I can't even ask," she said, blushing.

"Ask what, Annie? Why I never acted… um, why you and I… Oh God, why we never got together that way?"

She nodded, too embarrassed to speak.

He let go of her hand and put his arm around her.

"I admit it crossed my mind, Annie. Many times," he said quietly. "But you and I both know… we aren't meant to be together. Not as husband and wife anyway. You're meant for another."

"Sometimes I'm not so sure, Michael. And since we're baring our souls here… Well, I've thought about it too. I look at you and think, 'it's him. He's the one I've been waiting for all my life!' Your face, your hair… even your build are what I've seen in my dreams… what I've felt in my heart. And then you touch me and there's nothing. You're him, but you're not him, Michael. Why is that? And I do love you, but as a brother and a very dear friend. I just don't understand…"

"Don't even try, Annie. And for what it's worth, you're that third woman. And now you know why I… why I can't."

She stopped walking and turned to him.

"It's really too bad, isn't it? We're such good friends and… It's just too bad. But Michael, I do hope you can find someone to love someday…"

"I did, Annie, and there will never be another. But don't you give up, hon. You'll find who you're lookin' for. May not be tomorrow or next week, or even next year, but you'll find him."

"Oh? You can be so sure?"

"Yep. Sometimes I know things and this I know…"

"Do you have a crystal ball or something that you can see into the future?"

she asked, laughing just a little.

"Funny you should say that."

She raised an eyebrow at him.

"My brother used to ask me that all the time," he explained. "Kind of a runnin' joke with us even if some of it wasn't very funny."

"Your brother again," she muttered, wondering how this mystery sibling could shut someone as nice as Michael out of his life.

"Aw, Annie… It isn't his fault. And I know you'd love him if you ever met him."

"Is he anything like you?"

"Very much like me… even if he calls himself my evil twin. Okay, enough talk. Let's hike up to the clearing and spend the rest of our time together sittin' on that bench and watchin' the stars. No talkin', just bein' together."

"I'd like that, Michael."

He smiled down at her and gently took her face into his large, rough hands.

"I do love you, Annie Benton," he whispered, and kissed her lips. Not with the passion of a lover, but not much like a brother either…

Chapter Eleven

Late Summer, 1991

"Annie-bananie, you're back! How was your vacation? What exotic places did you visit?"

"Exotic? Jeez, Marti, you know I stayed home."

"You did? I thought you were kidding!"

"Nope, I was serious, I'm afraid. I was tempted to go to Montana but… I don't know…"

"To find him?"

"Like I'd be able to. And he'll show up again when he can. He said he would and he never lies…"

"So you sat home and did nothing? What a waste of two weeks…" Marti sighed.

"I kept busy. Gosh, I can't believe how much work Michael did around the place. Now that he's not there anymore I have to do it all. I enjoy it though…"

"Sure… Weeding the garden and taking care of all of those animals you have? God, it's a freakin' zoo anymore!"

"They're my family, Marti. And guess what?"

"What…"

"I have a new member."

"You're kidding. What now, a giraffe?"

"Hardly. Marti, I finally have a horse!"

"You do? Oh wow… You've wanted one forever."

"I know. It was weird… I never read the newspaper, but I was coming home the other day and passed a black truck. I didn't see who was driving, but he *was* wearing a cowboy hat and I suddenly thought of Michael…"

"Like he's not always on your mind anyway…"

"True, but at that time he wasn't. Anyway, I turned into that convenience store by that park with the stinking duck pond, and bought a paper."

"What does that have to do with Michael?"

"I don't know… cowboy hat, cowboys… horses… One of those things when your mind wanders. Anyway, I was flipping through the classifieds, in the farm and garden section… and *why*, I still don't know… But I saw an ad for a horse auction – that same night."

"So you went?"

"And found the perfect horse. Marti, he's beautiful, and so smart and gentle and… and I just love him!"

"Do tell…"

"Oh stop. I couldn't believe he went so cheap either. He'd been trained as a jumper but didn't do well in the arena, so they were dumping him! Jeez, he could have ended up as dog food!"

"Probably a reason…"

"Not that I've found so far. I've ridden him quite a bit and he'll do anything I ask. He jumps like a dream, every gait is so smooth; he'll even do flying lead changes."

"I'll pretend to know what the heck you're talking about. And how do you know all this stuff?"

"I've been horse crazy ever since I was a kid, and I read a lot. Michael used to talk a lot about it too. Did you know he used to *train* horses? And students… Mostly for roping and reining, but he had a few that wanted to compete in Western Pleasure…"

"Again I'll pretend…"

"Thanks for indulging me," Annie grinned.

"But I didn't know you rode all that much. Jumping?"

"Mmhmm. It's like Adonis is teaching me…"

"Adonis?"

"My horse."

"Fancy name…"

"Beautiful horse. And I can't believe how much I've leaned over the last week. We do a lot of trail riding… That woods is huge!"

"Well don't get lost in it!"

"I did. And you know what?"

"Let me guess… Adonis the wonder horse found the way home."

"Well… yeah! Dog helped. But only a little…"

"You and your critters… I suppose you'll become a recluse again? Not that you ever really abandon it, but you and Tyler did manage to get out once in a while. Still seeing him?"

"Once a week. He's seeing someone else now, and it's sounding kind of serious."

"And he still dates you? Whoo… Does she know about you?"

"According to him, yes. But Tyler and I are just friends, and I'm certainly no threat to her. I'll fade away gracefully if it becomes a problem though… or if they decide that they're meant for each other."

"You're too nice, Annie. If it were me I would have married him right away!"

"Marti! It was never like that with us! Besides, I couldn't 'settle'."

"Then you'll die an old maid. I'm beginning to think I will too," Marti moaned.

"Something to look forward to, huh," Annie sighed.

"Great. Now I'm all depressed," Marti laughed.

"And it's time to punch in. See you on break?"

"Assuming I get one. I'm floating over to labor and delivery tonight…"

"Ick. I'll stick with Pediatrics and NICU."

"My first choice too, but… Hey, when do you want to get together again? We haven't been out in ages. First it's Tyler and then Michael… You just don't have time for poor ol' Marti anymore. God, I haven't even been invited to your cabin since you moved in."

"You don't need an invitation, Marti. You're welcome any time…"

"Tomorrow?"

"Ooh… I have plans."

"A date?" Marti sighed.

Annie just smiled. *Sure was…*

✦ ✦ ✦

"Gabe?"

"Hey Tyler… Where the hell have you been? Christ, I haven't heard from you in weeks!"

"Busy, busy! I heard that Deirdre's play is opening tonight and wondered if the two of you would like to stop somewhere for drinks beforehand."

"We already have a table reserved at Brody's. Five o'clock? I know it's early, but…"

"Five is fine. Mind if I bring a date?"

"Not at all. Actually, I'd be rather disappointed if you didn't, Ty," Gabe said, thinking back to their last aborted dinner engagement. He smiled, hoping he'd finally get to meet that nurse Tyler was half in love with. She must be something…

"…Nee and I will meet you there," Gabe heard, catching only half of what his friend said.

Annie? Did he say Annie?

"Uh, yeah. Later, Ty…"

Annie… green eyes and autumn hair… Oh God, just when he thought he'd finally purged that specter from his mind, she came dancing back in. His body began to tingle and his vision to fade, and he dropped his head to his desk. *Aw God…*

"Geoffrey? Are you all right, dear?"

It wasn't her voice, but the aroma of flowers that jolted him back to reality. *Roses.*

"Geoffrey…?"

"I… I'm fine, Deirdre. Just catching a quick nap…"

"Save your lies for those who can't see through them, dear," Deirdre murmured, giving him a gentle caress on his head.

"You know me too well, Dee. And I'm fine… really. All set for you debut tonight?"

"Hardly a debut… I've done dozens of plays… before I met Steven. But yes, I'm ready. And excited! I do love Shakespeare…"

102

"Taming of the Shrew… Deirdre, I can scarcely imagine you as that acid-tongued Kate…"

"I'm an actress, Geoffrey. I can be anyone I care to be…"

Except a true wife…

They both looked at each other and glanced quickly away, reading each other's thoughts.

"I… I suppose I should go put these in water and get ready," Deirdre murmured, glancing down at the bouquet in her hand.

Gabe stared at the flowers, and then plucked one of the white roses from the bunch. He ran a finger along the velvet petals as green eyes stared at him from the back of his mind.

Deirdre turned quickly away and left his den.

Gabe sat there, staring at his white rose, until a knock on the front door interrupted his sad, confusing reverie. He laid his precious bloom on the desk and went to let the twins' babysitter in.

Annie threw the last of her "necessities" into her bag, and left for her "date." Her excitement was building with each moment, although she had no idea why. But tonight was going to be special, that much she was certain of.

"Good afternoon, Mr. And Mrs. Evans," Abby said, giving them her professional smile. "Your guests are already seated… your usual table."

"Thank you, Abby," Gabe replied, and escorted Deirdre to a very intimate table towards the back of the restaurant.

Without knowing why, he grabbed a white rose from the bouquet on the hostess' stand, and gave Abby a wink.

She smiled back, changing her professional façade to a warm, sincere one.

Tyler looked up and saw his friend heading towards them.

"They're here," he whispered to the redhead at his side. "You finally get to meet the famous Gabe Evans."

She smoothed her hair back, making sure she looked no less than perfect, and eagerly anticipated his arrival.

"Hi, Tyler," Gabe mumbled, trying not to stare at Ty's date.

Aw God, this was his nurse? She was beautiful…in a plastic sort of way. Her dark red hair was smoothly plastered to her skull, and pulled back into a tight knot low on the back of her head. Her make-up was somewhat heavy – although appeared to have been applied by a professional hand, and her long, well-manicured nails were painted a dark burgundy that matched the color of the long, sparkling sheath of a dress she was wearing. Diamonds glittered at her ears and throat, and Gabe could not possibly imagine her ministering to the sick and injured.

The rose in his hand seemed to wilt just a bit, and Gabe handed it to Deirdre along with a quick kiss to the top of her head.

"Hi Gabe, how've you been?" Ty said, rising to shake his friend's hand.

"Not bad. You remember Deirdre…"

"Mrs. Evans, you look lovely tonight."

"Thank you, Mr. Howe," Deirdre acknowledged.

"This is Deanna Montgomery," Tyler said, introducing his date.

Not Annie… Gabe felt unwarranted relief. *But who the hell was Annie in the first place?* He shook his head to clear his whirlwind of thoughts.

"Call me NeeNee," Deanna laughed, her voice sounding like tinkling crystal.

Gabe and Deirdre both nodded, and took their seats.

The foursome made small talk about the weather, Deirdre's play, and how they wished they had time for a decent dinner instead of merely drinks and appetizers.

"So, you're a nurse?" Gabe asked, turning to the sleek woman on his left.

"A… A nurse?" she nearly choked, being in the middle of a sip of wine. "Oh dear God no! That's Tyler's other little 'friend'…"

"Oh! Um… sorry."

Tyler tried not to glare.

Had Gabe been capable of blushing he would have. Never blushed in his life though…

"No no," Deanna continued, "I'm a buyer for women's fashions at Le Elegance… you know, that large boutique over on…"

Deirdre nodded. Very trendy, very ritzy, and very expensive… she never shopped there.

Deana looked at the smaller woman and continued. "And I'm also the fashion editor for the Waterston Watch's Sunday edition. I have a four page spread in their weekly magazine…" she smiled, but it didn't reach her smoky gray eyes.

Snooty bitch… Gabe's opinion of her dropped a few more points. Why the hell did Ty hook up with a fake like her in the first place?

"Fashion, hmm…?" Gabe teased. "Tell me, am I a fashion 'do' or 'don't'?"

Deanna gave him a long look, taking in his expensive black suit, dark royal blue shirt, which almost exactly matched his eyes, and the subtle yet distinctive tie he was wearing. She took another long look, imagining him without those clothes…

"Well?"

"Oh! Definitely a 'do', Gabe. Deirdre, you do a marvelous job dressing your man…"

"He dresses himself, NeeNee," Deirdre said, not liking this woman very much. She'd seen the look Geoffrey had gotten, and it very nearly made her jealous. She was glad that she had no romantic feeling for her husband or she may have been tempted to scratch Deanna's big smoky eyes right out of her sleek red head.

"Then he certainly has good taste, Deirdre. Tell me, Gabe, do you ever do any modeling? You're quite photogenic..."

"Aw God," he burst out laughing, "Me? You've got to be kidding!"

"I never kid about such things. And I've seen your videos; the camera loves you..."

"Well I can't say it's reciprocal. I hated doing those damn things."

"And yet you did so many," Deanna purred.

"It was something to do at the time."

"Well, should you happen to change your mind..." Deanna pulled her card from her purse and slid it over to him. "Call me any time," she murmured, letting her hand brush his.

Gabe gave her a cold smile but totally ignored the card.

"Good for you, Geoffrey," Deirdre thought, feeling sorry for poor Tyler. Imagine the nerve of that woman... flirting so openly with another man, and right in front of her date! Not to mention the other man's wife...

She felt Geoffrey's knee nudge her under the table.

"Deanna dear, let's go powder our noses," Deirdre suggested, gathering up her handbag.

Tyler was giving her a rather nasty look, so NeeNee thought it might be a good idea.

"God, Ty, I'm sorry about that," Gabe sighed, picking up Deanna's card and tucking it under a plate of half-eaten snacks.

"Happens all the time, Gabe... to you anyway. And she's not all that I thought she was," Tyler murmured, pulling the card back out and ripping it to shreds. He dumped the pieces into an ashtray on the vacant table next to them.

"I have to admit, I was surprised to see you hooking up with someone like that. I figured you'd go for a more 'down to earth' type," Gabe told him. He absently picked up Deirdre's rose and spun it in his fingers.

"I do. Did anyway, but I wasn't *her* type..."

"The nurse?"

"Yeah..."

"What happened? Or didn't happen as the case may be..."

"Oh, we still go out but only as friends."

"Ouch. I take it you wanted more?"

"Wanted it all, Gabe. Cozy little house, white picket fence, dog, cat... two-point- two children..." Tyler said with a sad smile.

"Well don't give up on her, Ty. You never know."

"Oh, I know. I've told her enough that I want to further our relationship, but she's holding back. I know she cares for me though and I keep plugging along... Besides, she's living with some guy..."

"Oh God... You sure can pick 'em!" Gabe chuckled.

"Now wait and hear me out. Annie and I…"

Gabe felt himself grow cold.

"A… Annie?"

"Yeah, you know… the nurse? Anyway, Annie and I are pretty good friends, and she told me all about this Michael character…"

"Michael being the man she lives with?"

"Lived. He moved on… job related, apparently. I was a bit stunned at first, but she was so honest about her relationship with him. Strictly platonic. She loves him, but he's not the one for her either. 'Him but not him', she told me."

"And you believe her? Oh Christ… Ty! She *lives* with a guy and…"

"She told the truth, Gabe."

"Uh huh…"

"Annie can't lie. It's just not in her to do it! I guess that's why I feel the way I do about her… honest, down to earth… calls 'em as she sees 'em, but will do it in such a way that it won't hurt. Too bad anyway…"

"So why didn't you bring Miss Perfect tonight instead of Miss All That?"

"She had other plans, Gabe, or I would have. But then again, she might have dumped me on the spot once she saw you," Tyler laughed. "She likes the tall, dark, and cowboy type…"

"Then she wouldn't be worth it after all, eh Ty? Subject change. Our ladies approacheth…"

Gabe stood and welcomed them back, giving Deirdre a very loving kiss and Deanna a smirk of a smile.

Snooty bitch…

He also found himself wishing that they'd taken a bit longer with their nose powdering, because he really wanted to hear more about Tyler's Annie. Like… what color were her eyes, and was her hair reminiscent of autumn…?

Better that he never found out though. Knowing she might actually exist and not being able to have her would literally kill him.

Michael sat high up in the balcony of the little community theater and enjoyed the heck out of the Shakespearean comedy. He'd seen the blonde actress who played Kate before, but she was Juliet at that time.

He sighed and sniffed the single, blood-red rose in his hand, wishing like hell he could deliver it to her himself. Couldn't though, and had already recruited an usher to do it for him.

The play ended with a standing ovation and several curtain calls, and many bouquets handed to the various cast members.

Deirdre took the single rose handed to her and added it to her already flower-laden arms, but then hesitated. She gazed deep into the spiral of the petals, and then glanced at Geoffrey.

He shrugged his shoulders, denying that he'd sent it to her. Didn't know who had either.

Oh God… Steven was the only other one to have ever handed her such a gift… that single, blood-red bloom. She scanned the audience, knowing how foolish it was to hope, but hoping just the same.

Reality hit hard, remembering that her Romeo was dead, and it was all Deirdre could do to exit the stage and hide in a dressing room as she collapsed into tears.

Gabe found her moments later, recognizing that split-second look of unfathomable sorrow on her face, and then followed the trail of dropped and forgotten flowers in the labyrinth of halls behind the stage.

"Dee," he said quietly, taking her into his arms.

She clung to him, sobbing as if she'd never stop.

"Oh God, Geoffrey," she moaned, "I miss him. I miss him so very much…"

He held her and kissed her, and even cried a little himself.

"I miss him too, love…"

Gabe picked up her trembling hand, which still held that single rose, and brought it to his lips.

"God, I miss him…"

Annie saddled her horse and was off on her first overnight adventure. Camping adventure anyway. After finding Michael's abandoned bedroll in the barn, and missing him as much as she was, she decided to take a little trip to the woods and spend the night. Although a little apprehensive at such an endeavor, Annie felt safe enough with her rapidly growing Dog to protect her. It was just a night in the woods…

After a long ride along the road to reach the other side of her property, Annie turned into the woods and followed a deer trail, hoping like heck it would take her where she wanted to go.

Adonis took her to place she had been dying to visit ever since she moved in. She could see the waterfall from across the lake, but never had the time or the energy to make the long hike. Now she was finally there… and it was beautiful.

She could pretty much see the entire, crescent shaped lake from her vantage point nearly one hundred feet above the water. She never realized how long the lake was, more like a river actually, but land-locked. She could see her beach, the hill with the clearing, and the swamp off to the northeast… Wow. It wouldn't be long and she'd see the sunset too.

Annie found a place she thought suitable for her bed, and unrolled Michael's sleeping bag. It was close enough to the tiny stream that fell over the flat rocks to the lake below, but far enough away from the edge of the cliff so that she wouldn't have to worry about rolling to her death in her sleep. As if…

She probably wouldn't sleep a wink when all was said and done. Regardless, it was an adventure for her, small though it was.

She and Dog shared some sandwiches, and then settled down to enjoy the sunset and the late summer evening. Annie sat there for hours, just enjoying Mother Nature and thinking of nothing in particular. Well, not entirely true. Her mind was on Tyler and Michael, and why if she loved them both, she couldn't go further than friendship. Oh well... but she sure was wishing that either of them were with her at that moment, sharing the beauty of the night. Of course Tyler and his new love were at the theater, and Heaven only knew where Michael was.

Maybe she should have taken Tyler up on his offer to go to the play. She found it amusing that he asked her to go before he asked Deanna, even if it wasn't very nice to think such things. Still... a play would have been fun. Annie had never been to one in her entire life. Yeah, she should have told him she would go. Darn it. Then again, she would have missed this absolutely wonderful night, watching the fireflies dance through the trees, watching the stunning sunset, watching the stars pop out one by one... all by her lonely self. To think she thought this would be special...

Darn it.

Annie climbed into the sleeping bag and snuggled deep into its warmth. It smelled faintly of Michael, and his serene scent of horses, leather, and a cool pine forest. It made her smile, and she felt as if she were wrapped in his loving arms. Lord, she missed him.

A loud shriek had her bolt upright in seconds, torn from a deep sleep and a most wonderful dream. She couldn't remember the details, but she felt almost as if she... she was about to be kissed... What the heck had woken her up? She shivered in the cool air of the late night, and looked around.

A shadow moved in the trees, high in the branches, and then an owl swooped after its prey. Must have been the owl... Annie had heard them before, but not nearly so close. Kind of creepy, actually. Dog was awakened by the bird too, and left his bed by Adonis to join Annie. He gave her face a quick lick and sat next to her.

"So, Dog, are you enjoying our wilderness adventure?" she asked, ruffling his fur.

He let out a short whine and licked her again.

"Yeah...I know what you mean. Not as much fun by ourselves, is it? Oh well... we can chalk it up to experience. Now get off my blankets and go back to your own bed, and let's get some sleep." She gave the pup a little nudge, and snuggled back down.

It was then she saw another shadow, but this one was no owl. *Oh jeez...*

The fur on Dog's back rose as he saw the movement of the uninvited camper, but the changed his attitude when the scent of the intruder hit his nose. His tail went into a happy wag, and he ran off to greet the man.

Annie couldn't believe it. How on Earth did he ever find her? She sat, stunned, and watched as he made his way over to her.

Long, denim clad legs stopped a few feet in front of her. Annie just stared, taking in his scuffed boots, bits of chaff from the summer grasses clinging to them, and then let her eyes travel up.

He hadn't changed a bit. He still wore those faded jeans, the same gray tee shirt, and that beat up leather jacket. His Stetson still had that dark dust clinging to it, and his eyes were just as bright, his smile just as serene as ever. She hadn't realized how much he had missed him until he was right there in front of her.

Neither of them said a word. Annie flipped back her blankets, inviting him to share the warmth, and he lay down next to her and took her into his arms. He gave her a light kiss on her forehead, and they watched the stars move overhead.

She wanted to ask him the million questions she had, like where had he been and how long was he staying, but she sensed a very deep sadness in him and ended up not saying a thing. Not one single word... Just held him as tightly as he was holding her, taking comfort in one another and just being there.

Annie wasn't sure what time she dozed off, still in his arms, but she did remember hearing the birds begin their morning song. When she woke... he was gone again, and the only proof that he had been there were the fresh tracks his boots had left in the early morning dew, and a single, blood-red rose petal.

Chapter Twelve

Christmas, 1991

"Annie, do I really get to come to your cabin for Christmas?"

"Of course, Eric! The party wouldn't be complete without you there. Besides, I need someone to hand out presents," she said with wink.

"Presents? For... for everyone?"

"Not everyone, just the most important people in my life, Eric."

"Oh." Eric dropped his eyes and looked away.

Annie figured she knew why, and put his mind at ease. The poor kid didn't have any money to get her anything.

"Eric, my house is nearly all decorated, but I don't seem to have enough ornaments to make it complete. Um... Did you get me anything yet?"

"I... No, not yet."

"Good. Then the perfect gift would be for you to make me some more decorations. Think you could do that?"

"I might be able to..." Gosh, he sure hoped she didn't want anything fancy. Her house was always so pretty.

"I'm sure you can. Let's see..." Annie reached into her tote bag and pulled out a large box. "Here you go, kiddo. This should keep you busy..."

Eric took the package and looked inside. Oh jeez... There were dozens of little clear glass balls with hooks in them, and bottles of paints in every color. Did she want him to paint them? He dug a little further and found some instructions. Just pour the paint into the balls and swirl it around... instant ornament! Yeah, he could handle that!

"There's more, Eric. Check under the cardboard."

He did, and found several squares of glass with pictures outlined in black metal, and a few brushes. Wow, when he was done it would look just like the stained glass windows in the church Annie took him to sometimes.

"Well?" Annie asked, giving him her sweet smile.

"Gosh, Annie, thanks! But this is kind of more like a present for me than for you."

"Mmm... perhaps, but that's what Christmas is about... giving? I give to you and then you give to me."

"Yeah... Annie, thank you so much! Gosh, I can't wait to get started!"

"Well you'll have to wait until tomorrow after you're discharged, and then you'll have plenty of time at home. Do you think your Aunt Irene might like to help?"

"I doubt it," Eric laughed. "She says she can't even draw a straight line, and she has no idea where I get my... my..."

"Artistic ability?"

"Yeah, that's it! Anyway, she doesn't know why I'm so good at drawing and painting and stuff."

"A gift from God, Eric. He didn't give you perfect health, but blessed you with a special ability not too many people have. Jeez, you're only eight years old and already you have an eye for detail that leaves me in awe. I still can't get over that picture you drew of Adonis. It looks just like him!"

"Yeah… I don't mean to brag or anything, but it was kinda good…"

"I framed it, Eric; it was that good. I have it hanging on a hook, right next to his stall. Well, I'd better get back to work and you'd better get some sleep. I *don't* want you to get sick again and miss my party! Now remember… I'll pick you up at four sharp on Christmas Eve, and you may spend the night."

"Wow… Um, will Santa find me there instead on my trailer?"

"I'm sure he will, Eric."

"Then that will be a first," the boy laughed, although a bit sadly, "because he still hasn't found the trailer!"

That tore at Annie's heart like nothing ever had before. She knew his tragic history, but Santa never visited either? Well, he sure as heck would this year… It would probably be the last as well as the first. Not too many boys Eric's age still believed…

"Maybe he's been saving up and you'll get it all at once. Anyway, bed time, mister…"

Eric adjusted the oxygen tubing in his nose for a more comfortable fit, and then snuggled down into his scratchy hospital sheets. He couldn't wait to spend the night at Annie's again. The bed in her guest room was big and soft, and the blankets always seemed warm and smelled so good… just like cinnamon or something spicy like that. Spike and Dog would always sneak in and keep him company too. Only four more days…

Annie gave him a hug and a kiss, and tucked him in. The rest of her patients that night only got a tuck in.

"Tyler, you can bring whoever the hell you want to the party as long as you show up! Deirdre is really looking forward to seeing you again."

"It would be Deanna…"

"I figured as much, given your tone of voice… and your hesitancy."

"Partially. I was invited to another party too."

"It won't be as much fun as mine," Gabe laughed.

"Probably not, but I have to at least make an appearance. She'd be hurt if I didn't show…"

"Who, your mother?"

"No… my 'nurse'. She's having a little get-together Christmas Eve for her handful of friends. Rather a holiday-housewarming combination. She moved into a new home this spring and she's just now getting around to showing it off."

"Well then, make her day and make an appearance, and then finish up the night at my place. Is that do-able?"

"I think so. See you then, Gabe."

"Later, Ty."

Gabe hung up, wishing that he could trade places with super-bitch Deanna for a while and join Tyler at the nurse's little housewarming. Why the hell hadn't he met her yet? Christ, he and Deirdre, and Tyler and his dates had been out together a dozen times over the last few months, but the nurse had never been able to make it. Gabe wondered if Ty was deliberately hiding her. Or did she really even exist…?

Annie's party wasn't quite a failure, but it sure wouldn't be high on her list of successes. The blustery, cold weather kept most of her casual acquaintances from venturing so far out into the country, and the ones that did show stayed only long enough for a cup or two of Christmas cheer. By eight o'clock, only Marti and Eric remained. Tyler had yet to show up, and Michael… Annie wondered if she'd ever see him again.

She touched the crystal angel he had given her the previous year, and tried to conjure up his face in her mind. Couldn't though. Just how strange was that? After all the time they spent together, the most she could come up with was a vague image of a tall, dark haired man. Couldn't remember the shade of blue that colored his eyes or how his smile looked. Kind of remembered that he was lean and well-muscled, but couldn't remember what he felt like when she hugged him. What she did remember was that she loved him and missed his serene presence filling her days… and those long, long nights.

Annie sighed and joined the remnants of her guests.

"Well, we might as well open our presents and call it an early night," she said, giving Eric a little nudge towards the tree.

His eyes lit up and he hurried over, thankful that he wasn't dragging his portable oxygen tank for a change. His mouth dropped open in awe as he looked at the small mountain of gifts and saw his name on the majority of them. Santa Claus had come, but disguised in the form of Annie.

"Go ahead, Eric," Annie laughed, "Dig in!"

He could hardly wait, but pulled out gifts for Annie and Marti first. The ones labeled "Tyler" and "Michael" he discreetly set aside, knowing how hurt Annie must have been that her two boyfriends never showed up.

Marti was touched by Eric's gift to her: a comical statue of a nurse with a big red smile on her face and an even bigger red heart on her chest, done in air-dry clay and painted with her coloring.

"Annie helped me pick it out," Eric said, just a little shy, "but I painted it. Gosh, I hope it's dry…"

"You did this today, Eric?" Marti gasped. The detail was incredible for such a young kid.

"Uh huh. Do… do you like it?"

"I love it, Tiger. I'm going to put it right on top of my television, and then you'll know I'll see it all the time."

Eric grinned and blushed just a little bit.

"Now open yours, Annie," he said, sitting next to her.

"But Eric, I already did! You even helped me put them up!"

Annie waved a hand at the brightly colored ornaments, hung on a gold tinsel garland and strung along the hearth behind the woodstove. The stained glass pictures of the Nativity hung in her windows.

"I know, but this is special… Aunt Irene and I went shopping this morning," he grinned.

"Oh Eric, you didn't need to do that."

"Yeah, I did, Annie," he answered quietly. "Open it."

So she did, and could barely keep from crying when she read the little poem on the plaque.

"…And all that really matters is that I made a difference in the life of a child…" Annie whispered, reading the last line aloud.

"Annie?" *Oh jeez, didn't she like it?* Eric thought for sure she would; it said exactly how he felt about her.

"It… it's beautiful, Eric. Thank you." Annie hugged him close, and hugged the inexpensive – yet priceless - plaque closer.

"Okay," she sniffed, "Marti, open your gift from me."

"Do I dare?"

"It's harmless… and you're so darn hard to buy for that I thought I'd let you shop for yourself. Enjoy!"

Marti loved the gift certificate from the mall, even if Annie spent way too much, but it was perfect. After all, she did have the reputation of being a shop-aholic!

"And now mine," Marti laughed, wadding up some wrapping paper and throwing it at Annie. She missed, and Dog went after it. Brought it back to her and waited patiently for it to be tossed again.

"Ooh… Marti, these are great!" Annie said, opening a box of scented candles. "I know just where to put them too."

"As if there were ever a question. In the bathroom, right?"

"You bet. Oh, and bubble bath too?" Annie sighed, pulling more goodies from the box. "I don't suppose there's a good book in there too to round out a perfect evening…"

"No, but there is a gift certificate to a book store. I wasn't sure what you *haven't* read yet," Marti answered dryly.

"Me neither, but I'll have fun looking! Okay Eric, it's your turn."

Eric grinned and went back over to the tree and all his wonderful presents.

Gosh, he felt just like a kid at Christmas… for the first time ever.

"Annie, you're one in a million," Marti whispered after Eric had opened nearly everything. "I don't think he'll lack for a thing now. God, a new coat, gloves, a hat… clothes that actually fit him, and that art set… He about cried when he opened that."

"Yeah… But he's so gifted that way and I want him to have every opportunity to use that talent. Now he has oils, watercolors, charcoal… canvases and paper. And I've arranged for him to have a tutor, an art major from Western, come to his school twice a week. Instead of suffering through a gym class he'll never survive let alone excel in, he can enjoy himself in art."

"Irene is okay with that?"

"She doesn't much care what happens as long as she doesn't have to be involved. She loves him, but she's so overwhelmed with his care and her jobs… the poor woman needs a break."

"Which is why Eric spends so much time over here?"

"It's only one day a week, and I love having him here. It gets pretty lonely at times…"

Marti put an arm around her friend and gave her a hug.

"Well, I'd better be going, Annie. It's almost ten, and I have to get up early tomorrow. Jill and I are driving to Midland for dinner with the folks."

"Tell them I said hello, and you be careful!"

"Will do. Eric, Merry Christmas!" Marti gave him a hug and a kiss, looked at her gift from him, and gave him an extra hug.

Annie and Eric sipped hot chocolate, and soon the boy was nodding off. She carried him to the guest room and tucked him in, and even looked the other way when Spike and Dog joined him on the bed. Hey, it was Christmas… or nearly so. Only an hour and a half to go.

She curled up in her favorite chair and covered herself with a fuzzy afghan, and watched the lights twinkle on her Christmas tree. The crystal angel sparkled at the top, and Annie never felt more alone in her life than she did at that moment. A tear slid down her cheek, reflecting the festive colors shining around the room. It was joined by another, and then a few more.

"Where are you, cowboy?" she whispered, not even aware than she had spoken.

✦ ✦ ✦

"Hell of a party you have here, Gabe. Valet parking, caterers… and the guest list! God, it looks like the 'who's who of Waterston'! I can't believe the mayor showed up!"

"Thank you, Tyler, although Deirdre was in charge of the guests. She travels in uh… slightly different social circles than I do."

"I wondered. So where are all of your rowdy friends tonight? Besides Davidson, of course."

"They'll be here after the snob patrol leaves. And speaking of Davidson, he'll be hosting a poker game around eleven. Can we count you in?"

"Ooh… sounds tempting, but I'm afraid not. I don't plan on staying that late."

"Oh? Going to go home and 'stuff Deanna's stocking?'" Gabe laughed.

"Hardly. Well, not tonight anyway," Tyler grinned. "No, I'm dropping her off and paying a little visit to someone I should have spent the evening with after all."

Gabe raised an eyebrow. "In other words, my party is *dull*?"

"I didn't say that, Gabe. Actually I'm having a wonderful time! Deanna certainly is…"

They both glanced over to where Miss Montgomery had a collection of gentlemen hanging on her every word. Either that or her impressive and exposed cleavage held them captive. Regardless, she was basking in their attention.

Deanna looked over at Tyler and blew him a kiss, and then threw a suggestive wink at Gabe. Now that she and Tyler were clear on their relationship, that it was physical only, she went out of her way to flirt with other men. Secretly she hoped to make him jealous enough to commit to her alone, but so far it wasn't working. *Ah well…*

"I still can't understand what you see in her, Ty," Gabe sighed.

"She looks good on my arm, and that's pretty much it, Gabe."

"That's it?"

"Well, that and…" he gave Gabe a sly grin.

Gabe literally shuddered at the thought of bedding Deanna. Christ, he'd remain celibate if it were a choice between NeeNee or nothing.

"You're welcome to her," Gabe sighed.

"She'd be disappointed to hear you say that."

"Her loss. Anyway, how long before you leave?"

"I have time for one more drink."

"Then let's do it!" Gabe smiled and slapped his friend on the back, and they snuck off to the den.

"So you're really ditching Deanna to spend time with…"

"I know… crazy, isn't it? I feel terrible for not calling her sooner and telling her I wouldn't be there, but Deanna… When I suggested going over there she looked like she would rather have her fingernails pulled out with a pair of pliers. She doesn't mind me seeing Annie, but she doesn't want anything to do with her…"

"I could imagine! What woman wants to meet her man's other girlfriends…"

"Gabe, Annie is not my… well, we don't have that kind of relationship."

"Still love her, don't you."

Tyler gave him a half nod. "I think I do, Gabe. Christ, I even bought her a ring on the off chance there'd be a … a Christmas miracle and she'd find that she loves me too."

"You're fucking kidding."

"I wish I was. But I also bought her a bracelet… just to have something to give her. Doubt she'll accept it though."

"And yet you spent all that money, knowing…"

"Have you ever been in love, Gabe? God, it makes you crazy! Of course you have… You and Deirdre have the perfect relationship."

Gabe could only smile at *that* comment.

"…So you know what I mean. The crazy part anyway. I don't know what the hell to do…" Tyler sighed.

"Yeah, I do know what you mean, Ty. Sometimes I… well, never mind. Anyway, I hope you get your nurse… Annie…"

Gabe felt ill all of the sudden, and excused himself. He raced to an upstairs bathroom and splashed some cold water on his face, and took slow, deep breaths to try and quell the nausea rising in him. *What the hell had brought that on?*

Once he was back in control, he slipped into his bedroom and looked out at the snow -covered park across the street. Great, fat flakes of snow drifted by his window, and even though his house was filled with hundreds of people who knew and loved him, Gabe had never felt more alone in his whole wretched life. His Annie… would he ever find her?

"Gabe?"

Christ, it figured…

"Miss Montgomery," he said, turning around.

"I saw you leave… aren't you feeling well?"

"Just needed a moment. May I help you with something, or is you presence here merely concern for my well-being?"

She smiled and moved into his bedroom, dropping her miniscule handbag on the bed and then seating herself seductively next to it.

"A little of both, Gabe. I thought maybe I could help you… feel better…"

"I'm sure you could, NeeNee. And for starters, you can get the hell out of here."

"Oh come on now, Gabe, you don't need to continue with the games. Your show of indifference might fool Tyler and your wife, but I can see right through it. You want me just as much as I want you…"

"Out, Deanna. The party is downstairs… go party."

"I'd much rather stay and…"

She reached behind her and began to unzip her dress.

Even though she repulsed him, Gabe found that he couldn't move away. She was beautiful, and if one looked beyond her personality…He found himself thinking things he hadn't thought about in quite a while.

Deanna smiled, recognizing that glazed look in his eyes and the lust beginning to show elsewhere. She slipped the thin straps of her dress from her shoulders.

"A little help here?" she whispered, running a finger along her lower lip.

Gabe took a step towards her, but stopped when a gust of wind hit the window and brought him back to reality.

"Merry Christmas, Miss Montgomery," he said coldly, and went to join his guests. *Dear God… what had he been thinking?*

He bumped into Kyle halfway down the stairs.

"Dude… are you okay? Dee sent me up to run interference but I couldn't get away in time…"

"I'm fine, Kyle, and I can fight my own battles. Been turning women down for a long time now," Gabe said, giving his buddy a lop-sided grin.

"I know, but she's… Christ, she's a snake!"

"You're telling me. Well then, my mongoose friend, let's get downstairs and have some fun. Oh, I have to tell Ty where his date is… He wanted to leave shortly."

"If he had any sense he'd leave her and get out while the gettin's good."

"I all but suggested that to him on several occasions, yet he… Hell, I don't know what he is, Kyle! He's in love with a seemingly decent woman, and yet he tolerates the likes of NeeNee the Nasty. Anyway, it's not my problem. Hey, go break out the cards and I'll see you in a few."

"So soon? But Gabe, the cream of the Waterston crop is still havin' a snooty good time down there. Won't they…"

"Who the hell cares? They can join in if they want to. We'll clean 'em out and donate all of our winnings to Deirdre's charities. That would get their shorts in a wad…" Gabe laughed. The wealthy society bunch had no problem soliciting for charities, but when it came to opening their own pockets they suddenly were short on ready cash. He'd seen it all too often lately when he helped Deirdre host one of her fund-raisers. Pissed him off to no end, and he always ended up donating far more than he could really afford.

"I'll see you in a minute, Kyle."

"Gabe? Is everything all right? You looked a little peaked there…"

"I'm fine. And I'm glad you could stop by tonight, Tyler."

"Me too. Well, I'd better be going…"

"Deanna was just upstairs…"

"Like I care. She can find her own way home…"

"Tyler…?"

"I know… not a very gentlemanly thing to do, but at this point I don't much care, Gabe. I need to get over to Annie's… I feel compelled or something, and that extra hour it would take to run super-bitch home… well, I just don't want to take it."

Gabe smiled. He was finally beginning to see the light…

"I'll see that she gets home safely, Ty."

"Uh… you don't plan on taking her, do you?"

"Of course not! We do have a taxi service…"

Ty grinned, and headed for the door.

Annie dried her tears and tidied up her home, putting away the leftover snacks and washing up the dishes. Once those tasks were completed, it would be time to "play Santa" and put the rest of Eric's presents under the tree. Most of the toys she had were stashed in her bedroom, but the biggest gift was out in the barn. She threw on her boots and coat, and went to fetch it.

Tyler pulled in just as Annie was muscling the bicycle up the steps to the cabin.

"Annie! Hold on... I'll get that for you," he called out his open window. He shut his car down and ran to help her.

"Tyler? I... I didn't think you were going to make it? The weather..."

"The weather is nothing. I had to go to another party... Well, I didn't have to, but he is a good friend... Anyway, I should have been here for you, Annie. I'm so sorry..."

"That's okay, Tyler. You're here now..."

He smiled and hauled the bike into the cabin.

"So he's spending the night?"

"Mmhmm. No one should have to be alone on Christmas Eve, and his aunt was scheduled to work a double shift today. But I would have let him stay anyway... Gosh, I can't believe you're here this late."

"Is that a problem?"

"No, not at all! You know I'm up most of the night anyway... stuck in that third shift schedule. I... I just figured that you and Deanna would be... uh..."

"I left her there. She'll have just as much fun without me, assuming she even notices that I'm gone. Annie, I uh, I brought you a gift. Two actually, but I'm not sure..."

"I have one for you too, Tyler. Let me get it."

Annie gave his hand a squeeze and left her spot next to him on the sofa. She knelt in front of the tree, reaching for his gift, but her hand strayed to Michael's... Her throat tightened in sorrow, and she resumed her task.

"For you," she said, handing Tyler a small package.

He thanked her and set it aside, and then took her hand in both of his.

"Annie, I know that we've been friends for a while, good friends, and I think you know that we'd be more if I had my way about it. I don't suppose you... that your feelings have changed at all, have they?"

"Tyler, I..."

"No, don't say it yet. God, I just can't face hearing it... I should have known. But I have to ask anyway. Crazy..."

Tyler pulled two velvet lined boxes from the inside pocket of his jacket. The first was long and thin, and the second, small and square. Annie swallowed hard, knowing what at least one of them probably contained. *Oh jeez...*

"This first one," Ty said, setting the smaller box aside, "you have to accept. It's my Christmas gift to you. It comes with no strings attached, other than our friendship, and… well, here." He handed her the present.

Annie's hands were shaking a bit as she opened it.

"Oh wow…" she gasped, staring down at the diamond bracelet. "Tyler, this is way too much. I can't…"

"You can, Annie." He pulled the jewelry out and fastened it around her wrist. "See? Made for you… a perfect fit."

Annie couldn't help but agree, even if she'd never possessed anything so expensive in her life. She held up her hand. The diamonds glittered. But it was too much… to intimate. She shook her head.

"Tyler, I can't. This is…"

"Annie, I'm not taking it back. I'll pitch it in the lake before I do that. And like I said no strings… just our friendship. And I guess that pretty much answers the question of what you'd say had I given you this," he sighed, picking up the smaller box.

He ran a thumb along the line of her jaw, and kissed her gently on the lips.

"Annie, I love you. I've been fighting it, denying it for months now, but I can't any longer. God, I was sitting in Evans' den tonight, drinking a great drink and debating on whether I should even be with you tonight. Why should I put myself through the torture, wanting you and knowing I'll never have you? I'd already told him I was going to do it – to ask you, but I still wasn't all that sure myself until his wife came in looking for him. I saw the love she has for him… and he for her, and I want that too. I made up my mind to try for it one last time…"

"Tyler, I…"

"Not yet, Annie. I know what your answer will be, but I have to tell you this anyway. And I've had this for about a month now," Ty said with a little laugh, giving the box in his hand a little toss. "Would you at least look at it before you tell me no?"

Annie was at a loss. *Oh jeez, she did love him, could even consider marriage to him, but he wasn't the one! Gosh, she didn't even know if her dream existed! And what if he didn't exist? She'd spend the rest of her life waiting for nothing, all alone, and possibly giving up what could be a very nice life with a man who did love her… someone she would be content with. Content… did she want that? Should she settle for content, or continue to hope…*

"Annie?"

Tyler opened the box and pulled out the most beautiful diamond ring Annie had ever seen.

"Oh Tyler, it's… Oh my…"

Tyler's hopes soared. She hadn't said no yet, and he could sense that she was wavering a bit. Hell, he knew she loved him as a friend and even a little bit more. And they could build on that! He'd kissed her enough to know she enjoyed it even if she never let it go any further. And weren't the best marriages based on a solid friendship? He sure knew that the Evans' was! And the Davidson's. Hell, Kyle and Jenna had been friends since they were nine years old for Christ's sake!

"Annie," he whispered, taking her left hand, "I love you and want to spend the rest of my life with you. Would you at least give it some serious thought? And in the meantime…"

He began to slip the ring onto her finger, thrilled that she wasn't pulling away, even if her hand was shaking uncontrollably.

She should tell him yes. He was a good man, loved children, had a wonderful career, and Annie knew she could do a lot worse than Tyler Howe. Heck, hadn't Marti told her time and time again to marry him? Maybe he was the one she had been waiting for, just didn't realize it yet. It certainly wasn't Michael…

Michael! What she wouldn't give to have his advice right now. He'd tell her what to do. He never lied…

Annie glanced at the crystal angel glittering from the top of her tree. A heavy gust of wind hit the cabin, rocking the structure just enough to shake the tree. The angel spun around, catching the light and sending sparks of color shooting across the room.

Annie felt the warm metal of the ring touch the tip of her finger. Her vision began to fade, and once again intense blue eyes over a lop-sided grin filled her mind. She had her answer. Her hand closed and dropped to her lap.

"Tyler, I'm sorry, but I can't. It wouldn't be fair to either of us…"

"I figured as much," he sighed. "And save the 'we can still be friends' speech. We'll always be friends, Annie… and I'll do my best to let my heart move on. Um… but before we go back to what we apparently never left, I want one more kiss that I never got," he said with a sad laugh.

He took her into his arms and kissed her hard, kissed her deep. He knew then that there would never be anything more than friendship between them. It just wasn't there.

The ring went into the box and the box into his pocket, and he stood to go.

"Annie, before you ask me to stay longer… I'd love nothing more but I don't think it's a good idea tonight…"

She nodded. "I understand, Tyler. And I'm so sorry… I wish…"

"Not any more than I do. Well, have a merry Christmas, and tell Eric hello for me."

"I will, Tyler. And thank you…"

He brushed a hand along the bracelet on her wrist and gave her a smile.

"We'll always be friends, Annie."

With that, he left.

It wasn't until his car vanished into the night that Annie realized he hadn't opened her gift from her. She put it back under the tree and curled up in her favorite chair.

✦ ✦ ✦

It was nearly one in the morning before the last of Gabe's guests left. The party was a roaring success, sure to be reviewed in the Waterston Watch's society section. Deirdre was glowing with happiness, and Gabe was wishing he was halfway into a good drunk. He was thrilled that his wife's party came off without a hitch, but ever since he talked to Ty in his den, he felt… off somehow. Not even Kyle and his kick-ass poker game managed to lift Gabe's spirits.

He and Deirdre helped the help clean up, and by two the house was empty except for the Evans'. They put gifts for the twins under the tree, gave their children one last kiss goodnight, and then staggered off to their own rooms.

Gabe was already undressed when he heard a knock on his door.

"Geoffrey, may I come in?"

"It's open, Dee." He grabbed a robe and threw it over his naked body. Just in time…he hoped.

"Oh! I'm sorry, Geoffrey, I didn't realize…" Deirdre averted her eyes, but not before seeing pretty much all of him. Dear God, she had forgotten how incredible he looked… She pulled her own robe tighter around her small frame, hugging her arms around her.

"Did you need something, Deirdre?"

"Ah, only to thank you for tonight. I know you don't enjoy entertaining in this manner… Just a little too 'stuffy' for you. I appreciate you indulging me…"

"I'd do just about anything for you, Dee…"

"I know, Geoffrey. Goodness, you announcing that there was a high-stakes poker game going on in the family room, and that no one could leave without playing at least one hand for charity… A bold move, but we raised another nine thousand dollars! I… I hope it wasn't illegal…"

"It was for charity, Deirdre. Christ, the mayor was even there! I do believe Kyle got him for nearly a grand…" Gabe laughed.

"Anyway, thank you, Geoffrey dear."

Deirdre went to him and gave him a hug.

"You're welcome, Dee."

He held her close, very aware that there wasn't too much clothing between them. Aw God… it seemed that any female close enough to touch was sending his thoughts down roads he shouldn't be taking. Gabe pushed her gently away.

"Better get to bed, love. Those boys will be up early again…"

Deirdre nodded. She knew she should leave, but she was so damn lonely. Thanking her husband was only a pretense to come to his room. She was missing Steven more than ever, and desperately needed to be held, to feel loved… to fall asleep in strong arms and then be awakened with a kiss. However, did she dare ask to spend the night with him?

"Dee, was there something else?" Gabe asked, turning down his blankets. He sat on the edge of his bed and waited for the answer that seemed to be a long time in coming.

"No... Yes. Yes there is. Geoffrey, I... Oh God, I don't know if I can say this..."

"Deirdre, what is it?" He stood, alarmed by the distraught look on her face.

"I... I don't want to be alone tonight," she whispered, unable to meet his eyes.

He didn't either, but didn't want to risk ending up in a situation that neither of them really wanted... Yet his physical need for affection was rapidly shoving aside any thoughts of possible regrets he might have in the morning.

"Deirdre, I don't know... Christ, the last time this happened we were miserable in our guilt."

She nodded, but moved closer to him anyway.

"...Although why we felt the need for guilt, I'll never know," Gabe continued. "We love each other... we're married..."

He pulled her close to him when she was within reach.

"And there's no reason for us not to have this... this physical side, right?"

She nodded again, and put her arms around him.

"So why doesn't it feel *right?*" Gabe asked in a ragged whisper.

She shook her head, unable to answer him.

"Christ, I used to take any woman I wanted into my bed," Gave murmured, leading her over to his bed. "Never even thought twice about it... just took what I wanted. Day after day... night after night. Didn't even know their name half the time, and never even cared most of the time."

They sat down together, and she let her robe fall from her shoulders. Gabe brushed her long, pale blonde hair away from her neck.

She shivered under his touch.

"And here we are, Deirdre," he whispered, his breath warm on her skin, "so alone... You miss Steve, and I haven't found *her*... I don't think you want to make love to me anymore than I want to make love to you, but I think we... we *need* this... It isn't right, but... oh God..."

He just couldn't take it anymore, and let himself go. They didn't speak, didn't even kiss, just satisfied their needs and fell asleep in each other's arms.

Chapter Thirteen

Spring, 1992

Annie managed to bury her feelings of loneliness by keeping just as busy as she possibly could. She arranged her schedule so that she could work three days in a row, and then have a four-day stretch to enjoy herself. She labored in her gardens, planting rose bushes in the shape of a spiral with her favorite white ones in the center, and then changing from yellow to peach and then pink to the darkest shades of red. When she was done there were nearly a hundred bushes in the floral maze, and she couldn't wait to see what it looked like in full bloom.

She planted perennials around the cabin, and then began work on her vegetable garden. It was hard work, digging up all that soil, and she'd have thought that she would have remembered that fact from last year. But wait... she hadn't done it last year. Michael had. Funny how she only thought about him on a rare occasion anymore, like when something triggered a memory. She couldn't remember at all what he looked like, but she always felt that gaping hole he left in her life, like part of her was missing. Tyler tried very hard to fill it, but their relationship began to fall apart a bit after Christmas. He called her a little less, and she found more reasons to be busy on the nights he wanted to take her out. It was rumored that he was now dating one of the doctors at Brighton, although Annie didn't hear who it was. Marti and her gossip... Not that it mattered; Annie just wanted him to be happy, no matter who it was with.

Once the task of planting was finished, Annie spent her free time riding Adonis. Dog was always with them, and they began to explore more and more of the property in the high hills.

Annie had been watching a pair of domestic geese that had found their way to her lake. They built a nest near the beach and it wasn't long before eggs appeared. Dog was kept away from the new family to insure that they would remain undisturbed. Annie looked forward to the hatching.

On a warm morning near the end of April, it began.

Annie observed from behind a bush about twenty feet from the nest. The gosling was almost completely out of the egg when Annie began her vigil so she didn't have long to wait.

The proud parents stood at the edge of the nest while the gosling struggled to free itself from the confines of its shell. The head appeared, followed by one webbed foot and then another. A yellow wing was next, and the gosling was free. It wobbled in its attempt to stand, weaving drunkenly and emitting a small, scared "peep."

The mother goose bent her head towards her offspring, and to Annie's horror, the bird grabbed the chick by the neck and flung it from the nest.

Annie stared in shock.

The male goose ran to where the baby had landed and gave it several vicious pecks. Annie felt nauseous as she witnessed the unwarranted, brutal attack.

The geese settled back into their home as if nothing had happened. Annie took a deep breath and went to check the damage done to the gosling. Maybe it could be helped.

Or not. Too late to be of assistance, Annie buried the murdered baby on the hill next to the woods. She wondered if her presence had caused the disturbing behavior in the geese. She didn't that they had noticed her, but couldn't be sure.

Four eggs to go.

The following day the next egg began to hatch, but this time Annie stayed at the top of the hill and watched through binoculars.

Same scenario: gosling hatches, gosling murdered. It was awful, and Annie was very tempted to remove the last three eggs from the nest. She made a half-hearted attempt until a wicked bite on her arm from the gander caused her to reconsider. Probably better to let nature take its course anyway. Maybe the two dead goslings were defective in some way and this was the geese's way of making sure only the healthiest of their species survived. Regardless, Annie had to work the next two days and wouldn't be around to witness any more hatchings – or killings.

✦ ✦ ✦

"Gabe buddy! Miss me?"

"Only about as much as the plethora of potholes perforating the pavement and plaguing our driving pleasure. Goddamn annual rite of spring passage… So, how was your vacation? Vegas was it?"

"It kicked ass, buddy! The weather was great, the food was great, the shows were great…"

"And the gambling was great?"

"…The weather was great, the food was great…"

"Kyle, are you trying to tell me that you *didn't* gamble? Dear God, is the world coming to an end?" Gabe laughed.

"I gambled," Kyle muttered.

"Ah… Then am I to take it that you merely broke even this time?"

"I wish."

"Oh God… Kyle, you *lost?*"

"Big time."

"And you played poker, right?"

"Tried. Sure as hell couldn't get a decent hand the whole time I was there. I couldn't believe it, Gabe! I've never had such bad luck in my life! Kept tellin'

124

myself that the next one will be it. I'll clean up. But nope. Jesus, I sat there for ten hours one day and never won a dime!"

"Whoa. And Jen let you get away with that?"

"She doesn't know, Gabe. After the second day of hangin' with 'Kyle the loser' she figured she was bad luck and hung out with the nanny and the kids for the next ten days."

"Oh God... Kyle, just how much did you lose?"

"Enough. Thought I could win it back..."

"How much, Kyle?" From the look on his buddy's face, it must have been a hell of a lot.

"Enough, and leave it at that," Kyle snapped. He'd maxed out every single one of his credit cards, cleaned out the savings, and lost nearly everything in the checking account too. There was just enough left to get by for the next month or so.

Not knowing any of this, Gabe was already planning to sneak a few grand into Kyle's battered bankbook.

"Got some good news though," Kyle said, his face brightening up again.

"Do tell! Is Jen pregnant again?"

"God, I hope not! I mean, I'd love another kid but it's not a good time right now..."

"So what is it?"

"Well, I was talking to some people down there and it seems we haven't been forgotten after all."

"We?"

"SD. The band. They wanted to book us for ten shows, dude! Ten! I told him we split up a few years ago, but he said..."

"He?"

"Ivan somebody. Weird last name... you'd remember him though. We played at his casino in eighty-six."

"Vaguely. Anyway..."

"He said call the guys and get back together, and it would be a cool million for us to split, Gabe! Can we? God, I sure could use the cash..."

"No."

"No? Why the hell not? Jesus, Gabe, a million bucks! And I want to get back into it so bad..."

"No. I have neither the time nor the desire to start that shit again."

"Don't have the time? The hell you say! Dude, you got nothin' but time anymore! Christ, all you do is spend a few hours at the studio doin' practically nothin' and then go home and... and hide. You and me haven't gone out and done shit since Christmas! Don't go bowlin', don't play pool... haven't even gone out for a goddamn beer after work together! What's up with that, pal?" Kyle snapped.

"Well, excuse me for causing such a boring rift in your life, Kyle. Perhaps it's time you found someone else to play with…" Gabe shot him a deadly glare and turned away.

Kyle got his uncharacteristic anger under control.

"Gabe, what's wrong? You and Dee aren't having problems, are you?"

"No."

Not problems, but ever since they shared a bed – and each other, on Christmas, their relationship had suffered. Gabe felt tremendous amounts of guilt for using Deirdre as he did, and pretty much shut himself off from any affection she offered him in any capacity. In turn, she felt rejected and confused, leaving the emotional climate at the Evans' decidedly chilly.

Gone were the hugs, the smiles, the laughter, and the simple joy of best friends sharing their life together. Replacing all of that was a feeling of tension coupled with uncertainty as Gabe and Deirdre attempted not to offend each other with unwanted attention.

Gabe knew he should try and end it and recapture the wonderful relationship they had once shared, but quite frankly he didn't much care to. Didn't much care about anything anymore except surviving one more goddamn lonely day.

"Gabe?"

"Gabe!"

"What?"

"What's buggin' you, man?"

"Nothing," Gabe muttered.

"Dude, we've been friends – best friends for eleven years now, and I *know* when you've got some heavy shit goin' on. You wanna talk about it?"

"Kyle… There's nothing you can do. Nothing anyone can do. I'll survive… have so far… Christ. Hey, would you mind finishing up the payroll for me? I… I need some air." Gabe shoved the company checkbook across the desk, and tossed his pen on top of it.

"Dude, I don't know how to do this!" Kyle moaned, hoping his partner wasn't serious.

"Then it's goddamn time you learn, Kyle. Until we can afford an accountant and office staff again, we *all* have to do our fair share of work around here. And it's simple… Write in the date, the employee's name… check the list for their salary and fill in the fuckin' blanks! And don't forget to scrawl your name at the bottom…

"You don't have to get so pissed about it. And can't Jen do it when she comes in tomorrow?"

"No. Would you like to wait an extra day to be paid?"

"No…"

"I doubt our hard-working staff would either. Now write the damn checks, hand them out, and then find something else useful to occupy your time. I'll see you later…"

"Later as in today?"

"Later as in later," Gabe snarled, and slammed the door on his way out.

"Gabe!"

He stuck his head back in.

"What!?"

"Fuck you, man."

Gabe slammed the door even harder the second time he left.

Kyle flipped him off, and then sat behind his partner's desk.

"Jesus, Chet," he mumbled to the bird next to him, "he's the moodiest son of a bitch I've ever seen. What's wrong with him anyway?"

"Noannie!" Chet squawked, fluffing his feathers.

"No wannie?" Kyle mumbled, wondering what the hell that meant. Aw, who cared? Just bird babblin'…

He picked up the pen and carefully began printing dates, names, and numbers on checks. His penmanship had always been less than legible, so it took him far longer than it would have taken Gabe.

When he was finished he sat staring at the balance…

SD Productions wasn't doin' too bad… and just maybe he could borrow a little from the company to tide him over. Hell, he owned half of it anyway, right? And to make sure Gabe didn't find out, Kyle would volunteer to do his fair share, meaning the payroll, from now on. Or at least until he was back on his financial feet again.

With a pounding heart and sweaty palms, Kyle wrote out one more check. He tore it from the page and tucked it into his back pocket, and then took the payroll book to his office where he locked it in a desk drawer.

Gabe found himself sitting in the parking lot of a bar, more than ready to revert to his old, undesirable ways and drown his sorrows in a bottle of very expensive scotch. Oh, to be that young, wild, carefree Gabe again, stoned out of his mind with a warm, willing female sharing his bed. Sex, drugs, rock and roll, and not a goddamn thing in the world to worry about.

He unbuckled his seatbelt and opened the door of his truck, ready to dive back into that decadent world, but before his foot hit the pavement he was cursing himself for even thinking such things. He was a man with a family and responsibilities now, and no way could he ever forget that. He needed to be a positive role model for his sons, a promise he made to his late brother before the twins were even born. He also needed to be the best husband he could be to Dee, a promise he made to her on their wedding day. And poor Kyle… Gabe had been less than a friend to him again too. And he'd damn well better get his shit together and remedy the situations.

Gabe hauled himself out of his pool of self-pity, and drove home to his Park Street mansion. Stopped off at a flower shop first and bought a dozen dark red roses for Deirdre… and one white one for himself.

"Geoffrey, you're home early…"

"I had some errands to run and thought I'd stop by to say hello. I'll be going back to the studio shortly, and then Kyle and I are going out for a beer. I'll be home in time for dinner…"

Deirdre nodded and turned back to the counter where she was stirring cake batter.

"Deirdre?"

"Yes, Geoffrey?"

"I… I'm sorry."

She waited for more, as in what he was sorry for, but he remained silent. After a long moment she turned to face him.

"Sorry, Geoffrey?"

"Yes, sorry. I've been… I don't know. I haven't been a very good husband – or friend lately, and I want to apologize."

"Geoffrey… you don't need to. I think I understand…"

"I don't know how you possibly could when I don't understand it myself. And if you don't mind, I would rather not try to analyze or even discuss it. I love you, Deirdre. I hope you know that, but… but I can't…" He shook his head, not at all sure what he was even talking about.

"I know you do, Geoffrey. And I'm afraid this has all been my fault. If I hadn't gone to your room that night… well, I just shouldn't have."

"Probably not, but it happened. I regret it… and then again I don't. God, I'm so weak…"

"You're human, Geoffrey, just as I am. Why should we deny ourselves a basic need? And why should we feel guilty if we fulfill that need?"

"Because it's not right, Deirdre! Sex without love… Oh God, listen to me! Of all the hypocritical bullshit…"

"You've changed since then, Geoffrey."

"Not all that much, Dee. Jesus, do you know what I nearly did today? I was so damn close to… to reverting back…"

"But you didn't. Obviously, since you're here right now with me and *not* smelling of alcohol or another woman's perfume."

Gabe sighed and nodded, and hugged his best friend for the first time since they'd shared his bed.

"I really don't deserve you, Deirdre. You know every one of my dark, shameful secrets… You know how weak and insecure I am… spoiled and moody, and yet you're still willing to love me."

"How could I not love you, Geoffrey? And you're not all that horrid of a person. Actually, this world would be a far better place to live if more were like you. I'd list your virtues but it would take far too long, and I need to get this cake into the oven."

Deirdre hugged him and went to resume her baking, but then turned back around and melted against him.

"I do love you, Geoffrey," she murmured, wiping away a few tears. "And

I'm sorry too."

"So we're friends again?"

"Just like before."

"Deirdre?"

"Yes Geoffrey?"

"Um… what if… Well, what if we find we're 'human' again, and… and…"

"And we need each other? That way, I mean…"

"Yes. Oh God, should we…"

"I've thought about that quite a bit, Geoffrey."

"You have?"

"I have. And… and I can't think of any reason to deny ourselves should the… the situation arise again. I don't plan on making a habit of it, but… Oh dear, this is awkward, isn't it?"

"To say the least. But I think I know what you mean, and how you feel, and I'm of the same mind… And having said that, I'd like to drop the subject for now."

"As would I," Deirdre sighed.

"I brought something home for you," Gabe grinned. He dipped a finger in the cake batter and stuck it in his mouth, looking very much like a mischievous child.

Deirdre laughed and slapped at his hand.

"Be right back." Gabe skipped into his office and grabbed the box of flowers, feeling better than he had in months.

"For you, love," he said, bowing low as he offered her his gift.

"Oh Geoffrey, they're beautiful!"

Deirdre pulled out the roses, tossing the box aside.

"But Geoffrey dear…"

"Yes, Deirdre love?"

"You left yours in here." She plucked the odd white one from the bunch and held it out to him.

Gabe stared at it as if he'd never seen it before… although he vaguely remembered ordering it. How strange…

"You'll find her someday," Deirdre murmured, placing the bloom in his trembling hand.

"What? I'm sorry…?"

"Nothing, Geoffrey." She kissed him and sent him on his way.

Chapter Fourteen

Dog held the geese at bay until he heard the slam of the cabin door, and then gave the foul fowl one – and only one warning never to be seen in the area again. He turned and jogged up the hill, giving a backward glance to them as they fluffed their feathers and honked in annoyance.

Annie let Dog into the cabin and gave him a hug of thanks. He wagged his tail in response but never took his eyes from the stolen egg.

"Well, Dog, I guess since you rescued us you are entitled to see what you saved," Annie laughed.

She held the egg down for him to examine, hoping he wouldn't decide that it was an early morning snack.

Dog sniffed the egg thoroughly, and then sat back on his haunches and cocked his head. His ears were at full alert and his golden eyes glittered.

Annie felt movement from inside the smooth white shell of the egg. Oh jeez, it was hatching! She nestled it on a soft towel and placed it into a large plastic bowl, and then set the makeshift nest under her desk lamp to keep the egg warm. She hoped the temperature was right; after all she went through she sure as heck didn't want to cook it.

And as much as she wanted to watch it hatch, she needed to get to bed. Eric was due to visit later, and she had a special surprise for him – other than the egg of course. It was too bad he couldn't come over earlier and watch it hatch himself, but he had school and wouldn't be out until two, and then dropped off at the cabin by Irene at three.

Annie yawned, gave the egg a gentle caress, and went to bed.

When she awoke at two and checked her egg, the hole in the shell wasn't any larger. She feared the worst, seeing no progress in the hatching process. Eric would be so disappointed if this baby didn't make it, especially after hearing about the other eggs. He'd all but convinced Annie that she should at least try to save this one. She'd be heartbroken too; she'd grown quite fond of that lone egg and the gosling it contained.

"Annie, did it hatch yet?" were the first words out of Eric's mouth as he labored up the cabin steps.

"No change yet, kiddo. I... I'm not all that sure if it will, seeing how it's taking so long. Eric, don't be disappointed if..."

"It *will* hatch, I just know it!"

Annie wasn't so sure.

Eric pulled a chair next to the table where the egg lay, and Dog took his position as official guardian next to him. Eric's hand automatically went to Dog's head. The two had become close friends ever since their meeting last summer.

The egg wobbled, and several cracks appeared around the hole.

"Annie!" Eric yelled, "Come see!"

She ran over, grabbing her camera on the way, and was just in time to see a tiny orange beak protrude from the shell, and began to photograph the momentous occasion.

A webbed foot poked out, followed by another.

For the next hour, the gosling painstakingly struggled to escape the confines of its oval prison. Eric took pictures as each limb was freed, and Annie did chores around the cabin, occasionally coming over to watch as the hatching progressed.

The gosling was finally free. Annie and Eric looked down at it, dismay showing openly on their faces. The poor chick looked dead. Instead of a fuzzy yellow ball of peeping fluff, there lay before them a thin, gasping imitation of a bird. Its eyes were closed and its down lay in wet strings around its bony body. Wings were splayed and its feet seemed to be facing the wrong way.

"I'm so sorry, Eric. I didn't want you to have to see something like this…" Annie could barely keep her voice from trembling.

"Don't worry about me, Annie, it's this poor thing. Can't we do anything for him?"

"I don't know what, Eric. He doesn't appear to be suffering though. Let's just cover the bowl with a towel and leave him under the light; at least he'll be warm. And we gave him more of a chance to survive than is parents would have," she said sadly.

"Yep. I'm going to clean out his house a little… Would that be okay?"

"I'm sure it would be. You could probably put him in a more comfortable position too."

Eric carefully picked the pieces of the shell out of the bowl, and then straightened out the gosling's feet and folded its wings to its pathetic little body.

Dog watched the process, looking from the gosling to Eric, and then back again. He gave the boy's hand an occasional lick of encouragement.

A towel was placed over the bowl, and Eric went into the kitchen to where Annie was packing a picnic supper for them.

"Are we going to eat by the lake again?" he asked. "I really don't want to if those geese are still there."

"I don't blame you… and they're gone. I think Dog had something to do with it," Annie answered, looking over to her pet and smiling. "And I had another place in mind for dinner. Go call Donny and I'll be out in a minute."

Eric's eyes lit up despite his sorrow over the tragedy of the gosling. He was going to ride Adonis! He called to Dog and the two of them ran to the barn. By the time Annie arrived, Eric had the bridle on the horse and was struggling with the heavy saddle. She lifted it onto the back of Donny, but allowed Eric to fasten the girth strap.

Annie tied the saddlebag to the cantle, and gave Eric a leg up. He settled himself in and turned the horse to follow her as they walked uphill along the tree line next to the meadow. Dog, and Annie, had recently discovered a less difficult route to the marble bench clearing. It was little more than a deer trail, but so much easier to use than climbing the step hill by the lake.

As Annie followed the new trail to the clearing, she wondered how Michael had gotten there before. The trail he said he came in on was nowhere to be found, and even if it was there it would have been a very far journey to the nearest road.

Michael… would she ever see him again?

When they reached the clearing, Annie and Eric's eyes opened wide in amazement. The area looked as if it had just been groomed and the smell of fresh-cut grass still hung in the air. A ray of sunlight knifed down through the trees, illuminating the marble bench, and two long-stemmed white roses were placed carefully in the center. Several drops of moisture clung to the blooms, creating a prism effect as the sun hit it. Sparks of color decorated the clearing and all that surrounded it.

It was like walking into a fairy tale.

"Wow!" exclaimed Eric as he slid off Adonis.

"Yeah, wow…" echoed Annie, but for entirely different reasons.

"Did you do this for me?" Eric asked her.

"Nope. Wasn't me."

"Well whoever it was, they must be magic or something!"

"Or something…"

Adonis dropped is head to graze in the thick grass. Dog ran to the bench and sniffed at the roses. He turned to look across the clearing and into the woods, nose quivering as he tried to catch a scent. He took a few steps forward and stopped. A low growl formed in his throat, and Annie moved towards Eric to protect him if need be.

Dog growled again.

Annie heard a rustling in the bushes.

"Who's there?" she called out, looking around for a weapon of some sort. She picked up a thick branch, ready for action.

Dog growled again, and then changed to a happy whine as his tail went into a low, relaxed wag.

Michael Anthony stepped into the clearing.

"Oh… thank God it's you," Annie sighed in relief. She dropped her club and stared at her friend, not quite believing he was really there.

"My dear Miss Benton… How nice to see you again," Michael said, holding his arms out to her.

She didn't even hesitate, but ran to him and hugged him tight.

He picked her up and swung her around, kissing the top of her head as they laughed together. God, he had missed her…

"I can't believe you're here, Michael!" Annie cried, hugging him some more. Jeez, she hadn't realized just how much she had missed him until she was in his arms again.

"I'm here, Annie, and hopefully I can hang around for a while. Who's your friend?" Michael asked, nodding to the broadly smiling Eric.

Annie introduced them; the boy had found a new hero. They ate the dinner Annie had packed and talked about nothing in particular. Several times she attempted to ask Michael about the roses, but he would just smile and change the subject. He directed much of his conversation towards Eric, asking about school, his artwork, how he was coping with his illness, and just life in general.

Eric had just began telling Michael about the gosling when a loud clap of thunder interrupted the tale. All eyes looked heavenward to where a huge black cloud was blocking out the sun.

"Party's over, kids," Annie laughed as she threw the remnants of their meal into the saddlebag. She hoped like heck Adonis could get them home before the storm hit. Eric ran over to the horse to tighten his cinch, and then Michael helped him into the saddle.

"Will you be all right?" Annie asked him as she climbed up behind Eric.

"I'll be fine, Annie. A little water never hurt me, and I have my own transportation," Michael replied. He grinned and gave a short whistle.

Lightening flashed on the other side of the lake.

"It's not the water I'm worried about…" Annie's voice trailed off as she saw an immense black shape move through the woods. The form took the shape of a horse and trotted over to Michael.

"My ride," he laughed. "You get Eric back to the cabin and we'll follow you down, and then you can fix us some dessert and we'll watch the storm."

She gave him a doubtful look but didn't waste any more time leaving the woods. With Dog leading the way, they raced for the cabin and the usually-congested trail seemed to open up before them. Annie didn't remember it being that wide, and the low-hanging branches and exposed roots seemed to have vanished.

Adonis' hooves flew over the fern-covered forest floor, and then down the hill through the meadow. They reached the cabin as the first raindrops fell. Annie dropped Eric on the porch, and then took the horse to the barn. Michael rode up behind her, and together they brushed the sweat from their mounts and made them comfortable in their stalls.

Hand in hand, Annie and Michael ran through the rain to the cabin, becoming soaked to the skin in the process.

He opened the door for her, bowing low and sweeping a hand in front of her.

"Ladies first!" he said with a grin.

She curtsied and entered the cabin through the door being held open for her.

Annie saw Eric sitting next to the table that held the egg. His hands were clasped between his knees as he stared, unblinking at the bowl. Dog sat with his head on the boy's knee, alternating glances between Eric and the bowl. The cabin was unusually quiet.

Since she had sensed that a bond had formed between Michael and Eric, Annie asked if he could comfort the boy while she went to get some towels for them to dry themselves.

"Eric, do you believe in miracles?" Michael asked, sitting next to the kid.

Eric shrugged a shoulder in reply.

"Look under the towel," Michael whispered.

Eric looked at him, and his new hero nodded encouragement. He carefully peeled the towel back from the top of the bowl and heard a faint "peep" as the light hit the gosling and he came to life. A fuzzy yellow head with bright, light blue eyes popped over the rim, and several more peeps followed.

Michael smiled, Dog barked, and Annie came running in from the bathroom. Eric lifted the gosling from the bowl, unsure whether to believe it or not. Jeez, he was dead just a few minutes ago!

Being a good gosling, he imprinted on the first living thing it saw. Eric, Dog, Michael, and Annie were his new parents. He peeped again and nibbled on Eric's fingers.

"Oh, Annie... look! He didn't die after all!" exclaimed Eric. "I think he's hungry..." The boy giggled as the goose continued to nibble his fingers.

"Well, there's strawberry shortcake on the menu. Think he'd like that?" Annie laughed.

"I saw some chick feed in the barn. I think he'd prefer that over strawberry shortcake," Michael said. "I'll run out and get some after the rain lets up."

Annie threw him a towel and changed the subject.

"You're dripping all over my floor. I don't see you in forever, and the first thing you do is mess up my house. Where the heck have you been anyway?"

"Annie... you know I can't tell you. But you were always in my thoughts and I came back to you as soon as I could. I missed you."

"I missed you too, Michael. Oh jeez, and I have so much to tell you!"

"I can imagine! You can start by filling me in on that fine horse you have out there, and work your way back..."

He gave her a wink and she blew him a kiss.

"Oh jeez... look..." Annie laughed and nodded over at Eric, who was lying on the floor and letting the gosling walk all over him.

"Annie, can I name him?" Eric asked, giggling as the goose pecked at his buttons.

"Sure. He thinks you're his papa..."

"I think I'll call him... McDonald."

"McDonald it is! Would that be like Old McDonald or Ronald McDonald?"

Eric made a disgusted face at Annie. *Really!*

"Neither. It's a mix between Michael and Adonis. Kinda sorta. It just popped into my head," he explained.

Michael folded his towel and draped it over a chair. "The rain is letting up so I'll go get McDonald his first dinner, and I think I'm ready for some of that shortcake."

Annie handed him a pie plate to bring some feed in on.

"Whipped cream on it?" she asked.

He looked at the pie plate and grinned. "Sure!" he said, and pretended that he was going to throw the pan back at her.

"The shortcake, you dolt!" she laughed.

He kissed her nose.

"Yes, I would love whipped cream on my shortcake, Miss Benton," he said seriously. Under his breath but loud enough for Annie to hear he mumbled, "Some people just can't take a joke."

She gave him a poke in the ribs and he left, laughing.

Annie watched him walk to the barn and hoped it wouldn't be another year before she saw him again.

She spread some paper towel on the floor, and then placed a shallow pan of water on it for McDonald to drink from. Michael returned with the food and set it next to the water, after which Eric put the little goose next to the feed. The gosling wasn't sure what it was all about until Annie tapped her finger into the meal. The baby reacted to the pecking-like motion of her finger and began to eat. Annie was more than relieved; she knew that trick worked for chicks, but wasn't at all sure about goslings.

While the humans enjoyed their strawberry shortcake, with whipped cream, McDonald ate chick feed until his bulging crop would hold no more. He moved to the pan of water and drank, tipping his head back to let the liquid slide down his throat. When he had enough, he stepped into the pan of water and plopped his fuzzy goose bottom down. He flapped his bony little wings; splashing Eric and Dog who were sitting a little too close.

Eric laughed and returned McDonald to his bowl to dry off, and then rest. The boy had never been happier in his life than he was at that moment. Ever since that magical minute when they entered the clearing he had felt different. He was sure there was a word for it, but he didn't know what it was. Elated maybe? And then he met Michael. He felt as if he had known him all his life. And Annie... she wasn't just his nurse or even just a friend. Eric loved her like a mother. Every time he was in the hospital she would read him stories, and when he was little she used to hold him in her lap. She even kissed him goodnight, even when he was in isolation and she'd have to wear that ugly yellow gown and mask when she touched him. His aunt hardly even visited him.

Annie let him come to her house all the time too. She told him stories about her grandmother and the gardens, and Eric hoped that they could visit there someday. He was thrilled that she had found a new trail to the magic place with the stone bench. She had told him about that too, but he never expected to see it, as the hill from the lake was too steep for him to climb.

Eric gazed at Michael, and then at Annie, wishing that they were his parents and all living in the cabin together. Maybe he could even get his own pony, just like Michael's horse only smaller. He would exercise every day and get stronger, and his lungs would get better and he wouldn't have to take all those pills all the time. And then maybe he would get a brother or a sister... He yawned and shut his eyes as his dream mother covered him with a soft blanket and kissed him. Such a beautiful dream...

Michael lifted him to the couch and covered the sleeping boy with a blanket, and then placed his hand lightly on Eric's head before planting a kiss on him. The smile on the man's face was replaced by a look of profound sadness, and Annie caught a glimpse of it as she returned from the kitchen with two cups of steaming tea.

"Is everything all right? Eric...?" she asked, handing Michael a cup.

"Fine for now... he just fell asleep. He's had a pretty busy day."

"That he has," Annie agreed. She kissed Eric and then smiled at her friend. "Let's go out to the porch."

The two of them sat on the steps and sipped their tea. The storm was over and the first star of the evening could be seen in the purple sky.

"Beautiful, isn't it?" Annie asked, nodding to the heavens.

"All that and more, Annie." He put his arm around her and pulled her close.

They remained there, just silently being with each other until Irene came to pick up Eric.

"Michael, um... are you staying for a while?"

"As in tonight or are you thinkin' future..."

"Either or. Your room is still available if you want it," she said, blushing just a little.

"My room?"

"Well, the guest room. Yes, your room. I... Oh jeez... Michael, after you left I... Well, I kind of went shopping for you. There're new clothes in the closet and... and other things... socks and stuff in the dresser. You never seemed to have very much, nothing at all actually, and I wanted you to... well, I was so hoping you'd be back some day!" She knew she was rambling on, but she was so very happy to have him back even if she was embarrassed to admit to hoping that he would be – and living with her again.

"Annie... I don't know what to say! Uh... thanks, I guess... I can really stay here?"

"Unless you have other plans..."

"No plans at all. Not for a while anyway."

"You brother...?"

Michael shook his head, fighting to keep the sadness from showing.

She saw it anyway and changed the subject.

"Oh yeah… and your Christmas present is in there too," she laughed, nodding towards the bedroom.

"You're kidding."

"No I'm not. Michael, I was so sure you would show up…"

He looked away, not sure if he should confess.

"Michael?"

"I… I was here, Annie. I was heading in and saw your boyfriend pulling into the driveway. Figured it would be awkward with both of us there, so I kind just kept goin'."

"Oh no… Michael, why? You know you're always welcome here! And he's not my boyfriend… wasn't my boyfriend…"

"He proposed, didn't he?"

She shot him a sharp look.

"How would you know something like that?"

"I… I saw him give you that ring. I'm sorry, Annie, but I… I couldn't help myself and watched through the window. I can't tell you how relieved I was when you turned him down, too."

"I suppose I should be furious that you were spying on me, but somehow I get the feeling that it wasn't spying but more of 'watching over'. Is that what it was, Michael?"

He nodded.

She took his hand.

"And I suppose I should confess that you were on my mind at that very moment, Michael. I was wishing that you were there telling me what I should do…"

He smiled. He already knew that, and had answered her plea in his own way.

"Do you still see him, Annie?"

"No, not really. It just wasn't the same after that…"

"Do you miss him?"

"A little. Sometimes more than others, but I keep too busy to think about not having anyone in my life."

"Still hoping to meet your 'dream man'?"

"I'm not sure how to take that, Michael. Joke or serious…?"

"Serious, Annie. Matters of the heart should not be made light of. Do you still see him?"

"I do, Michael, and it makes me crazy! How can I possibly be in love with a… a fantasy or whatever the heck he is? Jeez, he was the reason I turned down what could have been a great life with Tyler! I was so close to saying yes, and then there were those darn blue eyes filling my head and looking at me like… like…" She shook her head, unable to continue. It was all so stupid and crazy…

"You did the right thing, hon," he said, giving her a hug. "You weren't meant to be with Tyler."

"Apparently I'm meant to be with no one," she sighed.

"Don't give up hope, Annie. And in the meantime, you have me," he said chucking her lightly under the chin.

"As long as you don't vanish again."

"I'll be here when you need me most, Annie. That's a promise. Well, I guess I'd better check on my horse and then turn in. It's gettin' late…"

"Your horse! Gosh, I'd nearly forgotten about him! What's his name, Michael?"

"I just call him horse…"

"Kind of like 'Dog'?"

"Kind of. Care to walk to the barn with me?"

"I'd love to."

Michael pulled her to her feet and put his arm around her, and they slowly made their way through the warm night, happy that they were once again together, but still all alone.

Chapter Fifteen

Autumn, 1992

Annie had never had a better summer in her life. Michael had stayed, and the two of them were closer than ever. They took long rides on horseback, exploring the woods and the acres beyond. Michael would talk about his days in Montana then, telling her of his camping adventures in the mountains with his brother. He told her about his years riding the rodeo circuit, and how one summer his twin had joined him. They'd always been an unbeatable roping team in high school, and did nearly as well when they reunited years later.

Michael told her about the ski trips they used to take and how the wild brother nearly fell off a cliff and was saved by the gentle one, and then related how his sibling had once saved him from a deadly fall into a pit after Michael stumbled into it and dislocated his shoulder. It seemed they were always there for each other, and shared a bond that would never be broken.

Yet during all those conversations Michael had not once referred to his brother by name. Annie didn't pry though. It was obvious that he loved his mysterious twin, and perhaps saying his name aloud was more than Michael could bear, even if he loved to talk about him.

Eric was a frequent visitor to the cabin, and early in the summer Michael suggested that he teach the boy to ride. Of course Eric was thrilled… And after a few weeks of very productive lessons, Annie bought him his very own horse.

Wanda was a perfect mount for a young boy. At twenty years of age she had a calm wisdom and a gentle spirit, and was more than happy to carry the youngster around on her swayed, bony back.

Michael had raised an eyebrow when he saw the old Palomino being unloaded after Annie informed him of her purchase.

"Annie, what were you thinkin'?" he laughed, counting the ribs poking through Wanda's golden hide.

"I wasn't. She was heading for the slaughter house and looked at me from the trailer… And I just couldn't let her die, Michael! I handed the driver a check for five hundred dollars and gave him my address… And here she is. She has a few good years left in her…"

"You did good, Annie," he said, running a hand down the mare's neck. "With some good feed and some decent groomin', you'll have yourself a nice horse here. She's got a kind eye and seems bombproof. She didn't even bat an eye when Dog came tearin' around the corner there, barkin' his fool head off, and he's darn near as big as she is!"

Annie laughed at Michael's exaggeration of the canine. Sure he was big, but his back only went up to Annie's waist… Wanda's was at least two feet higher than that.

So life went on at the cabin… peaceful, pleasant, and almost fulfilling. Michael still spent far too many nights alone on the beach, thinking of his lost ladylove.

Annie still had way too many dreams of her blue-eyed, dark-haired cowboy.

✦ ✦ ✦

"Geoffrey dear, please hurry! I don't want to be late! Photographs are at six, and the reception and dinner are at seven. Oh, and the awards are at eight-thirty," Deirdre called out from her bedroom.

"Jesus Christ," Gabe mumbled, yanking the tie from his neck and then searching among the dozens on the rack for a more suitable one. Deirdre had bought him the shirt he was wearing and it was the hardest damn color to match! If she hadn't raved so much about how good it looked on him, he would have just chucked it and worn something of his own choosing.

Just why the hell did he have to go to the goddamn awards banquet anyway? Dee could have easily gone without him, picked up his stupid little plaque for him, and then read the lame-ass speech he had written only ten minutes ago. Meanwhile, he and Kyle could be out in Kyle's boat, tippin' back some cold ones as they did some evening fishing and tried to land a few big ones.

Oh well, it wasn't like Kyle was going to be free to enjoy himself either, being the co-recipient of the humanitarian award he and Gabe were being honored with that evening.

Although… it might be worth wasting a few hours at the high-society shindig just to see his goofy buddy in a suit. Gabe wondered if it would be the blaze-orange three-piece or the "Tux in a can." Most likely the tux… After all, it was a high-class affair…

Gabe gave the tie rack a spin, grabbing at something that just might work. Too bad the entire contraption crashed to the floor.

"Goddammit" he yelled, wishing that just one thing would go right for him that day.

"Goddammit!" Jeremy echoed, grabbing a handful of the fallen ties.

"Jer… don't say that," Gabe mumbled absently, kicking around in the pile of silk and other fine fabrics. Still nothing to match… and when had Jer wandered in?

He smiled and picked up his son, and gave the toddler a noisy kiss on his bare belly.

Jeremy laughed and held a tie out to his papa.

"Pretty," he said, and draped it around Gabe's neck.

Gabe glanced down.

"And it matches perfectly! Thank you, Jeremy! You have saved me from being a laughingstock of a fashion disaster this evening."

"No, Papa," Jeremy said, shaking his head, "you look good all the time!"

Once again, Gabe marveled at how articulate his son was. Not quite two and a half, and already had a vocabulary that left Gabe in awe. James was still trying to string together a complete sentence.

"But I like your cowboy clothes best," Jeremy continued.

"Me too, Jer, and for two cents I'd be wearin' 'em tonight," Gabe laughed.

He set the boy down and moved over to the mirror on his dresser so that he could tie his tie. And he had to admit, that shirt looked pretty fuckin' good on him after all. It was a shimmery royal blue, but the tones changed with the lighting. No wonder it had been so hard to match… the colors kept changing. Matched his eyes exactly though.

"Papa?"

"Yes, Jeremy?"

"Will you tuck us in tonight?"

"Of course I will, Jer! I tuck you in every night."

"I know, but you're going away. I wanted to know if you'll do the secret tuck in."

"Secret…? I don't follow, Jer."

Uh oh… The secret tuck- in was a secret, and Daddy said not to tell anyone. Which left Jeremy plenty confused. Daddy and Papa were the same, right? Well, pretty much anyway. The Daddy late at night was kind of fuzzy-looking and didn't say much. He came after everyone was asleep and just sat next to the bed. Jer had seen him and asked his Papa why he was there. Papa said, "I'm Daddy right now, Jer, but don't tell anyone. Keep our tuck- in times like now a secret…" And Daddy was there pretty much every night after the world went to bed. But Papa didn't seem to know about it…

"Never mind, Papa." Jer didn't have to say anymore because Mamma was on her way in.

"Geoffrey, are you nearly finished?" Deirdre asked, fastening a diamond earring to a delicate lobe.

"Ready and waiting, Deirdre love." Gabe turned around and held his arms out to her.

She gave Jeremy a quick hug, and then went to her husband.

"Geoffrey, you look magnificent! I swear you become more handsome every day."

"You're aging, Deirdre, and your eyesight is beginning to fail," Gabe laughed. "And I must tell you that you have never looked more beautiful, Dee."

He spun her in a slow circle and got his money's worth of the view. Her long, pale blue dress clung to her petite figure like a second skin, and her hair was piled high on her head to show off her delicate neck where an impressive diamond necklace glittered. Her cheeks had a rosy glow, and her blue eyes shone with excitement. She was so proud of Geoffrey…

"Well, we should be going. I want to get there before Kyle shows up and spills something down his shirt," Gabe sighed. "If we must be photographed, I'd prefer it to be with someone who isn't wearing his dinner…"

"His dinner would probably be preferable to whatever the heck he decides to wear tonight, Geoffrey. I simply cannot understand why Jenna puts up with his antics the way she does!"

"Aw, he's harmless, Dee, and he's just out for a good time. Nothing will make his day more than to see the looks on the faces of all those hoity-toity snobs when he shows up in a wet suit or cammo fatigues."

"He wouldn't…!" Deirdre gasped. She feared he'd opt for jeans and a tie-dye tee shirt…

"We'll find out pretty soon," Gabe said, giving her a wink.

He draped a faux-fur wrap over her shoulders and gave her neck a quick kiss. God, she really did look beautiful tonight… He wondered if she was feeling "human" like he was. He hoped so as much as he hoped not. But Jesus, he hadn't had that basic need met since Christmas, and it was beginning to consume his thoughts once again.

Kyle went with the "Tux in a can," and was very pleased with the disgusted looks he was getting from the white-collar set. Yep… he was dressed for success. But Jenna sure looked good… He literally drooled every time he looked at his beautiful wife. God, now she knew how to dress! She wore a long black evening gown, low in the front and even lower in the back, and made it look respectable enough to be worn in church. But she oozed sex appeal, and all the guys in the room could barely keep their eyes off of her. She let her long, wavy, honey-gold hair hang loose, held away from her face by tiny ebony clips. Her only jewelry was her wedding rings and a golden bracelet dangling two golden hearts. Gabe had always told her that she never needed jewelry to add to her appearance, it would be like gilding the lily. Jen was beautiful enough already.

So… Kyle rocked back and forth on his heels and waited for his partner to show up, and then they could get the pics done and go schmooze with the champagne and caviar set. Ooh! He was on his way in… Kyle slapped on a pair of glasses, complete with fake mustache and bushy eyebrows, and went to greet his buddy.

"Gabe buddy! Miss me?"

"Only about as much as finding out your children's babysitter is being featured on 'America's Most Wanted'. Hey Kyle, do you have a pair of those for me?" Gabe gave Kyle's 'stache a flick.

"Sure do!"

"Geoffrey, please don't…" Deirdre moaned.

"I'll only be naughty until the reception, Deirdre, and then I promise to do nothing more to embarrass you in front of all your friends." He took the glasses Kyle offered him and slapped them on. *Oh yeah…*

Deirdre sighed and went off to socialize.

Gabe and Kyle skipped over to where the photographer from the Watch was waiting to do the publicity pictures of them. He did manage to get a few good shots with and without the disguises, and planned to run a picture of each in Sunday's weekly magazine.

The buddies high-fived each other and went to see what kind of trouble they could get into before they had to behave themselves again.

"Gabe!"

"Tyler? Ty! Where the hell have you been, man? Christ, I haven't seen you since… since Christmas!"

"I know… I got real busy for a while there, and… and I've been on my honeymoon for the last month," he grinned, pulling a very lovely woman up next to him.

"Ooh… she said yes, eh Ty?" Gabe grinned. *So this was Annie… Nothing at all like he'd pictured her though, and that thought left him very relieved.*

"Huh?" Ty said, rather confused. *Oh well.* "Gabe, I'd like you to meet my wife, Doctor Ann Marlowe-Howe. Ann, Gabe Evans and Kyle Davidson."

Ann held out her hand to Gabe. "Very pleased to meet you, Mr. Evans," she said, giving him a very friendly, very sincere smile.

"Ann Howe," Gabe winked, playing on her name. He liked her immediately. So much nicer than that snake NeeNee… who was staring at him from across the room.

Kyle liked her too, and swept her away in a dramatic tango as Tyler and Gabe tried to suppress hysterical laughter at the always-goofy Davidson.

"She's great, Tyler," Gabe said, watching the new Mrs. Howe laugh at her "dance partner" as he lowered her into a dip.

"She is, Gabe. I sure got lucky…"

"But I thought you said she was a nurse, man. That doctor bit kind of threw me."

"What? A… a nurse? Gabe, I never even *told* you about Ann! God, I didn't even meet her until February."

"Now I'm confused! You told me on Christmas Eve that you were going to ask Annie to marry you… Annie the nurse?"

"Oh God… Annie," Tyler sighed, looking more distressed than he should have, for a newlywed anyway…

"Not the same one?"

"No, Gabe. And I did ask Annie to marry me but she said no. It took her a minute though… and I was so hoping, but it wasn't meant to be…"

"The doctor isn't a rebound, is she? Ty…"

"God no! When I met Ann… Gabe, I found out what love really is. Annie… well, I'll always love her, but it's no where near what I feel for Ann."

"Glad to hear it, Ty. Um… does Annie know you're married? You don't still 'date' her do you?" Gabe laughed, sending a smug look over at the simpering

NeeNee. *God, what a bitch.*

"I'm not sure if she knows, Gabe. I haven't talked to her in months. I did call over there one day, but a man answered and I hung up before I said anything."

"Didn't take her long either then, did it?"

"I'm pretty sure it was that Michael she was living with before."

"Oh? Clairvoyant are we…?"

"No, but when he answered he said 'Annie's place, this is Michael'. Not rocket science, Gabe."

"Whatever. Well, Kyle has decided to bring your bride back, a bit flushed-looking but no worse for wear. And congratulations, Ty. My best wishes for a most perfect marriage."

"Thank you, Gabe."

"Hey Ty, I'll take her if you ever decide to dump her," Kyle said, handing Mrs. Howe over to her hubby.

"I'll keep that in mind, Kyle. Jen wouldn't care?"

"Nope. She'd probably welcome the help. I got five kids you know," Kyle grinned at Ann.

She faked a swoon, and they went their separate ways, laughing their asses off.

At seven, the fake glasses were stashed away and Gabe and Kyle became "respectable" once more. They chatted, they socialized, they signed a few autographs for some die-hard fans, and when it was time for the ceremony, they took their seats at the overly decorated table in the front of the room.

Gabe would have rather been anywhere than there. He hated recognition for doing what he did, be it selling a million records with his band or raising a million dollars for the Children's Hospital like he was being lauded for that evening. He liked the applause from the fans when he was on stage and performing, but other than that… He wanted to be no more than Gabe Evans, just a regular guy with a regular life. And now he had to stand up before all of Waterston and be thanked publicly… He'd tried so damn hard to keep his name out of it all, but Deirdre, bless her little heart, felt that he had accomplished something so great that she let it slip to some members of the fund raising committee that it was him behind the whole idea. Well, and Kyle too…

Gabe and Kyle pasted attentive little expressions on their faces as the president and CEO of Brighton Memorial Hospital gave some long-winded, time-consuming speech about the community and the need for bla bla bla… To the audience it appeared as if the duo were glancing humbly at the table, but what they didn't know was that Gabe and Kyle were in a heated game of tic tac toe, the squares drawn on the table cloth earlier and the X's and O's bits of paper blown into position by the combatants. So far they were tied at three games each, and hoping to break the standoff to see which one of them had to accept the award. The winner got to do the speech.

"Ha!" Gabe whispered, blowing his O into the winning square. "Loser…"

"Fuck you," Kyle whispered back, hoping that the microphone didn't pick up any extraneous noise.

Gabe kicked him under the table, and then stood and smiled as his name was bellowed out into the room.

"...And I am thrilled to present Mr. Geoffrey Evans and Mr. Kyle Davidson..."

The applause was deafening and cameras flashed like lightening.

"Thank you..." Gabe said, nodding around the room and holding up a hand for quiet.

Kyle stood next to President "Brighton" and took the bronze and teak plaque from him. He was touched by it, but he'd had so much fun with his fund-raising that an award was just plain silly.

"...Thank you, everyone. And I'm not only thanking you for this lovely memento of our hard work, but thanking you for your contributions to the hospital, to the community, to the children... We couldn't have done it without you... and all your money," Gabe grinned. "When we first came up with this different concept of fund raising, we questioned its morality - given that the proceeds would be used for the children, but upon further reflection we decided to go ahead and pursue it. And it worked. Never in Waterston's history has such a large amount of cash been raised in so short of a period of time. One point two million dollars, ladies and gentlemen... That's a lot of jack! And this was done in only five short months... I commend you..." Gabe gave them all a nod, blew them a quick kiss off his hand, and took his seat.

"I guess I should say thanks too," Kyle said, taking his buddy's place at the podium. "I really got a kick out of our weekly 'Vegas Daze'... I want to thank my wife for putting up with me and my passion for poker, and Deirdre Evans for doin' all of the publicity to get this thing rollin', and Gabe here for suggestin' that I put my skills to good use and get a few bucks outta you in a fun way. And did you have fun losin'?" he laughed.

The audience applauded and cheered.

"Yeah, I thought so," Kyle said, looking around the room.

Every Saturday night they set up a miniature casino in the Waterston township hall, and people from miles around came to piss away money at the tables, the roulette wheel, and the slot machines, knowing damn well they'd lose but not minding too much since it was for a good cause. So that it wasn't a total loss, there were prizes given away, including a year's lease on a new car and a tropical vacation on a cruise ship. The word spread from Waterston to the outlying towns, and before too long the "casino" had to be moved to a larger area, namely the empty half of the SD Productions building. Fortunately it had all been warehouse space at one time, and after a quick renovation it was suitable for their needs.

Kyle had seen many of these faces in front of him now, only they had been across a poker table and he was takin' 'em for every penny they cared to bet.

Most of the serious gamblers would come just to see if they could beat him, but few walked away any richer. Not that they actually would… The chips and slot tokens were purchased with actual currency, but winnings could only be turned in for food and entertainment vouchers at a penny on the dollar.

"So anyway, thanks, everyone," Kyle said. He raised the plaque in the air and flashed his goofy grin, and then joined Gabe.

"Thank God that's over," Gabe sighed, tossing off his last glass of champagne.

"No shit. God, I hate standin' in front of people unless I got a guitar in my hands, dude. Speaking of… are we ever gonna…"

"No, Kyle, and I don't want to discuss it again."

"So what are we gonna do now to fill up our time, buddy? Not much happening at the studio, and it's getting' too cold to fish… No more casino nights and…"

"I don't know, Kyle. Sit home and stare at the goddamn TV like I've been doing, I guess."

"Find anything good to watch yet?"

"Nope. Just Ash's show. Do you still keep in touch with him?"

"Yep. We e-mail every month…"

"E-mail. Interesting concept. I think I should probably invest in a personal computer for home, Kyle…"

"Dude, they rock! God, they got all kinds of cool games, and surfin' the net… oh man… endless amounts of things to do!"

"And yet you whine about having nothing to do, Kyle…"

"Kiss my ass. That's just time filler anyway. I'm talkin' about something with substance… some project we can really sink our teeth into…"

"I'll think about it and let you know, Kyle. But right now I'm taking my wife home and…"

"Oh ho… gonna get lucky, Gabe?" Kyle grinned. He knew for sure he was…

"Get lucky? Kyle, must you be so… adolescently crude?" But Gabe found himself rather hoping to "get lucky" as he watched Deirdre float over to him. Didn't help that he'd drunk so much champagne… Now he was feeling a little more "frisky" than usual.

"Later, Man," Kyle said, wrapping his arms around Jen and kissing her neck right where her pulse beat under her jaw. Aw God…

Jenna threw a hasty goodbye to the Evans' and literally pulled her husband along behind her as she ran from the building. She couldn't wait to follow up on that kiss…

"Geoffrey, you were wonderful tonight."

"I didn't embarrass you, Deirdre?"

"Impossible. No, everything you do seems to be the right thing for some reason, Geoffrey dear. Even those horrid glasses were a roaring success…"

"Kyle's idea…"

"But you can both pull it off. Oh dear, here comes that awful Deanna. Geoffrey, would it be rude if we…"

"Who the hell cares? C'mon, Dee…" Gabe put an arm around her and they raced out of the building before they had to put up with the likes of NeeNee.

Deirdre was breathless and laughing by the time they reached her car. Gabe opened the door for her and she got in, thanking him for his consideration. He was always considerate…

Gabe got in next to her and put his key in the ignition. Her hand closed over his before he could turn it on, and he looked over at his wife.

"Deirdre?"

She said nothing, but he recognized that look in her eye. It was pretty much the same one he had in his. He grasped her hand and brought it to his lips, and then dropped it so that he could use that hand to pull her towards him for a kiss.

Later that night he lay in his bed, wrapped in her arms and again fighting guilt. Yeah, this time they'd kissed and even murmured little words of love, but he never meant a bit of it. It was all just physical gratification to him, no different than years ago when he bedded any available female that captured his fancy. There was no love in his lovemaking, and Deirdre didn't deserve such low treatment. Not that she was complaining… he knew damn well he'd satisfied her over and over again, but the emotions that should have been there… the all-consuming love, the passion, the joining of two souls as they expressed their devotion… Gabe had never in his life experienced that and he found that he desperately wanted it. Wanted to find his soul mate, wanted to find that one woman that he lived for… that he'd die for. Wanted to find his green-eyed dream.

Deirdre lay in Geoffrey's strong arms and fought back her tears. During the two and a half years they'd been married, she found that she was deeply in love with her husband. It would never compare to what she had with Steven, who she still missed desperately, but it was close – very close. It hurt her more than she ever could have imagined that Geoffrey would never love her that way. He loved her, there was no doubt about that, but she'd never be the "one" for him. His best friend and confidant, yes, but never the wife he wished he had. Even now he was thinking about his dream woman, wishing she were in his arms instead of Deirdre… And yes, Dee would keep her promise to Geoffrey should he ever find her. She would release him from their marriage and quietly fade away…

Chapter Sixteen
Late winter

Michael filled the wood box on the porch, and then brought in an armload of the split oak logs to fill the stove. Annie would be home from work soon and he wanted the cabin all warm and cozy for her. She'd been working a lot of overtime lately and it was really wearing on her.

He stoked the fire, hung the afghan close to the stove to get it toasty, and then fixed a mug of hot coco as soon as he heard the truck pull into the driveway. Yep, this should make her feel a little better...

Annie dragged her tired self from her truck, swore when the door didn't shut tight and she had to trudge back through the snow to close it properly, and then made her way to the cabin. Thank God Michael had already shoveled a path for her. It had snowed at least six inches during the night, and she had not been looking forward to clearing it away before she fell into bed. And thank God Michael was back again after having been gone for nearly two weeks. She couldn't wait to see him again.

He helped her out of her coat as soon as she hit the door, and then lifted her into his arms and gave her a kiss.

She smiled up into his eyes as her arms twined around his neck, and let him carry her to the favorite chair.

"Good morning, Miss Benton," he said, tucking that toasty afghan around her.

"Good morning, Michael," she said, snuggling down into its warmth and accepting the steaming mug handed to her. Jeez, it was hard to believe she hadn't seen him in weeks, and now it was as if he'd never left. "How was your trip?"

"Same as always, Annie. Get sent somewhere, finish the assignment, and come back here to wait for more orders."

"Mmhmm. You know, one of these days I'm going to tie you down and force you to answer my questions. I'll want to know who you work for, what you do, how they contact you... how the heck you get there! And if you don't tell me I shall be forced to tickle you with one of McDonald's feathers until you talk..." She gave him a playful look, but there was a little seriousness behind her threat too.

"And you know what? One of these days I'll be able to tell you without fear of that threat, Annie. But not yet, so please don't push."

"I've learned not to, Michael. So how are you? You look great!"

"Same as always, hon; I never change..."

She gave him a long look, surprised at how true his words were. During all the years she'd known him his hair never changed, he never seemed to age, never gained or lost weight… still wore that nasty, dusty hat, although he did let himself take advantage of the new wardrobe she provided for him… But other than that he looked the same as that first day she had met him in the clearing. At least she thought so… During his frequent and sometimes long absences she would completely forget what he looked like other than a vague memory of tall and dark. Weird. But who cared? He was back with her where he belonged.

"You look kinda tired, Annie. I know you've been working too much again…"

"How? You haven't been around…"

"But I still keep track of you. I watch over you, remember?"

"How could I possibly forget? And you take care of me pretty good too." She lifted her mug and rubbed a cheek against the soft blanket wrapped around her.

"It's the least I can do, hon."

"Thank you. I have the next three nights off, Michael; are you going to be around?"

"No plans until after the holidays…"

"Good. I know you don't like to go out, but… well, I have tickets to a play and I was wondering…"

Michael stiffened. "Uh… which one, Annie?"

"The Nutcracker. The Children's Theater and Ballet Company is putting it on…"

"Sounds like fun, and I'd love to go."

"You would? Really?"

"Really." Of course if it was "Colors in the Wind," he wouldn't have even thought about it. No way could he show up at that theater with Annie at his side… although he would have loved to see the play considering who was in it.

"Great! Tomorrow at seven…"

He smiled, planted a kiss on her nose, and went outside to see to the horses.

Annie watched him go. Her mysterious Michael… She loved him more and more every day, but never developed those romantic feelings for him that she'd so hoped she would. He was so much like the man in her dreams… Him but not him. And his feelings for her… He loved her too but never did more than hold her or give her a brotherly kiss. He mentioned once again that friends were all they could ever be since she was meant for another. She accepted it although it left her beyond confused.

"Kyle, you are so dense! I would have thought that after weeks of rehearsal you would at least get more than two lines in a row correct! God! If you fuck up tomorrow night I'm going to kick your ass! This means a lot to Deirdre and

I won't have you spoiling it for her!"

"Aw, I was just messin' with ya. I'll get it right, Gabe, I promise!"

"You'd better. I took a hell of a chance allowing her to use that stupid play I wrote years ago… And to let you co-star? I must be insane…"

"Dude, just 'cuz I flunked out of drama in college doesn't mean I can't do this now. I got a lot of experience doin' those music videos…"

"Live theater is nowhere near the same thing, Kyle. You get one chance… one shot. No one will yell cut so that we can do another take. You fuck up, everyone knows it."

"I *know*, Gabe. God! And I promise no less than perfection… I could never do anything to hurt Deirdre…"

Gabe could only pray. He still had second thoughts about the whole affair, starring in his own play, Deirdre and Kyle at his side, but she had found the script in a box of his old papers and fell in love with the story. She took it to her fellow actors in the little community theater company, and it was decided that they would do the play for their Christmas special.

Auditions were held, choices made, but no one seemed to fit the main character. Gabe had gone in to support Deirdre during her audition, and nearly died when he saw actor after actor slaughter his script. Unable to take another minute of the horrible interpretation of his words, he jumped on stage, grabbed the handful of papers from the stunned man doing the reading, and after tossing aside the script, Gabe went on to show them how it was meant to be. He poured his heart into his words, and the director wouldn't even sit through another audition. Gabe was the one and only choice. Yeah right… Acting was the last thing on his list of favorite activities, and he put up a hell of an argument until Deirdre quietly asked him if he would please do it for her. Of course he could deny her nothing, and resigned himself to the fact that he was committed to the play for the next two months.

To be fair, he was having a good time with the whole thing, especially when Kyle came on board after the original actor hurt his back in a fall. And tomorrow night it would all come together…

Gabe made one last inspection of the stage, making sure everything was in place, and then retreated to his dressing room. Well, not entirely his, he shared it with about six other guys. Still, it was a place to chill out for a few before the curtain was raised.

"Oh Geoffrey, I'm so excited for you! Imagine… starring and co-directing a play you wrote yourself! And you will be wonderful…"

"Thanks, Deirdre, although I'm afraid I can't share in your enthusiasm," he sighed, tapping a knuckle on his chin as he sat slumped in his chair.

"Geoffrey? Why not? The story is superb, and…"

"And it's dredging up too many memories of Steve, Dee. God, what the hell was I thinking when I agreed to this? I figured enough time had passed… and it wouldn't hurt so much to relive our last Christmas together, but… I honestly don't know if I can do it, Dee!"

"Oh my… so this is a true story? Oh Geoffrey…"

"But I have to, don't I? I'd be letting far too many people down if I backed out now… Not only you and our colleagues, but the audiences… and all those kids. We made quite a bit of money off the ticket sales, Dee, and there was enough to pay for that entire Christmas party for the community center's annual Kids-Fest."

"You forgot one person, Geoffrey, the one who would be most disappointed…"

"I mentioned you first, Deirdre…"

"Not me, Geoffrey, you. You must do this for yourself. Deep down you must have wanted this… this story to be known to the world, or at least our little corner of it, and that's why you let me read it after I found it. And why you allowed me to let my friends read it… Why you jumped on that stage during auditions and opened your heart… And now I understand why you had such passion… And the characters… Ben is you, and Mike is Steven, right?"

Gabe nodded.

"I'm surprised I didn't pick up on it long ago. Ben is so much like you, and Mike… yes, he's Steven. Quiet and gentle, so loving… Oh Geoffrey, I'm so glad we're doing this! I can have him back for just a little while… even if Kyle is playing Mike. But he does a pretty good job. Does he know who he is playing?"

Gabe shook his head. "No, he doesn't, Dee. I never told him about any of this. And don't you tell him either. He's still not over Steve's death. Poor guy…"

"I won't. Well, it's nearly time, Geoffrey dear." Deirdre kissed him and went to change into her costume. Given this new bit of information, Deirdre's character was actually her mother-in-law, Marie.

"I don't understand, Michael! I thought for sure it was tonight! What's this 'Colors' play anyway?"

"Not what we came to see so I guess we're out of luck. How about if we take in a movie instead?"

"I don't know… nothing I want to see right now. Should we see if there are tickets available for this?"

"I don't think so, Annie. I heard it's… well, rather a tear jerker at times and I'm not into anything like that at the moment."

"So… any suggestions?"

"Old movie at the cabin and a big bowl of popcorn?"

"Perfect." Annie pulled away from the curb and drove to the video store.

Annie fell asleep before they were even five minutes into their movie. Michael covered her up with her blanket and kissed her, and then went to see his tearjerker play after all.

He arrived just at the first act was underway, and took a seat high up in the corner of the balcony where it was darkest.

Davidson did a great job portraying the Mike character, and Evans… well, he was playing himself. How could he not give the performance of a lifetime?

Michael Anthony sat back and absorbed the drama and emotion of brothers spending one last Christmas together after a long estrangement. Granted, the script drifted a little from the actual story, but it was wonderful nonetheless.

The second to the last scene showed Ben and Mike sitting in the darkened living room of their parents' home. The only lights on were shining from the Christmas tree, and the brothers had just ended yet another argument. Ben was arguing anyway… Mike was just trying to save his brother from himself again.

And then Mike dropped the bad news on his sibling. This would be their final Christmas together, as he had just found out he had an incurable disease and time was growing short. Ben couldn't accept that – wouldn't accept that, and vented his pain and rage on Mike… and then collapsed into tears as reality hit.

Of course there was the usual seven stages of grief, all portrayed within a twenty-minute scene, and finally Ben accepted the inevitable.

He waked to the tree and touched the angel gracing the top, and then turned to his brother.

"Mike, I don't know what I'm going to do without you," he said in a voice choked with emotion. "My God…"

"Ben, my body may be leaving but my spirit will be with you forever. I'll still be by your side… laughin' when you laugh, cryin' when you cry…"

"Just allow me a few minutes of privacy when I'm with a lady," Ben said with a sad chuckle.

Mike gave him a serene smile and led him back to the sofa.

"It'll be hard for a while, Ben. I need you to help Mom through it though. Dad too, but Mom…" Mike trailed off, shaking his head.

"I know. And I have to be the strong one again, right?"

"Right. So… Let's have one last drink together before we hit the sack, eh Ben?"

Ben poured two glasses and handed one to his brother. They touched the glasses in a silent toast and stared at the Christmas tree as they sipped their whiskey.

"This was always my favorite part of Christmas," Mike said with a sigh. "I'd sneak out here after everyone went to bed and just stare at the tree. I love all those colors… Hey Ben, would you like to see a trick?"

"Sure, Mikey, whatever makes you happy," Ben murmured, lost in his own sad thoughts.

"Watch." Mike stood and waved his arm through the air, smiling down at his brother as he did so.

The tinsel on the tree began to shimmer and dance, sending sparks of color shooting around the room

Ben looked up in awe. "How… how did you do that, Mike? My God… We're at least twenty feet from that tree! No way could you have…"

"Been doin' it for a while now, Ben. Surprised the heck out of me too the first time it happened, but… well, pretty cool, don't ya think?"

Ben spun in a slow circle, raising his hands in the air and watching as the colors danced around him. A miracle for sure…

"You'll see this again after I'm gone, Ben. You'll see the colors in the wind and know I'm right there…"

The lights dimmed for a moment and the scenery changed, and Ben was standing in a cemetery on a cold, gray blustery day in autumn. He was standing in front of a headstone, a rose in his hand and tears in his eyes.

"Mike… God, I miss you," he murmured, raising the rose to his lips. A teardrop fell on a rose petal just as the wind kicked up and a ray of sun escaped from a cloud. The light hit the moisture on the flower, and once again the air was filled with a kaleidoscope of colors. Ben raised his face to the sky and smiled, knowing his brother had never left him after all.

The curtain dropped and the audience sat in silence. Gabe, on the other side of that curtain, was terrified that his work had been nothing but a disaster. *Oh well…*

He jumped when a thunderous applause broke out, and the curtain opened once again.

Oh God… they were all on their feet! He took a bow and then welcomed his fellow actors on stage. With Deirdre on his left and Kyle on his right, they held hands and bowed again.

"Geoffrey, you were wonderful," Deirdre whispered, squeezing his hand.

"They liked it, Dee!" he whispered back.

"They fuckin' loved it, Dude!" Kyle said, not as quietly as he should have. The audience members in the first few rows heard him, and nodded enthusiastically as they applauded and wiped away a few tears.

Michael was wiping away his own tears, and slipped out of the theater as soon as the curtain closed on the actors for the final time. He went straight back to the cabin and joined the sleeping Annie, holding her in his arms as he stared at the Christmas tree. Knowing he shouldn't but doing it anyway, he waved a hand through the air and immediately shut his eyes. He wasn't sure if his battered heart could handle the colors as they danced around the room.

~Part Three~
Winds of Change

Chapter Seventeen

Summer, 1993

Deirdre sat up on her heels and wiped the sweat from her face. It wasn't all that warm in the garden yet, and the weeding certainly wasn't difficult work, and yet she felt as if she had just run a marathon. Her muscles ached, her head spun, and she felt just a little nauseous. And her period was now officially two months overdue. She let herself smile a little in spite of her discomfort. Pregnant... and she was thrilled about it. She hoped that Geoffrey would be just as happy.

Dropping her tools into the wicker basket she used while gardening, Deirdre abandoned her chores to go make a phone call. It was time to see her doctor and confirm her suspicions. And after finding out for sure, she'd make a special dinner for her husband and tell him her most wonderful news.

Gabe sat in his office at the studio, once again staring out the window as he faced another goddamn unproductive boring day. Business was still slow, and there was just enough of it to keep SD's doors open. Kyle had enthusiastically volunteered to take over the pathetic payroll and Jen was doing the rest of the accounting, leaving Gabe very little to do. Sure there was still all the work involved in running a recording studio, but there just wasn't all that much recording going on... which resulted in a lack of related activities like promotions and sales, and all the rest of those fun little chores Gabe had once loved to do.

God, something needed to happen to pull him out of his rut! It would take a lot of pulling though as his depression was beginning to take over again. Ever since that goddamn Christmas play...

Steve was forever on his mind, and the nightmares had started up again in earnest. Several times a week Gabe would wake screaming for his brother after dreaming of the choking smoke and the heat of the flames. Same dream he'd had for years before Stevie died, and the same one he'd had for nearly a year after. And just why the hell was it starting up again? Poor Deirdre... having her sleep interrupted to rush in and hold him until his trembling subsided. He felt terrible for putting her through it. Especially lately. Instead of going back to her room she was staying in his, and occasionally they'd end up having sex. It had only happened a few times, but Gabe still felt just as guilty afterwards as he had the first time. He still didn't love her as he should, but because he did love her it made it so very wrong. He shook his head and sighed, and then got up to wander through the quiet halls of his studio. He couldn't wait until Kyle and his family got back from their vacation in Jamaica so he could liven things up a bit.

Maybe he should just leave early and take Deirdre and the boys out for nice dinner and then a walk in the park. The twins loved outings like that, and Gabe loved to take them. They were full of curiosity about the world around them and asked their papa question after question. Gabe was a near genius and had an answer for everything. Deirdre would laugh, loving her little family more than she ever thought possible…

Yeah, he'd do it if for no other reason than to get his mind off his own misery.

Deirdre's hands trembled as she picked up the ringing phone. The news from her doctor was nothing at all like she expected, and the possibilities… No. No way. She slammed her mind shut on her doctor's suggestions and answered the phone.

"H… Hello?"

"Dee? Got dinner on yet?"

"Geoffrey? Uh… no, not yet…" She was barely able to function let alone cook…

"Good. Pack up the boys and be ready for me in about half an hour. We'll pick up a bucket of chicken with fixin's and head for a picnic in the park. Sound good?"

"Uh… wonderful, Geoffrey…"

"Dee? Something wrong? Oh God… are the boys all right?"

"Just… just fine, Geoffrey. I'll see you soon." She hung up and went to her children.

"Deirdre?" Huh. Oh well, probably hormonal or something… although in the three years they'd been together he'd never seen her that way. She was always bright and sunny, happy and content, except for those rare moments when her memories of Steve would bring her down.

"Michael? Are you alright? You seem a little distracted today…"

"I'm fine, Annie. Just got little disturbin' news is all."

"Are… are you leaving again?"

"Not right away, but don't be surprised if I have to up and go at a moment's notice…"

"And I was so getting used to having you around again," she smiled. Ever since January he'd been home every day. Every single wonderful day… They rode and hiked, and went for long, quiet rides on her lake in the canoe she had bought early that spring. And when Eric would come over it was just as if she had a real family… Mom, Dad, and the kid. She'd never been happier in her life, and dreaded the day when Michael would leave and end it all.

"Are you going to share or hold it all in again, Michael?"

"I suppose I could tell you a little… God, it's tearin' me up inside, Annie!"

She went to him and held him, surprised at the emotion in his voice and the horrible sorrow on his serene face.

"What is it?" she whispered, hugging him to her.

"Aw God… Annie, it's awful. I… I heard today that my fiancé, my ex-fiancé has… has cancer."

"Oh no… Michael, I'm so sorry! Is… well, did they catch it in time? Will they be able to treat her for it?"

"She went in time, but she has that long, long road ahead. All of the suffering…"

"Are you going to go to her, Michael? Is that why you might have to leave?"

"No. God, I would give anything to be able to be there for her, but I can't. Not in this lifetime… not yet anyway."

"Why not? If she needs support and still loves you… Or is it her husband? Would he be upset?"

"No, he'd probably just as thrilled to see me as she would. But I can't, and leave it at that, Annie."

"Anyway, I'll be here for you, Michael. Never doubt that."

"I know, Annie, and you're the best friend I've ever had…"

He raised her face to his and gave her a tender kiss, and together they walked up to the cabin.

She made him a special dinner to cheer him up.

He ate very little, and then took his big black horse for a very long ride, not returning until well after dark and Annie had been long asleep. He looked in on her, gave her a kiss, and then left again.

"I don't know what the hell's wrong with her, Kyle! She's like a shadow of the woman she once was. She quit the theater, has all but given up her charity work, and hardly ever smiles anymore. The twins can wring one out of her but not me…"

"Don't know what to tell you, Gabe. Um… you two are still okay, right? I mean your… personal life?"

"No changes there, Kyle." *As if… There had never really been anything to change!*

"Whoa dude! I just thought of something! Maybe she's pregnant! Jen always got a little moody the first month or so."

"Pregnant? Kyle, that's impossible."

"Why? She on birth control or something?"

"No, but… Never mind. Pregnant?"

"Sure, why not? 'Bout time you had another kid, buddy!" Kyle grinned.

"I don't have any now," Gabe mumbled.

"Do too! Oh yeah… I keep forgettin' that James and Jer are Steve's. But dude, you're their papa now and you're a damn good one too. And I think it would be great if you and Dee had a baby together. You want more, right?"

"Nothing would make me happier than to have a child of my own, Kyle…"
Just not with Deirdre.

Even though he'd all but given up on finding his Annie – yes, that's how he thought of the woman haunting his dreams now, to share a child with Deirdre would forever bind him to her. Not that he'd ever leave her, but it would irrevocably dash any hopes he ever had of finding true love.

"So ask her!"

"Huh?"

"Ask her, dude! Come right out and ask her if she's gonna have a baby. Maybe she's kinda scared to tell you."

"I don't know why. I've never given her any reason to fear me, Kyle!"

"Not on purpose, no. But Gabe, sometimes you get a look on your face that even scares the hell outta me!"

"I do?"

"Yep."

"Huh. Well then I apologize for that…"

"Nothin' you can do about it, buddy; it's just you."

"Just me…" Gabe mumbled, contemplating a possibly pregnant Deirdre. And his latest mess…

He did some quick calculations, estimating the possible moment of conception, not that it was all that difficult to figure out. June fifteenth was the last time they had relations, which meant that she was just a little over two months gone. The time before that was early March, and she'd be showing by now if that was when it happened.

"Gabe?"

"Huh?"

"Anything wrong?"

"No, not really. I think I'll head out early today, spend some time with Deirdre…"

"Let me know, man," Kyle said, shaking his best friend's hand and giving him a wicked grin.

"You'll be the very first, Kyle."

"See ya later, Daddy…"

Gabe gave him a pathetic smile and left the office.

Kyle's breath was released in a whoosh of relief, and he sat down at his desk. The hastily stashed checkbook was pulled out, and Davidson "borrowed" a few grand to get him by. His vacation bills were beginning to pour in and Jen was bitchin' about him gamblin' again. She nearly shot him when she found out about his little financial fuck up in Vegas, but he managed to smooth the waters by tellin' her that Gabe was helping out a bit. He also told her not to say anything to him, given his need to be the anonymous savior. *So anonymous that even Gabe wasn't aware.*

And all was well in the Davidson house…

"You're exceptionally quiet tonight, Geoffrey."

"And you've been that way for weeks now, Deirdre. Is there something you need to tell me?"

She shivered a little bit at the look he gave her... so dark and foreboding, and demanding an answer. *Not that she had one to give him.*

"Deirdre?"

"There's nothing, Geoffrey..."

"Are you sure? Dee... Aw God, Deirdre, are you pregnant?"

He didn't look all that happy about it, and his negativity along with her unspoken fears caused her to burst into tears.

"Dee? Jesus, what brought that on?" he asked, taking her into his arms.

She shook her head and cried all that much harder.

"Christ, you are, aren't you? Well, when may we expect our little bundle of joy?" he sighed. He didn't mean to sound so sarcastic though. And goddammit, she was all-out sobbing now...

Deirdre totally lost it. Thank God she wasn't with child, not when his own father didn't appear to want him very much. Which was very strange since Gabe loved children! He doted on the twins and treated the Davidson's brood as if they were his own.

But her child, and his, meant nothing to him...

"Dee, I'm sorry," Gabe whispered, kissing her gently. "Stop crying and tell me..."

"I... I'm not pregnant, Geoffrey," she sniffed.

She stifled fresh bouts of weeping when she felt him relax in relief.

"Then what is it, love? Why all of this..."

He wiped away her tears, gazing deep into her eyes for an answer.

"I... I thought I was, Geoffrey, but I found that it was a mistake. I guess I'm still a little upset over it all." And it *was* the partial truth, the only truth she was willing to deal with anyway.

"You want another child, Dee?" Weren't the twins enough? And how could she even contemplate having a baby with a man she didn't love – not that way, anyway...

She only shrugged a shoulder in response. To deny it would be more of a lie than she could utter, but to admit that it was her fondest wish, no, not with his apathetic attitude.

"But your quiet demeanor of late... because you were upset about not being pregnant?"

She nodded.

"Then I truly am sorry, love. I've been so wrapped up in my own woes that I've failed to notice you were suffering from your own. How can I make it up to you?" *Besides getting her pregnant...*

"Just be here for me, Geoffrey. Just be here..." *And give her the child she so desperately wanted...*

Fearing what they would see, they avoided looking into each other's eyes for a long time to come.

So life went on as usual. Week after goddamn week of same shit different day for Gabe, although he did spend more time with Kyle.

Kyle was happy, happy, happy… He'd hooked up with Jerry, an accountant he'd met over a game of pool, and his new buddy had turned him on to some sure-fire investments. He was already starting to see a little return, and began paying SD Productions back. He still "borrowed" every month, but not nearly so much. He even included Jen in on is plans. She was pissed at first, then skeptical, but after telling her that Jerry knew his business and they were seein' some cash comin' in, she let him continue. It still scared her though – Kyle hadn't been very good with managing their money ever since they were married.

Kyle was even happier about Gabe. He was sad that his buddy wasn't gonna be a daddy, but thrilled that Evans spent so much time with him lately. And Kyle did his goddamn best to cheer his moody partner up.

Deirdre called upon her acting skills, becoming the happy homemaker during the day, but at night after the boys were asleep, she'd lock herself in her room. She cried, she prayed, she begged for a quick death and then begged to live another day, another month… or even long enough to see her boys grow into men.

She did her best to ignore the nameless sickness growing in her. She feared that to have it diagnosed… given a name, it would be her death sentence. Her subconscious told her that ignoring it *was* a death sentence, but she slammed her mind shut on that horribly prophetic little voice.

Deirdre would still go to Gabe when he woke screaming in the night, but spent as little time as possible in his room. There was one time he asked her to stay, brushing a trembling hand along her cheek and then along her breast, but she fled the room before he could see her tears. Never again would she share his bed knowing that he could never really truly love her. She began to understand just how Danni felt, and joined the sisterhood of the women used by Gabe.

Chapter Eighteen

Autumn was rapidly losing its glorious blaze of colors, the reds and golds turning to russets and dusty browns.

Annie's garden fought the coming of winter and held its blooms, brightening an otherwise dead landscape. She wandered through the spiral of her roses, snipping a flower here and pruning a branch there, and when she reached the small square of grass in the center, amidst the white roses, she sat and let the vision come.

It had been an almost daily ritual for a few months now, her sitting there with closed eyes and a heart beating out of control, but one she was loathe to give up. And she was there again, waiting…

Her eyes closed, the aroma of roses filled her nostrils, and he was there. It was always the same thing…just like her dreams. She would feel lost, alone, and scared, and there he was, taking her into his arms. She'd look into his intense blue eyes and know that was where she belonged… His head would bend to kiss her… and she'd wake up to reality. Still lost and alone, but with no man to bring her home.

She sighed and stood, and began her way back through the spiral.

"Annie! Annie, you out here?"

"Over here, Michael."

She stepped from the flowers and waved to him.

He sent his horse off to the barn with a slap to the rump, and walked over to her.

She wanted to turn right back around and run away from that look on his face.

"How… how was your ride, Michael?"

"Short. Annie, we need to talk."

"I figured as much…."

"I have to leave, Annie. My brother needs me right now. His wife is ill… I'm going to help out with the kids. I'm not sure when I'll be back."

"Your brother's wife? I… I thought you'd be leaving because of your fiancé…"

He looked away as if he didn't want to think about anymore horrible things.

"Is it something serious?" Annie asked, her heart breaking for him.

"I'm afraid it is, hon. I… I have to leave soon. Tell Eric I said goodbye, will you?"

"I will, and Michael, let me know if I can do anything."

He took her into his arms, hugging her as if it would be the last time ever. The intensity of it sent a chill of foreboding through her.

"Annie, you'll do more than you can possibly imagine. I have a feeling that the next year or two will be very hard on us all. I can't explain now, but remember that I'll always be there when you need me most."

"Be here for me? But it's your brother who…"

"Just remember what I said and be strong. You can give in, but don't ever give up."

He raised his face to hers and kissed her lips, gently at first, and then with some passion.

"I love you, Annie Benton," he whispered. He took a white bud from the basket in her hand and tucked it into her hair.

"You are so very, very special…" He kissed her one last time and ran to the barn.

She stood there staring after him, trying to make sense of what she had just heard.

"Michael! Michael, wait!" She ran after him, flinging open the door to the empty barn.

"Michael?"

Where was he? She had seen him walk in not ten seconds ago, and now neither he nor his horse were anywhere to be seen! Her mind began to buzz with questions about him… Just who was he really? She plucked the rose bud from her hair and stared at it. Her fingers began to tingle…

Eric took the news about Michael much better than Annie had expected. His health had been declining over the last few weeks and he had been unable to visit the cabin, but just after the first snow of winter he was able to visit.

He sat by the woodstove, holding McDonald in his lap while he and Annie chatted about their missing friend.

"You know," Eric said, "Michael will always be here with us even if he isn't here. He has magic."

"Magic?"

"Sure! Remember that spring? The day McDonald was born?"

"Yes…"

"Well, it was Michael that made all the colors come from the flowers. And he brought McDonald back to life too."

"Eric, he didn't bring him back to life! McDonald was just… delayed."

"Annie, he was stiff and cold! I peeked just before you guys came into the cabin and he was dead! I've seen dead… I know dead, Annie. McDonald was dead and Michael brought him back." Eric was silent for a moment, petting the soft white feathers of the goose in his lap. "He was dead… But everything was so right when Michael was around… And you know what? I've seen him disappear into thin air too. He didn't know I saw him, but I did!"

"C'mon, Eric… you're a little too old to be believing in fairy tales. Magic… The colors came from the sun reflecting some water that was on the roses. McDonald… well, I still think he was just delayed, and no one vanishes into thin air!" But some of the conviction left Annie's voice as she remembered the last time she had seen her friend.

Eric said nothing else. He knew Michael had special powers and he had seen him do a lot more than he told Annie. Like when his breathing would become so labored and Michael would touch him, and all of a sudden the air would flow into his lungs as it should. And the time when they were out in the canoe and saw the baby rabbit trapped on a floating log... Michael had paddled right over to it and picked it up like they were best friends. The little bunny snuggled into his lap until they reached the shore, and then Michael lifted him to dry land. There were so many other things too... And Eric could see the blue light around the man, just like he could see the white one around Annie. But Michael's was a whole lot brighter and a whole lot stronger.

He had Magic.

Chapter Nineteen

Spring, 1994

"Deirdre, I don't care what the hell you say! You're seeing a goddamn doctor today if I have to drag you there kicking and screaming!"

"Geoffrey, I'd thank you to not use such language in front of me."

"Don't change the subject. Now, will you call or will you be hauled in…"

"Geoffrey, I'm fine. Just a little under the weather…"

"A little under… Jesus Christ, Deirdre, you look like hell!"

She shot him a sharp, hurt look.

"Well, you do," he said, softening his tone a little. He ran a hand down her hair, wincing a little at the feel of the rough tresses. It used to feel like silk…

"Deirdre, something is seriously wrong. You've lost so much weight, not that you ever had any to spare, and you have no energy anymore. You're pale, and your eyes have shadows… Please, please see a doctor!"

She nodded. There was no way she could deny it any more, and the pain was becoming more than she could take – and hide. But to hear it said… to know for sure… Dear Lord, would she be able to bear it?

Gabe didn't wait for her, but made the call himself. He was appalled when the doctor herself was on the phone, telling him that she'd see Deirdre right away. She couldn't give him all of the details over the phone, but promised to explain everything, with Deirdre's permission of course, when they met in her office in an hour.

"Deirdre, what have you been keeping from me?" he asked quietly, kneeling next to her.

"I… I don't know what you're talking about, Geoffrey."

"Don't lie to me. I just spoke with Dr. Geering."

"You did?"

"I did. Deirdre, why? Why in God's name didn't you follow her advice and return for tests?"

"I… I don't know. I was so hoping that I was pregnant, and when I found I wasn't…"

"Deirdre, she all but begged you to come back so they could determine the problem. And yet you didn't… Why?"

She shook her head and looked away.

"Was it fear? Deirdre, are you frightened of what might be wrong?"

She gave him a small, scared nod.

"Oh God… And you have been living with this… dealing with this all of this time? All alone?"

She looked at him and a tear escaped, slowly trickling down her pale, drawn cheek.

"Oh God," Gabe moaned, and took her into his arms. He rocked her slowly as she cried, and then helped her up the stairs so that she could prepare for her appointment.

"It's not good, Kyle..."

"You want me there, dude? I can be there in fifteen minutes..."

"Would you mind? You need to know, but I... I can't tell you over the phone."

"Aw God... It's that bad, Gabe?"

"That bad, Kyle..."

"Cancer? She has cancer? Oh... oh God!" Kyle felt dizzy and fell into a chair.

"I'm afraid so, Kyle."

"For sure? I mean, it might just be one of them fake tumors or something..."

"For sure. After her appointment she was taken to Brighton for an immediate biopsy, but Dr. Geering already knew for sure. Hell, she was suspicious last summer but Dee never went back. Anyway, she has ovarian cancer with probable metastasis to her uterus and cervix, and God only know what else. It's been in there growing for nearly a year... maybe even longer. Christ, I just can't believe this..." Gabe mumbled, dropping his head into his hands.

"Oh man... Gabe, is... is she going to die? She can't die, Gabe! Oh God..."

Gabe went and sat next to his friend, putting an arm around him for support. Poor ol' Kyle... Always Mr. Sunshine and good times until the health of a loved one was threatened, and then he'd turn into a basket case.

"She won't die, Kyle. She's going to have a little surgery and some chemotherapy and radiation, but she'll survive this. She's strong, buddy, and she'll do anything to stay with her sons. If nothing else, they'll keep her going. Would you like to go see her?"

"Could I? I mean, she won't mind, will she? Oh God, Jen's gotta know..."

"I'll tell her, Kyle. Come on. You visit with my wife for a while and I'll go see yours. Is your useless nanny over there today?"

"Uh... yeah. Until five or so..."

"Good... One less mess. I'll uh, bring Jen back with me, okay?"

"Yeah... bring Jen back..."

"Kyle, are you with me? Hey buddy..." Gabe gave him a little slap to the face to bring his somewhat catatonic friend back around. Couldn't have him "checking out" right now...

"Gabe? Aw God... Deirdre..."

"I'll take you to her, Kyle."

Jeremy woke to see his papa standing at the foot of the bed. The moon was low in the window so Jer knew it was very, very late at night.

"Papa?"

The man moved a little closer and took off his dust-covered hat.

"Daddy?"

"Hey, Jer, how's my little man tonight?"

"Not so good, Daddy. When will Mamma be home?"

"Not for a while, kiddo. She's not feelin' too well right now and has to stay at the hospital until the doctors can make her better."

"How long? I miss her, Daddy. James does too."

"Me too, Jer. And she'll be home before you know it. But Jeremy, she won't be the same Mamma she was before she left..."

"She won't? But I want *my* Mamma..."

"No, not like that. She uh... Well, she had to have medicine that will change her a little. She won't laugh as much, and she might look a little different..."

"But she'll still be Mamma? She'll still love us, won't she Daddy?"

"She'll always love you, Jeremy."

"Will you always love me, Daddy?"

"For ever and ever, son..."

"And Papa? He'll always love me too?"

"Just as much as I do. Jer?"

"Yes, Daddy?"

"Just when was it that you figured out that your Papa and I were not the same person?"

Jeremy thought for a minute, and then said, "The night he went to that party and got that award. He didn't know about the secret tuck in. I thought about it for a long time, and then I knew. You were really Uncle Steve, and not Papa. But then you said you were my daddy... not 'papa', but daddy. And then I knew..."

"You knew..."

"Uh huh. Sometimes I just know things and I know this. It's Papa who's my uncle, isn't it? He's my Uncle Gabe and you're my daddy..."

Steve sighed and sat next to his son. His most wonderful, far too intelligent son. Such a burden to be put on such young shoulders, knowing this not-so-well-kept family secret, but he knew nonetheless. And seemed to be handling it just fine, too. Maybe his age was in his favor... seeing the unbelievable and being able to believe...

"I'm your father, Jeremy, but we have to keep this a secret."

"Can I tell James? He should know too."

"Not right yet, son. And by no means should you tell any adults, okay?"

"Not even Mamma? She misses you so much..."

"I know. But she'll find out when the time is right, and in the meantime it's just between us, okay?"

"Okay, Daddy. Daddy?"

"Yeah, Jer?"

"Are you an angel? Do you live with God? Mamma said you did..."

"Off and on... but I'm not quite ready to spend all my time there yet, Jer. I have some unfinished business here, and then I'll be goin' home for good."

"Do you have to?"

"Yep. I was lucky to even get to come back at all, Jer."

"I'm glad you did, Daddy. I see your pictures and Mamma talks about you a lot, and I always wished I could meet you... and I got my wish!"

Steve hugged his boy and gave him a kiss.

"Well, I have to go, kiddo. You get to sleep now, and I'll be back when I can."

"Daddy?"

"Yeah, Jer?"

"Can... can you visit Mamma like you visit me? She must be very lonely right now..."

"I'll see what I can do, son..." Steve ducked into the shadows when he heard footsteps in the hall.

Jeremy ducked under his blankets.

Gabe opened the door and looked around the room. James was sprawled sideways in his bed, as usual, and Jeremy... more than likely awake again. He went in and put James back to bed, pulling the blankets up to his chin and giving him a tender kiss.

"Jer? You awake?" Gabe whispered, sitting on his bed.

"Yes Papa..."

"Were you just talking to someone? I thought I heard voices..."

"Yes Papa. I was talking to my guardian angel. I... I asked him to take care of Mamma..."

"Aw God..." Gabe murmured, taking the boy into his arms. The poor kid...

"And he said he'd try, Papa."

"Thank you, Jeremy," Gabe said, his voice choked with sorrow. "Now you get to sleep, okay?"

"I will. Papa?"

"Yes, Jer?"

"I love you..."

Gabe crushed the boy to him in a fierce hug.

"I love you too, Jeremy... God, I love you..."

Steve watched from the shadows, his heart breaking for each and every one of them. Breaking for the losses they had suffered, and the suffering of losses yet to come.

When Gabe left the room, Steve kissed his boys goodnight and vanished in a flash of blue.

"Mr. Evans, visiting hours were over long ago," said the nurse coming in for Deirdre's four a.m. vitals.

"I know, and I don't plan on stayin' for long. I just had to see her..."

"I won't tell," the nurse smiled. It was obvious that he loved her, and given the woman's prognosis he probably wouldn't have her much longer. Far be it from Nurse Smith to forbid him any time he wanted to spend with Mrs. Evans.

"Thank you," he said quietly, giving her a serene smile.

"I'll tell you what. I'll go see the rest of my patients and be back in oh… say twenty minutes. Okay?" She gave him a wink.

"That's plenty enough time," he answered. "And thanks again."

"She probably won't wake though, Mr. Evans. She has some heavy-duty drugs on board," Smith added. She smiled and left the room.

He smiled back and immediately went to Dee's bedside. He took her limp hand and raised it to his lips, kissing it long, kissing it lovingly.

"Ah, my lady," he whispered, gazing down at her. "I could end it all now with a touch of my hand. No more pain, no more suffering… no more disease. But I won't. I can't. This is your fate… all of ours. And for me to interfere… well, there's things meant to happen that have been in the works for a long time now and I have to let them happen. God, I hate the thought of you havin' to suffer, but I have let you live with this even though I could take it away. You'd be cancer-free and live a long, happy life. Anyway, it won't be much longer, my love, and we'll be together again."

He plucked a blood-red rose from the bouquet Gabe had left earlier, and placed it in her hand. He kissed her cool lips and vanished in a flash of blue.

The door opened and Nurse Smith stuck her head in.

"Mr. Evans? I forgot to tell you…" Huh. Gone, and she hadn't even seen him leave. Oh well, it would save her the trouble of kicking him out a little later.

Deirdre smiled in her sleep, dreaming of her Steven.

"She's coming home today, Kyle. God, I'm terrified and yet I can't wait."

"You're scared? Why for, Gabe?"

"She's still so sick. You'd think that after nearly a month in the hospital she would have recovered some, but she's still so weak and frail."

"I thought so too, but I didn't want to say anything. Um… anything I can do to help?"

"No, but thanks anyway. I hired some full-time help, and I've arranged for a nurse to come in and check on her every day."

"Does she still have it? The cancer, I mean."

"We're not sure. There's no sign of it now, and yet it could come back at any time. But she's survived so far, Kyle, and I thank God for that every day."

Kyle nodded, too choked up to say anything more.

"And I think that once she's home with the boys and me it will be good for her. She misses them so damn much," Gabe sighed.

"Yeah… Those poor little guys not bein' able to see their mama for all that time, well, it breaks my heart, Gabe."

"Mine too, Kyle. James is having a hell of a time coping with it, but Jeremy… well, he seems to be doing just fine. He said…"

Gabe took a ragged breath and tried to keep the tears at bay. "Kyle, he said that his guardian angel has been with Deirdre every night, and touches her to make the pain go away. Where does he come up with that? We're not all that spiritual of a family! Deirdre taught them the basics, but we've never really practiced any religion. God, the only time I've been in a church since I moved away from my patents' home has been on Christmas."

"Probably saying it to ease his mind, Gabe. Yours too."

"Perhaps, but he's so convinced that it's true. He almost has me believing…"

"So believe it. Can't hurt."

"Unfortunately I reside in reality, Kyle. Cold, harsh, ugly, fucking reality. I see her pain, I see her suffering… and there's not a goddamn thing I, or anyone else, can do about it. And do you know how that makes me feel? What that does to me? My God… she's my wife and it's my duty to protect her… and I can't. I can only sit by and watch… just sit there and watch her waste away in a slow, miserable death.

Gabe lost his battle with his emotions and the tears slid down his cheeks.

"Aw, Gabe… don't," Kyle murmured, going to his buddy and slinging an arm over his shoulder. "You said yourself that she's gonna be fine! And you're always right, right?"

"Have been so far," Gabe sniffed. "Sure as hell hope I am this time."

"You will be. Now c'mon… perk up, pork chop! I know! Let's dress the twins up in those little cowboy outfits and go get Dee. She'll get a kick out of it…"

"Kyle, what would I do without you? You're the best friend…"

"Hold it right there, pal. Don't you go gettin' all mushy on me…"

Gabe wiped a hand over his eyes and smiled at his buddy.

"Alrighty then. Kyle?"

"Yeah?"

"Fuck you."

"Much better! Let's go, dude…"

Of course Gabe was right. Only a few days after Deirdre was home she began to improve. Her color was better, her appetite was almost back to normal, and her strength returned.

Two weeks after her return she was well enough for visitors, and the Davidson family paid a visit. Deirdre was thrilled to see them, although quite embarrassed by her appearance. She deeply mourned the loss of her long, beautiful hair, which had fallen out in clumps shortly after her treatment had begun. Jenna knew what her friend might be feeling, and helped out by supplying her with an assortment of large, colorful scarves. Deirdre tied one on her head and flipped the tails over her shoulder, laughing in delight. Gabe said she looked rather like a gypsy, and good ol' Kyle produced a pair of oversized, gold hoop earrings. Deirdre gave him a wink and put them on, wrapped a scarf around her waist, and did a quick, fast stepping dance.

"Time for a party, Gabe!" Kyle howled, jumping in to dance with Dee.

"Give me an hour," Gabe grinned.

By dusk the back yard had been transformed into what appeared to be a gypsy camp, complete with torches and a bonfire. Gabe invited a few of his musician friends over, and soon the sounds of a fiddle, guitar, and tambourine were echoing down Park Street.

James, Jeremy, and the Davidson children had a ball as they laughed and danced around the fire, and then roasted hot dogs and marshmallows over the open flames, with help from the adults, of course.

Gabe and Kyle took the "stage" for a while, singing some of the tunes that made them famous, and then Kyle played a Spanish song while Jen did a rather seductive dance for him. Minutes after she finished, Mr. And Mrs. Davidson vanished for nearly an hour… and no one dared to look for them.

Deirdre lounged in a comfortable chair, enjoying all the love and laughter surrounding her. Yes, this was the best medicine ever – her family.

The children were tucked in for the night, and the adults returned to the yard to enjoy the warm summer evening.

Kyle and Jenna lay on a blanket, whispering to each other and exchanging tender kisses.

Deirdre looked on, just a little envious of their love, as her own husband sat quietly by her side. He held her hand, although it was more out of friendship and support than the love she craved from him.

A movement in the shadows caught her eye and Deirdre strained to see it. Dear God… she was hallucinating again. There was Steven, standing there with his serene smile and raising his hand with the "I love you" sign. She smiled at the vision and her free hand made a small movement, signing back to him.

Hallucination or not, she felt much better and it didn't seem to matter quite so much that Geoffrey didn't return her love. Steven's memories were alive and well…

"Annie Benton, this is the first night we've had off together in ages, and if you back out on me now I swear I'll… I'll…"

"You'll what, Marti? Come over here and kick my butt?"

"Well… yeah! Come on… please go out with me. You've been a hermit all year…"

"I don't know, Marti. I don't feel very social…"

"Only because you've forgotten how. When was the last time you left the cabin? Other than work, I mean."

"I ride every day…"

"Still at the cabin, Annie-bananie…"

"I don't know. Does grocery shopping count?"

"Nope. That falls into the 'work' category. And I'll tell you when it was. It was last freakin' summer! Michael was off doing whatever it was he did, and you and I went bowling."

"Yeah…"

"And we had fun, right?"

"That we did…"

"So let's do it again. Big Ten Lanes has a live band tonight and beers for a buck. Come on, Annie…"

"All right, just so you'll stop begging…"

"Great! I'll see you at eight."

Great. She had until eight to dredge up a little enthusiasm. It wasn't that she didn't want to see Marti, but ever since Michael left it was as if Annie's world had fallen under a shadow. Colors weren't as bright, sounds weren't quite so clear, the flowers seemed to lose their fragrance, and tasteless food was only consumed so that she'd stay alive.

Yet she didn't think about him all that much. Heck, she couldn't even remember what he looked like, and when she pulled out that picture she had taken of him and his horse, it was faded and indistinct. Must have been bad film.

Then again maybe it wasn't Michael's absence that left her feeling so alone and empty. Maybe that was how she had always felt but hadn't thought about it when he was around. Well duh… that would make sense.

Regardless, she needed something more in her life, or someone. Someone tall, with black hair and intense blue eyes… Someone she seemed to know forever and yet hadn't met. Someone she lived for… someone she loved enough to die for.

Oh God… when would she find him?

"We've got about a two-hour wait for a lane, Annie. Did you want to wait here and have a few beers or do something somewhere else?"

"It doesn't matter much, Marti."

"You're a lot of help. Okay then, if you leave it up to me we'll stay. I already put our names on the waiting list anyway."

"Whatever."

"Oh snap out of it, Annie! God! Hey, they have karaoke tonight until the band starts. Let's get drunk and sing 'Girls just wanna have fun'."

"Marti, I'll never be that drunk," Annie laughed. "But feel free…"

"I just might. Anyway, I got you smiling…"

"I still remember how! Jeez!"

"Well leave it on… if it disappears for even a second I'm dragging you up to sing with me."

Annie pasted on a Cheshire cat grin and gave her friend a light punch on the arm.

"So who's the band?" she asked, glancing up at the stage.

"Heck if I know," Marti answered. "But who cares? Loud music, cold beer, and tons of guys to pick from... God, is this place crowded or what?"

"Yeah, but I didn't come here to meet guys, Marti."

"Why not? We're not getting any younger, Annie, and I don't want to spend the rest of my life alone. Do you?"

"Of course not! But meeting your future mate in a bar? Really, what kind of low-life would be looking for a wife here?"

"Are you saying the guys here aren't decent? We're here, and we're good people, Annie. You're sounding a little snobby..."

"I didn't mean it like that..."

"Then what did you mean?"

"I don't know. Just drop it. So how do you want to kill the time until our lane is ready?" Annie sighed, looking around the huge playroom in the bar. Jeez, they had everything there!

"I don't care. Pool, darts, air hockey, pinball... You pick."

"How about darts? The windows are open and it's not quite so smoky over there," Annie said, wrinkling her nose as some jerk blew cigar smoke in her face. Great, now she'd probably get a stupid headache.

"Darts it is!"

The ladies shoved their way through the crowd and claimed space at the dartboards in the corner.

"Kyle, I'm really not in the mood..."

"Christ, Gabe, you need some entertainment. You've been home every night since Dee went to the hospital and then came home, and you need a break. Hell, she all but kicked you out tonight, right?"

"Actually she did. I still have a footprint on my ass, Kyle. And it hurt! Kiss it and make it better..."

"Gabe?"

"Yes, Kyle?"

"Fuck you."

"Feeling better already. But I don't plan on staying long."

"Deal. A few beers, shoot some stick, and listen to the band for a while. Might be someone we want to sign, Gabe. We need some new talent..."

"True, true... All right, but I'm out of here by eleven."

"Cool. You find us a table and I'll grab a pitcher."

"Only one?"

"Table?"

"No, pitcher, you ass!"

"Oh yeah... I meant one for each of us," Kyle grinned.

Gabe slapped his buddy upside the head and shoved his way through the mass of humanity that decided to spend their Friday night at Big Ten Lanes. He nearly got in a fight when some drunken asshole blew a cloud of cigar smoke in his face, and Gabe removed the smoldering stogie from the man's lips with a flick of his wrist.

"Hey!"

Gabe glared.

"What the fuck was that all about?" the man snarled, puffing up his chest a bit.

"I don't appreciate your exhaust deliberately sent my way," Gabe said, stepping up to the moron.

"Free country. Don't see any 'no smokin' signs, do you?"

"Who could see through the smog in here if indeed there were any? And I don't begrudge you the right to indulge; I just don't want to indulge with you. And you know what I think?"

"Like I fuckin' care…"

"I'll tell you anyway. I think you are lacking in the basic intellect to function in polite society, and for that reason alone I won't haul your ass out back and kick it clear into Sunday."

"Like you could," the dude laughed, poking a finger into Gabe's sternum. He regretted it though.

Gabe grabbed that hand and applied just enough pressure to bring tears the drunk's eyes and force him down on one knee, right on his smoldering cigar.

"Catch my drift?" Gabe said, releasing him. He didn't wait for an answer, but walked away.

He received a round of applause from the closest bystanders fed up with the dickhead's smelly cigar.

Kyle watched, glad that the fight didn't happen quite so soon. Hell, it was way too early to be rockin' that way, way too much fun to be had partyin' first!

"Annie, you suck! I've beat you three games in a row!"

"I let you win…"

"Oh bull. Your aim isn't what it used to be."

"Sorry. I'm just a little 'off' tonight. Must be the noise… and the smoke. How long before we can bowl?"

"Should be anytime. I'll go check…"

"I'm heading to the ladies' room. Two beers sure go fast…"

"Lightweight. I'll be right back."

Annie leaned against the sink in the relative quiet of the bathroom, and rubbed her temples. Her threatened headache had blossomed into a whopper, and she was miserable.

She pulled a few Tylenol out of her purse and washed them down with a handful of water from the tap before she splashed a little of the cool liquid onto her face.

After wiping away the moisture with a paper towel, she wadded it up into a tight ball and then chucked it into the trash barrel across the room. Yeah… two points for Annie. She ran her fingers through her mass of curls, and with a sigh, stepped back out into the bedlam of the bar.

"Annie, over here!" Marti called, waving her over to where she was standing with two very nice-looking men.

Oh jeez… Annie pasted on a little smile and joined them. This she did not need…

"Annie, this is Liam and Kent. We're going to share their lane with them," Marti grinned. She tucked a hand under Kent's arm and gave him a melting look.

Annie raised a questioning eyebrow at her.

"I was checking at the same time they were, and their lane was ready. Kent asked me if I wanted to share," Marti explained.

"Ah…" Annie nodded. Her head pounded unmercifully with the movement.

"So let's bowl! Guys against the girls or mixed doubles?" Marti laughed, squeezing Kent's arm.

He slung that arm over her shoulder and pulled her into a quick hug.

"Mixed doubles," he said, feeling like he was gonna score both on and off the alley that night.

"Shall we?" Liam asked, offering Annie his arm.

She smiled at his heavy Irish brogue. Charming, but it was going to be rough carrying on a conversation. Headache, the crash of the pins, and that noise from the band starting in the bar… and an Irishman to boot.

Yee-freakin'-ha.

"See Gabe? They're not half bad! Told ya…"

"Not half bad is only half good, Kyle; but they do have potential. We could talk to them. Who are they?"

"Brown Rear Egress"

"Christ… what a name! The 'brown back exit'? Sounds rather… sick."

"You're sick. And your point? Lotta stupid names out there…"

"Amen. Order one more pitcher, Kyle; I have to make a pit stop."

Kyle nodded and waved to the waitress.

Gabe escaped to the john.

He splashed some water on his face to try and quell the throbbing in his head. God knows the beer didn't help like it usually did. He sure as hell didn't want to be in that goddamn noisy bar anymore either. Sure, it was fun for a while playing pool with Kyle and then watching him hustle a few people who thought they had a chance at beating him, but now… Christ, he'd love nothing more than to be sitting on a quiet lake somewhere out in the middle of nowhere, just him and the moon and the stars… and his Annie.

He sighed and dared to look in the mirror at the imitation of the man he'd become. Didn't appear any different, still had that wild black hair of his and eyes that could intimidate or seduce anyone, still had that strong, perfect face and that lop-sided grin… but under it all he was nothing. Just goddamn nothing…

"Dude? Gabe, you okay?"

"Of course, Kyle, why wouldn't I be?"

"Because you've been in here for fifteen minutes, man! Thought you fell in or something…"

"Now that's just absurd. Given the size of… and… Oh, just shut the hell up."

Kyle grinned and went back out to their table.

Gabe couldn't believe he'd been standing there for a quarter of an hour and hadn't even used the facilities yet. He did so, washed his hands, and chucked his paper towel into the basket behind him. He didn't bother checking to see if it went in; he never missed.

Annie only half listened as Liam blathered on about his beloved country of Ireland, especially after she made the mistake of telling him that her Great-grandmother Delaney was born there.

She sipped her beer, nodded and smiled at the appropriate intervals in his conversation, and wondered just how soon she could make her escape. There were four frames left in their second game, maybe after that. Marti sure wouldn't care, as it looked like she might be spending the night with good ol' Kent. Kent sure had a hopeful expression on *his* face…

"Marti, I think I'm going to head home after this game. My head is pounding…"

"No way, Annie-bananie! We were going in after this and watch the band!"

"I don't think…"

"But you have to, Annie! Kent and Liam were going to buy our drinks for the rest of the night. I think Liam likes you…"

"Goody for him."

"You don't like him? God, he's gorgeous! And that accent…"

"He's nice enough, but I'm not like you, Marti. I can't just hop into bed with a guy because I like him."

"Too bad. You're missing out, chica…"

"My loss. But I really don't feel very well, Marti."

"You do look a little pale. Okay, I'll let you slide, but you might be missing out on the best night of your life!"

"A chance I'll have to take. Well, I'm up. Last two frames…"

"Go get 'em, girl! You get a spare and you'll have at least a two hundred game goin' on!"

Annie nodded, and let her ball fly.

She got three strikes in a row and ended up with a respectable two twenty-nine.

Marti ran right up to the counter to have it announced.

Annie blushed and gave a little wave when the other bowlers looked over to see who had done so well.

Minutes later she was in her truck and heading home.

"Dude, did ya hear that?"

"What's that, Kyle?"

"Some chick just bowled your average… and they announced it like it was a big deal," Kyle snickered.

"Perhaps it was to her. My average, eh? Maybe I should buy her a drink in congratulations…"

"Go for it. Annie something on lane thirty."

"A…Annie? Did you say Annie?"

Gabe's head began to spin.

"I think that's what he said. Dude, you okay?"

But Gabe was up and out of the bar before Kyle could even finish his sentence. He ran to the far end of the building, shoving bodies out of his way and receiving more than his share of curses and rude gestures. A thrown beer glass nearly missed his head, but he didn't give a shit.

Annie… Could it be?

He stood behind the rail, staring down at the woman and her companions.

"A… Annie?" he asked, panting a bit from his mad run.

Marti answered before she looked up.

"Just missed her, man. Can I tell her… Oh… oh God! It's you!" she gasped, finally looking to see who was asking for her friend.

"Me?" Gabe squeaked. *Did Annie know him?* Oh God, now he was feeling dizzy. He slumped down on a bench.

"You! You're Gabe Evans!" Marti gushed, hopping up the few steps to meet her idol's partner.

Gabe's heart sank. Goddammit, just another fan. And just what the hell had he been thinking… His Annie was no more than a dream. Even if she did exist he could never have her, especially now with Deirdre so ill. He'd be the lowest form of life on earth to abandon his sick wife.

"Oh God… I can't believe it!" Marti gasped, standing in front of him and clapping her hands together.

"Believe it," Gabe muttered, and stood up.

"Mr. Evans… Gabe, uh… would Kyle happen to be here too? I've been wanting to meet him forever…" Marti loved Kyle.

"He's in the bar, Miss…"

"Marlett. Marti Marlett. Oh God… Do you think he'd give me his autograph?"

"Buy him a beer and he might even give you his firstborn, Marti," Gabe laughed. It was hard not to be taken in by her high spirits and sunny demeanor. Christ, she even reminded him of Kyle in a way.

He took her hand and led her in to meet his buddy. Kent and Liam followed along behind, pissed that they were forgotten but feeling pretty cool about maybe sharing a beer with actual rock stars… even if Gabe and Kyle were kinda "has been."

Gabe wanted so very much to ask about the mysterious Annie, but didn't dare. Kyle would start bitching about it, Gabe being married and all, and if there was no Annie he'd feel beyond stupid. After all, Kyle may have misheard the announcement. But then again, Marti had said she'd left...

Then again, Gabe would never know. Could never know. Couldn't ever get his hopes up again.

At precisely midnight he left Kyle and company and went for a very long drive.

He found a deserted lake in the northern part of the county. Well, not quite deserted, there was a lone house on the other side.

He parked his truck on the street and hiked through heavy brush until he came to the edge of the dark, deep water. Gabe lay on his back, staring at the stars as he listened to the soft lapping of the waves, and thought about what his life should have been.

Annie sat on her beach with Dog and McDonald at her side, and stared at the stars overhead. The quiet peace of her little slice of heaven had helped her feel better, and her headache was nearly gone.

The breeze whispered through the trees and the water made a gentle sound as it kissed the shore, and it very nearly put her to sleep until a stupid truck went roaring past and interrupted her privacy. She thought she heard the slamming of a door a few minutes later, but it was across the lake and not her concern, even if it was still her property. Probably teenagers out parking or something, and Dog would sound the alarm if she were threatened.

Ah well... it was nice while it lasted. She chucked a pebble into the lake and went up to her dark cabin for some sleep. Maybe she'd dream of her cowboy again.

◆ ◆ ◆

"Oh my God. Annie, you should have stayed the other night. You won't believe what happened!"

"Kent proposed?"

"Who? Kent? Oh yeah... and no! Kyle David Davidson actually bought me a drink! Me! And then we played pool together! Oh God... I nearly died from happiness."

"And this is big news because..."

"Jeez, Annie! Kyle Davidson! *The* Kyle Davidson!"

"I have no idea who you're talking about."

"Oh yeah... you live in a cave. So I guess my enthusiasm and excitement is wasted on you..."

"Sorry. So who is this Kyle that has sent you into orbit?"

"Only the man I've been dying to meet for most of my life. Since nineteen eighty-two anyway. Annie, I want to bear his children," Marti said in the most serious voice Annie had ever heard come out of her friend.

It did her in. She began to laugh hysterically.

"What? I mean it, Annie! If he wasn't already married I'd kidnap him! I just might anyway. He's gorgeous; he's nice, and so funny! He had us cracking up. Joke after joke… and the stories! Oh my God…"

Annie got it back together and asked, "But *who* is he? Did you go to school with him or something?"

"Hardly, he's way older than me. At least five years. And he's the guitar player in my favorite band. I've told you about them…"

Annie shook her head.

"I haven't? No, I haven't because you wouldn't care. All you ever listen to is classical and bluegrass…"

"I listen to everything, Marti! Those are just the CD's I have, but I don't like jazz."

"Me either. But Kyle's band plays kind of a rock-country-folk music. They can go any way with it. At least they did before they broke up. And guess what?"

"What?"

"Kyle actually got on stage and played a song for me! Me! I nearly died I was so happy," Marti sighed.

"And I missed it…"

"See? Told ya so… and you don't have to be so sarcastic and rain on my parade."

"I didn't mean it bad, Marti. I'm glad you had a good time. Maybe we can do it again…"

"Won't be anytime soon. We don't have another night off together for weeks."

Maybe by that time Annie would be ready to socialize again…

"Well, time for work. Where are you tonight, Annie-bananie?"

"NICU. You?"

"Peds."

"Have fun."

"You too."

They punched the clock and went their separate ways.

"Gabe buddy! Miss me?"

"Only about as much as getting stuck behind a diesel truck with a faulty exhaust during a traffic jam. What brings you over here tonight, Kyle?"

"My Jeep, dude!"

"Smart ass."

"Naw, it was you. Feelin' any better yet? What was it, a cold or something?"

"Yeah… goddamn things."

"How'd you get it? You were fine Friday..."

"Hell if I know." *But he'd slept on that beach all night and the weather had turned damp and chilly... And it was more of an emotional ill than a physical one.*

"Well, you're better, right?"

"As good as I'll ever be." *Which wasn't all that great...*

"Cool."

"So... did you have fun with your girlfriend after I left?"

"Huh? My girlfriend?"

"Yes, the lovely Marti Marlett. She's quite taken with you, Kyle."

"Christ, tell me about it. She all but ditched her boyfriends. That one was ready to kick my ass too!"

"You da man, Kyle."

"But yeah, I had fun. She was pretty fun! And dude... she told me to play her a song..."

Gabe raised an eyebrow. Kyle had that look in his eye...

"So I did! I jumped right on stage with the band! Now that kicked ass!"

Gabe had a sudden flash of guilt for terminating his own band and depriving Kyle of one of the great joys in his life. But he couldn't do it again... couldn't tour or even perform in front of a crowd ever again. Just didn't have it in him anymore...

"Gabe?"

"Huh?"

"You were spacin' out. And I said 'Brown Rear Egress' is coming in for an audition tomorrow. You gonna be there?"

"I'll be in. Time for me to get my ass in gear again and get back to work. I've been neglecting it horribly lately..."

"No argument from me. How's Dee doing?"

"Much better," Gabe said, his face lighting up in a smile.

"Good. I worry about her, buddy."

"No more than I do, Kyle. She's in the yard with the boys. Would you like to say hello?"

"Was hopin' to," Kyle sighed. Next to Jen he loved Deirdre best.

Gabe knew what that look on his friend's face meant, but didn't think it appropriate to comment.

"C'mon, Kyle, let's go see her," was all he said.

Chapter Twenty
Winter, 1994

"Deirdre, calm down. They'll do just fine. After all, you spent hours rehearsing with them… and it's in their blood!"

"I know, Geoffrey, but I'm still nervous. What if James forgets his lines? Oh dear…"

"Then Jeremy will cover. And the audience won't even know the difference. God, I can't even tell them apart sometimes!" Gabe laughed.

"Don't be silly, Geoffrey. James and Jeremy are like night and day. I've never seen two children *more* unlike each other…"

"Except Steve and me. He was the good twin and I'm the evil one… But Dee, if you sit our sons down side by side, and they remain quiet of course, it's nearly impossible to tell who's who. Even Mom couldn't tell the difference! Pop did, but it was a lucky guess."

"I'm glad they decided to join us this Christmas, Geoffrey. I do love your parents…"

"They love you too, Dee. Now hush… the program is about to start."

The lights dimmed and the curtain opened, and a choir of small children dressed as angels began to sing. Gabe took Deirdre's hand and brought it to his lips for a kiss as their sons stepped forward to recite a Christmas poem.

Marie took Al's hand and gripped it tight when her two precious grandsons stepped into the spotlight. They were so very much like Steve and Gabe at that age…

Kyle kicked the seat ahead of him and waited for his buddy to turn around.

"Kyle, not now!" Gabe whispered.

"Just wanted to tell you congrats, man. They're doin' great!"

"It just started, you moron!"

"But they're facin' the audience! So far so good…" Kyle snickered.

Gabe glared and turned back around, and then scratched an imaginary itch on the back of his head with his middle finger. *Take that, Kyle…*

Jenna punched her husband and raised a finger to his lips, warning him to be quiet.

Kyle took that finger between his teeth and ran his tongue over the tip, giving her a look full of promise of good things to come later.

She shivered in anticipation and folded her hands in her lap, before she was tempted to run them all over his body.

James impressed everyone by remembering his part of the poem. Especially himself. He'd practiced and practiced, but some of the words were hard to say. At least Jer could say them all and was thinking them as James said them, and that helped a lot. He liked it when his twin helped him think…

Jeremy took his turn as the "star," reciting the poem about Baby Jesus that his papa had written for them. It told of joy and love, peace and hope, and it made Jer feel very happy. What made him even happier was Daddy peeking in the window of the doors way in the back of the auditorium. He smiled at Jer and made the "I love you" sign with his hand.

Jeremy signed back, but then looked at Mamma and Papa, and then Gramma and Grandpop so they wouldn't wonder who he meant.

When the poem was over, the Evans "angels" joined their little friends from the pre-school, and the choir of cherubs stumbled their way through the singing of "Away in The Manger."

Gabe was the first to stand and applaud when they were finished, and was soon joined by dozens of proud parents.

The Christmas program continued on with the elementary, middle school, and then high school kids, but the most memorable of all were the little twin boys who opened the show.

"Are you sure you don't want to go with us, Annie? You're more than welcome…"

"Thanks, Marti, but I need to stay here with my critters. Even two days is too long to be away from them."

"Yeah, I guess. But you shouldn't be alone. God, it breaks my heart, Annie!"

"I'll be fine, Marti. And I won't be alone; I've got Spike and Dog… and McDonald."

"But they're animals, Annie."

"They're my family. And Eric might be well enough to visit too."

"I hope so. Well, I have to pick up Jill by three. I should get going."

"How's she doing in school?"

"She loves it. She wanted to be a veterinarian all her life and now her dream is coming true."

"I'm glad for her. Everyone should be able to have their dream," Annie sighed.

"I know I got mine!" Marti laughed. "I still relive those wonderful hours with Kyle…"

"Lord…" Annie groaned, and then hugged her friend. "You drive safely, okay?"

"Will do, Annie-bananie. See you next week."

Annie nodded and went to the locker room to get her coat.

Yippee… another Christmas alone. She wondered if Michael would show up. She hadn't heard a word from him since he told her good-bye so long ago, and she missed him so much. She'd even gone through the phone book, looking for his brother, but not knowing his first name she didn't call any of the six "Anthony's" listed. Oh well, he'd get back to her when he could. He *did* say he'd see her again, right? She just hoped it would be in this lifetime.

Annie went home to her lonely little cabin and fixed herself a cup of tea. She snuggled into her favorite chair, covered in her afghan and with Spike purring in her lap. She stared at the crystal angel dangling at the top of her tree and willed the prism to spin a little, catching the light and sending colors dancing around the room.

Didn't happen, though.

She gave up trying to cheer herself up and went to bed.

Merry freakin' Christmas, Annie…

"Deirdre, that was a wonderful dinner," Marie said as she helped with the dishes. "I just don't know how you do it."

"Cook?"

"No, keep up around here. Well yeah, cook too. Steve… Steve told me you didn't know how when he met you."

"I didn't," Deirdre laughed. "But I learned! I learned just as much as I could to please him, Marie."

"You did well, honey. But the rest of this place… My goodness, just pickin' up after Gabe is a full time job! And the twins… and this house is huge!"

"I love it, Marie. Everything from dusting the knick-knacks and wiping peanut butter fingerprints off the walls to picking up Geoffrey's trail of clothes. It's the simple things I've learned to appreciate."

"Hard to believe," Marie murmured.

"What's that, Marie?"

"How you've changed my opinion of you, Deirdre. I never really gave you a fair chance… Had my own thoughts about you, and I'm ashamed to say they weren't very nice."

"And now?"

"I couldn't have picked a better daughter-in-law, honey."

"Thank you, Marie, but you're not just saying that because… because I was ill?"

"Heavens no! Deirdre, you've done wonders for Gabe. I'm not sure if you knew, but he used to be a little on the wild side. Well, a lot on the wild side. I can't tell you how many sleepless nights I had worryin' about him… But he's changed into a son I can be proud of and it's all your doin'. He's such a good husband and father…"

"Marie, I…"

"Nope. He's finally grown up, honey. Lord… I was terrified he'd kill himself with his wild ways… smokin' and drinkin'… But he hasn't touched a cigarette in years and I haven't seen him drink more than one or two beers a day, and no hard liquor. And the women… Oh, I'm sorry…"

"I know all about them, Marie. Geoffrey told me everything."

Deirdre wasn't so sure there wasn't another woman in his life right now. Ever since that night last summer when she insisted that he go out with Kyle and he never made it home until morning, well… it had happened many times since. Geoffrey would say he was going for a drive and then be gone for hours – if he came home at all. And then for days after he'd be quiet and withdrawn, and she knew darn well he was fighting to control his temper. He had that look of a trapped animal in his eyes, and he was tense and moody.

She never found any evidence pointing to him having an affair, other than his frequent absences, but she knew he couldn't live without a woman for very long. He'd proven that by sleeping with her even as he fought the guilt their lovemaking brought. She actually dared to confront him about it once, but he looked at her as if she'd lost her mind and curtly told her he'd never entertained such absurd thoughts. Furthermore, he was merely driving around to "get his shit together"; sometimes it took far too long, being as messed up as he was. Deirdre wished that she could believe him even though he'd never lied to her before.

She never mentioned it again since she had no right to claim those particular affections from him in the first place, but she was still hurt beyond words.

"Deirdre, what is it? Did I say something…"

She wiped away a tear.

"No, Marie, it's nothing…"

Marie dropped her dishtowel on the counter and sat her daughter-in-law down in a chair. She gave her a long look and said, "There's something really botherin' you, Dee. I'll listen if you want to talk…"

Deirdre could only look away. Even though Marie knew her son's faults, she thought the sun rose and set by Geoffrey and Deirdre didn't dare say a word against him.

"Oh honey… was it his past with women? He's not like that anymore! He'd never…"

Deirdre stifled a sob.

"Lord… Deirdre, you think he's having an affair, don't you?"

Her silence was her answer.

"Oh no. Gabe would never… Nope. You just get that thought right out of your head," Marie scolded. "Gabe may be a lot of things, but never an unfaithful husband. Absolutely not!"

"How can you be so sure?" Deirdre whispered between her tears. "I can't provide what he needs anymore."

"Like that would matter to him? Deirdre, he loves you! Anyone with eyes in their head can see it!"

"I know, but…"

"But nothing. Deirdre, do you remember your wedding vows – and his?"

"Yes…"

"Didn't he promise to love, honor, and cherish you, and forsake all others?"

"Yes…"

"Have you ever known him to break a promise like that? To take a solemn vow before God and toss it aside?"

"No…"

"Well I haven't either, especially something as sacred as marriage," Marie said in a firm voice.

"But Marie, you don't understand how it was… how it is with us. It was… was never…"

"Deirdre, that's enough. You love him and he loves you, and as long as you both draw a breath he'll never break that promise he made to you. Now you dry your tears and join your husband, and I'll finish up in here. Do I make myself clear?"

"Y… yes, Marie."

"Deirdre, do you ever see your mother? Talk to her?"

"What?"

"Your mother, dear; are you two close?"

"Not… not really. We never had much of a relationship."

"Then it's about time…"

Deirdre shook her head. "Marie, I don't think she's capable even if she were interested."

"I was talkin' about me, Deirdre. I… I like to be a mother to you, if you'll let me."

Fresh tears of a happy nature filled Deirdre's eyes, and she looked up at Marie and nodded.

"Oh honey…" Marie sat next to her and wrapped her arms around the poor girl, and let her know that she did indeed have a mother's love.

Gabe quietly stepped away from the door where he'd heard pretty much the entire conversation, and then ran upstairs to his room. Aw God… he'd never meant to hurt Dee like that! She was way off base in her suspicions, and his mother was right on the mark about him. He had no interest in any other woman, and had barely even thought about sex since Deirdre had fallen ill. In some skewed way, Gabe felt that the cancer was some sort of punishment for the sin they'd committed together, even if they did it under the blessing of marriage, and he'd had no desire for that particular act again.

"Deirdre, may I come in?"

"One moment, Geoffrey."

Deirdre threw on her robe over her shoulders and pulled her blankets up a little higher. She didn't want him to see how thin and ugly her body had become.

"Come in, Geoffrey."

He did, and sat next to her on the bed. He took her hand and kissed it, and turned her face so that he could look deep into her eyes.

"She's right, you know."

"Who, Geoffrey?"

"Mom. Dee, I overheard the two of you today and she's right. I would never break the vows I made to you. You're the only one, love."

"I suppose I believe you, Geoffrey, but does it really matter? Our marriage was never a true one..."

"I know," he sighed, "and you don't know how sorry I am about that. But I tried, Dee, God, how I tried. For years I had hoped that I... that I'd find the love for you to make it so."

"Geoffrey, don't. Don't lie to me and for God's sake don't lie to yourself. As long as she haunts your dreams you'll love only her."

He nodded and looked away.

"I'm sorry about that too, Dee. Christ, I've tried so hard to exorcise that... that demon, but I can't! Sure, I'll go for days – weeks even, without thinking about her, and then it happens. That same ol' dream will come and hold me prisoner... and it seems nothing matters but to try and find her. Oh God... why can't I be free of it?" he cried, dropping his head to the bed. "Why can't I let go and love you like I should?"

"I don't know, Geoffrey," she said quietly, and ran a gentle hand through his forever-messy hair. "But I envy her, your Annie; I envy her. To have that kind of love from you..."

"My Annie..."he murmured, raising his head to look at his wife. "How... how do you know her name?"

"You say it in your sleep, Geoffrey dear. I've heard you when you have your nightmares and call out for Steven... You'll calm down and whisper her name before you are awake. And I've heard you when... when we've shared a bed. You would hold me close and... and I'd hear it again."

"Oh God... Deirdre, I'm so sorry..."

"For something you're not even aware of? No, Geoffrey, I'm sorry. If it wasn't for me perhaps you would have found her by now and been truly happy instead of trapped in our sham of a marriage."

"Deirdre, don't say that..."

"It's true, Geoffrey. You look deep inside yourself and you'll know."

"I married you of my own free will, Deirdre. I made a lifetime commitment to you, to our children, with eyes wide open and knowing..."

"Out of a sense of duty to your brother, Geoffrey," Deirdre said, growing somewhat angry.

"Bull. I asked you because I loved you..."

"Oh God!" she cried, yanking her hand away from his. "Love? Perhaps, but not the kind of love a marriage should be based on. And I'm just as guilty of it as you... I felt it was wrong from the very start, but I was frightened, Geoffrey. I didn't want to be alone... raising my children without a father."

"*That's* why you agreed? I was under the impression you felt the same as I..."

"I did, Geoffrey. We share a very deep bond, and we do love each other, but I'm afraid we both made a very tragic mistake. The guilt you've suffered… Perhaps we should end it now. Perhaps we should divorce…"

"Absolutely not!"

"Why? What do we have anymore?"

"What we've always had, Deirdre! We've made a home together… you and I and the kids…"

"This isn't your home, Geoffrey, you merely reside here."

"How the hell can you say that? My God…" Gabe jumped up and spun around to glare at her.

"Because it's true. You think I don't know? Geoffrey, I know you so well. You dread having to come home here, knowing that it isn't what you truly want. Walk through this house… look close. Geoffrey, where are you? Where is your mark… other than your office?"

"My mark?"

"You, Geoffrey. Where are signs of you? Other than your piano in the family room, there is nothing of you in this house. Even your bedroom is merely functional. It has no more character than a… a room in a hotel."

"That's insane. This place was nothing but a dump when I bought it. Christ, half the walls were knocked out, the wiring was a hazard, the plumbing non-existent, and I poured myself into this place! I hung board and plastered and sanded and painted… How can you say…"

"It was a crutch at the time. You had just 'cleaned up' from the drugs, and all the labor you put into this place was merely another addiction. Once the last coat of paint was on, you were finished. You wanted nothing more to do with it."

"Bullshit! I love this place!"

"Like you love me, Geoffrey. It's a good friend that got you through the hard times, but it doesn't command any passion from you. Nor do I. This house and I…"

"Deirdre, I…"

"This house… this home. Geoffrey, I was the one who made this house a home. I chose the furniture, the décor… drapes and linens. When I asked for your opinion you had none to give. 'This is your home, Deirdre', you said, 'Do what you like with it', and then you handed me the credit cards. Does that sound like a man who cares about where he lives?"

"It sounds like a man. What do I know about decorating?"

"You have excellent taste, Geoffrey! Your office – and the SD Productions building show it."

"Dee…"

"Hush. Geoffrey, you've always said that you live in the 'real world'. Well, it's time to put your money where your mouth is and admit that I'm right."

"I suppose," he said after a few moments of painful contemplation. "But I have to ask… Why? Why are you telling me this? And on Christmas of all days…"

"Because it needed to be said, Geoffrey. Ever since I talked to your mother

I've been doing a lot of thinking, and I've dealt with reality myself. I don't know how much longer I have, and I don't want to spend my remaining days living a lie. I love you, Geoffrey. I love you as a wife should love her husband. But even if I weren't ill, and able to… to be with you, I still wouldn't. Not unless you shared those feelings, and we both know you don't and never will. And I still think that we should divorce."

"Over my goddamn dead body, Deirdre."

"Geoffrey, you language…"

"…Is fucking reality. Deal with it. There will be no divorce if for no other reason than I won't have *my* sons living in a broken *home*!"

"Why are you so angry, Geoffrey?"

"Christ…"

Gabe wandered over to the window seat and flopped down onto the soft cushions. He stared out at the park below, watching as the moon shown down on the blanket of snow covering the ground. The light reflected off the ice crystals and colors glittered all around. It was mesmerizing, and he couldn't tear his eyes away. He thought of Steve… and his dream.

"Geoffrey?"

"I'm fine, Dee. And I'm angry because… because the truth hurts. I'm angry at myself and I took it out on you. I apologize."

"Don't, Geoffrey. Just tell me goodnight and leave me be, and we can discuss this tomorrow."

"Nothing to discuss. There will be no divorce. Neither of us will leave this house to live elsewhere, and we'll continue on as before – now that we know where we stand. And Dee… I really don't know what I'd do without you. Mom was right about that too. You've changed me for the better. I can say in all honesty that I owe you my life… and I really do love you."

"As a friend."

"As a friend, but it doesn't lessen my feelings for you. I suppose it's terribly selfish on my part, but would you just forget the idea of divorce and stay with me? I need you, Deirdre…"

"I will, Geoffrey. And to tell the truth, I don't know if I could live without you."

"Friends again?"

"As always, Geoffrey. Now scoot. I've had an exhausting day and I'm very tired…"

"Aw God… Are you in pain? Dee, are you okay?"

Gabe ran to her bedside and dropped to his knees next to her, taking his hands in his and kissing them.

"I'm fine, Geoffrey, just tired. Now tell me goodnight.

He lifted her face and brushed his lips on her forehead.

"Merry Christmas, Geoffrey."

"Merry Christmas, Deirdre."

She turned off her lamp as soon as he left, and gave into the pain. Her tears flowed unchecked as her broken heart took another blow, and the cancer in her body continued to grow. And she was so very, very tired.

Sleep took her despite the pain, and before long her nightly dream of Steven began.

He sat next to her on her bed and placed his hand over her heart. Her misery was lifted from her body with the blue light that rose from his calloused fingers, and floated away.

They gazed into each other's eyes. She couldn't actually feel his touch and he never spoke, but was there for her nonetheless, in her dream, and was more than she could ever hope for.

Gabe waited until he was sure everyone in the house was asleep, Mom and Pop included, and then he changed into his sweats. He grabbed his jacket and stepped outside. He only meant to take a quick run in the park across the street but soon found himself in his truck and miles from home.

Home… Yeah, Dee was goddamn right about that. He still felt like an outsider in that house. The furniture was mostly antique and very expensive, and he was almost afraid to sit in it. The rest of the furnishings… the artwork and knick-knacks, the drapes and the carpets, the flower-filled vases and wall hangings… They were all fitting for a mansion, and the place resembled a museum in Gabe's opinion. Dee had done a wonderful job decorating and had even been featured in a "celebrity homes" magazine…

Yet it just wasn't Gabe. Nope, he preferred his office-den with the cluttered desk and the overflowing bookshelves. He loved the wall of pictures and his old, worn leather sofa that he had picked up at a second-hand store over on Main. That couch was the most comforting piece of furniture he'd ever rested his body in, and he'd always enjoyed tossin' his colorful quilt over him and indulging in a good book on it.

Then there was the "abused" wall where Gabe had chucked, and smashed, many different objects when his temper his critical mass. That hadn't happened in a few years though. Maybe he'd go home and chuck something for old time's sake. Maybe a shot glass… after he'd tossed back a stiff drink from it.

Or not.

And goddammit, Dee was right about their relationship too. It may have been a mistake to marry, but what was done was done, and it was forever.

Yet he meant it when he said he needed her. Without her calm presence and unconditional love he was sure to fall back into his old, undesirable lifestyle. Not that he wanted to, but it was certain to happen if he had no one to be responsible for other than his sorry self. His spoiled, arrogant, moody, good for nothing, shit, sorry self.

Dawn was breaking when he pulled into the garage and snuck by his mom in the kitchen, and then went to hide in his office for a while.

Yep… Merry fucking Christmas, Gabe…

Chapter Twenty-One
Spring, 1995

"Good news, Kyle!"

"What's that, Gabe? You've decided to go ahead and have the sex change operation after all?"

"Kiss my ass. And I won't do it because then you'd want to date me, and Jen would get pissed and kick my ass!"

"God! Ya freak! Ew…"

"Yeah… Jen kicking my ass is pretty scary."

"So what's got you in such a good mood, dude…"

"SD Productions if finally functioning financially fit, friend!"

"Far-freakin-out! Finally! Future?"

"Fantastic. Formerly fallow faculty forthcomingly fruitful."

"Fabulous!"

"Kyle, I've hired back pretty much everyone, and…"

"And?"

"And we can hire an accountant. You and Jen will no longer be required to tax your brains as you do our taxes."

"Uh… we don't mind…"

"I'm sure you don't, but Jen will be free to… well, to sit in the lobby and look beautiful should she choose to continue her volunteer services, and you, my friend, will have more important duties to attend to."

"Such as?"

"Do you still want to start up that guitar clinic?"

"Are you serious? God yes!"

"Then you shall."

"But Gabe… we don't have the room."

"Of course we do! There are thousands of square feet of empty space next door… I'm beginning the improvements next week, and by mid-summer it should be finished."

"You as in 'you', or are you hiring it done?"

"Me as in me. Most of it anyway. I'll have the wiring and the plumbing done by professionals, but I'll handle everything else."

"Dude… Big job."

"Something I need to do, Kyle. Hell, I did pretty much all of this," Gabe said, sweeping a hand down the hall of offices.

"True. Can I help?"

"You may hold my tool…" Gabe grinned.

"Jesus, Gabe! Ya queer!"

"Homophobe. My tool belt, Kyle. You're far too dangerous with a hammer."

"I am not!"

"Are too."

"Am not."

"Are too. Case in point: When we built that 'fort' of plywood cubes for your children, what happened?"

"Which time?" Kyle mumbled.

"Pick one. There was the smashed thumb – I still have a scar, the bent nails pounded flush with the surface instead of being pulled out…"

"Covered in carpet anyway."

"Details. And you broke three ceiling tiles, Kyle! I still haven't figured that one out…"

"Me either…"

"So you see…"

"Yeah, I guess. Stupid to even suggest it…"

"I'd be happy to have you assist me, Kyle. It's far too big a job for just one man, even if that man is me, and this is your place too. You love it as much as I do…"

"Seriously? Aw God… Thanks, Gabe! And just for that I got a guy who can do the books for us."

"You do?"

"Yep. He's pretty good, buddy. Can I hire him?"

"After I check his references. Name?"

"Jerry Packard. His office is over on Briarcliff."

"Ooh. High-rent district. He must be doing well. I'll check him out, Kyle."

"Cool! Well, I'm off to *work*," Kyle grinned.

"As if. Play-Doh or Battleship today, Kyle?"

"Neither, Gabe. I found a new game I'm gonna download on my computer. 'Duke Nukem'…"

"How… thrilling," Gabe sighed, rolling his eyes.

"Fuck you. Lunch?"

"Doable."

"Twelve-thirty?"

"Place?"

"Root Beer Stand?"

"Hot dogs with the works?"

"And extra chili."

"Perfect. Later, Kyle."

"Later, dude."

Kyle whistled a happy little tune as he strolled into his office. Yep, with Jerry on board he could continue his 'borrowing'. He hated like hell to do it, but just as he'd almost get caught up his investments would go sour and he'd have to cough up a little more jack to tide him over. And since Jerry was now aware of Kyle's source of funds, he wouldn't say a word if the books didn't balance once in a while.

Ooh… and Gabe was expanding the studio, and there was the guitar clinic to look forward to, and things were finally going their way!

Far-freakin'-out!

Gabe whistled a happy little tune and flopped into his desk chair. He grabbed a few bits of dried fruit and spun around, waving a chunk of dried apple at Chet.

"What's the word today, you feathered fart factory?"

Chet lifted a leg and made a rude noise.

Gabe laughed and gave him his treat, and spun back around. God, Kyle was always teaching that damn bird something new. None of it was very nice, though.

Life was pretty good again. Dee was nearly back to her former self, both mentally and physically, and without the question of "sex-no sex" hanging between them, their relationship was back on track as well.

Gabe's nightmares had all but gone away, suffering from them perhaps once a month now, although his other dream still haunted him.

The twins were growing stronger in body, mind, and spirit, and were a constant source of joy for their proud parents.

The Evans family had started attending services on Sunday evenings at a pleasant little non-denominational church across town. The pastor begged him to join the choir but Gabe declined, saying that his fame might detract from the true reason the other folks attended. It may have sounded a bit egotistical, but the good Reverend Avery had to agree. Gabe Evans was a draw, but a full church meant nothing if the people were there to hear him and not the word of God.

Gabe was more than happy to be spiritually fulfilled, merely listening and not having to concern himself with performing. He did tithe generously to make up for the lost income he might have generated though. And it did feel good to attend services again; he hadn't realized how much he missed it – and needed it.

On the down side, his creativity still eluded him. He hadn't written a single song – not a lyric, not a word – nothing, since the Christmas poem for his sons. And before that it was his play, "Colors," shortly after Steve died. But that was it. He'd have to work on that, even if it couldn't be forced.

His company… SD Productions was finally producing again, signing on a dozen or so unknown bands with endless potential. Album sales were picking up daily and Gabe was busy playing manager and booking his new talent all over the country. A few were even opening for some big name, mega talented bands.

He still had the shadow of Steve's loss surrounding him, but was learning to cherish his memories instead of mourning them.

And his Annie… his green-eyed dream. Yeah, she still haunted his slumber, but he was learning to cope with that too by sleeping as little as possible. He took long runs after his family had retired, his feet pounding the pavement until he was totally exhausted. He'd fall into bed around two in the morning and sleep until six. Sure, he was sleep deprived again, but he'd never been in better physical shape.

Gabe beat a quick little tattoo on his desk with his fingers, and then went to grab a cup of coffee to start his day.

◆ ◆ ◆

Annie was exhausted. She'd been working extra shifts for months now and it was catching up with her. But it kept her mind occupied so the loneliness she felt wasn't quite so devastating.

She fed her critters, set her alarm, and fell onto her bed – still wearing her work clothes. Moments later she was jarred awake by the phone. She groaned and rolled over to answer it.

"Mmm… H'llo?"

"Annie? Good, I caught you before you passed out. Guess what."

"Marti?"

"Who else? Annie, you won't believe what happened!"

"Probably not," Annie yawned.

"This is the best thing ever!"

"Mmhmm. Did that Kyle dump his wife and ask you to run off with him?"

"I wish. Okay, this is the second best thing ever. Have you put in for vacation time yet?"

"Yeah… I've got two weeks; the first of June."

"Oh jeez… even better! Perfect! Pack your bags, chica, we're going to New York!"

"Mmhmm… that's nice," Annie mumbled, sinking back down into her pillow. She couldn't even keep her eyes open any more.

"Nice? Annie, this is a dream vacation! And it's all free!"

"Free…"

"Annie, wake up and listen! I won!"

"Won…"

"Annie!"

"Marti…? Oh yeah… What was that?"

"I won that contest the Watch was sponsoring! You know… in the fashion section of the Weekly?"

"Vaguely." Annie didn't give a hoot about what was in style, but tried to listen to her friend anyway.

"Anyway, all I had to do was write in fifty words or less why I needed a fashion makeover, and I won!"

"That's nice…"

"Oh God… Annie, don't bring me down…"

"I'm sorry, Marti. I'm awake now." Annie sat up so that she wouldn't be tempted to doze off again.

"Good. Anyway, I wrote about what I wear most of the time, nursing scrubs and a raggedy ponytail, and they took pity on me! A week in New York for two, a fashion makeover, and two grand in cash. We're gonna have a ball, Annie!"

"Have a good time, Marti, and congratulations."

"You're going with me, chica."

"I'd love to but I can't."

"Can too."

"Impossible. I can't leave my critters…"

"Taken care of. Jill said she'd love to critter-sit for you. She's out of school and would jump at the chance to run your little zoo for a week."

"That's only half the problem. I have to get my gardens ready and planted."

"Oh God… You've never heard of the produce section at the market?"

"Funny. But it's veggies *and* flowers."

"So I'll help. Can you do it in a week?"

"Maybe."

"Then it's settled. I'll be over to play farmer next week, and then we're heading for the Big Apple! Oh God, I can hardly wait!"

Annie figured it would be useless to argue, and her reasons for not going had just been blown away by an ecstatic Marti-breeze. And she sure as heck needed a vacation. A real one, not just hanging out at the cabin and waiting for her days off to be over.

But New York? Even Waterston and its fifty thousand souls were too crowded for her. Oh well, it would be an experience…

"You talked me into it, Marti. You're sure about Jill?"

"Her idea, Annie."

"And you won't back out on the gardening?"

"If I don't show, you don't go…"

"Okay. But *New York*?"

"The city that never sleeps…"

"Sleep. I need some. Call me later, Marti."

"Sweet dreams, Annie."

"With any luck…" And Annie was out before she could even hang up the phone.

He was back…

Standing in front of her and smiling that lop-sided grin. Annie smiled back and raised her hand to touch that hint of a dimple under his lower lip. He took her hand and kissed the fingertips… A tingle ran through her, radiating up her arm and exploding in her very core, sending little shocks to every cell in her body.

"My Annie," he whispered, "I love you. Always have, always will…"

She was stunned that he knew her name, and that he'd even spoken!

She wanted so much to say his name, to have her own voice tell him that she loved him too, but she didn't know who he was... Only that she'd known him forever.

He took a step closer and bent his head to kiss her.

She raised her face for his kiss...

And he was gone.

Annie spun around, looking for him, but there was nothing but a gray mist surrounding her.

"Where are you?" she cried, groping about as the mist grew thicker and all but blinded her. "Who are you?"

From far away she heard him say, "The dream, Annie. You'll know when you find the dream."

"Wait! What dream?"

She sank to the ground and felt something pierce her skin, causing her to cry out. She picked up the white rose, staring at the drop of blood clinging to a wicked-looking thorn. Such beauty hiding such treachery...

Michael was there before her, smiling his serene smile and holding a red rose.

"I know it hurts, hon, but don't give up. Nothing is as it seems..."

Annie held up the rose that had caused her so much pain.

"He left that for you. His symbol of love, Annie."

"Who? Who is he, Michael?"

"My evil twin. And now I'm off to give this to my lady... A symbol of my love."

Michael brought the bloom to his lips and vanished in a flash of vivid blue.

Annie blinked in surprise.

"Oh God," she moaned finding herself in her own bed.

Spike lay on her chest, his amber eyes staring into her emerald ones.

"Cat," she said, stroking his fur, "I just had the strangest dream ever. It was about... about..."

The harder she tried to remember the details, the faster the memories faded. All that was left of the dream was a pair of intense blue eyes gazing at her over the petals of a white rose.

Annie hauled her luggage out of her truck, and joined Marti and a snooty-looking, sleek redhead at the baggage check in counter.

"Annie! About time you got here! They just called first boarding..."

"Sorry, Marti, but Dog chased me. I was nearly a mile from home before I noticed and took him back. Before that it was Adonis breaking through a fence and I had to fix that, and..."

"No matter. Dog," Marti laughed, turning to the woman next to her. "NeeNee, her dog is nearly as big as her horse!"

"How... nice," Deanna nearly sneered.

"Annie, this is Deanna "NeeNee" Montgomery. She's going with us...

kind of like a tour guide. NeeNee, this is Annie Benton."

"Miss Montgomery," Annie said, dropping a bag and holding out her hand. *Oh jeez… Tyler's old girlfriend.* It was going to be one long, hellish week.

"Annie," Deanna purred, "It's so nice to finally meet you. Tell me, do you still date Tyler? I know he's married, but the fact that he had another woman never seemed to matter to you…"

"As a matter of fact we had lunch the other day."

"You did?" Deanna nearly gasped.

"Mmhmm. Actually I had lunch with his wife, but Tyler tagged along. I think he wanted to brag about becoming a father pretty soon," Annie said, giving NeeNee a sweet smile.

"A… a father? His wife? Oh, God…"

"The baby is due around September. Anne and Tyler are thrilled, of course…"

"You *know* Anne?"

"Mmhmm. She's a doctor at Brighton. She recently transferred from adult oncology to pediatric oncology, and we've been working together. She's a wonderful woman."

"Oh. Well, let's get going before we miss our flight," Deanna chirped, somehow feeling as if she'd just been bested by the little hick in the faded jeans.

Dear God, she even had the smell of a barn about her! Deanna wrinkled her nose in disgust and stalked off to the gate.

"Way to go, Annie!" Marti laughed, thoroughly enjoining the little encounter between Annie the Angelic and NeeNee the Nasty. "You sure put her in her place!"

"I didn't mean to, but… Marti, there's not too many people in the world I don't like. None actually, but she'd be right on the top of my list.

"Why's that? Because of Tyler?"

"No… well, a little but she's just… not nice sometimes. And don't ask because you know I don't gossip."

If she did, Marti would know what Tyler told Annie about Deanna, and how she practically tried to seduce another man right in front of him, and how she followed that same man up to his bedroom at a party, leaving Tyler downstairs all alone. Tyler hadn't cared a bit, not liking NeeNee for more than a casual date, but the idea… Annie just couldn't get over it.

"Spoilsport. But I know what you mean. Unfortunately she's part of the package."

"And I think I'm going to be sorry for crossing her. She's going to chew me up and spit me out, Marti."

"Let her try. I'll protect you, Annie," Marti laughed.

"You'd better; you got me into this…"

"Ooh! They called our seats, Annie. Uh… did you notice NeeNee got first class and we're ridin' the tail?"

"Then we have a better chance of surviving if we crash."

"Oh God… You're serious!"

Annie grinned and walked to the boarding gate.

NeeNee had big plans for Little Hick Annie, oh yes she did! It was bad enough that Tyler preferred that wild- haired peasant to Deanna, but to have that little bitch get the best of her by being nice? Unforgivable!

She'd have a hell of a good time humiliating her in New York, on her own turf, so to speak. NeeNee could hardly wait. She ordered another martini and relaxed as they winged their way east.

Annie sipped a tepid, flat Coke and tried to read a book. She hated to fly and couldn't wait until the trip was over, the entire trip, not just the flight.

Marti flirted with the man across the aisle. He wasn't her type at all, a slick hustler who said he was an accountant, but Jerry was a little more fun to talk to that Annie the Terrified was at the moment.

Jerry let the brunette with the big blue eyes think he was interested in her, although if he was planning on a little female companionship he would have taken that shy little redhead next to her. He loved a challenge… But he was on business investing a little of Davidson's ill-gotten funds. First he was going to invest in a very expensive hotel room followed by a very expensive dinner. After that he'd invest in a little entertainment of the kinky kind at a private club, and the remaining five grand would be invested in his bank account. He'd cut Kyle a pittance of a dividend check from one of his fake companies and keep that dumb son of a bitch satisfied a little longer.

"Good God, Kyle! I leave you alone for four days and… and… What the hell is this anyway?" Gabe asked, looking around the room in a mixture of anger and awe.

"You like it? I wanted to surprise you," Kyle said proudly.

"I uh… Jesus, Kyle, you did all of this while I was gone?"

"Yep. You said, 'paint your new room, Kyle,' so I did."

"I meant slap a few coats of semi-gloss latex on it, not pretend this is the Sistine Chapel and you are Michelangelo," Gabe sighed. But he had to admit it was a work of art.

He stepped closer to the mural covering an entire wall.

"You don't like it?" Kyle moaned, crestfallen. And he'd done it just for Gabe…

"I didn't say that, Kyle, I'm just surprised is all. I wasn't expecting…"

"I know. And it's a present for ya, buddy," Kyle mumbled.

"And it's wonderful."

"You mean it?"

"Of course I do! The detail…"

Gabe ran a finger over his own face, standing on stage as he played his guitar and belted out a tune. Kyle's image was next to him, goofy grin on his face and his own axe in hand. The rest of the old SD band was behind them. Aw God... there was Wolfe and his violin and Mick on the drums, Jarred on keyboard and Billy pluckin' his mandolin. Randy was kicked back with his Dobro and Dalton played bass.

God, Gabe missed those guys. They'd had some great years together touring the country as they entertained the masses.

A bit of fresh paint came away on his finger and he wiped it on his jeans.

"Sorry, Kyle, I didn't realize..."

"No problem, buddy! Just a quick touch up."

Kyle pulled out a brush and made the repair.

"Good as new, Gabe."

"Kyle, this is great. And just perfect for your room. I know how much you miss playing..."

"But this if for you, Gabe, not me! I know you miss it as much as I do even if you won't admit it."

"Whatever..." But Kyle was more right than Gabe cared to admit.

"So dude, how was your trip?"

"Sucked, but productive. We now have someone to fine-tune our proposed video productions. There have been so many new innovations since we did ours and I want to start out with the best we can get. And I could use a little updating myself," Gabe sighed. He'd been away from that part of the business for too long, and the technology had passed him right on by.

"Wish I could have gone," Kyle said, putting an extra foot of hair held down by a headband, and bushy mustache on the painted "Gabe." He'd fix it in a minute, but messin' with his buddy was too tempting.

"I wish you could have too, Kyle, and I could have stayed here. Oh for God's sake, is that really necessary?" Gabe exploded, turning around to see himself turned into a member of a "hair band." He despised that look.

"Dude... you rock!" Kyle laughed, painting in a joint danglin' from his buddy's lips.

"Not funny, Kyle. Don't make me kick your ass. And I hate New York."

"New York is cool!" Kyle grabbed his palette and mixed some more paint. Time to fix it... but it was fun while it lasted.

"Too goddamn many people. Oh God... and of all the things to happen... Kyle, guess who I ran into at La Guardia?"

"Elvis?"

"No, that was in Memphis. Ha ha. It was NeeNee the Snake. I sat down, ready to tip back a cold one while I waited for my flight, and she slithers up and plops her skinny little ass right next to me!"

"Aw God... think she followed you?"

"To New York?"

"Whatever."

"No she didn't. Apparently she'd just arrived and was waiting for her limo."

"Limo? Well shee-it! Too good for a cab?"

"Probably, but her story was that she was 'babysitting' for two 'dreadfully clothed, horribly coiffed' women who were winners in a makeover contest or something."

"Horribly what?"

"Hairstyle, Kyle. Anyway, she was really rippin' on 'em. Said one was reasonably pretty and had some potential – the winner of the contest, but her friend was hopeless, and poor NeeNee was embarrassed to be seen with her."

"What a bitch."

"No shit. I feel bad for those two gals forced to spend the week with her, hopeless or not."

"Did you see 'em?"

"The women? No, although I'd rather hoped to. I was curious as to what the snake's interpretation of hopeless was. She didn't sound all that bad…"

"Oh?"

"Yeah… Faded jeans and tee shirt, 'barn boots' – NeeNee's description, and an obese size ten…"

"That's fat?"

"According to size four Deanna, yes."

"I'd better tell Jen! She's up to a size six!" Kyle laughed.

"Indeed! Anyway, 'hopeless' has crazy red hair and swamp eyes. Kyle, 'swamp eyes'?"

"Green?"

"Ah. You know, I think Deanna was jealous of the hopeless hick. She went on and on about her and never even mentioned the friend."

"Jealous? Miss All That was jealous? Dude, the hick must be gorgeous then! I've never seen All That jealous before!"

"Good point. But alas… my flight was called before the ladies in question arrived."

"Too bad, buddy."

Gabe shrugged a shoulder, thinking about wild red hair and swamp eyes. Wild as in untamed or the wild, varied hues of autumn… all red and gold and brown, shining in the sun and blinding him with its beauty. And the eyes… like gazing into a deep, clear pool of water, the green color a reflection of overhanging willows.

His Annie…

Goddammit, just when he'd gone for a week without the vision plaguing him, here she was again.

"Gabe?"

"Huh?"

"Where were ya, dude? You just checked out."

"Hmm? Oh… just thinking. Are you finished in here? I'd like to hang board in the new conference room and I could use your help."

"Do I get to help nail it up?"

"I'll nail; you can play in the mud."

"I get to tape? Cool!"

"And sand… God, I hate that part."

"So hire someone."

"No. I need to do it, Kyle, and don't ask why."

"'Nuff said, buddy. So let's go!"

Gabe nodded and went to work on his latest addiction, the absolute perfection of SD Production's new space.

Deirdre took advantage of Geoffrey's absence to do a little "house cleaning"… namely in the attic. If he knew she was attempting to climb the steep steps he'd have a fit and forbid her to do so again, but she knew he had stored several boxes of his old works up there and she was curious as to what went on in the extremely complex mind of her enigmatic husband.

She'd read the three books he had published and she knew the words to each and every song he had ever recorded, but there was still so much that he never shared with anyone, and Deirdre knew that it was hidden away in the dusty room overhead.

It was three days before she could find the energy, but once she did and the twins were at pre-school, she took a few pain pills and made her exhausting ascent into the forbidden attic.

Deirdre turned on the light and sneezed from the dust in the stuffy room, and then went to open a window. The late spring breeze blew in, scenting the air with the smell of lilacs. Much better…

She gazed around the room, wondering which one of the many boxes to explore first. Goodness, there were so many of them! All but a few were labeled with dates, and she decided to peek into the unmarked ones first.

She was quite surprised at what she found. Dozens of leather-bound books were uncovered, along with a very old family bible – and a small, porcelain horse. Geoffrey certainly hadn't penned any of this! She looked at the glass equine in her hand. How odd…

Deirdre opened a book, but the light was just too poor to see the faded ink on the paper, and she took the bible downstairs to read. The names written in the front were rather intriguing. She'd come for the rest of the books later.

"Oh my God! Annie, I'm so sorry! I can't believe what a bitch she is!"

"I figured it would happen, Marti, I was just hoping it wouldn't."

But she felt terrible nonetheless. After exploring a bit of the city and doing some shopping at a few exclusive boutiques, Deanna took them to a salon for the first leg of their makeover. She obviously knew the owner, and after exchanging "air kisses" and a cold hug with Rupert, he gushed in a lisping falsetto how delighted he was to see her again, and all was ready.

Marti gave Annie an elbow in the ribs, and both women fought to contain their laughter at his exaggerated French accent and flamboyant gestures.

Deanna introduced her charges.

"Rupert, this is our contest winner, Martha Marlett…"

Rupert took Marti's hand in his soft, well-manicured one and kissed it.

"Welcome…welcome, Miss Marlett," he sighed, already deciding to turn her raw beauty into stunning glory.

"And this is her… companion, Annie Bottom," Deanna said in a cold, bored voice.

"Benton," Annie corrected quietly when Rupert took her hand.

Jeez, she could see her reflection in his buffed fingernails. It kind of creeped her out. *This was a man?* Such a waste… he was otherwise someone she'd look twice at with his height, shiny black hair, and the look of ruggedness under his effeminate persona.

"Ah… Miss Benton." He stood back, raised a delicate finger to his full lips, and appraised that marvelous hair of hers.

Deanna glared, and in a loud voice announced, "Rupert, don't waste your time on that mop. Obviously she has no idea… no sense of style. She wouldn't know how to manage even the simplest cut."

Several of the patrons stared and a few snickered.

Annie blushed in embarrassment and wished she could have died right then and there.

Marti turned red too, but she was furious. For the first time in her jovial, carefree life she experienced the emotion of hate.

"*Au contraire*," Rupert sighed, twirling a lock of Annie's silky curls around his finger, "she has already attained perfection. I shall not touch it! To do so would be sacrilege. No… I shall merely allow myself to shampoo and dry… and perhaps a light condition, but to change this? Absolutely not!"

Annie gave him a smile of thanks but felt he was just patronizing her. After all, she'd never been able to control her wild mane. It was forever escaping any restraints she put it in, and the colors changed with every turn of her head. Maybe she should just shave it all off and buy a wig.

Rupert touched a finger under Annie's chin and turned back to Deanna.

"NeeNee, run along while I work my magic, and you may return to collect your beauties after four. We can display them for all of New York to see this evening when you shall be my guests for dinner."

"I'd like to stay, Rupert. After all, I *am* covering this story…"

"And you are now an unwelcome distraction. Be gone!" He waved a limp wrist at her.

She gave him a smirk and turned to Marti.

"You heard the... *man*, Marti, I'm being evicted. But I'll make it back and we'll have a quick snack before we shop some more."

"Deanna, I said you were to be my guests for dinner. No argument or I shall tell the world about your little problem..." Rupert said, nonchalantly examining his fingernails.

She turned as red as her hair and glared.

"Marti, I'll see you at four," she spat.

Marti nodded but didn't smile. It was all she could do not to punch the bitch.

Deanna looked at Annie; a quick, derogatory head to toe glance coupled with a sneer, and walked away shaking her head with the futility of it all. *Hopeless... just plain hopeless.*

Her unspoken opinion was not lost on the other occupants of the salon, and they looked at "Miss Bottom" with a mixture of superiority, pity, and just a hint of sympathy.

Annie was mortified.

It was then Marti made her apologies.

"Ladies, this way," Rupert snapped in a crisp, no-nonsense voice.

He led them to his private workroom, sat them in comfortable chairs, and then smartly clapped his hands together.

Two assistants in lilac-colored smocks appeared, and Rupert gave them orders in French. They gave him a nod and a curtsey, and vanished.

Annie and Marti shared a glance, wondering about his personality change. Minutes later they were sipping a marvelous cup of cappuccino while Rupert gave Marti a comb-out.

"I simply cannot stand that creature," he sighed, losing his lisp and sounding very masculine and sexy in his newer, deeper voice. He still had the accent, although now it was lighter and much more authentic.

"Deanna, you mean?" Marti asked. She shivered in delight as the comb was traded for fingers, and she received a delicious scalp massage... and wondered what those fingers would feel like elsewhere on her body.

"Yes, NeeNee the Meanie as she's known to a select few. But I have to act the part... she does throw a lot of business and free publicity my way."

"Act the part?" Marti asked, melting into her chair as those magic fingers relaxed her. *Oh God... he was so good!*

"Yes. When I first started in this business – in this country, I was me – the man you see now, but for some reason the women shied away from my salon even though I was the best. I'd never had that problem in Canada and was dumbfounded! I did a little research to see where the 'money' went, and found that they preferred the stereotypical 'gay male' as far as stylists went. Stupid, yes, but I guess it's part of the game. Anyway, I adopted my 'Rupert' persona and they have been flocking in ever since. Deanna happened in one day and 'took me under her wing' as she put it, and she's been popping in regularly ever since. Apparently I am the only one to ever give her a style she liked."

"But she lives in Michigan, Rupert! Rather far to drive for a haircut," Marti said, even she'd do it every month just to have this gorgeous man's hands run through her hair… gay or not. Mmhmm…

"Call me Anton when we're alone. Rupert exists out there; Anton lives back here. And Deanna spends a lot of time in the city on business. She's a buyer, you know."

"Oh yeah. So Rupert – uh, Anton, why the split personality? With us anyway?"

"Because you and Miss Benton are *real* women, Miss Marlett. Rare as precious gems and just as beautiful, and I knew it as soon as I saw you. Would you prefer 'Rupert'?"

"God no!" Marti gasped, and winked at an oblivious Annie. *Jeez, where was her friend now?"*

"As I suspected," Anton laughed.

"Um… so you aren't… uh,"

"Gay? God no! But how many straight males do you know in this business," he laughed.

"None… But then I usually cut my own hair," Marti sighed.

"Unfortunately that's obvious, Miss Marlett."

"Marti. Call me Marti. Anton, are you from France?"

"Quebec. I moved here around five or six years ago. A little more lucrative financially, and I don't have to put up with my parents comparing me to my brother. I love him, but I'll never measure up."

"Your brother?" Marti grinned. *There were two of them?*

"Ashton DeLaCroix."

Annie's head snapped up. *Ashton?*

"Ashton's your brother? I love his show," Marti sighed.

"He's good… so you can see why I felt the need to escape his shadow."

Annie felt that his acting skills rivaled Ashton's after having seen his performance as Rupert.

"Now, Marti, tell me about yourself. Your work, your hobbies… I have an idea of what I want to do, but to know you… I can better match a style that will suit you best.

That, and he just wanted to get to know her a little better too. Perhaps she was free after dinner…

Marti grinned and filled him in.

Annie half-listened, thinking of Ashton. From there her thoughts moved to cowboys in general, and then one in particular. Would she ever find him?

"Miss Benton…"

"Hmm? Oh… Anton. I'm sorry, I was just…"

"The picture of a woman in love, deep in thought and dreaming of good things to come," Anton said, waving her to his chair. "He'll be so very thrilled to see the 'new you', even if not much will change. I was serious when I said you had reached perfection. Have you been together long?"

"I uh... There is no 'he', Anton," Annie choked out, sitting down and wishing she were anywhere but there.

"No... But I saw... I'm so sorry. No one?"

"No."

"Then that will change soon, Miss Benton. Too bad Ash married recently... I can picture the two of you together. But I'll change the subject and discuss my ideas for what you and Miss... uh, Marti should wear tonight."

Annie nodded, more than happy to get off that particular topic. *She and Ashton? Oh jeez...*

"I have already sent my assistants to purchase your wardrobe. I have a few friends... Well anyway, Marti will be Air in ice blue and sapphires tonight. Light and breezy, cool and crisp, and yet smoldering underneath. You, Miss Benton, will be Earth. The gown I have selected for you is the colors of autumn to match your hair. Muted yet vivid, warm and inviting, innocent... but very, very sexy."

"Oh no... I couldn't wear anything like that!" Annie cried.

"Of course you can!"

"Not... not sexy, no way. I'm not built for that, Anton."

"Says who? Deanna? That skinny bitch. She reminds me of a ferret... same width from head to toe, smelly and sneaky... "

Annie burst out laughing at his description. He hit it right on the head that time!

"It wasn't her," Annie said, maintaining her composure once more. "I'm just not the type. Jeans and a tee shirt..."

"Is very attractive on you, but Annie – may I call you Annie?"

She nodded, liking Anton very much despite his choice in her attire.

"Good. Annie, you have a beautiful body. Granted it's not what the modeling agencies are looking for, but what man really wants a manikin anyway? Real women... a real woman with real curves and..."

He spun the chair around to look at her, flipping off the drape that covered her.

"Look at yourself, Annie. What do you see?"

"Anton, I..."

"You can't see yourself, can you? Your wall is too high, your shell too thick... But that's only part of it. You've never seen yourself in a man's eyes, have you?"

"I... I have..."

"No, not the way you should see yourself. You've seen friendship, infatuation, even lust, but never love. Never true love..."

He spun her back around and replaced the drape, and began to carefully run a comb through her curls.

"I don't mean for my words to seem harsh, Annie, but I say what I see to those that need to hear the truth. The women out there…"

He jerked his head to the door. "Those women are told what they want to hear. 'Yes dear, you're beautiful', or 'yes love, it's sooo you'… I feel like mirror mirror on the wall half the time and I'm dealing with a vast army of wicked witches," Anton chuckled. "Annie, tonight you will begin your metamorphosis. It won't be a sudden change, you have too much to work through for that, but I hope to give you a little confidence… let you find the courage you need to take that next step. I know you have it in you, right? You couldn't do the job you do without believing in yourself… your skills."

"How do you know what I do?" she asked, truly surprised.

"If you had been paying attention you would have heard your best friend as she bragged about your awards in nursing excellence, Annie. She admires you very much."

Annie glanced over at Marti, snoozin' under the hair dryer as she enjoyed a manicure and a pedicure.

"She does?"

"She does. She talked quite a bit about you. Anyway, tonight will be your new start, and when you return home… I see nothing but the brightest of futures for you my dear."

"Anton, how do you know so much about me? About women… Like what you said earlier about seeing myself…"

"You don't do my job without learning human nature, Annie. You wouldn't believe the conversations women have with me. Dear God… I know their love lives, their affairs, their 'female' problems… They tell me anything and everything! When I'm not a 'mirror on the wall', I'm a therapist! I don't offer advice – too often, but I do listen. And learn. And I probably shouldn't say this, but you and Ash would have made quite a match. I wonder if that crazy friend of his ever married…" Anton mused. "Now *he* would have been the perfect partner for you. Looked very much like my brother… No, on second thought never mind. He's too complex for any woman… And enough chat. I want to get you shampooed and conditioned before Marti is finished under the dryer. That color I put on is very temperamental and one minute too long could be the difference between triumph and disaster…"

The color was a triumph, changing her plain brunette hair into a shining cascade of rich brown with auburn highlights. The cut was a simple one, framing her face with bounce and body. Marti loved it and gave Anton a hug when she saw the finished product.

Annie's hair was stunning too. He gave it the promised light condition, and then pinned the mass of curls up onto the back of her head with the promise that only a few select tendrils would escape until she took it down for bed. Or had someone take the pins out for her, he said with a wink.

Their dresses arrived and were tried on, and appropriate make up applied.

"Oh Annie… can you believe us?" Marti sighed, looking at themselves in the mirror. "I feel like freakin' Cinderella! He even got us jewelry…"

"Which turns back into the shop it was borrowed from at midnight, Marti. But we do look good, don't we?"

"Good is hardly the term I would use to describe you, ladies," Anton said, coming back into the room to see his creations complete. "Actually I don't think a word has been invented yet to describe the visions that you are…"

Marti turned from the mirror to face him.

"Anton, this is the best… the best… Ooh…" She ran to him and hugged him.

He hugged her back, but was careful not to crush her dress. She still had a few hours to look her best, and perhaps he could help her out of it later. He did let his fingers linger on her a little longer than necessary, though, and she got his message.

Deanna sauntered uninvited into the back room and nearly dropped in her tracks when she saw her hopeless hicks. Marti… well, she had expected as much, but that goddamn bitch Annie… NeeNee hated her more than ever.

She waved an impatient hand to her charges and herded them out to the limo before they could even change into their comfort clothes. Deanna would get a sick thrill out of watching them try not to soil their gowns or muss their hair until dinner that evening. And it was going to be a long four hours; she'd make sure of that.

Chapter Twenty-Two

Summer, 1995

"Dude, did ya hear?"

"I believe the song goes, 'Do you hear what I hear…'" Gabe sang, chucking a can of beer at his buddy.

"Kiss my ass. Too early anyway. God, it's hot out tonight!"

"I know. Ninety-five and muggy as hell. What was I supposed to have heard, Kyle?"

Kyle popped open his beer and sat down on the worn leather sofa beside his buddy.

"Dude, why didn't you bring everyone out to my house? It's a lot cooler on the lake…"

"Because Deirdre isn't feeling well, Kyle. I don't want to be too far away if she needs me. Now either quit bitching or go home."

"At least turn the air on in here. Damn! You're richer than God and don't spend money…"

"The air is on in the rest of the house but I prefer it off in my office. I like the smell of the flowers coming in the window…"

"And the mosquitoes. Can't even put up a fuckin' screen?" Kyle growled, slapping a little bloodsucker.

"You brought that one in. Probably did it on purpose just for something else to bitch about. Now what is your news, Kyle?"

"Huh? Oh yeah… The snake!"

"Snake?"

"NeeNee the Nasty. She's in the loony bin, dude!"

Gabe very nearly choked on his beer.

"She's *what?*" he gasped.

"Yep. Crazy as they come…"

"Oh God… Tell me the fuckin' story!"

Kyle grinned and stretched, and took another slow, frustrating-for-Gabe sip of his beer.

"Kyle…"

"I'm tellin', I'm tellin'! I guess it started when she went to New York a few months ago. You remember, you saw her there?"

"How could I forget?" Gabe groaned. "But first, from whom were you told this titillating tale of towering tastelessness?"

"Vince at the Watch. We're buds, you know."

"You're buds with everyone, Kyle."

"Yeah… comes in handy. Anyway, them girls she brought to New York?

One of them was that Marti chick! You remember her?"

"She's as unforgettable as you, Kyle."

"Not touchin' that one. Anyway, her friend is the one that made NeeNee nutso."

"Let me buy that woman a beer," Gabe laughed. Although as much as he disliked Deanna, he never would have wished ill health, mental or otherwise, on her.

"Yep. I guess from the moment they hit the airport NeeNee was out to get her, but that chick never let her. Was just as nice as all get out and never let the snake win – and didn't even try!"

"No one is that nice, Kyle."

"Well this Annie chick was. Oh man… to have seen that whole week… Dude, they went and got them makeovers? Never even touched that Annie… didn't need to! Deanna got her panties in a wad over that and they never unbunched. Period! She tried harder and harder to piss Annie off, get her mad, ruffle her feathers even, but ol' Annie never wavered. Ooh… and that Marti chick? Turned her gay hairdresser straight! Can you imagine? NeeNee had been after his… uh, well, she wanted him, dude, but he never gave her a second look. And then Marti…"

Kyle sipped his beer and paused for effect.

"Kyle…"

"Marti goes and gets her hair done, has dinner with the fruit, and ends up going home with him! God!"

"This Annie person, Kyle… She uh…"

"Oh yeah. Well, no matter where they went or what they did, ol' Annie would shine without even tryin'. Just stayed shy and quiet in the background, and ended up being the center of attention before it was over. You didn't see her pic in the magazine?"

"I don't read that shit!"

But he sure as hell was wishing he had. Annie again… His Annie. He just knew it had to be her, the way she kept popping up in is life. So why in the hell couldn't he find her? But he just might be able to now… He'd check on it first thing in the morning.

"Should have, dude." Kyle frowned a little, thinking that perhaps it was better that he didn't though. It just dawned on him where he'd seen Annie before. But he continued… "Great article and even better pictures. NeeNee didn't end up writing it though. She wrote one but Vince threw it out and had her committed. She trashed Annie so bad, and even threatened her! Loony-toon…"

"So uh… who wrote it, Kyle?"

"Vince. Deanna sent him notes every night, pictures too, and he talked to Marti to piece it all together. It was a big contest and he just couldn't blow it off because his reporter tried to use his computer as a suppository on him."

"She didn't!"

"Yep. He told her that her article was a biased piece of shit and she could just shove it right back where it came from and give him something he could use. She screamed something about shoving it, and grabbed his monitor off his desk. Swore she was gonna shove it up his ass right after she took his head off with it."

"And I missed it," Gabe sighed. "Um… did Vince talk to … to Annie?"

"Nope. He wanted to just to get her side of the story, but she wouldn't. Said that the contest was all about Marti and that Marti should tell the story. Annie wanted nothing to do with it. I guess she really felt bad about NeeNee too. Wanted to know if she could do anything to help her."

"Guilty conscience?"

"Not according to Vince. Annie didn't know a thing about anything until he told her, and he didn't tell her that she was the one that sent the snake slithering to Sillyville. Just told her that Miss Montgomery had a bit of a breakdown from overwork and would be taking a therapeutic vacation."

"And the article? He didn't tell her about that?"

"Nope. After he met her he decided not to and just asked to interview her along with a few photos. She declined to do both, and the pic in the paper was one that Marti took in New York. It's the only one of Annie. I guess she's pretty good about escaping the lens too. Always managed to be just out of the frame or looking away."

"As if she really didn't even exist," Gabe murmured.

"What was that?"

"Nothing, Kyle. You ready for another beer?"

"Will be by the time you get back with some."

Gabe nodded and left his den. *Annie… she was out there somewhere, goddammit, and he was determined to find her. He had to… Was meant to! Why else would he keep hearing about her?*

He grabbed two more beers from the 'fridge and went to check on Deirdre before he joined Kyle.

"Dee? You here?" he asked, poking his head into the family room where she liked to sit in her favorite chair by the window and read.

No answer. Must have gone to bed already, even if it was a little early. Oh well, she had been a bit more tired than usual lately.

He popped open his beer and sipped it on the way to the den.

"Gonna make it over tonight, Gabe?"

"I think so, Kyle. Dee's feeling much better and the summer's nearly over. I'd like her to have a little time relaxing on the beach before the snow flies."

"Cool. Well, the boat's gassed up, I'll light the charcoal, and we'll see ya in a few!"

"Sounds like a plan. God, I can't wait to ski again."

"Gonna try the jump?"

"Ever known me not to?"

"I meant that dumb-ass back flip you never seem to be able to do."

"I'm no quitter, Kyle, so yes I will be attempting it again today. Got the paramedics on speed dial?"

"Of course. But dude… you won't try anything stupid, will you?"

"That's your department, Kyle."

"Fuck you. Oh! Bring your guitar, Gabe!"

"I don't know… I don't feel much like playing, Kyle."

"Jesus, Gabe, you never feel like it anymore! When was the last time you even picked it up?"

"I don't know," Gabe mumbled. He glanced over at his guitar – an anniversary gift from Dee. A light coating of dust covered it, but he just didn't care anymore.

"I'll tell ya when, pal. It was last summer right after Dee got home from the hospital. You haven't touched it since. Not the ones at work or the ones here, and probably not there at your house either. Dude, you have got to snap out of it! Life goes on…"

"Spare me the lecture, Kyle, and until you've walked a mile in my shoes I'd thank you not to assume… Aw hell. I'll see you later."

"At least leave your pissy attitude home."

"I'll leave it, don't worry. I won't spoil Jen's birthday party."

"Better not or I'll kick your ass – after her party. I'm not gonna spoil it either."

"What was your gift to her, Kyle?"

"Which one?" he laughed. "And I'm not tellin' you about one of 'em… But she's been smilin' ever since I put it to her… uh, gave it to her!"

"Lord… then I don't *want* to know. See you later, Kyle."

"Later, buddy."

Gabe tossed the phone aside and lay down on his sofa. He bunched up the quilt, rested it on his chest, and folded his arms around it. Christ, why was he so miserable again?

The studio was still busy enough to keep the doors open and the staff employed and occupied, no problem there, and his home life was doing well again too. Deirdre's last stint in the hospital, beginning the morning after Gabe heard about Deanna, had only lasted a week and she was pretty much recovered from it. She was still weak and frail, but assured Gabe that she was otherwise fine and it had only been a temporary setback. He chose to believe her.

So why the depression? What in the hell did he have to be miserable about? And yet he was. If only he could talk to his brother again. Steve had always been able to pull him out of his pool of self-pity… but no more. Gabe was on his own.

He sighed and rolled to his side, hugging the quilt to him and wishing it were a warm body that could offer him comfort. Even Deirdre didn't do that anymore, saying that it brought her pain. He missed being held.

"Geoffrey?"

He sat up quick when she knocked on the door and called him.

"Yeah?"

"Are you ready? The twins are waiting."

"I'll be right there, Dee. Go ahead and get in the car."

She opened the door and looked in, saddened to see that expression his face again. *Poor Geoffrey…*

"Was there something else, Deirdre?"

"Uh… no. Yes."

"Which is it, Dee?" Gabe sighed.

She went in and sat next to him.

"Geoffrey, don't worry about me. I'm doing fine… better than ever actually. And I know what you're thinking so don't deny it."

He raised an eyebrow in question.

"Your face, Geoffrey," Deirdre said, running her fingertips along his jaw. "When you let your guard down your face is so expressive, and your emotions are plainly seen. And the look you just had…"

He took her hand and kissed it, not having the heart to tell her that she hadn't been anywhere in his thoughts for the last ten minutes.

"Anyway, don't worry about me, Geoffrey dear. Come now, let's go celebrate Jenna's birthday. Thirty-four years old and still looks like a teenager," Deirdre sighed.

She was glad that she thought twice about what she had planned on saying to her husband, that he would find his Annie someday. He had been thinking about her again…

"Thirty-four," Gabe murmured. Christ, where did the years go? Jenna *had* been a teenager the first time he had seen her sitting on his bed in the dorm room he was to share with Kyle. He'd fallen a little in love with the feisty blonde that day, and the years hadn't lessoned his affection for her.

He picked up his gift to her, a tape he made compiling photographs and home video of her husband and children over all those years. He hoped she'd like it.

"Let's go, Deirdre," he sighed, and helped his fragile wife to her feet. And yeah, he did worry about her.

"I can't believe you bought her that Cherokee, Kyle! What was wrong with the van? It held your tribe, was in good condition, and it was paid off!"

"Nothing, buddy, but she liked it and…"

"I can well imagine! It's a top of the line vehicle. But Kyle, I know your funds aren't enough to support those payments. And I know it's none of my business either, but I just hate to see you fall behind again. You just got caught up."

211

"You're right, pal, it's none of your business. And I'm doin' okay money-wise. Have been for a while now."

Gabe had to agree although he didn't know how it was possible. Christ, the payments on Kyle's castle of a house were over a grand a month, and the taxes on that large bit of lake property weren't all that small either. Their grocery bill for all those children was nearly enough to finance a small country, and Gabe hated to think of how much it cost to clothe the rapidly growing Davidson bunch. Kyle was still purchasing high-ticket toys too. He'd recently shown up to work on a new Harley; Gabe nearly shit when he saw that. And the gambling... Kyle was into it heavier than ever.

Yet Gabe's monthly inquiries into his friend's bank balance showed no more deficits so perhaps Kyle had finally figured out a budget.

Still seemed impossible, though.

"My apologies, Kyle. Well, I think I'm ready for a turn around the lake. How about you?"

"Been ready, dude. Who's first?"

"You can ski first. Hell, if I do and kill myself on that jump, who will haul you around?"

"Will could. He's drivin' the boat now."

Fourteen year-old Will grinned and nodded.

"Then how about if we ski together, Kyle?"

"Cool!"

"And the lovely Miss Hannah Claire may spot for us. You're old enough, aren't you, hon?"

Thirteen year-old Hannah blushed and nodded when her hero, "Uncle" Gabe, gave her that special smile and brushed his fingers under her chin.

"Good enough! Then let's go!" Gabe slung his arms around Hannah and Will, winked at Kyle, and took them all down to the lake.

Once again his back flip was unsuccessful, but he was always relieved just to have survived at all.

Kyle's jump was nothing fancy and he landed it with no problem. He let go of the rope as soon as his buddy wiped out and swam over to see that he was still alive. He was always grateful when Gabe survived his stupid tricks.

✦ ✦ ✦

"Annie, are we really going to make our dinner out of these?" Eric asked, holding up his basket of vegetables.

"We sure are, Eric. You like stew, don't you?"

"Oh yeah! But we always have it out of a can at home. Aunt Irene doesn't have much time to cook and I'm not very good at it yet."

"Then you'll have your first official lesson today, kiddo."

Annie checked the basket to see that they had enough. Yes... late carrots and early potatoes, a few onions and some herbs snipped fresh from the garden.

Chunks of beef were already simmering on the stove, and Eric's birthday cake was cooling on the counter.

After the veggies were cleaned, peeled, diced, and dropped in the stew pot, Annie was taking the birthday boy on a special ride. Irene was planning to join them for dinner, and the day promised to be perfect.

"McDonald, stop!" Eric laughed when the goose snapped some greens, and a carrot, out of the basket.

He bent down and gave the bird a hug, and gave Dog one too when the canine shoved his head under the boy's hand.

Annie smiled at the scene. Eric was always so happy when he visited her home, and it was almost as if he left his chronic illness back at the trailer. His breathing was less labored and his cheeks took on a bit of color, and he looked at the world around him as if it were a glorious new surprise each and every time.

And today was so special… his twelfth birthday. Annie wished Michael were there to share it with them, and sent a little prayer heavenward for a miracle. She was rather surprised when she realized that it was the first time she had thought about her friend in weeks. Must be all the overtime she was working… It left her exhausted and numb, and not caring much about anything at the end of her night except a soft bed and a deep sleep.

She tried to conjure up Michael's face in her mind, but could only manage a vague image of a tall man in a cowboy hat, and the feeling of serenity he always left her with. Jeez, she missed him.

"Annie?"

"Hmm?"

"Are we ready to go?"

"I don't' think so, Eric," she teased, "I've changed my mind. Let's stay here and watch television."

His face fell.

Oh man… she went too far; he looked like he was ready to cry. Annie hugged him and pushed him out the door.

"Just kidding, Eric. Go saddle Wanda."

His face lit up like the sun breaking through the clouds, and he ran to the barn.

Dog and McDonald followed, barking and honking in sheer joy.

Spike sat on the top step of the cabin, purring contentedly and surveying his kingdom. *Yes indeed, today would be a very special day for Eric Thomas and Annie Rose…*

He brushed a silky paw across his whiskers, and with a kitty sigh, went to snooze in the favorite chair.

"Are we really going all the way to the waterfall, Annie?" Eric sure hoped so. He'd seen it from the lake but never from the top.

"If you're up to the ride, Eric. Are you tired yet?"

"Only a little. How much farther?"

"Two miles. Maybe we should go back to the clearing and rest."

"I can make it, Annie," he assured her.

He patted Wanda's golden neck and told himself that he could do it. He hoped.

"Are you sure? Remember, we have to ride all the way back."

Eric nodded, too afraid that if he spoke again she'd hear how tired he really was. *Only two more miles…*

"Oh, Annie… this is beautiful!" Eric cried, standing on the edge of the earth and watching the waterfall into the lake below him.

"It is, isn't it? How about if you sit for a minute while I get us a snack."

He flopped down and let his legs dangle over the edge of the rocks. *This was so cool…*

Annie pulled two bottles of water and some peanut butter and crackers from Adonis' saddlebag. She also pulled out Eric's bottle of pills and shook a few into her hand; he'd need them to help digest his food.

"Thanks, Annie," he smiled, downing his stupid medicine and then munching a cracker.

Dog let out a little whine and was tossed a tidbit by Annie. He caught it and then went off to explore.

Annie and Eric sat in silence as they ate, enjoying the beauty of the day as they thought their separate thoughts.

Michael was on both their minds.

"I sure miss him," Eric sighed after a few minutes.

"Me too, Eric," Annie answered. She didn't need to ask who he was referring to.

"Annie?"

"Yes, Eric?"

"Can I make my wish early? You know, the one I get when I blow out all my candles?"

"I don't see why not. You *will* get them all on the first blow, right?" Actually he'd be lucky to extinguish a third of them…

"You bet, especially if it means I get my wish!"

"Eric, some wishes don't ever come true."

"I know, but this one isn't impossible. I'm not wishing to not be sick anymore, just…"

They both turned at the sound of hoof beats crashing through the forest. Wanda and Adonis looked up from their grazing and whinnied as the newcomer approached.

Annie and Eric reached for each other's hand at the same time. *Could it be…?*

The black horse and his tall rider broke through the trees, galloping up to the woman and the boy, and then came to a sliding stop only feet away.

"Did I miss the party?" Michael grinned, hopping down from his mount.

"I got it, Annie!" Eric cried as he jumped up to hug his hero. "I got my wish and I didn't even really wish it yet!"

"Happy birthday, Eric!"

Michael dropped to one knee so that he could return the boy's hug. He loved that kid…

"Oh Michael… you're here! This is the best birthday ever!" Eric hugged him one more time and turned to smile at Annie.

She just stood there, stunned, surprised, and happier than ever to see him.

Michael stood up, staring back at her.

Annie…

He held out his arms and she ran to him.

"God, I missed you," he murmured, kissing the top of her head.

"No more than I missed you," she replied, clinging to him.

She buried her face against his chest, taking in his special scent of horses, leather, and a cool pine forest. It was so good to feel his arms around her again. Odd though… she didn't feel the hardness of his muscles or the tightness of his grip, only the warmth and love that surrounded him. She felt total peace.

"Ahem…" from Eric. He popped another cracker into his mouth and grinned at the couple.

They smiled back and separated, although still holding hands, and went to sit on the edge of the rocks.

"I guess I don't need to tell you that I have a million questions for you," Annie said, running her free hand along his jaw and looking into his eyes.

"I pretty much figured you would, Annie. I'll answer what I can but I'm sure you know I can't answer them all," Michael replied, putting his arm around her once more.

"Then I won't pry. You look wonderful."

"I never change. You look good too. Lost a little weight, though."

"I don't eat much; no appetite."

"And you work too much, hon."

"Still watching over me?"

"As always. I saw your picture in that magazine. Did you have a good time in New York?"

"For the most part, yes. Marti had a ball. She's gone back twice now to see a man she met there. I do hope it works out for them, but I'll sure miss her if she marries him and moves away," Annie sighed.

"It's that serious?"

"She'd like it to be, but I don't know… Wouldn't be good for Anton's reputation. He'd have to kill off poor ol' Rupert."

"Rupert?"

Annie laughed and filled him in.

"Now I want to hear about you, Michael. How have you been?"

"The same. Still on assignment."

"And your sister-in-law? How is she? I feel so bad…"

"She has her good days and bad days. I spend a lot of time with her at night."

"That's good. So you and your brother are back on track?"

Michael looked away. "I don't speak to him."

Annie didn't dare ask why.

"Oh… I'm sorry. Um… how about your ex-fiancé? You said that she was ill too…"

Michael let out a harsh breath and chucked a rock as hard as he could out into the water.

Annie flinched at his show of disconsolate emotion.

"Michael?"

"Annie… God, I suppose I should tell you. You'll find out soon enough anyway."

"Oh jeez… I shouldn't have said anything."

"No, that's okay. My… my ex and my sister-in-law are the same person," he murmured.

"Oh! Oh no… Michael, I'm so sorry. Oh jeez, no wonder you and your brother don't…"

He shook his head. "That's not the reason. Their marriage had my full blessing, Annie. I kind of suggested it to him shortly after it was clear that I'd never be able to marry her. And she needed him…"

Annie could feel his pain and put her fingers over his lips to prevent him from saying anymore.

"Don't," she whispered. "I'm sorry I brought it up."

"It was something that was meant to be, Annie, just like her illness is now. Fate, destiny…predestination… all woven together and coverin' us up with love and joy and separation and heartache. God, I'd give anything to be able to change things, probably could even, but just can't. Yet in the end it will all work out. We'll all be happy…"

"I don't know how," Annie sighed. "You lost her and now… well, she's ill."

"Terminally ill."

"Oh no…"

"Annie, it's Eric's birthday. Let's drop this depressing talk and make a day of it for him. Think he'd like to ride Wh… uh, Horse?"

"He'd love it!" She gave him a quick kiss on the cheek and stood.

Michael whistled for his steed and then placed Eric high up in the saddle.

"Take him for a spin, Kid," he smiled.

"All by myself?"

"Sure! He's the safest horse you'll ever ride, Eric. Just down the trail a ways and back though, and then we should head home. Miss Benton, do you have plans for dinner?"

"Already on the stove, Mr. Anthony. Do you like beef stew?"

"My favorite! Hurry up, Eric."

Eric grinned and turned the big black horse around, kicking him into a canter.

"Eric, no!" Annie cried. The boy was nowhere near ready, nor strong enough, for a fast ride on the huge stallion.

"Let him go, hon; he'll be fine."

Hearing that come from Michael, Annie knew she needn't worry.

Eric managed to blow out all of his candles in a single breath, much to his delight and Annie's surprise. Irene was a little stunned, but the day had been full of surprises.

Eric had come back from his ride looking stronger and healthier than she had ever seen him. She watched from the porch as he unsaddled the mare and then ran up to the cabin when he was finished. He was barely out of breath. She commented on it, and Eric informed her that Horse was magic and took away his sickness for a little while. She smiled… he was still such a child in some ways.

Another very pleasant surprise was Michael's return. Irene had been infatuated with the man ever since the first time she set eyes on him, and if she were twenty years younger she'd make a play for him herself. Heck, Annie didn't seem to want him even though they lived together for a while. They were close though, and Irene felt jealous when the couple walked from the barn hand in hand.

It was the best day of Eric's life. Well, almost. It tied with the day McDonald was born. He'd never forget it though, and gave Annie and Michael extra hugs when it was time to go home. And Aunt Irene was in an extra good mood so it wouldn't be nearly so bad having to go back to the trailer.

He sighed on his way home. Looking from one present to the other. Annie had given him a picture of him and McDonald standing next to each other in the lake, and a card with five twenty-dollar bills in it. She told him he was getting pretty hard to buy for since she had no idea what grown-up kids like him preferred; he could choose whatever he wanted. Wow… a hundred dollars for anything he wanted. But it still wouldn't buy him what he really wanted, and that was Annie and Michael as his parents.

Michael's present was pretty cool too. Eric stuck his new hat on his head and pulled it low over his eyes, feeling just like the cowboy his hero was. It was a real Stetson and not one of those fake kinds he saw in the grocery store. Too cool…

Michael helped Annie with the dishes, and when they were finished they went to the porch to relax.

"Will you be staying, Michael? Your room is still available… I haven't changed anything."

"I can't, Annie. I shouldn't have even come today…"

"Oh yeah. Your sister…"

"She's not the reason and leave it at that."

"When are you leaving?"

"I wish I didn't have to… but around ten or so. Is that okay? If I stay until then, I mean."

"Okay? Jeez, Michael, this is your home for as long as you want it! You know that!"

"I'll stay until eleven then," he said, giving her a wink. "And I'll be wantin' seconds on that cake too."

"Take it all, Michael. I won't be eating any more of it."

"I just might. My… nephews would get a kick out of a little contraband sugar. Oh wait… not tonight. They're already at a birthday party and sure to be sugar-buzzed already."

"Then give it to your horse," Annie laughed. She was still sad about him leaving so soon, but he was with her now and the world was so right.

"Annie, are you up for another ride?"

"To where?"

"The clearing. I think we have just enough time to catch the sunset."

"I'd love to. Race ya to the barn!"

He smacked her on the butt and took off running.

She caught up with him halfway there and tackled him.

"Cheater!" he cried, rolling her over and pinning her down.

"All's fair," she laughed, and yanked his hat over his eyes.

He let her go and sat back on his heels as he watched her run to the barn. Yep, her cowboy was gonna be a lucky man before long.

They didn't bother to saddle the horses, choosing a carefree bareback ride instead.

They sat in silence at the clearing, awed by the beauty of the spectacular sunset. Afterwards they let the horses find their way home, the couple still not saying but a word here or there.

He walked her to the cabin and held her once last time before he had to go.

"How long before I see you again, Michael?"

"Wish I could tell you, Annie. Might be a while. Just remember what I told you last time…"

She looked up at him, not quite remembering.

"It's gonna be hard for a while, hon, but things aren't always as they seem…"

"And I can give in but don't give up?"

"Never forget that, Annie Benton."

"I'll try not to, Michael Anthony."

He smiled a sad smile and kissed the tip of her nose.

She watched him vanish in the dark as he walked back to the barn and his horse.

She never heard him ride away.

Chapter Twenty-Three

Winter, 1995

Michael's last words to Annie were sadly prophetic. After he left that summer night she'd gone down to her lake and sat on the beach. Her head spun as question after question about her mysterious friend streaked through her mind. Just who *did* he work for? Where did he stay – and with a horse? How did he manage to ride miles and miles to get where he was going? And for that matter, how did he always know where to find her? And know the details of her life! And the fact that his fiancé married his brother… very strange. How did he spend time with her and manage to avoid the "evil twin"? And why, not even a half hour after he kissed her goodbye, could she not remember what he looked like… how he felt in her arms?

Just who was he?

It was all downhill from there. Annie sunk into a deep depression, not giving a hoot about much of anything anymore. Her flowers went untended, growing wild as they fought the weeds for control of their little bit of earth, and the vegetables rotted on the ground. Her critters were cared for, but they missed their daily doses of affection from the female they loved so well. Adonis fretted and paced, waiting for her to come and take him for a ride, but it wasn't to be; Annie rarely came to the barn except to feed her family and clean up after them.

Eric's health took a bad turn, keeping him either confined to his pathetic trailer or spending too much time in a bed at Brighton.

Annie still worked her overtime, but it had turned into actual work instead of a fulfilling career. It didn't help that Marti quit and took a position with a traveling nurse agency, and was committed to employment elsewhere for at least three months. At least she was in New York and near her Anton…

The cabin began to show signs of Annie's apathy too. A light coating of dust covered the furniture and her bed went unmade. The refrigerator and cupboards never seemed to be stocked with food and her plants wilted and turned brown in the greenhouse.

Annie's appearance wasn't all that great either. Since she no longer had the desire to cook, let alone do anything else, she began hitting the McDonald's and Burger King for her meals. Bacon, egg, and cheese biscuits on the way home from work, and a burger and fries on the way in. Days off, she usually popped a TV dinner in the microwave and then nibbled chips or popcorn late into the night. Her best friends became Ben and Jerry, and the Cherry Garcia ice cream they so thoughtfully provided.

Needless to say, she gained back the weight she had lost, and it brought friends. Her jeans were suddenly too tight, but her work scrubs and their elastic waistband were a little more forgiving. It didn't matter though; she always wore sweat pants and baggy tee shirts at home, and if she did need to go shopping it was usually on her way home from work.

The Christmas season was miserable at best. Annie didn't even bother with a tree, she bought Eric only a little token gift, and she volunteered to work every night she could. She did dredge up a little holiday spirit on Christmas Eve though, not having to work after all, and pulled out the box of her most-special ornaments. The stained glass pictures were hung in the windows and the colored glass balls were strung along the mantel, and Annie kept the crystal angel clutched in her hand. She sat on her sofa, sipping tepid wine until the bottle was empty and she had cried herself to sleep.

✦ ✦ ✦

"Sucks, dude."

"Eloquently put, Kyle, and I agree. Christ, Christmas in the hospital? At least the twins are allowed to visit this time."

"So it's back? For sure?"

"I'm afraid so. The tests came back this afternoon... and it's more involved."

"Involved?"

"It's spread, Kyle. Liver and lungs... pancreas... God, it's just awful."

"Whoa dude... Gabe?"

"Yes, Kyle?"

"Is... is she gonna die?"

"Don't even think that! No, they are treating her very aggressively, and when I spoke to her earlier she sounded very positive. She didn't look all that bad either. Tired, but not... well, she looked almost at peace or something. I think she's thinking she's going to beat this horrid disease, Kyle. She certainly doesn't look as if she's given up."

"I sure hope so! Hope not. Well, you know what I mean. Gabe, she means a lot to me... and Jen and the kids too."

"I know, Kyle. God, I don't know what I'd do without her."

"I'm glad you found her though, buddy. She's good for you."

"You'll never know, Kyle..."

"So what are you gonna do?"

"Do?"

"About tomorrow... presents and stuff. And Christmas dinner!"

"Hell, I don't know. My head's spinning..."

"You're welcome to spend the day with us. We'd be glad to have you, Gabe."

"Thanks, Kyle, but Christmas is for family."

"That hurt, man. We're *not* family?"

Gabe gave his friend a long look. Yeah, Kyle was family and nearly as much of a brother to him as Steve was. The happy chaos of the Davidson house would help keep his mind off his own sorry state of affairs.

"What time, Kyle?"

"You'll come? Aw God… that's great! Um… dinner's at three, but come before if you want. After you visit Dee…"

"We'll be there, buddy. Uh, Kyle?"

"Yeah?"

"Thanks."

"For what?"

"Pretty much everything…"

"Mushy…"

"Fuck you then."

"Much better. Later, man. Have a good night."

"You too, Kyle."

Gabe hung up the phone and went upstairs to check on his sons. They had been pretty upset when Mamma had to be left at Brighton again, and James asked if Santa would find her there. Jer punched his brother and called him a dolt, and said that her angel would be there so she didn't need Santa. Gabe was about to reprimand him, but Deirdre smiled and stopped him and said that Jeremy was right. Gabe backed down and let them have their little fantasy.

The twins were asleep – thankfully, and Gabe sat between their beds, looking from on boy to the other. God, they were so sweet in their slumber and his heart nearly burst with love for them.

"Steve," Gabe whispered, "I sure wish you could see them. They're fine boys… you and Deirdre did a great job. I suppose I should thank you for them. I always wanted kids… Even when I was nothing but a partyin' hell-raiser, I knew deep down that I was meant to have a family… to be a father. I guess a step-father-uncle will have to do though. I love them, Stevie… love them like they were my own."

He stood back up and leaned against the wall, thinking back to the most horrible day in is life.

"Steve, I still remember that dream I had so long ago too. It was the night after you died… I got blind drunk and passed out on a roadside, and yet I remember that dream so goddamn clear. You came to me and said to take care of her… take care of them. I had no idea who you were talking about at the time, but I'm so glad I figured it out. They're the world to me, Steve, all three of them. If you have any pull with God, being the saint you were when you were alive, could you ask him kindly to spare Dee? I need her, Stevie. I only wish I could return her love…"

Gabe stood quiet for a moment and the kissed his boys goodnight. He stumbled down to his den and pulled out a long-forgotten bottle of scotch. He filled a glass and toasted his reflection in the window.

"Merry fuckin' Christmas, Gabe…"

Steve stepped from the shadows of the twins' room as soon as his brother left.

"You weren't meant to love her, Gabe. She's mine. I'm hers. Always have been, always will be." He wiped a rough hand over misty eyes and vanished in a flash of blue.

In Deirdre's dream she smiled when she felt his presence, and opened her eyes.

"Hello, Steven," she said, anticipating what was to come.

He smiled his serene smile and sat next to her on the bed.

"I'm so glad you came... I thought perhaps the drugs I was given would rob me of my dream tonight," she sighed.

He nodded, and laid his hand over her chest.

She could feel the warmth begin, originating in her breast and then spreading through her body with each beat of her heart. The blue light grew brighter and the pain faded away.

Deirdre whispered, "I love you," and closed her eyes once more.

Steve sat there with her until he heard the nurses begin morning rounds. There was a vivid flash of blue, and he was gone.

Annie woke to a horrible pounding in her head. She moaned, cursing herself for drinking that entire stupid bottle of wine. Dog whined and scratched at the door, and Spike sat on her chest, his amber eyes staring into her bloodshot emerald ones.

The pounding intensified and Annie realized that it was coming from the front door as well as her alcohol-abused brain.

"Just a minute," she mumbled, and tried to stand up.

Didn't make it, though. She stepped on the fallen wine bottle, it rolled under her foot, and she fell right on her butt. It was instant tears as soon as she hit, and then ran down her face unchecked when her hand was sliced open by the broken wine glass.

"Ready or not, here I come, Annie-bananie!" Marti chirped as she opened the never-locked door.

Dog shot out to relieve himself; he was hours overdue.

"Annie?" Marti called, sensing something was very, very wrong.

She tossed her coat on the rack, stomped the snow off her shoes, and hurried into the living room to see what had Spike so agitated. She'd never seen him so upset, thrashing his tail from side to side and pacing back and forth near the sofa.

"Annie?" Marti cried, dropping down next to her friend. "Oh God, what happened?"

Annie shook her head and tried to control her sobs.

"Can you walk?"

Annie nodded and tried to stand, but her stomach churned and she fell back onto the couch.

"Stay put," Marti sighed, and went into the bathroom.

She returned with a few aspirin, a glass of water, a cold cloth, and some first-aid supplies.

Once Annie was medicated, bandaged, and able to sit up straight without barfing, Marti started in.

"Mind telling me what's going on?" she asked.

"I'm hung over… isn't it obvious?" Annie moaned. Lord, she felt like crap.

"Well duh. Jeez, Annie, I leave for three months and come back to find… find… Well, this!" she said, sweeping an arm towards the messy room.

Annie raised an eyebrow at her and then looked away.

"What's up, Annie? My God! You look like hell, your house looks like shit, and…"

"So what."

"So what? Hello… where's Annie Benton? She sure as heck isn't in here." Marti gave her a poke in the arm.

Annie shrugged her shoulder.

Marti got pissed.

"That's it. Hangover or no hangover, you're going to straighten up right now, Annie."

"Why bother…"

"What? Good god, Annie! What happened that was so damn bad that you'd turn into a… a pig! Yes, a pig. You live in a sty and… well, you're porkin' out, chica."

The truth hurt, causing Annie to cringe under the painful words.

Still didn't care though.

"Well?"

"I don't know, Marti. I woke up one day and nothing seemed to matter anymore. I'm still functional at work, and…"

"Hoo-freakin'-ray. You sure aren't around here. Jeez, you don't even have a Christmas tree up, Annie! Not that you'd be able to see it through all this dust, but it's your favorite holiday! Girlfriend, I'm going to fix us a pot of coffee and a kick-ass meal, and then we're going to spend the day cleaning this dump up. Now you go get dressed, feed the barn bunch, and get back up here. Uh… can you do that with your hand? It's a pretty nasty cut."

"No less than I deserve, and I'll make do. Marti?"

"Yeah?"

"Why are you here? It's Christmas… Why aren't you with Anton or you parents?"

"Several reasons. First of all, Anton and I didn't work out. I hate New York and he loves it. I can't live there and he refuses to even consider leaving. But we parted on friendly terms, and I always have a place to stay when I'm in town," Marti grinned.

Annie was happy that her friend wasn't dumped.

"My parents, my dorky brother, and Jill are in Florida, and my stint with the agency is up until next month."

"Oh… And then where?"

Marti grinned. "Three months at Brighton Memorial, Annie! Their staffing always did suck, and I'm filling in at ten bucks more per hour. Cool, huh?"

"That's wonderful!" Annie began to feel better already.

"Now maybe you won't have to work so much OT."

"How did you know?"

"I know you. Or at least I thought I did," Marti sighed, glancing around the room.

As for the first time, Annie saw the mess too.

Oh God…

"And…" Marti continued.

"And?"

"And I need a place to stay until Monday. My apartment won't be ready until then."

"You want to stay here? Oh Marti, you're more than welcome!"

"Not sure if I want to anymore. The health department hasn't shut you down yet?"

"Touché. Jeez, what happened to me?" Annie moaned.

"You were Marti-less, chica! But I'm back to kick your depressed butt into Happytown again. Now get dressed, feed your menagerie, and we'll have lunch."

"Lunch?"

"It's just after noon, Annie."

"Oh jeez…"

Marti gave her a hug, pulled her off the couch, and sent her to her room. Then she went to tackle that hellhole of a kitchen…

It was nearly midnight before the girls finished turning the cabin back into the sparkling clean home Annie loved so much. Even the greenhouse was taken care of; plants that could be salvaged were, and the ones beyond hope were taken to the woods to be turned back to the earth. Annie was grateful that her roses and more exotic flowers were saved, although she was furious with herself for letting her life go like she did.

They collapsed on the sofa in front of the toasty-warm wood stove and sipped hot cocoa.

"Annie?"

"Yes?"

"I just missed him again, didn't I?"

"Who?"

"Michael. I saw his things in the guest room."

"They've been in there for years. The last time he was here was on Eric's birthday, and not a word since."

"That long? Huh."

"Why?"

"He left something for you. You didn't know?"

"I haven't been in there in weeks. Months even. And how do you know…"

"Because it's wrapped in Christmas paper and has a card with your name on it. I didn't see it at first… don't know how I missed it, but… I'll get it." Marti jumped up and went to the bedroom.

"Weird," Annie said, taking the package.

"Why's that?"

"He never went in there. He hasn't been in that room for over a year."

"But you have?"

"Oh yeah. Eric stayed here quite a bit this summer."

"But it's from Michael, right?"

"Mmhmm. That's his handwriting."

"He writes pretty well for a man. Almost like script."

"He's different…"

"So open it."

"I'm almost afraid to."

But with shaking hands, she did.

"What is it, Annie?" Marti asked, leaning over for a better look.

Annie could only stare in stunned wonder.

"A horse? Kinda cheesy…" Marti said, losing interest.

"M… Marti?"

"Yeah?"

"This… this horse; I've seen it before."

"Yeah… Zorro rode one just like it. Black horse, cheap ceramic… big deal."

"No, you don't understand. Remember when I told you about my grandmother dying? Why I wasn't close with my parents for a while?"

"Something about books…"

"This horse," Annie murmured, "I put this horse in the box to guard them. Oh God…"

"Uh huh. Annie, they made tons of these things back in the sixties and tried to sell all the leftovers in the seventies. I was a little young then, but I remember seeing them on the shelves at the dime store. The cost a buck and a quarter, and I wanted to buy one for Jill for her birthday. Mom said no; she was only a baby and couldn't have glass toys."

"No… See the bottom? The 'S' and the 'E' scratched between the front legs?"

"Oh yeah… A trademark?"

"I didn't think much of it then… but I'll bet whoever it belonged to did it. More like a mark of ownership. S E… I wonder who it was. Not my gramma, that's for sure. Wait a minute… Marti, I used to see this horse at a friend of my grandmother's house. Mrs. McCallum… Sophia McCallum was her name. She was part Chippewa Indian, and I used to love to listen to her talk about her life when she was a little girl. She had two grandsons… I wonder if this horse belonged to one of them."

"Beats me. Creepy, though."

"Creepy?"

"That you'd end up with it again after all this time, and from your mysterious boyfriend, who I still haven't seen…"

"Strange, but not creepy. Michael… never creepy. Amazing, wonderful, perceptive, loving… perfect, but never creepy. He always seems to be there, kinda sorta, whenever I need him. And out of the blue I get this… my horse. I'm beginning to feel like *me* again, Marti!"

"Well I feel like death warmed over. First that flight and the spring-cleaning a few months early… I'm beat."

"Oh Marti! You came here right from the airport? Why didn't you say anything?"

"Minor detail, and you needed me more than I needed some sleep. So you owe me," Marti grinned. "I'll expect breakfast in bed and a rose on my tray."

"We're lucky that there are any left, and you got it. Thank you so much for helping me… Well, for everything."

"'Cuz I love ya, Annie-bananie. Sweet dreams!"

They shared a quick hug and Marti went to her room.

Annie sat on the sofa for a few minutes, staring at her surprise gift. She set her 'angel' horse on the mantel next to the crystal angel and stood there staring at them once more. A rare car heading up the hill flashed headlights into the room, and for a second the colors the colors danced around her.

"Merry Christmas, Michael," she whispered, "and thank you."

~Part Four~

Colors in the Wind

Chapter Twenty-Four
The New Year, 1996

The few weeks after Christmas passed quickly for Annie. She and Marti had little time to socialize as a nasty flu virus hit Waterston and kept Brighton Memorial's beds full and the staff on mandatory overtime. Annie found herself picking up shifts on the adult wards as well as Pediatrics and NICU, just to help out with the staffing shortages.

Yet despite her heavy work schedule and Marti's cheerful companionship, she began to feel that depressing loneliness descend upon her. She fought it, forcing herself to avoid those convenient fast-food places and cook her own meals. She also vowed to ride on her days off and to keep her home spotless. No way could she ever fall back into her life as a "pig."

On those rare days away from Brighton, Annie and Adonis would ride into the woods, more often than not only going as far as the clearing. The place had a mesmerizing effect on her and she'd sit on the marble bench for hours, either staring a nothing in particular or experiencing the vision of the cowboy, until the cold air drove her back home for a steaming cup of cocoa in front of the woodstove.

The cowboy...

Thoughts of him filled Annie's every waking moment and continued on into her slumber.

The dream...

That same ol' dream. But it had changed slightly since Annie had found Michael's Christmas gift to her. The cowboy would still appear, standing in front of her, and as always Annie felt lost and alone. Now he seemed to share her emotion and was asking for her help with his expressive, intense eyes. She sensed a profound sadness in him and that feeling would linger on into her waking hours, leaving her confused and melancholy.

If only Michael were there for her to talk to about it. Sure, Marti would listen and sympathize, but Michael would understand completely.

Kyle flipped off the lights in his office and bopped on down to his partner's. Hated to do it again, but he needed a little cash and Gabe had the checkbook. He hoped his buddy had just written a few checks and wasn't takin' a good look at the numbers. Regardless, he whistled the catchy music to Ash DeLaCroix's TV series, "The Sky's The Limit," and did a little two-step through Gabe's door. Flipped on the light and... *Oh Shit!*

"Dude! You... you're still here!"

"No, I'm a hologram, you dip-shit," Gabe snarled, angry at having his privacy interrupted.

"No need to get so pissy…"

"Can I help you with something, Kyle?"

"Uh… no…"

"And you came to my office, thinking I'd left, for what reason…?"

Kyle sure as hell had a guilty look on his face. Gabe glared.

"I uh… Chet! I got a new song for Chet…"

"Bull-fucking-shit. What the hell are you up to, *pal*?"

"Nothin', Gabe! And for that matter, why the hell are you sittin' here in the dark? Weren't you supposed to go visit Dee?"

"Hmm." Gabe muttered.

"Dude? Aw God… she's not worse, is she?"

"No better, no worse, and no more pleasant than she has been. Kyle, it's all I can do anymore to go see her."

"The meds still makin' her whacky?"

"If 'whacky' refers to angry, accusing, depressed, and all-out nasty, then yes. It breaks my heart to see that sweet, gentle woman turned into the psycho-bitch from hell. I… I just can't take it anymore, Kyle!"

"Aw come on… She's not that bad! I saw her last night and she was… well, a little snippy and couldn't remember much, but a psycho-bitch? Dude…"

"A personality trait that's apparently reserved for me only, Kyle. Christ, you wouldn't believe…" Gabe muttered, trailing off.

"Believe what?"

"Deirdre, and the things she… she says. Kyle, have you ever known her to swear?"

"As in like your favorite words?"

"Uh… pretty much, yes."

"Nope. She wouldn't say 'shit' if she had a mouthful of it."

"Not anymore. I didn't want anyone to know… Kyle, promise you'll keep this to yourself! Don't even tell Jen…"

"I promise, dude."

"I just can't hold this in any longer. God, if only Steve were here…"

"Still got me, buddy."

"Yeah, I do."

"And we're best friends, Gabe."

"That we are."

"So talk. I can be serious for a minute."

"I know… It's just so difficult to… to actually speak of it. But Kyle, she's so different! Any love I ever felt for her is rapidly slipping away…"

"No, Gabe! She's sick… she can't help it! And you can't blame her and stop loving…"

"That's not what I meant. I'll always love her, but… Christ, every goddamn time I walk into her room, alone anyway, she starts in. First it's the accusations that I'm sleeping around, and then she moves into the name-calling. Moves right on through the alphabet… asshole, bastard, cocksucker…"

"Oh man… Even the 'F' word?"

"Her favorite."

"I can't believe it. No way."

"Kyle, please. I thought you were here to listen."

"I am, buddy. Sorry."

Gabe nodded.

"And after her little litany of lewd language she gets personal."

"Personal?"

"Yes. And no, I won't repeat what she says but it certainly doesn't do much for my battered self-esteem or me. I guess what hurts the most is to hear her say how much she… she hates me. I know she doesn't mean it, but to hear it day after day… Kyle, I just can't take it anymore."

"Gabe, I am so sorry. I didn't realize… Hey, is there anything I can do for ya?"

"You just did, Kyle. Merely listening…"

"How about the kids? Want us to keep 'em tonight?"

"I already talked to Jenna. She picked them up from school and is taking them to see their mother. Thank God Deirdre is reasonably normal around her children…"

"Okay. You wanna go grab a beer then?"

"Not tonight, Kyle. I need a few more minutes of alone time and then… then I shall go see my… wife."

"This won't last forever, man," Kyle said, giving Gabe a pat on the shoulder.

"God, I hope not. Forever is a fucking long time. I'm just frightened as to the possible resolutions…" Gabe sighed. "Goodnight, Kyle."

"'Nite, Gabe."

"Shut off the light on your way out, would you?"

"Sure."

Kyle walked to the door and gave his friend a long, sad look, and then left the studio. Christ, he hadn't seen his buddy lookin' that bad in years! His hair was messier than usual and seemed a little grayer around the ears, he hadn't even bothered to shave that morning and a thick shadow of a beard darkened his tired face. His eyes were red-rimmed and desolate, and his whole demeanor was that of a dog beat one too many times by its beloved master.

Christ, poor guy…

Gabe sat staring at nothing in particular for a full ten minutes after Kyle left. He opened his desk drawer and reached in, hesitated, and then muttered, "What the fuck," as he pulled out a box of Marlboros. He didn't really want to start smoking again, but he'd bought two packs that morning on the way into work, it helped take the edge off his frustrations of late. He tapped one out and lit it, and sat back to not really enjoy his smoke.

Thank God Jen had the boys for a while. He'd called her earlier and said he'd be working late, and asked if she could watch them for a while. Of course she would, and told him to let her know when he'd be picking them up. Gabe hated to lie to her about working late, but he desperately needed to psyche himself up to visit Dee, and the twins would be far too distracting.

He lit a second cigarette off the butt of the first, putting off his visit just a little bit longer.

✦ ✦ ✦

"Annie-bananie!"

"Hi, Marti."

"Back for more, I see. What is this, night number five?"

"Six. I was supposed to have it off but they're desperate for warm bodies again."

"No kidding. Where to tonight?"

"Three west; Oncology."

"Ooh… ick!"

"Not my favorite either. Least favorite, actually."

"Are you taking an assignment?"

"Are you nuts? No, just 'helping hands'. I wouldn't know the first thing about what to do with those meds and crap."

"I know. Give me kids and give me babies, but keep those adults away from me!" Marti laughed.

"Rather funny though…"

"What's that?"

"The general public's perception of a nurse."

"Mmhmm. Just because we have an 'RN' after out name we should know it all."

"Show me one who does. Even the doctors are clueless sometimes. Two nights ago I was helping out on the cardiac ward. Some doctor jumped all over me because I wasn't familiar with a cardiac med. Like we use them in the NICU… And I was just over it enough to stand my ground and gave it right back to him. I asked him, since he was so omnipotent, what the caloric intake for a fifteen hundred gram preemie should be. Simple enough…"

"Oh God… You didn't!"

"I did. Boy, did that set him off! He screamed, 'how the hell should I know? I'm a cardiologist, not a neonatologist!' 'My point exactly,' I told him, and reminded him again that I was just helping out with the busy work and not a regular staff nurse on the floor."

"Oh man… And then what?"

"Jeez, you won't believe this…"

"Try me."

"He asked me out."

"No… Are you going to? Wait… who was it?"

"That creepy Lester Putnik."

"Oh God… Short, fat, bald, lethal-breath Lester the Molester?"

"That would be him."

"Then I'm assuming you turned him down."

"Actually, we're heading for a weekend in the Pocono's… Of course I turned him down! He's weird. Creepy, watch-your-children-around-him weird."

"No kidding. So… are ya lookin' forward to changing diapers tonight?" Marti laughed.

"Marti! That wasn't very nice… And no."

"And turning all those people every two hours… my back hurts just thinking about it!"

"I know. I'll consider it part of my exercise program. But I do feel bad for them, Marti. Can you imagine how awful it would be to not be able to do a thing for yourself? Can't roll over or re-position yourself, not capable of even using the toilet without help – assuming you could even walk to it, and then having to be cleaned up by a total stranger? Well, it would be just awful. And I really can't laugh about the diaper thing anymore… My mom was in that position just before she died."

"Annie… I'm so sorry."

"No, it's okay. Nurse humor… and usually I'm right in there with you when it comes to rude, crude, and socially unacceptable jokes, but not tonight. I don't know… I've felt so off-kilter lately. Like something is really, really wrong, but then again something big is right around the corner…"

"Look out! It's Lester!" Marti howled.

"I said big, not creepy! Dork. I don't know…" Annie sighed.

"Well, chica, I hope you have a good night. I'll be on Peds if you find time for lunch. Toodles."

"Bye, Marti."

They punched in and went their separate ways.

Annie was assigned to help out another nurse with a very full, very busy load of twelve patients. Annie would do vitals and all the physical work while the "regular" staffer did assessments and administered medication. They just might be able to manage between them.

Annie checked out her list of patients and went to the first room to introduce herself and get started for the night. Just as she was reaching to knock on the door, it flew open and two young boys burst from the room. A blonde woman looking totally frazzled was hot on their heels.

"James and Jeremy!" she yelled after them.

They stopped dead in their tracks.

"You come right back here and apologize to this lady. You darn near knocked her over! You're in a public place now and I expect you to use your manners in the way you were taught."

The boys glanced at each other and made their way over to Annie. They stood in front of her, and as one raised their heads to look at her. Two sets of bright blue eyes widened in surprise, or maybe even shock, and Annie wondered if she had grown a horn out of her forehead given their astonished expressions. *Jeez, she never had that effect on children before…*

The twins glanced at one another and then back at Annie.

"We're sorry, ma'am," they said in unison.

"And I apologize too," said the blonde. "My name is Jenna, and these two hellions are James and Jeremy. Their mother is in there." She nodded towards the room. "I'm keeping them for a while until their father gets off of work, which I hope is soon. I've got my own brood back home and they aren't as easily controlled as these two."

"I'm pleased to meet all of you," Annie smiled.

She held out her hand to Jenna, whose grip was firm and friendly. Annie liked her immediately. She then offered her hand to the boys, which they took at the same time.

A tingle ran up her arm with the contact.

Three pairs of eyes met. Bright blue ones held a mysterious gleam; emerald… déjà vu.

Annie felt very strange.

"Uh… so how old are you?" she asked, not knowing what else to say. "You have very nice manners for such young children.

"We're not *that* young," Jeremy said.

"We're this many," James informed her.

Each twin held up three fingers.

Annie wondered at that; they looked much older than three. She glanced at Jenna, who understood her confusion.

"They're six," Jen explained. "They share everything… even a brain it seems. For some strange reason they think that they should split their ages between them for something like that. I don't know… weird. But they're great kids. I've known them since the day they were born. My husband and their father are partners and best friends… actually we're all like family."

Annie nodded.

"Aunt Jenna?" Jeremy said, taking her hand.

"Yes, Jer?"

"May we get some ice cream now?" James finished, taking her other one.

"Sure. But remember, no running! This isn't a playground."

Jenna let go of her charges and looked at Annie.

"Take good care of their mom. She's a very special lady."

"I will. Are you coming back after your ice cream?" Annie asked.

"I don't know. It depends on their papa. I have to check in with him to see if he will be here in time to take them home or if they should just spend the night with us. Anyway, it was nice meeting you," Jenna smiled.

"Thank you, and likewise. Boys, enjoy your ice cream!" Annie said to the twins.

They smiled and winked at her.

"Bye, Annie..."

They skipped off down the hall.

She watched them go, her heart filling with joy at meeting such wonderful kids, even while it was breaking for them too. She knew their mother's prognosis was poor.

Annie was just about to enter the patient's room when the twins' last words came back to her. They'd called her "Annie." Sure it was her name, but she never told them. Had they read her nametag? She glanced down... Nope. It had flipped around like it was prone to do and all that was visible was the magnetic strip used for identification in the time clock.

Oh jeez... She shivered and went to meet their mother.

A frail, petite woman lay in the bed, eyes closed and in a deep sleep, so Annie took a moment to observe her.

Her head, hairless from chemotherapy was wrapped with a bright red scarf. Her pale complexion enhanced the dark crescents under her eyes, and her bones were prominent under her thin, dry skin. A milky bag of fluid hung on a pole next to the bed, and dripped into an IV line that disappeared under a dressing on the woman's chest as it delivered nutrients directly into her blood.

Annie moved closer to the bed while she checked her assignment sheet for the woman's name.

Deirdre Burnside. Ovarian cancer with mets to lung, bone, and brain. The poor soul didn't have much time left on the earth. And those poor little boys...

She saw that Deirdre had a paper clutched in her hand; the picture drawn in crayon. Annie looked closer. Two adults and two children were holding hands at the bottom, while two angels, a winged male and female, hovered in the background. The children had black hair and blue eyes – James and Jeremy? The father, she thought, shared the same coloring as the kids. The mother, she assumed once more, had green eyes and hair colored in alternating red, yellow, orange and brown crayon, which caused Annie to wonder what color Deirdre's hair had been.

The angels interested Annie most. The male was wearing blue pants – jeans perhaps, and what looked like cowboy boots. His shirt was gray and he wore a brown jacket. A halo circled his cowboy hat. The female angel was dressed in a long blue gown, and her blonde hair flowed from underneath a halo-adorned red scarf. Strange attire for angels... They both had big smiles on their faces as they gazed at the family below them. If the twins had drawn this picture, they certainly had artistic talent. The best most five year-olds could manage to do were stick figures.

Deirdre stirred.

"Jenna?" she murmured in a faint British accent.

"No, Mrs. Burnside, I'm Annie. I'm a nurse helping out your assigned nurse for the night. I came in to do your vitals and to see of you need anything."

"Call me Deirdre. Is Jenna still here?" she asked as she sat up and flipped on the light over the bed.

"She took the boys for ice cream. She wasn't sure if they'd be back or not. I can page them in the cafeteria; they just left."

Deirdre waved her hand in a theatrical way, dismissing the idea.

"No, that won't be necessary; I'll see them all soon enough. How about my husband? Has he been here yet? I can't seem to remember much anymore," she sighed, looking at the picture in her hand.

"I don't think so," Annie replied. "Jenna said she was going to call him…"

"Mmhmm," Deirdre interrupted. She held the picture out to Annie. "Did you see this?"

"I did. It's wonderful."

"It is, isn't it? The twins were working on it when I dozed off. James supplied the crayons and Jeremy did the drawing. He's quite talented," Deirdre smiled, studying the picture again.

"Very talented," Annie agreed.

"And he's sure I'm going to Heaven. Look, I'm an angel already," she chuckled as she tapped a delicate finger on the celestial blonde. Her smile faded and was replaced by a look of unfathomable sorrow. "Hmmm… and darned if that isn't Steven. He was never too far from a horse. I always said they'd be the death of him, and I was right. So tragically right… I'm sure he's an angel now… he was always such a saint on Earth."

A tear slipped from Deirdre's eye and slid down her cheek. It hung for a moment on her bony jaw, and then fell onto the paper with a plop.

Annie felt herself choking up too. Deirdre must have really loved this "Steven" person.

Deirdre wiped a hand over her eyes and glanced at Annie. "What I'm wondering is who this is," she said, flicking a finger at the woman with the wild hair. "Geoffrey's latest mistress, no doubt." She stared at the drawing, gave Annie a measuring look, and went back to the picture.

Annie was taken aback. What kind of a man would be so cruel as to flaunt a mistress in front of his sick wife? And his sons? How else would they know about it and include her in the family portrait?

"Well, Annie dear, let's get on with it."

Deirdre tossed the paper aside and rolled up her sleeve for the blood pressure cuff.

After Annie had seen the rest of her dozen patients she returned to Deirdre's room. For some reason she felt drawn to the poor woman. Perhaps it was only pity, but she couldn't seem to get her out of her mind.

Deirdre was awake, standing at the window and staring out at the city lights below.

"Deirdre, can I get you something? Annie asked quietly.

"No, I'm fine," she answered without turning around.

"All right then. Let me know if you need me for anything... anything at all." Annie turned to leave.

"Wait, please. Do you have a few minutes?" Deirdre asked with a catch in her voice. She turned away from the window and made her slow way back to her bed.

Annie hurried over to assist her, taking the IV pole in one hand and placing the other around Deirdre's overly thin waist. Good thing too, because the frail woman nearly collapsed before she was halfway back.

Annie tucked her in and chucked the idea of taking a much-needed break. Her heart went out to this woman and she could not deny such a simple request.

"Thank you," Deirdre gasped, fighting for breath after her exertion. "Would you stay for a moment?"

"Sure, Deirdre, I have plenty of time."

"Then have a seat, dear."

Annie pulled a chair closer to the bed and sat facing her.

"Geoffrey didn't come," Deirdre sighed, close to tears. "My loving husband couldn't find the time to visit me today."

"I'm sorry," Annie murmured, glancing at the table next to the bed where a big bouquet of blood-red roses in a beautiful cut-glass vase resided. Nestled in the blooms was a card with the message, "I miss you, Deirdre. Come back to me soon. Love, 'G'."

"G"... *Geoffrey?* Annie was sure the flowers hadn't been there a few hours ago when she was last in the room. It would have been difficult to miss something that spectacular.

"Maybe he came while you were sleeping and he didn't want to disturb you," she suggested.

"I doubt it. He doesn't want me anymore, Annie; his girlfriends told me. They were all in here today, wearing those horrid white coats. They stood around my bed and were talking about me as if I weren't even here! Dear God..."

As Deirdre rambled on, Annie knew the woman was confusing the "girlfriends" with the med students and residents making rounds. She was so addled by either her medication or the cancer in her brain that she probably had no idea what was real anymore.

Annie listened, which was the only thing she could do.

The patient dozed off and her nurse rose to leave.

"Mistakes!" Deirdre blurted out. "Mistakes... both of them."

"Mistakes?"

"Geoffrey and his brother. I loved them both and they left me... Mistakes..." she mumbled, and fell into a deep sleep.

Annie felt this would be an excellent time for a break; listening to Mrs. Burnside had unnerved her. Was what she said true or was it the meds talking? Her husband had never shown up as far as Annie knew, but she'd been extremely busy for several hours and could have easily missed anyone going into the room. Was he still working or with the mistress Deirdre had mentioned and the children had drawn?

She checked her watch - midnight, and the ward was finally quiet. The nurses and aides were congregated around the main desk gossiping, but Annie felt the need to be alone for a while. She barely knew anyone who staffed this floor and didn't feel comfortable intruding on their conversation, which seemed to revolve around a fellow staff member and an intern and the compromising situation that they had been found in. Annie let the ward clerk know that she was leaving for a while, and to page her if she was needed.

Annie passed the elevators and took the stairs the three flights down to the basement to where the cafeteria was located, and walked down the deserted hallway. She loved the hospital at night. It was so quiet, and suited her solitary nature. During the day hundreds of people filled the corridors, each performing his or her own task. Patients and visitors wandered the bright halls, usually lost as they stared at the "You Are Here" map and wondered just where the heck "here" was in the sprawling facility. But at night... at night the lights were turned down, the halls were empty, and the silence was almost overwhelming. The only sound was the soft hiss of air as it moved through the ventilation system.

She sat on a bench in an alcove in a hallway just outside the cafeteria, leaned against the wall and stretched her legs out, crossing her feet in front of her. She closed her eyes and enjoyed the peaceful moment. Time ceased to exist. Annie didn't think. She didn't feel. She just "was."

"Excuse me?" a most pleasant male voice cut into her non-reverie. "Ma'am?"

Ma'am? Good God, she wasn't that old yet was she? Annie turned her head towards the voice and opened her eyes, a bit embarrassed at having been caught with them closed. She hoped this person didn't think that she was sneaking a nap. And just what was he doing here anyway? This was a service hallway that was only used during the day, and then only by staff.

She looked up into intense blue eyes that would have been described as gorgeous if they hadn't been surrounded by a face so fatigued and full of distress.

"Can I help you, *sir*?"

Ooh... maybe she put a little too much emphasis on the word "sir." She didn't want to appear rude, but can't take it back now. Make nice with a sincere smile, which wasn't difficult. Despite his haggard appearance, he looked like someone who smiled a lot himself; the lines radiating from the corners of his splendid eyes were a dead giveaway.

Annie guessed that he was a few years older than she was. A touch of gray hair frosted his temples and the rest of his thick black hair sprouted wildly from his head as if he had absently run his fingers through it, and it was just long enough in the back to brush the collar of his worn leather jacket. One hand held a Stetson and the other was shoved casually into a front pocket of his jeans. A shadow of a beard was beginning to darken his handsome face.

She dared a quick look at the rest of him. Under the brown leather of his jacket he was wearing a tee shirt, and of course he had cowboy boots on - what else had she expected? *Hmm, smelled woodsy-spicy too.* She had an eerie sense of deja vu and rose from the bench. The man was quite a bit taller than her, standing a few inches over six feet. Jeez, he looked familiar… An image of him holding his arms out to her flashed through her mind. *Where did that come from?*

"Yes *ma'am*, I'm hoping that you can." The extra emphasis that he put on "ma'am" was softened by a lopsided grin.

Annie felt her knees go a little wobbly when the cowboy looked at her.

"Would you happen to have change for a fifty?"

"A fifty?" she choked out. *Oh yeah, right buddy. Welcome to the First National Bank of Annie.*

"I'm afraid that's all I have. I gave the smaller bills to my buddy at lunch today; I didn't realize this was all I had left."

"I'm sorry, I don't usually carry quite that much cash on me. I can loan you a couple of dollars though." *Knowing she would never see it again…*

"No, thank you. I was just going to get a cup of coffee. I was upstairs to see my wife but she's asleep. I thought I'd grab a cup and wait for her to wake up."

"How about if I buy you that cup of coffee," Annie offered.

"No, that isn't necessary," he said.

"I insist." *Was she actually flirting?* He was married with children for heaven's sake! No, she was just being nice. She kind of felt sorry for him; life didn't appear to have been very nice to him lately.

Annie turned down the hall, heading to the cafeteria.

"I was on my way down there anyway before that bench jumped out and held me prisoner. The cafeteria is closed, but the coffee is still available."

"I know. I spent some time my share of time here over the years. I had the misfortune to lose several wars and a substantial amount of money in those vile vending machines," he joked.

"Oh, things have changed since then. The machines are no longer vile; they are possessed by the demons from snack food hell. I've never seen one actually deliver the goods once they are in possession of one's hard earned money… just a whiff of brimstone and the sound of maniacal laughter for your trouble," she joked back.

He gave her a grin, loving her sense of humor.

"Hmm, that bad? Perhaps we should obtain some holy water and a cross from the chapel, just in case an exorcism is called for. I really need some caffeine!"

They entered the cafeteria and walked to the coffee station, where large sign over the coffee urn welcomed them to Brighton Memorial's cafe and wished them a pleasant dining experience. The sign went on to explain the new policy of complimentary coffee and tea during the hours in which the cafe was closed.

Annie poured two cups while the cowboy read the sign.

"You led me to believe that you were actually *buying* me a cup of coffee," he said, nodding towards the sign.

Annie handed him a steaming Styrofoam cup.

"So I'm cheap," she said as she poured creamer into her coffee. "Cheers!" Her drink was lifted in a mock toast.

Why was this guy so familiar? She felt as if she had known him forever. Even the faint smell of his cologne triggered memories. Not only memories, but also a sense of... knowing? Strange... But she had to get back to the ward.

"Well, I hope you have a nice visit with your wife," she told him.

"Now that would be a pleasant change," was the slightly bitter reply.

The look on Annie's face caused the cowboy to explain.

"I'm sorry, I didn't mean it like that. She has been very ill and some of her medication has... well, changed her personality. It's been very difficult."

Annie nodded in understanding but had nothing to say at this point. She had no idea of what the woman's condition was, and she didn't want to patronize him with some "feel good" phrase. She just smiled and told him goodbye, and then returned to the ward.

Gabe sat in a corner table at the back of the cafeteria and sipped his coffee. He wished he could have a cigarette as he stared at the No Smoking sign. He thought of the nurse who had let "buy" him the coffee, him knowing darn well it was free in the first place. He remembered another time in another hospital when he looked into green eyes, but of course it wasn't the same person. That nurse he had seen so long ago had been rather bitchy and not nearly as attractive as... Christ, Gabe hadn't even gotten her name.He would never forget her though... she was rather refreshing - didn't even recognize him! If she did, she did a wonderful job of hiding the fact.

He took another swallow of coffee. God, he was so tired and nothing had gone right today. Three much needed contracts were cancelled, two of his musicians had gotten into a knock-down, drag-out fight and had damaged some expensive equipment, and Gabe still hadn't come up with any new material. He was just about ready to chuck the whole goddamn business and go back to Montana.

The mess with Deirdre... Thank God she had been asleep when he dropped off his guilt-induced gift of roses. She probably would have accused him of hiding bees in the blooms or some ridiculous shit like that. Yet she was recovering physically, although still very weak. Her nurse that evening told Gabe that she was to be discharged quite soon. Yep, now he'd have to hire a home health care nurse again. Deirdre was still sleeping, didn't seem about to wake up for a while, so he went in search of coffee.

Gabe thought back to his first glimpse of the green-eyed nurse all relaxed on that bench. Christ, what he wouldn't have given to join her. Just close his eyes and let his troubles float away… He wanted to take her hand, and together they could share the simple pleasure of a quiet moment away from their own private hell. But, such things were not to be. He could have at least looked at her ID badge, gotten a name to go with those eyes.

Those eyes... Aw God, he knew those eyes... and that hair too! He'd been seeing them in his dreams forever! She was the one!

"Annie!" he called out as he jumped up from the table - spilling his precious coffee in the process, and ran into the hall. But she was gone. Just like that. Been waiting for her his entire life, and just that quick, gone. He swore, and then slowly trudged up the three flights of stairs to his wife's room.

Swore again as he reached for the door to the hall, only to turn and trot back down to the main floor. Hell, she wouldn't miss him for just one night. And he did drop off the flowers to prove he'd been there in case she got bitchy about it… Besides, autumn hair and green eyes were filling his thoughts.

He needed some air and went for a very long drive.

Annie returned to the floor where a message was waiting for her that the patient in room 320 wanted to talk to her.

Deirdre.

Annie went right in.

"Annie, look," Deirdre said, pointing to the bouquet of roses. "He was here after all and I missed him. Geoffrey is such a sweet man... He knows how I love these." She pulled a bud from the bouquet. "Red roses. Steven always preferred red roses and yet Geoffrey prefers white ones."

Annie was only half listening; her mind was on that cowboy drinking coffee downstairs. Why had she run off so soon? Jeez, and why did she feel it was the stupidest thing she'd ever done, leaving before she learned his name? *Stop thinking about him, he's off limits! Listen to Deirdre... What is she saying about roses?*

She turned her attention back to the woman. Deirdre seemed to be coherent at times, and then would talk to a Steven as if he were in the room. Ah, the magic of modern pharmaceuticals… *Wonder how much morphine she was on?* She listened as Deirdre chatted about her life in the theater, her children, and her friend Jenna. She then asked Annie about herself; her hobbies, her likes, dislike, did she have a husband? No? Boyfriend? Annie answered her questions until the medication took over again, and Deirdre slept.

✦ ✦ ✦

Annie arrived at work an hour early to attend a staff meeting, but the supervisor of the department had cancelled at the last minute due to illness so Annie and the other nurses who had come in early had some time to kill. But what to do? Maybe wander down to the cafeteria and write. Ever since the night when she had worked on the Oncology floor, her mind had been working overtime. She had written three poems already, and she felt another one coming on. Actually, they were more like lyrics to a song. She was very un-musical, so any melody to the song was forever trapped in her head but she could get words on paper! Michael's birthday was coming up, and she had the beginnings of a birthday poem that needed to be written immediately.

Michael...

Annie shut her eyes for a moment in yet another vain effort to conjure up his face in her mind. She could still imagine his serene smile, and enjoy the peace that accompanied his memory, but that was it.

She sat at her favorite table in the back corner of the cafeteria and was so engrossed in her writing that she didn't see her visitors until they spoke. In unison.

"It's her!" they whispered.

She looked up. James and Jeremy stood on the other side of the table.

"Hi guys, how are you doing today?" She glanced around for Jenna, or some other adult who might be looking for missing twins, but no luck. *Better keep them with her for a while then...* "Have a seat."

The boys exchanged glances, smiled, and sat across from Annie.

"What'cha writin'?"

"Hmm? Oh, a poem. It's a birthday present for a friend of mine."

She put her pen down, again scanning the cafeteria for a responsible adult.

"Papa's having a birthday too."

"Mama said she would make a cake, and Jenna and Kyle and Sarah, Jack, Em, Will and Hanna will be there."

"Chet will sing Happy Birthday."

"And everyone gets presents."

"Except Chet."

"He can be naughty sometimes and Papa laughs at him."

The boys nodded in agreement, having alternated the sentences in their conversation.

"Um, is Jenna here? Or maybe Kyle or Chet?" Annie asked.

The boys found this question hysterically funny although she had no idea why.

"Chet is a bird!" they said as one.

"My mistake!" Annie laughed. "Well then how about Jenna, or is she a pony in disguise?"

She looked around again, becoming concerned.

Jenna appeared in the doorway, frantically looking for her charges. It took her several seconds to locate the twins, and then relief - followed by anger, washed over her face. She squared her shoulders and walked up to the trio.

"Here's Jenna!" The boys chirped, stating the obvious.

"Hello again."

Annie smiled at the other woman, hoping she wouldn't be too hard on the kids.

Jenna returned Annie's warm smile, and then replaced it with a look of anger as she addressed the twins.

"Excuse me, gentleman. What were you thinking, running off like that?"

The boys gave her a benign look. Why was she so upset? They were fine! They only came down here to see Annie... but better just apologize; Jenna wouldn't understand.

"No harm done, I think," Annie commented.

"We're sorry," said the twins.

"Well, don't let it happen again," replied Jenna.

"So, how is Deirdre?" Annie asked.

"Actually, I'm glad we ran into each other. She has been asking for you. She said she had a message for you... from Michael? She said you would know him," Jenna told her.

Annie glanced down at the poem she had just written and the hair stood up on the back of her neck. Deirdre knew Michael? Okay, so that's possible. Then why did she have this twilight zone feeling?

"I've got a few minutes before my shift starts. Is she able to have visitors now?" Annie asked.

"Sure. She's much better than she was the other night. She might even be discharged in a few days; just in time for her husband's birthday."

"Will Chet be singing?"

Jenna looked surprised, and then began to laugh.

"God forbid! That bird is a terror! My husband, Kyle, has taken it upon himself to teach it every naughty little ditty he could think of. The bird is *not* fit for polite company. He hides in the boss' office most of the time," Jenna laughed again.

Annie was curious about the details, but time was running short. She glanced at her watch.

"I'd better run. Will you be coming up to Deirdre's room with me?"

"No, going home. It was nice seeing you again," Jen said, holding her hands out to the twins.

"Likewise. Bye, boys."

They waved.

She knocked on Deirdre's door.

"Come in!"

Annie opened the door and poked her head in.

"It's Annie."

"I know; the boys said you would be here. Come in and sit down," Deirdre said.

It took Annie a moment to realize what Deirdre had just said. *The boys knew she was coming? How?* The day was getting stranger by the minute.

"I hear that you're feeling better. Will you be going home soon?"

"Yes, in two days. It seems I've recovered much quicker than expected, although I'm afraid it won't last very long. But we cannot always have our own way," Deirdre said with a melancholy smile. "How have you been, dear?"

"Fine, keeping busy."

"Doing a little writing, I see?"

"What?"

Annie saw that Deirdre was looking at her notebook, still open to the new composition.

"Oh, yes. Just a collection of words that may or may not make sense, but more often than not will rhyme." *Where on God's green earth did that come from?*

"My husband is a writer. He has other talents as well, but the writing is the most important to him... next to his music that is. You haven't met him yet, have you?"

"I'm afraid not." She was in no hurry to meet the man who may have stood up his wife for a girlfriend.

"May I?" Deirdre asked, indicating that she would like to read Annie's work.

"I don't know. I'm really not very good, and it's..."

"Oh bother," Deirdre smiled. "I'm sure it is wonderful. Please, let me?"

Annie felt very awkward. Of all the people to see her first attempts at writing... the wife of a real writer for heaven's sake! She hesitated, and then held the notebook out to Deirdre. She could have sworn her hand was being pushed forward.

Deirdre quickly glanced at the poem, then read aloud,

"I want you to know what you've done for me. You've shown me how wonderful my life can be. Your words, you music, your kind gentle way. You live life to the fullest every day.

To be an inspiration to those who don't stand tall. To never overlook the insignificant or small. To share a word, a laugh, a smile with those you see each day. To be happy and fulfilled; to be able to play

To always see the wonder of the world in which you live. To share the warmth of family and the love in which they give. Every morning a bright sun, a sky forever blue, clouds with silver linings... My birthday wish for you."

Deirdre looked up at Annie. "He does make one feel that way, doesn't he?"

Annie was totally confused. "Who?"

"Why, Michael, of course! That is who you wrote it for, am I right?"

"Yes, but how...?"

"He told me that soon, very soon, the circle would begin to complete itself. Difficult days ahead for all, but he wants you to remember that you may give in, but don't ever give up."

Annie's knees were so weak by this time that she had to sit down before she fell down. The day was now officially beyond strange.

"How do you..."

"Know Michael?" Deirdre finished Annie's question. "I've known him for quite a while, although he went by another name then."

"Have you seen him recently? Is he in town? How does..."

"Oh no, Annie. I haven't actually seen him; he came to me in a dream."

Annie thought it was the meds talking again. But no... how did Deirdre know that she knew Michael in the first place? She had told very few people about him.

"Annie dear, some things just shouldn't be questioned. You are here in this room for a reason. My life will be ending soon for a reason. I'm not sure what that reason is, but I know it is inevitable, and I've come to accept it."

Annie began to protest; Deirdre raised a hand to quiet her.

"The circle will be completed, the course is set. Follow your heart. Michael will be there when you need him."

"What circle? What are you talking about?" Annie didn't know if she was scared, annoyed, or both. This woman was talking like a third-rate psychic.

"That's all I can tell you. I don't even understand it all myself, but the information came from a most reliable source," Deirdre smiled.

She seemed to be looking at someone Annie couldn't see.

James, Jeremy, and Jenna could be heard out in the hall. Annie thought that they had gone home... Probably forgot something. She retrieved her notebook from Deirdre, who was somewhat reluctant to give it back.

"I should be going, my shift starts soon," Annie said, standing. "Thank you for the, uh, message."

She didn't know what else she could possibly say.

"I'm glad you stopped by. I wish we could have had more time together to chat, though," Deirdre said, holding her arms out to her sons who had entered the room.

Annie was thinking that they had chatted a bit too much; the whole episode was a bit unnerving. She nodded and smiled at Jenna as she left the room.

As Annie walked down the hall towards the Children's Hospital wing, she heard footsteps rapidly approaching.

"Annie, wait up!"

She turned to see Jenna trotting towards her and slowed so that the other woman could catch up. They began walking together.

"Did Deirdre seem strange to you today?" Jenna questioned.

Annie thought that she had never seen her not strange. *She would surely go to nurse hell for thinking such things...* but replied, "I've only met her twice, and she's been on narcotics both times. I couldn't possibly give you an answer."

"Could the medication be causing her to have hallucinations?"

"Not usually, but then everyone reacts differently."

"Hmm. I don't know what's going on. She was really out of it last week, but for the last couple of days she was fine. Almost back to her old, sweet self. Then this morning, she started talking about Steven - that was her fiancé before he died. She said he had visited her. Gabe had just left, so I thought she got the two of them confused. 'No,' she said, 'it was Steven.' She was glad to see him so that she could apologize."

"Gabe?"

"Her husband. Oh gosh, I'm sorry. You probably have no idea what I am talking about," Jenna said.

"No, I have an idea. Deirdre was talking quite a bit the other night, but she called her husband 'Geoffrey'."

"That's him. Everyone but Deirdre calls him Gabe."

Annie still looked a bit confused.

"Gabe is for his real name. Geoffrey Alan Benjamin Evans… He used to joke that his mother found his name in the 'Acronyms-R-Us Book of Baby Names'. His brother is the same."

"I see," said Annie, but really couldn't see what any of this had to do with her.

"Well, it was just strange, not at all like Deirdre." Jenna changed the subject. "Can you make it to Gabe's birthday party? It's Friday night. Nothing big, just family and a few friends."

Annie was taken aback by the invitation. She hardly knew these people and had never even met this Gabe person.

"Thanks, but I'm not sure if I can make it." This was too much... but she had to ask even if it seemed rude though. She stopped and faced Jenna.

"Jenna, I hope you don't take this the wrong way, but why did you invite me? I barely know you - or Deirdre, and I've never even met, uh, Gabe.

"Well, to hear Deirdre and the boys talk, you sound like a member of the family. The twins go on about you non-stop." Jenna gave a short laugh. "You should hear some of the things they come up with. They were supposed to be napping yesterday, and I peeked in their room to check on them. They were talking about Goose-Mother and all of her kids. She had goats, cats, a dog, chickens, and some other stuff. And they all live on McDonald's farm. I can't remember it all. Well, they saw me so I went in. I tried to explain that it was Mother Goose. 'No,' they said, 'it was Goose-Mother. She has red-yellow hair and takes care of sick kids.' Again I tried to explain that's not how the storybook goes. They looked at me like I was a complete idiot and said, 'Not a book! Annie!' I thought it was cute."

Far from cute. The day had passed strange, drove by weird, took a left turn at bizarre and was parked in Stephen King's driveway. Thank God Annie had finally reached the pediatric wing.

"I've got to get to work. I don't want to be late."

"Sure. Didn't mean to talk your ear off. Hey, if you can make it Friday everyone would love to see you there."

"Thanks." *But not bloody likely!*

Annie went through the double doors.

Straight into the locker room.

Right into the bathroom.

She felt ill and splashed cold water on her face, then tried to shift into her professional nurse mode. She almost succeeded.

"Gabe buddy! Miss me?"

"Only about as much as finding that the milk I've just poured on my cereal has turned to cottage cheese. You're in early, Kyle, what's the occasion?"

"You're birthday, dude! God… thirty-six years old. 'Bout ready for your social security to kick in, huh."

"Fuck you, and you're only a year and two weeks younger, pal, so I'll be seeing you in line to be cashing that check."

"I got you a present."

Gabe glanced at Chet, who was mumbling obscenities under his birdy breath.

"I do hope it's one of a non-verbal type, Kyle," Gabe sighed, turning back around.

"Nope. It don't talk. Makes noise though."

"Christ, a customized whoopee cushion?"

"Nope. Guess again. But that's an idea for next year…"

"Spare me. Makes noise… doesn't talk… Hell, I don't know!"

"Want it now or at the party tonight?"

"Might not be a party, Kyle. The weather is turning to shit and I seriously doubt that anyone will want to venture out just to see me get older."

"I'll be there…"

"Laughing and pointing, no doubt."

"Probably. Want your present now?"

"You brought it in?"

"Well duh… can't very well give it to ya if I ain't got it."

"…Logic according to Kyle. Alrighty then, give it to me. I could use a little cheering up," Gabe sighed. *Lord, what an understatement…* Ever since his close encounter of the nurse kind he'd been unable to think of nothing else, and it was driving him fucking nuts.

"Cool! Be right back!"

Gabe drummed his fingers on his desk and wondered just what the hell his goofy buddy had seen fit to purchase for him *this* year. They were never ordinary gifts, and sometimes even bordered on the bizarre.

"Here we go," Kyle said, dropping a box wrapped in the Sunday color comics onto the desk.

"Nice paper, Kyle."

"Read it later. Goddamn funny funnies!"

"I just might. Um… is this safe to open or should I have the bomb squad on standby?"

"Safe. I found it in one of those weird little shops in Chicago. You know… a lot of junk inside and a hand-painted sign outside?"

"Indeed! I'm flattered that you shop for my gifts in such an upscale setting, Kyle," Gabe grinned. And very thankful his buddy didn't shop in those expensive stores with over-priced crap Gabe didn't really want or need. "Well, here goes!"

He carefully pulled off the "Bugs Bunny" Band-Aids holding the paper closed while he raised an eyebrow at Kyle's choice of tape.

"Couldn't find anything else, Gabe, and Jack brought me those. Hell, they work good enough!"

"That they do." Gabe laid the paper aside and slowly… very slowly lifted the lid on the box. He got a sick thrill out of making Kyle crazy with anticipation.

"C'mon, man! Open it!"

Gabe grinned and did so.

"Wind chimes?"

"Cool, huh?"

"Different…"

"Very different. They were hangin' outside the shop and the breeze blew through… Dude, they play kinda like a song! Not just those notes, but a song!"

"Impossible, Kyle. They bump each other at random and it cannot be predicted which sounds will be produced when. So there."

"It pays a song, dude…"

"We shall see…"

"Right now? You gonna take 'em outside? Windy enough…"

"Nearly gale force at times, and would most likely ruin your gift, Kyle. No… I think I'll wait until spring and then hang this outside the back window of my den. I always have that window open in the summer…"

"But Gabe, you gotta hear the song! You fuckin' wrote it, man!"

"Oh for God's sake… Now that *is* impossible!"

"That you wrote a song? Dude, you wrote hundreds of 'em!"

"No, that it would play one of mine."

"Does though."

"Does not."

"Does too."

"Does not."

Kyle glared and pulled the chimes from the box. He hung them from his raised arm and pulled a folder off the desk, and waved it in the air, creating an impressive breeze. High, tinkling notes filled the room and Gabe's jaw dropped in awe.

"Well son of a bitch…" he muttered, totally stunned. ""The Dream"…"

"See? Told ya…" Kyle grinned.

"The Dream"… Gabe had written that song when he was only eighteen years old, and then recorded it after he and Kyle got the band together. It was the title cut on their second album, and made them very rich men. And now Gabe had fuckin' wind chimes that played the first few bars of the chorus!

"Kyle, were there more of these in that store?"

"Nope, that was the only one. I asked the dude in there about it and he had no clue. Said it came in with a box of assorted junk and he just hung it up 'cuz he like the tune."

"Huh. Well, I can't say that I've ever received a more unique gift, Kyle! Thank you."

"You like it then?"

"Of course I do! And I'll hang them in my office until spring, buddy."

"No breeze in there."

"Will be if you visit. You're so full of hot air…"

"Gabe?"

"Yes, Kyle?"

"Fuck you. And happy birthday, man…"

"Thanks, Kyle. Now get the hell out… No, wait. Let's shut down early today, weather related of course, and head for my house. If you plan on partying with us anyway, you might as well get there early before the snow closes the roads and you're stuck at your place. Call Jenna…"

"Cool!" Kyle grinned, and ran off to his office.

Gabe followed him out and went through the studio, telling his staff to pack up and go home. He'd see them all again on Monday… at least the ones that didn't make it to his party that evening.

He went back to his office and sat at his desk, still just a little depressed and lonely. She had invaded his thoughts once again, dancing through his mind to the tune of "The Dream." He'd written that song about her so many years ago…

Michael sat on the marble bench and looked at the ice-covered lake below the hill. The snow was beginning to fall a bit heavier now; it looked as if it might turn into a full-blown blizzard before long. He heard the sound of muffled hoof beats coming from the woods, must be Annie, and then he melted into the shadows of the pine forest.

Annie rode into the clearing, and as always Dog was at her side. She had taken advantage of a break in the weather to come up here and leave Michael his birthday present. She wasn't sure if he would get it, but she had to try. And just why she felt compelled to leave it there and not keep it at the cabin, she had no clue.

Darn, it was starting to snow again. She would have to hurry; it looked like it might be bad this time.

She halted her horse at the edge of the clearing as if she didn't dare enter it. She took a deep breath and dismounted. Again, she hesitated, and then pulled a small package from the saddlebag. Another deep breath... and walked slowly to the marble bench and placed the package in the center of it. The accumulated snow all but covered the present as she set it down.

Annie took a backwards step and scanned the woods, looking for... she wasn't sure. Was he here? Had he been here? Would he ever come back? She turned to look at the frozen lake. Dark clouds were piling high above the trees on the opposite shore, and the snow falling now was nothing compared to what was heading her way.

A gust of wind blew through the clearing creating a small blizzard around her. Ice crystals caught in a small sliver of sunlight shot sparks of color through the air, and once again the clearing had been transformed into something magical.

"Michael, are you here?" Annie whispered.

No answer.

"I brought you something. Nothing much, but it comes from... I... we miss you Michael, Eric and I. He doesn't ask about you, but I can tell that he is thinking about you. He... he hasn't been doing very well lately. I was hoping that maybe you could call him, or even visit him. He's back in the hospital again. Well anyway, happy birthday."

She looked around her one last time. The wind had died down, the clouds had totally obscured the sun, and it was becoming very dark. The snow was beginning to dangerously decrease visibility. Annie mounted Adonis and they turned into the woods, rapidly disappearing into the snow-covered trees.

Michael watched them leave from where he had been standing behind a large blue spruce, and it was all he could do not to go to Annie and take her in his arms. He missed her just as much as she missed him.He left his hiding place and walked to the bench to where the package was almost entirely covered by the heavily falling snow. He picked it up and shook the white flakes from the blue wrapping paper, and then pulled at the darker blue cord which secured his present.

Inside was a box containing a handmade card. On the front was a picture of the lake as seen from the clearing; Eric had drawn it. Inside the card was Annie's poem. There was a second item in the package - a picture of Eric and McDonald standing knee-deep in the lake, and the smile on the boy's face told more than any words could ever say. A frame decorated with macaroni shells spray painted gold surrounded the photo. Michael put the card and picture back in their blue wrapping and re-tied the cord around the package. He then placed the present in the interior pocket of his leather jacket, right over his heart. He would treasure this modest gift forever.

He felt a hot puff of air on the back of his neck.

Another puff of hot air, followed by stiff hairs that poked him. He reached behind him and felt the velvety muzzle of the horse. It nudged Michael's empty hand, disappointed that it held no treat. The prehensile lips of the animal moved to nibble the man's ear, shoving the man's hat into his eyes.

"Whiz, how many times have I told you not to do that?" he chuckled as he repositioned the battered Stetson. With a last look at the trail Annie had taken, he mounted the great black horse and vanished.

Annie, Adonis, and Dog raced through the woods, trying desperately to get home while they still could see where they were going. She trusted her animals to find the way, regardless of the conditions, but there was always that fear...

Wanda whinnied when she sensed the trio's return.

Adonis answered back. He could no longer see landmarks, trees, or the damn trail for that matter... *Guide him in Wanda.* He called to her again, she answered. It took the horse several minutes to travel the last quarter mile to the barn, but he finally made it. Annie patted him on the neck and told him what a wonderful animal he was. He already knew that, but accepted the complement gracefully. Dog barked him a thank-you too, even though they both knew Dog could have easily found the way home himself. Give and take.

Adonis sighed deeply as Annie brushed his sweaty coat. He always itched so after a hard ride, and the brush felt wonderful. He was given his water and an extra portion of sweetened grain before she left for the cabin.

Annie struggled through the knee-deep snow to the safety of the cabin. McDonald honked a hello from his little house on the porch, but she only gave him a quick wave as she opened the door and then fell inside the warm comfort of her own house. She made it. For a while, she wasn't quite sure that she would.

The storm was increasing in its intensity. The wind had picked up and blew against the cabin, rocking it on its foundations. Annie went to the woodstove and stoked the fire, threw a few more logs in the firebox, and shut the door. After making herself a cup of tea she went to the porch window to watch the snow fall. It wasn't actually falling; it was more like blowing straight across. Even if she had wanted to attend Gabe's party, it would have been impossible to get there.

Gabe's birthday party was a roaring success despite the blizzard deterring all of the other guests from coming except the Davidson's, who practically lived at the Evans' anyway. Kyle, Jenna and their brood were enough to keep everyone entertained. The children raced through the halls playing hide and seek; their energy seemed limitless. Gabe glanced at Deirdre, afraid the noise and activity would be too much for her. Hell, she'd only been home from the hospital for one day now... but he needn't have worried.

Deirdre smiled as she watched her children - and Jenna's, play. So uninhibited and carefree... Every few minutes James and Jeremy would go to the window, Deirdre was sure they were looking for Annie. She had hoped that the nurse would attend tonight's festivities but doubted that she would. Jenna had told Deirdre that Annie was acting very strange after their conversation about Michael. She wasn't surprised; if Annie had known the full story, God only knows how she would have reacted.

She turned her attention to Geoffrey and gave him a loving smile. He was such a good man. He had taken her in when she was desperate and he had nursed her through a difficult pregnancy. He had held up the remodeling of the rest of his house and concentrated on finishing off two of the bedrooms - a nursery, and a beautiful room for Deirdre, never asking for a thing in return. And if that weren't enough, he offered to marry her to give her sons the stability of a two-parent home, and the name that was their birthright.

She hesitated to say yes to his proposal at first, she missed Steven terribly and couldn't imagine being with another man, not that the issue would come very soon. Lord, she would soon be as big as a house! Geoffrey understood her feelings and let her know he would place no demands on her as far as the more intimate side of marriage went. They had grown to love and respect each other over the last few months and that was enough.

Impending motherhood had softened Deirdre. She abandoned her arrogance and pettiness, and became the woman Steven had first seen: soft, vulnerable, and beautiful. Her selfish heart had transformed into one of extreme generosity, and was as happy and content as she could possibly be without her Steven.

She threw her energy into raising her children. She did a little acting in Community Theater and sat on committees for several charities, and whatever free time Deirdre had left was spent improving the gardens surrounding their house. One day Geoffrey found her on her knees in the middle of a flowerbed, wearing an old tee shirt of his, cut-off jeans and a red scarf tied around her head to keep her long blonde hair in check. He told her how she reminded him of a friend of his grandmother's. She too, had loved to garden, and had the most beautiful flowers Gabe had ever seen. Even as a young boy he had been impressed, especially by the white roses she had grown.

Deirdre had heard about that woman from Steven. He had told her how he, his brother, and grandmother would visit the lady. Gabe and Steve would play hide and seek in the maze of trees and bushes behind the gardens while the two ladies had tea. There was some romantic little story that involved roses and a table or something, but Deirdre couldn't recall exactly what it was. She regretted not listening closer to him as he told the tale.

Two pair of bright blue eyes brought her back to the present. James and Jeremy stood before her, a solemn look on their little faces.

"Goose-Mother isn't coming, is she?" the twins asked.

"I'm afraid not babies," replied Deirdre. "I think the snow may be too deep for her to go out in, and that's why our other guests couldn't make it."

"No no," James shook his head. "Her horse could bring her."

Jeremy nodded in agreement. "He can go through anything. They took Michael a present today."

"Way up the hill," James added.

Such imaginations they have... And what big ears! Earlier in the evening, Kyle had made a birthday toast to Geoffrey and included a toast to Steven. A moment of silence followed. True silence. Even the children were quiet. Deirdre realized that they had been listening when a little while later the James and Jeremy came into the room and asked her about Steven. Deirdre gave Geoffrey a questioning look. He smiled sadly and nodded, indicating that she could tell the boys whatever she felt they needed to know. She had told them about him before, but now the story was shared with the Davidson's too.

Deirdre told the tale of the hero cowboy who had saved her life that day at the rodeo. She talked of his great, black horse, and how the two of them would rope cattle and wrestle steers, and how he would ride the bucking horses. She choked back tears as she told the children how Steven had died a hero, saving many valuable horses from a fire.

"And now he's an angel!" said the twins.

"Yes," Deirdre said quietly, "He always was."

"And he guards Papa and you and us and the Goose-Mother," added the twins.

Gabe raised an eyebrow at this last statement.

"Who is 'Goose-Mother'? Isn't it Mother Goose, or am I not remembering my nursery rhymes correctly?"

"The Goose-Mother," Deirdre explained, "is a nurse I met while I was in the hospital. The boys took quite a liking to her."

"Does she have a long orange nose and white feathers?" teased Gabe.

"No!" shouted the twins, laughing.

"Must be webbed toes..." mused Gabe.

"No!" giggled the boys.

"Well then, how did she come by such an interesting title?" Gabe asked them.

The twins shared one of their famous conspiratory glances. "She had an egg and a goose was inside and now she's the mommy!"

"*An* egg," corrected Deirdre.

"Hmm... And all I've ever found in an egg is breakfast! What a truly extraordinary woman she must be!"

The boys laughed. Papa was silly. He knew baby birds came from eggs. Only the eggs from the market were breakfast eggs.

Jenna joined the conversation. "Actually, she is very nice, but rather quiet. She's great with kids..."

Deirdre agreed, and the topic of conversation changed. "Let's go blow out the candles and cut the cake," she said with a mysterious smile.

Chapter Twenty-Five

The Monday following the birthday party, Gabe sat in his office, idly picking at his guitar. He'd dreamed of his brother the night before. The details of the dream were fuzzy, but the feeling he'd had during the dream followed him into his waking hours... just like they always had. He remembered a lake and a hill. He had been exhausted from climbing the hill, but once he reached the top he knew that he would do it over and over again, as the reward at the top of the hill was worth any sacrifice he would ever have to endure. It was odd, but now that he was awake he couldn't remember what that incredible reward was. But he'd sure as hell climb that hill for it!

Then the dream changed. He was in a white room, or so he thought. Everything around him was white. He couldn't tell where the floor turned into wall, or where wall turned into ceiling, but it was definitely a room. Hoof beats thundered overhead, and then echoed all around him.

Steve was there. He held his hand out to Gabe, palm up. He looked at Steve's hand and then down at his own, which was holding a red rose. He handed the rose to his brother. Steve smiled, and then offered him his other hand. Gabe looked down to see that Steve was handing him a white rose. He reached out to take it, and as Gabe touched the flower a tingle raced through his fingers and up his arm.

He could hear music. His music. "The Dream"…

A feeling of total contentment settled over Gabe.

He felt complete.

His long wait was over.

As Gabe sat in his office, that wonderful feeling stayed with him. He couldn't understand why he felt so good; his world was beginning to fall apart around him. His brother was dead, his wife was very ill, and if that wasn't enough, his career was just about over. He hadn't written anything for years. Nothing. Not a chapter, phrase or lyric. Not a word. At first he blamed his lack of creativity on concern for Deirdre, but he realized that wasn't the case. There was just nothing left in him. He felt empty... dead. Until this morning anyway - now he felt great! Ideas for songs were fighting for position in his mind.

His fingers picked out a new tune on his guitar and he began to hum the melody. Better call Kyle in so that they could work on it together. No, maybe later. He wasn't ready for his euphoric feeling to go away just yet and the distraction of Kyle's boisterous personality would surely put an end to it.

Gabe set the guitar on the floor next to his chair. He kicked back and put his feet up on his desk and folded his arms across his chest, contemplating the toes of his well-worn boots for a moment. His feeling of wellbeing was beginning to fade so he closed his eyes, hoping to recapture it before it was lost to him entirely. He heard the music from his dream... slow and sad. He could almost feel his arms wrapped around a feminine form. Green eyes and her hair the color of autumn leaves, all russet and gold and... He bent his head to kiss the soft lips...

The door of his office burst open, shocking him from his daydream. He opened his eyes just in time to avoid the paper airplane flung at him by good ol' Kyle, and caught the aircraft just before it cleared his left shoulder. He glared at his partner who stood in the doorway, hands in pockets and whistling innocently. Gabe shot the paper jet back at him, catching him directly in the center of the forehead.

"Hey, what did I ever do to you?" Kyle said, rubbing the red mark caused by the impact. "You're pissed cuz I caught you sleepin'?"

"I felt the need to test my aeronautical skills vicariously through that pathetic little piece of origami," Gabe replied.

"In English?" Kyle grumbled.

"I was not sleeping. Just enjoying a moment of creativity."

"If you say so. Well, I don't know what the hell you were creatin', but from the look on your face you were..."

"So, Kyle, what's on your mind other than an accumulation of dust do to inactivity?"

"Yeah, whatever." Kyle picked up the fallen plane and once again took aim at Gabe. Thinking better of that idea, he walked to his buddy's desk and handed him the paper. "Here, read this."

"What is it?" Gabe asked, opening the paper.

"Found it on the floor outside of your office. The handwriting looked familiar but I can't place it. Didn't know if it might be important. Cute little poem. Corny, but okay."

Gabe stared at the paper in his hand, which was beginning to tremble. Oh, he recognized the handwriting all right. He had hundreds of letters with the exact same script, the last one being an invitation to a wedding that never took place. He could not focus on the words before him.

Kyle snapped his fingers under Gabe's nose.

"Yo, buddy! You all right? Gabe?" He was becoming concerned; Gabe was almost as pale as the paper he was holding.

"Where did you get this?" he asked in a hoarse, harsh whisper.

"Uh, I told you. It was on the floor outside of your office."

Kyle went to Gabe's side and looked at the paper. "What is it? You look like you've seen a ghost."

Slowly, Gabe raised his eyes to meet Kyle's. He raised the crinkled paper. "That would explain this."

Kyle was confused. He took the paper from Gabe and read each word aloud, beginning with the date at the top of the page. "January 16, 1996. I want you to know what you've done for me. You've shown me how special my life can be..."

When Kyle had finished, he looked at Gabe, "Yeah, so?" He looked back at the paper and then he too paled with the realization of what he was seeing. This was Steve's handwriting. With last Friday's date written on the top.

"Good God almighty!" he exclaimed, dropping the poem on the desk as if it were going to bite him. "Is this someone's idea of a joke? Sick bastards!"

"I don't know," whispered Gabe.

His mind whirled with images of green eyes, autumn hair, and her soft body in his arms. There was a large black horse carrying a red rose in its teeth and a white rose on its saddle. A lake, a white marble table gleaming under a full moon...

Green eyes, hair the color of autumn...

A roaring sound filled his ears. Bright flames leapt before his eyes. He couldn't breathe... and then silence.

Gabe was back in his office, sitting in his own chair. He took a deep ragged breath. The beads of cold sweat that had formed on his forehead began to slowly trickle down the side of his face. Absently, he wiped them away with the back of his hand and stared blankly at the wall opposite him.

Kyle didn't know what to do. He was still in shock over seeing what appeared to be a message from beyond the grave. Gabe looked terrible; Kyle hoped he wasn't having a goddamn heart attack or a stroke or something.

"Gabe... Gabe." He gently shook his friend's shoulder.

Gabe returned to reality.

"I think I'm going to go home a little early today, Kyle; I don't feel very well," he said in a flat voice.

"That would be a damn fine idea, partner." Kyle didn't feel so well either. "Want me to give you a lift?"

"No, that won't be necessary. I may drive around a bit first. I need some air."

Gabe picked up the poem, and without looking at it, jammed it into his pocket.

"Uh, call you later?" Kyle asked.

Gabe ignored him and walked out of the office, grabbing his leather jacket from the coat rack.

Kyle watched him leave, and then slumped down in his buddy's chair. He swiveled around to look at Chet, who had been uncharacteristically silent throughout the whole morning.

For once, Kyle, too, was at a loss for words.

Gabe walked out into the bitter January cold. Iron-gray clouds billowed above him and it looked as if it was going to snow again soon. He crossed the parking lot and unlocked his car, and as he reached in to start the vehicle and grab the ice scraper he heard someone whisper his name.

"Gabe..."

He whirled around, nearly giving himself a concussion when his head hit the roof of the car.

There was no one there.

He scanned the nearly empty parking lot. There were no cars near enough for anyone to hide behind and still be within whispering distance. Gabe rubbed his head and checked for bleeding. A small knot had already begun to form. A goose egg. Mother Goose. Goose-Mother. Green eyes. Oh God… now he was becoming unhinged. Nucking Futs.

He scanned the parking lot one last time and entered his car, starting it on the first attempt. *Well, at least one thing went right today.*

He turned on the defroster and freezing cold air blew into his face. His breath crystallized into tiny ice particles, creating a miniature blizzard in the car. Gabe closed his eyes and could feel the ice melt has it hit his face.

He needed to get away… If only he could drive until he ran out of road like he used to when he wanted to escape his demons. He knew he could never do that, wouldn't abandon his responsibilities now, but a short drive wouldn't hurt a thing. Deirdre wouldn't miss him; he was still at the office as far as she was concerned. His head began to clear, and he put the car into gear and pulled out onto the snow-covered road.

He had no destination in mind; he just drove.

Gabe found himself in an old driveway; the house it belonged to had burned down years ago. He couldn't remember what the house had looked like, but he did remember playing in the gardens behind it and wondered if any of it still existed. Wouldn't be able to tell now though, too much snow on the ground. He backed the car out of the drive, realizing how insane it was to pull in in the first place. It was amazing he hadn't gotten stuck. There were no other houses around for at least a few miles either way.

He continued on down the road. He wasn't quite a mile from the driveway when a deer ran in front of him. Gabe slammed on the brakes and the car went into a skid, stopping only when it became buried in a snowdrift.

Shit.

He put the car into reverse, gently pressing on the accelerator. The wheels spun but he got nowhere, so he tried rocking the car out; forward, reverse, forward, reverse… Still no luck.

"Goddammit," he grumbled, wishing he would have taken his truck today instead of Deirdre's car. It had four-wheel drive and his cell phone, but it was in the shop with repairs being made to the hydraulics of his recently installed plow.

What to do… He drummed his fingers on the steering wheel, weighing his options. It was a long walk back to anywhere. A long, cold walk and all he had for winter wear was his leather jacket and his pretty-much useless Stetson. He turned the car off and tossed the keys into his coat pocket, and enjoyed one last moment of the warmth of the car before he opened the door.

An icy blast of January wind took Gabe's breath away as he exited the vehicle. Good God it was cold! He jammed his hands into the pockets of his jeans, and then hunched his shoulders to bring his jacket collar up around his ears. He was certain his efforts were indeed in vain, he was going to freeze to death before he found help or shelter. He shoved his hip into the car door, closing it, and then glanced down to see if the door had shut completely. Didn't want snow blowing in.

A spot of color on the floor of the back seat caught his attention. A blanket? Maybe one of the boys left something in here that might help keep him warm on his upcoming arctic journey. He opened the back door. It wasn't a blanket, but a scarf. What luck! Well now, the gods were definitely looking favorably upon Geoffrey Alan today! And what's this? Why, under the scarf was a bag from a sporting goods store. Impossible, but yes; it contained a pair of ski gloves. Men's... size large. He didn't even dare question the reason for the clothing being there... and maybe he wouldn't freeze after all. He donned the winter wear and closed the door.

Gabe studied his surroundings. The hilly road was long, straight, snow covered, and desolate. To his right were barren fields, probably corn or soy beans in the summer months. He climbed to the roof of the car and looked past the field. No signs of life out there, not even power lines that might lead to a house. No sense in going that way... He knew what was behind him, nothing for at least three miles. He looked to his left and saw a large meadow with a rolling terrain and a forest just beyond. It looked huge. No help that way unless that damn deer had a phone. And just what the hell was deer doing out this time of day anyway? It was just past noon.

Gabe jumped from the roof of the car into the snow and began to walk. Not down the road, which would have been the sane thing to do, but into the meadow, following the tracks of the deer of misfortune. *How "Alice in Wonderland..."*

He felt strange again. It wasn't unpleasant, just odd - light-hearted even. He felt like falling down onto his back and making a snow angel. Now that was something he hadn't done in years... not since he was a kid having snowball fights with Steve. Gabe reached down and scooped up a handful of snow, formed it into a ball and threw it at nothing in particular. He fashioned another snowball and pretended to take aim at an imaginary foe. He let it fly, followed in quick succession by two more.

"Gotcha!" he yelled at no one.

He dove to the ground as if dodging a return volley, and lay in the snow, laughing like hell. He rolled onto his back and spread his arms out, then began to move them up and down through the snow as his legs moved back and forth.

"I'm going insane," he said to himself. "Here I am, a grown man, lying in the middle of some godforsaken wilderness, making a damn snow angel!"

He never felt better. Bits of snow found their way beneath the scarf and under his jacket, and the cold bit into his flesh before it melted into icy drops of water and absorbed into his shirt. He didn't even care.

His arms and legs ceased their motion and he lay still, looking at the sky. The sun peeked out from behind billowy gray clouds and the surrounding sky was a pale blue. Clouds of steam rose over Gabe's face with every breath he took. It was so peaceful... he could just lay there forever. And he probably would if he didn't get moving.

He rose to his feet, brushing snow from his jeans, and thought he heard a goose honk in the distance. Once again, he began to follow the tracks of the deer across the snow.

He was almost to the woods when he saw that the tracks vanished behind a large fir tree. Just stopped. He looked around to see if he could pick up the trail but there was nothing, so he began to follow the tree line, heading west. He didn't know what he expected to find or why he was even out there, but hell, nothing had made sense all day. Why start now?

Gabe came to a small break in the trees. Ah, now this was interesting... hoof prints in the snow, from a horse. Heading in and out of the woods. The wind had erased the prints once they had reached the open field, so he had no idea where they went from there. And yet there was a definite trail into the woods.

Okay, Alice, let's follow it…

So he did.

Right into wonderland.

Gabe felt compelled to follow the trail. The feeling of euphoria he had felt this morning was beginning to come over him again and his speed increased with each step. Soon he was running, not even looking down to follow the horse's path.

He knew this trail. How he knew, he wasn't sure, but he knew it... *Around that big oak… Right between that copse of blue spruce. Watch out for the bushes... raspberries and thorns. There - the clearing!*

Gabe burst through the brush, almost tripping over a white marble bench. His eyes widened in amazement as rays of sun shot down through the trees, reflecting rainbows of light off of the ice crystals in the snow. Flecks of color danced through the air and the scene had a kaleidoscope effect; the moving, changing colors dizzied him.

He sat heavily on the bench, just missing a square object covered in snow. Absently, he picked up the box and placed it in his jacket pocket.

"Oh my God," he murmured as he raised his hand in front of him, watching the colors whirl and change on his borrowed glove.

"Oh my God..."

A cloud blocked the sun and the world returned to normal. Gabe blinked. *Did that really happen, or was he still in that field, freezing to death and having one final hallucination?*

Nope. He was sitting on a bench in the middle of some forest.

Wow, and it was some view! About twenty feet ahead of him the earth dropped away. He stood, walked to the edge of the clearing, and looked down at the frozen lake below him. Gabe wondered what this place was like in the summer; must be beautiful. He could almost hear the chirp of the crickets, the soft lap of the waves as they met the shore, the whisper of the warm breezes blowing through the pine boughs, and if one sat on the bench, the full moon would shine right down on one's self. *A warm breeze, a pale form floating gently in the calm, dark water... Autumn hair, green eyes. A lonely soul, yet fiercely guarded by...*

Gabe heard the honking of a goose again, followed by the half-hearted snarl of a dog. Another hallucination? Probably hypothermia setting in. His feet were past freezing and now officially numb. Cowboy boots were not meant for a trek through the tundra.

That goose... it seemed out of place. The lake was completely frozen, so he knew it wasn't a Canadian - they preferred open water. So, it had to be a domestic? And it lived with someone? On a farm?

The breeze picked up again and Gabe caught a whiff of wood smoke. Oh, now that would be heaven. Sitting in front of a roaring fire, sipping on a mug of hot, spiced rum...

So, go for it! But where was that smoke coming from?

The goose honked once more, followed by the bark of a dog; things were looking up again. The animal noises came from below him, and to the right... down the hill. Damn, but it was steep! He could make down just fine, but he didn't think he could make it back up. At least not today, in these conditions, and with frozen feet. He prayed his trip wouldn't be in vain and made his descent.

He only slipped once on the way down. An obliging tree broke his fall, exacting only a few bruises in payment. Hey, it could have been worse, could have been that boulder at the bottom of the hill stopping his forward motion.

Gabe reached the lake, looking for signs of life, but saw nothing except snow and ice, trees and rocks. He turned to his right and followed what he thought might be the shoreline. The snow was deep and the going was slow.

The lake was long and crescent shaped, and it seemed that he could never see around the next corner. Dammit, now his legs were becoming numb. Would it have been too much to ask to have a pair of ski pants along with the gloves? He laughed, but there was no humor in it.

The quarter mile he walked along the lake seemed much longer and he couldn't go much further. Where the hell was that damn goose? It hadn't sounded so far away. Well, he'd walk to that big rock up ahead and then rest for a minute.

Gabe sat in the snow, leaning against the boulder and shivering uncontrollably. What had ever possessed him to leave his car in the first place? He had to admit it was beautiful out here. Pristine white snow covered

259

the ground and the lake was surrounded by steep hills, decorated with outcroppings of layered rock. Evergreens broke the monotony of winter-gray, leafless trees.

He closed his eyes and waited for inevitable. At least his last glimpse of life would be that of something beautiful.

Something was bumping his arm, up and down, from wrist to elbow. Weakly he tried to wave it away, and then a cold, wet sponge hit his forehead. *What the hell?* His eyes flew open and he found himself staring into golden eyes only inches from his own. Hot breath washed over his face, followed by a warm tongue.

The dog licked him again and then sat back on its haunches. Gabe just stared until something bumped his arm again. A large white goose nibbled on his jacket... up and down his arm it went, the large orange beak biting gently.

Gabe jumped to the top of the boulder he had been resting against. Christ, a carnivorous goose! A freakin', man-eating goose!

The dog rose to its feet and barked twice. The goose looked up at Gabe, and then lowered its head and spread its wings in a courtly bow as it gave a short honk. Once over his initial fright – or surprise - Gabe began to chuckle.

The goose ruffled his feathers and placed his wings in their proper resting position against his body. He tilted his head and with one pale blue eye looked up at the man. The dog barked again and circled the rock.

"What is it Lassie, Timmy fall in the well again?"

Shit, he was definitely ill if he was making lame jokes like that. Gabe slid down from his perch, and the impact of landing on frozen feet jarred him to the top of his skull. He took a quick breath through clenched teeth... *Let's end this nightmare.*

"Lead on, Lassie," he said to the dog.

The dog began walking around the endless corner, and the goose kept pace with him in a most dignified manner, head high and with a slight waddle. As the dog and goose walked along, they gave each other frequent looks and made little noises at each other. Gabe thought it looked as if they were arguing. *Felix and Oscar...*

Gabe gave a last look around him and with a shrug of his shivering shoulders began to follow the odd couple.

Another fifty feet. That's all it was, and the cabin came into view. Gabe had always scoffed at the stories he heard of people dying mere feet away from rescue, and yet he was nearly one of them. And oh, what a lovely site the cabin was, located halfway up the gentle slope of the hill. A curl of smoke rose from the chimney and a covered porch surrounded the front and sides of the light colored logs of the home. Off to the left of the cabin stood a pole barn, right next to the steep hills that sheltered the homestead. Two horses poked their heads from a large window in the barn. The big bay horse nickered when Gabe came into view.

The dog trotted up to the cabin, turned to face Gabe, and barked twice. It then turned back to the building and shot up the steps. The goose waddled to the bottom of the steps and flew to the porch. He honked and flapped his wings at the nearly frozen man.

"An invitation if ever I heard one," Gabe laughed.

He slowly made his way up the hill, and as he reached the bottom of the steps the dog barked again and disappeared into the cabin through a doggie door. The goose retired to a small, straw-filled house at the edge of the porch.

Gabe climbed the stairs.

"Hello? Anyone home?"

Silence.

He knocked on the door.

No answer.

"Hello?"

Nothing.

There was a movement in the window to his left. A large, orange tabby cat was staring at him from between the lace curtains, with a paw placed on the pane of glass. Impulsively, Gabe reached over and touched the glass opposite of the cat's paw. *Damned if the feline didn't just nod!* He pulled his hand away in surprise, and the cat yawned and jumped from his perch.

Gabe smiled. If nothing else, at least the critters were friendly.

There just had to be someone home; he didn't want to think he came all of this way for nothing. He knocked on the door again, a little harder this time, and the door moved… opened just a fraction of an inch. Obviously, security was not an issue here.

Gabe opened it a bit more and stuck his head in.

"Hello? Anyone here?"

Nope. He didn't think that they would appreciate a frozen corpse on their porch so he went inside.

The cabin was warm and smelled faintly of sweet spices, and a woodstove radiated heat. Not the fireplace he had imagined, but it would suit his needs for now. Painfully, Gabe peeled the boots from his stiff feet and limped to the woodstove.

A chair and ottoman sat a few yards from the stove. Gabe eyed it longingly.

"What the hell," he muttered, dropping into the chair and putting his feet up.

The numbness was beginning to wear off as warmth seeped into his legs, and his toes tingled and burned when the circulation returned to them. His fingers sank into a soft afghan that was draped over the arm of the chair. He folded it and placed it in the crook of his arm, using it for a pillow.

God, he was so comfortable… Maybe he had died in the frozen field and this was Heaven. It was his last thought before he drifted off to sleep.

✦ ✦ ✦

Annie could barely keep her eyes open. She hadn't slept well since Friday, and here it was Monday. To make matters worse, she was working a day shift. What the heck had she been thinking when she volunteered for that? Must have been sleep deprivation starting early.

She had worked Thursday night, the night Eric was admitted, and spent some time after her shift to visit with him Friday morning. She went home around noon and took a short nap. She slept deeply, and if she had any dreams, she couldn't remember them.

When she woke, her mind was filled with thoughts of Michael; it was his birthday. Eric had made him a little picture frame for a present and Annie had finished the poem.

The poem. It made her think of Deirdre and the mysterious writer husband. It was his birthday also. And what was with that party invitation? Annie hardly knew those people, and they were acting like she was a member of their family. She hoped that they would understand if she didn't attend the night's festivities. It wasn't that she didn't like them, it was just, well, kind of weird.

It had been snowing pretty hard, accumulating quite rapidly. Good, she could blame her absence from the party on the weather should the subject ever come up. Which she doubted that it would... Deirdre had been discharged from the hospital and Annie had no plans to ever see her again. That thought saddened her though; she really did like Mrs. Burnside. Jenna too... and the twins. There was just something about those kids that touched her heart - as long as she didn't think about their strange comments to Jenna.

She realized that she had been pacing back and forth in her kitchen. Her cup of tea had grown cold, untouched. Why was she so restless? Maybe a ride on Adonis would help calm her down. She'd ride up to the marble bench and take Michael his present. If only he would be there, she had so much to tell him and she missed him so. Annie carefully wrapped the frame and card she had made in a small cardboard box. She dressed in her warmest clothes and went out to saddle her horse...

Annie dragged her attention back to the chart she had been working on. She could barely make out the scribble, also known as doctor's orders, which were written there. It was no use. She would have to page him and ask him what he had written. She dialed his pager number and punched in her extension after the tone sounded. Hopefully, he would call back soon. She leaned her head on her hand and closed her eyes. Oh, for a nap!

After Annie had returned from her ride Friday night she sat on the porch for a while, watching the snow. It was terribly cold, sitting there in the storm, and she really should have gone in before she froze to death but the thought of Michael possibly showing up kept her out there for a while longer. She could have sworn that he was at the clearing, he had such a strong presence, yet he never showed.

She was scheduled to work Saturday night, so she had planned to stay up for most of Friday night and sleep during the day on Saturday. She kept herself busy with household chores, and then started reading a Patricia Cornwall novel. However creepy

262

it could be, she was fascinated with forensic pathology. Becoming deeply involved in the intrigue of Kay Scarpetta's life would help take Annie's mind off of her own lonely existence.

Around five a.m. she reluctantly closed the book and went to bed. She had to get some sleep. She spent three hours tossing and turning in bed before giving in to the fact that sleep would not come. Back to the book? Better not, so she dressed and went out to feed the livestock.

Annie shoveled snow from the porch and filled the wood box on it with split logs. She baked a pan of brownies to take to the girls at work that night. Organizing the bedroom closets, re-arranging the furniture and finishing the book she had started filled the rest of her day.

And finally, it was time for work.

The night seemed to drag on forever. She only had three patients to care for, and they needed very little attention other than the routine nursing. Eric had been discharged earlier in the day, so he couldn't even distract her. Then at last, shift change. Annie gave her report to the day nurses, went home, and went to bed. She felt that she could finally sleep, but just as she dozed off, the phone rang.

Wrong number.

She rolled over and tried to return to her slumber. The phone rang again; same caller with the same wrong number.

Annie unplugged the phone.... and back to bed again. Dog began barking and she could hear a commotion in the chicken coop.

Dog ran through his recently installed doggie door and went to save his chickens. Annie threw on a robe and boots and joined him at the coop, but whatever had upset the fowl was long gone. Dog sniffed around the base of the hill next to the pen, but failed to pick up a scent and returned to Annie's side. She threw some grain to the ground, and when the chickens came out to eat, she counted heads; no one was missing.

Back to bed again. She dozed fitfully for an hour before she gave up, thinking that she wasn't scheduled to work that night so she could sleep then.

Annie turned on her rarely used television and watched an old movie. During the commercials she surfed the channels, looking for something that might be a bit more interesting. A music video on a country station grabbed her attention. She only caught the last ten seconds or so, but what she heard of it really moved her. The music was different than the usual Nashville fare, not too twangy and with a lot more rock than country. And the vocals... what a voice that man had! The singer had finished the lyrics and was facing away from the camera, and she could only see the back of him. His crisp black hair was cut just above the collar of his leather jacket. Faded blue jeans and worn cowboy boots... Dear God, he looked just like Michael from the back! The singer gave the guitar he was holding a final strum and began to turn around. Annie held her breath, waiting to see his face. Just as his profile was about to be revealed, an obnoxious VJ broke in, babbling about the latest Hollywood scandal. Annie felt like throwing the remote control at his smirking face. Oh, this was way too much! And who was that singer?

She wondered if they would play the video again, or did they play them on a schedule like some of the radio stations did with music? She chided herself for paying so little attention to both types of media. An idea formed in her brain, and she programmed her VCR to tape for three hours at this time tomorrow. An hour before, an hour during, and an hour after. With any luck...

Annie thought of calling Eric. He watched music videos, but if he had seen this one, surely he would have told her. Michael was his hero! Any one resembling him...

She shrugged off the thought.

The phone... It was still unplugged. She took care of it and began making dinner. Annie wasn't really hungry, but it would help pass the time. Dog always enjoyed leftovers anyway. The phone rang and she sighed, probably that stupid wrong number again.

It was the staffing office at Brighton. They were shorthanded and things were getting busy, and wanted to know if Annie could work an extra shift.

Why not?

A day shift? And half a shift tonight?

Sure, no problem. Seven to one that night, then seven to seven in the morning. She would survive somehow.

Now she wasn't so sure. She had only slept for two hours, as her anxiety over possibly sleeping through her alarm had kept her awake for most of the early morning hours.

Annie heard a ringing. She reached out for her alarm clock; instead her fingers met the phone.

The phone. She was at work, and it was probably the doctor with the appallingly poor handwriting calling back. She pulled her thoughts together and answered.

Gabe attempted to roll over but something was jabbing him in the hip and preventing pretty much any movement at all. *What the hell?* He opened his eyes, blinking the sleep away.

This wasn't his bed, this wasn't even his chair. It took him a moment to realize where he was. *Ah yes...* He was the uninvited guest of the cabin with the benevolent dog and goose. (Said dog was asleep at Gabe's feet.)

Christ, how long had he been sleeping? He glanced around the room, looking for a clock. There was a time display on the VCR: 5:30. He then wondered what time he had arrived. He thought it had been around three, but he wasn't his usual alert self at the moment.

Damn, something was jabbing at his hip again. He reached down into the chair and pulled out a small package partially wrapped in blue paper, although he didn't recall seeing it in the chair when he had sat down. He turned the object over in his hands. Under the torn paper he could see a cardboard box... *Happy birthday to someone.*

The bench. He remembered shoving a box into his pocket while he was in the clearing above the lake.With a mixture of curiosity and guilt, he opened the package. Inside was a card that looked handmade. Pretty good job of it too. Under the card was a picture of a small boy standing in water with a goose floating next to him. A gold-painted, macaroni-encrusted frame surrounded the picture. It made Gabe smile. He looked at the front of the card again. Nice drawing; somebody had some talent. He opened the card and read.

"Dear Michael," it began.

Gabe read the now familiar words. "I want you to know what you've done for me..."

He felt as if he had just been kicked in the stomach, and began to tremble from head to toe. His mind went blank and he stared, unseeing, at the paper he held in his hands. *Just what the hell was going on?*

"Oh God," he choked out, thinking that he had to get out of there. He dropped the card and the picture to the floor as he jumped from the chair, and then staggered to the center of the room and looked around him.

Where *was* he?

A phone. He needed a phone.His mind was beginning to clear. If he could get the number of the phone there, he could call information and maybe get an address, and then call a wrecker. If he couldn't find his car today, well, he'd think about that later.

Christ, where was the damn phone? Aw shit, what if there wasn't a phone? He could not recall any power lines running to the cabin, but there had to be. The VCR was working, wasn't it? He walked into the kitchen area and noticed a bowl of red and yellow apples set in the center of the small dining table. The kitchen counters held some small appliances, but no phone. He saw a door just to the left of where the counter ended. It was partially open, so he didn't think it led outside. Maybe it was an office or something.

Gabe walked through the door and blinked in surprise. It was certainly no office! The air was warm and humid, and smelled of freshly turned soil and flowers. He took a deep breath. *Ahh... summertime.*

Plants were everywhere. Flats of seedlings lined the floor, baskets of flowers hung from the ceiling, and a gardener's bench ran along one wall. Pots of roses in various stages of growth shared space on the bench with pots of herbs. There were also geraniums, pansies, petunias, and impatiens... daffodils and tulips. *Was that an orchid*? Whoever lived here certainly had a green thumb.

He walked across the floor to where he had seen the roses. Several of the plants were sprouting buds. He touched a blood-red flower, and then moved his hand to a bud of the purest white, which he plucked and held it to his nose. The scent was very faint.

Reluctantly he dragged himself from the room. The shock of seeing all of that greenery had made him forget his dilemma for just a moment.

The poem... He tried to block that whole thing from his mind. Gabe heard a soft meow and looked up towards the loft where he saw the cat sitting on the corner of a desk. Now that looked promising. As he climbed the narrow steps he heard a sound behind him. Aw jeez, that freaky dog was coming up too. Whatever.

Gabe walked to the desk. *Yes!* A phone, complete with dial tone! He called his office, just in case Kyle or Jenna were still there but got the answering machine. Figures. And there was nothing on the phone that looked remotely like the number.

So, what now? A phone book? Address book? He could see neither lying on the desk and he really didn't want to open any desk drawers; it was bad enough that he was trespassing already.

He heard the dog give a low whine. *Oh shit... Was the homeowner back?* Gabe froze, listening for a car or a door opening or closing... and heard nothing, just another whine from the dog. He looked at the animal, which was standing in a shadowed corner of the loft. The dog was wagging his tail in a low, slow motion, never taking his golden eyes from Gabe.

He walked towards the friendly critter.

Dog opened his mouth in a doggy smile, wagging his tail a little faster. He sat down next to a pile of books.

Gabe walked over to the stack and picked one up. Notebooks... Journals? He was tempted to peek inside, but the animal growled and Gabe hastily put the book back.

He then noticed a photo album lying open next to the stack of journals; it must have fallen from the pile. As he picked it up, he noticed pictures of the cabin. He read the caption written under the center picture. "My New Home. 140359 Hidden Lake Road. A Little slice of Heaven"

Bingo! He knew where he was... kinda sorta. He knew where Hidden Lake Road was anyway; his car was buried on it. He called information for the number of a towing service.

After talking with the overworked driver of the wrecker, he wondered what he should do during the hour wait he would have until help arrived, and descended the stairs. One little matter to take care of before he left though. He needed desperately to use the bathroom facilities. He hoped the resident of the cabin wouldn't mind.

Found the bathroom easy enough... One certainly could never get lost in this place; it was only about a quarter of the size of his house. Gabe looked at the bathtub and chuckled. Might get lost in that thing though, it was huge!

He felt he should leave a note for the owners of the cabin, thanking them for their unexpected hospitality, but needed some writing materials. So back up to the loft, and this time into the desk. Fortunately, he found paper and a pen in the first drawer he checked.

At the kitchen table, he sat down and composed a letter explaining his becoming lost and of the dog coming to his aid. He apologized for entering uninvited, but it was, after all, a matter survival. He thanked them again, and signed the note 'G', wanting to remain anonymous for several reasons. As an afterthought, he thanked the unknown host for the apples, and then grabbed two of them - one red and one golden. He left the note on the kitchen table, and then threw a few more logs on the dying fire in the woodstove. As he walked towards the door to leave he saw the blue wrapping paper on the floor by the chair.

He stopped.

He stared.

He couldn't just leave it, but he was loath to touch it again.

Oh Lord, not the dog again... The creature had come from somewhere and was now sitting next to the picture of the boy and goose. He placed his paw on the card and barked, and then removed his paw.

Gabe picked it up and looked at the card.

He read the words.

He read the signature.

"Love, Annie"

Annie. He liked that name.

Annie. Soft, yet strong. Comfortable. Self-sufficient. Smart. Green eyes, autumn hair, and a shy smile.

Annie. He'd been hearing that name in his mind forever.

A cold wet nose pushed at his hand. The dog. Gabe closed the card; he would keep it. He gave the dog a few absent strokes on its head and thought about her some more.

Annie. Did she live here? This is how she would live, he just knew it. He was almost tempted to stay and wait for her return... but that was a bit insane. For all he knew the person who lived there could be some psychopath with homicidal tendencies, although Gabe didn't think so.

He gave a last look around the room. The honey-oak paneled walls were decorated with framed watercolors, similar to the one on the front of the card in his pocket. Colorful rag rugs were strewn about the polished hardwood floor. Potted plants were at each window, and the whole interior of the cabin made one feel as if they were home. Kick off your shoes, put up your feet and relax. Leave your worries outside... Nothing but peace and contentment in this house!

He wanted to stay... God, did he ever want to stay. Stay forever and ever here with his Annie... Instead he put his boots back on and went out into the bitter cold evening.

Dusk had fallen and Gabe hoped that he wouldn't get lost again. He followed the long driveway up the hill until he turned a corner and saw a break in the trees. Looked like a road...

He was right; he had reached the street, but none of the area looked familiar in the gathering twilight. He figured his car must be south and began to walk up the high hill. Dog joined him and he felt better with the large canine at his side.

He found his car about a mile from the cabin's driveway, and as he was throwing a snowball at the offending vehicle he could see headlights heading towards him. The wrecker. Now that was good timing!

After driver hauled Gabe's car from the snow bank, he waited around to see if it would start. It did, and then he was paid an added another fifty as a tip. The shocked driver thanked him several times until Gabe hinted that maybe he had some more people to haul out of drifts... maybe?

The dog turned and trotted for home, and Gabe felt a little silly as he yelled a thank you to the retreating hound. He heard an answering bark.

Gabe shivered as he sat in his car waiting for it to warm up. It was about then that he realized he'd left his hat back at the cabin. *Dammit...* But it would give him an excuse to go back. Maybe tomorrow... Didn't think he'd better until then; the clock on the dashboard glowed the time: 7:30 and he'd better get home. Deirdre would be worried sick and she didn't need any more stress in her life. He put the car in gear and carefully pulled out. The road was icy and there would be no hurrying home tonight. A truck passed him, making Gabe think of the card in his pocket.

Annie. Who was she? What was she like? Thoughts of the mystery woman occupied his mind for the remainder of his drive home.

Annie could not wait to get home. She knew she would sleep; sheer exhaustion would take care of that. She only hoped she could stay awake during the thirty minutes it took to get there.

It seemed to take forever before she turned down Hidden Lake Road and had only another five miles to go. She passed a wrecker and then a car, marveling at the excessive amount of traffic for this out of the way place. Annie slowed the truck as she neared her driveway and saw Dog waiting for her near the driveway's entrance. That was odd; usually he was on the porch when she arrived home.

"Hey, Dog, what brings you so far from the house?" she asked, opening the passenger side door to let him in. "You're usually on the porch waiting for me."

She ruffled the hair between his pointy ears and finished her drive home.

Annie went straight to her favorite chair in front of the woodstove, sat on the ottoman and kicked off her boots, too tired to care about a little melting snow. She shrugged out of her coat and let it fall to the floor as she leaned back in her chair. *Ahhh...bliss.* Closing her eyes, she reached for the afghan. Her fingers found the soft, fuzzy material and she pulled it close to her face. Hmmm, it smelled good.

It had a kind of woodsy-spicy.

Rather like a man's cologne she had once smelled.

Like the cowboy.

"Okay Annie," she said to her, "why would this blanket have this scent?"

Slowly she opened her eyes and glanced around the room, looking for an intruder. Wouldn't Dog have alerted her to anything or anyone unusual though? Apparently not, he was sound asleep in front of the woodstove. That was quick... poor, tired watchdog. She brought the afghan to her face again and inhaled deeply. She felt kind of tingly all over - a warm, fuzzy tingly.

She rose from the chair and draped the blanket over her shoulders; might as well see if the nice smelling stranger robbed her blind. She looked about the room but nothing seemed out of place. No, wait, the pyramid of apples in the bowl on the table was different. She went over to investigate and sure enough, two apples were missing. In their place was a folded piece of paper. Annie snatched it up, eager to read the note written there. Maybe Michael had finally stopped by.

She unfolded the paper and looked for a signature. Not from Michael, and who was 'G'? A man, judging from the scent of the cologne left on the afghan. Annie read the note. Jeez, it figures that she would pick today to work a different shift. Then again, maybe it was better that she hadn't been home when this person came to her door. What if he was some psycho with mayhem and murder on his warped little mind? She rubbed her cheek against the soft blanket around her shoulders. No, she didn't feel threatened; quite the opposite in fact. She longed to feel strong arms hold her close, to run her fingers through wild, black hair, to gaze deeply into intense blue eyes... And she was sure he would smell woodsy-spicy too. She sighed. If only there was such a man.

Annie fixed a light dinner for herself, and halfway through her meal she realized that she hadn't loaded the woodstove. She didn't want it burning out, so she grabbed a couple of logs and opened the door of the firebox to find that it was already full. Mystery man must have loaded it before he left. He couldn't have been gone for more than an hour, judging by how much the wood had burned. Could that have been his car she passed on the road? Darn it, why hadn't she paid more attention? She finished dinner and washed the few dishes she had dirtied, and then went to feed her critters.

Dog and McDonald followed her out to the barn. She flipped on the light, and horses, goats, and chickens looked at her expectantly. It was then she realized that she was two hours late with their feed. She'd never work a day shift again, totally messed up her day in more ways than one.

With the goats and chickens taken care of, Annie turned her attention to the horses. She fed Wanda and then Adonis. She grabbed a brush and slowly groomed the big bay as he munched his feed.

"Hey, Donny boy. Did you happen to see anyone strange here today?"

The horse sneezed and continued eating.

"Like you could tell me if you did. I wish I had seen him. I wonder what he looked like. And what's his name? G. Greg? Gary? George? Maybe G is for his last name... Oh, this is too frustrating. You know, Donny, I should be terrified that a stranger was in my house today. I should have locked the doors... and be thankful nothing was stolen except a couple of apples. Big deal. But instead I feel like a teenager who just had her first kiss, except that I haven't been kissed in a long time."

Adonis turned to look at her. One ear was cocked forward and the other back, giving him a rather skeptical look. He snorted and went back to his dinner. Annie gave him a playful smack on the rump.

"Don't you look at me like that, buster," she said with a laugh. "I've been a good girl. Not necessarily by choice, mind you, but I still haven't met Mr. Right. Oh God! Did I just say that? Now I'm sounding like a darn soap opera! I wish Michael was here, I could really use someone to talk to."

Adonis stomped a front hoof.

"No offense, hay-burner, but you never answer me back."

She returned to the cabin and made herself a cup of chamomile tea, and then went into her greenhouse. Nothing out of place there. She plucked a miniature white rose from the plant nearest her and held it to her nose. All she could smell was woodsy-spicy.

That's it. Time for bed.

Annie stuck the white bud in a small vase and then placed it on the table next to her bed. As she climbed into bed she hoped it would bring her good dreams, it could serve as a botanical dream catcher. She turned out the light and was instantly asleep.

"Annie. Annie, wake up."

She waved the annoying voice away. Didn't he see that she was trying to sleep?

"Annie, it's Michael. Wake up."

She sat bolt upright. A male figure sat at the foot of the bed.

"What? Who?" she stammered.

"Michael. C'mon, you haven't forgotten me already!"

"Michael? Where have you been? What time is it? How did you get in?" She was sure that she had locked the doors this time.

"It's late... and I've been around. I can't stay long though; I just came to give you a message."

"A message? I don't understand... Wait, let me get up and I'll make us some tea, and then we can have a proper conversation. I have a million things to tell you!"

Annie started to rise from the bed.

Michael raised his hand to stop her.

"Sorry, but no time for that, I can't stay. Now please listen to me, will ya? I need you to help Deirdre and the kids, and especially Ga..."

"Deirdre! And the twins? Why? I barely know them, and I don't feel 'right' when I am around them. It's like I'm in the twilight zone or something."

"You mean you don't *like* them?" Michael was shocked.

"No, no... I like them just fine. Deirdre is the sweetest person, and the twins... I've seen a lot of kids, but those two are really special. It's just that..." Annie searched for the right words. "They seem to know me a lot more than they should. I've hardly spent any time with them and well, you should hear what they say. It's creepy. I like to read King and Koontz, not be a character in one of their stories. And Deirdre, she gave me a message from you. Can't you two work this out between you? By the way, what was the name she knew you by?"

"Annie dear, rest assured that there aren't any malevolent forces at work here. You'll be quite happy with the end of the story if you follow your heart. Things aren't always what they seem."

"Care to explain, Mr. Cryptic?"

"If only I could. I've got to go... Please help Dee and her family. They need you... And you need them." Michael reached across the bed and took Annie's hand. "Please? For me?"

He kissed her forehead and left the room.

She blinked in surprise. She had seen him take her hand, and had seen him kiss her, but she never felt a thing. She lay back in the pillow and closed her eyes. Had to be dreaming... that was it. After all, the door was locked; she was sure of that. And Dog, he would have barked had anyone entered the house. Where was he, anyway?

Annie flipped off her blankets and sat on the edge of the bed. She shivered. The woodsy-spicy afghan was at the foot so she grabbed it and wrapped it around her.

"Dog?" she called softly.

An answering snore came from the door where Dog was sprawled half in, half out of the bedroom, sound asleep. He was too large for Annie to step over and she gave him an annoyed nudge with her bare toe. How'd Michael get by him? Oh yeah, it was a dream.

"Move, you useless pile of canine carcass." She nudged him again.

Dog stretched and broke wind.

"Oh, jeez... Dog, you are disgusting!"

Annie gave him a gentle shove with the ball of her foot; he finally got the hint and moved from the doorway.

"I think you need to go visit a tree. C'mon, outside."

Annie opened the door for the animal. He trotted to the edge of the porch and sat, looking at the sky.

Strange creature... She slipped her boots on and joined him on the porch.

It was a bitter cold night, and she wrapped the blanket around her a little tighter. She sat on the top step of the porch next to Dog and wrapped the blanket around him too. He gave her face a quick lick and they both looked at the night sky.

It was beautiful. The black velvet dome was studded with a million white diamond stars, and crystals of ice glittered in the air. The stillness of the night was almost palpable. Annie shivered and wondered just how far below zero the temperature was.

Dog let out a low whine. Above them a meteor soared across the sky. The beauty of the shooting star mesmerized Annie.

"Did you see that, Dog?" she whispered.

He whined and looked behind him. Annie continued to stare at the sky until she felt a warm hand on her shoulder. She spun around, only to find no one there. *Michael?*

"This is getting to be a bit much," she said as she rose to her feet. "Dream, awake, hallucinating? I mean, I could understand if it was flashbacks from the seventies, but I never did those drugs. So tell me, Dog, what the heck is going on here? I don't think I'm going insane. I mean I don't feel crazy or anything... Shouldn't this all be, oh… freaking me out or something? Somehow it seems perfectly natural though. Of course, next thing you know, I'll be seeing ghosties! Oooweeeoooooo!" She wiggled her fingers at Dog.

They went back into the cabin and she double-checked the locks on the doors, used the bathroom, and then crawled back into bed. As she reached to turn out her light, she noticed a small note propped against the bud vase.

"Oh now what? Are the ghosties leaving notes for me?"

She read the note.

"Not ghosties. How about angels, Annie? I forgot to answer one of your questions. My real name is Steven Anthony Michael. Sleep well!"

Annie sighed in exasperation and flipped the note over her head, where it fell to the floor behind the headboard of the bed. She turned out the light and pulled the blankets over her head. Soon it would be morning and this freaky, weird dream would be over.

Deirdre was waiting at the door when Geoffrey finally made it home. It was after eight and she was worried sick. She hugged him as soon as he was inside.

"Geoffrey dear, are you all right? Where have you been?" she asked him as she helped him remove his jacket.

"I'm fine. Just a little mishap on an icy road and it took a while for help to arrive." Gabe felt guilty for not calling her from the cabin.

"Kyle called me this morning. He said that something had upset you, and that you went for a drive. Oh God, Geoffrey, we were so worried! Are you sure you are all right? You look so pale." She placed her hand on his cheek.

Gabe covered it with his, and then kissed the palm of her hand. He didn't know how much to tell her. Oh, he'd tell her about his adventure in the wilderness and the cabin, but what about the poem in Steve's handwriting? She still loved his brother with all her heart, and Gabe was loath to upset her any more than he had to.

"I'll tell you all about it; it's really quite a story. Are the boys in bed yet?" he asked.

"No, they're in the dining room with Jenna and her children. Kyle is in your office. He's been rather busy on the phone calling everyone he knows, looking for you. You had better let him know that you're back. Oh, and don't let him see those gloves you're wearing. They were supposed to be for his birthday!" Deirdre winked and grinned at Gabe as she yanked the scarf from his neck and walked into the dining room.

Gabe turned the opposite way, into his office.

Kyle was perched on the edge of the old leather sofa, the phone in one hand and a glass of scotch in the other. Bleary eyed, he looked at Gabe.

"Gabe old buddy old pal!" Kyle slurred. "Where the hell have you been?" He raised his glass in a mock toast.

"Kyle, my friend, I've been to hell, heaven, hell, and back again," Gabe replied, remembering his recent adventure. "Pour me a drink, provided you are still sober enough to comprehend such a simple request."

"Comprehend and honor," laughed Kyle, handing Gabe what remained of the bottle of scotch. "Cheers!"

"Thanks," Gabe replied dryly. He took both the bottle and glass from his buddy. "I think that you are officially cut off, man. The bar is closed."

"Hmm," Kyle mumbled. He fell back onto the sofa and began to snore.

Gabe threw a blanket over him; he could spend the night right there and sleep it off. Jenna and the kids could stay too; there was plenty of room. He took a sip of Kyle's scotch and joined his family in the dining room.

"Papa!" yelled the twins in unison. They ran to Gabe and hugged his legs.

Gabe put his glass on the table and picked up the boys. Two pairs of arms squeezed him about the neck and he made a realistic choking sound. His tongue waggled out and his eyes rolled back, showing only the whites.

"Arggghhh!" he gurgled.

The boys laughed. He kissed them both and returned them to the floor.

He walked around the table, tickling each of the Davidson children as he passed them, and Jenna received a peck on the cheek. Gabe stopped behind Deirdre's chair. He placed his hands on her shoulders and looked at this wonderful group of people.

"To share the warmth of family and the love of which they give," he whispered to himself.

Only Deirdre had heard him.

"Every morning a bright sun, a sky forever blue, clouds with silver linings… this is my wish for you," she replied, then looked up at him and smiled.

Gabe's legs turned to jelly and he leaned heavily on her chair for support. His mouth was dry as dust and a roaring sound filled his ears. He took a few slow, deep breaths as he fought for control. Aw God, he felt like he was going to faint. He glanced around the table to see if anyone had noticed... *Good, only Deirdre - and she was looking at him with alarm.*

"Geoffrey dear, what is it?" she whispered.

She stood so that he could take her seat.. Gratefully, he did.

"What you just said; where did you hear that?" Gabe asked slowly.

"What I just said? Do you mean the poem?"

"Yes. How do you know it?" He grabbed her hand a little tighter than necessary.

She winced.

"I read it last week. A nurse at the hospital wrote it for a friend of hers, for his birthday."

Deirdre wondered how much to tell him. When would be the right time to reveal all she knew?

"What nurse?" Gabe was almost afraid to hear the answer.

"The one we invited to your birthday party, but she couldn't make it. You remember, don't you? The boys called her Goose-Mother."

Gabe just stared at Deirdre. His thoughts whirled about in his mind... The goose, the cabin, the poem, Goose-Mother. Red hair, green eyes, white roses, Steven, Michael. *Oh God! Steven Michael! What was going on?*

"Geoffrey?"

"This nurse, her name... What is her name?" He could barely get the words out.

From across the table he heard the twins answer.

"It's Annie, Papa!

Gabe continued to stare at Deirdre. "Did they say Annie?"

He nearly choked on her name.

Annie.

It was his Annie... It had to be. He knew who she was. Green eyes... That crazy dog and his pal the goose.

Annie. A bowl of apples and a soft, warm blanket.

Annie. Coffee shared in a deserted hospital cafeteria.

Annie. Because of her he had come in from the cold. She had rescued him.

The metaphor was not lost on him. He didn't know whether to laugh or cry.

"Geoffrey dear, why don't you go to bed? You can share your adventure tomorrow," Deirdre said as she helped him to his feet. "Children, tell your Papa goodnight."

James and Jeremy ran to Gabe for a goodnight kiss.

Jenna also gave him a quick hug.

"Stay home tomorrow and I'll handle everything at the office. I have a feeling Kyle won't be in either," she said, glancing towards the den.

"Thanks, Jen, I do appreciate that. Today's events have taxed me more than I could have imagined," he replied, returning her hug.

Deirdre took her husband to his room and helped him change into warm pajamas. He still had a chill, and she didn't want it progressing into anything worse. She tucked him into bed, just as she did her own sons every night, foregoing the bedtime story in exchange for giving Gabe a chance to unburden himself. She could see that his emotions were in turmoil.

"I'll listen to anything you want to say, Geoffrey," she said quietly as she sat next to him on the bed. "We have been very close, very dear friends for a long time now. You know that you can tell me anything. Anything at all."

Gabe wondered if that included telling one's wife that one felt he had finally found his true love, which didn't happen to be one's wife. Better not say anything, not just yet.

"How well do you know this, uh, nurse… Annie?" he asked.

"Hmm…" Deirdre pondered. She knew her well, but not in the conventional way. "She spent quite a bit of time with me while I was hospitalized. I fear I may have talked her ear off in one of my little drug-induced states though. She is a very sweet person, very patient. The twins and Jenna also took quite a liking to her. I wish she could have made it to your party, and then you could have seen for yourself what a wonderful person she is."

Deirdre hoped she wasn't overdoing it.

"Yes, but do you know anything else about her besides the fact that she is super-nurse? Is she married? Have kids? For all we know she could have a second career as an axe-murderer."

Gabe didn't want to appear *too* interested.

"No, I don't believe she is married. I did get the impression that she may have been at one time, but that was long ago. Her only children have either fur or feathers. She does like human children, though; she's a pediatric nurse."

"So then why was she taking care of you?"

"Occasionally she helps out on adult wards. Annie called it 'expanding her skills'. I called it a Godsend. The regular nurses were impossibly busy with all those other patients… I just don't know how they do it," Deirdre sighed, shaking her head. "Anyway, Annie spent the better part of the night with me, listening to me ramble on. I felt so much better with her there. And seriously, I doubt that she would know how to wield an axe!"

She gave Gabe a playful punch on the arm.

He smiled to himself, thinking of the piles of split logs Annie used for firewood. Oh, she knew what an axe was for.

"So, you know all about this woman just from spending an evening with her?"

"Well, you know how you can meet someone, and things just click? There is an understanding… a chemistry? That's what I felt when I met her," answered Deirdre. "I'd love to call her, but I'm afraid I don't know how to find her. The hospital was very reluctant to give out any information when I called to see if I could contact her. They don't reveal last names, or any personal information for that matter, nor do they release work schedules. They would only tell me whether or not she was on duty, which she wasn't, and I'd really like to see her again."

"So would I, thought Gabe, so would I."

More questions nagged at his mind. What was the connection between Steve and this Michael person? And what about that poem and the card he had found. The card... It was still in the pocket of his jacket. What about the box and the picture? He couldn't remember what he had done with those. The picture of the little boy and the goose... He knew who the goose was; maybe the boy was Michael. But why was the box way up there on that bench?

Gabe longed to tell Deirdre of these things but something held him back. He shook his head. Better to just sleep on it tonight, and maybe tomorrow things wouldn't seem quite so strange. He'd sleep a little longer in the morning; the ever-efficient Jenna would handle anything that came up at the studio. Not that it would, nothing much had happened there for quite a while. Great. Another mess.

Deirdre was looking at him. Was she expecting an answer to something? If so, he had none to give... just an unending amount of questions. He feigned a yawn.

"I think I'd better get some rest, Deirdre," Gabe sighed. "We'll talk in the morning. By the way, how are you feeling? You are looking a bit tired yourself."

He felt guilty about the temporary lack of concern for his wife.

"I'm fine. And you're right; I am tired but otherwise doing quite well." She kissed his forehead. "I'll put the children in bed and then turn in myself. Jenna is taking her family home, except for her lout of a husband, and I'll check on him before I go to bed," she told him.

"Thanks. You're a good person, Deirdre. I'm sorry things aren't better for you. If I could only..."

"Who ever said that life is fair?" she interrupted. "I have known great love and have two beautiful children from that union. And I have you. I *do* love you, Geoffrey. I've had a very full life although not a very long one and I can die happy, for I have truly lived."

Gabe felt tears burn in his eyes. Despite all the suffering she had endured, Deirdre remained strong, never complaining and always putting others before herself. Except for her last stint in the hospital of course... but she was back to her old, sweet self again.

He reached for her and she lay beside him on the bed. They held each other for a while... two lost souls brought together by fate.

She felt him relax in her arms, he was finally asleep. Gently, she released herself from his embrace. Pain shot up her spine, every joint in her body ached, and her head throbbed with each beat of her heart. The cancer was eating at her bones... It wouldn't be much longer now. She prayed that she could hang on until the circle was complete, as Steven had told her that things were going as they should.

Ah, Steven. She couldn't wait to join him. She smiled a sad smile and went to her children.

Chapter Twenty-Six

Annie awoke with a start. She felt disoriented and looked at the clock next to her bed. Great... One o'clock and she had overslept.

Her critters! Oh jeez, they must be starving! She quickly threw on a pair of jeans and a sweatshirt, and hobbled to the kitchen while trying to put on a pair of socks. She was halfway through the living room and sat on the floor to finish the job. A piece of blue paper under the chair by the woodstove caught her eye; she'd throw it away later. She grabbed her barn coat from the rack next to the door and jumped into her boots, and noticed that Dog was nowhere to be seen; must be outside already.

The sun reflecting off of the white snow momentarily blinded her when she opened the front door. Well, at least it was nice out, and considerably warmer than last night. Why, it must be almost ten degrees now!

Annie skipped down the steps and trotted to the barn. She felt wonderful despite the bizarre dream last night. Once she had finally gotten to sleep, she made the best of it.

She heard McDonald honk from the lake. He must have seen her, and she knew he'd be up for his breakfast in just a moment.

There was quite a symphony of animal noises coming from the barn. The rest of the critters had heard McDonald and knew Annie would be in shortly. As she opened the barn door, the noise became deafening.

"Quiet!" she hollered.

Instant silence. One by one, the animals began their clucking, bleating, and nickering again, but at a much lower decibel level.

"As it should be," Annie laughed.

Each critter was fed and apologized to for the lateness of their meal, and Annie was forgiven. Now for her own breakfast. She collected what eggs she could find in the barn then returned to the cabin.

She put a pot of coffee on to brew, and sipped a glass of orange juice as she prepared her breakfast: hash browns, green pepper, onions, diced ham, mushrooms and scrambled eggs all cooked together in a cast iron skillet. A bit of seasoning and some melted cheddar cheese over the top completed her early afternoon feast.

Dog had returned from whatever adventure he had been on and lay at her feet, waiting for a rarely dropped morsel of food. Spike decided to make an appearance, and the cat jumped on the chair opposite Annie, and then gave her a nonchalant look with his amber eyes.

She picked a chunk of ham from her breakfast and tossed it to the cat, which caught it lightning-fast. Spike ate the ham and then washed his soiled paw and face. Annie knew she was probably breaking some rule, feeding a cat at the table, but who cared?

She hummed along to the bluegrass music that was quietly playing on her stereo as she re-read the note in front of her.

"G. Hmm... Gary, Greg, Glenn, Goober, Gabe... Gabe." Funny how that name seemed to fit. Couldn't be Deirdre's hubby though.

Woodsy-spicy, jeans, leather jacket... The cowboy in the hospital, desperately seeking coffee... He wore the same scent as what was on her afghan. And he did say that he was visiting his wife who was very ill. Could he have meant Deirdre? Oh Lord, she hoped not. Annie was already in love with her unseen visitor from yesterday. Her over-active imagination had merged the man in her dreams with the cowboy, and was now melding him with the woodsy-spicy stranger. And if he was married... oh, this was not good.

She thought of what Michael had told her in her dream last night - it was a dream, wasn't it? He said that things aren't as they seem. What did he mean by that? Annie was beginning to feel confused and very frustrated. She needed to get out for a while.

In an uncharacteristic lapse of good housekeeping, she left her unfinished breakfast on the table and the dirty dishes in the sink. She changed into some warm riding clothes and went out to saddle Adonis.

Spike watched her go, a Cheshire cat smile growing on his feline face. As soon as he heard the click of the closing door, he sauntered across the table to enjoy the rest of Annie's forgotten breakfast. His purring echoed through the empty cabin.

Annie and Adonis took a different route than usual. She wanted a hard, fast ride, but the snow in the meadow was too deep, and the trails through the woods were too full of twists and turns. She trotted her horse up the driveway and turned onto Hidden Lake Road. She usually avoided riding in the street, but today she felt the need for a change and safety be damned. Adonis cantered along the side of the street where the snow was packed down from the plows, but where there was no ice.

They crested the first and highest hill. From this vantage point Annie could see clearly for almost a mile in each direction. Not a vehicle in sight... as if there would be, she was usually the only traffic on the entire street. She tightened down her riding helmet.

"Let's do it, Donny!"

Annie squeezed the horse with her legs while giving him a tap on the rump with the reins. Adonis exploded beneath her. Rarely was he allowed to run full out with his rider, and now he was going to make the best of it.

She leaned forward in the saddle, her heart racing with a mixture of fear and exhilaration. The cold wind beat against her face, blurring her eyes and tearing her breath from her body. She didn't think, she just felt.

Adonis slowed on his own about half a mile from the driveway, and Annie wiped the wind-induced tears from her eyes. What a rush! She gave him a pat on his sweaty shoulder and decided to walk him for a while; he wasn't used to such speedy rides.

She rode past an oddly shaped pile of snow with tire tracks leading straight into it. That must be where her visitor lost it on the ice. She dismounted for a closer look and saw deer tracks heading into the field, which would explain the accident… although why he was on this road was a mystery; there was nothing on it but her cabin. Annie remounted and turned Adonis into the snow-covered meadow, following the tracks of man and deer.

They came upon the snow angel. She smiled, imagining a grown man making it. He'd neglected to add that little tidbit in his note to her.

"How about angels, Annie?"

She could almost hear Michael speaking the words. That was certainly a vivid dream she'd had last night.

The trail led to a huge pine, and then turned to follow the tree line. The guy must have been insane! No wonder he was freezing. The tracks led into the woods, and Annie could see the distance between the boot prints lengthen. He ran through there? Either he knew where he was going or he was totally unhinged; the trail was anything but straight.

As Annie suspected, the trail ended at the clearing. She dismounted and walked to the bench, and touched the spot on it where she had put Michael's present. The snow around it had been recently disturbed, as if a snow-covered box had been removed. Who had taken it? Michael or the cowboy?

She walked across the clearing towards the lake and could see where someone had gone down the hill, not always in control from the looks of the tracks. She wanted to continue on down, but Adonis would never make it. Well maybe he could, but why risk it?

She gave a short whistle, calling the horse to her.

Adonis looked over the edge of the hill and then gave Annie a doubtful look.

That settled it. She mounted up and they retraced their steps through the woods, taking the usual route back to the cabin instead of taking the road again. Her slightly reckless spree had spent itself.

Annie gave her horse a quick grooming before going back into her messy cabin. As she entered her home, she glanced at the dirty dishes strewn about. They'd wait; they'd have to because all she could think about was a nice, relaxing bath and a nice cold beer. She shed her clothes, tossing them towards the bed. They'd get picked up later.

Wrapped only in a towel, she grabbed a beer from the 'fridge and took it with her into the bathroom. She threw some bath salts into the tub and turned the water on full force. Lavender scented steam rose from the scented foam forming in the huge tub. She wished it smelled woodsy-spicy. While the tub filled, Annie lit the dozen or so candles that lined the shelf surrounding the tub. They reflected off of the thick glass blocks that formed the entire back wall of the bathroom. Dusk was falling outside, turning the blocks a leaden-gray behind the flickering candles.

Annie turned off the bathroom light and slipped into the steaming tub, and then took a healthy swig of her beer. Eyes closed, she slid down in the water until it reached her chin. Behind her closed eyelids she could make out the flickering of the candles' flames.

She fell into a half-sleep, awake enough not to lose it and drown, but unconscious enough to dream. She was still aware of her surroundings, the fragrant scent of the bath salts, the dancing flames of the candles, the warm, silky water, but her mind also took a break from reality.

Images formed around her. She could see Michael standing next to Deirdre, with the twins standing in front of them. Deirdre was holding a bouquet of red roses, and a large black horse stood just behind Michael.She could see her cowboy from the hospital, surprised to see how much he resembled Michael. They could almost be twins, except Michael was more on the wiry side, where as her woodsy-spicy cowboy was more heavily muscled. Still, the resemblance was...

The cowboy was holding something in his hand. He was reaching out to her, handing her the object. Annie extended her hand to accept the offering. A rose bud... pure white and perfectly formed, the flower just beginning to open.

Their fingers touched. Electricity shot through Annie's hand, raced up her arm, and spread through her entire body. The room began to spin and sparks of color whirled and danced around her. The cowboy's other hand was reaching out for her. She moved into his arms and felt... a sharp pain in her leg!

Annie's eyes flew open. She was back in her bathtub. Her beer bottle had slipped from her fingers and bounced off of her raised knee. *Damn, that hurt!* And the bath water was positively freezing! How long had she been sitting there anyway?

She found the offending beer bottle and climbed out of the tub, shivering uncontrollably. She wrapped herself in the towel and went out to stand next to the woodstove to thaw out. *Hmm, that was better.*

She glanced around the room, and saw dirty dishes still in the sink, paper on the floor, half-empty wood box, and clothes all over the bedroom, all needing to be taken care of.

Hello reality.

Annie slipped into a pair of sweat pants, tee shirt and fleece-lined moccasins, her at-home uniform. It would never make the cover of Vogue, but who the heck cared? Silk and satin wouldn't wear very well when one was carrying an armload of wood.

She filled the wood box and then went for the dishes, raising an eyebrow when she saw that Spike had done an excellent job of cleaning the breakfast plate left on the table. It was tossed it in the sink with the rest of the dishes. Once that task was finished she grabbed the broom for the floor in the living area. She knew there was paper under the chair, so what else might lurking about? She swept up the inevitable scatter of wood chips one had to endure with a wood stove, and then poked the broom under the chair. When she heard the crinkle of paper she scooped it out.

But it wasn't just paper, it was the paper she had use to wrap Michael's present in. Inside the paper was the box the picture had been in, was still in. How did that end up there? Oddly enough, she wasn't surprised. After the events of the past few days, nothing surprised her any more. Aliens could dance the can-can naked through her kitchen and she wouldn't even think twice about it.

Annie moved to the bedroom, leaned against the door, and sighed. Clothes lay scattered on and around the unmade bed, of which Spike lay sprawled in the center. She picked up a sock with the toe of her slipper and gave it a quick flip. The sock sailed across the room and landed next to the laundry basket.

Better luck next time.

A second sock followed.

Missed again.

She'd get it this time... She picked up the flannel shirt she had worn during her ride and wadded it up into a tight ball. Annie took aim and fired the shirt towards the basket.

Ha! Got it that time. Jeans were next... Another score!

"Well, that was fun, now what to do you want to do, Annie?" she mumbled to herself.

"Why, make the bed, of course! Never mind the fact that I'll be crawling back into it in a few hours. Oh, but it's ever so much fun to smooth sheets and fluff pillows. Some people even make a career of it! Good God Annie, get a life!"

She yanked the blankets from the bed, causing it to bump the bedside table which rocked just enough to tip over the bud vase. Water ran across the surface and dripped onto the floor. Several one-syllable, four letter words - none of them very nice - came to Annie's mind. She couldn't decide which one to scream in her exasperation, so she said nothing. Just clean up the mess and then get dressed. Drive into town and buy the biggest bar of chocolate she could find.

And a bag of chips.

Yes, junk food was definitely the answer.

When the water mess was taken care of, Annie turned her attention to the unmade bed…

Screw it. It could stay unmade.

She changed into some semi-respectable clothing and grabbed her truck keys.

Dog and McDonald jumped into the cab with her and the trio headed for the nearest convenience store... nearly twenty miles away. The critters argued over who got to sit next to the window. Canine and goose jockeyed for position until McDonald ended the fur verses feathers with a well-placed nip to Dog's backside. Dog settled in the center of the seat, he could still see out the front window.

The goose would pay later.

Fat chance, Dog.

The odd couple glared at each other.

"Knock it off, you two," snapped Annie. "I don't need your crap right now. Jeez, sometimes you're worse than children."

She gave them "the look," and once again peace was restored between the unlikely friends.

As Annie drove, she wondered why she was feeling the way she was. The lack of patience, the labile emotions, and God forbid... the sloppy housekeeping! It just wasn't like her. Not again! Couldn't blame it on PMS - wasn't the right time, and she had never suffered from it in the past.

"Maybe I need a vacation," Annie muttered to herself as she climbed the steps to the cabin. She set the eight-pack of soda on the porch and attempted to find the key to unlock the door.

The massive Dog squeezed by her and went in through his doggie-door.

"Well now that makes a lot of sense. I go to all the trouble of locking the darn door and totally ignore this breach of security."

She found the key and let herself into the cabin, and then put the soda in the 'fridge and dumped her cache of junk food on the kitchen table. It didn't sound nearly as good as it did an hour ago. *Well, maybe some of the chocolate.* She took a Hershey bar, putting the rest of the chocolate and assorted bags of chips into the cupboard.

What to do now?

The phone rang.

Saved by the bell...

Annie looked at the clock to see that it was after eleven. Who could be calling so late?

"Hello?"

"What's up, girlfriend? Marti's perky voice sang into the receiver.

"Obviously you are. You work tonight?"

"That I am. When are you coming back?"

"Tomorrow. I work Wednesday and Thursday, then I have a wonderful five-day stretch off."

"Got any plans?"

"Not really. I thought about painting the ceiling and then watching it dry."

"Ooooh...sounds tempting. Cancel it, you're going skiing!" Marti laughed.

"Oh, no no no. I tried that once. At least I went down a big hill with long strips of fiberglass strapped to my feet. I doubt that anyone, by any stretch of the imagination, would call it skiing," Annie joked.

"That was years ago. Here's the deal: my brother rented a villa in Canada for the weekend, lift tickets included. Non-refundable. Anyway, the dork broke his ankle falling down some steps so he gave me... *gave* me the tickets! A free weekend! You've got to come!"

"Wow, that's great! Not your brother's ankle, of course... but how's he doing?"

"He's fine. Really, really pissed off, but otherwise okay. So, are you interested?"

"Gosh, I don't know. I'm curious though, Marti, why ask me? Why not one of your ski bum friends?"

"Ya know, I'm not sure. Other than you're my best friend. Duh! Not to mention... as soon as my brother told me about this, your name just popped into my head. You've been working your ass off around here lately and you need a break. So, you gonna come?"

"I don't know, but I do appreciate the offer. Jeez, I have no ski equipment, and more important, I can't abandon my critters."

"No problemo. You can use Jill's stuff. And speaking of Jill, she said she'd baby-sit for you again, she has another paper to write anyway. So now you have no excuse not to go."

"I thought she would be back to school by now," Annie said.

"She's here for another two weeks. Came down with mono over vacation, and is still recovering. She talked to her instructors and they were actually human enough to let her come back late, provided she doesn't fall behind in her studies," explained Marti.

Annie was severely tempted to go. Wasn't she just thinking that she needed a vacation? But skiing? What the heck... she wasn't getting any younger, life wouldn't wait much longer.

And she needed to get one.

"You talked me into it. I'll go." Annie was excited, maybe this weekend would help her get back to normal, whatever that was.

"Great! Get your bags packed. I'm driving the van, so the ride up won't be too bad," Marti laughed.

"Where is it we are going? Canada?"

"Just over the border in Sault Ste. Marie. River Ridge Resort... It's beautiful. I've been there a few times. Um... plan on about a seven-hour drive."

"Sounds great... and I'm looking forward to it."

"Okay. I'll see you at work tomorrow. G'night."

"Goodnight."

Annie hung up the phone. Skiing, huh? Now that should be interesting. Well, it was about time she did something besides work all of the time.

She went to the loft, sat at the desk and pulled some paper from the desk drawer to write out instructions for Jill. It dawned on her that this was the same type of paper that woodsy-spicy had used. He must have been up here.

Annie glanced around but nothing seemed out of place. She wondered if it was indeed Gabe that had been here. She thought about calling him and asking.

She put aside the paper and picked up the phone book. What was Deirdre's last name again? "B" something... Burke, Bird, Burns, Burnside. That was it, Burnside. Annie ran her finger down the page of B's, but no Geoffrey Burnside was listed. Wait... Gabe's name was different; 'E' something. She thought it was Evans although she couldn't be sure. She tried it, but couldn't find his name listed either. Darn! She could get Deirdre's number from the computer at work, but that would be violating the company's confidentiality policy, scratch that idea. Besides, if it wasn't Gabe she would be feeling mighty foolish. Best to just forget about him. If only she could.

She stood to head back downstairs and caught a whiff of woodsy-spicy again. *Oh man...*

It was then she noticed something out of place after all. Next to the chair in the corner was an odd lump in the shadows. Annie walked over to it and picked it up.

A hat.

A Stetson, to be exact, and it did not belong to Michael. Smelled like her mystery cowboy and it looked just like the one he was wearing in the cafeteria.

Oh God... he had been there!

"Geoffrey Alan Benjamin Evans! It's barely ten o'clock, and here you are, sound asleep already!"

"So sue me," Gabe grumbled at the annoying voice. Couldn't his brother see that he was trying to sleep?

His brother? He opened one eye.

A familiar figure was perched on the edge of the chair across from the bed. Gabe's other eye opened up. *Yep, it was Steve all right.*

Both eyes closed again. Can't dream with 'em open, and it had to be a dream.

"Sleeping Beauty!" Steve said in a singsong voice, "Wakey, wakey!"

"I'm as awake as I need to be," Gabe snarled. He rolled to his back and put his arms behind his head, but his eyes remained shut. "Say what you have to say and then be gone. I want to dream that I am sleeping, not being subjected to your inane chatter."

"Same ol' Gabe. Always had a way with words. So bro, how've you been? Anything interesting in your life lately? Gold records? Movie deals? Beautiful women willing to do anything for the merest scrap of your attention?"

Steve walked over to his brother and smacked the bottom of his foot.

"Seriously Gabe, I need to talk to you." He sat on the edge of the bed. "Hey! Open your eyes!"

Gabe deserted the idea of undisturbed sleep and complied.

There was Steve, only two feet away from him. He looked great, just as Gabe remembered him.

"Good to see you, Steve. I guess. So, how have you been?"

"Other than dead? Fine, just fine. Keeping busy... I do a little gardening here and there. Made a few new friends. Work a miracle every now and then."

Gabe decided to go along with it. Hey, it *was* his dream after all.

"Gardening? What, pushing up daisies?"

"Now that's just sick, Gabe!" Steve joked. "Actually, I've developed a certain fondness for roses."

"Roses. Why am I not surprised? Have you taken up any other hobbies? Say... poetry?" Gabe was beginning to enjoy this dream. He was in complete control... maybe even come up with some satisfactory answers.

"You must be referring to your little 'find' of this morning. I must admit it was rather naughty of me but I needed a catalyst. Things just weren't movin' fast enough. We don't want to run out of time now, do we?"

"What the hell are you talking about, Stevie?" Gabe was getting pissed. That is not what he expected to hear.

"The poem... What did you think I was talking about?" Steve replied. "Hey, sorry about Kyle too, didn't mean to shake him up so bad. Boy, did he tie one on! Hate to be him in the morning!" he chuckled.

"Yes, the goddamn poem. You really need to explain that to me. First I find it in my office, and then I find it written on a card out in the middle of nowhere... and if that wasn't enough, I hear my wife reciting it! What catalyst? What isn't moving fast enough?" Gabe was seriously pissed now.

"Settle down, bro," Steve said quietly. "You'll wake everybody up. As much as I'd like to explain, I'm not allowed to do so, and I can't stay for very much longer either. Just remember to follow your heart. At first it may not seem like the right thing to do, but it is. The sooner, the better. Those that know you best will understand."

"Care to explain, Mr. Cryptic?"

It would be a good match...

"I have an idea. Why don't you find a horse somewhere and go for a ride. I'd let you ride Whiz, but, well, he's dead too!" Steve laughed again. "Seriously though, think about it. You meet some of the nicest people on horseback."

"You are truly insane. You talk gibberish, you will not answer a simple question, and now you feel I should once again indulge in equestrian pursuits?" Gabe sat up in his bed and glared at his brother.

"I've got to go. I miss you, man... Follow your heart."

Steve tipped his sooty-looking hat to Gabe and turned towards the door, and then turned back again. "Have an apple." He tossed a bright red one to his brother.

Gabe tried to catch it, but there was nothing there. When he looked up, Steve was gone.

"I miss you too, brother," he murmured, and sank back into his pillows.

Gabe rolled over and looked at the clock. Almost nine... better get up. He returned to his position on his back and scratched an itch on his well-muscled abdomen as bits and pieces of his dream teased his memory before the whole episode came back in a mind-numbing rush. *Aw God, it had been so real!* He wished that he could go back into the dream; he wouldn't be so hard on Steve this time.

He took a quick shower, and went downstairs to find Kyle already in the dining room, staring into the dregs of his coffee cup. His red-rimmed eyes glanced up at Gabe when he entered the room.

"Mmm," he mumbled.

"And a good morning to you, sir! How are you on this fine day?" Gabe asked with a cheerfulness he didn't feel, he only wanted to harass his buddy.

"Kiss my ass," Kyle mumbled, a little clearer this time.

"Ah, sir, your mastery of the English language is no less then awe-inspiring! I commend you!" Gabe gave him a deep bow.

"Fuck you, ya bastard," he said, not looking at Gabe but at the coffee cup that he was holding upside down, hoping for that last drop.

"Again, pearls of wisdom flow from his bewhiskered lips. Plato, Aristotle, nay, even the Bard himself cannot even hope to..."

His speech was cut short when Kyle's empty coffee cup rocketed towards him. He caught it just before it smashed on the wall behind him. *Ewww... Kyle was in some kind of mood this morning!*

"Sorry, man, didn't mean to piss you off. Just trying to cheer myself up at your expense," Gabe apologized.

"Accepted. Any more coffee?"

"If not, I'll make some."

Gabe went into the kitchen and returned with two steaming cups. He wished he had a cigarette.

"Other than the hangover from hell, any other reason for your particularly foul mood?" he asked, handing Kyle a brew.

Kyle was silent for a moment. He stared at a spot on the table just past his cup and then raised his eyes to Gabe, uncertain if he should confide or not. Things had been so mixed-up and crazy lately... Deirdre had cancer, Jenna was talking non-stop about some nurse she met, the twins were acting stranger than they normally were, and even his own children were talking about angels and talking dogs and ducks... or something like that. Then there was that paper with Steve's handwriting on it. He didn't know what to think about that. And the more he thought about it, the creepier it got. And Gabe... taking off like that!

He wasn't sure what to do, so he'd had a drink, then another and another.

Jenna came into the office and he told her what happened. She never said a word; just grabbed their coats and they went straight to Deirdre's - where he had many more drinks. He couldn't stop thinking about that handwriting!

As if that wasn't enough already, he'd had one hell of a weird dream last night. Kyle figured it was a combination of the day's events and nearly lethal amounts of alcohol, but it had been so real! He rarely dreamed and when he did he could barely remember them... but this one! Every moment was etched in his memory; he could recall every word said. And the details! ...The way Steve's hair was messed up from wearing his hat, just like it used to be, and the scratches in the leather of his jacket. Christ, he could even smell that faint horsy smell Steve always had.

He placed his throbbing head in his hands, slowly shaking it in denial of he knew not what.

"Kyle, what is it?" Although Gabe had a feeling he knew.

Kyle let out a deep sigh and ran his fingers through his hair, and then looked up at his friend.

"Have you ever had something really weird happen to you?" Seeing the look on Gabe's face he quickly added, "Other than yesterday, of course."

Gabe had to laugh; it was without humor. Look up weird in the dictionary, and the past few days of his life would be right there.

"Yes, Kyle, other than yesterday I have had quite a rash of strange occurrences. Why do you ask?"

"Well, I was thinking about Steve all day yesterday after, well, you know." Gabe nodded.

"Anyway, as you know I got a little trashed last night."

Again Gabe nodded.

"Well, the combination made me...gave me... I had the strangest goddamn dream last night. To tell the truth, I don't know what to think or where to begin."

"Let me guess," Gabe began, "Steve came to you in a dream. He sat on the edge of the sofa, made a few jokes, then gave you some sage advice about say, oh...follow your heart?"

Kyle's eyes grew wide as he listened to his buddy. *This was too much*! He was ready to trade his coffee for another shot of scotch.

"Well, how close am I?"

"Uh, pretty damn close. Except the last part, he didn't tell me to follow anything. He said... let me think a minute. He said, 'True friendship doesn't question or criticize. Things aren't always what they seem.' Then he said he had to go and vanished."

The two men sat in silence for a while, each immersed in his own thoughts.

Deirdre took a quick peek into the dining room; Steven must have paid them both a visit last night. Good... she was running out of time. She thought about making breakfast for them but changed her mind. Kyle looked in no condition to eat, he looked absolutely dreadful! She felt sorry for him, yet at the same time felt that he deserved what he got. He should know better than to drink so much.

Painfully, Deirdre climbed the stairs to the second floor. She checked to see that her sons were behaving themselves, and then considered making her way up another flight of steep stairs to the attic. Once again she had taken an interest in the books she found up there. Geoffrey didn't know a thing about them, so they had most likely been there when he had purchased the house.

What excited her most were the journals, dozens of them. All written in a very lady-like script by Mrs. Rosalind Charles, nee Delaney, and were dated from 1920 to 1977. Deirdre had thumbed through a few of them, reading a bit here and there. Oh, it was too good... and what a history lesson it could be! Maybe even an idea for a play; she had wanted to try her hand at writing a script for a while now.

Deirdre had organized the journals by date from oldest to the most recent and placed them into two boxes, with the classic books going into a third. She wished she dared tell her husband about them and have Geoffrey carry them down later, but he'd be furious with her for daring the climb to the attic in the first place. She would have done it herself, but it was all she could do to get herself down the steps.

On second thought she went back to Geoffrey's office.

She flipped on the desk lamp and opened cover of the bible she had found so long ago, and then read the names written there.

The Charles' family tree went back five generations... Fascinating! It began with Peter Charles and his wife, Martha, and ended with Amanda and Ann (Annie) Benton. It also included names from relatives of the immediate Charles family.

Something had been inserted in the center of the huge bible. Deirdre opened it to the mismatched paper and pulled out a very old envelope. She carefully lifted the flap and saw a dried flower, flattened from years of being compressed between the pages of the scripture. The once white petals of the rose were now a sickly yellow-brown, the leaves a dull gray-green. It was so old and fragile that she feared it would turn to dust at any moment. She wondered what significance it had, being preserved in such an important book. The memento was carefully replaced in the bible, and Dee slipped the bible into one of the few empty spaces on the bookshelf.

Once again, Deirdre was in the attic, pouring over the journals. She had skimmed though several before her hospitalization and they had meant nothing to her at the time other than an interesting read. A few names caught her attention, having known people by the same name, but that was all. But it was certainly different now; the names meant something to her. She was anxious to finish the journals before she turned them over to their rightful owner.

She just had to find a way to reach Annie.

Annie Benton.

The same Annie whose name was the last one entered in the bible downstairs. Deirdre knew that Geoffrey knew where to find her, but he wasn't quite ready yet… still trying to be the good, faithful husband. She longed to tell him to go to Annie, which was who he belonged with, but it was not up to her. This had to progress at its own pace. It began well over a century ago; a few more weeks weren't going to make a difference.

Gabe went back to work late Wednesday morning although he wasn't sure why. They were between projects and he was suffering from a serious case of writer's block.

He didn't care. All he could think about was Annie.

Kyle had finally, well nearly, accepted the unreality of reality. After Gabe had shared his dream with him they decided that maybe it wasn't a dream after all, maybe more of a visit. After all, Steve wasn't one of those chain-shaking, sheet-wearing ghosts that ran around killing people. He was Stevie, full of practical jokes and unusually good manners. At least they had a good laugh over the ghost theory, far-fetched as it was.

Gabe seemed pre-occupied, but not freaked out.

Or maybe he was just numb.

Kyle went back to work Wednesday afternoon. As usual, Chet blew him bird kisses when the man entered the office.

"Yeah, kiss this," Kyle told the bird, and aimed his ass right at him.

Chet gave Kyle a wolf-whistle in return.

Sometimes he really regretted buying that bird.

Jenna emerged from the washroom.

"Morning lover," she said as she kissed her husband.

"Morning. Or is it afternoon?"

"Depends on when you get up, I guess."

Kyle nodded towards Gabe's office. "He here?"

"More or less. His body is there but his mind is miles and miles away."

"I shouldn't wonder," he muttered, and then louder said, "Coffee, woman!"

"Coming right up!" She was glad to see Kyle back to his old self.

Gabe walked out of his office, coat in hand.

"I need to talk to the two of you for a moment," he told them.

Kyle and Jenna glanced at each other; it didn't sound good.

"I'm going to take some time off," Gabe began. "Things have been a bit… strange lately and I need some time to sort it all out. I'm sure you two can handle everything around here."

"Uh, how long will you be gone?" asked Kyle.

"I don't know. Maybe a day, maybe a year. I'm not even sure where I will be," Gabe answered, shaking his head.

"You're leaving town?" Kyle gasped, hoping like hell he wouldn't.

"What about Deirdre and the kids?" Jenna said quietly, laying her hand on Gabe's arm.

"They'll be fine. Actually, it was Deirdre's idea. She seems to think I have been 'stressed' lately, and suggested that I go, get this, skiing. I haven't skied in years!"

"Skiing?" the Davidsons said in unison.

"Skiing. Don't sound so surprised. I *can* ski, you know."

"We know. You were poetry in motion on the slopes," Kyle said with just a hint of jealousy.

"It just seems strange for Deirdre to suggest such a thing," Jenna mused. "I mean, with her being so sick and all. Is she going with you?"

"No. She said she would make all of the necessary arrangements for me and I wasn't to worry about a thing. She wants a few days to herself too. She's even sending the boys to my parents' home for a week."

"I wonder if she has a boyfriend," Kyle snickered. "Hey Jen, you want a few days to yourself too? I'd be glad to chaperone Gabe!"

Jenna looked from Kyle to Gabe and back again. "You know, that may not be a bad idea. Maybe a change of scenery would get you two losers out of your creative rut. If this dry spell continues we'll be fighting over positions in the unemployment line."

She walked over to her husband and poked him in the chest with a well-manicured finger. "Go and have a good time, just send me a postcard from whatever exotic locale you happen to land in. I'll call Deirdre and tell her to buy two tickets to paradise."

"Ooh, I can feel an idea for a song coming on already!" quipped Kyle.

"Been done," Gabe quipped back.

Deirdre closed the door to the lab behind her. The blood tests every other day were becoming quite tedious, and she saw no reason for it, other than to appease her worried husband and placate the numerous doctors following her case.

As she pulled her car keys from her purse and turned towards the parking ramp, she felt a hand on her shoulder. She stopped and turned around, yet no one there. But she did see a poster advertising the Children's Hospital on the third floor.

Why not? Annie just might be working, and if she wasn't, maybe Deirdre could find a way to contact her. She would at least leave a note; it was time for Annie to know about the journals.

The Children's Hospital was brightly decorated with murals and pictures, and cartoon animals painted every few feet along the wall held signs indicating where to find the various rooms and departments on the floor. Children in hospital gowns wandered the halls with parents or nurses, and Deirdre could hear video games being played from a room down the hall near the reception desk.

She walked to the room and peeked in the door. It was a child's paradise, all provided by Geoffrey and Kyle's large, somewhat anonymous donation from Vegas Daze.

In addition to the video games, the room included a playhouse, dolls, blocks, and toy trucks and cars big enough for small children to ride on. There were crayons and a chalkboard, play-clay, and watercolors for painting. In one corner of the room set up as a kitchen, a family of four was taking fresh-baked cookies from an oven.

Deirdre watched as one of the children carefully took the cookies from the cookie sheet with a spatula. Tears pricked her eyes as she observed the child working around the IV tubing hanging from a pole and attached to an access port on the girl's chest. Her bald head shone in the florescent light of the room and her pale skin had a faint yellowish tint. After the child removed the last cookie she sank into a chair, exhausted from her efforts but wearing a brave smile on her little face.

Deirdre could watch no more. She dabbed the tears from her eyes and moved on to the reception desk. Several children were clustered around, exchanging knock-knock jokes. All were wearing hospital garb. They moved aside as she approached, allowing her access to the desk.

"May I help you?" inquired the ward clerk.

"Good morning. I was wondering if Annie was working today," Deirdre answered.

"No, she isn't here today; she usually works nights. Would you like to leave her a message?" the clerk asked, reaching for a pen.

"Yes, thank you." Deirdre took the proffered writing materials and jotted down a quick note. "Will she be in tonight?"

The clerk glanced at the schedule behind the desk. "I'm afraid I can't give out that information."

"Oh dear. Is there any other way I can reach her?"

"I'm sorry, I can't help you," replied the clerk.

"Well, thank you anyway." Deirdre smiled and turned away from the desk, colliding with an older boy.

He looked to be around eleven or twelve, but was rather small and thin for his age. He grabbed the handle of a portable oxygen tank to prevent it from tipping over. Clear tubing ran from the tank to the boy's face and he was breathing quite hard.

"Oh, excuse me!" Deirdre said, putting a hand on the boy's thin shoulder. "I wasn't aware that anyone was behind me... Are you all right?"

"I'm fine," he replied. He glanced at the ward clerk who was back to sharing knock-knock jokes, and then smiled at Deirdre. "I know where to find Annie," he whispered.

"Do you now?" asked a surprised Deirdre. She doubted that he really knew, and yet if he did, would it be proper to ask him?

The boy took her hand and pulled her away from the desk. "Annie is my best friend," he told her. "Annie and Michael."

"M... Michael?" Goose flesh covered Deirdre's arms.

"Mmhmm. And McDonald."

"McDonald?"

"Mmhmm. He's my, uh, Annie's goose."

"Can we go somewhere and talk?" asked Deirdre, smiling.

Goose-Mother. This was too good to be true.

Eric led her to a small waiting room not too far from the elevators. They sat together on a plastic-covered sofa.

"My name is Deirdre," she said.

"Eric." He extended his hand.

She shook it.

"So, you and Annie are friends?"

"Yeah, for quite a long time now. I spend a lot of time at her lake in the summer."

"You said you were friends with, uh, Michael?"

"Yeah, he's the best. He used to be a cowboy and he taught me how to ride a horse and rope goats. He's really good." Eric smiled at the memory.

"Hmm... I remember it well," Deirdre murmured, more to herself.

"Oh good! You're the lady... I was hoping you were the right one. He told me to look for you," Eric said, quite relieved.

"You've seen him? Recently?"

"Sure! He was here last night. He visits me here when Annie isn't working but he usually comes after I'm sleeping. Sometimes I think it's a dream at first, but I know I'm awake. He told me to tell you where Annie went."

Typical Steven. But he must have abandoned the dream scenarios with Annie and Eric, roping goats wasn't something one normally did in bed. Interesting... And she would have given anything to have him in her dreams again.

"Where did Annie go?"

"Nowhere yet, but she's going skiing with Marti on Friday. In Canada."

"And Michael told you this?"

"No, Marti did. She asked me if she should kidnap Annie and go skiing. I said sure! I don't really know if she should or not, but jeez, she needs a vacation. You wouldn't believe how much she works. I'm here a lot, so I know."

"Do you know where in Canada?" Deirdre just had to find out.

"'Fraid not. Michael does though, you can ask him."

"Yes, I'll do that." She wondered how Eric knew of her connection with

Michael.

Steven.

She looked into Eric's eyes and saw that they held the same knowledge that Deirdre possessed regarding herself, he was aware that his time on this earth was severely limited. He also knew that Michael's time had been over for a long time.

"Eric, I would love to visit with you again sometime; I think we have a lot in common." She gave his hand a squeeze. "Would that be all right with you?"

"I'd like that. Annie needs us and Michael can only do so much." Eric returned the squeeze.

"Here is my phone number." She handed him a pre-printed card. "Call me anytime, day or night, if you want to talk. It was very nice meeting you."

"Me too. And I'll call you if uh, anything else comes up." He flicked the card with a thickened finger.

Deirdre went straight to a pay phone to call Geoffrey, and caught him just as he was leaving for the studio. She asked him to stay at home until she returned; she had something important to discuss with him.

After they had talked and Geoffrey went to work, Deirdre went to the attic to bring a few more journals down. She would have liked to bring them all at once, but she only had enough strength to make one trip a day up the steep stairs, and then only bring two down at a time. She was reluctant to let anyone else in on her secret.

She stood at the top of the steps to catch her breath. Damn cancer had taken over her lungs now. What a horrid disease it was... Her back ached with a dull, heavy pain.

With great effort, she walked to the box of journals and looked down into it to see that there were still dozens of books in there. Maybe she could shove the box to the top of the stairs and push it down... let gravity work for her. With any luck the damage to the journals would be minimal. She had to do something though; she didn't have many more trips up there left in her.

Deirdre reached down and grasped the box and gave it a good tug. Sharp pain shot through every bone in her body and she sank to the floor, moaning. Tears ran down her face as she grit her teeth against the agonizing torment. Dear God, she couldn't take much more.

She heard the scuff of boots on the dusty floor behind her. *Oh no... Geoffrey was there?* She didn't want him to know how sick she really was.

Strong, masculine arms lifted Deirdre from the floor and held her tight. She looked up into bright blue eyes, and then raised a shaking hand to caress his beloved face.

"My lady," Steven said as he bent to bestow a kiss upon his Juliet.

As he kissed her, Deirdre's pain faded to nothing but a distant memory. The kiss ended and again she gazed into his eyes.

"Oh, Steven, have I finally died? I must have, for I can feel you... This is truly heaven!"

He allowed her to regain her feet and they stood together in a tight embrace. He kissed the top of her head.

"No, not dead yet. Close to it, but you're already well aware of that," he said, smiling down at her.

"But I can feel you!" Deirdre released her arms from around his neck and gently squeezed his biceps. "And you feel so good! Why couldn't I ever do this before when I saw you?"

"Don't ask me to explain it. Even if I knew, I'm not allowed to divulge much information regardin' the afterlife."

"So much for the million questions I was going to ask."

She hugged him again, scarcely able to believe that it was actually happening. He had been coming to her in dreams since her diagnosis of cancer, but she had never touched him - or even tried. It was enough just to be able to see him, to talk to him. And on her last admission to Brighton he had begun to talk to her while he eased her pain.

It was Steven, who had told Deirdre about Annie, but much of what he had said was vague and she didn't quite understand. What was clear to her was that she had to get her husband and Annie together.

Deirdre sighed and pulled him closer to her.

He returned her embrace and began to slowly waltz her around the room as he hummed a tune his brother had written. The song never made it to the charts, but the couple had heard it on one of the demo tapes Gabe had sent Steve, and it became "their song."

When Steve got to the chorus, Deirdre sang the words.

"We've known each other forever, since the dawn of time. Two lives linked together; two souls, yours and mine. Our love is enduring, no other is as true. Two loves joined for a lifetime; two souls, me and you."

The song ended and once again they shared a kiss.

"I just realized that my pain is gone," Deirdre whispered.

Steve smiled. "We're allowed to perform a small miracle every now and then. Unfortunately, I can't make it last."

"I understand. Even this small respite was too much to ask for. Thank you," she said gratefully.

"We've some business to discuss."

"Yes… Annie. Just where is she going in Canada? Eric said that you would tell me."

"Ah, Eric. Great kid. He'll be joinin' the ranks of our angelic army before too long."

"It's so sad. Not only him, but all of those children I saw today." Deirdre choked back a tear and added, "So much suffering."

"I know," replied Steven. "But once you cross over you never feel pain again. I can't even remember what it felt like."

"Steven, did you suffer before you died? I... I'm not sure if I really want to know, but the horror of what you must have endured has been plaguing me since the day I found out what happened."

"Well, let me think; I haven't thought about it for years… I remember thick smoke, it was almost impossible to breathe, and it was the horses... They were sufferin' and I had to get them out. Then I saw Bud, he owned the stable in the barn, and I yelled for him to help me. He not so delicately told me to have intercourse with myself... and he kept mutterin' about what a loser he was and…something about 'Matt'. He was flickin' lit matches into the straw and I thought I saw a gas can on the floor behind him. I was torn between savin' him or savin' more of the horses. My misfortune was trying to save him. Son of a gun hit me over the head with a pitchfork handle... or was it a shovel? Whatever. Anyway, that was all she wrote and I was headin' for the light. So, in answer to your question… no, I didn't suffer." He finished his speech with another kiss for his ladylove.

"Thank God. Now about Annie... Do you actually know where she is going?"

"Yep. Little place just north of the Soo. I've been there, real nice."

"You never told me that you skied. You were there to ski, weren't you?"

"Yep, we went there to ski. Whenever Gabe and I would visit our grandmother over Christmas vacation, we would drive up there. Couldn't ride much in the winter so we had to find a new hobby. If memory serves, Gabe was quite good. Always had a flock of ski bunnies hovering around him too. I usually got the leftovers," teased Steve.

"Now he has yours," Deirdre teased back.

"Ha ha. I know how it is between the two of you; I'm dead, I'm not blind. You are still hopelessly in love with me and no other man will do, and Gabe is too much of a gentleman to inflict his beastly marital rights upon your oh-so delectable person," Steve said with a smile.

"And I love him for it." But she did feel a twinge of guilt at loving Geoffrey like she did… and making love to him like she had.

"Back to Annie. I think she'll need some ski lessons... Know anyone willin' to instruct her?" he asked with a gleam in his eye.

Deirdre tapped her chin with her index finger, appearing to be deep in thought, and then raised the finger over her head. "Aha! I have just such a person in mind. I think Geoffrey needs a little vacation. He's been a little off his mark lately."

"Splendid idea my dear!" exclaimed Steven. "I'll leave you to attend to the details." His expression saddened as he said, "I'm afraid I have to go."

Deirdre nodded. "I know. I love you, Steven."

"I love you too, my lady."

They wrapped their arms around one another and shared one last kiss. She watched as he faded into the darkness of the attic. There was a bright flash of blue light, and then he was gone.

Deirdre could feel the pain creeping back into her joints. Better finish getting those journals down before it was too late. It took five trips to and from the attic before she had transferred all of the books, but they were now safely hidden away in her bedroom closet. She went to the bathroom and pulled the bottle of Vicodin from the medicine cabinet. Typed under her name, were instructions to take one to two capsules every four hours as needed for pain.

"That's a good one," she mumbled as she read the label. She swallowed six of the pills and hoped that it would be enough.

Deirdre called Al and Marie and arranged for them to take James and Jeremy for the week. They would love to fly to Montana for a visit with their grandparents, and the senior Evans' were happy to oblige.

She called four hotels in Sault Ste. Marie before she could find a room for Geoffrey, not at all surprised that the resort at River Ridge was booked up. She had no sooner hung up the phone when Jenna called, wondering if Kyle tag along.

Sure, why not? Deirdre called the hotel back and changed the reservations to two rooms, Thursday through Sunday.

She was exhausted by that time. She fixed lunch for sons, and then went to rest in her room. Thank God those boys were well under control; it was almost as if they knew she wasn't well enough to handle any bad behavior.

As she lay in her bed, she could hear their voices in the next room.

"Tell us another story, Daddy."

"Yeah, tell us the one about how you met Mamma."

"And tell us the one about the Goose-Mother again."

Well, that explains it. They had their very own guardian angel for a babysitter. Their father would never let them come to harm. Not right now, anyway.

Smiling, Deirdre closed her eyes and slept.

When Gabe arrived home, the house was unnaturally quiet. Deirdre's car was still parked it the drive so she must be home... He hung his jacket in the closet and noticed that the boys' coats were still there.

"Deirdre?"

No answer.

"James? Jeremy?"

Silence.

Aw God...

Gabe began to worry. He ran up the stairs and burst into the twins' room, only to find it empty. Deirdre's room was next, and his sigh of relief was audible when he saw them.

She lay on her bed, a sleeping child in each arm. The boys lay cuddled against their mother, each with a hand clasped to his brother's and resting on Mama's tummy.

Gabe stood in the doorway looking at his family.

His brother's family.

As much as he loved them, he longed for a true wife of his own... children of his own. Yet James and Jeremy were his own as far as they knew and it would stay that way. Maybe when they were older they could be told the truth, but not for a while. Not for a long while.

Deirdre stirred and opened her eyes, and smiled when she saw her husband in the doorway. She had been dreaming of Steven - a real dream this time. She was happy.

Gently, she moved the boys away from her so that she could get up.

"Hi, Geoffrey," she whispered.

They went downstairs into the office-den. Deirdre told him the details of his weekend trip and Gabe began to look forward to it. *She was certainly enthusiastic about it – hell; maybe she did have a boyfriend coming over. Well if she did, good for her!* But he knew better. There would never be anyone for her but Steve.

The Evans' invited the Davidson's over for take-out pizza from T.J.'s. After they ate, the kids watched a video and the adults played cards, men against the women. The ladies won of course, only because Kyle let them...

Kyle and Gabe went into the den to discuss travel plans, while the women went upstairs to Deirdre's room. Dee stopped for more Vicodin on the way, all too aware that she'd need a stronger narcotic before too long.

"Jenna, I have a huge secret that I need to tell you. You have to promise not to tell a soul until I say, or unless I... well, just don't tell anyone. Promise?"

"Promise. Scout's honor." Jenna held up two fingers in a salute.

Deirdre opened the door of her walk-in closet. As she entered she motioned for Jenna to follow, and then pointed to the boxes of Rosalind's journals. The leather-bound bible sat atop the closest box.

"Open the cover," Dee said, indicating the bible.

Jenna picked up the heavy book, and with questioning look at her friend, opened it. Inside she saw what appeared to be a family tree. Names and dates spread their roots down the paper.

"So, what's the secret?"

"Read the last name entered. There, at the bottom." Deirdre pointed a finger towards the lower half of the book.

Jenna found the two names. "Amanda Claire Benton. Ann Rose Benton." She looked at her friend. "I don't get it."

"Annie Benton. It's Annie... our nurse?"

Jen walked to the bed. She sat down and began to read the rest of the names. When she reached the top names, her eyes widened.

"Wow! Where did you get this? Does she know about it?"

"No, she doesn't; I plan to tell her next week. But that's not all."

Deirdre walked to the closet again and brought out several of the earliest journals.

"These belonged to Annie's grandmother. I haven't read through all of them yet, but so far they are quite a history lesson."

"Whoa! How did you get them?" Jenna put the bible next to her on the bed and picked up a journal.

"They were in boxes in the back of the attic. They must have been here when Geoffrey bought the house." Dee eased her aching body onto the bed.

Jen flipped through the journal. "Anything juicy or scandalous?" she asked.

"Not the way you think. I doubt the National Enquirer would be interested, but I think it will explain a lot of what has been going on around here lately. I'm hoping this will give us some insight on the names in that bible." Deirdre was silent for a moment, the continued. "You can see why I don't want you to say anything?"

"I think so, but shouldn't Annie know? I mean, if this is her grandmother..."

"I've already left a note for her at the hospital, asking her to call me. The rest is up to her." Deirdre placed her hand on Jenna's. "One more thing. If anything should happen to me before Annie gets these, could you see to it that she does get them? It's very important."

"Sure, Dee, you can count on me," Jen assured her. "Well, it's getting late and we should be going. I want one last fling with my man before he's freed among the savage beauties in tight ski pants. I want to give him something to remember me by," she winked. "You'd better do the same for Gabe. He might be tempted by some fresh young thing out on the slopes."

That's exactly what Deirdre was hoping for.

Gabe was packed and ready to leave by nine o'clock Thursday morning. As soon as Kyle arrived they would be on the road – fortunately for Davidson, he was only thirty minutes late, and therefore spared much of the wrath of Evans.

He sat out in his Jeep, honking the horn until Gabe glared out of the window at him, so Kyle went up to the house to help him with his newly purchased gear.

"New stuff, buddy?"

"Yeah... might as well. My old skis had way too many miles on them and were hopelessly outdated... wouldn't want to embarrass myself on the slopes now, would I?"

"Then I'd stay off 'em if I were you," Kyle chuckled.

"Kyle?"

"Yeah?"

"Fuck you. I can ski..."

"Used to, anyway."

"Always kicked your ass..."

"Whatever..." Kyle trailed off when he spotted Deirdre coming towards them.

"Kyle," she said, giving him a hug, "You're looking much better than the last time I saw you."

"And you're always beautiful, Dee. Can I get a kiss too?"

She gave him a very nice one on the cheek.

Kyle blushed.

Kyle rarely blushed.

"Lord..." Gabe mumbled, thinking about how his pal always had a little thing for Mrs. Evans - not that he minded, of course.

Gabe hugged the boys and told them to be good for their grandparents, and then gave his wife a kiss on the cheek, instructing her to call him for anything; he'd be back as soon as he could. Charter a jet if he had to. She smiled up at him... *What a dear man he was.*

As he turned to leave, she touched his shoulder and then pulled him around to face her. She gently held his face in her hands, forcing him to look at her. She had to choose her words carefully.

"Geoffrey, I want this weekend to be really special for you. As of this moment, you are a free man. I want you to have fun. Live, laugh... and love. Follow your heart."

He searched her face, trying to understand the meaning of her words. Steve had said the same thing to him in the dream.

Follow your heart...

"Deirdre..."

"I mean it, Geoffrey. You go and have a wonderful time." She kissed him on the chin before she gently shoved him out the door. She waved until they were out of sight and closed the door against the January cold.

As she was turning around, she heard a familiar voice say, "Do you think he will?"

"I certainly hope so."

She took Steven's hand and they went to join their children.

For the first time since high school, Gabe was on his way to River Ridge. Since then he had skied in Aspen, Vail, Breckenridge, Banff, and even Europe, yet compared to those mountains, River Ridge was not much more than a bunny run. He wondered why Deirdre had chosen to send him there. No matter; he'd always liked the small resort. It was never crowded and the runs were pretty good. The Canadians were a friendly bunch, even if they did end each sentence with "eh?" Yes, it might prove to be a good weekend after all.

To pass the time on the way up, Gabe and Kyle sang medleys of the songs they had written and recorded together. Gabe played his guitar while Kyle drove and used the steering wheel as a percussion instrument. It was rather amazing the range of sounds produced by the simple wheel.

Eventually, they ran out of their old material.

They glanced at each other.

"So," said Kyle with false sadness, "Does this mean the relationship is over?

Have we gone as far as we can go? Do you want a divorce?" He pretended to burst into tears.

"You wish. No, actually I was coming up with something promising earlier this week. At least I was until I was hit with a paper airplane. What do you think of this?" Gabe began plucking out notes on the guitar to give him the melody, and then switched to chords.

Kyle hummed along.

"Any lyrics yet?"

Gabe thought for a moment then said, "Let's see... You told me you'd love me forever; I believed every word that you said. I built my whole world around you; I followed wherever you led..."

"Hey, I like it so far. Maybe we're not dead after all!" Kyle was more excited than he had been in months.

They worked on the lyrics some more, Gabe jotting them down in his ever-present notebook. By the time they had reached Cadillac, the song was finished. They high-fived each other and pulled into Burger King for cheeseburgers and chocolate shakes.

The rest of the trip was spent in either idle talk or comfortable silence. SD was back on the creative track again, both men could feel it, and now they could really enjoy themselves.

Gabe and Kyle checked into their rooms, not the best they'd ever had, but comfortable enough.

Kyle threw his gear on the bed and began to dig through his suitcase, looking for his swim trunks. There was a hot tub downstairs and he could not wait to get into it. Just as he was about to damn Jenna to hell for all eternity for not packing something to swim in, he found them...wrapped inside an 8 x 10 picture of his provocative little wife - and she wasn't wearing very much. The note attached said, "'behave yourself or you will never touch this again!" Kyle's eyes moved back to the picture... to the perfect breasts barely covered by her long, wavy blonde hair, and then to the slim, strong thighs barely hidden by a bit of silk.

His pulse beat faster. *Damn her*! He'd behave himself all right, as if it was ever an issue in the first place.

Gabe found his buddy relaxing in the outdoor hot tub, already surrounded by bikini-clad women. Jen was damn lucky that she could trust him. The females looked up as he approached and immediately made room for him to join them. He groaned inwardly and hoped that he would not be recognized. He didn't think it likely that they would be known this far north, but one never knew. Sometimes he truly regretted making those music videos.

The ladies in the water flashed Gabe bright smiles and shifted position to better display their other assets. He was sorely tempted to turn and run... *Maybe if he ignored them they would go away.*

"Gabe buddy! Miss me?"

"Only about as much as finding one's reservations have been misplaced and there's no room at the inn. How's the water?"

"Mighty fine… mighty fine. Dive on in!" Kyle laughed, glancing at the women surrounding him.

They smiled encouraging smiles, scarcely able to believe their luck at having not one, but two gorgeous men joining them.

Gabe sighed and stepped into the pool. The hot, bubbly water was too much to resist after the long ride he'd recently endured in the cramped Jeep.

He handed Kyle one of the beers that he was holding.

"So, buddy, how's the wife doing?"

Two of the women in the pool nonchalantly moved away from Kyle, not that he really cared. He grinned as he watched the ladies turn their attention solely to Gabe. The partners had played this game before.

"She's fine, buddy, and yours?"

"Better than fine. A veritable Venus! A magnificent Madonna! Ah, the mere thought of her blinds me to all others of the fairer sex." Gabe kissed his fingertips and stared off into space as if he could see the love of his life hovering before him. It didn't seem to deter the women, so the duo moved on to plan B.

"Yeah right, buddy," Kyle snickered. "You're only blind to the others 'cuz deep down you prefer your own… kind."

"Kyle! Jesus… not here!" Gabe groaned, rolling his eyes and glancing to see if the women had heard. He snuggled close to his buddy and whispered, "You swore to God you'd never mention our… relationship in front of anyone!"

"As if it would stay a secret… God, you're hot!" Kyle winked.

Gabe simpered.

One by one the disappointed women made their excuses and exited the pool; maybe the bar had easier pickings. Who needed those weirdoes anyway? But damn, they were good-looking!

When the last female left, the duo clinked their beer bottles together and toasted a night free of estrogen. Sure, the attention was nice, but they'd had their fill of it early in their career.

"To Deirdre, and her kind generosity in arranging these fine accommodations for us," toasted Kyle.

"To Jenna, for allowing you - of all people, to chaperone me - of all people, on our snowy voyage of discovery," toasted Gabe.

"Christ, that was so damn lame... Can't you do better?" Kyle took a swig of beer and started to laugh. "Wait until you hear this!" he choked.

He told Gabe of Jenna's little warning note, leaving out the most intimate details of course.

Gabe found it highly amusing, and laughed nearly as hard as he did when he had first been introduced to his bird, Chet.

The two men had dinner in the hotel's restaurant. The Texas theme seemed a bit out of place in the great white north, but the food was excellent and the service just as good. After dinner Kyle said that he was tired from the drive and was going to turn in early because he wanted to be on the slopes as soon as the resort opened in the morning. And he wanted to call Jen.

Gabe figured he knew what would be involved in *that* conversation and wished his buddy a most pleasant night. He ordered one more beer and kicked back in his booth. But Christ, he was restless. He'd been trying to keep thoughts of Annie at bay since his unexpected visit to her cabin, with little luck. Now that he had actually seen her, the visions of her danced through his mind with an intensity that left him frustrated as hell.

He didn't even finish his drink before he stomped off to his room.

He sat on his bed and flipped through the channels on the TV. And as usual, nothing interesting there even with the fine Canadian programming.

It was no use, he needed to get out and move around. He grabbed his jacket and went for a long walk in the cold, northern air.

The night was crisp and clear; the sky was incredibly beautiful. He was now far enough from the city lights to see the aurora borealis. It never ceased to amaze him.

A meteor split the sky... Wish upon a shooting star. He wished for...wished for... He wasn't sure what to wish for and hoped he could save it for later.

Better get back to the hotel though; too bad he wasn't tired yet. He began to jog; thankful he had the good sense to change from his customary cowboy boots into a warmer pair of sneaker-type hiking boots.

His feet hit the snow-covered pavement in muffled thumps.

One two one two ann nee ann nee.

He moved faster.

Annie Annie Annie.

He was running full out. His breath burned in his lungs, his eyes blurred from the sting of the frigid wind, and he ran until he could run no more. He stopped, stooped over and gasping for breath while her name still raced through his mind.

Gabe walked the rest of the way back to the hotel, happier than hell that the bar was still open.

He needed a drink.

And another...

And another.

He sat alone in the deserted bar, staring out of the window and getting drunker by the minute. Bet ol' Deirdre hadn't planned on this when she sent him there.

He ordered yet another scotch and the bartender hesitated to give it to him, but the guy was a guest in the hotel. Not like he'd be on the road tonight. He observed Gabe for a moment and decided that one more wouldn't hurt. It was last call anyway.

"Thank you..." Gabe looked at the bartender's nametag, "Jay."

He toasted Jay and downed the drink in one swallow then attempted to slide the empty glass from one hand to the other and back again across the table. He missed and it fell. From far away in his boozy haze Gabe waited to hear the smashing of the glass on the hard surface of the floor. It never came. There was a roaring, buzzing sound in his head - maybe which had drowned out the sound of the crash. He didn't really care though because he was comfortably drunk.

He was jovial.

He smiled at no one in particular.

Gabe closed his eyes when the room began to dip and sway, working up to a wild rotation. His hands went to his head, supporting it with elbows digging into the table. As soon as the spinning stopped, he opened his unfocused eyes back up and looked at his reflection in the window. He grinned and waved at it. Three seconds later his reflection waved back - with the opposite hand. Aw God… how was it that he was still sober enough to notice the difference? He blinked and looked closer. His reflection grinned, putting the unbroken scotch glass back on the table.

"Steven Anthony!" Gabe cried, his voice breaking into two octaves. "And to what do I owe the pleasure of your company?"

"Hey, bro. Thought you might want someone to talk to. You seemed a little down earlier."

Jay was wiping down the bar and watching an old music video on the country-western station; two dudes singing about dreamin' up some chick. He wished he could turn it to something with a little more hard rock. He glanced at the lone drunk. Damned if he wasn't talking to his reflection in the window. What a freakin' loser, he thought, turning back to watch the video. Hey, that dude looked kinda like that drunk over there. He looked at the drunk again and then back to the video. Damn, it was the same guy! Not only was he a freakin' loser, he was a freakin' washed-up loser. Wait until he told his buddies about this one!

"Hey loser!" Jay yelled to the drunk.

Gabe turned to face him, his expression darkening.

"Skooze me?" he slurred. He didn't take kindly to people calling him names. Maybe he should teach the little punk a lesson. Christ, it had been forever since he'd been in a goddamn good fight, and tonight… well, it sure as hell wouldn't take much.

"Um, sir? It's closing time. I'll have to ask you to leave now." Jay's attitude changed dramatically when he realized that Gabe could probably do him great bodily harm.

"D'ja hear that Stevie? The barkeep sez we gotsta go." Gabe was beginning to weave in his chair as the recently consumed alcohol took full effect.

Jay watched him. *Damn… That drunk was having a regular conversation with himself in the window. Better get him to his room.* He turned the lights in the bar off and walked over to Gabe.

"C'mon, sir, I'll help you to your room."

He walked up behind Gabe, ready to assist but even readier to move quickly out of the way should the man take a swing at him. Jay watched the man's reflection carefully. It continued to smile a serene smile that belied his condition.

"Not nessr'y. My good brother here will deliver me safely to my room." Gabe slurred.

Oh God... he could hear the drunk talking, but he couldn't see his mouth moving! Wait... where was *his* reflection in the glass? Jay couldn't see anything else except the drunk in the window, still smiling serenely.

He began to back away from the eerie scene.

The reflection stood and walked around the table to help his drunken twin to his feet, and the duo slowly made their way to the door.

Or was it two? Jay wasn't quite sure. It looked as though the drunk was definitely leaning on someone, but that someone never took a solid shape. He thought that he could see tables, chairs, even the wall through that someone! Oh, man... he didn't know whether to roll up and smoke a big ol' doobie, or quit smoking it completely! Pot didn't cause hallucinations, did it?

Steve saw to it that his brother was safely delivered to his room. He wasn't sure where Gabe's key card was, so he just materialized on the other side of the door and unlocked from there.

Gabe staggered in and fell onto the bed.

"Whoa, Stevie! I do believe that I am indeed intoxicated! I can't be sure though… too goddamn drunk to know! Any thoughts on the matter?" he said with a short laugh.

"Oh, you're drunk all right. Sloshed, blotto, smashed, lit, inebriated, intoxicated... drunk," Steve assured him.

"You left out shit-faced. Thank you for clearing up *that* little matter," Gabe sighed. "I'm so relieved."

He began moving his arms back and forth as if he were making a snow angel.

"Stevie? When was the last time you made one of these?" he asked as he began making whooshing sounds to coincide with his arm, and now leg movements.

"And what would that be, Gabe?"

"That would be a snoooow angel," Gabe drawled. "A snow angel with green eyes and autumn hair, all red and gold." He stopped moving his limbs. "A snow angel who keeps apples on her table and a talking dog. A snow angel that can split a log with an axe and break my heart should I never find her."

"Am I to assume that you are referrin' to the fair Annie?"

"You are correct, sir. The fair Annie." Gabe sat up and stared at his brother. "Do you know her?"

"Indeed I do," Steve replied, "Indeed I do."

Gabe lay back down on the bed. He grabbed a pillow and held it close to him. "I know her too. I've never met her... at least I think I haven't... maybe I have. But I know her. I've known her forever. Since the dawn of time."

"Two lives that are linked together?"

"Two souls, hers and mine."

"Is she the 'green eyes' from your dream, do ya think?"

"Aw God... Stevie! Is that where I know her from? Is she the one I've been waiting forever for?"

Steve just smiled and tossed a pillow at his twin.

Gabe woke with a splitting headache. Oh God, did he actually drink that much last night? And that far out dream about Steve...

He smiled in spite of the pain. What fun they'd had. Steve told him about going to Heaven and then coming back again, and Gabe said he want to see his angel brother fly around the room on his golden wings. Well, he never saw any wings, but Steve did a damn good imitation of flight, and Gabe had laughed until his sides ached. He had almost forgotten what fun his brother was.

The dream faded with Steve's promise to show him a first class, angel-grade miracle, only because Gabe had begged him non-stop.

Christ, what was that infernal banging? He rubbed his eyes and massaged his temples... *Make that goddamn pounding go away...*

"Room service," called a voice from the hall, followed by another knock.

"Hold on!" Gabe snapped.

Oooh... big mistake. He took a deep breath and sat up. His stomach lurched. Another deep breath... and the nausea went away - for the moment. It was about then he realized that he was wearing nothing at all. With a groan and a near gag, he bent, retrieving his boxers. Putting them on in his condition was akin to rocket science, he thought with a pained grin.

Another groan was wrenched from him when he pushed off the bed, headed for the opened the door, and opened it a crack.

"Yes?" he whispered through the narrow opening. Christ, his head hurt.

"Room service, sir. I brought your coffee."

"Didn't order coffee." Gabe grumbled, sounding a little curter than he intended. He still wanted that coffee, though.

"Ah, no sir. This is compliments of a Steven Anthony. He said that you had requested it last night," said the disembodied voice from the hall. "Should I return it, sir?"

"No, I'll take it." Gabe didn't care if the devil himself had sent it; he needed caffeine. He grabbed his pants and pulled a couple of toonies out of the pocket for a tip. Crazy play money... Who ever heard of a two-dollar coin?

Coffee and money exchanged hands, and he leaned against the closed door and took a sip. God, that was good. It had an odd aftertaste, but it was hot and strong and he could feel the caffeine ripping away the cobwebs in his brain.

As Gabe went to replace the cup on the saucer he noticed a folded paper with his name on the front, in Steve's handwriting. It hardly bothered him in the least this time... Probably still just a little drunk.

He read, "Here is that little miracle I promised you. Say good-bye hangover and hello overhang - which you'd better not try and ski off of today. Remember what happened last time!"

"All too well," Gabe muttered.

When he was in college they'd made a trip to Alberta, and one of his buddies had skied out of bounds trying to get 'big air' from off of an overhanging rock. The only big air he ended up with was the pneumothorax he suffered when he crashed into some trees. Well, he did get big air when the helicopter transported him to the nearest trauma center too.

By the time he finished reading the note, his headache was gone and his stomach felt fine. In fact he was hungry. Ravenous even! He drained the rest of the coffee in three large gulps. Hardly dignified, but he was in a hurry... He had to get on the slopes.

Gabe took a quick shower, put on his ski clothes and went to find Kyle.

Before she realized it, Annie was heading north in a minivan with Marti. It was great to be heading out on another little vacation with her, and this one was thankfully NeeNee-free.

Marti had popped a CD into the player and began singing at the top of her lungs. The music was vaguely familiar; a mixture of rock, country, folk, and something Annie couldn't even describe.

It had its own style.

It worked.

The male singer had an incredible voice, his partner sang harmony, and they were perfect together. It made her feel... feel what? She couldn't describe it, but it was just "right." She pulled her new, borrowed Stetson over her closed her eyes and listened to the lyrics.

He sang of searching for his true love and finding her, only to find out the whole thing had been a dream.

Again with the dream. Except for the one about Michael the other night, all of Annie's were always the same. The dark-haired, blue-eyed man, reaching for her... And now she had a name to put with that face. Kind of. Was it Gabe? Was he the cowboy she had met in the cafeteria? Was this really his too-big hat she was wearing?

Questions whirled about in her mind, one after the other, until she felt like screaming.

The song about the dream ended and a new one began, something about love gone wrong. Never meant to be.

"Who is this?" Annie asked Marti.

"What, this group? They're called SD, short for Sleep Deprived. Like 'em?"

"Yes, I do; they're different. Strange name though. I wonder how they came up with the name."

"You're asking the right person, Annie-bananie. I just happen to be the local authority on them," Marti grinned. "Heck, I've told you about them time and time again! Kyle...?"

"Well, enlighten me once more." She was more than curious now.

"They're a local duo, originally from Montana. Why they relocated here is beyond me, but anyway... They had a bunch of big hits about six or seven years ago. Did some music videos. Quit touring about six years ago, but did some local concerts. Both of them are married with children." Marti made a disappointed face. "Lucky wenches that snagged 'em. These guys are gorgeous, for older men. I think that they're pushing forty."

"Yes, that is positively ancient," Annie said dryly to the late-twentyish Marti.

"Oops... sorry. I forget that you saw twenty-nine a long time ago,"

"Forgiven. So what about their name? Sounds like they've pulled a night shift or two."

"Actually, they did. Or at least one of them. Kyle, he's mostly the back-up singer, use to work at a recording studio, night shift of course, doing scut work that wasn't finished during 'normal' hours. His buddy would hang out with him sometimes and they would goof around with the equipment doing songs that they wrote. One night they recorded some stuff with a few of the studio musicians who were hanging around later than usual. Kyle's wife called about a sick kid and they left. They left the tape there in the machine. The boss found it the next morning, played it, *liked* it, and the rest is history."

"Rags to riches, huh?" Annie mused.

"I guess so. They haven't done much lately though. I think they moved more into writing and producing. I sure wish they'd do another CD - or at least another video. I could look at Kyle all day."

"That good? What does he look like?"

"About time you asked – and mean it. He's tall, blonde, gorgeous... Their picture is on the cover but I don't have it with me." Marti tapped the CD wallet. "Too much to haul all those cases around."

The women lapsed into silence, listening to the remainder of the CD, and Annie made a mental note to find all of the music that SD had recorded and add them to her sparse collection. She enjoyed many different kinds of music, but SD's really spoke to her.

The trip north was uneventful, except for maybe Grand Rapids. The heavy traffic was moving through the infamous 'S' curves twenty miles an hour faster that the posted forty-five miles an hour and Annie felt like an unwilling passenger in a grand prix race. Marti was having the time of her life. She thrived on any adrenaline rush-producing activity.

The white-knuckle ride was over in minutes and the highway straightened out. Annie dozed off for a few hours, tired from working the night before and no sleep for almost twenty-four hours. She woke when they stopped in Cadillac for burgers from McDonald's. She had never been this far north in Michigan, and vowed to stay awake for the remainder of the drive.

The Mackinaw Bridge loomed ahead and Annie couldn't wait to ride over it. She had seen pictures of it, but it was even more impressive than she could have imagined.

As they crossed the five miles of bridge, she looked to her right. She could see the Grand Hotel on Mackinaw Island; it made her think of the movie "Somewhere in Time." The cloudless sky reflected in the partially open water of Lake Huron, giving the color of that water a most incredible shade of blue. Annie had seen eyes of the same color many times in her dreams, and once in a hospital cafeteria.

An hour later they had crossed the Upper Peninsula. One more bridge to go and they would be in Canada.

On Annie's left was the ice-covered lake, Superior, and to her right were the Soo Locks. She was going to have to come up here in the summer; there was so much to see.

Her first view of Canada sickened her. As they crossed the International Bridge, she got a good look at the city below her. A steel mill belched smoke into the bright blue sky, and across the street a paper mill did the same. Row upon row of identical houses surrounded the steel mill. Row upon row of logs filled the yard of the paper mill. *Now there was some firewood!*

Where was the Canada she had heard about... the pristine wilderness, the unspoiled beauty?

"Just past customs," Marti told her.

As they sat in line at the checkpoint, Marti warned her that the agents had no sense of humor. As many times as she had been through, she had never seen them smile. They'd search your vehicle at the slightest provocation.

Annie thought that her friend was exaggerating, but as she watched the agents in their tiny cubicles repeating the same questions ad nauseum, she began to think maybe her friend might be right. Warning signs regarding illegal weapons were posted every few feet. She laughed to herself and hoped Marti wasn't packing any heat.

It was finally their turn.

The stern-looking agent glared. "Citizenship?"

"U.S." Marti replied.

"Purpose of visit?"

Marti raised her eyes towards the roof of the van where two pairs of skis were strapped. The agent looked at the skis.

"Uh… skiing?"

"Where?"

"River Ridge."

"What is in the van?"

"Just clothes… luggage."

"Anything else?"

This was too much for Annie; she had never seen Marti so serious. And that agent, he looked like a poster child for constipation. She tried to stifle a giggle.

"A camera?" Marti was getting nervous. She did have a bit of weed stashed in the toe of her ski boot.

"Anything else?"

Before she could stop herself, Annie blurted out, "It's over Marti, he knows about the circus midgets."

Marti stared at her for three full seconds then dissolved into laughter.

The agent's left eye twitched in angry spasms.

"Oops," Annie mumbled, sinking down into her seat.

"Have a nice trip, ladies," grumbled the agent. The corner of his mouth was beginning to twitch into an unfamiliar grin.

The girls wasted no time in leaving the checkpoint. Forty minutes late they pulled up to their rented villa.

The sun was just setting over the trees, the clouds were moving in, and the snow was taking on a grayish hue. Gabe was on the triple chair lift, making his last run before dinner. Kyle was two chairs ahead of him, raising hell with a hot-dog snow boarder and having a grand old time. Gabe hoped the boarder knew that his buddy was not serious in his criticisms; it could get ugly.

He looked behind him at the rocky terrain. Not quite big enough to be mountains, but definitely larger than hills. To his right was the deserted bunny run. The chair stopped with a lurch and Gabe swung back and forth, wondering how long this delay would take. He glanced back at the beginner slope. Ah, some brave soul had decided to tackle it. He watched as woman in a white jacket and matching ski pants dropped her skis. Aw God… that hair! Its red-gold highlights sparkled in the setting sun and he stared, willing the girl to turn around. *It couldn't be, could it?*

The chair lift started again. *No!* Not till he found out…

The lift stopped again and Gabe looked below him… Too high to risk jumping out, goddammit. He turned back to the woman in white.

Another skier came up rapidly behind her, stopped quickly, and sprayed the redhead with snow. The woman laughed and "died" in a dramatic death scene, falling to her back at the bottom of the hill. Gabe still couldn't make out her features, it was getting too dark with the clouds rolling in, but he did watch as the woman didn't get up right away and instead began to move her arms back and forth, making a snow angel.

The sun chose just that moment to make one last appearance, throwing rays of rose-gold light down upon the female in the snow, like a heavenly spotlight. He couldn't see the green eyes, although he could make out that smile, it was the same one that had once bought him a cup of free coffee.

The skier was now pelting the "angel" with snowballs until she jumped up to return the volley. The chair lift started up again. *Aw no... not yet...*

"Annie!" Gabe shouted.

The woman's arm stopped in mid-throw as she looked about her.

Gabe lost sight of her when the chair went between a grove of pine trees.

Annie completed her throw, catching Marti dead center in the gut, and then brushed snow from her borrowed outfit. Jill was just a bit smaller than her, but the jacket and matching pants fit well enough. She turned to face the hill, feeling just a bit intimidated. It looked terribly high even if it was the beginner run.

Marti had given Annie a quick instruction about how to get her ski boots in and out of the bindings. She placed the toe of her boot in the front binding, then pressed her heel down on the back one, and heard a solid "click" as the binding caught. So far, so good... and repeated the process with the other ski.

Marti stayed put just long enough to see that Annie could handle her equipment before took off for the real slope. Annie was grateful; she didn't want any witnesses to her impending humiliation. Well, there was the lift operator but he looked too jaded to notice anything. She wondered what horrible thing he had done to tick off the boss who had relegated him to this lowly position on the bunny hill.

She looked at the lift. Long poles hung from the ever-moving cable... up the hill and back down again. A small disc was at the end of each pole, and she wondered how to use these contraptions. In answer to her prayers, two young girls skied past her to the lift and stood in the tracks to wait for a pole to reach them. The operator caught the next one and handed it to the first girl in line. She straddled the pole and the disc pulled her up the hill. The second girl did the same. Seemed easy enough. Annie watched the girls dismount at the top of the run, which didn't seem all that difficult either.

The girls began their descent, legs wide apart and snowplowing to slow down as they turned to traverse the hill. Moments later the skiers reached the bottom. They giggled as they passed Annie, and once again they were on the lift.

Well, better do it; daylight was fading fast.

Annie shuffled to the loading station, which wasn't nearly as easy as it looked. She watched behind her, waiting for the next pole. The operator handed it to her and she slipped the disk under her tush. With a sudden jerk, she was heading up the hill.

This wasn't so bad, just terribly slow. That was a good thing; she felt a little safer. She thought of when Marti sprayed her with snow. Now that girl could ski. What had possessed Annie to fall into the snow, and then do the angel thing? What a totally undignified activity for a woman of her age to do... But it felt good! And then the strangest thing happened. Just as she was about to flatten her friend with a snowball, she had heard someone call her name. The voice seemed very familiar, yet she couldn't place it. She had looked around and saw no one, the place was practically deserted. There were a few people on the chair lifts, but they were far up the hill.

Annie had reached the top of the hill and prepared to slip the disk form between her legs. *Ready... now!* She held the pole for a few seconds longer before it was pulled from her grasp and it shot ahead, swinging wildly as the internal spring retracted. Lord, she felt embarrassed. Was that supposed to happen...? At least no one was around to see.

So... here she was at the top of the hill. It looked huge. Actually, it had about the same slope as the meadow surrounding her cabin, sans the level area where the cabin actually stood, but Annie had never stood at the top of her snow-covered meadow with boards strapped to her feet.

She shuffled towards the center of the hill, away from the large supporting poles of the poma lift, and aimed her ski tips down the hill - and took a deep breath. Oh jeez... She dug her poles into the snow and pushed forward.

She began picking up speed. With a sigh of dismay, she knew she was going way too fast, but how to slow down? She remembered the girls pointing their tips together to form a 'V' to decelerate. Annie tried it. Thank God, it was working. She slowed to a stop, surely diverting a disaster.

She turned to look at the top of the hill. Lord… she'd only gone about thirty feet and the rest of the hill loomed below her. She straightened her ski tips and began to move forward again. By shifting her weight and the angle of her skis, she was able to traverse the hill and control her direction. Wasn't long before she was almost to the bottom. Good thing too, because she could barely see anything; the clouds had completely obliterated any remaining sunlight.

Just about there... one more turn and... Annie found herself face down in the snow. The edge of her ski had caught, flipping her over.

Yep, this was too much; she'd have to see about lessons in the morning. Annie tried to stand but couldn't seem to be able to get her feet under her, so she released the binding and stood up. Enough for one night. She picked up her skis and returned to the villa Marti's brother had so kindly given them.

Gabe passed the grove of pine trees then turned in the chair to look back at the beginner slope. Two young girls were riding the poma lift, but he didn't see Annie anywhere. He hoped the reason was because she was standing behind the lift operator's shed.

The chair lift stopped again with a lurch. He nearly fell out and grabbed the safety bar over his head. It was meant to be pulled down to lap level, but was rarely used. Gabe swore as his ski poles fell into the deep snow far below him. Goddammit, now he'd have to ski down there to retrieve them.

He looked back to the beginner hill and there she was... Her white ski suit shown brightly against the graying snow.

The chair lift started up again.

Gabe watched her until he was lifted out of sight.

Once he reached the top of the hill he jumped from the chair and flew down the hill, locating his poles before racing to the bunny hill.

She was gone.

Gabe called to the lift operator, who was in the process of shutting down for the evening.

"Hey! Buddy!"

No response.

He skied closer.

"Excuse me? Hello!"

Still no response.

He skied to a point only two feet away from the operator.

"Hey, Sparky! Helloooo!"

The operator responded with a blank stare.

"Excuse me, the woman in white; where is she?"

The operator shrugged a shoulder. "Dunno who you're talking about."

Gabe's frustration level was beginning to reach critical mass. He was about to deliver a scathing comment regarding the man's genetic makeup and the resulting mentality, but figured it would be a wasted effort considering said mentality. He turned and skied back to the lounge.

He placed his skis and poles on the conveniently located rack outside of the clubhouse then kicked the snow from his boots and went in to see his buddy holding court near the fireplace. The table was filled with equal amounts of men and women, and Gabe felt a little better upon seeing that. The group around Kyle burst into laughter as he entertained them with one joke after another.

"The man certainly has a gift," Gabe mumbled.

The bar wasn't very crowded, as most of the patrons were seated around Kyle's table. Gabe scanned the room, hoping that Annie would be there, but didn't see her. Maybe it was just his imagination running wild... After all, his mental state had been rather questionable lately.

He went to the bar and ordered a Corona; no more scotch for him for a while! He squeezed the lime into his beer and turned back towards Kyle, who looked up to see his friend looking at him.

"Gabe! C'mon over!"

Might as well.

Room was made for him at the table and he sat down.

"Everyone, this is Gabe. Gabe, this is everyone!" laughed Kyle.

Gabe raised his beer to the crowd and nodded while he watched the door, willing Annie to walk through it.

There! A feminine hand appeared on the door's handle.

Come on, open it...

The door began to open and a young woman pushed it halfway in, only to stop and turn to speak to someone behind her. Gabe lost interest when he saw that the woman wasn't his Annie, but then a flash of white outside of the door recaptured it. He half stood; hoping for a better view... only to find it was gone.

The girl at the door came into the lounge and went straight to the bar. Gabe watched her as she ordered her drink and looked around the room as it was being made. Her gaze landed on Kyle and her eyes widened. Aw shit, what was Marti doing there? Marti... and her friend... Annie? *Aw God...*

Marti saw what Kyle was drinking and added it to her order. She paid the bartender and walked to his table, and then placed the bottle in front of him.

"I believe I owe you a drink, Kyle." She couldn't believe her luck.

"Hey Marti!" He smiled his thanks and invited her to sit.

She squeezed in between him and Gabe, mumbling a quick hello to Evans. It was Kyle that had captured her heart so many years ago; he held it still. She couldn't believe that she was actually sitting here next to him! Next to both of them! God, wait until she told Annie!

Marti wished her friend would have come with her tonight, but the poor thing was exhausted. After all, she hadn't really slept since Thursday afternoon and here it was Friday night. Well, she was not about to let a perfectly good Friday night go to waste, and this was turning out to be too good to be true!

Kyle turned to Marti, and being a gentleman (ha!) made polite conversation. Gabe half listened as he asked her what she was doing there, did she like the resort, and the usual bullshit. He was at full attention when he heard Marti say "Brighton Memorial Hospital."

"So, are you a doctor there? Kyle laughed.

Hardly," she laughed back. "I'm a pediatric nurse."

"Well, you look all grown up to me!" he teased, looking her up and down.

She gave his arm a playful punch, thrilled to be accepted as his friend. Too bad he was married...

Gabe was dying to ask if she knew Annie. *The woman in white had to be her, he just knew it!*

Kyle ended the conversation with Marti and turned to the person on his other side.

Damn. Marti turned to Gabe.

"Hi," she said.

"Hello again."

Ask her! Christ, what have you got to lose?

"So... taking a little vacation away from the states, Miss Marlett?"

"Little is right. We're only here for the weekend. How about you?"

"The same. I overheard you say that you were a nurse at Brighton. My wife was recently a patient there."

Marti nodded.

"While she was there, she grew quite fond of a certain nurse. I was

313

wondering if you may know her."

"Probably not. It's a huge hospital, and we don't associate very much with the nurses from the adult wards," she told him.

"Oh?"

"Nothing against them, don't get me wrong, but pediatrics rarely has contact with adults. We see them in the halls or the cafeteria and stuff, but we don't really know them," she explained.

"I see. Well the nurse I am speaking of is a pediatric nurse, but I believe she also works on the adult floors. Apparently, she likes the overtime?"

"Oh sure, you must mean Annie. She's the only one I know crazy enough to volunteer for that. And on adult floors... Ick!" Marti was disappointed that he wasn't interested in her. Oh well, he was married anyway. And old. Although he didn't look it, she knew that he was closer to forty than thirty.

"Yes, Annie is her name." Gabe could scarcely believe his luck. It had to be her that he saw, it just had to be! "My wife was quite taken with her... Talked about her for days. Unfortunately, I never had the chance to meet her."

"Then you're in luck! She's here," Marti grinned. Won't Annie be surprised to find out whose wife she had had as a patient?

Gabe closed his eyes. *Thank you God, thank you...* When he opened them, he could have sworn that he saw Steve across the room, giving him the "thumbs up" sign. He blinked and the image vanished. He swallowed. His mouth felt dry as dust.

After a sip of beer, he said to Marti, "She's here?"

"Well, not *here* here," Marti grinned, indicating the room they were in. "She's at our villa. Sleeping. If you're here tomorrow you can meet her."

"I'd like that very much," he replied, when actually he was thinking that there was nothing on God's green earth that would keep him away.

Marti chattered away about nothing in particular and Gabe only half listened. He was thinking of Annie. *She was there! Really there!*

Marti noticed that wonderful lopsided smile on his face and mistook it to be for her alone. She rattled on about what a big fan she was of SD and bla bla bla...

He wasn't even listening anymore. That wonderful, warm, giddy feeling he'd had Monday morning washed over him again. Monday seemed like a lifetime ago, and Gabe's world had completely, irrevocably changed since then.

The sound of applause and cheering brought him back to reality; damned if someone hadn't produced a couple of guitars. Kyle was tuning one of them up, and the other was being shoved into Gabe's hands. Instead of feeling angry at the imposition, he actually felt like singing.

From the rooftops!

"Kyle, let's do this right!" Gabe said to him, and then leaned over and whispered into Marti's ear.

She smiled and ran over to the bartender, talked to him for a moment, and then went back to join the duo from SD.

While Gabe whispered his plan to Kyle, the bartender and another resort employee were setting up a makeshift sound system. When they had finished, what the audience heard being sung in the bar could also be heard on the slopes.

The impromptu concert began. Even without back-up percussion and keyboards, they sounded great. They warmed up the crowd with some of their lesser-known songs and the audience loved them. They then moved into their most popular songs - the songs that had made them wealthy men. The bar was beginning to fill up as the skiers heard the music on the slopes and came in to investigate.

Gabe and Kyle were in the zone. It had been a very long time since they had performed outside of a studio, and the duo gave the audience everything they had.

The mood was infectious. Ski boots piled high as the skiers kicked them off so that they could dance, and the surprise party at River Ridge was soon in full swing.

Ten songs later it was time for a break. Kyle returned to his table for a beer while Gabe grabbed his and went outside.

It was beginning to snow. Great, fat flakes fell from the clouds above to land gently, yet heavily, all around. Gabe caught one and watched it melt in his hand. He looked up at the small mountain in front of him as the snowfall became heavier. It would be great skiing in the morning.

"Kyle, do you think you're ready to do that song I wrote on the way up yesterday?"

"Uh, I can handle the music, but can't remember all the words, why?"

"I'd like to introduce it here... what do you think?"

"Sure, as long as you don't fuck up and forget the lyrics," he grinned.

"Never happen. You know my mind is like a steel trap..."

"Uh huh... kinda rusty and sportin' a dead animal?"

"Kyle?"

"Yeah?"

"Fu... uh, you know." Gabe didn't dare finish his comment that close to the microphone.

He turned around and faced the crowd.

"Hi, all, having a good time?"

The audience clapped and cheered.

"Good! Kyle and I want to try something out here. This next song is new... barely even twenty-four hours old; you'll be the first to hear it."

More clapping and cheering, louder this time.

"All we ask is that if you don't like it, please don't throw ski equipment or apparel... You ever have one of them boots upside your head?" he laughed, running a hand through his forever-messy hair.

The crowd laughed with him as a ski boot bounced onto the makeshift stage.

Gabe raised his hand for quiet, and then began to strum a few chords. Kyle joined in, and Gabe began to sing…

"You told me you'd love me forever, I believed every word that you said. I built my whole world around you; I followed you wherever you led…"

Kyle joined in.

"I opened my heart and I let you in. You couldn't lose, and I couldn't win…"

Gabe finished the first verse alone.

"There's a place in my heart created by you; you made it when you set me free."

He strummed a few more chords and started the second verse. Kyle joined him.

"What did I say to turn you away? Or was it something that I didn't do? I begged for a reason; what went wrong? But I got no answer from you. I fought through the wasteland of your icy stare… looking for warmth, but it wasn't there. There's a place in my heart abandoned by you. You don't know what you've done to me."

Gabe looked around.

Several couples were slow dancing and the rest of the audience was entranced. He threw Kyle a quick thumbs up and began the last verse.

"There's a place in my heart and only you know it's there. It's hidden, no others can see. A small place, a dark place, a secret place where your love, it used to be. An emotional void, a desert of dreams, a river of tears that endlessly streams. There's a place in my heart and only you know it's there. You left it when you walked out on me…"

The last note died away. The room was completely silent except for the crackling of the logs burning in the fireplace, and Kyle and Gabe exchanged a worried glance. Then as one, the audience rose to its feet. Whoops, whistles, cheers and applause rocked the rafters.

Kyle asked Gabe if they thought they should include the song on their next CD. Gabe just grinned his lopsided grin.

They finished the set with their hit "The Dream," and waved to their new fans as they left the stage. The owners of the guitars begged them to autograph the instruments, and were rewarded with the signatures of Gabe and Kyle. The duo signed a few more autographs, escaping to the Jeep as soon as possible.

The partners began the twenty-minute drive back to the hotel. Snow was falling fast, making the drive become more dangerous with each passing mile. Visibility was almost nil. Kyle slowed the Jeep down well below the speed limit; he had no desire to hit one of the rock walls that lined the roadside to his left, or veer off the road into the river to his right. His trusty Wrangler could only handle so much.

Gabe hoped that no large, hoofed animals would get the urge to wander the streets tonight. A moose would not make an attractive hood ornament.

"We probably should have stayed there," Kyle sighed. "This could prove to be hazardous to one's health. Christ, this road is shit!"

"You'll get no argument from me," Gabe mumbled. "You know, I'll bet that Marti would have let you bunk with her. She's got it bad for you, man."

"Hmm. I noticed. Imagine, coming all this way, to another country even, and meeting someone from Waterston... Not to mention that someone being a loyal fan of SD. What are the odds, dude? Hey, do you think she followed us up here?"

"Highly unlikely," was Gabe's reply. He was just thankful that she had come. And brought Annie. Dammit, this was going to be the longest night of his life. It was about then the terrible thought hit him. Aw God, what if she wanted nothing to do with him? He'd never thought of that before. Their being together seemed so right, so inevitable, that her rejecting him... well, it just would not - could not - happen.

Don't think about it, Gabe. Think about something else. Come on Gabe...

"Tell me, Kyle, how did we end up entertaining the masses tonight?"

"You're asking *moi*? It was your idea, man. Shocked the hell out of me!"

"My idea?" Gabe was confused. "How was it *my* idea? I don't seem to recall anything about that."

"You and Marti were talking. Well, Marti was talking; you were noddin' and smilin'. I was kinda half listening. She was going on about what a big fan she was, and how she played our CDs all of the time and wished we'd start doin' some concerts - or at least do something new. The next thing I knew she's askin' if you'd play tonight if she could scare up some guitars. You were over there nodding to everything she was saying... You don't remember any of this?" Now Kyle was confused.

"I'm afraid I don't remember a word she said, my mind has been elsewhere for most of the night... But you must admit, we were a roaring success. I actually enjoyed myself! I like the smaller crowds... Maybe we should start doing some local gigs when we get back home."

"Maybe we should, but nothing more than an hour's drive away. Jenna..."

"Agreed."

They drove a few more miles in silence.

Gabe's eyelids felt heavy. Just a short doze…

His eyes flew open when he felt something hit the Jeep. *Christ, what the hell was that?*

Kyle was steadily pumping the brakes, hoping to bring the vehicle back under control as it slid downhill.

There was another thump on the passenger side of the Jeep.

Gabe looked but could see nothing. He knew from the angle of the terrain they were on that the river wasn't very far away.

Another thump and the Jeep seemed to be heading uphill now as their speed was decreased.

The vehicle came to a stop and both men jumped from it as if it might take off out of control again.

Kyle was visibly trembling.

"Oh my God! Oh my God! Oh my God!" he repeated over and over as he walked around in a stunned, tight circle.

Gabe went to him and put his arm around his friend's shoulders, although he was shaking nearly as bad as his buddy.

"It's okay man, we're okay." He gave Kyle a little shake. "Take a deep breath..."

He did, and calmed down a bit.

"Better?"

Kyle nodded.

"It's freezing out here. Let's get back in the Jeep," Gabe said, trudging back to the vehicle.

Again, Kyle nodded, but hesitated when he reached the driver's side door. He stared at the Jeep as if it were some malevolent beast waiting to devour him.

"What is it, Kyle? You want me to drive?"

Relief flooded Davidson's face, and in a hoarse whisper he answered, "Yes."

The men got back into the Jeep and buckled their seatbelts. Gabe put the vehicle into gear and began to slowly pull uphill. Oddly enough, they were not too far from the road.

The snow wasn't falling nearly as fast and the visibility was much better. Once they were back on the icy pavement, Gabe stopped the Jeep and got out to look at where they had been. He felt his knees go week when he saw where they could have ended up. Fifty feet from the sloping roadside, the world ended. He could see nothing, but could hear the river rushing far below. A morbid sense of curiosity led him to follow the hair-raising path that they had just made through the deep snow.

He told Kyle that he'd be right back and grabbed a flashlight from under the Jeep's rear seat.

Gabe walked along the roadside until he found where the Wrangler had left it. The tire tracks veered to the right, onto the shoulder, and continued on down. He wondered if Kyle had fallen asleep at the wheel.

The tracks led straight towards the river, and Gabe found the large rock that they had run over. From there the tracks took a sharp turn to the left, Kyle must have woken up about then. The tracks then fishtailed and were aimed towards the river once again. Another jog to the left - that must have been when Gabe was jarred awake by the first impact, but he could find nothing that may have caused it.

He continued to follow the path of the Jeep. Two more times it had been headed for the river, coming within yards of the steep cliff, and he could see where the tracks looked as if the vehicle had been pushed back uphill.

Sideways.

He didn't know what to think about that.

Gabe joined Kyle and saw that some of the color had returned to his friend's face, and his breathing was more on the normal side. He debated on whether or not to tell him what he had seen.

Better not. He put the Wrangler into gear and headed for the hotel.

"Gabe?" Kyle mumbled.

"Hmm?"

"Do you believe in, uh, divine intervention?"

"I'm beginning to."

"Me too," Kyle sighed, and told him what had happened.

He had indeed fallen asleep and veered off the road, and when the Jeep ran over something it woke him up. Kyle had seen the cliff rapidly approaching and tried like hell to steer away from it. Just as he thought that they were finished, something hit them, pushing them away from certain disaster. He never saw anything that could have explained it. Then it happened two more times! Although thankful, it scared him almost as much as the thought of ending up in the river.

"Maybe we have a guardian angel," Kyle nervously joked.

"Maybe we do," Gabe mumbled, lost in thought.

Steve smiled, unseen, from the back seat.

Annie had fully intended to join Marti in the bar for a few drinks after the ever-so-chilling slide down the bunny hill. She took a quick shower and changed into jeans and a sweater... and yawned; the warm water had made her even sleepier than she already had been. Well, maybe a noisy, crowded bar would perk her up a bit.

By the time Marti was ready to go, Annie could barely keep her eyes open. She'd been awake, except for the nap in the van, for over twenty-four hours. Maybe she could stay awake long enough for just one quick drink.

She threw on her borrowed white jacket and followed Marti across the snowy yard between the villas and the lounge. Her eyes felt scratchy and she was beginning to feel a bit nauseous on top of it. When they reached the lounge, Annie knew she would never make it. She made her apologies to her friend and went back to the villa where a pair of warm flannel jammies and a soft bed awaited her.

She was asleep before her head hit the pillow.

She heard someone singing. It was the same song Marti had played on the way up... the one about the dream lover. Annie smiled and snuggled deeper into the blankets, not wanting to wake up yet.

Ahh... that voice. She knew it, but not from hearing it earlier. From where?

Her dark-haired cowboy from the hospital had entered her dream. He was singing to her.

"Each night I have the same old dream, the one in which you say, 'You'll be mine forever, until my dying day. Come my love and take my hand; wake and you shall see... I am real, I'm not a dream. I'm not a fantasy."

The cowboy reached out towards Annie. She took his hand and he pulled her close. She could smell the leather of his jacket and the woodsy-spicy scent of his cologne.

She looked into his intense blue eyes.

He bent his head to kiss her.

Oh God, was it really going to happen this time? Annie's entire body vibrated as she anticipated the feel of his lips on hers...

And the dream faded.

She opened her eyes for real this time. She looked about the bedroom in the villa, forgetting for a moment where she was. *Oh yeah... the resort.*

She could hear someone singing. It really was SD, and she wondered who was playing their music so loud. Actually, it sounded like it was coming from the resort's PA system. Strange...

Annie listened to the lyrics and felt the song was meant just for her.

"But now the night is over. The sun brings the dawn. I reach out to greet you, but you've already gone. With each waking moment, the truth becomes too clear. You haven't really left; you were never really here.

"As I lay here, amid my tears and an empty glass of wine, I pray our hearts will meet again in another place and time. I come back to reality. Life is still the same. The fantasy's gone forever, but the dream... it still remains."

The song ended.

Annie lay in her lonely bed, staring at the ceiling.

She made no attempt to wipe away the tears as they slipped down her face.

Al and Marie came for the twins early Saturday morning. Deirdre had a nice visit with them, and then had the house to herself.

It was so quiet; she couldn't remember the last time she'd been entirely alone... but she didn't think about it for very long, as she was on a mission.

She made herself a pot of tea, and with some difficulty carried it up to her bedroom. She retrieved several of the journals from the closet and brought them to the bed. The bottle of Vicodin was now on the bedside table since there were no children to get into it. She took four of them and started in on the journals.

Rosalind wrote of her childhood, living on the outskirts of Detroit and hating it. The city was dirty, ugly, and grossly overpopulated. She wanted to move back to the other side of the state where her grandparents, Anne and Michael still lived. *Deidre felt the first hint of a connection.*

At least let her visit, Rosalind begged her father. He conceded to a short holiday for a few weeks every year.

In the summer of her sixteenth year, Rosalind attended a charity ball with Grandmother and Grandfather Killington. It was to be her first real dance. She had no lack of partners and danced almost every dance, but as the musicians struck the chords for the final waltz of the evening, she realized that she had no partner. She sighed and began to look for her grandparents.

Behind her, a most wonderful voice said, "May I have this dance?"

She turned and found herself looking at the most handsome man she had ever seen. They danced the whole dance, never taking their eyes from each other and never even saying a word.

Deidre could understand that...

When the waltz was over, William bowed low before Rosalind and asked if he could call upon her the following day. She would like that very much, and they spent two oh-so romantic days together before she had to return to Detroit.

William Charles wrote to her every week. Once a month he would take the train across the state and visit with her. At first Rosalind's father did not approve of her romance with the much older man, but as time went on he grew to respect and even admire William. The man was hardworking, respectable, and obviously deeply in love with Rosalind.

Deirdre continued to read…

Rosalind told of the courtship and of the most romantic marriage proposal near a lake by her grandparents' home. William and Rosalind were married soon after, and set up housekeeping in a cozy cottage not far from that very lake.

Deirdre drifted off to sleep.

She never felt the bed move when the man lay down beside her.

Steven slipped his arms around her and kissed the back of her neck.

She sighed in her sleep and snuggled closer to her lost love. *Ahh...what a delicious dream…*

"My lady," he whispered in her ear. "Wakest thou from thy slumber, for I have news for thee."

He produced a rose bud of the deepest shade of red and gently caressed her pale cheek with the flower.

Deirdre smiled and rolled over to face him.

"Pray, kind sir, what news hast thou?"

Steven kissed the tip of her nose, and then sat up on the bed and pretended to examine his fingernails.

Deirdre punched him on the arm.

"Don't tease me like that you wicked, wicked man!"

"Hey, is that anyway to talk to an angel?" he laughed.

She sat up next to him, and once again her pain had vanished. She felt wonderful.

Steven grinned at his ladylove. "Guess who Gabe will be running into shortly."

She looked at him expectantly.

"She has green eyes and red hair, and lives with a goose."

"Annie? She made it up there? Oh, good... I was so afraid something might happen, what with all of the snow and ice up there."

"She's there, and she's fine," confirmed Steve. He then filled her in on all of the details, including the new song, Gabe's foray into extreme intoxication, the impromptu concert, and the near disaster on the snow-covered highway.

"Oh, Steven! Are they all right?"

"They're fine, but I can almost imagine my shoulder bein' sore from pushing that damn Jeep away from the cliff," he chuckled. "Kind of reminds me of bulldogging a steer."

To demonstrate, he wrestled Deirdre to the bed. He lay above her, pinning her wrists with his large hands.

She offered no resistance when he kissed her.

He rolled onto his back and picked up a journal. "Doing a little light reading, I see," he said, flipping through a book.

"Well, I'm trying to, but it seems that I am to be plagued with constant interruptions," she teased.

"I can leave..."

"Don't you dare. Oh, Steven, these journals are fascinating! Annie's grandmother wrote them, and I'm hoping that perhaps I can discover the reason for all of this happening. I know it's destiny, but I think part of the answer might be in one of these. I've already found what I think may be a connection."

"You'll have your answers, my dear. Be patient."

She gave him a searching look. "You already know, don't you?"

"Maybe I do, maybe I don't."

"Oh, you are wicked. I'm surprised you don't reek of brimstone," she grinned, turning away from him.

"Now, Deirdre, is that..."

"I know, any way to talk to an angel."

"Yep, I know the answers. I also know the connection, but I'm afraid I can't tell you. More of those silly rules from upstairs." He raised his eyes skyward.

"Then I guess I'll have to read faster," Deirdre sighed, but she didn't want to do anything to take away from her precious time with Steven.

"Would you mind if I read over your shoulder?" he asked, resting his chin on said body part.

"I'd like that very much," she sighed, raising her hand to caress his beloved face.

✦ ✦ ✦

In southwestern Ontario the morning dawned bright and clear, with three inches of fresh new snow sparkling in the sunlight. Annie stood at the bottom of the beginner slope, giving herself a pep talk. She had planned on taking a lesson, but do to a mix-up in the scheduling there would be no instructor until early afternoon.

"Okay, Annie, you can do it. It's just a little hill, and you did it last night. C'mon feet, move."

She shuffled to the poma lift, and just as she grabbed the pole she heard another skier come up behind. Maybe it was Marti. It certainly didn't sound like a beginner, judging from the speed at which they had approached.

She gave a quick glance behind her, but the glare of the sun on the snow momentarily blinded her. She'd have to get some goggles, and soon.

A sudden breeze whirled up the hill. A small vortex of snow blew across Annie's path, bringing with it a whiff of woodsy-spicy. A tingle raced through her as she remembered her dream from last night.

Oh no, not now... Once that cowboy invaded her thoughts he was impossible to evict.

She was almost at the top of the hill and prepared to release the pole. *Okay, let go...now!* She opened her hand and the pole swung wildly away. Now, to get out of the way of that skier behind her. She shuffled awkwardly to the center of the hill.

The only other skier on the lift watched her, thinking that she could use a few instructions on the basics of skiing, and he was just the man to do it.

Annie stood at the top of the hill, admiring the panorama before her. The gray of the miniature mountains enhanced the whiteness of the fresh snow that had fallen, and evergreens added a dash of color. The nearly cloudless sky was the most incredible shade of blue, only occasionally interrupted by a wisp of white.

Someone skied up behind her, just a little too close she thought. She was about to move away when she caught the scent of woodsy-spicy. Again.

A familiar voice behind her said, "Beautiful isn't it?"

She whirled around in surprise.

Not a good idea; she lost her balance in the confining skis and fell into an undignified heap.

"Are you alright?"

She looked up into the intense blue eyes of her cowboy.

The man from her dream.

Her mysterious 'G'.

Deirdre's husband.

"Buy you a cup of coffee?" he asked, giving her his best lop-sided grin.

For the first time in her life, Annie was truly speechless. It wasn't that she couldn't think of anything to say, but it was her brain, it just shut down.

Emotions were at war within her. Oh, how she had dreamed of this moment, and now that it was here she almost dreaded it.

She wanted this man in every way, shape, and form.

She felt drawn to him.

The two of them together seemed so right...

But he wasn't hers to have.

Annie swallowed the lump that had formed in her throat and could feel the tears as they burned her eyes; she blinked to clear them. She went into her "Annie the professional" mode and extended her hand.

"A little help here?"

"My pleasure."

Gabe grabbed both of her hands and pulled her to her feet, using a little more muscle that necessary. Still anchored in her skis, Annie lost her balance again and fell against him. He wrapped his arms around her to steady her.

She didn't want to move.

He didn't want her to move.

Another gust of wind tore around them, blowing snowflakes from the ground up into the air and creating a miniature blizzard. The sun caught the ice crystals, causing the tiny prisms to shoot sparks of color.

They had both seen this before, and yet were still awed by the phenomenon. Although only moments, it seemed that hours passed as they stood embracing in the wintry kaleidoscope until Annie reluctantly pulled away from Gabe.

This wasn't right no matter how right it felt.

As difficult as it was for him, Gabe let her go. He gave in - for the moment, but he wasn't about to ever give up.

"I think that we should probably introduce ourselves," he said, offering her his hand. Gabe Evans."

"Annie Benton," she said, returning the handshake. So, it was true, this was Gabe.

Deirdre's husband.

Why did this have to happen...? Her heart was nearly breaking.

"Pleased to meet you, Annie Benton."

It was Annie.

His Annie.

Gabe's heart sang.

She managed to choke out a thank you before she repositioned herself to face downhill, although skiing was the last thing on her mind. Yet she couldn't stay up there forever... so planted her ski poles in the snow and pushed off.

Gabe was right behind her.

"Lean forward just a bit more... good. Now let's turn. Point the tips of your skies together to slow down. Great! Now, shift your body around into the turn and bring your skis in line... You did it!"

His instruction continued until they reached the bottom of the hill.

Annie smiled up at him, her face beaming. She had made it to the bottom in one piece... and it felt good! Gabe had given her the confidence she needed and she wanted to try it again. They made several more runs down the beginner slope as Gabe taught her several turns and showed her different ways to stop on the hill. By mid-morning she was quite proficient at her new sport; it was time for a break.

"I think I owe you a cup of coffee," Gabe told her.

"Well, you did, but I'm willing to write it off in exchange for you instruction in the fine art of skiing. Thank you."

"You are most kind, madam. Shall we?" He waved a hand towards the lounge.

"We shall... I think. It takes me a while to move around on these things," Annie sighed, looking at her skis.

"Horizontal movement takes a bit more effort," he laughed. "You have to skate. Push off with you poles and the ball of your foot."

He demonstrated, skating forward for about twenty feet, and then turned and motioned for Annie to follow. She tried but just couldn't get the hang of it. She took off her skis and carried them to where Gabe was waiting, shaking her head.

"Don't worry about it; it will come to you with a little practice." He removed his skis and picked them up. "Let's go get that coffee."

Business was picking up at the resort. Fresh snow on a sunny Saturday... who could resist?

Gabe and Annie found a seat in the crowded cafe, and she was surprised at how many people seemed to know him. Several of them came up to him and complimented on the great job he'd done last night.

She had no idea what they were talking about.

A tall blond man wearing a bright orange ski jacket walked up to their table, glaring at Gabe. He picked up Gabe's coffee and took half of it in two gulps, never taking his eyes from his victim, who just sat there smiling benignly. Annie stared in disbelief as the blond man set the cup back on the table, removed a snowball from the pocket of his jacket, and plopped it into the half empty cup.

She was shocked. Who was this loony-tune?

Gabe just sat there and smiled.

The man sat in the chair across from him and continued to glare.

"Annie, I would like to introduce you to Mr. Kyle Davidson. I apologize for his appalling lack of manners, but it appears that he is angry with me for not joining him on the slopes as I promised him I would," Gabe said, the smile never leaving his face.

Kyle turned to look at her, and the glare on his face transformed into one of sheer delight, as if he had just found a long-lost friend.

Kyle, thought Annie. Wasn't that the name of Jenna's husband? And the name of that singer Marti was crazy for?

"Kyle, may I present Miss Annie Benton," Gabe said, looking at her.

"Very pleased to meet you, Miss Benton," Kyle said. Actually, he was not pleased at all as he saw how his very-married pal was looking at her. *Deirdre, honey, you are in big trouble!*

"Annie!" someone yelled from across the room.

She looked up to see Marti running towards her in the stiff-legged gait one has when wearing the cumbersome ski boots. She joined the three of them at the table.

"I see you met Kyle and Gabe of course," Marti said.

"Uh, yes. You've met them already?" a surprised Annie asked.

"Mmhmm... last night. They throw a heck of a party!" Marti winked at the men.

"Now I'm sorry I missed it." Annie wasn't sure if that was quite true. She wouldn't have given up that dream for anything... but now here she was having coffee with him.

"Figure out how to ski yet, Annie? Marti asked.

"Yes, I did... No thanks to you," Annie teased.

Marti rolled her eyes and shook her head. "Hey, I got you here... what more do you want?"

"Marti, that was more than enough, and I thank you," Gabe chuckled. "And she found herself a most-willing instructor..."

This could be trouble. "Gabe, I'm going to call Jenna. You want to come with me and call Deirdre?" Kyle gave his partner a very meaningful look.

There it was. Annie could no longer deny the Deirdre issue. She made a pathetic attempt at a cheerful smile.

"Kyle, I thought your name was familiar. I've met Jenna... and Deirdre, too." To Gabe she said, "How is your... your wife doing? I've thought about her quite a bit since I last saw her."

"She insists that she's fine, although sometimes I'm not so sure. She is a very proud, very brave woman." Gabe decided to come clean. "So, you must be 'her' Annie. She talks about you non-stop, and as a matter of fact, I believe that she has been trying to find a way to contact you. She wants to thank you."

"For what?" Annie was surprised but pleased.

She had wanted to talk to Deirdre too, not to mention seeing the twins and Jenna again. The creepy feeling she once had about them was now a distant memory. But Gabe... Gabe who had just solved this little problem was now a major complication. How could she ever face Deirdre again, knowing that she... that she...? Admit it - she was in love with Deirdre's husband. This was all too complicated.

"Gabe? Comin'?" Kyle was getting very impatient.

"Be right there. Excuse me, ladies." Gabe smiled at the women, letting his gaze linger a little longer on Annie.

Kyle poked him in the ribs with his finger. "Come on!" he whispered harshly.

As Marti watched the men walk to the lobby, she said to Annie, "Wow! How'd you do that?"

"Do what?"

"Get him to look at you like that? Rumor has it that he hasn't looked at another woman since his marriage."

"Like what?" Annie wasn't sure she wanted to know.

"Like he wanted to scoop you up with him on a big white horse and ride off into the sunset... And live happily ever after," Marti sighed. "If Kyle looked at me like that, wife or no wife, I'd never let him go."

"No," mumbled Annie miserably, "No, this isn't good."

He couldn't be interested in her, but it seemed so right.

But it wasn't. What about Deirdre? How could he treat her like that? Her first impression that she had of him in the hospital was right. He was a creep.

No, he couldn't be.

Sure, look at the facts.

Wait a minute...

"Marti, did you say Kyle? Like Kyle from SD?"

Marti was still staring down the hall, waiting for the men to return.

"The one and only, Annie, the one and only."

She had to ask…

"Gabe wouldn't happen to be the other half of SD, would he?"

Marti turned and looked straight at Annie.

"Well, *duh!*" she said, smiling.

Oh, God, this was just too much to comprehend. That had to have been Gabe singing the night before. Annie couldn't take any more; she had to get away. She made a quick apology to Marti and ran to the villa as fast has her stiff boots would allow.

Annie threw herself on the bed and dissolved into tears, crying until she heard a knock at the door. She sniffed and wiped her face with the back of her hand.

"W... who is it?" she stammered.

There was no answer, so she walked to the door and peeked out.

Nothing.

She sniffed again and added crybaby to her newly formed list of character flaws, which also included hopeless dreamer and potential home wrecker.

Annie sat back down on the bed. Jeez, she wished Michael was there, he was the one person she could always talk to. She thought back to the weird dream she had... What was it he had said?

"Follow your heart."

Yeah, right. Follow it right straight to disaster.

"Things aren't always as they seem."

No, they were much worse.

And surely she couldn't forget, "Help Deirdre and the kids."

Oh sure. As if it weren't already complicated enough.

"Well screw you, Michael-who-said-he'd-always-be-there-for-me. Screw you!"

Annie picked up the glass ashtray on the bedside table and threw it across the room, smashing it against the heavy oak dresser. She burst into tears again, horrified and shocked by her outburst and lack of control. Add vandal to the list. With a sniff and an unladylike wipe of a sleeve across her nose, she fought for some semblance of calm.

Her anger and self-pity drained away as she picked up the shards of glass.

Another knock on the door...

She ignored it.

"Annie?" Marti said from the other side. "You in there?"

Annie sighed and walked to the door, depositing the broken glass in the wastebasket on the way. She wiped away any remnants of tears with the palm of her hands.

Deep breath, open the door...

"C'mon in."

"Why did you take off like that? Gabe's waiting to take you..." Marti stopped speaking when she caught sight of Annie's face. "Annie honey, what's wrong?"

She shook her head. "Nothing. Just not feeling well at the moment."

"Try again. You look like you just lost your best friend, which you didn't, cuz I'm still here."

Marti put her arm around Annie's shoulders and led her to the bed. They sat together on the end of it

"Now, tell your ol' Auntie Marti what the problem is..."

Tears formed in Annie's eyes again. She wanted to open up to her friend, but it was all just too complicated and she shook her head again. "I'm sorry, Marti, but I can't talk about it... not yet anyway."

"I'll let it go for now, but you have got to cheer up, chica!" She gave Annie's shoulder a squeeze. "Come on, let's go ski. It's not even noon yet and the conditions are more than perfect... don't waste it! Besides, Gabe wants to take you on a real hill."

Annie flinched at the mention of Gabe's name.

Marti noticed but didn't say anything. Things were beginning to make sense though. She wasn't sure if she liked it or not.

Marti was right. Annie couldn't stay in here for the rest of the weekend; she would just have to face Gabe. Treat him like she would treat any other husband of a friend.

Don't think about those dreams, or how hearing him sing made her feel. Definitely don't think about what his touch did to her. She wasn't sure if that would be possible.

Steven and Deirdre read journal after journal, and then Deirdre pulled out the bible so that they could match names on the family tree.Rosalind had been quite an historian; clearly Annie needed to see this!

The phone rang. Steven picked it up and handed it to Deirdre.

She answered it and looked at him, mouthing Geoffrey's name.

He gave her the "thumbs up" sign, listening to her side of the conversation.

"Hello, Geoffrey dear... I miss you too."

"Really? How wonderful!"

"You did what? Sang?"

"And Kyle?"

"You're having me on. Annie is there?"

"Then give her my best... and tell her that I need to speak with her as soon as possible. I've made a little discovery that she will be most interested in."

"Don't worry. I'm fine. I will... Bye, dear."

Deirdre handed the receiver back to Steven and giggled. "Can you imagine the look on Geoffrey's face if he knew who had picked up the phone?" she asked.

"Well, after recent, um... events, he just might be a little more accepting of my presence here."

"That remains to be seen, Steven. Back to the task at hand." She picked up another journal, tapping him playfully on the knee.

"For just a bit longer, then I have to go. Things to do, places to go, people to get together..." He added a wink to his statement.

"If you must, you must," she sighed. She hated for him to leave, but knew that it was necessary. Anyway, it wouldn't be much longer and they would never be apart again.

"I must. I'll be back when I can." Steven gave her a quick kiss, and they returned to Rosalind's journals.

✦ ✦ ✦

Annie rinsed her face in cool water and ran a brush through her russet curls. It helped; she felt a little better now.

"Let's go," she said to Marti.

Gabe was waiting for them outside of the café, although his buddy was nowhere to be seen.

Marti looked around for him. "Where's Kyle?" she asked.

"He once again found himself in a heated discussion with a few snowboarders regarding the superiority of skis over boards. I believe they went to the slopes to settle the debate," Gabe grinned. "I do hope Kyle survives, as I'm not sure where he put the keys to the Jeep!"

"I'll keep an eye on him," Marti grinned mischievously. She jumped onto her skis and headed for the lift.

"That's what I'm afraid of," Gabe mumbled under his breath.

"I'm sorry, I didn't catch that...? Annie gave him a puzzled look.

"Nothing... just thinking out loud. So, are you ready to tackle that hill?" He nodded at the slope in front of them.

"I guess..."

Come on Annie, get over it and return to your pre-Gabe personality.

"One thing though; if I shouldn't survive this mad dash down the hill, could you see to it that my animals get taken care of?"

"Certainly, but you'll do fine, and I won't let anything happen to you." He thought of the odd couple, the dog and that goose; it made him smile.

As they walked to the lift, Gabe explained the finer points of getting on and off of the chair. Simple enough, she found out, and once they were on the lift Annie relaxed a bit. At least for a few moments anyway.

The chair swayed gently as it carried them to the top of the small mountain. The scenery was breathtaking in its new blanket of sparkling snow, the sun was shining in a cloudless sky, the air was fresh and pure, and she was sitting with...

No. Don't go there. Think of... Deirdre.

"Gabe, did you speak to Deirdre earlier? How is she?" Annie asked.

"Yes I did, and she is well. She had a message for you. She would like you to call her as soon as you return home; apparently she has something important to show you."

She wasn't sure what to say to that.

They were near the top of the lift and it was time to get off. If she could just do this without falling...

She scooted forward, a death grip on the chair; poles clenched in her other hand, a prayer on her lips. Skies scraped over packed snow...

And success! Spared from embarrassment once again.

They made their way towards the center of the hill where it wasn't as steep, and Annie looked around her. If the view from the bunny run was beautiful, the view from up here was nothing less that spectacular. She could see forever.

"Awe inspiring, isn't it?" Gabe said quietly.

"Yes, it is."

"If you think this is beautiful, you should see the Rockies. God, I can't wait to take you to Colorado; the skiing there is incredible... and then we could go to Montana and meet..." He caught himself; trailed off.

His enthusiasm to give Annie the world threw him off guard and he was getting ahead of himself.

She treated his comment as casual conversation, although she had a feeling there was more to it than that. Hoped anyway. But then again, there was reality to consider.

They admired the panorama before them for a moment longer.

"Ready?" asked Gabe.

"As I'll ever be," Annie murmured with more determination than she felt, and began her descent.

It was even more wonderful than she could have imagined. She could see how people could get addicted to the sport. She traversed the hillside, making the turns as Gabe had taught her. Then feeling a little braver, she picked up speed. She went down the hill, leaving a serpentine trail in the new snow behind her. Gabe skied a few yards behind her until they reached the bottom of the slope.

She made it! And she was ready to go again...

After their third trip down the run, Annie told Gabe that she felt confident in skiing by herself, and he could find Kyle and do some real skiing. She insisted.

Gabe didn't want to leave her though. Ever. But, it might be beneficial to let her try it on her own; build her confidence.

"All right, I'll let you go... but could we meet for a late lunch?"

"I don't think so..." She made it sound as if she already had plans.

Gabe said he understood and reluctantly skied off.

Annie was relived; she didn't think that she could spend another minute near him without screaming in frustration. She made another two runs before heading off in search of lunch.

In her villa, she made a cup of tea and a bowl of soup. She wasn't hungry, but she felt kind of shaky and thought that she had better eat something.

Annie took her meal out to the balcony where she had a pretty good view of the runs. She thought she saw Kyle in his bright orange suit racing some snowboarders down a hill full of little jumps. The man was insane! It sure would be a while before she tackled a hill like that!

She looked for Marti, thinking that she would be tailing Kyle, but didn't see her. She tried not to look for Gabe.

Annie thought of Deirdre's message, although she couldn't possibly imagine what the woman might have to say that was so important. Well, she would find out on Monday.

She yawned. Fresh air and exercise... do it every time. Maybe a short nap and then back to the slopes. Annie went to her room and lay across the bed. Just a short nap... She closed her eyes.

The foot of the bed dipped as someone sat down on it.

Annie mumbled in her sleep. "This had better not be one of those weird Michael dreams."

"Annie, I'm offended!" Michael laughed. "I thought you missed me."

She opened her eyes. Yep, there he was. She closed them again and said, "If you are referring to the ash tray I chucked across the room earlier, hoping you would appear at just the precise moment and get beaned with it, then yes. I missed you. Now go away... I'd rather be dreaming of, oh... turtle races or something thrilling like that."

Michael grinned. "Annie, listen. Remember when I told you that things aren't always as they seem?"

"Vaguely. I also seem to remember you telling me that you would always be there when I needed you. Do you know how long it's been since I've actually *seen* you? Other than these tiresome dreams of course."

"Ah! But I am here when you need me, just not when you want me. Back to my question. You do remember, don't you?"

She nodded, eyes still closed.

"Good. I'm talking about Gabe, Annie. Things aren't what they seem with him and Deirdre. Follow your heart, hon."

"You're beginning to sound like a broken record, Michael. Not what they seem... follow your heart. Bla bla bla. I have no idea what you are talking about. Explain, please!"

"I only wish I could. It would certainly make it much easier for all involved here. Just remember what I said. Oh, and have fun tonight!" Michael gave her a playful tap on the foot.

"Whatever," she mumbled.

She rolled to her side and tried to get back to sleep.

Wait... back to sleep? Was she awake through all of this?

Her eyes flew open and she sat up on the bed. No, she must have been asleep and dreaming that she was awake. Regardless, the nap was over.

Annie gathered her ski gear and returned to the runs.

The rest of the day passed pleasantly. She skied with Marti for a while, and even made a run with Kyle. She got the impression that he didn't care very much for her and that he was just being nice. She wondered what she had done to make him feel that way. Not that it mattered... she would probably never see him again after this weekend.

Even though she wasn't looking for Gabe, she saw him. He was never very close, but he always seemed to be on the same run as her.

She wanted him to go away.

No she didn't.

She didn't want to see him again.

Yes she did.

Annie wondered what terrible thing she had done in her life to warrant such torment.

After a full afternoon on the slopes, her legs began to ache and a hot bath was beginning to seem like the only thing left in life with any real meaning. She went to her villa and replaced her ski boots with a pair of boots more suitable for walking. Her feet felt very light in the new footwear as she walked across the yard to the lounge.

She wanted a great big alcoholic beverage to sip as she soaked in the tub. Hmm... what sounded good?

"Yes ma'am?" smiled the bartender.

"I'm not sure…" Annie mused, "But I'd like something sweet and potent."

"And warm?"

Annie grinned and nodded.

"How about a B-52 coffee? They're very good…"

"What is it?"

"Kahlua, Bailey's and Gran Marnier. Some coffee and a bit of whipped cream on the top."

"Make it a double, to go."

He smiled again and made an extra-special good drink for her.

Annie took a sip before she returned to her room. Perfect.

She sat in the tub, watching the steam rise around her as she sipped her drink. That bartender certainly knew his business. The drink was pretty potent and she was already beginning to feel a buzz.

She swished the water around in the tub and thought that maybe she should go back to the lounge and socialize. Yeah, she was beginning to feel like partying.

Annie picked up a handful of bubbles and blew into them, sending white foam spraying in all directions. She laughed and took another sip of her drink. Her head felt lighter and the buzzing in it was a little louder. Sure, she'd do it. Maybe she would meet a guy who would take her mind off of Gabe for a little while.

She knocked back the rest of her drink; it hit her like a truck. She stepped out of the tub and almost, but not quite, staggered to the bedroom, leaving a wet, bubble bath trail behind her.

She flopped on the bed.

Better get dressed…

She stared at the clock until the numbers came into focus. 6:30.

Where's Marti? Haven't seen her in hours…

Better get dressed…

Whoo… dizzy! She hadn't felt like that in a long time.

Better get dressed…

But what to wear? Jeans and a sweater - anything else was too complicated. Not that she had a choice; all she brought was jeans and sweaters.

She giggled.

Better get dressed!

Annie heard a door close.

"Marti? That you?" she called out.

"Yeah. Hey, you want to go over to the lounge and grab some dinner or go into town?"

"Not too hungry, but let's go to the lounge. I want to get another one of those bomber drinks." Annie's head was beginning to clear and she wanted the buzz back. She quickly finished dressing.

Marti walked into Annie's room and saw her sitting on the bed, with a silly grin on her face. A nearly empty mug of tan liquid was on the bedside table.

"Annie, have you been drinking? Who'd have thought?" Marti laughed. "So, are you plastered yet?"

"No, not hardly. Hummin' right along though. Get changed so that we can get going. These are quite tasty, and I do believe I would like another," Annie giggled, playing with the cup.

"So you said. Okay, just give me a few minutes." Marti smiled to herself.

Annie Benton, all liquored up... It might prove to be an interesting evening after all! She took a quick shower and changed into jeans and a sweater, which seemed to be the local costume, and wondered if Kyle would be there again tonight. She hoped so. She knew that he was off limits, but just being around him made her feel so... so good.

"Let's go Annie-bananie."

Annie was sitting on the sofa, staring out the window and humming a nameless tune. Marti was glad to see that her friend's spirits were much improved. She grabbed that cowboy hat Annie had worn up and plopped it on her friend's head. *Yeah... now she was ready!*

Annie was about to protest but figured what the heck. She needed to return it anyway, assuming it was his.

Gabe and Kyle stood at the top of a black diamond trail; it was the first run they had made together all day.

"Glad to see you finally ditched the baggage," Kyle said with more than a little sarcasm.

"Excuse me?"

"That Annie bitch. She's been hangin' on you all day."

Gabe's face darkened. "And from what source did you obtain this bit of misinformation?"

"Every time I've seen you today she's been right there next to you. What's her angle?"

"Kyle, we have been friends for quite a long time, correct?"

"Yeah..."

"Have you ever, ever known me to tolerate unwanted company, be it male or female?"

"Nope."

"So what makes you think the she is 'hanging' on me?"

He didn't answer. He didn't want to think that Gabe was seeking out the company of another woman other than Deirdre, who was perfection itself as far as Kyle was concerned. So, it *had* to be Annie that was after Gabe.

"Forget I said anything," Kyle mumbled.

"I don't know that I can. Don't you *ever* speak like that about Annie again. Understood?" Gabe's voice was low and dangerous.

"No, I'm not sure that it is!"

It was Kyle's turn to be angry. *Why the hell was Gabe defending Annie so fiercely*? He thought of Deirdre again. His damn buddy can't be treating her like that, chasin' after another woman. What the hell was he thinkin'?

"What's so special about Annie?" he asked, and then quietly added, "Are you forgettin' you're married?"

Gabe fixed him with a long look. Of course Kyle didn't understand what the truth was behind his and Deirdre's marriage. No one did. To the rest of the world they were the perfect couple.

"No, I'm not forgetting that I am married. Believe me, it's been on my mind the whole goddamn day." The anger was leaving Gabe's voice. "But Annie is... well, special. She's a good person and I will *not* tolerate you speaking of her that way. And for the record, I would be skiing with her right now but she sent me packing."

"If you say so. Sorry," Kyle mumbled, but he still wasn't feeling any better about the situation.

"I'll see you at the bottom," Gabe muttered.

He pushed off with his poles, skiing with reckless abandon down the hill. He hit every mogul and every jump he could see, taking out his anger out on the slope. When he reached the end of the run, he made a quick stop, spraying snow in a high, white arc, and then stood there panting as he waited for his partner.

Moments later Kyle caught up with him.

"Christ, Gabe, what the hell was that all about? Planning on trying out for the freakin' Olympics?" he said sarcastically.

Gabe ignored the question. "Let's go get a drink."

"Fine by me." He wondered what the hell had gotten into Gabe. The weekend was beginning to turn to shit... and it had started out so good.

The two men sat at a table next to a corner window; most of the ski area could be seen from there. Kyle idly watched the people in the room while Gabe watched Annie walk to her villa, carrying a steaming mug in her hand.

He had just missed her. Stifling a sigh, he turned his attention back to Kyle. "What are your plans for dinner?"

"I dunno. Any suggestions?"

"No. Did you want to eat here or head back to town?"

"Head back. But not yet, there's still some damn good skiing left. Did you want to come back here tonight or see what the Soo has to offer?"

"Doesn't much matter," Gabe told him, even though he was thinking that he wanted to be with Annie. "Let's see what happens."

Kyle nodded and finished his beer. He stood and looked at his buddy. "Comin'?"

"No, just breathing hard..."

"Smart ass..."

"I'm going to sit here for a while and do a little 'people watching'." Gabe smiled up at Kyle. "Be gone," he said, waving him away.

Kyle wasted no time in returning to the lift.

Gabe watched Marti maneuver her way into the lift line so that she could share the chair with Kyle. *Talk about baggage...* He moved from his table to one closer to the fire, where he sipped his beer and stared into the flames.

He thought of Deirdre.

He thought of Annie.

He thought he would go insane.

"Excuse me, Mr. Evans?"

He looked up to see several young people looking at him.

"May I help you?" he asked.

"We were wondering if you were going to play again tonight. Last night was so cool, and I... we told some friends and they want to hear you too."

Gabe looked at the eager faces gathered around him. How could he say no? Also, it would give him an excuse to be here tonight.

He smiled.

"Sure, why not? Let me clear it with management first. Can you check back with me in about twenty minutes?"

"Wow, you bet!" The group dispersed, talking excitedly to anyone who would listen.

Gabe finished his beer and then went to find the resort office.

The manager was thrilled to have free entertainment and told Mr. Evans that he would arrange to have sound equipment set up. What time did they want to start?

When Gabe left the office, the manager made a quick call to his friend at the radio station, who made several announcements an hour about the American duo known as SD who were doing a free concert at the resort.

He hoped that Kyle wouldn't be too pissed off about the plans he had made. He didn't think that he would, his buddy had enjoyed playing last night. They both had, and it had been far too long since they had done something like that.

He sat back down at the table by the fire and glanced out the window. It was beginning to snow again. He looked at the fire and thought of Annie, and a new melody began to shape in his fertile mind.

Here come the words...

He borrowed a pen from the bartender and wrote the lyrics down on a napkin. *God, now to locate Kyle so that they could rehearse this before tonight.*

Gabe went outside to find his partner.

Kyle was more than willing to perform again, and they rehearsed the new song on the way to the hotel. They showered, changed into fresh jeans and tee shirts - their every-day attire anyway, Gabe grabbed his guitar, and they returned to the resort.

The parking lot was full when they arrived - so much for anonymity, so they drove around looking for a space large enough for the Jeep to squeeze into.

Nothing.

Kyle said he'd risk getting towed and parked in the reserved villa parking, blocking in a minivan with Michigan plates. He took a chance that it was Marti's and she'd have no problem with it.

Marti and Annie walked over to the lounge, which seemed to be more crowded than usual. Several employees were setting up sound equipment in a corner by the fireplace. *Cool... live entertainment!* The women managed to claim a table in the front near where the band would be, and they wondered who would be playing; they hadn't seen any advertising promoting the night's performance.

Annie was working on another B-52, only a little slower this time. The alcohol had affected her normally reserved personality and she came alive. Her green eyes sparkled and she wore a perpetual smile, and that Stetson perched on her curls gave her an irresistible air of carefree and cute. Several unattached males began spending more time at their table; the fact that Annie was several years older than them didn't seem to matter. Marti was glad that her friend was finally letting herself loosen up a bit. Still, she felt that Annie's new sociable persona wasn't genuine; she was trying too hard to have fun.

Two very attractive young men asked to sit with the women. Marti, being Marti, made them feel very welcome. The men brought a round of drinks and the ritual of short-lived courtship began.

Marti was having a fine time, contemplating different accommodations for the night, yet having a hard time deciding which suitor would be the lucky one.

Annie was almost having a good time. The hunky blond skier sitting next to her seemed to be quite attracted to her, although she had to question why. She was at least ten years his senior, and there were dozens of other younger, prettier women wandering around. Absently she smiled and nodded at the appropriate parts of the conversation.

She wondered if Gabe was still around.

Her attention shifted when a man walked up to the microphone in front of them. He thanked them all for coming and then wanted to thank the evening's entertainment before he introduced them.

"Ladies and gentlemen... and snowboarders," he began.

...A groan from the crowd mixed with an occasional obscene suggestion about what he could do with himself...

"We want to thank these guys playing here tonight for their kind generosity in doing this for free!"

A cheer from the crowd.

"But, we do want to make a little money off the deal, so we will be passing the hat a little later in the evening."

Another groan from the crowd.

"Everything we collect will be donated to the 'I Can Ski' program for under privileged kids in the Soo City."

Another cheer from the crowd.

"Okay, enough out of me. All the way from the US of A...Let's hear it for Kyle and Gabe! SD!"

The crowd cheered and applauded.

They came in from around a corner, smiling and waving to the audience, and then picked up their guitars and took their positions on the makeshift stage.

Gabe scanned the crowd for Annie. *Aw God... she was right there in front, staring at him like she'd seen a ghost.* Sitting with some goddamned ski bum too. He was so surprised that he missed his cue to start singing.

Kyle covered for him by repeating the intro, and discreetly poked Gabe in the back with the end of his guitar.

Gabe snapped back to attention and began the song.

Annie had in fact seen a ghost. As surprised as she was to see SD performing, the resemblance between Gabe and Michael left her dumbfounded. She always thought that Gabe, her dream man anyway, looked a little like Michael, but until she saw him up there in that jacket, holding that guitar... well, my God! They were twins! Gabe looked a few years older, but... jeez! He had a brother named Steve, but he was dead wasn't he? So how...?

Gabe began a new song about the misfortunes of a man and his mail-order bride, and its tongue-in-cheek lyrics and fast beat had the crowd laughing and stomping their feet. It had always been one of his favorites, but he couldn't enjoy it tonight. *Christ, why was Annie sitting there staring at him like that? And just who the hell was Mr. Nordic sitting next to her?*

Too close to her.

By God, if he touches her arm again like that I swear I'll smash this guitar... Gabe was surprised at his anger. Jealousy? He'd never experienced it before and he didn't much care for the emotion, and yet he couldn't seem to control himself.

Annie noticed Gabe staring at her. His expression didn't match the humor of the song he was singing. He looked so angry. Too angry. And he kept glancing at the guy sitting next to her. *What was his name again? Brian? Brad? Butthead?* Didn't matter. He really was an ass.

Still buzzing right along from her B-52, she smiled as she pictured his blonde head turning into a giant pair of buttocks, complete with orifice. She pushed her hat back from her face a little and stared at the man on the stage...

Gabe saw her smile. *At him?* He felt a thrill at the thought and it made him smile back at her. He began singing the song as it was meant to be sung.

He began to smile. *At me? Oh God... Gabe, if you only know what that look did to me!* Just for a little while she would pretend that he wasn't married and that he did love her. Everyone is entitled to a little fantasy, right? Anyway, she was a little drunk and could blame it on that. It would seem like yet another dream in the morning and she could blame being miserable on a hangover. *Okay, back to the fantasy*!

Unknowingly, Annie let the love she felt for Gabe show in her eyes.

The blond ass next to her noticed.

Marti noticed.

Kyle noticed.

Gabe noticed.

The blond went to mingle, trying to find someone who might be less of a bitch and much more available.

Marti looked at Annie in a whole new light.

Kyle was extremely worried and getting more pissed off by the minute.

Gabe was beyond happy. Beyond thrilled! Beyond ecstatic! It was true; she did love him! *Thank you God, thank you.*

He finished the song with a flourish and looked out at the crowd, thanking them. A man at the bar held up his glass in a congratulatory salute. Gabe saluted him back. It didn't surprise him to see Steve here. In fact, he almost expected it, even if it was only his imagination…

Kyle picked out a random tune while Gabe spoke to the crowd.

"Hi! Everybody doing all right?"

A collective affirmation from the crowd.

"Great! Glad you could all be here tonight. I'm Gabe, that's Kyle, and we are SD - Sleep Deprived, and we hope that you are too by the end of the night."

Cheers and applause.

"This next song, well, we just wrote it today. Hope we don't forget any of the words…"

More cheers and applause.

"It's a slow song, a love song… so grab that someone special and get out on the dance floor"

Kyle changed from picking at random to the slow sound of the new song. Gabe took a seat at the piano he had ordered and began to play.

After hearing the new music, dozens of couples moved to a cleared area in the bar and began to dance… including Marti and her new companion.

Gabe pulled the mic down to him, looked directly at Annie and began to sing.

"Cold wind blowin', snow falling down. The frozen night lies all around. But I don't care what's out there; my whole world is here in my arms.

"The candlelight plays on your face, and your touch makes my heart race. I want you to know… I love you so. All that matters is you're here in my arms."

Gabe went into the chorus.

"I've waited so long for a night like this. I've waited so long for our first kiss. And now we're together to share our love… I can't believe you're here in my arms."

He moved into a piano bridge and then started the next verse.

"Empty nights; I've had my share… too many days without you there.

Now you're here with me where you should be... held close here in my loving arms.

"Time stands still, and then fades away. Day turns into night, night into day. I want you to know I'll never let you go. Stay forever right here in my arms..."

Gabe never took his eyes from Annie throughout the entire song. The majority of females in the audience wished it were them that he was looking at that way. Who was she, anyway? Wife? Girlfriend? Whoever, she was damn lucky!

Annie was transfixed. It was if he was singing that song just for her. Well, it *was* her fantasy; she could think whatever she wanted. She took another sip of her drink, but the warmth that spread through her body and centered below her belly had nothing to do with the alcohol.

Steve moved through the crowd until he stood behind Annie's chair, and then placed his hands on her shoulders as he bent to whisper her ear.

"Follow your heart, Annie." He kissed the top of her head and vanished.

Annie could have sworn she just heard Michael. "Follow your heart," he had said. Well dammit, she would. If only for tonight, she would. God help her... she was about to do the unthinkable, but if Gabe offered to spend the rest of the night with her, she would accept.

Gabe forced himself to look around the room as he finished the song.

The crowd was visibly moved, not so much by the mediocre lyrics, but by the passion in which with they were delivered. Not a person in the room could admit to ever before hearing a song sung with such heart-felt meaning. Those still seated in the audience rose to their feet and applauded, joining those who were dancing.

Kyle whispered to his partner that they should add this one to the next CD too. Gabe beamed, nodding to his new fans.

The duo sang four more songs and finished the set, and then went to Marti and Annie's table. Beers were delivered to them as soon as they were seated.

Marti introduced Gabe and Kyle to her new friend Jason, another Nordic-type ski bum... *She did like 'em blond*!

Kyle was relieved, while Gabe was polite but indifferent. Annie was the *only* thing on his mind. He wanted to talk to her, but for the life of him couldn't think of a thing to say. He had so much to tell her. He was touched, and just a little stunned that she was wearing his hat. Had she known to whom it belonged?

Annie's fantasy was getting better. Gabe was there, sitting right next to her with his arm thrown casually over the back of her chair. It was all she could do not to lean into that arm, to feel the hardness of the muscle press into her neck...

Her head buzzed with a combination of Kahlua and Gabe. Her fingers tingled and she had a quick memory of finding the white rose bush in Gramma's garden so many years ago. The tingle, the vision... now there it was again. Right next to her.

She closed her eyes and took a slow, deep breath.

Woodsy-spicy…

He was still right next to her when she opened them back up again. She could not stop smiling.

Marti looked from Annie, to Gabe, then back again. This wasn't good. Did Annie know what she was getting herself into? Good God, he was *married* for Christ's sake! Even though Marti talked a good game, she would never actually mess with a guy if she knew he was married. Not even Kyle. And speaking of Kyle, he looked like he was ready to kill Gabe. What was that all about? *Ooh... this could get ugly.*

He sat across the table, glaring at his pal. *What the hell was the man thinkin'*? Gabe wasn't even trying to hide the fact that he was attracted to Annie, and Kyle prayed that Deirdre wouldn't find out about this; it would just kill her.

Kyle would never let Deirdre be hurt. He had to get Gabe out of there, away from that bitch. But how? He felt that if he spent one more minute - no, one more second - watching those two acting like lovesick teenagers, he would do great bodily harm to Gabe... and his little Annie too.

He excused himself and stalked off to the bathroom.

Kyle splashed cold water on his face in hopes that would help calm him down, and then studied his reflection in the mirror. His usually handsome face was twisted in anger; his blond hair was spiky with drying sweat from performing under the hot lights. His soft brown eyes were red-rimmed from a day of exposure to sun and wind.

He looked ugly.

He felt ugly.

He wanted to punch something, but couldn't risk hurting the hands. As an alternative, he kicked a stall door with such force that it hit the doorframe, bounced, hit the wall behind it, bounced back and cracked him in the head.

Kyle's eyes opened wide in surprise and he fell to the floor, unconscious.

Thank God... Kyle left. Marti hoped he'd cooled down before he came back. She looked at Jason, who was oblivious to everything except the possibility that he might get lucky tonight. But she had to try to talk some sense into Annie.

"Annie, I need to go to the little girls' room. Come with."

She gave Annie's shoulder a little push with her fingertips. The light pressure forced her to sway and that, combined with Annie's slightly intoxicated state, caused her to fall right back into Gabe's waiting arm. She didn't even try to pull away. *Oh shit, that is not what was supposed to happen.* Marti wondered what to do next.

Annie fell up against Gabe. *Ooh, this was heaven.* Did Marti actually push her? Not that she cared... Gabe was warm and hard and soft at the same time. His woodsy -spicy scent surrounded her and she took a deep breath, pulling him in. She felt a rush of warmth spread through her and a tingle ran up her spine. She wasn't about to move; Marti could damn well go to the john by herself.

Annie moved a little closer to her fantasy.

Gabe was only vaguely aware that Kyle had left the table. Annie was still there. Still there and sitting very, very close to him. He moved his arm from the back of her chair and settled it around her shoulders. She moved a little closer to him. *God, she smelled good.* He moved his head closer to hers, to whisper in her ear, to tell her...

"Mr. Evans! It's Kyle... come quick!"

Someone was behind him, yelling at him. The urgency in the voice brought him back to reality and he turned in his chair, trying to locate the speaker.

An employee of the resort was standing near the door of the washroom, waving and trying to get Gabe's attention. *Kyle? What the hell did he get into now?* He excused himself and left the table.

Kyle's head felt like it was about ready to split in half and fall clean off of his neck. He groaned, and could feel a trickle of blood slide down his face. *Aw shit... what the hell happened? And where was he?* He could feel a cold, hard surface under and behind him. Must be sitting up, against a wall? Very slowly he opened his eyes. Bright light blinded him and he slammed them shut again. *Was he dying? Heading towards the light?*

"Kyle."

Yeah, must be dying. Steve was there to get him.

"Kyle, open your eyes, man."

Kyle was scared. He shook his head. No. No fuckin' way. If he ignored it, maybe it would go away. *Damn, but his head hurt.*

Something hit him in the face and he looked down at the offending object, which had dropped into his lap - a wad of paper towel. He looked up and saw that he was in a bathroom. There were the toilets, the urinals, the sinks, and Steve sitting on the sink with his boots waving in Kyle's face as he slowly kicked his feet back and forth. He was looking down at Kyle, smiling.

"Well now... And how are we feelin' tonight?" Steve asked.

Must be a trauma-induced hallucination. Maybe if he answered it, it would go away. "We are feeling like shit," Kyle answered weakly.

"Well then, perhaps we shouldn't have assaulted an innocent door."

"Go to hell."

"Sorry, not in the game plan... But I digress. You a little upset there, big guy?" Steve laughed.

The recent events of the evening came back to Kyle. Gabe, Annie, that damn stall door... He looked at the door. It was hanging by one hinge and his boot print could clearly be seen in the center of it. His anger returned with the memories.

"Yeah, I am." Kyle's voice was tight with rage. "Your brother is out there, as we speak, puttin' the moves on his wife's friend. His wife's friend and I use

342

that term loosely - is just as anxious to hop in the sack with him!"

"My brother - your *friend* - happens to love Deirdre very much, and she loves him. But things aren't always as they seem, Kyle. Trust Gabe."

"Yeah yeah, whatever." His head was throbbing and he felt like he was gonna puke. "Do you hand out aspirin with your bullshit advice?"

"Sorry, no. But really, Kyle, trust Gabe. It's meant to be." Steve touched two fingers to his brow and gave him a quick salute. "Later."

Kyle closed his eyes again and hoped that he wouldn't puke.

A door opened.

Footsteps...

"Hey dude... you okay? Man, what happened...? Hey you're that singer dude; I'll get some help!"

From out in the hall, "Mr. Evans!"

It was the last thing Kyle heard before his world went dark. Again.

Deirdre sat up in her bed, watching a late night talk show and sipping on a cup of hot cocoa as she wondered how things were progressing up north. She could hardly wait until Annie returned; she had so much to tell her.

She had finished reading the journals. What an historian Rosalind had been, and Deirdre felt as if she knew everyone on that family tree in the Benton bible. She also knew what the connection was. Speaking of connections, she wondered if Geoffrey and Annie had "connected" yet. And how would Geoffrey act when he returned? Would he be up front and tell her everything, or hide certain little details... like maybe a new romantic figure in his life? She had to figure out a way to let him know that she approved of Annie as his new wife and mother to her sons. Deirdre knew that Geoffrey would never divorce her, and she doubted that he would have an affair - even with her blessing. Well, she would just have to take things as they came.

She picked up the remote control and flipped through the channels. Geoffrey's music video was playing on a country station. Seemed to be popping up quite a bit recently, given that it was nearly seven years old. She watched it, and then found an old movie that captured her interest somewhat before she dozed off.

Steven kissed her awake. She sighed and snuggled in his arms, and told him of her discoveries.

He nodded; he already knew what the journals contained.

She asked him if there was any good news from Ontario.

"Well, yes and no. There was a definite chemistry between Gabe and Annie, but good ol' Kyle pulled a little stunt that might curtail the evening's anticipated events. I did as much as he could do, now we can only wait and let destiny have its way."

"Oh dear... But Geoffrey and Annie... They *are* attracted to one another?"

"Dee, if it were possible, I'd say that when they finally realize it, their love will equal yours and mine."

"Impossible, Steven… but encouraging!"

He hugged her and kissed her, and they dozed off in each other's arms.

Gabe stalked down the hall towards the washroom, trying not to glare at the employee who was waving for him to hurry. Several people were clustered around the door, trying to see what was going on. He pushed his way through the crowd and entered the room.

Aw shit… there was Kyle on the floor, holding his bloodied head and groaning.

Gabe saw the imprint of a boot on the stall door. *What the hell happened?* He knelt beside his friend.

"Are you alright?"

Kyle gave him a quick nod and attempted to rise to his feet, and with help from Gabe was successful. The resort's manager arrived, first aid kit in hand. Gabe asked if there was a more private place where Kyle could rest; they were escorted to the employee lounge.

"So tell me, Rambo, what happened?"

Kyle was lying on a sofa, holding a cold compress to his head. Marti had appeared in the room and was dabbing at his wound with a gauze pad as Gabe stood over him with his arms crossed. He didn't know whether to be extremely annoyed or sorry for his injured friend. More likely annoyed, unless he succumbed to his injury.

"I had a sudden urge to kick the door and it fought back," Kyle mumbled. Gabe's attention to Annie was still pissing him off.

"Did this door do something to offend you or was it something else?" Gabe made no attempt to keep the sarcasm from his voice. He knew that he should probably drop the subject and let Kyle recover, but he felt that things needed to be said. He wasn't sure what, but there was definitely something wrong.

Kyle looked up at him. *Well now, didn't he look all holier-than-thou, standing there ripping on him?* He gave Gabe a hard look and closed his aching eyes again, and then winced as Marti poured disinfectant over his wound.

It was bullshit. The whole night was turning to bullshit.

"Just leave me the hell alone, pal," he growled.

"Hmm… Seems the blow to your head as affected your normally jovial personality. Let's hope the condition isn't permanent; it's most unbecoming…" Gabe knew that he was pushing it. Didn't care.

Kyle extended the middle finger of his right hand towards his pal and refused to say anything else.

Marti finished dressing the wound and then took Gabe aside.

"I think he should be seen by a doctor," she whispered. "He seems fine now, but he did lose consciousness, he may have a concussion and it's better to be safe. A few sutures wouldn't hurt, either."

Gabe agreed. Now, if only Kyle would.

"Kyle, where are the keys to the Jeep? Let's go get you checked out."

"I'm fine," he spat. "Just leave me the hell alone."

Marti and Gabe looked at each other.

"Can't force him," Gabe shrugged.

Aw God... Annie! He'd forgotten all about her! For the first time in days, he had forgotten about her. "I'd better go find Annie and let her know what's going on."

"Annie again," Kyle muttered. Here he was, practically dying from head trauma and his best friend was thinking about getting laid.

"Marti, could you excuse us for a sec," Kyle said, struggling to sit up on the couch. *Christ, he felt dizzy. Maybe he should go to the hospital.*

She said she'd be right outside if they needed her, and left.

Kyle forced himself to look at Gabe. The throbbing in his head increased with his rising pulse rate as his rage became full-blown.

"So, you want to know what's wrong?" he exploded, throwing the compress from his head to floor at Gabe's feet.

Gabe looked from Kyle, to the compress, and back to Kyle. He nodded for him to continue.

"Fine, but remember, you asked me. It's you and Annie... How can you do something like that to Deirdre? Christ, Gabe, the woman worships you! She's your wife, goddammit, or did that happen to slip your mind?" He was on a roll and there was no stopping now, no turning back. "And if that isn't enough, she's dyin'! That sweet, beautiful, gentle woman is dyin'..."

Deirdre was dying. He felt tears sting his eyes and turned away from Gabe to hide his emotion.

"She's dyin'. Are you lookin' to replace her so soon? And with her nurse even! God, you make me fuckin' sick, both of you." Kyle's dizziness returned. He sank to the sofa and closed his eyes.

Gabe said nothing. *Christ, what could he possibly say? Tell Kyle the truth? And what exactly was that anyway? That he loved Deirdre like a sister, and Annie like... like he had never loved anyone before? And Deirdre... she was ill but hardly dying. She would have told him, wouldn't she? And he certainly wasn't looking to replace her.*

Nevertheless, Kyle's words were a big reality check that Gabe was about to cash. He was a fool to pursue Annie; he couldn't have her. As his buddy not so gently reminded him, he already had a wife, even if in name only.

A numbness settled over him. He stood, staring at the wall just past Kyle's head, making no movement other than a muscle twitching in his jaw.

Kyle went on. "What, no comment? Pleadin' the fifth?" He let out a bitter laugh. "'Trust Gabe', your brother says. 'Things aren't as they seem', he says. 'It's meant to be', he says."

Gabe found his voice and interrupted Kyle's tirade. "My brother?" he whispered.

Kyle's eyes snapped open. *Steve!* It was only now that he remembered the hallucination. That was the second time he had "seen" Gabe's twin. Again, the vividness of what he experienced left him deeply disturbed.

He raised his hand to stop Gabe from asking any questions. He didn't want to discuss it or even think about it.

"Forget it... Forget I said anything. Forget this whole fuckin' night ever happened." Kyle shook his head. "Let's go back to the hotel; I wanna leave first thing in the morning."

"I'll go make our apologies to the audience out there, and then we'll go," Gabe said quietly. His mind was whirling with all that had happened this evening. Now add Steve into the mix. What was with the sudden appearances lately? And to so many people... Even the twins spoke of him. He sighed and went to address the noisy crowd in the bar.

Marti met Annie and Jason halfway down the hall to the employee lounge. She shot him a quick glance and turned to her friend. "Everything's fine. Kyle's got a nice head lac and possible concussion, but I think he'll live. I'm hoping Gabe can convince him to go to the ER; he could use a few sutures and maybe even a CT."

Annie was almost completely sober by now and grabbed Marti's arm, asking, "What happened... how did he get hurt? Is Gabe all right?"

She gave Annie a long look. "Gabe is fine. Why wouldn't he be? And Kyle... well, it seems that he was hit by a bathroom door. I think he kicked it or something."

Annie continued to walk to the employee lounge until Marti stopped her.

"Not a good idea," she told her. "I think they have some issues to discuss. C'mon." She pulled Annie back towards the bar.

Jason tagged along like a forgotten puppy.

The trio returned to their table, where several people approached Marti for news of Kyle.

"What happened?"

"When will they be back out?"

"Will they be back out?"

She waved her hands at them. "Settle down. Kyle is fine, but I'm not sure if they'll be back. Gabe..."

Gabe interrupted her as he went to the stage and asked for the attention of the audience. "Excuse me... "

The crowd became silent, giving him their full attention.

"Thank you. It seems my partner has had a slight mishap, and I regret to inform you that we will not be able to continue our performance tonight. My apologies to all."

He stepped down from the stage before they could start asking questions... or throw things.

There was a mixture of applause and boos from the crowd. Oh well, what did it matter? It wasn't as if they paid to see SD.

Gabe walked over to the bar and talked with the bartender for a moment, who then called the waitresses over. Instructions were given. Gabe would pick up the tab for everyone for the remainder of the evening, and anyone who was interested would receive a free CD from SD. The waitresses would take the information and it would be relayed to him in the morning. It was the best he could do. For good measure he also made a rather generous donation to the "I Can Ski" program.

Now, to get Kyle home.

No, a quick drink first. Gabe realized that he had been avoiding talking to Annie as he toyed with the small glass of scotch in front of him, and wished he had a cigarette. Goddammit, this was getting way too complicated. What the hell was he going to say to her?

He downed the whiskey in one swallow.

Let's do it.

Annie was totally confused. One moment she was being held close to Gabe, now he wouldn't even look at her. Now that she had sobered up, she was horrified at what she had almost done. Oh, she still wanted to, but face reality - he was married. He obviously loved his wife, with the exception of his behavior tonight, and she knew that Deirdre loved him too. Annie had no right to intrude. But then why did it feel so right sitting with him like that? And that song… she would have bet her life that he had been singing only to her, and that he meant every single word. She wished she had never left the quiet, although lonely, comfort of her cabin.

The weekend had been a huge mistake.

Gabe slipped into the chair next to her. She couldn't look at him. She sat there with her hands in her lap, staring at nothing across the room.

"Annie," he said softly. He reached under the table to take her small cold hand into his large warm one.

Her fingers tingled. The sensation traveled up her arm and spread through her entire body, and her heart beat so loud in her chest that she thought the whole room would hear it.

"Annie," Gabe repeated, "I'm sorry, I want… I never… I… I…" He was at a loss for words.

She continued to avert her gaze from him, but nodded in what could have been understanding. It took all of her effort to pull her hand away from his.

"I've got to go. Kyle… well, I think he needs medical attention. I'll get in touch with you later," he told her as he rose, touching a finger to a tendril of her autumn hair.

It took all of his effort not to kiss her goodbye.

Annie slowly removed the hat from her head and held it out to him.

Gabe's hand lifted to take it, but with a quick shake of his head he walked away. She could keep it. At least a little of him would always be with her.

Marti watched the couple from across the table and had to blink back tears. This was truly a tragedy. If ever two people were meant to be together, it was these two. The way Gabe had looked at Annie during that one song... *My God!* It made Marti half-crazy with jealousy, and she really didn't even like Gabe! Well, not as much as Kyle anyway. Poor Annie... She had the same look in her eye that he had. Ya know, it was almost as if they had loved each other forever and were being torn apart... separated against their will.

Again.

Really weird. Marti wasn't sure how she knew these things, but she knew.

Jason leaned over and whispered something in her ear. *Jeez... was that all men ever thought about?*

Marti leaned over to him and whispered that he could take his little suggestion and do it to himself.

Jason's face grew red with surprise and anger. *Was she serious? After all of the signals she had been sending him all night?*

Marti glared at him.

Yep, she was serious all right. Jason wasted no time in leaving.

After Gabe left the table, Annie turned to watch him walk away.

Good-bye, Gabe. Maybe our hearts will meet in another place and time.

Just before he turned the corner at the end of the hall, she left for her villa.

Gabe reached the end of the corridor and turned for one last look at Annie. She wasn't there.

Goodbye, my Annie. Back to reality.... Life is still the same. The fantasy's gone forever... The dream... it still remains.

But did it really? He didn't want to think about it.

Kyle required, and received, ten sutures to his split scalp. The CT scan of his head showed nothing. Under other circumstances, Gabe would have commented on the lack of anything in the cranial cavity, but this time just left his not-so-witty remark to no injury to the brain.

They returned to the hotel in silence.

Annie and Marti sat in the living area of the villa. Marti wanted to comfort her friend, but wasn't sure how, or if, it was even possible, and after several minutes of strained silence, the women retired to their bedrooms.

Marti fell asleep right away.

Annie lay on her bed, watching the snow softly falling outside of the window.

The words of Gabe's song came back to her.

Tears burned a path down her cheeks.

"Rise and shine, Annie-bananie," Marti chirped through the closed door of Annie's room.

She pried her eyes open. Pain shot through her already pounding skull, and her mouth felt dry and... ick, like water buffalo had been wallowing around in there. Her stomach roiled.

Hangover.

Reason number four hundred and three *not* to drink to excess.

Maybe a shower would help.

Slowly... very slowly she put on her robe and walked to the bathroom.

Marti handed her a glass of Pepsi and Annie gave her a confused look.

"Drink it; it will help."

Annie sipped the dark liquid. It was cold and sweet, and the carbonation chased some of the fuzziness from her brain.

"Thanks, it does," she mumbled, giving Marti a painful smile.

Annie stood in the stinging spray of the hot shower until she thought she would melt. She felt a little better - physically, anyway.

Marti called into her to let her know she was heading out for a few more runs before they went home.

"...So did you want to come too, Annie-bananie?"

Nope... Not a good idea.

"Marti... oh God, no," Annie groaned, fighting nausea at the very thought of the chair lifts.

"Okay. Oh, yeah... There's a little something on the kitchen table for you. It was delivered this morning. Enjoy!" Marti said as she was leaving.

A little something? Delivered? Now Annie was curious, and headed to the kitchenette as soon as her shower was over.

The scent reached her before she saw what it was.

Roses.

Her knees felt weak.

Oh God, oh God, oh God...

On very shaky legs Annie walked into the kitchen, and there they were on the table.

White roses.

Dozens of them.

She saw a card peeking out of the buds. She didn't want to know who they came from, but she knew already. She had almost expected it, and her hand seemed to have a mind of its own as it reached out to take the card. Annie's mind screamed in denial, but before she knew it she was reading the inside of the card.

"Annie,

Each morning a bright sun, a sky forever blue, Clouds with silver linings... This is what I wish for you.

'G'."

Gabe. So it *was* him that had been in her cabin that day. Deep down she had known it, and this confirmed it. He wanted her to know it. Annie pulled a rose from the vase and walked to the sofa, absently stroking the velvety white petals of the flower on her cheek. She sat down, and the aroma of the rose brought back memories... of late summer... of their first kiss long ago. Hand-in-hand they walked and for hours they talked, until they knew all there was to know...

What was this? What memories? Annie was trembling. Powerful emotions washed over her: love, passion, contentment and the deep pain of loss overwhelmed her.

She walked to the desk and found pen and paper, and began to write.

When she had finished, she read what she had written. *Jeez, where had this come from?* She had no conscious memory of writing the words.

She reread the poem, a sad tale of lost love. How appropriate...

She set the paper down and picked up the rose. There was something else going on here.

Something big.

Something powerful.

Something out of her control.

Michael's serene, smiling face flashed in her mind. And that man was involved somehow.

Annie had to get home.

Chapter Twenty-Seven

"Geoffrey... you're home so early," Deirdre said, trying to hide her disappointment at his sudden arrival. "How was your trip?" She took his jacket from him and hung it in the closet.

"Interesting. Somewhat productive. Good snow," was his terse answer.

This could not be good; he was in such a foul mood. She was dying to ask him questions but didn't dare. Although... maybe one safe one about Annie.

"Did you give Annie my message?" she asked.

Gabe stiffened. Without turning around he said, "Yes I did."

She wasn't sure whether to pursue the issue, but might as well - what could happen?

"And what did she say?"

"I don't think she said anything." Gabe hesitated, and then said, "Dee, do you think it wise to get closer to Annie? You hardly know her and she doesn't seem to very receptive to the idea."

He didn't think he could bear it if Annie were underfoot in his house, not that she'd care to come over in the first place.

"Oh, dear! Geoffrey, it is very, very important that I speak to her. I... I found something that she should know about. Did she give you any indication that she might call?" Deirdre was getting worried; things weren't working out at all.

"I think it highly unlikely. I'm sorry," Gabe said shortly. "If you will excuse me, I have some calls to make." He went into his office and shut the door.

Deirdre realized that Geoffrey hadn't once looked at her since he had arrived home. No, this wasn't good at all. Where was Steven when she needed him?

Marti and Annie pulled into the driveway at the cabin, and Dog and McDonald ran out to greet them.

Spike managed to tear himself away from his ever-so-choice spot by the fireplace and waited on the porch for the female. He was very glad that she was finally home; he'd missed her. He disguised the fact by being totally engrossed in grooming his face.

Dog and McDonald had no such reservations. The odd couple raced up the driveway to meet the van, nipping at each other and wanting to be the first to receive Annie's attention. It was a tie. She stepped out of the vehicle and both animals were on her. She caught McDonald in mid-air as he struggled to fly up to her, and he nibbled up and down her arm. Dog leaned up against her leg, pushing his muzzle into her hand.

"Quite the welcoming committee!" Marti laughed. She could never get over the strange friendship between the two creatures.

Jill stood on the porch, her packed suitcase next to her; she hated to leave. Maybe someday she would live in a place like this.

Annie grabbed her luggage from the back of the van as Jill put hers in.

"Jill, thanks for critter-sitting for me," she said, giving her an envelope containing cash for her efforts.

Jill thanked her, and gave her a quick rundown of the weekend – everyone was fine and nothing exciting had happened. Spike had moved from one end of the sofa to the other, but nothing else out of the ordinary.

The women laughed at this. Good ol' Spike; an endless source of entertainment.

Spike resented being the butt of their little joke and stalked back into the cabin. He gave his tail an impudent flip at them just before he disappeared through the door.

The women said their goodbyes, all three waving as Marti and Jill drove away.

Alone at last... As much as Annie enjoyed Marti's company, she couldn't wait to be by herself for a while. She changed into some riding clothes and went to see her horses.

Adonis and Wanda nickered at her approach, happy to see her. Annie was just as happy to see them, and indulged in a few long minutes of just looking at them before she began the tasks of grooming and mucking out stalls. Tasks she very much enjoyed, so time flew by, and before she knew it she was done, and it was time for a ride. Adonis practically crawled under the saddle when Annie held it up, so eager was he to go.

She put her mind on autopilot, letting her horse pick the route. She didn't want to think about a thing, not even where to ride.

Adonis tore up the hill next to the tree line, only to turn abruptly into the woods, nearly unseating his rider. They followed the trail to the clearing and the marble bench.

Oh, big surprise... Annie dismounted and sat down to look at the frozen lake. She could hear Dog and McDonald in the distance, arguing as usual. She turned to her horse when he nickered. He was looking off towards the woods, ears at full alert. She followed his gaze to see a huge, black shape moving through the trees. The horse was enormous, easily seventeen hands, with his rider sitting tall in the saddle. He stopped next to her, his bright blue eyes shining over the serene smile on his face.

"Michael!" she cried, jumping up. It was no dream, no hallucination. He was actually there!

He kicked a leg over the saddle horn and hopped down, then picked Annie up and swung her around in an exuberant hug.

"My dear Miss Benton," he grinned when he put her down, "As always, you are a vision..."

"Funny you should mention visions," she mumbled under her breath.

Michael raised an eyebrow. "Oh?"

"It's nothing," she replied. "I'm so glad you're here. I've really missed you!"

Again, his eyebrow shot up. "Oh? You... missed me?"

She gave him a sharp look. *No... he couldn't know, could he?* Annie felt a chill, totally unrelated to the weather.

Michael took a seat on the bench, waiving her over to join him. "Have a seat, Annie, and let's enjoy what's left of this beautiful day."

They sat together, gazing out at the lake. The sun would be setting within the hour, promising to dazzle them with a visual feast. Annie shivered again, although this time from the freezing weather. Michael put his arm around her, and as he did so she felt a curious warmth spread through her body. She felt safe and protected; the emotional turmoil she had endured seemed to melt away. So peaceful here... And Michael had come back to her.

"Care to tell me about it, Annie?

She startled at his voice when it disturbed the tranquility. "Hmm? What...?"

"Talk to me."

She looked deep into his eyes, and what she was there both thrilled and frightened her.

He knew.

He knew about Gabe.

He knew so much more...

She allowed herself to be pulled into the bright blue depths. She saw insurmountable joy and unspeakable pain. She saw love, passion, and loss. She could see the past, present, and future. She saw a light in his eyes that seemed... unearthly.

Annie jumped slightly when a faint blue aura formed around him. *Must be a trick of the light.* She blinked. The aura was gone.

"Annie...?"

She slumped against him. "Michael, I don't even know where to begin," she sighed.

"Begin at the beginning." He pulled a white rose bud from the inside pocket of his leather jacket and placed it into her gloved hand.

She stared at the flower. The beginning. It all started with the rose bush at her grandmother's... seeing Gabe's image. Yes, the beginning... or was it? Maybe it began long before... when time began.

Annie told him everything. Although he knew most, she told him of the visions, the strange tingling, meeting Deirdre and the twins. She told him about the cowboy at the hospital and the visitor to the cabin. She told him of her disastrous weekend.

She told Michael of her feelings for Gabe, and how she thought he felt about her. Her words poured from her, as did her tears.

He held her as she purged her troubles, and when she had finished, he turned her to face him.

"Annie, you need to listen to me, really listen. Understand?"

She nodded.

"I know Deirdre very well. Better than anyone…"

Annie blinked in surprise. "You what?"

"Just listen. Go to her. You need her and she needs you. The twins need you. Gabe needs you."

"I… I don't understand," she stammered. "You've said that before, but I still don't understand. I can't go over there and see Deirdre! Not with him there! And after what I just told you, how could you even suggest such a thing?"

Michael forces her to look into his eyes again. She saw them change. The blue became more intense, and then changed to a deep green. Annie could see herself reflected there. She could see into her own eyes. She could see joy, love, passion… Gabe.

"Annie? Do you trust me? Complete trust… no questions?"

She swallowed hard. "Yes. You know I do, but…"

"Then go to her, Annie. You've got to!" He gave her a long, tender kiss to the forehead.

"This feels like good bye, Michael…"

"It could very well be, Annie. My job here just might be done and I'll be heading home for good."

"I can't talk you into staying?"

He sighed, framed her face with his large, calloused hands, and looked deep into her eyes one last time.

She saw he had no choice. Her hands covered his, squeezing slightly, turning to bring her lips to his palm. "Go," she whispered into it. "Go before I beg you stay."

Michael swallowed hard, whistled for his horse. "It's time, Whiz," he said in a choked voice, swinging up into the saddle.

Annie gave him a moment before moving to him, placing her hand on his worn boot. She looked up at him. "You never told me where home is, Michael."

He raised his eyes heavenward, blinking rapidly to clear his vision. "Let's just say it's Big Sky country, hon." He blew her a kiss, turned Whiz towards the trees, and vanished in the early winter twilight.

"Good bye, my angel," Annie whispered.

She sat in the darkened cabin where the only light present was the glow of the fire through the vent in the woodstove, sipping a cup of tea and reviewing the weekend's events. She was so glad that Michael had been there for her to talk to, and she was feeling much better, even though life was still the same. The fantasy was gone forever… did the dream still remain? Wait. Where had she heard that before? Gabe had sung those words at the ski resort, hadn't he? She was sure of it.

Another thought came to her. The singer she had seen on the television the other night… could that have been him? Setting her cup aside, she hurried over and tuned in to the country channel, rather disappointed to see a talk show.

"Crap. Well, it was worth a try," she shrugged. Then again, hadn't she taped that station in hopes she would catch the video again?

The tape was still in the VCR, waiting to be rewound. She did so, sitting back down with the remote and her cooling tea. Leaning forward in anticipation, she fast-forwarded the tape, watching the images at warp speed until she found what she was looking for.

There was Kyle standing in the foreground playing his guitar while Gabe stood in the background, facing away from the camera. White mist swirled around him, and far off in the distance Annie could see a female form standing next to a bare-limbed tree. Her long blonde hair waved about her, as did her flowing robes, in a manufactured breeze.

Gabe turned around. His intense blue eyes bored straight into Annie's soul. He began to sing "The Dream" as the camera moved closer to him. The video jumped from one scene to the other, the only constant being Gabe's face in the upper corner of the screen, just slightly out of focus as he poured out the pain and passion of love lost. Annie never took her eyes from his. Towards the end of the last verse he was once again standing in the swirling mist, holding his guitar and facing away from the camera. Kyle and the woman were no longer in the picture.

The song ended. Gabe turned to face the camera one more time; this was the part of the video that Annie had just missed before.

Once more she played the video, closing her eyes while she listened to the lyrics. They moved her as nothing ever had before. It inspired her to take pen in hand, pick up her notebook, and write.

Spike watched from the back of the couch. *This is pathetic! Something had to be done, and soon.* He would watch closely for his opportunity to intervene.

Chapter Twenty-Eight

Annie slept deeply that night, with no dreams to interrupt her slumber. When she woke Monday morning, the terrible heartache was gone, replaced by a sense of waiting, of anticipation. The talk with Michael had done wonders for her, although she had to wonder how he knew Deirdre so well. So many mysteries surrounded that man... Perhaps Deirdre would have some answers?

She would call right after breakfast. No, maybe not. No phone number. Try Gabe's office? Hopefully Jenna would answer. If he did, Annie planned to hang up and try later. Now, if she only knew the name of his company. Marti would know for sure, and hadn't she mentioned something about Mr. Evans being in the recording and producing business?

Annie poured herself another cup of coffee and sat at the kitchen table, dropping the phone book down with a solid thump. Little good it would do without any clue where to start, but she had to do something. As she was opening to a random page in the yellow pages, Spike jumped into her lap for his daily dose of adoration.

"Where do I start, cat? Recording? Studios? Production? A? B? Why am I doing this to me?" she sighed.

Spike moved from her lap to the table, making himself cozy on the phone book and purring in utter contentment. His amber eyes studied Annie through half-open lids.

"Get your fuzzy butt off the table, cat," Annie sighed, waving a hand at him. "Absolutely no manners..." She ended up giving him a small shove, sending him to the floor. He replied with a flip of his tail and a feline snort of disgust. "Whatever...." She brushed a few stay cat hairs, and there, right under her hand.... SD Productions. It had to be. The ad said that Geoffrey Evans and Kyle Davidson were the owners. It had to be Gabe!

"Thank you, Spike!" Annie called out, already focusing on nothing but seeing Gabe once more...

Spike was no longer listening. He sat near the woodstove, grooming himself and thinking how that woman's gratitude was sadly lacking.

Thinking how insane she must be, Annie punched the seven magic numbers into the phone. It rang three times. She was about to hang up when a warm female voice answered.

"Good morning, SD Productions. This is Jenna speaking."

Thank God it wasn't Gabe.

"Good morning, Jenna. This is Annie. Annie Benton...? Do you remember me from the hospital?"

Jen's voice cooled considerably. "Annie. Yes, I remember." She remembered now much Deirdre had liked the nurse. She also remembered what Kyle had told her about Annie and Gabe's behavior over the weekend. "What can I do for you?"

"Well, I'm trying to reach Deirdre. Her husband told me that she was trying to contact me, but I never got a chance to get their phone number. Would be kind enough to give it to me?"

Jenna was torn between loyalty to her friend, and loyalty to her friend. Protect Deirdre or honor her wishes? She looked over to the family portrait of Dee, Gabe, and the twins; their perfect picture of the perfect family. Her gaze rested on Dee's smiling face.

Deirdre winked at her.

Jenna blinked in surprise.

Annie heard only silence as the answer to her question.

"Jenna? Hello?"

"Huh? What?" Jen continued to stare at the portrait. Must be stress, pictures did not move!

Dee's smile grew wider beneath happy eyes. Jen quickly looked away, rubbing her fingers over her forehead. Annie… What to do about Annie?

"Jenna, are you there?" Annie asked, concerned.

"Wha…? Yes, I um… I'm fine."

"The phone number?"

Jen thought of Dee's excitement over the journals. *Honor her wishes…*

"Got a pencil, Annie?"

Annie stared at the phone number she'd written down. 555-2783. It burned into her memory. She'd taken the first step into… Into what? Why was she even doing this in the first place?

Because Michael told her to, and from what she saw in his eyes. That was reason enough.

So… call Deirdre. *But what if Gabe answered?* Then ask to talk to his wife.

And get over him. Don't waste time wanting what she could never have. She'd lived relatively testosterone-free for this long and done just fine, so why change now?

Because.

Because…

Annie looked at the bouquet of white roses on the kitchen table.

Because of that.

Deirdre sat at the dining room table, sipping a cup of tea. It was already nine in the morning and Geoffrey had yet to come down for breakfast. She could hear him in his bedroom, pacing like a caged animal. There was a moment of silence, and then more pacing. Silence again. Her heart went out to him. She wanted to open up and tell him everything: that she was dying, that he and Steven had returned, that Gabe and Annie were meant to be together…

Why not? What was stopping her?

Enough of this nonsense. Geoffrey had to know, and soon.

A noise in the kitchen captured her attention; he had finally left his room. Odd thing though, she hadn't heard Geoffrey come down the steps. The double doors opened and Dee turned with a bright smile on her face. "Geoffrey!" she beamed at the man walking through the door, and then choked out, "Steven? What are you doing here?" The surprise in her voice was evident.

"You'd rather have Gabe? I can leave," he teased.

"No, you know better than that. But Geoffrey... What if he comes down?"

"Not to worry. At this very moment he's staring out of his window in a semi-comatose state, contemplating the mysteries of the universe. A little divine intervention," Steve answered with a wink.

"You wicked man!" Dee laughed. "And to what do I owe the pleasure of your most unexpected visit?"

He turned serious. "You can't tell Gabe about any off this."

"Why not? The poor man is miserable and I hate to see him hurting so. I don't have all that much time left, Steven, and I want to see him truly happy before I die."

"I know, but this has got to happen when it will happen, Dee. We can't interfere any more than we already have. Rules, you know." He put his arms around her and pulled her close, pressing his lips to her forehead. "And you have more time than you think, love."

Deirdre felt her pain melt away and strength return to her wasted muscles. *Thank you, Steven...* "If you say so, but I must say that I'm growing very impatient!"

"Understood. Think Gabe is ready for breakfast yet?"

Dee shook her head. "No, probably not. He's been acting very strange ever since he returned home. Just what happened up there? I thought things were working out."

"They were. At least I thought they were. After Kyle knocked himself out everything fell apart. I tried to do a little damage control although I'm not too sure it was very successful."

"We can only hope. From the way Geoffrey is acting, I think we're back to square one."

"Well, they're aware of each other now. Very aware." Steve gave her a sly smile.

"Do tell!" Dee laughed. She was about to further question when she thought she heard the nicker of a horse, and instead gave her love a bemused look.

"I've got to go. Whizbang calls."

"That horse again," Dee sighed. "Give him a hug for me?"

"Will do. Good bye, love." Steven kissed her again, vanishing as he walked through the double doors.

Deirdre giggled. He could have at least opened them up first, the show off.

She sobered a bit when she heard movement from upstairs. Geoffrey was on is way down. She started a fresh pot of coffee for him. She reached for a mug, interrupted by the ringing of the phone. Her heart skipped a beat. *Annie?* No, just Jenna calling to tell her that she gave out Dee's phone number to the nurse and wondering if it was alright.

More than alright, it had made Deirdre's day. Jen was still torn; sure she hadn't done the right thing at all.

Gabe stumbled into the kitchen, walked straight to the coffee pot, and held a mug under the filter basket to let the coffee brew directly into his cup. He was in no mood to wait around any longer than he had to. He stared as it filled, replaced the pot, and mumbled a hello to his wife. He wouldn't look at her. If he had, she would have seen misery in its purest form attempting to hide behind an unshaven face and bloodshot eyes.

"Geoffrey dear, are you ill? Should I call a doctor?" Dee placed a light hand on his arm, very concerned; although she knew all he really needed was a good dose of Annie.

"No, I'm fine. Although I'm not going to work today. Kyle already knows," he replied in a voice void of emotion.

"Can I get you anything? Do anything for you?"

"I don't think so. Maybe a walk… I think I need some air." He placed his unsipped coffee on the counter and left the room.

Gabe grabbed his favorite leather jacket before he left the house, shrugging into it as he went down the stairs. He hadn't worn it since his unscheduled visit to Annie's cabin. He shivered, zipped up, mumbled, "Christ, it's freezing out here…" *Big surprise, Sparky, it's January.* Wandering over to the park, he shoved his hands into the pockets of his coat. His hand met with the stiff resistance of a folded piece of paper and it took him a moment to remember that the card he'd found at the cabin was still there. He pulled it out, and as he did so, a crumbled bit of paper fell to the snow. Gabe picked it up and carefully smoothed it out. It was the poem written in Stevie's handwriting. He sat on the picnic table, wishing he had a cigarette. Held the card and the poem next to each other.

"To Michael."

Stevie's handwriting.

The truly unthinkable thought that had been lurking in the back of his mind finally fought its way to the front and Gabe was forced to face it.

Michael.

Steven.

Steven Michael.

"Steven Michael Anthony Evans…" he murmured, feeling a tremor of awe and fear course through his body.

How? And why? Of course it couldn't be possible. People don't come back from the dead, right? Maybe in vivid dreams, but in reality? Not goddamn likely!

"Ghosts… ha!"

Ghosts... Angels.

Snow angels... angels in the snow.

Could Steve's nocturnal visits be trying to tell him something? There was a definite connection with Annie, that much Gabe knew, but just how much did Deirdre know about all of this? More than she let on, he was sure of that too. After all, she was the one who sent him to River Ridge. So was Annie in on it too? No, he didn't think so. She had no idea who he was until they'd been introduced. Although by now she'd probably figured out that it had been him in her cabin, seeing how she'd had his hat on. That particular thought brought a small smile to his troubled face. He thought about the roses he'd sent her. Yep, he'd been walking by a flower shop early Sunday morning and had gone in on a whim, amazed that such a place was even open on a Sunday. The scent of roses drew him to the back of the building, and before he knew it he'd ordered white ones to be delivered, and was staring at a blank note card in his hand. But what to say to her? With a sigh, he'd turned to look out the window to see the sun breaking through dark gray clouds edged in silver and behind them a brilliant blue sky. That was it. He quickly scratched out his message and deliberately signed it the same as the note he'd left in her cabin.

So, Gabe, now what do you do? You love Annie. You always have and you always will. You're pretty certain that she feels the same about you, but she knows your wife and will not do anything that would harm your marriage.

Deirdre... She sent you off to a weekend at a ski resort. Could she have possibly known that Annie might be there? God, man, she's offered several times since you've been married to release you from your vows if you found someone you truly loved as a wife, but until now the issue had never come up. Until now. Now, when your wife is so ill and you'd be the lowest of the low to leave her.

And mixed liberally throughout this little drama is your brother Steve. Kyle has seen him, you've seen him, there was evidence the twins had seen him, and Dee was acting like she'd seen him too. She'd been so happy lately. Radiant even. Gabe, it's all just too bizarre.

He rose from the picnic table and wandered deeper into the park, thinking that it was time to make some decisions. Tell Dee everything? Contact Annie? Continue on as if nothing had ever happened? No, that last idea was not an option.

Talk to Dee. She was his closest friend, other than Kyle of course, even if he'd been less than friendly lately. Yeah, Dee. She'd always been there for him after Steve died, getting him through his nightmares, and keeping him from falling back into his depression and the alcohol-drug haze that would inevitably follow. She knew his every secret, every sordid sin, and loved him regardless. He loved her too.

Gabe stopped in his tracks and turned to face his house. He could see bits of its mellow brick through the trees in the park. A curl of smoke rose from the chimney; Dee must have lit a fire in the hearth.

Yeah, go home and talk to Deirdre. She'll know what to do...

Dee felt chilly. She turned from the window where she'd been watching Geoffrey, rubbing her hands along her arms in an attempt to warm herself. A fire... that's what she'd do. Build a cozy fire for him to come home to, and brew another pot of coffee as well. He'd yet to have his first cup of the day. Once that was accomplished she returned to her post at the window to see that he was on his way back, running up the path on powerful legs. She sighed, thinking of what a specimen of manhood he was. Strong, handsome, and even a bit rugged-looking with the shadow of a beard darkening his face. Annie was indeed a very lucky girl. With a smile, Mrs. Evans returned to the living room to wait for him.

The front door opened and closed, followed by sounds from the closet door as Geoffrey hung up his coat. Dee looked up as he entered the living room, carrying what looked to be a card of some sort.

"Deirdre, we need to talk, "Gabe said, his voice serious.

"Yes, Geoffrey, we do," she replied, her voice soft. She smiled at him and patted the sofa beside her, indicating that he should sit.

He hesitated for a moment, and then joined her, blinking in surprise when she stood just as he flopped down next to her.

"I'll go get some coffee, Geoffrey. I have a feeling this might take a while." She cupped his unshaven chin in her hand, and with another smile, disappeared into the kitchen.

Gabe nodded absently, his mind already wrapped around the mystery of Steve. He barely noticed when she returned with a tray bearing two cups and an insulated carafe of steaming coffee, which she placed on the table in front of the sofa. She poured, handed him his cup, and flitted back out with an excuse of forgetting the cream and sugar. He didn't care. He liked his black anyway.

Just as he was about to enjoy his first sip, still thinking of Steve, the phone rang. It jangled on his already frazzled nerves, causing him to spill hot liquid on his leg. The pain was intense, although brief.

"Goddammit!" he squealed, nearly dropping his mug and reaching for the phone in the same motion. Biting back more obscenities, he gasped a, "hello?"

There was no reply.

"Hello?" he repeated, considering one of his favorite obscenities.

"Is... is Deirdre there?" asked a very familiar voice.

"Annie?" he managed to choke out. *Oh God, it was his Annie!* "Uh... yeah. One moment." With a hand over the mouthpiece, he called out for Dee.

She entered the room at the same time he said her name. "Yes," she said, placing the sugar bowl and creamer on the tray.

Gabe said nothing, merely handed her the phone.

"Hello?" Her face brightened. "Annie! I'm so glad that you called. Could you hold?" Deirdre turned to Geoffrey and said, "Could you excuse us for a moment?"

He nodded, picked up his coffee, and went upstairs to change before sneaking off to his office.

Oh jeez... Gabe was there! Oh, and it was so good to hear his voice again. Annie shut her eyes and pictured him singing to her all over again, but snapped back to reality when she heard Mrs. Evans' voice on the other end of the line.

"Annie, thank you for holding. How have you been?"

"Um... fine. G... Gabe said you wanted me to call?" Annie could barely get the words out.

"Yes, I did. Oh, where to begin?"

No answer from Annie. What could she possibly say to the wife of the man she loved?

Dee continued. "Annie, I'll just come right out and say it. I found some journals that were written by your grandmother Rosalind. There is also a family bible. Forgive me, but I took the liberty of reading through them. I think you need to do the same. It's very important."

Annie was stunned. Of all things possible that she may have expected to hear, she never ever expected that. *The journals!*

"Annie, are you still there?" Deirdre asked after a prolonged silence.

"Uh... yes, I am. I'm sorry, I'm just so surprised! Stunned, actually. Are you sure that they are my grandmother's?"

"Yes, I'm sure. Your name is entered in the bible, along with your sister Amanda and several generations of the Benton-Charles-Delaney clan. When can you come to collect them?"

"This is unbelievable! I... I thought I'd never see the again. I um... Well, when is convenient for you?" The shock was still evident in Annie's voice.

"Any time is fine. I have no plans for today or tomorrow. Why don't you come for lunch today?"

"Lunch? I... I suppose I could," Annie said after a long moment of contemplation. What if Gabe was still there? She didn't know if she could handle it. Dare she ask? Would it really make a difference?

Dee took care of the little dilemma. "It will be just the two of us. The twins are with their grandparents for the week and Geoffrey will be at the office." Now all she had to do was convince him to go, they could talk later. "Here's my address, Annie..."

Annie jotted down the info, surprised by the location. She had imagined that they would have lived in one of the newer pseudo-mansion recently built on the south side of town, not in the neighborhood of old, rundown structures on Park Street. She remembered driving by the park on that road with her grandmother so many years ago. Rosalind was giving her a little history lesson, telling Annie about some distant relatives who had lived in the area many years ago. Had the neighborhood changed that much?

"Annie? Say right around noon...?"

"Yes... I'll be there. See you soon, M...Mrs. Evans." Annie hung up before she lost it, not knowing whether to laugh or cry. What an unexpected turn of events. Gramma's journals. Lunch with Gabe's wife.

Deirdre found Geoffrey in his office where he was lounging on his leather sofa, idly picking at his guitar and singing softly. She listened until the song ended before she interrupted his reverie. "Geoffrey, what a lovely song. Did you write it?"

Gabe jumped. He'd been lost in his memories of Saturday night, singing to his Annie and dreaming of the night when she'd actually be in his arms. He looked up at Dee, set his guitar aside, and sat up. He hoped his face wasn't too red at being "caught in the act." "Mmhmm. Saturday," he answered, dropping his eyes.

"Well I love it, and you sing it with such passion!" Deidre told him, hoping he would open up to her.

Gabe was thinking that now would be a very good time to tell her - everything. "Do you have time to talk now?"

"A few minutes. Annie is coming for lunch and I should get it started." She smiled and sat next to him.

Now was his chance to bare his soul. He looked down at his wife who was smiling up at him, her eyes sparkling. Pity… he had no idea where to begin.

She reached over and took his large, rough hand into her small, soft frail one. "Geoffrey, you know you can tell me anything… anything at all. There is absolutely nothing you can say that will shock or upset me. Do you understand?" His hand was given a small, reassuring squeeze along with her words.

Gabe nodded, but still didn't know where to start. "It's Annie," was all he said.

Dee raised an eyebrow. "Go on…"

"As you know, we spent some time together at River Ridge. I… she… We seemed to um… get along quite well together."

Dee nodded, encouraging him to continue.

"I think… No, I know… Oh God, I'm in love with her, Dee!" Gabe finished in a rush. *There. It was out.*

Dee could barely contain her excitement. "Oh, Geoffrey… I'm so happy for you! That is… if… Does she feel the same way about you?"

"I think so," he replied with a quick nod. "Or at least I thought so. It's all so damn complicated."

Dee agreed. "I believe that I'm the major complication?"

"What am I going to do, Dee?" Gabe sighed.

"Let me think about it for a while. Can you hold on for one more day?"

"Have I any choice?"

"Come now, Geoffrey, cheer up. I have a feeling that things will work out just fine," Deirdre smiled.

"And you base this assumption on what…?"

"Hmm… I cannot reveal my sources," she teased.

Gabe made a pathetic attempt to smile. "Are you holding out on me? Do you have a crystal ball tucked away some where, or did a little birdie tell you?"

A wry grin was his only answer.

They sat in silence for a few minutes, and then Deirdre stood and faced Geoffrey. "I really should start lunch, Annie will be here soon. Might I suggest that you go elsewhere and find something to keep yourself occupied for a while? I have some important matters to discuss with her and we don't need you around as a distraction."

"Kicked out of my own home," Gabe mock-pouted and stifled a hint of a grin. "Oh, and the mystery surrounding these matters. Will I be let in on your big secret?" The grin became more obvious as his depression lifted.

"Perhaps. I'm sure you'll find out in some form or another," Dee replied, smiling back.

Gabe attempted to speak again until she stopped him with a finger to his lips. "Not another word about it. Now go. Go to your studio and record that lovely song I just heard. Oh, and give Kyle my love." She pulled him to his feet as she spoke.

Gabe let out a short laugh. "That's a good one. The man won't even speak to me, let alone accept any show of affection, no matter who sends it!"

"Really? And his reason would be…?"

"I'm not certain, but I think he thinks that I betrayed you… with Annie. Saturday night."

Deirdre raised an eyebrow. "And?"

Gabe sighed and confessed. "I spent Saturday morning teaching her how to ski. She sent me packing before noon, but I uh… well, kept a close eye on her after that." Another sigh. "And Saturday night we were sitting rather close together in the bar."

Deirdre gave him a stern, although far from angry or serious look. "You wicked, wicked man, you! Such behavior… and in public!" Her hand floated dramatically to her forehead. She continued, "Ah sweah! Ah will nevah be able to show mah face in po-lite so-ciety again! Oh, Geoffrey… I'm about to swoon in mah dis-tress…"

Gabe caught her in his arms, dipping her backward. Assuming a perfect Rhett Butler persona, he begged her forgiveness. "Miss Deirdre, please, please forgive my most ungentlemanly behavior. I'm a cad, a rogue, a scoundrel… and as your husband I should call myself out!" He smacked a loud kiss on her forehead and let her up.

She leaned against him, laughing at their theatrics. "I'm not sure if you'd win or lose that duel, Geoffrey; you've always claimed to be less than adept with firearms."

He gave her a quick hug. "Then I suppose I'd have to chuck rocks at myself until I cried 'uncle', eh? I do love you… you know that, right, Dee?"

"I know, Geoffrey. I love you too. Now scoot. I have things to do." She released him, smacking him smartly on the butt on her way to the door.

Gabe walked her to the door, thinking. Something was so different about her. "Dee? How are you feeling?"

"Hmm...?"

"Feeling. You seem..."

"Funny you should ask, Geoffrey," she interrupted. "I feel wonderful! I haven't had a pain pill since... oh god, since Sunday morning."

"Not smoking weed, are you?" Gabe joked. "I mean, I wouldn't mind, but not to share it with me? Unforgivable!"

Dee favored him with a smirk. "You've missed your calling, love; you really should have been a comedian. Seriously though, let's chalk my feeling so well up to divine intervention."

Her comment triggered something in Gabe's mind. He suddenly remembered what else he had wanted to discuss with her. With a furrowed brow he asked her to give him another moment or two of her time, and retrieved the card and note from his desk. "What do you make of this, Dee?" he asked, handing them to her.

She took the papers, biting her bottom lip as she looked at them. "This will take too long to discuss now, Geoffrey. After dinner tonight." With a nod, she handed them back and left the room.

He stared after her. Jesus, she didn't even seem surprised! Was Stevie making the rounds? Was he Annie's Michael? Should Gabe go see a shrink for having such crazy thoughts? *Tune in tomorrow for the next episode of "As Gabe's World Turns... into a stint at the funny farm..."*

Lord, dinner was going to be a long, long time away.

Annie pulled up to the curb in front of the Evans', noticing that the neighborhood had indeed changed. All but a few houses had been restored to their former glory, and this one was by far the largest and most elegant. She felt a bit dwarfed by the structure, never having been in a home nearly as large as this. Jeez, her entire cabin would just about fit into half of the first floor!

She parked, turned off the engine, and made her way through the decorative iron gate and up the sidewalk. She forced herself up the steps; her hand shook when she pressed the doorbell.

Deirdre answered right away. "Annie!" she cried, "I'm so glad to see you! Let me take your coat."

Annie was pulled inside, given a hug. "Thank you," she mumbled, handing over her jacket.

Dee took the nervous woman's hand, tugging her through the spacious foyer. "This way, dear..."

Annie stumbled along behind, discreetly peeking into, and admiring, the rooms they passed. Whoever had decorated the place had excellent taste; understated elegance with a touch of whimsy. She slowed a bit to look at the framed photos lining one wall. Family pictures... the twins at various stages of their young lives, Gabe, Deirdre, some older people (grandparents?), and a picture of a smiling cowboy standing next to a large black horse. His hat was pulled low over his eyes, but Annie would know that smile anywhere. Michael. She stopped to take a longer look at the photo.

Deirdre noticed who Annie was looking at, but decided not to tell her a thing just yet. "Come along, dear. We don't want our soup getting cold..."

Annie nodded, tearing her eyes away from the cowboy, and followed.

The light was better in the living room, allowing Annie to get her first really good look at her hostess, which very much surprised her. Deirdre looked wonderful! Although pale and far too thin, she seemed strong and vibrant, and it was difficult to believe that she was in the end stages of cancer. Impossible to believe, actually.

"Deirdre, I must say that you're looking much better than the last time I saw you."

"Hmm... I must agree, and I'm feeling just as good. I don't know how long it will last, so I'll enjoy it as long as I can," Dee smiled.

"Let's hope it lasts for a very long time," Annie said sincerely.

"I suppose you're wondering about the journals? There are about two dozen. They're all upstairs in my room right now; we can bring them down later. Annie, you won't believe the history recorded in them! Generations of Charles' and Delaney's... and others. Let's eat and then I'll show them to you."

Annie wasn't all that hungry and would have preferred to grab the books and run, but Deirdre was already ladling out bowls of homemade vegetable soup and passing hot wheat rolls around, and apologizing for not serving a more lavish lunch.

"It's just fine, Mrs... um... Deirdre. Perfect, actually. I'm a little too nervous to be very hungry."

"Thank you, Annie. My appetite is still a bit lacking, so this..." Dee waved at the spread... "is pretty much all I want most of the time."

They spent the next hour chatting about everything, and Annie found that she liked Deirdre very much. Even though Annie had heard some of the stories before when Dee was doped-up in the hospital, it was even more interesting now that they were told with a clear and perfect memory. Deirdre was witty, clever, and Annie was sure she'd been a wonderful actress, and wished she had known her longer. Despite the difference in their ages, she felt that they would have been great friends.

"It's not too late, you know," Dee murmured, cutting into Annie's little reverie.

"What? What's not too late?"

"Us... being friends. That is what you were thinking, am I right?"

Annie blushed a bit. "Well, yes, but how did you know?

"I felt it the first time I met you. There was a bond there... Couldn't you feel it too? Even the twins felt it. Surely you must have, Annie!"

"Well, I did feel kind of like there was something different about all of you," Annie replied evasively. Gabe was the only one she really felt a deep bond with, or so she thought.

"Good. Now let's go up to my room and meet your relatives."

Gabe walked into the offices of SD Productions, surprising Jenna and nearly stunning Kyle. Neither had expected to see him. The Davidson's mumbled a cool hello when he blew by them on his way to his private office.

Chet screeched his own greeting; Gabe ignored the bird and began sifting through the many messages littering his desktop. Most were from the skiers at the resort, thanking the duo for their generosity Saturday night. Gabe nodded in satisfaction as he read each note. Mmhmm… he'd be happy to make SD's music available to anyone who wanted it, and given the collective nature of what he was reading, it was a relief to know that they could still be a draw – especially with a new CD in the works.

Assuming Gabe still had a partner, of course. Kyle was still acting a little pissy, and Jen wasn't all that friendly either. Evans admired their loyalty to Deirdre, but wasn't he entitled to a little bit too? Why couldn't they trust in him, that he'd never willingly hurt his wife? That thought pricked at him, making him want to tell his friends the truth about his marriage, but that was for Dee to decide. He hoped she wouldn't take too damn long to do it.

Chet screeched again, forcing Gabe to acknowledge him this time. Man swiveled around in his chair to glare at bird.

"What is it, you worthless pile of feathers?" Gabe snarled playfully.

"What?" Chet answered.

"I asked you first."

"Whatever," mumbled Chet.

"What?!"

"Whatever," whispered Chet.

Gabe leaned forward in his chair, musing at the bird's odd behavior. Had Kyle been in there again, teaching him obscenities?

Chet made a sound very much as a whoopee cushion in use.

Gabe chuckled and then moved a little closer to the cage. "Speak up, o' eloquent one," he demanded.

Chet sidestepped on his perch until he was up against the bars, lowered his head in a conspiratory way as if he were about to divulge a deep dark secret, and repeated his famous fart noise.

Gabe also put his head down, right next to the bird's head. Sounding very threatening, he said, "Listen, you overgrown budgie, you tell me what you said or I'll sell you… no, I'll *give* you to that dumb-ass pirate who runs the fish and chips down the street. You'll spend the rest of your days perched on his stooped old shoulder, and be allowed to say naught but 'Polly want a cracker?'"

Chet's pupils expanded and contracted in fear. To a bird with a vocabulary such as his, that was worse than death at the paws of a toothless but enterprising cat! Ripping, gnawing, ripping, gnawing... He shuddered, thinking that perhaps Gabe just might do it. He had been acting rather odd lately.

"Well...?" Gabe sighed, losing interest in the bird's mindless game.

"Annie!" squawked the parrot.

Gabe's mouth flew open in surprise. That was by far the last thing he ever expected to hear!

Chet spread his wings and warbled.

"DogMcDonaldAdonisWandaSpiiiiike!!!"

"What the hell?" Gabe choked out, and then yelled – very loudly – for his partner.

"He bellows," Kyle sneered to Jen. "I'll go see what the bastard wants, and then we'll get the hell outta here. 'Kay?"

Jen nodded and began clearing her desk.

Kyle stormed off to his ex-buddy's office, kicking the door open when he arrived.

Gabe fixed his friend with a long look, trying not to flinch at the hatred flashing in Kyle's eyes when he burst in.

"Yeah?" Kyle snapped.

"Just a quick question, Kyle. Did you teach Chet any new words lately?" Gabe asked, ever-so politely.

"Not unless he called you a motherfuckin' bastard," Kyle shot back. The more he thought about it, the more he couldn't stand to even be in the same room as his cheatin' former friend.

"That was a little uncalled for. Where is all this hostility coming from, Kyle? I haven't done a thing to warrant it!" Gabe was truly baffled.

Kyle merely glared.

Gabe tolerated it for exactly one minute before enough was enough, and his confusion turned into anger. Kyle had no right to judge him on a few actions and too many assumptions. The hell with that....He stood, stalked across the room and kicked the door shut.

Kyle jumped in spite of himself. *Uh oh...*

Gabe pointed to a chair. "Sit!" he commanded.

Kyle sat without a second thought, although he maintained his belligerent attitude by crossing his arms over his chest and continued to glare at Gabe.

Gabe sauntered over to Kyle, and placed his hands on the arms of the chair, trapping his buddy where he sat. He lowered his head until he was eye to eye and only inches from that pissed off face. He snarled, sounding very lethal. "Now you tell me exactly what crawled up your ass this time. You've been on my case all weekend, and I'm fucking tired of it!"

No answer from Kyle other than a slow exhale of the breath he'd been holding.

"Is this animosity related to Annie?"

Kyle's eyes shifted momentarily then returned to glare at Gabe, who took the gesture as a yes.

"Fine. Christ… Now you listen to me, Kyle. I'll explain this one time, and one time only. What I do with my life is my business. You don't judge me, you don't condemn me, and if you can't trust me, then we're through. Done. Fuck the friendship, sell the company. Finished!" He poked a stiff finger in Kyle's sternum for emphasis, and went on with his rant. "I'd never hurt Dee. You don't know how things really are with us, and out of love and respect for her, I can't go into detail. But remember, *friend,* things aren't always as they seem. If I ever… EVER hear you so much as utter one more derogatory remark about Annie, you'll be sorry. Very, very sorry… "Gabe moved closer to Kyle with his last words, so close that their noses were touching. "Is.that.understood?"

Kyle had never been so scared in all his life. Gabe had fuckin' lost it! *God, Jen, call the fuckin' cops before he kills me!!!*

"Well…?

Kyle managed a short nod. More of a neck twitch, but still a nod. It satisfied Gabe.

"Good." Evans moved away from Davidson and sat back down in his chair. He kicked his feet up on the desk and crossed his boots at the ankles, then pulled out a long-forgotten pack of Marlboros from the drawer. Slowly he removed the cellophane wrapper and tapped out a smoke.

Kyle's nerves shredded with each crinkle of the wrapper. He was too frightened to stay, but didn't dare leave.

Gabe never took his eyes from Kyle's as he dropped the cigarette butt first on the desk a few times, packing the tobacco. Putting the smoke to his lips and striking a match, he mumbled a "dismissed" to his partner.

Kyle shot out of the chair and fled the room, slamming the door behind him.

Gabe blew out the match and tossed the unlit cig into the trash, his body shaking with laughter. Oh God, he really did miss his calling as an actor! Kyle was scared shitless! This frightened Gabe in a way, when he realized he'd meant everything he said to his partner.

With a sigh, he glanced at the cigarette in the trash; he really would have loved to have lit that baby up and enjoyed a good smoke. With another sigh, the remainder of the pack was tossed in as well.

Chet ruffled his feathers, thankful for the lack of bloodshed.

"Thank you for reminding me, pea brain. Just where did you learn to say Annie? And who the hell is DogMcwhatever?"

"You have a lovely home, Deirdre, "Annie remarked after a quick tour of the house.

"Thank you. You should have seen it when I moved in," Dee chuckled. "It was a disaster! Some of it had been remodeled, but for the most part it was a disaster. Geoffrey worked so hard to bring it back... restore it to what you see now, and handed me the checkbook. He told me I could decorate any way I wished. I thought it very generous of him since he barely knew me. We'd only known each other for a few days when I arrived, and married a few months later."

Annie processed this information, not quite sure what to make of it.

They climbed the stairs to the second floor for another tour.

"These are the guest room, here is Geoffrey's room, this is where the twins conspire and then retire, and this is my room. The journals are in here," Deirdre pointed out as they walked the long hall.

Mr. And Mrs. Evans didn't share a room? More information for Annie to process, leaving her beyond confused.

Dee opened a door, inviting her guest inside.

"Oh, Deirdre, it's beautiful!" Annie sighed, looking around. The bedroom was the very picture of feminine grace and charm. The canopy on the bed matched the drapes on the windows, which complimented the fabric of the window seat and its pillows. A mellow, dusky-rose colored carpet cushioned Annie's feet. She marveled at how thick and soft it felt. An antique vanity with a large, round mirror stood against one wall, and two overstuffed chairs flanking a small table resided in a cozy corner. An armoire stood opposite the bed; the partially opened door revealing a stereo system and television. The entire room was faintly scented with Deirdre's exclusive, expensive perfume.

Annie walked to the window and peered out. Jeez, she could see almost the entire park! What a gorgeous view it would be in the summer. She sighed and leaned forward for a better look, bumping something dry and rustling. She looked to see a dried rose hanging from a bit of lace. The once brilliant red bloom had faded to a dirty tan, which was hardly beautiful any longer. She wondered what the significance was, but other than ask a question hardly her business, she merely repeated, "It's beautiful."

"Thank you, Annie. It's the one place in this house where I can feel free to be me."

Rather a cryptic comment, thought Annie, when no more explanation followed.

"Come." Dee waved her over to the walk-in closet. "They're in here."

As Annie moved to join her, she noticed a picture on the bedside table, framed in decorative silver. At first it was the frame that drew her eye, but then the horse captured her attention. She knew that horse. Curious, she took a closer look, smiling when she saw Deirdre dressed in a period costume, perched proudly upon the steed. "Juliet" gazed down at her Romeo, who was standing next to his horse.

Annie felt a tremor run through her. She knew Romeo, alright, but he'd introduced himself as Michael. And he bore a very striking resemblance to Gabe, now that she thought of it. Were they brothers? Twins? What was the other's name…? Steven, that was it. But didn't he die in a fire years ago? Yes, that's what happened. Dee's stories of the twins gelled in Annie's mind, and she nodded slightly when things fell into place.

Then again, her logical mind seemed to explode with the implications. That horse… he was Michael's, the same one she had seen yesterday. And that cowboy… how often had that very same smile been directed her way? *Here we go again, Annie… Stephen King's driveway.* It was a place she really didn't care to pull into.

"Annie…?"

"Oh! Deirdre, I'm sorry." Annie hurried to help carry the journals from the closet, but before she did so, she withdrew a book and opened it to see Gramma's handwriting on the pages. Her eyes misted as she thought of Rosalind. Yes, it would be better to go through these in private.

Deirdre placed a hand on her shoulder. "I'm sure you won't want company when you read these, so take them home. They belong to you, Annie. Read them…"

Annie nodded and wiped a quick hand over her eyes. "I will, and thank you so much…"

"Could I ask you to carry them down for me? I'm afraid I no longer have the strength to do it myself."

"Of course I will, Deirdre, and thanks again. You have no idea how much this means to me." Annie gave her a quick hug and a peck on the cheek which surprised them both.

"Annie, you don't know how much they really mean to you."

Another cryptic statement, but Annie didn't care. She couldn't wait to get home and start reading, and wasted no time in loading the boxes into her truck.

"Annie, before you go I need to ask you something," Dee said in a serious tone.

Annie felt a twinge of fear. Oh God, here it comes; Mrs. Evans had found out about Saturday night. She swallowed hard and managed to squeak out a "yes…?"

"In here." Dee led her to Gabe's den and they sat together on the worn leather sofa.

The woodsy-spicy aroma of Gabe's cologne enveloped Annie. She felt a bit dizzy. Every nerve in her body hummed, and her vision faded in and out. To steady herself, she placed her hand on the arm of the couch and in the process bumped the guitar that had been leaning against it. It fell to the floor with a crash and a medley of notes from the vibrating strings. She darn near jumped off the sofa in surprise. "I'm so sorry! I… I didn't see it there…"

"No harm done, Annie. Are you feeling alright? You look a bit pale… Can

I get you anything?"

"I… I'm fine now. I'm not sure what happened…"

Dee patted Annie's hand. "I do, dear." She didn't elaborate, but once again became serious. She had brought Annie to Geoffrey's den on purpose, knowing the effect it would have. "Annie, I need you to be totally honest with me. Will you do that?"

Annie moved her head in a way that could be either a yes or a no. She felt somewhat ill.

"I'll take that as a yes. Annie, I need to know what there is between you and Gabe. What are your feelings about *Gabe*?" Deirdre said gently, stressing the name "Gabe," and not Geoffrey.

Annie half expected the question. Nevertheless, the fact that Dee had actually asked left her stunned. "G… Gabe…?"

"Yes, Gabe. He… I… I need to know how you feel about him." Dee took Annie's hand into her own. "Annie, look at me, dear."

Annie raised her eyes to Gabe's wife. She felt the tears burn, threatening to spill.

"Annie, do you love him?" The question was a whisper.

Annie could not deny it, nor could she admit it – not this woman, anyway. Tremors shook her body and the first tear slid down her cheek.

"Annie, you can tell me. Don't be afraid…"

A sob escaped. Annie felt horrified.

"You do, don't you? You love him…"

Annie dropped her gaze, her tears falling freely now. Her head bobbed once in affirmation.

"Oh, thank God," Dee sighed, hugging her.

Annie remained where she was for a moment, in that frail yet comforting embrace. Had she heard right? No… how could that be? She pulled away, wiping her eyes with the heel of her hand, and stared at Deirdre. "Wh…what did you say?"

Dee gave her a wink and a grin. "I said, 'thank God'. Why, what did you hear?"

"That's what I heard, but hardly what I expected."

"I shouldn't be surprised," Dee murmured, more to herself than to Annie. "Gabe loves you too. He has been waiting a very, very long time for you. Not even he realizes how long."

"I… I don't understand…"

"I have a confession to make," Dee explained, glancing quickly around the room to see if Steven was around to interrupt. "Even though Geoffrey and I are married, we're not husband and wife."

Annie gave her a confused look. "Not…? Deirdre…?"

"We are married in name only so that the children would have their father's name."

Annie was still lost.

"Geoffrey is not the twins' biological father, Annie."

"He… he's not?"

"No. His twin brother is. Geoffrey took me in after Steven died. He gave me his home, his name, and my children a father, but he never gave me his heart. I… I never asked for it. He never asked that of me, either, knowing that I'd never stop loving Steven." Deirdre smiled, thinking of her lost love.

"Oh my God," Annie whispered, processing this latest bit of information. Gabe was free to love her! And she could love him in return! No, wait. He was still married, with children. Back to square one.

"Annie, listen to me. Please…"

"I… I'm listening." Annie raised her eyes again, daring to meet Deirdre's.

"Annie, I'm not going to be around much longer. I'm dying. No, don't argue. I know it, my doctors know it, and even my children know it. Geoffrey might suspect, but I really think he's in denial about it. Well, that and the fact I've neglected to inform him of certain details. Regardless, my children will need a mother, and Gabe will need the wife he's waited for all his life. You, Annie, are the chosen one."

Annie shook her head violently. This was crazy!

"I know it's a bit overwhelming, dear, you'll need time to absorb."

Annie, still shocked and stunned, merely stared. Dee suspected she'd have to try a new tactic to break though. "Tell me, have you seen Ste… er, Michael lately?" she asked.

Annie nodded slowly. "Yesterday…"

"Do you remember what he told you?"

Again, Annie nodded. "I… I do…"

"And he said…?"

"He… he said I should go to you. That I need you and you need me… and that the twins… need me. And…. And Gabe needs me! Oh… oh God…" A new feeling washed over Annie. Her heart raced and her breath came faster, and she felt as if she were about to hear something she didn't want to hear.

"Annie, I'm sure you have noticed the resemblance between Steven and Michael, am I right"? Dee asked, sure that Steven should be popping in any time now to either stop this or confirm it.

Annie's lips moved, soundlessly denying that it could be true.

"There's a reason for it, dear. One moment, and I'll…" Deirdre trailed off and went to the bookshelf, searching quickly until she found what she had been looking for: the tattered copy of *Romeo and Juliet*. The one Steven had read again and again. She sat down next to Annie and opened the book, pulling a piece of yellowed newsprint from the pages. "Here we are…" she smiled, placing it in Annie's shaking hands.

Annie didn't want to touch it. Nope, to do so would be the impossible becoming possible, and despite her open-mindedness regarding the supernatural, this… oh jeez, this was just impossible!! And yet, despite her trepidation, her hand reached out to take the paper, carefully unfolding it to read the headline. "Local Man Dies In Stable Fire." Her eyes focused on the smiling cowboy standing next to the big black horse. Michael. Her mouth felt dry and her heart thundered in her chest. She scanned the article until she found the name she'd hoped not to find…. "The victim, Steven Anthony Michael Evans, was…"

"Annie?"

She looked up into those familiar, bright blue eyes.

"It's me, Annie. Steven. Steven Michael…"

"Nooooo…." The paper fluttered to the floor, dropped by her numb fingers, and came to rest on the toe of a scuffed boot. She fainted dead away.

"She took that rather well, don't ya think?" Steve said to Dee, lifting Annie from the floor where she slid. He laid her gently on the couch and covered her with the colorful-yet-faded quilt.

"Oh, you are wicked, Steven!" Dee chucked a pillow at him, laughing.

Gabe quietly opened the door to his office and scanned the hallway. Good, no sign of Kyle or Jenna. He grabbed his guitar and ran down the hall to one of the recording booths. For the next three hours he wrote music for the songs he'd created the previous weekend, first for the piano, then guitar. He wondered how things were going at home. Did Annie show up? And just what was the big mystery surrounding Dee? Perhaps he should add a mandolin to "My Arms" for a little romantic flair. If so, he needed to get Dave on board, he was the best player around.

"Goddamn you, Kyle. Get over your little temper tantrum and get your ass back to work," Gabe grumbled absently, jotting down a few more notes. "We have a CD to burn!" He sighed and sipped tepid coffee, wincing at the taste.

"Probably crying on Jen's comforting bosom."

He wished he had a smoke.

"Well boo hoo, Kyle. Sorry. I'm ever so sorry that you feel this way…Oh God…" Gabe felt another burst of inspiration and turned back to his piano. Hit a few keys and smiled. "Oh yeah…"

Energized, he straddled the piano bench and wrote rapidly on the paper before him, mumbling the lyrics as his pen scratched out the words. "I'm ever so sorry that you feel this way. You won't change your mind, you've nothing to say. We've reached a dead end, there's no turning around. Such a shame what was lost… can it ever be found…"

Kyle kissed his wife one last time before he gathered up his clothes, which had been scattered around the office. He smiled, thinking that Jen always knew just how to make him feel better. Hell, he was hardy mad at that bastard Gabe anymore! He wondered where his partner was, and flipped on the intercom to his ex-buddy's office.

"Pretty quiet in there, Jen."

"He's probably pouting, Kyle."

"Yeah. I guess I should go check…"

"I'll go with you, just in case." Jen flashed Kyle a meaningful look as she dressed.

"Hmm. Not in here."

"I can see that, Kyle."

"Bitch."

"Pig."

Kyle sat on the desk, tapping a pencil on his knee. It was about then that he noticed the "occupied" light activated on the console, indicating that someone was in the booth. He flipped a switch and the sound of a piano filled the air. The Davidson's looked at each other. *Gabe?* In answer to their unspoken question, the man in question began to sing.

"I thought we had such a good thing, that we were ahead of the game. You never let on you were changing… everyday always the same. I soon found out I was mistaken… your still waters ran deep. I wasn't enough for you anymore. You turn away from me in your sleep…"

The voice faded, replaced by a piano bridge to the chorus.

Jen looked at Kyle and quirked an eyebrow.

Kyle fanned a hand in front of his face. "Goddamn! For a minute there I thought he was talkin' about me," he joked.

"Maybe he was," Jen teased back.

Kyle swished a hip at her and lisped, "If you tweat me that way, bitch, I'm goin' back to mah stud-muffin…"

She rolled her eyes, formed a W with her fingers, and shoved it at him. "Whut-evah…"

Their banter ceased when Gabe began to sing again.

Kyle turned off the intercom with a sad sigh. "I'm gonna go apologize, Jen. He was rough on me, but I think I had it comin'."

She nodded, kissed him, and shoved him out the door. After giving the men a few minutes of privacy to patch things up, she turned the intercom back on, curious about the song Gabe had been singing. To her delight, the unmistakable, magical, soul-searing sound of Gabe and Kyle was heard.

Jen felt tears prick at her eyes; "Us," written by Kyle for Gabe, many many years ago. A tribute to their strong bond and never-ending friendship. *They could have the world at their feet if they wanted it,* she thought. "All you need is a little exposure, a little promotion. It would take much for you two to do a comeback tour and be on top again," she murmured to the intercom. She was relieved they couldn't hear her, though. She wanted her man home with her every night, and the children needed a full-time father, and things were just fine the way they were. To suggest such a thing… Kyle would love to tour again. No way would Jenna allow him to go. Never again.

Gabe and Kyle finished their tune, gave each other a glance that spoke volumes, and turned back to Gabe's new song.

"Let's hear it, buddy," Kyle demanded, feeling better than he had in a very long time.

Gabe nodded and continued, happy to have Davidson at his side once more. "Is there someone else in your life at this moment? Or are there places that you'd rather be? Am I holding you back? Cramping your style? You want your life back; you want to be free…

"You say it's time for you to be leaving… I'll ask you one more time will you stay. You answer no, nothing's left… and don't call me. Just say goodbye and I'll be on my way…"

Jen turned the intercom back off. "You two… could have it all…"

Gabe pulled into his driveway, parked next to a pickup truck, and wondered just who the hell the owner was. Intrigued at the possibilities, he grabbed the bouquet of roses he'd picked up for Dee as a thank you, and walked to the Dodge for a better look.

Dried mud and road salt caked the lower half of the Ram's candy apple-red finish. Bits of straw and grain littered the bed of the truck, reminding Gabe of his days in Montana. A smile twitched at his lip as he peeked inside the cab. It was spotless except for a few boxes of leather-bound books and a single, downy white feather on the passenger's side floor.

Feather?

Goose?

Annie?!

He vaulted over the iron fence and raced up the steps to the front door, pausing for a moment to rein in his emotions. "Settle down, Evans," he murmured to himself, opening the front door. "Might not be her after all…" It had to be, though; he could almost feel her presence.

Hands shaking and knees weak, he hung his jacket in the closet. Muted conversation could be heard coming from his den. Dee's voice he recognized, but the other? Barely perceptible, almost as if it were coming from far, far away. Odd. Very, very odd.

With a shrug of frustration that it wasn't his dream after all, he called out a crisp "I'm home!" and opened his office door. The vision that met his eyes nearly sent him to his already weak knees. *Aw God… there she was.*

Gabe stared at his Annie. His Annie… curled up on her side on his sofa, a sweet smile on her sleeping face. He wanted to go to her, to touch her, to kiss her, to hold her forever… but was frozen in place.

Deirdre left her seat at the desk to stand behind her husband. Her arms wrapped around his waist and her cheek rested against his broad back. "There she is, Geoffrey, your Annie. But first, we need to talk."

Gabe felt himself dragged most unwillingly into the dining room.

"Dee…?" Gabe mumbled, glancing at his wife and finally finding his voice. He sank into a chair, a tremor shaking his body.

"Good afternoon, Geoffrey dear. I hope you had a pleasant day." She nodded to the flowers he was holding. "Oh, how lovely!"

His eyes dropped to the bouquet in his hand; he'd totally forgotten about it. "Um… for you. A thank you for today." He fought to keep his hand from shaking when he handed her the flowers.

"Geoffrey… really! You shouldn't have." She took the roses, and with a wry grin on her face and deliberate slowness, she walked into the kitchen. When she reached the door she glanced over her shoulder and said, "I'll see if I can find a vase worthy of these. They really are beautiful." With a wink, she slid through the double doors.

Gabe blinked in surprise. The wench was teasing him! She knew damn well that he was full of questions regarding their visitor, and she was prolonging the suspense. A chuckle escaped him. He jumped up and followed Dee into the kitchen.

Deirdre stood at the sink, humming a tune while she snipped the ends from the stems before arranging them in a cut-crystal vase of water. Totally engrossed in her work, she pretended to ignore him. She had to smile to herself; had Geoffrey entered his den a moment sooner, Annie wouldn't have been the only surprise there to greet him!

Gabe was able to tolerate a mere two minutes of the suspense. "Dee, why is…" he blurted out.

"…Annie sleeping on your sofa?" she interrupted, turning to face him.

"Uh yeah… that would be correct," he grinned.

Deirdre thought for a moment, carefully considering her words. "The poor girl was overwhelmed by the events of the day. I thought it best to let her rest for a while."

"Now I am curious. What could possibly have happened around here to be so overwhelming?" Gabe asked, sweeping an arm through the air for emphasis.

"Oh, that's not important now. Annie will come to… er; I mean she'll wake up anytime now. Go to her, Geoffrey. Be the first thing she sees when she opens her eyes." Dee gave him a little shove. "Go!"

His heart began to race. "Dee, what did you and Annie discuss today?"

"Many things, including you." She tapped him with the rose she was holding. "I think she's a bit taken with you," she winked, and turned back to her flowers once more.

Gabe spun her around, his hands firm on her thin shoulders. "What did she say? Come on, Dee, tell me!"

"Geoffrey, you sound like a lovesick teenager," she laughed. "Actually, she didn't say much of anything. She didn't have to. She couldn't hide her love for you any more than you can hide your feelings for her."

Gabe gave her a searching look.

"Geoffrey dear, it's all too obvious. I knew how you felt about her the first time I said her name and saw the look on your face..." Dee trailed off, swallowing back the myriad of emotions, and turned to her flowers. "Here. Take this to her," she murmured, handing Gabe a rose.

He noticed that it was white.

He'd purchased a dozen red roses.

He'd handed Dee twelve red buds.

How the hell did the white one get in there?

"Now for the last time, go!" Deirdre insisted.

Gabe gave her a short nod and left the room.

"Cute trick, Steven," she murmured under her breath. From far away she could hear him laughing. He really was quite mischievous at times.

Gabe stood in front of his office door and stared at the flower in his hand. He'd been waiting all of his life for this very moment, and now that it was here he felt that it was happening all too fast.

And he was terrified.

Annie loved him, though. Deep down he had always known it, and Dee had just now confirmed it. All that was left was for Annie herself to tell him.

But what then? What about Dee? She was pushing him towards Annie with both hands, yet what was her plan? Divorce? Christ, he wasn't sure he could even go through with that; he'd already denied her twice.

A soft moan from the den distracted him from his disturbing thoughts.

Gabe sat on the floor next to the sofa where his Annie lay, studying her face as she woke. He gently stroked the soft petals of the rose along her jaw and was rewarded with a hint of a smile.

Annie's eyes fluttered open to see her cowboy before they drifted shut again. *Good, she was dreaming. Maybe he'd get around to kissing her this time.*

"Annie..."

The man was speaking but his lips weren't moving.

"Annie, I'm here..."

"Just shut up and kiss me," she said in her dream.

That sounded like a direct order to Gabe, so he did.

The dream had never progressed this far before! She felt warm lips press against hers, and the familiar tingle spread like wildfire through her body, increasing in intensity as the kiss deepened. Her hand rose, brushing trembling fingers against the bearded jaw so close to hers. *If only it were real...*

Gabe reluctantly pulled away. If he didn't stop now, there's no telling where this would end up in a matter of a few minutes. Tracing his thumb along her lower lip, he studied her face once more, wishing she'd wake up. He wanted her to open her eyes, to see him reflected in their green depths. "Annie..." he whispered, "My Annie..."

378

He was speaking to her again, calling her form her dream. Annie opened her eyes and there he was. "G… Gabe…?"

"You were expecting…?" He sat back on his heels with a goofy, giddy, lopsided grin.

She was horribly confused. Where was she? And why was Gabe there? *Oh God… Gabe!* She tore her gaze from his and looked around the room. *Desk, books, more books, a wall full of pictures, guitar… and the scent of his cologne, strong and inviting on the pillow under her head. His den? And where was Deirdre?*

Deirdre! Handing her the newspaper clipping…

Annie sat up and began a frantic search for the yellowed paper. It had to be there, although why she wanted to find it and reaffirm the impossible, she had no idea.

"Annie? What is it? What the hell is wrong?" The worry in Gabe's voice was evident.

"It's here somewhere, I know it is. I read it! I didn't believe it but I saw it," she babbled, flipping the quilt aside in her search.

"What's here? What the hell are you looking for?" Gabe was very confused. He'd just kissed the love of his life, and she acted as if nothing had happened. Then again, she had been sleeping, although that little fact was hardly balm to his now-bruised ego.

"It *has* to be here! I was reading it and…" The fog lifted from her brain. Annie sank back down on the sofa, trembling. "*He* was here," she whispered as the events of the afternoon came rushing back.

"Who was here? Annie, you're beginning to worry and somewhat annoy me. What the hell is going on!?"

"M…Michael," she stuttered, still in shock. "Steven Michael…"

Gabe grabbed her by the shoulders, giving her a firm but gentle shake. "What do you mean… Steven Michael?"

"My friend… Michael. H… he's your brother! And he was here, Gabe!"

"Impossible," Gabe spat, wondering how she, of all people, could be capable of such a sick joke.

She shot him a hurt look, stung by his tone. "I… I saw him…"

"Explain." Gabe stood, hovering over her with arms folded across his chest, demanding an answer.

Annie looked away and tried to regain control of her emotions. Her palms ran over her thighs, wiping away the dampness in a nervous gesture. She took a deep breath and attempted to answer. "Okay… Um, Deirdre and I were in here talking about…." A look at Gabe and then a quick glance away. "Um, that's not important now, or maybe it is, but… Jeez, I can't believe it!"

"Annie, just get to the point," he sighed.

She nodded. "Alright. Deirdre was telling me about… about James and Jeremy's… about their real father. She handed me a newspaper clipping. It was about a fire, and how he died in it. His horse too. Years ago…"

"And...?"

"Earlier today I saw some pictures of a good friend of mine. Michael. There's one in the hall here, and one in Deirdre's room. His horse is in both pictures... The big black."

Gabe felt the hair rise on the back of his neck. *Impossible.* "Go on," he managed to choke out.

"The picture of Michael, Michael Anthony, is identical to the one in the newspaper. The man who... who died in the fire. Your brother, Steven Anthony Michael Evans. Gabe, Michael and I have been friends... close friends for years!"

Gabe's legs were no longer steady enough to hold him upright and he sank down on the sofa next to Annie. "Michael," he murmured, not sure if he wanted to hear the rest of her tale.

"Anyway, I think that's when I fainted or something, when I read that story. I remember dropping the paper and it landed on a boot. I looked up and he was standing right in front of me! It was him, Gabe! My Michael... Your brother!"

"This is insane," Gabe muttered, beyond confused and trying like hell to deny what Annie was telling him. Impossible! And yes she actually believed her words. At least she seemed to. He gave her a long, hard look.

"Gabe," Annie pleaded, "Please! Please... Ask Deirdre if you don't believe me. She was here! She..."

"Enough, Annie. Christ..." Gabe leaned forward, resting forearms on knees and attempting to make any kind of sense of the situation.

Annie shut up, fighting tears of hurt and frustration. It wasn't supposed to happen like this. Jeez, he should be holding her in his arms right now, telling her that he loved her. Had loved her forever, just as she loved him. But instead he was angry at her for all the craziness brought down upon them this afternoon. He probably thought *she* was crazy! She never should have told him about Michael... Swallowing back a sob, she stared at a white object on the floor.

Gabe, too, was staring at the rose near Annie's feet. Jesus, what the hell had happened? He should be holding her in his arms right now, telling her how much he loved her. Had loved her forever! Instead he was fighting the urge to shake her and force her to tell him that it was all just a joke – Steven Michael... just some silly joke...

She made a small, sad sound, drawing his attention back to her. Aw God, the poor thing. Whatever had happened certainly affected her. He sighed again and put his arm around her shoulders, pulling her close.

Annie resisted at first, but then melted against him, absorbing his strength. They remained that way for several minutes, until Gabe decided that it was time to talk to Deirdre.

He found his wife in the kitchen, still arranging the roses. She hummed a happy little tune as she played with the flowers, and turned to him when he entered the room.

"Geoffrey! Is Annie awake yet? How is she doing?"

"To be honest, I'm not all that sure. She seems to have suffered a bit of a... shall we say a bit of a shock? Dearest wife, just what the bloody hell is going on here?" he all but snarled.

Deirdre raised an eyebrow at his surly tone and took his hand. "I believe it's time we had our talk, Geoffrey dear. Come." She gave his hand a squeeze and pulled him towards the den.

"It's about damn time," he grumbled.

Dee stifled a smile.

Gabe perched on his desk while Deirdre and Annie sat on the sofa. He felt very strange at having his wife and the woman he'd loved forever in the same room. Could this possibly be any more awkward?

Annie felt even more uncomfortable.

Dee was the only one who didn't seem to mind. In a cheerful voice that belied the bizarreness of the situation, she said, "So where shall we begin?"

"Since you seem to be the only one who knows what's going on, why don't you begin?" Gabe shot back. He hadn't meant to sound so short, but damn! It was all so crazy, and his wife seemed to be enjoying herself! Perhaps the medication she was on was affecting her mental status. Again.

"You need not snap at me, Geoffrey dear," Dee scolded gently, and then turned to Annie. "Annie dear, I'm sorry about what happened earlier. I certainly didn't plan it that way. Things were just progressing too slowly and I needed you to understand the importance of what's happening. I wanted you to read your grandmother's journals before you found out about Steven... Michael. I think perhaps it would have lessened the shock a bit."

Annie was dumbfounded. "Lessened the shock?!" she cried. It was all she could say, being on the verge of hysterical laughter, totally without humor. *Dead people coming back?* It was too unbelievable... too absurd. How could anything possibly lessen the shock of that?

Gabe let an exasperated snort escape and glanced out the window, sorely tempted to get up and walk out on the whole silly conversation.

"You'll understand a bit more after you read them," Deirdre continued. "At least I hope so. I guess it is a bit shocking."

"Dee, what are these journals you keep mentioning?" Gabe asked.

Deirdre smiled and patted Annie's trembling hand. "Annie's grandmother has put the Benton-Charles' family history down in a collection of journals," she explained. "It's absolutely fascinating! The lives of generations are documented..."

"What does that have to do with us?" Gabe interrupted. "And Steve... We have no Benton-Charles relatives." With a glance at Annie, he thought, "not yet, anyway."

"Well, Steven is involved in a rather roundabout way. I can't elaborate at this time, so both of you will have to read them fully to understand. Quite honestly, I don't really understand it all myself." Dee looked from Gabe to Annie and back again. "Yes, Steven has come back, but not the way you may think. He's returned to help guide us through a very difficult time in our lives. Annie... Geoffrey... He is here to act as a catalyst in bringing you together. You are destined to be together as the fates have decided long ago. As for me... Steven will guide me home. Eric too."

"Eric? How do you know about Eric?" Annie murmured, finding her voice again.

"Steven told me. We've been spending some time together," Deirdre answered, smiling softly.

"Oh for God's sake!" Gabe spat, jumping up from the desk. "I've had enough of this bullshit! Dee, I strongly suggest that you contact your doctor. I think your medication is having an adverse effect on your mental status again." He felt like screaming in frustration. "I can understand if you're having hallucinations, but I don't appreciate the turn they're taking. Steve..."

"Geoffrey, I'm fine. Now sit back down and I'll tell you what has happened. It might take a while... Would either of you like some coffee? Tea? Annie, may I bring you something?"

Annie gave her head a quick shake. "No... Well, maybe something. I don't know..." she mumbled.

"I'll be right back." Dee left the room before Geoffrey could stop her.

Gabe was right behind her, ready to drag her back in for some more answers, until a small, scared sound stopped him in his tracks. *Aw God...* "Annie," he murmured, sitting next to her and taking her hand in his. "Are you alright?"

She turned to look at him. "Gabe, what is going on here? I feel like I'm in the middle of a vacuum. Everything is so distorted... so unreal. I'm scared and... and yet happy. I can't wait to hear what Deirdre has to say, but then again I don't think I really want to know! Then there's you... You and me... I don't even dare think about that."

"I know. I feel the same... except about you and me. I think about that quite often, ever since you bought me that cup of coffee, Annie."

She dared look into his eyes and began to feel a little better. "Yes, that was rather generous of me, wasn't it?"

Gabe's lopsided grin was her answer.

She blushed, and then unwillingly changed the subject. "Gabe, have you seen... Steve? I mean since... well, you know. Recently..."

Gabe sighed heavily and nodded. "In a way I have, Annie. Once in a dream a few days ago, although I was a bit drunk. A lot drunk. I didn't think much of it when I saw him at River Ridge, knowing how the mind can play tricks. Then I found a poem he'd written. Wait... I have it here in my pocket." He pulled it out and handed it to her. "Now that really got to me. Long story, but it's the reason I ended up as the guest of the odd couple," he chuckled.

"The odd couple?" she asked, taking the paper from him.

"Your dog and goose. They reminded me of Felix and Oscar... the way they argue all the time. I was on the verge of hypothermia, so it's quite possible that it was my imagination..."

"No, you're right there, those two are always going at it – even if they are best friends," Annie grinned. "The odd couple... how appropriate. That confirms it; you are the mysterious 'G' that took my apples."

"I thought my hat would have confirmed it, Annie. You were wearing it at River Ridge..."

She could only smile at that memory, no matter how painful it was at the time.

"Yes, that was me, and they were the best apples I've ever had." He brushed a few stray curls from her face, and with a soft voice he said, "It was then I knew, Annie... knew for sure. You're the one I've been waiting for. Waiting for so long now..."

Annie's breath caught in her throat at his touch. She blushed again and dropped her gaze from his, and it was then she noticed the paper held in her shaking hand. It distracted her enough to break the spell he'd been casting on her. That paper... so familiar. She opened it, trying to focus on the words written there. Sure enough, Michael had penned it.

"Hey, this is my poem! Where did you... Did Michael give... give it to you?"

Gabe shook his head, slightly dizzied by the implications of what might be happening, and trying desperately to remain in denial. Michael... Steve? Impossible. Fucking impossible! "I... I found it," he said quietly. At the studio... last Monday. This is Steve's handwriting." He tapped a finger on the paper. "It sent me on a near-death journey, and Kyle... Poor Kyle nearly drowned in a bottle of Chivas."

"I can see where it might have had that effect."

"Mmhmm. And speaking of Kyle..." Gabe was interrupted by the appearance of Deirdre.

"Here we are," she said, setting down a tray bearing three steaming mugs. "Coffee. Special recipe." She handed a mug to Annie and Gabe, taking the rest when she sat in the desk chair.

Deirdre took a sip and smiled at them. "You two are looking a little more composed. Good. I'm truly sorry about this... how you found out. If it could have been any other way..." She stopped speaking when she saw the look on Annie's face after having sipped the coffee. Obviously the woman hadn't been expecting the shot of liquor Dee had so generously added. "Like it?"

"I uh... yes. I wasn't expecting it is all," Annie replied, taking another sip.

"I thought it might help relax us a bit."

"Good thinking," Gabe muttered, taking a healthy swig of his.

"Then I shall begin." Deirdre shifted to a more comfortable position in the chair, her feet tucked up under her. "The last time I saw Steven – before all of this, of course – was a few days before the fire. We'd had a terrible fight. My entire fault, I must confess, and he left. I wanted to teach him a lesson, so I moved from the hotel where we had been staying. When I tried to return… Well, he was already gone. He died in that fire, along with his horse. Whizbang… who I later found out had given his life to protect Steven." She paused to wipe away the few tears trickling down her face. "I never forgave myself after that. If only I'd not been so selfish and jealous of… of a horse! I was certain my cancer was a punishment for being such a horrid person. As it turns out, the disease brought Steven back to me."

The couple on the sofa gave her a confused look.

"Let me explain. I had been feeling unwell for quite a while. Geoffrey, you know the details… and I'll spare Annie from hearing them, but as it turns out, it's terminal. There's nothing to be done about it, and quite frankly, my doctors are surprised that I've survived this long." Deirdre paused to sip her coffee, nearly wincing at the look of horrified surprise on Geoffrey's face.

"Oh God… I had no idea!" he blurted out.

"I know, dear. Wrong of me or not, I've been hiding my true condition from you. Jenn, and more than likely Kyle, are the only ones who know the truth. I made her promise not to tell you."

"That would explain Kyle's show of hostility," Gabe sighed.

"At least one of the reasons," Deirdre agreed, and continued. "The first night of my chemotherapy… I was so terribly ill. I wanted to die. I prayed that I would die! The pain and fear were unbearable and I knew it was all in vain, yet I felt I owed it to my sons to at least try. They were far too young to be without a mother." With that, she gave Annie a meaningful look.

Annie felt her heart breaking. Such a tragedy…

"I still wanted to die. I begged the nurses for more pain medication, hoping that I'd overdose. Of course they couldn't do it, and I cried myself to sleep.

"I think that I slept for maybe an hour, and when I woke, the room was filled with a beautiful blue light. I thought for certain I had gotten my wish; I had passed on. A man appeared. He had the most serene, loving smile on his face. It was my Steven. He had forgiven me and had come to take me home. He sat next to my bed and placed his hand over my heart, and for a few moments my pain was gone. When I woke the next morning, I found a red rosebud in my hand."

Deirdre stopped speaking and sipped her coffee, staring off at nothing with a sad smile on her lips.

Gabe and Annie shared a glance, waiting for her to continue. After three full minutes of silence, Gabe politely cleared his throat, bringing his wife back to the present.

Dee jumped. "Oh… oh yes, I'm sorry. My second round of chemo was even worse than before. I was violently ill, and even the medication I received for nausea wasn't helping."

Gabe was horrified. "Oh God, Dee, why didn't you tell me? I had no idea you were that ill! If I had known…"

"What could you have done, Geoffrey? Not a thing. Not one bloody thing. You would have worried and felt guilt over something which you could not control. No, I had no intention of telling you."

"I'm so sorry, Deirdre," Gabe said softly, shaking his head in dismay. She was right; he had to admit that much.

"To continue… Later that afternoon, after all of my visitors had left, I began to doze off. Steven came again, although without the light this time. I thought it was another dream, yet as I looked around the room, nothing had changed. You know what I mean – in a dream, even the most lucid of them, there is always some type of subtle change. This was no dream. He was actually in the room, looking the same as the last time I'd seen him before the fire. I thought that perhaps I should be afraid, but I couldn't think of a reason why. Steven would never, could never hurt me.

"He sat on the bed and held me in his arms, and once again my pain was gone. I had thousands of questions to ask him… I never said a word. I suppose I didn't want to break the spell and have him disappear. He began talking to me instead. Annie, he told me about you. He said that you had come back, and Geoffrey, you too had come back. I wondered to as what that meant, but I couldn't find my voice. I think perhaps that I felt I shouldn't ask. He told me to watch for Annie, as I was to give her a message. Which I did, by the way, although it was much later than anticipated.

"Every day Steven would come to me, and while he was there my pain was gone. The only time he wasn't there was the night you were, Annie. I wanted to give you the message then, but between my medication and the severity of my illness, I was quite confused. Geoffrey, I apologize for that. I know how hard it was on you to hear some of the things I think I said.

"After I returned home, Steven continued to appear. The twins have seen him, and I know that he has appeared to both of you. I have a confession… he told me to send you skiing, Geoffrey, and where. Annie, your friend Eric told me that you were planning the trip with your friend. The weekend wasn't what I was expecting, but I think the desired results were achieved." Deirdre gave the couple a knowing smile.

"Kyle has seen him too," Gabe said.

"I know," Dee replied.

Gabe thought for a moment, tapping his closed fist lightly on his chin. "What I would like to know," he said, measuring his words, "is why all the intrigue? Why the cryptic messages, the notes casually left lying around… and scaring the shit out of people? Why not just come out and say what needs to be said and be on his way?" Denial was still in full control, but slowly being eased aside by... by reality?

"I'm not sure why either, Geoffrey. I asked him the same questions. He was vague with his reply, saying only that he does what he can do. It seems that his return comes with restrictions on how much contact he is allowed... how much he may interfere in our mortal lives."

"That almost makes sense, as if any of this could make sense," Gabe smirked in a dry, somewhat amused voice.

Annie, who had been silent for most of the time, had to ask. "If he just recently began appearing to you... us... why is it that I've known him for years? My God... the man is... was... my best friend! We spent a lot of time together and he... well, he sure didn't seem very 'different'."

"Oh, that's easy. He likes you!" Deirdre told her.

"What, he just picked my name out of a hat, liked what he saw and hung around?"

"No, that isn't it, Annie. I'm under the impression that he was... looking after you. He never said much about it, but I do know that only the one meeting was planned, the first one. It was his decision to live... er... be with you after that. I think he felt that you needed him."

"He wouldn't have been wrong," Annie sighed, missing her friend.

"Now we all need him, and here he is," Deirdre smiled.

Gabe and Annie looked at her again, confused.

"Really! Here he is!" Dee repeated, glancing at the door.

Steven walked into the room.

"Steven! How nice to see you again," Dee laughed.

"M... Michael?" Annie choked.

"Holy fucking shit!" Gabe yelled, pressing back into the sofa in a vain attempt to escape the apparition before him.

"A pleasant good evening to you all," Steve grinned. He stood just inside the doorway, unsure of what his next move should be.

"Come join us. We were just speaking of you." Deirdre waved him to the sofa.

Steve hesitated, and then moved to sit on the arm of the couch, closest to Dee, and mere feet away from his stunned sibling.

For the third time in his life, Gabe was at a loss for words. *His brother! Right here in this very room!! Holy motherfucking shit!!!!* He could pass off the earlier appearances as dreams or hallucinations for whatever. And the poem? He really had no idea, but it seemed almost insignificant now. Christ, not now... now with his brother – his dead brother! – sitting right there next to him! He could no longer deny the fact that Steve was truly back. He couldn't decide whether to scream at the insanity of it all, or give his twin the hug he'd been aching to give him for the past five years.

Of the three people in the room with him, Steve knew that Gabe would have the most trouble dealing with the unreal. Dee, well, she couldn't wait to see him again, to pass over with him when the time was right. Annie, she'd been his friend for a long time now. She knew him, loved him. Ah, but Gabe... sensible, logical Gabe. It must be wreaking havoc on his sensible logical mind; Steve hoped it wouldn't push his brother over the edge in madness. He looked over at Deirdre for help, thankful when she picked up on his cue.

"Geoffrey, no need for that language. I'm sure you can find something far more appropriate to say. Greet your brother properly."

"Um... uh... St... Steve, how... how are you?" Gabe stammered.

"Well enough, I suppose. And you?"

"I'm afraid I've become unhinged. Any suggestions?" Gabe still had trouble wrapping his mind around the fact that he was conversing with a dead man, brother or not.

"Just go with it, bro. It's not so bad," Steve grinned.

"Good God, Steve, is it really you?" Gabe was nearly in control again. He reached a tentative hand towards his twin, and then quickly pulled it back again.

"It's really me, Gabe, in the almost-flesh. It's good to see you."

"Uh... yeah. Christ! I don't know what to do! Or say! This is so... so..."

"Unexpected?" Annie offered.

"Not what I was thinking, but it will do for now," Gabe sighed, staring at Steve.

Steve stared back at his beloved twin. "I can understand. Actually, I was rather shocked myself when I found that I had um... returned. I wasn't aware that unemployment was unheard of in the afterlife. They keep us busy, busy, busy!"

The trio gaped at Steve.

"What... did you think it all harps and clouds and little golden wings? Think again. I'm not allowed to say too much, but I can tell you that there is a Heaven, and there is most definitely a Hell. A few places in between, too. I'm kind of in between at the moment, although I've seen... Oh, what I've seen."

The trio continued to stare.

"No, don't look at me like that," Steve continued. "I won't be goin' to Hell. Honestly, Gabe, I won't! And that's all I can say... or I will go to Hell! And there are no horses in Hell, so there!" Steve snickered.

Annie blinked. Dee grinned. Gabe's mouth opened and closed like a fish out of water.

"You think I'm making this up? It's true!" Steve turned serious. "There are many kinds of Heaven and Hell; it's all a matter of perspective. You decide which is which. For example. Annie, you think your cabin is a little slice of heaven, right?"

Annie nodded. "I do, Michael."

"Deirdre, from what she told you about the cabin, would you agree?"

"Oh my, no! It sounds nice, but it's so far from everything and so much work. I don't think I'd be able to handle it. Chopping wood and mucking out stalls? No, not my idea of heaven," she said with a delicate shudder and an apologetic glance at Annie.

Steve nodded. "That's a very vague analogy. It's really much more sharply defined after... well, after you pass. Kinda strange... Some see what they think is Heaven on earth, only to find that it ain't quite the same when they pass. Likewise, not everyone has to do their penance once they cross over. Some are living a little bit of hell in this life." Steve glanced at his lady. "And if it's a self-created hell, something you have control over, it may very well continue on forever... this life and the next."

Annie nodded. Dee dabbed a tear from her eye with a linen napkin from the coffee tray. Gabe was still trying to accept the impossible, although he had been listening.

"Well, enough of my preachin'," Steve smiled, moving behind his brother and placing his hands on Gabe's shoulders. "I don't think that's in my job description." He gave the broad shoulders a loving pat and walked to the window to stare out at the blazing red of the setting sun.

"If only I could tell you all that I know," he whispered.

"Steven...?"

He turned to the voice he loved so well, blinking away a mist of tears. "Dee... Gabe, Annie... Don't be afraid of death. Don't seek it out, but don't fear it either."

Deirdre shook her head, feeling that his last words were for her.

Annie's head buzzed from the effects of the spiked coffee, and she leaned back into the sofa to review Steve's revelations. It made sense when she really thought about it – but then again, anything could make sense regarding the unknown. She felt she'd been living a little bit of both Heaven and Hell lately; what would the afterlife bring?

Gabe knocked back the rest of his coffee, silently thanking Deirdre for thinking of the booze. It had certainly come in handy as far as taking the edge of this most bizarre affair. *Steve... God it was all still so unbelievable!* Yet, believe he did, as well as accept.

He rose from the sofa, joining his brother at the window, once again pulling him into a hug. Gabe's throat closed with emotion. *Accepted and believed...*

Deirdre watched as the two men she loved most in her life embraced. She'd die happy now. Geoffrey had closure with Steven, and he would soon begin a new life with Annie. Although Dee was ready to move on, she'd been feeling far too good lately to think about death. Such a dilemma... Hope that Steven would continue to take away her pain and prolong her life, or ask him to help her along the way to a quick end? She shuddered at the memory of the pain she had suffered. No, she'd continue to take any respite Steven would offer, and cling to the time she had left – which brought up the issue of Geoffrey and

Annie. They couldn't truly be together until the current Mrs. Evans ceased to be. They'd have to discuss a possible solution, but not yet. The day's events had already taxed everyone's emotion, and introducing one more problem so soon would do no one any good.

Deirdre would suggest that Geoffrey see Annie home, and let them take it from there. They needed some alone time anyway.

Gabe released Steve, although held him at arm's length, taking a good look at his twin. Steve didn't feel so solid this time, but Gabe didn't care – didn't even think about it, just felt thrilled to have him there. Feeling much better about this miracle, he smiled and asked Steve again, "So, how are you?"

"Other than dead, you mean?"

"Smartass. God, you are one sick bastard! Kyle was right!" Gabe laughed, letting go and parking his butt on the window sill.

"Annie dear, would you mind helping me in the kitchen?" Dee asked with a meaningful look. The brothers would want a little privacy very soon.

"Uh… sure," Annie murmured, looking from Steven to Gabe and back again. Amazing. They were nearly identical, although Gabe was heavier in the chest.

Deirdre hustled Annie out before either man could protest.

Gabe watched them go; shocked that Dee would abandon him like that. And Annie… Although, he could understand her need to escape for a moment or two. Which reminded him… He turned back to his sibling.

"S… Steve? Is it really you?"

"The one and only, Gabe."

"Oh God, this is… is… Christ, I can't even think of a word for the situation!"

"How about long overdue, bro?"

"I uh… yeah. God, um… How are you?"

"Well enough, I suppose. And you?"

"We repeat ourselves, Stevie… but I'm stunned. In awe. My God…" Once again, Steve was nearly crushed in Gabe's arms. For a long moment they stood there, neither moving but for the tremor of a suppressed, joyous sob.

They let go and moved slightly apart. Gabe dared to look deep into his brother's bright, serene blue eyes. He smiled and wiped away a trickle of a tear making its slow way down Steve's cheek.

"Stevie… Aw God, don't cry, man…" Gabe sighed through a smile.

"I won't if you won't," Steve smiled back.

"Huh?"

"This." Steve's thumbs brushed away the tracks of Gabe's tears.

"Tell anyone I cried and I'll kick your ass," Gabe murmured, resting his forearms on Steve's shoulders. He was loathe to let him go, fearing that it was indeed all a dream.

"Just who am I gonna tell, Gabe?" Steve chuckled. His hands rested just below Gabe's biceps, then broke the contact between them with a firm pat on the back. "Dee knows you and Annie... Well, your secret's safe with me."

"Am I to assume that Mom and Pop don't know you're back?"

Steve shook his head. "No, and we have to keep it that way."

Gabe nodded and let a sigh escape. Sat back down on the sofa. "Stevie... God, this is just... Wow. I still have difficulty believing it."

Steve didn't reply, as Dee and Annie returned to the den.

Deirdre stifled a smile when she saw Geoffrey's eyes light up at the sight of Annie. She couldn't have been happier for him.

Annie dared a glance at her cowboy. Oh jeez... the look he was giving her sent her heart racing and turned her legs to rubber. She all but stumbled to the sofa and sank down on the worn leather before those legs failed her all together.

Gabe watched her for a long moment, and then turned back to Stevie.

"What about Kyle? He's seen you, or at least thinks he has. Should I tell him?"

"I don't know. Let's see how things work out. What is the situation between you two anyway?" Steve asked.

"He still thinks I'm a two-timing son of a bitch, but we did lay down some demo track on a new piece today. I think we might be back in business."

Steve laughed.

Gabe raised an eyebrow.

"I'm sorry, Gabe. I was just thinkin' about Kyle's little altercation with a bathroom door. You should have seen it!"

"You were there?"

"Saw the whole thing. I tried to explain to him about you and Annie – in a roundabout way, but I'm afraid he wasn't very receptive to my comments."

"You hit him? God, Stevie, you never hit anybody!"

"No... no... But I didn't prevent it from happenin' either. I do believe he ticked me off, Gabe. I heard what he said about Annie. Besides, I spoke to him after the door did." Steve grinned and whispered, "He thought I was a trauma-induced hallucination."

Gabe laughed. "Hell, he deserved it then!"

"Maybe so, but he was just tryin' to defend Dee. He's always had a soft spot for her."

"I figured as much. Nothing for Jen to be concerned about, is there?"

"Nope, absolutely harmless. I'm thinkin' Jen is pretty much aware of it anyway, but she's secure in her relationship."

"I'll say. She knows how to keep a tight rein on her man." Gabe chuckled at the memory of Kyle's swim trunks.

"Hmm. Those two are quite a pair."

Gabe gave Steve a long look. "God... this is incredible, man! How... um... How long will you be here?"

"Not much longer. I think I've done what I've been assigned to do. You and Annie have finally found each other."

Gabe's gaze wandered over to where his love sat on the sofa. She'd been so very quiet all night. Was that normal for her? It hit him how little he really knew her, despite the fact he felt as if he knew her forever. A small frown furrowed his brow.

Steve seemed to read his twin's mind, and said softly, "Go to her. Take her home and spend some time together. Alone."

Gabe turned back to Steve. "Yeah... Oh God, yes. Stevie... thank you." The sound of a small, pained cough pierced his thoughts. He glanced at Dee. "Jesus, Steve, what about her?"

"Don't worry about her, Gabe. I'll take good care of her," Steve whispered, adding a wink.

"Good God, Steve? Isn't that... kind of creepy?"

"Hey, I'm dead, not dead!" Steve laughed. "No, really, it's nothing like that. She's in a great deal of pain and I can help take it away for a while."

"One of your little miracles?"

"One of my better ones, yes."

Gabe nodded. "Then take care of her, brother mine. I... I hate to see her suffer, and I... I do love her."

"I know, Gabe."

Deirdre felt it was a good time to intervene. "Geoffrey dear, do you think that you could see Annie home? I'd feel better knowing that you got her there safely."

"On no, that isn't necessary," Annie protested. "I'll be fine... don't go to any trouble."

"No trouble at all, Annie. It would be my pleasure," Gabe insisted. He was not about to take no for an answer.

Annie had been hoping all along that he would make that particular offer, but did she trust herself to be alone with him? There was still Deirdre to consider as well, even though she'd been pushing the two of them together with both hands.

She looked at the Evans men, and then at Mrs. Evans, seeing identical looks of approval on all three faces. Annie nodded. "Alright then... I really should get going. I have to feed my animals; I'm a little late and they don't much care for deviations in dinner time," she joked.

"Then let's go. We can take my truck," Gabe offered.

"No, I have things in mine that I need to take home. Why don't you follow me?" Annie suggested.

"The journals?"

"The journals."

Deirdre gave Annie a light kiss on the cheek. "You're a very lucky woman," she whispered, and left the room.

Steve slung an arm over Gabe's shoulders. "Bro... yeah. She's worth the wait," he grinned. He gave his brother a quick hug and a long look before he went to Annie.

Taking her in his arm, he said, "Told you so," and pressed his lips to her forehead.

Gabe felt a quick, hard, totally unexpected stab of jealousy and had to turn away.

Annie slipped her arms around Steve's waist, just like she had done countless times before, and melted against his comforting strength.

"Thank you," she murmured, resting her cheek against his chest. It dawned on her that she'd never heard a heartbeat in all those times she'd held him like that. Now she knew why.

"I love you, Annie Benton."

"I love you too, Michael Anthony."

As one, they looked at each other with a bittersweet smile. Steve gave his friend one last, sweet kiss, and followed Dee out the door.

Gabe found that he couldn't watch him go.

Dog and McDonald were on the porch, waiting for Annie. Tails wagged and wings flapped when they saw her pull down the long driveway. Dog let out an excited bark when Gabe's black truck parked next to the little red one.

"Quite a nice little reception," Gabe chuckled, nodding to the critters as he opened Annie's door for her.

Annie laughed when Dog bounded up to Gabe, sniffing at him in the embarrassing way dogs are known to do. "I'd say that's a better one!" Instantly appalled at her risqué joke, she blushed and busied herself with a box of journals.

Gabe couldn't help but grin. Such an innocent, she was. He grabbed another box and followed her to the porch, setting it down next to the one she had just placed on the weathered wood.

With a flick of her wrist, Annie opened the door. She turned to pick up her package, and banged heads with Gabe, who was doing the same. Both fell in opposite directions, rubbing bruised noggins and giggling.

"It just keeps getting better and better," he said, still chuckling as he stood to help her up. "And still no security issues here, I see," nodding at the door.

"You'd try and get by Dog?" Annie favored him with a wink and invited him in.

Gabe glanced at the beast in question, who was heading onto the porch with his feathered companion. "Eh... perhaps not," he grinned, shutting the door. "He seems friendly enough to me, but I sure wouldn't want to tick him off. Those jaws of his struck fear in my heart for a moment, being too close to..." He trailed off, trying not to laugh at Annie's crimson blush. "Um... right. So, where would you like these boxes?"

"Next to the table if you wouldn't mind," was her reply. She hurried over to drop her burden. *Get a grip, Annie girl, you're both adults here and a little off-color humor is hardly anything to be blushing about!*

"Done and done." Gabe set his box next to hers, half listening to the dog and goose argue on the porch. "What is it with those two, Annie?" *Fortuitous change of subject…*

"Mac and Dog? I have absolutely no idea. It's been like that ever since the goose hatched," Annie sighed.

Growls and honks grew louder, more agitated.

"Hey!" Annie hollered, "Enough out there!"

The bickering ceased. Dog burst through the over-sized doggie door, heading for his mistress. She gave him a quick pat on the head, moving to ruffle his fur. He didn't wait around, but charged at Gabe, tongue lolling out in happy delight.

Gabe was nearly bowled over when Dog jumped him, placing mammoth paws on sturdy shoulders, bringing them eye to eye. Blue eyes widened in surprise, and then changed to relief when gold ones smiled back at him. A friendly lick on the chin from Dog assured the man he was safe.

"Dog! Get down!" Annie reached to haul him off. Again, Dog eluded her, and wandered off to annoy Spike with a wet slurp to the kitty's face.

"Gabe, I'm so sorry. He's usually not so ill-mannered…"

"I'm grateful he didn't eat me," Gabe joked. "Actually, we bonded when he rescued me. I just never realized how… big he is! You've got yourself quite an animal there, Annie."

"He's special. They all are," Annie smiled, looking from Dog to Gabe. "I'd like to thank you for helping me with the journals, and for seeing to it that I made it home safely."

"My pleasure." Gabe flashed her a wink and a grin.

An awkward silence filled the room. Annie was stricken with another attack of extreme shyness. *What should she do now? Here she was, alone with literally the man of her dreams, and she couldn't think of a word to say. Maybe invite him in to have a seat? Offer him a drink? Throw herself into his arms and asked him where had he been all her life?* She turned away to hide yet another blush. A seat was safe enough, and maybe a drink. She could certainly use a beer! Wouldn't hurt to offer a little hospitality, would it? They could leaf though the journals; that was safe enough.

"Um… Gabe? Can I get you anything to drink?"

Finally! He thought she'd never offer. "Sure, Annie, anything is fine."

Did that mean coffee? Soft drink? Something stronger? What was proper in this situation? Oh God, she couldn't think straight! It had been so long since she'd been on a date that she couldn't remember what to do anymore. But was it a date? Technically, no, so why was she so nervous? Jeez, her hands were shaking and her palms were sweaty, and she couldn't remember being so disconcerted in her life.

She found her voice and asked, "Any preferences? I've got coffee, tea, Pepsi… I think I have a few beers…"

"A beer sounds perfect." Gabe smiled to himself, enjoying the somewhat perverse pleasure at her nervousness. Such a refreshing change from the females constantly trying to attract his attention.

"Have a seat, I'll bring them out." Annie escaped to the kitchen while she could still remember why she was heading there. That cowboy was filling her head with nothing but thoughts of what his lips would feel like pressing down on hers.

Gabe wandered into the living area, feeling very much at home in the cozy cabin. He opened the flue on the woodstove, and then opened the door to the firebox to check the wood situation. A small pile of coals glowed red, changing to a bright orange when fed by the fresher air. He poked around, stirring them up a bit before shoving a few more logs in, leaving the door open so that he could enjoy watching the fire.

He'd barely parked himself on the sofa when he felt a light tap on his shoulder. *What the…?* He turned to find himself face to face with the strange kitty he'd encountered on his last visit to Annie's home.

Spike moved forward until his nose was mere centimeters from Geoffrey Alan's. He stared, unblinking, at the man, looking deep into his eyes, trying to detect any falseness or deceit.

Nothing.

Geoffrey Alan was as honest and noble as his brother Steven Anthony, whom Spike liked and respected very much. Very well, the man would not hurt Annie Rose. But would he protect her?

Spike twitched the tip of his tail and opened his amber eyes a bit wider, his pupils dilating, pulling Geoffrey Alan into another test. He allowed the human to catch a glimpse of his future-past. All very subtle, not allowing Geoffrey Alan to truly understand what he was seeing in his mind's eye – only that he must react to a situation without hesitation, without fear for himself.

Gabe looked at the cat. *Why the heck was it staring at him like that?* He tried to turn away, but was held captive by the feline's eyes. It was as if the cat were trying to crawl right into his mind! *Christ, just how absurd was that?*

The eyes opened wider, drawing Gabe deeper and deeper into the amber gaze. He felt himself becoming detached from reality, hurtling towards an unknown destination. And yet it seemed to be a place he'd been before. A horrible place. A place of nothing, a place of no return.

A nagging sense of anxiety washed over him, followed by an intense fear. He found himself on the edge of a gray void, and knew that if he didn't escape it right away; chances were that he'd never return to the land of the living.

Something shimmered near him. Close, but not close enough to touch. It was on the other side, caught in the grip of the void. Oh God, it was Annie! Gabe yelled her name, warning her not to go any further. She turned to look at him, and vanished.

"Anne! No…!!" He crossed over without another thought. He had to reach her, bring her out before it was too late…

Spike blinked, releasing Geoffrey Alan from the second test.

One more to go. Ever so gently, he extended his silky paw, brushing the pads along the beard stubble on the man's jaw.

Just as gently, Gabe reached up and ran a finger along the cat's face, smoothing back the long whiskers.

Spike felt himself begin to purr; Geoffrey Alan had passed.

What a strange cat, Gabe thought. First he was staring like he wanted brains for dinner, then a caress to the chin? He shrugged, stroking the kitty's soft fur. He never really had much use for cats before, but he rather liked this one. So different…

Annie returned with two bottles of beer, smiling when she was the cowboy making nice with the arrogant critter.

"You must be someone special," she said, handing Gabe his beer. "Spike isn't known for his social skills."

Gabe chuckled, sipped, nodded, and after another long swallow of the brew and a playful scratch behind Spike's ears, replied, "The cat and I have an understanding."

Annie raised an eyebrow. Gabe shrugged it off, not altogether sure what he meant by his comment either.

Spike jumped from the sofa to retreat to the loft. Geoffrey Alan would want to place his arm around Annie Rose when she sat next to him, and the cat didn't want it to appear as if he were being shooed away.

Annie wasn't sure where to sit. She knew where she wanted to be, but her shyness was still very much in control. She opted for her favorite chair near the woodstove, absently pulling the woodsy-spicy smelling afghan onto her lap. She turned the chair slightly so that it faced the sofa, and Gabe, and took a nervous sip of her beer. The next move was up to him.

Gabe was relieved when the cat cleared out before he had to move it aside. He kicked back, slung his arm along the back of the sofa, and waited for his Annie to snuggle up next to him. He blinked in surprise when she opted for a seat halfway across the room. Must be she was still pretty damn nervous, because she sure as hell knew how he felt about her! He knew how she felt about him, too. He sipped, smiled to himself, and contemplated different ways to take it from there.

He opened his mouth to speak then shut it abruptly when he discovered that he had no idea what to say. It had been a very long time since he'd had to play the dating game, if one could call his previous, short-lived encounters with women "dating." More like one-night stands. He'd never actually dated Deirdre, either.

But was this a date? No, not really. Not yet, anyway. Okay… Start with some light conversation. The weather? Too cliché. Politics? Heh. Like he'd bore her with that! Religion? Eh… no.

Her. Talk about her, Evans. Ask her… God, ask her what?

Spike sat on his perch in the loft, watching Geoffrey Alan. *Indeed! The man was positively pathetic! At his age, one would think that he'd know how to converse with a lady. The two of them hadn't said a word in nearly five minutes! Perhaps it was time to intervene…*

The cat glanced around the loft, looking for something… *Ah, perfect!* He padded over on silent paws, stopping at the desk. Jumped up, and found exactly what he was searching for, and with a nudge, sent it to the floor. He twitched his tail, peered between the rails and into the great-room, and with a smug feline grin, batted his prize to the floor below.

Annie and Gabe both jumped, startled at the smack-thump from seemingly nowhere. Gabe, already facing the loft, looked up to see the cat looking back down at him. A furry eyelid closed and opened. *Jesus, the cat just winked at him!*

Annie spun around in her chair to see what had fallen. Her notebook lay on the floor, the pages open to the lyrics of a song she had recently finished. She swallowed hard and raised her eyes to the loft. *Spike… She should have known.* But why the notebook? Usually he was tossing something small over the edge, like pencils and paperclips – something he could bat around when no one was watching.

It must be a sign… Gabe stood and went to retrieve the notebook, all but ignoring Annie's insistence that she would take care of it. He waved a hand at her, picked it up, and began to read. *Oh God…*

He read it again, out loud this time, turning to Annie as he did so. His voice was soft, melodic, picking up the tune in his mind, which went so well with the words on the paper.

"Dream Again… I thought the dream was over; a long-lost fantasy. But you came back again last night to give your love to me.

"Please go away, I beg of you. "I can't take any more." The pain was just too much to bear the time you left before…"

Gabe glanced at his Annie again. She was blushing fifteen shades of crimson. He smiled, charmed beyond words.

Annie's face burned like the fires of hell. Of all the people to read her pathetic attempts at writing! Why was he looking at her that way? Was he amused? Making fun of her? Angry? *Please, Gabe, just close the book and forget about it!*

He couldn't believe what he was reading, no matter that it was right there in his hands. She had written this? Of course she did. Who else? The music was in his mind again. Yep, it had to be. It was the sequel to his song "The Dream." It had to be. It would be!

He quickly read the rest of the words, and then softly began to sing the chorus.

"It's back again, the same ol' dream. The one in which you say… you'll be mine forever, until my dying day. You reach out to take my hand; I don't know what to do. The hardest choice I'll ever make… because I still love you…"

Oh God, he was singing her song! His song… her song. His music, her words.

She wanted him to stop. Her emotions were beginning to overwhelm her.

She wanted him to continue, to hear his voice bring life to her words.

Gabe…

Spike watched the little drama of Geoffrey Alan and Annie Rose unfold. *There, that should move matters along a little faster.* He licked a paw, and then smoothed his whiskers over his smug, self-satisfied face.

Gabe finished the song.

"Reality or fantasy? I can no longer tell. Yet to know the difference would deliver me from my private hell. Wake me if I'm dreaming, or let me escape into night skies. My tortured heart seeks refuge from the mirage of love's lies.

"I open my eyes and see your face hovering over me. Our lips meet, my world explodes, and time ceases to be. A whirling vortex, colors bright, a distant song I hear. The die's been cast, decision made; I see it all too clear.

"Long ago I prayed we'd meet in another time and place. Have we overcome the odds, defeated time and space? I'll take the chance this isn't real, that I'll be hurt again. You're here right now, you're in my arms, it's where you've always been."

Gabe closed the notebook and walked over to where his Annie was huddled in the chair. He placed his hands on the arms of the chair, one on either side of her, and then very slowly lowered his head to hers.

She looked up at him. Could feel his breath warm on her face. A tremor ran though her.

"It's where I've always been," he whispered, just before he kissed her.

It was no dream.

It was actually happening.

And it felt so, so right.

Annie raised her arm, placing a trembling hand on the back of his neck to pull him closer.

He offered no resistance, and gave in to what was meant to be. He damn near drowned in that kiss, but after a lifetime of a moment, broke it off. He lifted his Annie into his arms, again pressing his lips to hers. The chair was kicked aside, clearing the way to the bedroom, Gabe moving with purpose – again, losing himself in their kiss.

Annie felt herself being lowered to the bed. Somewhere in the back of her mind it registered that this wasn't the right time. Not yet, and yet, she wanted it so much… Wanted to finally discover what this side of love, the physical side, was all about. She moaned softly, meeting his eyes, before hers closed in near ecstasy.

Gabe's weight settled over her. Heavy, warm, gentle… Oh God, and so hard against her thigh. Every nerve in her body sang as his lips played over her face, moving down her neck to stop at the pulse point just under her jaw, sucking ever so slightly. Another delicious shiver ripped through her, bringing with it a ringing in her ears. It increased in volume until it penetrated the sensual fog engulfing her.

It took all of her willpower to push him away so that she could reach for the phone.

"Let it ring," he murmured, moving back towards her to nuzzle that tempting valley between her breasts. God, she was making him insane with desire.

Mmmm… she was so tempted, but felt compelled to answer nonetheless. *Something not quite right…*

Gabe ceded, rolling to his back and praying like hell the call would be a goddamn short one. Well, after one more searing kiss, anyway.

"H… hello?" Annie managed to choke out, still breathless from a most incredible kiss.

"Annie? Annie, I need help!"

"Eric? Oh jeez… What's wrong?"

"It's Aunt Irene. She fell and hit her head and won't wake up!"

"Eric, where are you?"

"Home. She was carrying groceries in and slipped on the steps. She won't wake up, Annie!"

"Eric, hang up and call 911 right now…"

"I already did. And I put a blanket on her. Annie, I'm so scared!"

"You did well, Eric. When they get there, you go to the hospital with them. I'll meet you there."

"I… Annie, I hear them coming. I'm going back outside now." He dropped the phone and scurried outside to wave down the ambulance.

"Eric, I'll see…" She heard a clatter, and then silence. With a sigh and a glance at Gabe, she hung up the receiver. The resigned look on his face indicated that he'd given up on returning to that kiss.

"You heard?" she asked.

He nodded.

"I'm sorry, Gabe, but I have to go. Eric is only twelve, and shouldn't be by himself."

"I understand, Annie. I'll drive," he answered, reaching for her. He brushed his thumb along her jaw, contemplating one more kiss.

She shivered under his touch. She fought, to focus on Eric instead of her lustful thoughts.

"Um… I… No, that's okay, Gabe. I'm not certain how serious this is. It might take a while, and…"

"It doesn't matter, Annie. I'll take you." He favored her with a sheepish, lopsided grin. "I'd planned on spending the night with you anyway. "

Annie felt yet another blush color her cheeks. "I... um... Oh God..."

Gabe grinned even more, totally charmed by her innocence. He planted a kiss on her nose.

"You're terrible, Gabe Evans!" She grinned back, totally under his spell. "Really, though, I have to go now. Eric must be terrified. He has no one else in this world other than his aunt."

Gabe ran his hands through her tangle of soft, autumn hair. "He has you," he murmured. After a gentle kiss to her forehead, he released her and went to start his truck.

Eric watched the medics put Aunt Irene on a cart then shove her into the back of the ambulance. She was so pale and gray... still hadn't woken up yet, either. He grabbed his portable oxygen tank and struggled to lift it in after her. Dang, it seemed so heavy tonight!

"Hey... What the heck...?" the medic started to protest.

Eric fixed him with a stare. "I'm just a kid, mister, and a sick one. You leave me here alone, and you'll be in trouble..."

The medic grinned, agreeing, and helped Eric into the back.

He sat next to his aunt, reaching under the blanket covering her to take her hand. It was so cold and stiff. He was scared that she was already dead. He was scared that Annie wouldn't be there waiting for him. He was just plain scared, and the wail of the siren as they sped through the icy streets didn't help much, either.

"Hey kid," the driver hollered into the back. "You doin' okay?"

Eric looked up, meeting familiar blue eyes in the rearview mirror. Looked just like Michael's. "Yeah, I'm doing a lot better now," he answered truthfully. He knew then that everything would be all right. Michael would never let him down. He hoped.

Annie and Gabe arrived at Brighton's ER minutes after the Peters'. Irene had been hustled off to a trauma room, leaving Eric alone and confused at the registration desk. The second he saw Annie walk in, he ran over to her, dragging his ever-present O2 tank behind him.

She wrapped her arms around him. Poor thing... he looked scared to death! Always the nurse, she glanced at the flow meter on the tank. His oxygen needs were up again, darn it. She then turned the boy around and introduced him to Gabe.

"Gabe, this is Eric Peters. He's a very special friend of mine. Eric, Gabe Evans... also a... a very special friend of mine."

Gabe felt a sense of déjà vu when he looked at Annie and Eric together. He smiled and extended his hand to the kid. "Very pleased to meet you, young man."

Eric's smile couldn't have been any bigger. Wow... Gabe Evans! Right here in front of him! He's seen him on TV, and had all of his music, and even had one of the books he wrote – even if it was a grown up's book. And Annie knew him! Jeez, and he sure as heck looked a lot like Michael...

He shoved his misshapen hand into Gabe's big warm one. "Very pleased to meet you too, sir!"

Gabe ruffled the kid's hair and slung an arm over his thin shoulder.

Annie smiled. Yep, they'd get along just fine. Now, to check on Irene. She went to the admitting clerk's desk and identified herself, and explained the situation. She was told she'd be informed and to have a seat. Couldn't ask for more than that!

She joined Gabe and Eric in the waiting room, and took the can of Pepsi Gabe offered her. "I see you had change for the vending machine this time," she teased.

"I can't count on anyone to break a fifty around here," he teased back, and patted the chair next to him.

Annie sat, thrilled when he took her hand into his. The familiar tingle raced up her arm and spread through her body. Would it happen every time he touched her? She sure hoped so...

Gabe chatted with Eric, asking him about his likes, dislikes, school, hobbies... It was as if they were old friends already, Annie thought, and Gabe was so much like Michael when he and Eric first met. Her mind drifted from the conversation around her, taking her back an hour to her bedroom. To Gabe in her bedroom. To Gabe kissing her and nearly making lo...

"Miss Benton?"

Annie jumped, feeling her face flush as if the ER nurse standing in front of her could read her wicked, yet delicious, thoughts.

"Yes?"

"You can come back and see Mrs. Peters now. She'll be going upstairs soon; you can stay with her until then. This way..."

The trio followed the nurse to the trauma room, Annie firing off questions all the way. "Can you tell us what her injuries are? Any idea on how long she'll be here? Any consults? We'll need social work involved... Oh God..."

Gabe slipped a comforting, supportive arm around his Annie. *Hey, any excuse, eh?* He didn't remove it when they stopped outside the door.

The nurse gave Annie a hint of a grin, and answered her questions. "She suffered a broken hip when she fell. It's not a big break, but more of a hairline fracture on the acetabulum. She'll have to stay off it for a while. She also received a concussion when she hit her head on the step. A CT showed a very small subdural hematoma."

Eric tugged at Annie's sleeve. "What does that mean?"

The ER nurse answered for her. "It's rather like a bruise on her brain, Eric. Kind of like... a blood blister."

"Has neuro been consulted?" Annie gave Eric's shoulder a light squeeze. *It'll be okay, kiddo...*

"Yes. She'll probably have another CT in a day or two to see if it's resolving, or if surgery is required."

"S… surgery?" Eric gulped.

"Possibly, but it's a very small bleed. It should go away on its own," the ER nurse assured him.

Annie knelt in front of Eric, her hands on his shoulders. "I think your aunt will be just fine, honey. She'll have one heck of a headache tonight, and it will be hard for her to walk tomorrow, but she should be good as new."

Gabe sure as hell hoped so. The kid definitely did not need any more crap dumped on him.

The group entered Irene's darkened room. She opened her eyes when she heard the visitors.

"Eric… Annie… I'm so sorry. I don't know how this happened," she said in a very tired, pained voice.

"You slipped on the ice, Aunt Irene. It's not your fault." Eric went to her, slipping his hand into her now-warm one.

Annie was right behind him. "How are you feeling, Irene?"

"I'll live, or so they say. But I won't be able to get home for a while. I… I don't know what…"

"Would you object if Eric stayed with me?" Annie knew what Irene's biggest worry was. "He's more than welcome."

"I couldn't ask that of you, Annie. It's too much. Besides, what about your work? He shouldn't be alone at night," Irene sighed.

Gabe stepped from the shadows, joining his Annie and Eric. He grinned his easy lop-sided grin down at the pale woman on the bed. "I could probably help out there," he offered. "He's more than welcome to stay with us, too. My boys would love an older brother for a while."

Irene stared in awe. Damned if it wasn't that singer Eric was so fond of. Played his songs all the time! What the heck was he doing there? Her eyes narrowed, noticing that he looked very much like Michael. She felt herself blush.

"Oh, I'm sorry? I've forgotten my manners… Irene, this is Gabe Evans. Gabe, this is Eric's aunt – Irene Peters." Annie stepped back, allowing Gabe to get a little closer.

He nodded, and gave Irene's hand a gentle squeeze. "Pleased to meet you, although I'm certain we both wish it could have been under better circumstances." He upped the wattage on his grin.

Irene could only nod, mesmerized by the sight of him.

"Gabe is Annie's special friend!" Eric smiled, very glad to see that his aunt was much better.

Irene continued to stare at Gabe. Lord, did he ever resemble Michael! Michael, her secret fantasy – even if she was quite a few years older. Could they be brothers? She'd be shocked if they weren't. And Annie's special friend, huh? Why not? Or… who'd have thought…?

"Mrs. Peters, I assure you…" Gabe's comment was cut short when a gurney appeared, pushed by a perky young nurse's aide.

"Here we go!" she chirped, and assisted by Annie, slid Irene from bed to cart.

Off to the fifth floor, where Irene would be for the next several days. She was exhausted and in considerable pain by the time she was finally tucked into bed.

"Aunt Irene, we're gonna go now," Eric said quietly. "I'll be back as soon as I can, okay? And Annie will take good care of me, so don't you be worryin' none. Gabe… Gabe too."

Irene was too tired to argue. She was asleep moments later. Eric kissed her forehead, and then left the room, followed by Annie and Gabe.

"Annie? It's kind of early yet. Would it be okay if we go see Austin? Please?" Austin was another CF kid, and very nearly Eric's best friend when in the hospital. They'd been spending way too much time together lately…

"Sure, hon. You go on up and we'll meet you there, but only a few minutes. We still have to go back to your trailer and pick up your things." Annie planted a kiss on the boy's forehead and sent him off.

"It's okay for him to wander around here alone, Annie?" Gabe asked, watching Eric drag off down the hall.

"He'll be fine, Gabe. He knows this place as well as I do," she sighed. "Comes from spending too much time…"

"Tell me about it." He'd spent far too much time there himself lately. "Well, Miss Benton, shall we find someplace quiet to wait for our charge?"

"Mmm… nurses' lounge," she grinned.

"Gabe, I want to thank you for offering to look after Eric. That was very generous of you, but what about Deirdre? Won't she mind? I mean… doesn't she have enough to deal with…? Her illness…?"

"Annie, I have a feeling that Dee would love to have young Mr. Peters as a guest. Just think of all the little plots they could hatch. After all, didn't they conspire to get you and me together?" Gabe laughed.

"Hmm… I guess they did! Still, do you think she's up to it?"

"If not, we'll work something out. I should hire some extra help again anyway." He took her hand and gave it a squeeze, and was contemplating kissing her again when the door to the lounge opened. Gabe nearly groaned in dismay when none other than Edith the Hag lumbered in. Not much he could do, though, when he saw her in uniform, complete with Brighton Memorial/ Housekeeping emblazoned on her name badge. Of all the shitty luck…

"Oh! Annie Benton… I didn't know you were in here! With… with… Sweet Jesus!" Edith was now speechless, seeing the man of her dreams right there in front of her. Her heart thundered in her chest, breath rasped through a dry-as-dust mouth. Her head spun and her knees turned to rubber, and she fell smack-dab right onto the floor.

"Edith!" Annie cried, rushing to her.

"Christ," Gabe muttered, going over to see if he could help.

"Gabe, hit the Code button; it's right over there…" Annie vaguely waved towards the wall, her main focus on the unconscious woman. "Edith… come on, hon… Wake up…"

Gabe turned, but was stopped by something clamped on his ankle. With a grimace, he looked down to see the ham-sized hand of the hag firmly attached to his leg.

"No… I'm fine," Edith wheezed. Sweet Jesus, she was actually touchin' him! Had right a hold of her Gabe Evans. He weren't movin' away none, either.

It was all Gabe could do not to shake his leg like a wet cat would, and rid himself of that oversized paw holding him hostage. "I think she's fine, Annie. Just fainted."

Annie sat back on her heels, quickly assessing the change in her patient. Pale had quickly turned to a patchy blush on Edith's face. Hmm… most likely Gabe was right.

"I'm fine, Annie, really I am!" Edith propped up on an elbow, took a deep breath, and righted herself like a ship recovering from a list in choppy seas. Her head bobbed up and down, her frizzy bleach-blonde hair looking much like an albino clown wig.

"You sure…?"

"Uh huh. I… I was jes' so surprised to see Ga… uh, Mr. Evans in here." Deep breath, deeper blush. "I been a fan for years," she sighed.

Jeez, was Annie the only one who didn't know who Gabe was? She shook he head in wonder. *You really need to get out more, Annie…*

Gabe held out his hand to Edith, helping her to her feet. Hell, he was a gentleman after all, eh? No matter that he had a sudden urge to run to the scrub sink and take a few layers of skin off his mitts to rid himself of her touch. He wondered why he was so repulsed by the woman. Wasn't her looks, even if she could scare the paint off walls. Looks never mattered to him; it was the inside that counted. Wasn't her size, either, which matched his six-foot-three frame. Nope, it was something deeper, something he couldn't quite place. He shrugged the feeling off and assisted her to a chair.

Edith sat heavily, tried to swallow, her throat thick and dry. He touched her! Gabe Evans had his hands on her!

Annie was already at the water cooler, fetching the poor woman something to drink. "Here you go, Edith. Are you sure you're okay?"

Edith's hand was shaking uncontrollably when she reached for the glass. Not even thinking twice about it, although still uneasy about her, Gabe's hand wrapped around Edith's to steady the glass.Damned if she didn't moan. Gabe glanced at Annie over the frizzy head, seeing that she was now amused instead of concerned for the mutant. Yep, just a fainting spell. They both fought to restrain a giggle, and now he was feeling a bit naughty. He knelt in front of his "biggest fan," looking up at her with a gleam in his eye.

"Edith? You're okay, right?"

She nearly swooned again, but managed to choke out an affirmation after a lusty, noisy gulp of water. "I... Yeah, better, thanks."

"Wonderful! I'll sleep much better tonight knowing that your health is no longer in jeopardy." He stood; ready to get the hell out of Dodge before she had a chance to pass out again.

Edith wasn't done with him yet, and stood quickly, nearly falling over again. Gabe instinctively grabbed her, more to keep her bulk from flattening him on the way down than to help. She fell against him, glancing at Annie as she did so. Her arms went around her sweetie, hugging him tight.

"Thank ya so much, Mr. Evans. You're a right nice man..."

Annie blinked, shocked at the look of lust and desire and possessiveness flickering over Haggins' face. Did she really just see that? Was Gabe aware?

Gabe's arms rose and fell, not at all wanting to hug he back, but felt somewhat obligated. It was quick, but the gesture made, and he gently pushed her away.

"Ga... Uh, Mr. Evans? Could I get an autograph mebbe?"

"I don't see why not." *Anything to get her the hell out!*

Edith beamed, lumbered to her locker, and began to paw through what Annie and Gabe could see were dozens of promo pictures of Evans and SD.

"Here we go! This is one o' my favorites." Edith shoved a dog-eared eight-by-ten glossy at him.

Annie took a peek. It was of Gabe, looking up at the sky. Dusk was falling, a deep red sunset on the horizon, and a single bright star winking in a royal blue sky. He looked as if he were waiting for his dream to drop out of the heavens. It was haunting and beautiful, and it took her breath away.

"Ah yes," Gabe sighed, remembering well when the photo was taken. It was the year before Steve died, and his last album ever. It graced the cover of the lyrics booklet. A similar one of Kyle was on the back. The pictures turned out so well, it was decided to send them to the fans when requested.

He found a pen on the table and murmured as he scrawled, "To Edith – After holding you in my arms, no other woman will ever be the same. Love, Gabe." He handed it to her and stood next to Annie, resting his arm around her shoulders.

Annie stifled another giggle. Oh, he was going to hell for that one, the scamp!

Edith read - awed, stunned, and still unable to believe she was even in the same room with him. "Oh, Mr. Evans! I... I don't know what to say! Thank you!"

"My pleasure, Miss Haggins."

"No, my...." Edith's reply was cut short, her pager buzzin' on her queen-sized hip. "Gotta get back to work," she groaned, clutching her precious prize close to her heart.

She all but floated out of the room.

Gabe and Annie burst into hysterical laughter the minute the door shut behind her.

"Do you often have that effect on women?" Annie giggled.

"I never really paid all that much attention. God, wasn't she a hoot?"

"Hmmm… But don't you think you were a bit… perverse? Writing what you did?"

"It made her day, Annie. Her life, even!"

"How do you fit that ego through a door?" Annie gave him a wink.

"Huh? Oh God, it's not like that at all. Nope. Annie, that woman has been all but stalking me for years. I sent her a few promo pics here and there, but it never seemed to be enough. Maybe now she'll back off and drool over that one. With any luck."

"I'll have a subtle chat with her if necessary."

"Let it go, Annie. I've got better things to think about now." He gave her a soft smile, and a gentle kiss. He sighed happily into her hair and held her close to him.

"Mmm… Much better, cowboy," Annie murmured.

A knock on the door interrupted them. Eric poked his head in. "Ready?" He grinned at the couple hugging. "Um… I'll be at the desk," he snickered, and shut the door again.

"Reality bites, Annie," Gabe sighed, not quite so happy this time. Dammit.

"We'd better go. I want to check on Irene one last time; it'll make Eric feel better to know she's sleeping comfortably."

After picking up Eric's necessities, the trio drove back to the cabin. It was very late; the boy couldn't help but nod off, using Annie's shoulder for a pillow. She put her arm around him, absently yet lovingly stroking his hair.

Evans watched them out of the corner of his eye as he drove, and found he was thinking about how marvelous the children of Annie and Gabe would be. She'd make a wonderful mother if how she treated Eric was any indication. Christ, why had it taken him so long to find her?

Gabe carried Eric into the house, placing him gently on the bed and leaving Annie to do the tucking in and seeing to the medical needs, as was her specialty. He'd do what he knew best and stoke up the woodstove. He sighed, poked at the coals. So much for tonight. Then again, maybe he was moving too fast. Jesus, he barely knew her and damn near had her in bed! Not that it ever mattered in the past with other women, but this was his Annie. He'd waited for her forever; a little while longer wouldn't hurt. Hell, they had to get to know each other anyway, right?

He shoved another log into the firebox and shut the door, then flopped in the favorite chair close to the stove. Mmm… the heat felt so damn good. He stretched, kicked his feet up on the ottoman, and let his head fall back. Yep, he could get used to this mighty fast. Gabe closed his eyes and drifted off.

It didn't take Annie long to get Eric settled into the guest room; he was nearly asleep before his head even hit the pillow. She spent a few extra minutes puttering around, thinking of the man in her living room. It wouldn't be long before she'd be joining him, and once again they'd be alone together.

She felt that awkward shyness creep up on her. Dear God, had he really expected to spend the night? In her bed? Annie shivered, remembering the scene in her bedroom a few hours earlier. Oh, she wanted to repeat it, but did she dare? Would that wonderful Spike intervene again?

Eric coughed in his sleep. Hello, reality. No way could Gabe stay, not with Eric there, it just wouldn't be proper. She hoped her cowboy would understand when she booted him out.

Dog flopped in the doorway, his idea of guarding Eric. Annie was careful not to trip over her overgrown canine on her way out. She turned, ruffling his fur in an attempt to put off "the moment" a little longer. Oh jeez, now her palms were sweating and her heart was thumping far too fast and loud... but from anxiety or anticipation?

She watched him from the doorway of Eric's room, thinking that he certainly seemed at home in her cabin. He stoked the fire and then settled in the favorite chair as if it were a long-standing routine before he finally went to bed. She wondered if he did the same thing in his house on Park Street. Just as she was about to say something, although she had no idea what it would have been, Gabe gathered the afghan in his arms, held it to his chest, and fell into an immediate, deep sleep. She fell in love with him all that much more. No, she wouldn't be waking him up to boot him out. He was harmless now. Kind of. She fought the urge to plant herself on his lap and give him one heck of a kiss to take with him into his dreams. Instead, she grabbed a blanket from her bed, flipped off the lamp in the living room, and curled up on the sofa with Spike. Together they studied the sleeping man, his face slightly illuminated from the reflection of the moon on the snow outside.

Annie thought that Gabe was the most beautiful man she had ever seen. Not glamorous beautiful, although he would certainly clean up that way. No, just... beautiful. Handsome, rugged... beautiful. His forever-messy black hair was just a little too long. It sprouted from his head here, curled in a tangle there, and frost at his temples shown silver in the moonlight. His face and chin were beginning to darken with a day's growth of beard, tempering that beauty with an air of roguishness. She could picture him as a pirate, or a stagecoach robber. The thought of him swinging from the mainmast and scooping her up in his arms made her giggle, and she abandon her assessment of him for another time; no way did she want to wake him. Best find another distraction until she could sleep.

Well, in a minute or two. Annie covered Gabe with the blanket she'd just been using, and stood near the woodstove, savoring the moment. It was after midnight, her favorite time of night. The world was asleep. Burning logs crackled and popped in the firebox, Spike purred almost imperceptibly, and Dog let out an occasional whine while he dreamed. The refrigerator hummed and the clock on the mantel marked off the seconds with a metallic click. Wind whipped crystals of ice against the windows, and sang across the shingles on the roof. Even with this cacophony of sound, silence reigned – with one exception. All Annie could really hear was the soft, even breathing of the man in her comfy chair.

Incredible.

Unbelievable.

For years and years she'd been dreaming of him and here he was hers for the taking. She loved him, she was sure of that, and that he loved her too wasn't in question. What she didn't know was *who* he was. What kind of a man was he? What about the little things? Food, sports, religion… what were his preferences? Did he like to travel? Hunt? Fish? Camp? Swim? Did he enjoy an active social life or prefer quiet nights at home? Republican? Democrat? Who the hell cared? Would he want children of his own? So many questions…

Her stomach rumbled, reminding her that she hadn't eaten since her late lunch, and even then she hadn't eaten very much. A glance at the clock told her what her body already knew – it was one-thirty, and lunchtime for a third-shift worker. Oh, and she was starving, but hesitant to wake Gabe by making too much noise in the kitchen. Cottage cheese and applesauce would have to do for now.

After a lingering glance at the incredible Mr. Evans, her heart so full of happiness she thought it might burst, Annie floated towards the kitchen. *Unbelievable!*

Her heart may have been floating, but her body was still earth-bound. She was brutally reminded of the fact when her foot impacted against something heavy and unexpected near the dining table. Her poor little toe bore the brunt of the assault, bringing tears to her eyes and rarely-used curse words to her lips.

"Ow! Shit! What the hell….?" She whisper-yelled, hopping awkwardly to the kitchen sink where a nightlight burned and she could better assess the damage to her must-be-broken toe.

Spike opened one eye, turning his head just enough to see Annie Rose bounce around before flopping to the floor and examine her hind… er, bottom…er, not paw, but foot. Well, at least she had ceased that bizarre dance of the smarting vestigial digit. Such displays… But his kitty heart hurt for her, so he padded in to see if she could use a bit of comfort.

"Owie," Annie moaned, lifting her kitty into her arms. "Talk about new adventures in pain, Spike! What on earth…?"

Spike jumped out of her arms and strolled over to where the humans had placed the boxes on the floor earlier. With a snort, he perched on the box which hindered Annie Rose's forward motion a short time ago.

"Oh yeah!" Annie sighed, remembering. The journals! Jeez, how could she have forgotten about them? Now there was an idea, she'd take them to her bedroom and read while she munched her nocturnal lunch. Heck, it would be at least two hours before she was sleepy anyway, right?

Spike slithered from his perch and vanished into the shadows. His tasks for the night were completed.

Her foot protesting in pain, Annie stood, and then hobbled over to the boxes, her hunger already forgotten. She carried the first box into her bedroom, and then went for the second. As she passed Gabe on her way into the kitchen, she couldn't resist the temptation to touch him, confirm that he was really, truly there. The throbbing in her poor smushed toe confirmed that she was definitely awake and not dreaming.

Just one little touch…

She knelt next to his chair, smiling at the soft rumble of an occasional snore. Moonlight danced across his face. Annie wasn't sure, but it looked as if his lips were moving. Dreaming? Mmm… Now those lips were twitching into that oh-so-cute lopsided grin.

Just one little touch…

Annie reached up and smoothed back a stray lock of his forever-tousled hair. There was that tingle again, racing up her arm to explode inside her. It left her silently gasping in delicious shock.

Just one more touch…

Nope, better not. With a soft sigh, she returned to the kitchen. The throbbing toe had morphed into sharp-pain-with-every-step toe. Yep, probably broken, and not a thing could be done to fix it.

The second box of journals was carried into the bedroom and placed next to the first. Annie noticed that the books had been arranged in chronological order, and she pulled out the oldest one to start with. Made sense, right? Yet, as interesting as it was to read about Rosiland's childhood, Annie couldn't get her mind off the man in the living room. He should be reading with her. The journal was replaced, and the boxes shoved into the closet.

Sleep, and an early morning, making breakfast for her men… The thought made Annie smile. She missed having someone to look after. Her loneliness began to fade. Of course it would take a while before it was gone altogether, but it was going. Going, going, soon to be gone forever and ever.

Gabe… He was really and truly out there. And she just had to have one more touch before she went to bed. After slipping into a pair of seldom-used 'jammies', she hobbled back out for a final good-night.

Her hand gently smoothed back another lock of hair. His lips twitched into another sideways grin.

Was he awake? No, still dreaming.

Ah, that smile… those lips. Her hand drifted along his strong jaw, her palm scraping lightly along the shadow of his beard. Her thumb slid over to nest in the dimple under his lower lip.

Just one quick kiss…

Annie squeaked in surprise when Gabe's arms captured her and pulled her onto his lap. "Finally," he whispered with a wink and a grin.

"You're awake!"

"Of course I am. You didn't know?"

"Of course I didn't! Otherwise I never would have…"

He shut her up with a kiss. Not that she minded, but she cut it short before it led to the bed.

"Don't go, Annie. Please… I've waited too damn long…"

"Shhh… Gabe, I… I'll stay for a while," she sighed, snuggling against him. He felt too darn good to give up so soon.

"How long is a while, Rose…?" His arms tightened around her, his lips brushed her forehead. He felt himself swell and harden underneath her.

Annie felt it too. "Um… not… not that long, Gabe. I… Eric… Not proper… Oh jeez…" She wasn't sure which was worse: her extreme embarrassment regarding their current situation, or the urge to drag him straight into the bedroom and take care of said current situation. *Rose…?*

"Just a few minutes, and I promise to let you go with your honor intact. Deal?"

She nodded. "Deal." She lay against him with her head on his chest, listening to his deep, even breathing and the beat of his heart. Apparently he was tired after all; the pulse rate, racing mere moments ago, had slowed to a strong, steady sixty beats per minute. He was asleep and not faking this time. Annie smiled and relaxed. Just a few minutes, and she'd sneak off to bed.

Heavy eyelids, a healthy yawn…

Just a few more minutes…

Chapter Twenty-Nine

Annie's nose twitched in appreciation of the mouth-watering aroma of fresh-brewed coffee. Ah, dreams... She was still asleep, right? Eyes were closed, snuggled comfortably with the cowboy... Yep, still dreaming, but the coffee? Had Spike finally evolved into a higher level of being, becoming somewhat useful? The thought of him in a butler's uniform, serving Dog and McDonald tea nearly made her giggle.

Mmm... coffee. And woodsy-spicy. *Oh God...*

Now fully awake, but not daring to open her eyes, Annie quickly assessed the here and now. Definitely a man underneath her, and from what she could feel, quite a man! Her face flamed with the thoughts of the male morning arousal... whatever the heck they called it. Jeez!! His arms were still around her, and he was nuzzling the top of her head with his lips.... "G...Gabe...?"

"I certainly hope so, Annie."

"I... Oh jeez... coffee. Who...? Eric? Eric!" She attempted to struggle out of Gabe's embrace. This was not something Eric should be witness too, no matter how innocent it all was.

Too late. A giggle drew her attention. She turned to see Eric sitting on the sofa, grinning from ear to ear, a grin unobstructed by O2 tubing. "Eric! Your oxygen.

"I don't need it today, Annie. I feel great! I um... I made coffee, is that okay?"

"It's just fine, Eric. Thank you..."

The boy just sat there, looking at the couple, his grin spreading.

Annie felt very conspicuous. Her face continued to burn with embarrassment, and she was sure her pajama top was pulled down a little too far under her blanket, if the heat of Gabe's skin against her was any indication. Just when did he shed his shirt, anyway? She shot him a green- daggered look of mock-chagrin.And what did he do? Gave her the most innocent, blue-eyed look of mock confusion right back, and with it, a devilish smirk. Oh, he was enjoying all of this!!

Eric remained planted on the sofa, getting the biggest kick out of it all. Michael said it would happen, that Annie would finally meet her cowboy, and Eric was right there to witness it all. Well, most. He didn't want to think of what "all" really was.

Gabe was quite content right where he was. Then again, he wouldn't remain content for long, not with Annie's most tempting parts nestled warm and soft over his most demanding part. Nope, not much longer at all. Despite the fact that he was having one hell of a good time teasing her, the fact that her nearness was more than teasing him. More like torture to not be able to...

Christ, it had to end before he totally lost control!

"Eric, is the coffee done yet?" Gabe all but groaned. Had to get the kid out of there for all their sakes!

"I'll check." Eric took the cue, and scooted into the kitchen.

"Here's your chance to retain your dignity, madam," Gabe chuckled. "Run like the wind!" He gave her a small shove.

"Me?" she said, raising an eyebrow, and feeling the wicked urge to tease back. "I'm not the one who's um… "She glanced down toward his belly; he'd get the hint.

"Touché!" he laughed, and sent her on her way, allowing her to remain wrapped in the blanket. He shot off to the bathroom for a quick clean up.

Gabe did a few stretches in front of the bathroom mirror, limbering up a bit and giving his physique a quick once-over. Yeah, still didn't look too bad for a man of his advancing years. Hell, he was in the prime of his life, right? That bit of gray at his temples, and the lines around his eyes sure didn't mean the rest of him was teetering on the top of the hill, ready to slide down into old age. Can't forget how quickly he reacted to Annie, either. He grinned at that thought while running a hand over his two-day old growth of beard. First a stop at the toilet, then seeing if Annie had what he'd need for proper morning hygiene.

Just as he was about to sneak a peak in her medicine cabinet, a fist thumped on the door, startling him, and making him wish he would have considered the toilet first. Christ, damn near scared it out of him!

"Gabe, look in the linen closet; you'll find everything you need in there."

Ah, his Annie… reading his mind already. Unless she was spying? As if. He chuckled and did, indeed, find what he needed, all still factory sealed. Disposable razors, half a dozen toothbrushes, three kinds of toothpaste, men's shaving cream? And women's? He wondered about the man it was intended for, wincing at the jealousy that came with it. His hand rested on a stack of towels and he contemplated a shower. Or a soak in that incredible bathtub built for two. Maybe Annie would wash his back for him! He sure as hell would wash her front. Oh God, lewd and lascivious thoughts creeping in again, and Mr. Happy was perking right up. Again. He couldn't remember the last time he'd had sex. Far, far too long ago. It wouldn't be just sex with Annie, though. No, it would be making love, probably for the first time in his life. Although he loved Danni, he was never really in love with her, and the sex was just that. Sex.

Gabe settled for the razor and toothbrush, and plenty of nice, cold water.

Annie raced back into her bedroom after the spontaneous rap on the bathroom door. Jeez, was that proper as far as being a hostess went? Was she too forward? Too casual? Too "too"? Not enough? She all but hid in her closet, picking out her attire for the day. Ha ha. Jeans and a sweatshirt, just like every other day. However, it was a good excuse to try and overcome her apprehension regarding her older guest. It was also a distraction from imaging her cowboy in the bathroom, most likely standing shirtless in front of the mirror while he shaved off that too-sexy bit of beard stubble. Mmmm… Or maybe he was wearing only a towel around his waist, water dripping from those very large biceps after a hot shower…

"Arrgh!!!" Annie groaned, wondering where her naughty thoughts were coming from. She barely knew the man! Loved him for forever, but knew so very, very little about him. She yanked a shirt from a hanger and shoved into it, then stomped off to find a pair of jeans that, although clean, weren't too torn or stained from her hours in the barn.

While Gabe and Annie were busy doing whatever they were doing, Eric had been busy in the kitchen, preparing the perfect breakfast for them. He set the table for two, poured OJ and coffee, had pancakes and sausage warming on the stove, and was now in the greenhouse, searching for just the right centerpiece. Every flower in the warm, sunny room was examined, and discarded for being too something. Too small, too big, too weird-looking, too pink, too smelly… too something. The sunlight glimmered bright-white on a plant in the corner. Eric grinned. Yep, just perfect. He didn't think Annie would mind if he snipped two of the flowers, and did just that, leaving the stems long enough to fit just right in the old vase he had found.

Breakfast and centerpiece hit the table seconds before Annie and Gabe hit the kitchen. Eric waived them over, holding a chair for Annie, who shared a look of surprise with Gabe. He grinned back at her. Uh huh, seems Eric had been waiting for them to leave the room!

Gabe offered Annie his arm. She took it with a shy smile, and was escorted most properly to the dining table. After Eric pushed her chair in for her, he handed her a napkin.

"Eric, thank you!" Annie said, truly amazed at the young gentleman and his manners. "Where did you learn…?" Sure wasn't from her. Oh, she had manners enough, but it had always been nothing but casual manners when Eric visited. She doubted very much that Irene had done much in the way of etiquette instruction, either.

"Oh, just a few things I picked up here and there," Eric grinned. Picked up from Michael, and his hours of lecturing on the proper way to treat a lady.

Gabe raised an eyebrow. Eric's actions had Stevie's influence written all over them. God, that man made the rounds…

"Eric, this is perfect! Coffee, juice, pancakes, sausage, even a centerpiece…" She trailed off, looking at Gabe.

He'd seen it too. Nothing on earth could have been as appropriate as the two white roses blooming in the cut crystal vase. He shivered slightly, feeling a strong sense of déjà vu wash over him. His eyes met Annie's, and he mouthed, "I love you."

Annie went from shock to numb to tingle to damn near floating out of her chair. He said it! Wasn't out loud, but the words were there! Close enough.

Oh God, it was overwhelming. She dropped her eyes back to the roses in her gramma's vase.

Eric cleared his throat, wondering where those two were now. Jeez, old people!

"Oh! Um, Eric, aren't you going to join us?" Annie found just enough of her voice to ask.

"No, I'm gonna eat with Dog and McDonald. It's pretty nice out this morning. Lots of sun. And I promise I won't stay out too long. Can I, Annie?"

"Ten minutes, that's it. And don't forget to take your meds, love."

"Give it a rest, Nancy Nurse, I know the drill."

Gabe's jaw nearly dropped in shock when, after Eric dished up his meal, he shook out nearly a dozen pills onto his plate. He threw on his hat and coat, and joined the furred and feathered duo on the porch.

"That's a lot of pills!" Gabe blew out in the breath he'd been holding. "Is he supposed to have that many?" Even Dee hadn't choked down that many in one sitting.

"'Fraid so. With his disease, he needs help with digestion. He has to take those with every meal."

"Poor kid."

"You have no idea, Gabe."

McDonald plopped his feathered butt next to Eric, sharing the top step, then reached over and helped himself to a pancake from the boy's plate. He thought it was about time the kid showed up again, the only time the goose ever got fun food was when Eric came to visit. MacD took his time with eating the syrupy treat since there was no competition. Dog new better than to interfere when he and Eric were dining. Ah yes, so much better than cracked corn and chicken feed. Almost as good as the fresh grass that grew down by the lake after the snow melted away. He did miss it. He nibbled a thank you on Eric's arm.

Eric's meal was further interrupted by the far-off whinny of a horse. Wasn't Wanda or Donny, they were too close. He set his plate down and walked around to the side of the cabin.

The second whinny determined where the animal was. A large black horse and his rider crested the hill at the top of the meadow. Eric waved and gave the thumbs up sign. Steven Michael tipped his hat, and turned Whiz around into the blaze of the rising sun. Eric returned to his meal.

"Where do we go from here, Gabe?" Annie asked. They had finished their breakfast and were working on a second cup of coffee. Very little conversation had gone on during the meal, and what there was consisted of the most general subjects such as Irene, the weather, and what a fine job Eric had done on breakfast. The rest of the time was spent in an almost uncomfortable silence, confusing both of them.

"Well, I should go back to Park Street, visit with Dee and the boys, and then head for the studio. I have a career to try and save. After that, Kyle…"

She was just a little put out by his smart ass answer. He knew perfectly well what she meant, and she felt pretty sure he knew the massive amount of courage it took to even ask him in the first place. She looked away, hurt and angry.

Oh God, he'd done it now. Annie could give as well as she got in witty repartee, but apparently not in matters of the heart. And this was a doozy... which was why he avoided a straight answer in the first place. He felt beyond terrible for hurting her. "I'm sorry, Annie. By this time of the morning I've usually harassed poor Kyle to near suicide. He wasn't here, so..." Shit! He was doing it again!

Annie didn't even bother looking at him. She picked up her dishes and went to the sink. Couldn't he see she was having a difficult time with this? Daylight had a bad habit of bringing reality crashing down on a person. So many issues came to light when the sun came up. Sure, it was all warm and cozy by the fire last night, when he didn't have to go home to the wife...

Oh God, why did she think this would ever work out? He'd hardly said a word to her during breakfast, they had only one friend in common, and on that note, did they have anything else in common? They worked different shifts; they lived in two different places – which brought up yet another issue: where would they live? No way did Annie want to leave her beloved cabin and pets any more than Gabe would be willing to give up his mansion and lavish lifestyle. Or his family.

His wife...

What about Deirdre, the most important issue of all? Jeez, and Gabe hadn't even called her to let her know that he wouldn't be home. How considerate – Not! Oh well, Dee probably figured it out by now anyway, which shot Annie's reputation all to heck. The husband plays sleep-over with the naughty nurse. Oh goody.

She ran water into the sink and added detergent, near to tears with the frustration of the whole Gabe situation. So much for finding true love. So much for her stupid dream. So much for... for everything!

Something soft touched her cheek. She looked to see the pearl-white of the half-open rose bud. Gabe's arm was sliding around her waist, pulling her close to him. She tried pulling away, but his voice stopped her. Or maybe she didn't really want him to let her go. She bit her bottom lip to keep it from trembling, closed her eyes to hold back her tears.

"Annie, I'm so sorry. I really am. God, I never meant to hurt you. I know this is hard... but I didn't realize just what it was doing to you." He pressed his lips against her temple, murmuring softly. "I promise, White Rose, no more smart-ass remarks. I... I just don't know where to go from here. It's all so sudden, and beyond being here with you right here and now, I haven't given much thought to tomorrow. We haven't had time to... to prepare for anything. I um... I think we need to talk to Dee."

She nodded, but couldn't answer; she was too close to tears.

"Annie, look at me." Gabe turned her around, hurt that she wouldn't meet his gaze. He placed his finger under her chin, lifting her face to his.

She took a deep breath, and allowed herself to look into his eyes. What she saw there nearly sent her to her knees. He did love her. Her arms went around his waist. His hand went behind her head, pressing her to his chest. Oh, if only they could stay like this a while longer. Pretend it was forever… But it could never be, and she told him why.

Gabe listened, feeling all of his hopes and dreams crushed by the weight of her soft, but honest words. Jesus, she was so right. What the hell had he been thinking? He was married, his wife was ill, and for them to take their new relationship any further would be beyond adultery, beyond immoral. No matter what Deirdre had said, it just wouldn't be right, no matter how right it felt.

Annie pulled away as soon as she finished her devastating little speech, even more despondent when he let her go. Deep, deep down she'd been hoping he'd argue, insist that none of that mattered, and he would never leave her side again. Yeah, right. He knew as well as she did what had to be done, and that was for him to go and never come back. She returned to her task of cleaning up the kitchen, scouring the countertop with a vengeance in a vain attempt to ease her frustration.

Gabe stifled a sigh, just as frustrated as Annie. Just as he was about to speak to her again, Eric chose that moment to interrupt.

"Um, Annie? Would… would it be okay if I go visit Aunt Irene a little later?" Eric had been watching the entire episode from the window. Gosh, things had started out so well and now they both looked like they were ready to start bawling. What had happened? Whatever it was, it wasn't good, and Deirdre needed to know. He hoped like heck she could help. Maybe Gabe would take him over there as soon as he was done visiting his aunt. He was supposed to spend the night at the Evans' anyway, right….?

"I'll take you over there, Eric," Gabe told him. "Annie has things to do here, and I'm heading that way anyway, not to mention you're to be our guest tonight. I'll call Dee and let her know."

Eric looked from Gabe to Annie and back again. Jeez, she looked even worse than she had a few minutes ago. Gabe was probably right… she needed time to herself. He nodded, and went to his room to pack his belongings.

Gabe went over to where Annie was assaulting the countertop. He wedged himself between her and her victim, forcing her to acknowledge him. Her hands dropped to her side, her head drooped. Damned if he didn't feel much the same. He placed his hands on her cheeks, framing her face and letting his thumbs brush the softness of her skin. "We will get through this, Annie. We have to, it was meant to be."

She gave him a quick, skeptical look. After what she had just told him?

Detailing exactly why it wouldn't work, and then he says it's meant to be? How could he possibly think that?

"You know I'm right, Annie. Why else would all of this be happening? My God… think about it!" He tried pulling her to him, ignoring her resistance. He wasn't about to let her go quite yet. Her words still rang in his ears with a horrible truth, but his heart wasn't listening. Nope, the hell with the brain, heart was in full control.

"I have thought about it, Gabe, and you know I'm right. Deirdre, the twins… your friends… What the heck will they all think? You can't just…."

He shut her up with a kiss that rocked them both.

Eric gave them a moment, and then coughed politely from the other room. He hated like heck to interrupt, but he had to talk to Dee. Things were still not as they should be.

Gabe reluctantly pulled away. "We have to get going, Annie. Lord knows I don't want to, but Eric… his aunt… studio… Jesus, so many things, so little time. I'll call you later; maybe we can meet for dinner tonight…?"

"I have to work, remember?" she answered in a small, tight voice, looking out the window. She couldn't even look at him. Her head was still spinning from his kiss; her heart was breaking because it was probably their last.

"We'll work something out, Annie. Come on… have faith in us." He took her hands in his, brought them to his lips. "Think about the song you wrote. 'You're here right now; I'm in your arms. It's where I've always been.' And where you'll always be."

Oh, she looked at him then, stunned. "You remembered the words?"

"How could I not? They're etched in my memory, burned in my heart, Annie. When I wrote "The Dream," I wrote it for you. About you. I was only eighteen years old, but I knew even then that you were out there somewhere. I nearly gave up trying to find you… but I did. We are meant to be! Not only did I find you, but you, Annie, wrote a song about me. For me. Am I right?"

She gave him a small nod, she couldn't deny it.

"If this isn't fate, isn't destiny, I don't know what it is. Have faith in us, my love. Can you do that?"

Another small nod.

He took a chance and took her in his arms again, more than relieved to feel her relax against him. "Good. But I have to get going… Eric is waiting by the door. I'll call you later, I promise." He kissed the top of her head and let her go. It was either that, or lift her into his arms and lock them in the bedroom, and damn the rest of the world.

Annie's fingers went to her lips, hoping to retain the tingle he left on them. She nodded again, unable to speak.

Gabe touched her cheek one last time, and went to find his jacket.

"Annie?"

She looked down, somewhat surprised to see Eric looking up at her. Jeez, she'd nearly forgotten he was there. "Yes?" she choked out, adjusting the scarf around his neck. He had that frail, beaten look about him again.

"Annie, everything will be okay. I know it will." Michael had said so, and he never lied.

"Thank you, Eric, I appreciate that. And thank you for breakfast; it was wonderful." She kissed his forehead and plopped his hat on his head. "Now scoot, and tell Irene I'll stop in later this evening."

"I will. Annie, um… thanks for… for looking out for me. I um… well, you know…." Eric felt himself blush a bit. He'd never actually told her he loved her, although he sure wanted to.

Annie smiled and tweaked his nose. "Yes, I know. Me too." She gave him a wink and pointed him to the door where Gabe was waiting, Eric's bag in his hand.

"Eric, take this out and start the truck. I'll be right out." He tossed the kid his keys before handing him the suitcase.

Annie took that moment to escape to her bedroom. She couldn't bear to say goodbye to her cowboy.

Gabe let her go. He wanted nothing more than to go to her, but he knew he couldn't push anymore. She needed time alone to absorb this new turn in her life. As did he, and he would call her later. Maybe they could at least meet for coffee… or a late, late dinner.

Spike jumped on the bed and sat next to Annie Rose, who was face down and hugging her pillow to her. What was wrong with this female? Couldn't she accept the inevitable? Why was she making this so difficult? He placed a paw on her arm and purred softly. Despite his frustration with her denial of the situation, he could at least attempt to comfort her.

Deirdre was waiting at the door when Geoffrey and Eric pulled up. After her husband had called to inform her of the situation, she had prepared one of the guestrooms before going back downstairs to wait. She was looking forward to seeing Eric again. He was such a nice boy, and he could keep her company until the twins returned on Friday.

As much as she wanted it to happen, Dee was surprised that Geoffrey actually spent the night with Annie. She never imagined the woman would… hm, how to put it? Move so quickly, allowing Geoffrey into her bed? Not that it was a problem, just quite unexpected. Dee ignored the tendril of jealousy curling in her belly. She wondered if Geoffrey would give her an update on their progress. Steven was certainly no help, not anymore, but no matter. Geoffrey was finally with his Annie, and they were now in possession of the journals. Dee could concentrate on spending the remainder of her time with her sons.

"Good morning, Geoffrey dear. Eric, how nice to see you again!" Deirdre said as the two of them came into the house. She took their coats hung them on the rack in the foyer, and then turned back with a smile.

Gabe grunted what passed for a hello, and stalked off to his den. Eric looked at Dee, and shrugged before glancing down at his suitcase and medical supplies.

"I'll help, Eric. Come along, your room is this way." She lifted a bag, motioning the boy to the stairs at the end of the hall.

Eric followed, his mouth open in awed wonder. He'd never ever been inside a house that big before! It almost reminded him of a museum where art and sculpture were displayed. He walked slowly and carefully as to not bump into anything. Jeez, there was fancy stuff setting on little tables all over the place! He looked up at the ceiling ten or twelve feet above. Aunt Irene's trailer would have fit right in with plenty of room to spare. He let out a surprised "whoa!" when he saw the staircase leading up to the bedrooms. Jeez, he figured a truck would easily fit on those, too. He was so stunned by everything in the house – including the house – that he only half heard Dee telling him to make himself at home, feel free to ask for anything, and she wouldn't take no for an answer. Then she giggled and said, "*Mi casa es su casa.*" He wasn't sure what it meant, but it sounded good. So yeah… he would make himself at home here. Even though it was big and fancy, it had a comfortable feel to it, just like Annie's cabin.

Deirdre set the bag in the closet, and then opened the door to the bathroom. "It's all yours, dear. You won't have to share with anyone. Now… lunch will be at noon. Do you have any preferences?"

"Huh? Oh, no, Deirdre. Anything is fine, thank you."

She nodded and sat on the end of the bed. "Now, about school. You may skip today, but I expect you to plan on going tomorrow. The bus runs right down the street, but if you would like, Geoffrey can take you. Agreed?"

He nodded. "Agreed."

"One more thing. Even though Annie and Geoffrey know about Steven… Michael, well, you and I know… more. And we shouldn't speak of it around them. Do you understand what I'm saying?"

"I do, and don't worry. But Dee, things weren't going too good this morning. I'm kinda worried."

She sighed and leaned back, propped on her elbows. "Tell me everything, Eric."

Dee paced in the living room, absently sipping a cup of lukewarm tea. Eric had filled her in on the morning's events at Annie's. It wasn't supposed to happen that way! It had started out so well, too. When she tried to ask Geoffrey about it before lunch, he mumbled how he didn't have time to discuss matters and stormed off to the studio. She was at a loss as to what to do next. She hoped like heck that Steven would return soon and help with some answers.

Gabe sat at his desk, flipping through his list of musicians and hoping like hell that he could reach Wolff and Mick, and that they would be willing to return. They'd both been with him, with SD, since day one. At least up until the band broke up on a whim of the almighty great and powerful asshole Gabe Evans.

He sighed, sipped his water, and jotted down a few more names and numbers, just in case his old violinist and drummer told him to take a flying fuck. God, he hoped not. He only wanted the best for this CD, already titled *Dream Again*, and Mick and Wolff were it. Alex and Billy and Dave, too, but what were the odds he could even find them, let alone convince them to come on board again? Damn, and if they did? Just might be what SD Productions needed to survive. Gabe hadn't told Dee or Kyle or Jen, but the financial situation wasn't nearly as rosy as they'd been led to believe. Most of the staff had long ago been let go in an effort to cut cost anywhere and everywhere, but with no work coming in? Nope, wasn't pretty. Only the sporadic sales of the few albums already under their label of Glazed Eye Music were keeping the company from locking the doors forever. Sales of SD's music barely trickled anymore. Sure, every now and then a die-hard fan would replace a worn out album or cassette with a new CD, but there weren't many new fans flocking to buy. Why should they? Promotion and touring were what sold music, bottom line. To do that, the fans expected something new now and then, not always rehashing the oldies but goodies.

Gabe could only blame himself for this mess. He hadn't written squat in years, other than the recent tunes, nor had he been out hustling up any new talent. Nope, he'd just sat around, playing family man and pretending all was just ducky. Probably why he'd been funneling his own funds into SD Production's accounts. Blood money, in a sense. Well, he could do it for a little while longer before he had to sell the farm, so yeah, they needed this new CD to survive.

Mmhmm. Now secretary, Jenna could call everyone on the new list and hopefully sweet talk the first four into coming back. They always did have a soft spot for the lovely Mrs. Davidson.

Moving on…

Gabe was certain that Annie would let him record and use her song, "Dream Again." That, along with the two he'd written at River Ridge were a good start. Maybe he would redo "The Dream" – have it be the first cut, and "Dream Again" the last.

He jotted down a few more notes and then called to see if Kyle had arrived yet. He wasn't surprised when there was no answer, which meant Jen wasn't in either. Which meant that they were most likely still lingering in bed. Worse than rabbits, they were, but at least it wasn't in his office this time. They thought he wasn't aware of their romantic little escapades in his personal space, although he knew better. Chet was quite the mimic, and the bird loved to talk.

Ah well, no sense in wasting any more time waiting for the dawdling Davidson's. Gabe picked up his notes and went to find his piano. He could at least start working on the music.

Kyle and Jenna arrived at the studio just before noon, having done just what Gabe had predicted – lingered in bed once they'd gotten the kids off to school. Their original intention was to snag another hour of sleep, but that only lasted long enough for them to dive under the blankets and snuggle for thirty seconds. One hour turned into two, then three, and after a very short nap they decided to head for work while they could still walk. It wasn't like there was anything pressing that needed to be attended to at the studio. Gabe was in a creative rut, and didn't seem even remotely interested in hustling any new talent, either. Kyle hadn't the ambition to even try, even if were capable of it.

The Davidson's were in the best of moods when they finally entered the doors of SD Productions. Kyle sent his wife off with a kiss before he went in search of his son of a bitch partner, who was not about to ruin his day. They'd been civil enough to each other yesterday, even kicking out some pretty decent material, but Kyle still couldn't forgive Gabe for cheating on Deirdre. Never ever ever.

Dee… God, what a woman she was. If Kyle had never met Jen, Deirdre would have been his choice in a mate. She seemed a bit stuffy at first with her lady of the manor airs, yet Davidson suspected something was smoldering just under the surface. That asshole Gabe was just throwing it all away.

He sighed, got his mind off of Dee, and knocked on his partner's door.

"Come in," said a voice from the other side.

Kyle peeked in. Huh. No Gabe. Just that damn Chet doing a very good imitation. Sometimes he really regretted buying that bird.

"Stupid critter," Kyle muttered.

"Ooh, baby," crooned Chet, sounding way too much like Jenna. "Ooh, yes! Yes! Oooh…"

"Shut the hell up," Kyle growled. *Stupid ass bird.*

"Come on, lover, give it to me," Chet purred.

That's it. The bird was dead. Kyle moved towards the cage, reviewing his options for parrot-cide, wondering which would look most like an accident. Or suicide. Could birds kill themselves? Maybe the damn thing would fly into a closed window.

"Gabe buddy!" Chet squawked in Kyle's voice.

Kyle moved closer to the parrot.

"Hi, Kyle." Gabe's voice this time. Goddamn bird.

"Kyle, helloooo…." Gabe's voice again, but from behind? Kyle turned to see his buddy standing in the doorway. He could hear Chet laughing behind him. Damn bird harassed him even more than Gabe did!

"I was wondering if you were planning on showing up today," Gabe said, straddling the end of the piano bench. He set his stack of papers in the center of it, and then leaned forward, resting his elbows on his thighs and lacing his fingers together. He had a feeling that the next few minutes wouldn't be pretty.

"I was um… delayed," Kyle mumbled. His mighty fine, fresh from the sack mood was rapidly vanishing. Now that he saw Evans again, all he could think about was the way Gabe looked at Annie, and he didn't like it one little bit.

"Hmm. I won't ask." Gabe tapped the papers in front of him and continued. "I've got some new material here. Actually, it's old music with different lyrics. From a new song writer."

"Another writer? Since when?"

"Since last night. This is her only one as far as I know, but there is potential for more."

Kyle wasn't sure he liked where this was going. "Anyone I know?"

"Mmhmm. Annie."

Kyle stiffened and gave Gabe that all too familiar glare.

Gabe slapped his hand down on the bench, anger rising in him. "Kyle, before you go off all half-cocked, there's something you should know about my relationship with Annie. It has Dee's full approval. She encouraged it. Hell, she even arranged it!"

"How convenient," Kyle muttered. "You expect me to believe a bullshit story like that?"

Gabe bit back his anger, taking a few deep breaths before he responded. "Whether you do or nor, it makes no difference to me. You'll either accept it or be happy for me, or you won't. I can't force you, nor will I waste my time trying to convince you. If you're truly my friend you won't question or judge me, Kyle. And if you can't trust me… can't believe in me, maybe we should call it quits right now. Done. Finished. It's your decision."

Kyle couldn't believe it. His best buddy was giving him an ultimatum? Jesus Christ! Over a woman? First he was throwing away a perfect marriage, and how he was ready to dump a perfect friendship? What the hell had Annie done to him? Must have been one hell of a good lay if she turned Gabe's head like that, the slut.

He sat silent for a while, torn between wanting to pound some sense into Gabe's head and wanting to believe this man he'd loved and trusted for nearly half his life. His hands balled into fists, white-knuckled and tense against his thighs. He felt sick to his stomach and sick at heart. He could feel Gabe's intense gaze burning into him, yet dared not look back. Not yet. *Oh God, what to do?*

Gabe stared at Kyle, willing him to give in to the inevitable. Lord, he hated doing this to him, but if it had to come to losing Kyle or losing Annie, was there really a choice? His heart nearly broke at the thought, spurring him to bend a little.

"Kyle, look at me. Please…"

Kyle gave him a short glance before he went back to staring at the floor.

Gabe sighed. "Kyle, I need to know. Now. Sit down and talk to me, or at least listen to what I have to say. Maybe if… if you hear the rest of it, your decision will be easier to make. I um… Jesus, I don't want to lose you, buddy. Please…"

Kyle sat, straddling the other end of the bench. He really didn't want to be without Gabe, either. Maybe there was more to it than he thought. Gabe wouldn't lie about something Dee said, not when it would be too easy to check. Things weren't always as they seemed, right? A quick flash of Steve's words shot through his brain. *Trust Gabe...* He jumped and tensed a little when he felt Gabe's warm, rough hand cover his own. A strange hint of a tingle ran up his arm and he quickly pulled away.

"Kyle, would you listen? Please?"

Kyle gave Gabe a short nod. "I'm listenin'. Um, Gabe? Are you plannin' on divorcin' Dee?"

Gabe bit his lower lip and closed his eyes. God, it was the only real solution so that he could be with Annie, but divorce was something he just couldn't force himself to do. He answered honestly.

"No, Kyle, I don't. I haven't even considered it."

Kyle chuffed a bitter laugh. "Might be a little awkward, won't it? Two women in your bed? Dee ain't no groupie, pal. Doubt she'd go for a threesome no matter if she supposedly pushed you and Annie together."

Gabe nearly snapped and punched his friend, but held himself to gripping Kyle by the chin and forcing eye contact.

"You said you'd listen, Kyle, and yet you blather on." Gabe let go and laced his fingers together again, more to restrain his hands than anything.

Kyle felt pretty bad when he saw actual pain in his buddy's eyes. Damn, this dude was hurtin', and he sure wasn't helping any. "Sorry, Gabe. Tell me what you have to say."

"Thank you. Like I said, there's something you need to know about Deirdre and me. I never said anything before out of respect for her, but now I'm free to tell you. Dee and I don't have a real marriage."

"Sure you do! I was there, remember?"

"No, no... I mean yes, we are legally married, but it goes no further than that. It's a marriage in name only. It always has been."

"Aw, come on, Gabe! I see how much she loves you and you love her. Or at least you did. You can't tell me..."

"But I am. We married for the sole reason of giving the twins a name and a two-parent home. There's no romance involved."

"The hell you say! You mean you never...?"

Gabe raised an eyebrow.

"Jesus! You're tellin' me that you and Dee don't... Haven't... Dude, I can't believe it!"

"She's never been in my bed, Kyle. Now drop it." Gabe dropped his gaze to the papers in front of him. It wasn't really a lie since any sex with Dee had been in her room, and Kyle certainly didn't need to know any details.

"Whoa. You and Dee never made love. Go figger. Man, if she was my wife, I'd..."

"Enough, Kyle. I said drop it. Although I'm sure my wife would be flattered to hear how you lust for her," Gabe said with a chuckle.

Kyle blushed. "I um… Ooh. Heh. Sorry…"

"Forget it. I've had similar thoughts of Jen. And before you get all in my face about that, it's time for a subject change. We have work to do here, and you still have to give me an answer. What will it be, Kyle? Accept my feelings for Annie, or do we say good bye right now."

"You really love her? Annie, I mean."

"I think I have since the beginning of time, Kyle, and I finally found her. And Dee… I love her too, you know. I love her like a sister."

"I guess I can't argue any of that. Hell, I remember a few times when…" Kyle shrugged. "Anyway, you found her, you love her, and… and I guess I'm happy for ya, Gabe. I don't much envy the position you're in, but it's your life. You gotta live it how you know best."

"Thank you for that."

"Gabe?"

"Yeah?"

"Got one more question."

"And that would be…?"

"You and Dee really never made love?"

"We never made love, Kyle." *Just had much needed sex a few times.*

"So you um… Jeez, you haven't done it since when? God, man!"

"I didn't say that…"

"So you cheated on Dee?"

"I didn't say that, either."

"You and Annie, eh?"

"Never have."

"Really? Whew. Man… This is… This is really fuckin' with my head. Give me a little time to get used to it, okay?"

"Take all the time you need. One thing, though."

"Which is?"

"You will treat Annie with every bit of respect that you show to Dee. Got it? No nasty looks, no innuendos, no rude comments… If you have anything bad to say, you'd best keep it to yourself. Got it?"

"Got it." To be honest, Kyle didn't think Annie was all that bad. She was pretty and sweet, and looked totally huggable – or so he would have thought if he hadn't have been so pissed off about her wrecking Dee's marriage. "Okay, so what potential hit did she write? Will it go gold? Platinum? Song of the year?"

"I don't detect any sarcasm, Kyle. Are you slipping, or was there none intended?" Gabe asked with a hint of a smile and a sigh of relief.

"Slippin'. C'mon, let me see." Kyle snatched up the papers from the bench. "Which one?"

"Right there on top."

"This one? "Dream Again"?" Kyle looked at the music Gabe had written for the new lyrics. "It's almost the same as "The Dream." Annie wrote this?"

"The lyrics, yes. What do you think?"

"Huh. Well, okay. Seems to work. Yeah, we could do it. Annie? Red Annie? Go figger."

"The one and only. She also wrote that corny poem you found in the office last week. I think she has more, but I'm not sure," Gabe smiled. "I'll have to ask her cat."

"Come again? Her cat?"

"Long story. I'll tell you about it someday, but for now, let's get to work, Kyle."

Gabe looked at his watch, shocked to see that it was already after four and far too late for even a late lunch with Annie. He was even more shocked when he realized that he'd gone nearly all day without even thinking of her. Blame the buddy. Once he and Kyle started working and the creative juices were flowing, the hours had flown by.

What a productive day it had been. The music was finished for two of the three new songs. Mick and Wolff both returned Gabe's calls, saying that they'd love to return to SD. Jenna was typing up a contract for a promising young mandolin player, and Gabe's band was nearly complete. Things were certainly looking up! Best of all, Kyle was Kyle again, and Gabe came very close to hugging the hell out of him.

Time to call it a day and call Annie, and apologize for him not contacting her sooner. Gabe reached for his phone, but ended up smacking himself on the forehead. Jeez, he'd forgotten to get her number! How stupid could he be? His useless phonebook was chucked across the room after it failed to yield those coveted numbers, there was no listing for any Benton whatsoever. It made sense, though, her being a single woman living out in the middle of nowhere. Way out in the middle of nowhere, which was the only thing that prevented him from jumping in his truck and driving out to see her. It was just too far, and he'd be very, very late for dinner. Not that Dee would mind, eh? And didn't she have Annie's number? He grinned and reached for the phone again, only to have it ring the second he touched it.

"Evans."

"Gabe! Tyler Howe, here. Long time no see."

"Tyler! How the hell are you? How's married life going?"

"Couldn't be better. I wish I'd met Anne years and years ago."

"Hm. I know the feeling," Gabe mumbled.

"What was that? Gabe?"

"Oh, nothing. So to what do I owe the pleasure of your phone call?"

"I haven't had any calls to bail you out of jail in a while and I wondered if you were still among the living."

"Ha ha. You know what a fine, upstanding member of the community I am! So, what's up?"

"We're having a little party next week, and we were wondering if you and your lovely wife would like to join us. Assuming Dee is up to going out…?"

"I um… She's doing better, Ty, although I don't think she's quite up to that yet. But thank you for the invitation. "

"Hopefully soon, then. Oh! Rumor has it that you're putting the band back together. That's wonderful, Gabe! What prompted this?"

"Many things, the main one being that if I don't get off my ass and get busy, I'll soon be unemployed. It looks promising, Ty." Gabe was eager to talk about this new turning point in his life, yet couldn't get Annie off his mind. He had to talk to her soon. "Hey, buddy, I hate to cut this short, but I was just on my way out the door…"

"Oh! I'm sorry. Well then, get on home to your family, and give Dee a hug for me. Anne just told me to tell you congrats on getting the band back together, too."

Anne… Annie. Could it be…?

"Tyler, not to bring up the past, but that nurse you used to date – her last name wouldn't be Benton, would it?"

"As a matter of fact, it is. Why?"

Gabe stifled a huge sigh of relief, and felt just a twinge of jealousy. "I recently met a nurse by the name of Annie… what are the odds? You um… you wouldn't happen to remember her phone number, would you?"

"Her number? Yes, I have it. Gabe…" Tyler felt his old uneasy feelings return, remembering that night in the restaurant and how obsessed Annie seemed to be with Gabe's rose.

"She um… she wrote a song we're thinking of using on our new album, Ty. I… I need to call her in regards to it."

"You're kidding. Annie? Well… alright then. Hold on and I'll look it up for you." Ty gave Gabe the number and they said their good byes. He wondered what his friend was hiding.

Gabe sat for a long moment, drumming his fingers on the desk. Annie and Tyler. Jesus, and they'd nearly gotten married! But she turned him down because she was waiting for … for the right man? Oh God, and her Mr. Right was married to Mrs. Wrong. He sighed again, in despair this time, and dropped his head to his desk. What a mess.

"Gabe! I'm headin' home, buddy!" Kyle called from the hall before he peeked into the office. "Gabe? What's up, man?"

Evans looked up, sat up. "Not a thing, Kyle. Long day and a bit of a headache are all. Go on home and I'll see you tomorrow."

"You sure? You look like hell."

"Probably. Headache… Go on. Get. Shoo. Vamoose." Gabe slapped on a happy little grin and waved Kyle away.

"Okay, but call me if you need to talk, okay?"

"I might even call you anyway. 'Night, Kyle."

"Later, buddy."

Gabe waited until he saw Kyle out in the parking lot before he dialed his seven precious numbers, all in vain. The phone rang twenty times before he gave in and hung up. Good thing he didn't waste his time driving all the way out there when she wasn't even home. Then again, where was she? She was scheduled to work that night, right? Oh God, what if something happened to her? Out there alone in the middle of nowhere...

He grabbed his jacket and ran to his truck, calling Dee from his cell phone to let her know he'd be a little late for dinner.

Annie woke to the ringing of her phone. Figures that it would be work calling, asking her to come in early. Might as well since she had nothing better to do. Gabe hadn't called for that lunch, hadn't called her at all for that matter. He probably realized that she was right after all. No matter how they felt about each other, it just wouldn't work out. She ruffled Spike's fur on her way to the shower, and within the hour she was on her way to Brighton and a night of baby care in the NICU. At least the mental stimulation involved would keep her mind off of her cowboy. She hoped.

Gabe was in a near panic all the way to Hidden Lake, calling Annie every few minutes from his cell. Horrible thoughts ran through his mind. What if she was hurt while riding her horse? What if she slipped and fell while walking to the barn? What if some psycho wandered into her unlocked cabin? Jesus...

He picked up speed, nearly becoming airborne every time he went over a hill on the long road. He needn't have bothered. Once he pulled into her drive way and saw that her truck was gone, he pulled back out and drove home. So much for that.

Once again, Deirdre was disappointed by Geoffrey's early arrival home. Couldn't those two just get it together? She knew she didn't have much time left; it was imperative that Annie and Gabe commit to each other before it was too late. She knew it would be easier for her husband if his wife was no longer in the picture, yet she couldn't go until she knew for sure that Annie would take her place, and then some. Her feelings of jealousy left her feeling somewhat guilty, but Gabe deserved to be loved by the woman he loved. It made her happy and sad at the same time.

And where was Steven? She hadn't seen or heard of him since the previous night. He wouldn't leave without telling her good bye, would he? The very thought depressed her even more.

It was difficult for her to remain cheerful through dinner. Geoffrey was sullen, hardly saying two words to her all evening, and Eric was acting very odd. Deirdre was worried about the boy. His color was bad, even for him, and he seemed shaky. It just didn't feel right.

After picking at his food for ten minutes, Eric excused himself and went upstairs. He felt icky… Dizzy and shaky, and felt like he had to throw up. His mind was weird too. He couldn't focus on anything. Maybe he was getting the flu. He hoped not, 'cuz then he'd have to go to the hospital and nobody needed that hassle right now. He'd probably feel better after a nap. He kicked off his shoes and fell onto his bed.

Gabe shoved the food he didn't even bother tasting around on his plate. Christ, where was Annie? Just before dinner he'd called the pediatric ward and was told that she wasn't there, at least not in their unit. She was scheduled to be in later, although no one would know where she'd be working until closer to seven.

He glanced at the clock. Another hour to wait, dammit. He nodded absently to Eric when the kid mumbled something about not feeling well, and then helped Dee clear the table. God, she was just this side of bitchy this evening. What was up with that? He told her to go put her feet up and he'd take care of the dishes. She gave him a curt nod, and slowly headed for the stairs. He couldn't bear to watch her leave. She looked to be in pain again, and it was easier if he denied it a little longer. Once the kitchen was tidied up, he slunk off to his den and picked at his guitar, waiting until he could call his Annie.

Deirdre sat at her window seat and gazed down at the park below. Any moonlight was blocked by a thick cloud cover, turning the snow on the ground to a dull gray. It depressed her even more. She thought it best, given her mood, that she take some pain meds and make an early night of it; neither Geoffrey nor Eric would be good company, either, given their sullen moods. She went to the bathroom and found her pills, and decided to check on Eric before she retired.

Annie checked the monitors over the babies' isolettes. The numbers looked good; everyone was stable, vital signs normal. She considered calling Gabe, just to check on Eric, of course. Sure, that would work! Consider quickly changed to decision, and she picked up the phone. As she punched in the numbers, she hoped that Gabe answered and not Deirdre, even if Mrs. Evans would hand the phone over to Mr. Evans. Given the changes in relationships, it was pretty darn awkward for Annie to speak to Dee.

One ring, two rings… only to be interrupted by a monitor alarm blaring across the room. Annie slammed the phone down and hurried over to find that it was no false alarm, unlike the dozens of other times already since her shift began. The infant was a dusky blue in color, with no visible respirations. Lisa, her co-worker, was called over to assist.

Annie quickly checked the baby's mouth for any signs of regurgitated formula while Lisa stood by, suction catheter ready.

"Suction," Annie nodded, slapping on a stethoscope and listening for the heart rate. It was low, but there.

As soon as Lisa cleared the airway, Annie applied bag and mask, pushing oxygen into the tiny lungs. The baby responded immediately and began breathing unassisted, turning back to a healthy pink color. Crisis averted, but the phone call to Gabe would have to wait. Annie would need to keep a close eye on this little angel for a while. She sat at the bedside, opened the chart, and documented the events of the mini-resuscitation.

Gabe reached for the ringing phone, only to hear the slam of the receiver on the other end before he could even say hello. Probably wasn't Annie anyway. She'd just be arriving at Brighton, and he figured he'd be the last thing on her mind about now. He returned to idly plucking at the strings of his guitar while he waited for seven o'clock to roll around.

The lure of a relaxing bubble bath drew Dee away from her thoughts of an early sleep. She was so miserable and achy; perhaps the warm, swirling water would help ease her pain.

She shed her clothes, wrapped a robe around her, and found a novel she'd been meaning to read, and then made her slow way down the hall to the bathroom with the Jacuzzi – namely the one in the master bedroom, which happened to be Gabe's room. He told her many times that she was free to use it.

As she reached for the door, she thought she heard a whisper.

"Geoffrey? Is that you?"

Finding herself alone, she smiled and tried once more.

"Steven...?"

The whisper came again, calling to her in a child-like voice.

"Eric... Is that you? Where are you, dear?" She glanced up and down the dim hallway. No one there.

She felt the same sense of unease they'd felt during dinner and moved a few doors down.

"Eric, dear, are you awake?" she asked, opening his door. "Eric?"

She could see him, illuminated by the nightlight, still dressed and sprawled on his bed as if he'd fallen there. A shoe dangled from his small foot.

"Eric!" she cried, dropping her book and rushing to him. "Eric, wake up!"

His skin felt cold and clammy when she touched his forehead, his body limp and unresponsive when she shook his shoulder.

"Geoffrey!" she screamed, running to the door. "Gabe, hurry!"

It took him only seconds to fly upstairs in answer to Dee's frantic call. He had never heard her sound so distressed before. She'd actually called him Gabe? Oh, this couldn't be good.

He found her in Eric's room, cradling the boy's limp body.

"Dee, what the..."

"Call an ambulance, Geoffrey."

"You call, Dee. I'll get him downstairs."

Gabe wrapped the child in a blanket and took him to the foyer, holding him close while he waited for help, rocking the bundle in his arms and praying like hell.

Within minutes, Eric was on his way to Brighton, with Gabe following the speeding ambulance. Dee went to the leather sofa in the office to wait for news of Eric's condition.

"Steven?" she whispered into the darkness of the room. "Steven, where are you?"

There was no answer.

After an hour's wait in the ER, Gabe finally received news of Eric. He stood to greet the solemn doctor heading his way.

"Mr. Evans? I'm Dr. Hunter. Where's Mrs. Peters?"

"She um… She's hospitalized with an injury," Gabe replied, shaking the man's hand. "He's staying with us in the interim. How is he?"

"In here." Dr. Hunter led Gabe to a small room, waving him to a seat. "Not good, I'm afraid. He's in a diabetic coma. The onset of this disease was rather sudden. We never picked up on it in the clinic." He paused, sighed, and continued. "It's not all that uncommon, though… pancreatic issues…"

"What?"

"It's detailed. I'm afraid I haven't the time to explain right now. We're swamped tonight. I can have one of the nurses print out some literature for you if you'd like." Hunter stood, indicating that he had to get back to work.

"I… yeah, I think I should review. So uh… Eric…? Will he recover?"

"He should, yes. We'll keep him in the intensive care unit for a while, and then admit him to the floor for education while he recovers. He's staying with you, you said? Do you have guardianship?"

"Yes and no. Not legally. Friend of the family is all. God, this is…" Gabe trailed off, nearly overwhelmed with this latest mess.

"Have his aunt contact us soon. We'll need her permission as far as releasing medical information to you, Mr. Evans. Until then… Well, you may visit, but that will be the extent of it. I'm afraid we really can't tell you much more than his condition."

Gabe nodded. "Thank you for that, Dr. Hunter. Can I at least stay with him until he's settled? He's a friend of Annie's, too. Annie Benton?" …?"

Hunter smiled. "I know her well. Friend of yours as well?"

"You could say that, yes."

"She's working tonight as far as I know. Will you be letting her know about Eric? I can call up there later if not."

"I'll do it. And thank you." Gabe shook the man's hand again and went to wait for Eric to be transferred from the ER to the PICU.

Annie… She had to be told.

Irene, also. Gabe would let her know that Eric had been admitted to the Peds ICU, and once that was done he would find Annie.

He followed Eric as he was taken upstairs, although he wasn't sure why. It wasn't as if he could do anything. The boy was still unconscious and intubated, and would be placed on a ventilator as soon as he was in his room. Gabe didn't know what else to do. He stood at the reception desk and watched Eric wheeled through the double doors of the restricted area.

"Mr. Evans! What'cha doin' here?"

Oh God, that grating voice. It was all he needed right now. Gabe did his best to put a civil look on his face and turned to face Edith Haggins. Edith the Hag.

"Hello, Edith, how are you?"

"I'm just dandy! You lookin' for Annie?" Edith asked, and then said, "She's not workin' in here tonight."

"Uh, yes, I am. Would you happen to know where she is?"

"Maybe I do, maybe I don't," Edith teased. She hoped he'd notice how witty she was.

Christ woman, spit it out! He actually felt like punching her. Instead, he said through ever-so-slightly gritted teeth, "Would you be most kind and tell me where she is? That is, if you know."

"Oh, I know! I know ever'thin' that goes on around here. The stories I could tell... Why just last week we had..."

"Please, Annie?" Gabe's hand was beginning to curl into a fist. He would never actually hit a woman, but he could still fantasize about it, especially this particular one.

"Okay," Edith sighed. "She's workin' in the NICU. I can take you over there!" Her blurry, pale blue eyes glittered in anticipation.

"The NICU? No, that won't be necessary, I can find it. Thank you Edith, you have been most helpful." *Not to mention an obnoxious ass.* Gabe made a hasty retreat to the elevator.

Edith was hot on his trail. "I'm headin' thata way anyhow 'cuz I got a few rooms to clean on that side of the hospital. There's only a coupla us workin' at night, so we goes all over the place."

What could he say? He gave her a curt nod and allowed himself to be escorted the opposite end of the huge building where the NICU was located.

Would this goddamn woman never shut up? She had been rattling on non-stop since they got on the elevator. Gabe didn't actually hear a thing she said, just was aware of the fact that her most annoying voice was akin to fingernails on a chalkboard, amplified through high quality headphones and projected into his aching head.

"Here we are!" Edith chirped. She hoped that Gabe had enjoyed her stories about some of the things she had seen around there. Especially the one about the intern and the nurse she had caught screwin' in the utility closet. Did he get the hint?

Gabe nearly dropped to his knees to give eternal thanks to God in Heaven when Edith finally left. Now, to find Annie. He took another elevator to the Neonatal Intensive Care Unit where signs on the doors proclaimed it a restricted area. Did he dare go in? Might as well, what was the worst that could happen?

He walked down the hall to the reception desk checking the layout of the unit. To his left, a long hall filled with doorways stretched out before him.

Nursing staff could be seen through the partially curtain-covered windows. Were these the baby nurseries?

"May I help you?"

He looked at the receptionist behind the desk. *Put on the 'ol smile, Gabe boy... this might take some doing.*

"Good evening. I was wondering if you could help me. I'm looking for Annie Benton, and the clerk in Pediatrics told me that I could find her over here. We missed our dinner engagement tonight when she was called in early, and I wanted see if maybe we could have a quick coffee together instead." He turned up the wattage on his best 'turn 'em to quivering piles of Jell-O' smile. He knew he was pushing it with the 'going in early' story, but he had to try something.

It worked.

The receptionist felt herself blushing from head to toe. Gabe Evans... right there in front of her! She had been a fan for a few years, but since there was nothing new lately she had nearly forgotten about him. And then damned if they weren't playing some of his old videos again.

"Annie. Uh, yes... She's in room six, just down the hall. Technically, you aren't allowed in there, but I won't tell if you won't tell," she flirted. "Just scrub up before you go down." She nodded towards the sinks.

"Thank you... very much," Gabe murmured, and gave her a wink.

After he had done as he was instructed, he found room six, but should he knock or just walk in? He peeked into the window, looking through an opening in the curtain. Oh God, there she was...

His Annie was standing at one of those incubator things and she was holding the tiniest baby Gabe had ever seen. Christ, that thing wasn't any bigger than a kitten!

Annie wrapped the baby up in a blanket and placed it gently back into the isolette. She made sure all the lead wires were plugged into the cable correctly, and then reached above her to turn the cardiac monitor back on. She made a few notes in the chart on the shelf behind the isolette, and then turned back around.

A movement in the door's window caught her eye.

Gabe moved closer to the window to get a better look. The way she handled that baby... She was so gentle! He feared that if it was him he might accidentally crush the tiny thing. Wow... How could anything that small survive? He put his arm on the glass of the window, and then rested his head against it as he stared into the room.

Annie looked at the man who stood on the other side of the door. Darn, now she was hallucinating. Every male who walked by was beginning to look like Gabe.

Their eyes met and she felt her knees go weak. It was Gabe. Thank God she had already put that baby back, as she would most certainly have dropped it in her surprise.

She regained her composure and walked to the door.

"Gabe! What are you doing here?" she asked, as she walked into the hall, leaving the door open so she could hear any alarms.

He raised his hand and placed it next to Annie's face, then ever so softly ran his thumb down the line of her jaw from chin to earlobe. Eric and the babies were forgotten. This is what he had come for.

She nearly fell over. Thankfully, she was holding on to the door for support.

"Gabe?" she whispered. God, she was tingling all over... She stared into his eyes and knew she could never really stay away from him.

"Annie, do you have a few minutes? I... I want to..."

He was cut short by the shrill sound of a monitor blaring a warning. Annie shot back into the room to see what the problem was. Fortunately, it was another false alarm. She returned to him right away.

"I can get away in a few minutes. Lisa will be back from her break soon, and then I can go. I can meet you in the cafeteria... Okay?"

"I'll be there. Maybe even buy you a cup of coffee," he grinned.

She just smiled and closed the door.

When Gabe walked back to the elevator, another nurse passed him. As she gave him a second, then third look, he glanced at her nametag. *Lisa*. Good. He wouldn't have to track her down and tell her to hurry her ass up! Now, to get to the cafeteria without running into the irksome Edith the hag. The mere thought made him shudder.

"Lisa, you're back. I'm going to take a break now, that okay with you?" Annie said as soon as the other nurse hit the door.

"Sure. You seem in a hurry. Any special reason?"

"A... a friend of mine stopped by. He wants to go get a cup of coffee, so I'll be in the cafeteria if you need me."

"This friend, he wouldn't happen to be that hunky guy in the jeans who just left here, would he?" Lisa said. *Boy, Annie, if it is, you are one lucky girl!*

"I didn't happen to see what he was wearing, but he did just leave. I'll be back in about fifteen," Annie told her.

"Oh hell, take a half hour. I'll cover for you. Have fun!"

"Thanks. See ya in a few." She could not wait to join Gabe. Instead of waiting for the elevators, she flew down the stairs to the basement cafeteria. She found him sitting at her favorite table in the corner with two cups of coffee in front of him. It made her smile.

Gabe stood when he saw her enter the room. In just a moment she would be right here with him and... aw God, he could hardly wait to take her in his arms. He quickly scanned the cafeteria, smiling to himself when he saw no one else there.

Annie walked up to where he was standing, but before she could even say hello, he had wrapped his arms around her and was giving her the most incredible kiss. She could not believe it! Right there in the cafeteria? What if someone saw? Well then, let them look. She returned his kiss, giving as good as she got.

From far away, Gabe heard a door open; they were no longer alone. Reluctantly, he pushed himself away from his Annie and they both sat down at the table.

"Gabe, I... you... what brought you out this way? I'm glad you're here, but it really surprises me," Annie said.

"I couldn't reach you at home. Where were you all day?"

"I was home but the phone never rang. Well, except once, but it was work. I was called in early. "

"No wonder you never answered. I called around four-thirty."

"Figures... But you're here now and that's all I care about." She smiled up at him.

Eric. He had just now remembered Eric! Gabe reached across the table and took both of Annie's in his. This was going to be very difficult.

"Annie, I'm afraid I have some bad news."

She froze. Oh God, here it comes. He changed his mind about her. She knew it was too good to be true.

"What is it?" she asked. She could feel a ball of ice forming in her stomach, spreading its frigid fingers through the rest of her body.

"It's Eric; he's here in the hospital. I'm not sure exactly what's wrong, but he's in intensive care on life support."

Annie's relief at not hearing the 'I love you, but' speech was short-lived. *Eric!*

"Oh no! Gabe, what happened? I've got to get up there and see him!" She jumped from her seat, bumping the table hard enough to tip both cups of coffee into sloshing their contents onto the floor.

Gabe was right behind her.

He took her hand and together they ran from the cafeteria to be with Eric.

Edith watched the couple from her hidin' place next to the vendin' machines. She had been disappointed when Annie had shown up and joined Gabe; she'd been thinkin' about joinin' him herself. After all, he did grab two cups of coffee. And that kiss! Sweet Jesus, what she wouldn't have given to be in Annie's shoes right then. They didn't even hang around long enough to drink their coffee. Talk about eager beavers! She didn't think that the shy Annie would be such a slut! Wonder where they was runnin' off to go do it? She'd follow 'em and find out.

Annie was updated on Eric's condition. He was critical, but would recover, thanks to Deirdre and Gabe. In addition to his CF, he did indeed have diabetes, which had gone undetected and resulted in a life-threatening situation. He would be treated in the ICU for a few days, and then be transferred to the pediatric floor where he would be taught how to live with his new disease.

From that day forward he would have to monitor his diet, his blood sugar, and more than likely give himself shots of insulin several times a day.

Annie had called NICU to let them know she would be back soon; she had a family crisis in the PICU. Not a problem, she was told, they could cover for her for a little while longer.

Gabe called Deirdre with the news. She was relieved that he would recover, but was sorry that his visit with her had been such a short one.

"Gabe, I've got to get back. I'm already almost a half hour late," Annie said, walking back to her ward.

"I know. When can we get together? I mean get together without any interruptions. It seems like every time..."

She cut him off. "I know, and I am sorry. I want to us to be together too, but... well, Eric... I couldn't just let him be by himself. My God, if he had been home alone he would be dead by now!"

"No, I didn't mean it like that; I'm thankful that we were there for him. I mean... when can we go... go on a date? You know, get to know each other. It seems like we have completely neglected that most important part of a relationship and jumped right to the next level. Not that I mind, but I want to know Annie. Who is she?"

She knew exactly what he was talking about; she wanted the same thing. This might work out after all! Now, if they could just get their schedules to mesh.

"I have to work tomorrow and Thursday, but I have Friday and Saturday off. Could we do something then?"

"Not Friday, the boys will be home. Wait, you could come over for dinner," Gabe suggested.

"That might be a little confusing for them. Children that age are very perceptive, and yours are more than most."

"That's an understatement. I love them more than anything, but I must admit that they are the strangest kids I have ever seen. Sometimes I just cannot understand where they get it from." Gabe hesitated, and then smiled. "Must be from their father. He is the poster child for strange... Especially lately!"

"Well, how about Saturday then. Would you like to come over for a ride? Donny will be raring to go by then, and maybe even Wanda will want to get out for a while. You do ride, don't you?"

Steve's words came back to Gabe. *You meet some of the nicest people on horseback.*

That did it. A ride it would be.

"Yes, I've been on a horse or two. A ride sounds wonderful. What time should I be there?"

"Any time. I'll make dinner for us afterward."

"No you won't. I think we should go out. I know a great little place not far from the studio. It's a microbrewery and restaurant, and the food is excellent.

What do you think?"

"Oh no, I can cook. We..."

"Annie, I don't want you to take this the wrong way, and please forgive me if it sounds, well, rude, but have you noticed that when we are alone together - truly alone - we don't have much to say?"

She nodded. Boy, did she ever notice.

"That's why I was thinking of going out. We never seem to lack for conversation when, uh, ooh... how to put this?"

"Don't try to explain. I know exactly what you mean, and you're right - a night on the town it is. I hate to think of you coming all the way out to my place then having to run back to your house to change into something not horsy, though."

"Would you object if I brought something not 'horsy' to change into? That is, if you will allow me to use your facilities to clean up."

"I think we could work something out. Spike will chaperone," Annie joked.

"Oh God, that cat? If I know him he'll probably have a bottle of champagne chilling when we return all 'horsey'. Where did you ever find him, anyway?"

"He found me. Strangest kitty I ever did see."

"Maybe he and the twins would hit it off," Gabe laughed.

Annie smiled. It was so nice just to talk like this; no pressure, no wondering what will happen next, was she doing the right thing...? Just as long as he didn't touch her. Not yet, at least, because that would be her undoing and she really needed to get to work.

They had reached the entrance to the NICU. Gabe looked around, and seeing no one, gave his Annie a quick but meaningful kiss. *Let her think about that tonight!*

"I will most definitely call you tomorrow. When is a good time?"

"Uh, any time after two. That's when I usually get up when I'm working." *The pig... Kissing her like that.* How was she supposed to concentrate on infants now? Annie thought she would die from happiness right there in the hall.

"Call you at two. Until then..." Another kiss, exactly like the first. *Ha! Think about that one too!* Gabe turned and disappeared into the elevator.

Annie practically floated back to her room and went back to work.

Chapter Thirty

The remainder of the week flew by. Annie was still working in the NICU where she would be there for a while as the preemie-baby business was unusually busy this winter.

Gabe and Kyle were having a great time. They had a full roster for their band, including several of their original members, and rehearsals were going great.

James and Jeremy returned from Montana on Thursday night, along with Al and Marie. The elder Evans' spent the night with Deirdre and Geoffrey, then returned home Friday evening. During their entire stay, neither Al nor Marie ever heard the names of Steve or Annie mentioned; it wasn't time yet.

Annie and Gabe talked on the phone at least once a day. The calls were always short, Gabe being busy at the studio, and Annie having her own chores to do. Besides, they wanted to save the more interesting conversations for Saturday.

The only two people not happy at the moment were Deirdre and Eric. She hadn't seen Steven since Monday, and her pain was a constant torment to her. She would need the stronger narcotics soon.

Eric was just plain pissed. He was on the vent for nearly two days, and then transferred out to the regular floor. He hated the idea of those stinkin' shots every day and poking his finger before every meal. The whole business sucked. And as if that weren't enough, his hormones were kicking in. He'd been having very disturbing dreams about girls lately, and they were getting worse - or better, depending on how one looked at it. Regardless, he thought it sucked.

His aunt came to visit him just before she went to the rehab hospital. She would spend a few days there until she could handle the stairs at home. That sucked too. She would be off of work for at least two months and there would be no money for a very long time.

Gabe and Annie's first date was disastrous. It started out well enough, being a beautiful day for a ride, and the horses were most cooperative. She insisted that Gabe take Adonis since he seemed so out of place on the placid Wanda, and could not take her eyes from her cowboy during the entire ride. As good as Michael looked on a horse, Gabe looked even better. It was hard to believe that he was the writer-musician, and his gentleman brother was the calf roper.

After the ride they showered - separately, of course, and changed into un-horsey clothes. It was all very proper and chaperoned by the hopelessly annoyed Spike, who had indeed been thinking champagne, served in a very cozy bubble bath built for two.

Dinner was as enjoyable as their horseback ride. The food was excellent, and the couple tried several of the beers brewed on the premises. They made small talk during the appetizers, mostly chat about the horses and the weather. Although Gabe loved hearing the sound of her voice, he soon tired on the inane chit-chat and decided to really dig in to who this woman really was. Lord, but he had a million questions to ask! Tyler Howe being on the top of the list...

Just as he was about to ask, the entrée was served. Just as he picked up his fork to dig into a mouth-watering salmon steak, he heard a voice he'd hoped to never hear again.

"Well, well... If it isn't the always delightful Geoffrey Evans," cooed Deanna. She sat, unwanted and uninvited at the table with them after dragging over an empty chair from a neighboring table.

Gabe's fork clattered to the table. He took a deep breath and gave Annie a look of apology before his face darkened and he turned to glare at NeeNee the nasty.

"Go away, NeeNee," he all but snarled.

"Why, Geoffrey? Oh! I see... You're here with your date. My my, you're taste in women is slipping a bit, love." Deanna gave him a smirk and turned to Annie. "You look familiar... Didn't I see you at the homeless shelter?"

"I... I volunteer there once in a while," Annie said quietly. Oh, she remembered Deanna and her venom all too well. She also knew darn well that the woman knew exactly who she was.

"No, I was thinking more... Oh, never mind." Annie was dismissed and Deanna turned her attention back to Gabe. "Does your wife know you're out slumming, Geoffrey?"

Gabe fought to keep his temper in check. Christ, he couldn't even answer for fear of exploding.

"Mrs. Evans knows we're here, Ms. Montgomery. It... it's a business dinner," Annie managed to choke out. She hoped she sounded convincing.

"Oh? Business dinner... Annie Bottoms, don't tell me you've turned pro!" Deanna laughed. "And here all this time I thought you gave it away. Is that why Tyler left you? Your price went up?"

Annie's face flamed in horrified embarrassment. She stared at her meal on the table, knowing that she'd never be able to eat it now.

"Oh for the love of..."Gabe growled. "Deanna, you have three seconds to get your skinny, snarky ass out of here or I'll do the honors myself by throwing you into the street."

"You wouldn't dare," she purred, helping herself to a grape tomato from Gabe's salad. "Oh, these are divine..."

Gabe never said a word. Just stood up, picked her up under his arm, and carried her to the door. He nodded politely to the hostess just before he tossed ol' NeeNee right out on her skinny, snarky ass.

He walked back to his table, nodding and smiling at the shocked diners who had witnessed the scene. Annie could only stare, even more embarrassed than before. Gabe sat back down as if nothing out of the ordinary had happened.

"I'm sorry about that, Annie, but that woman has been a pain in my... a thorn in my side for years now. Call this the straw on the proverbial camel's back." He smiled, picked up his fork, and took a bite of his salmon.

Annie could only stare at him in shock.

"Annie? Try your chicken. The sauce is marvelous!"

"Gabe how could you?" she cried.

"What?"

"How could you do that to her?"

"She's rude and disgusting, and I'll not have my first date with you ruined by trash like her. Now eat."

"That may be true, but that's no reason..."

"Get one thing straight right now, Annie. I do things as I see fit. You have no idea what that woman is like, and..." He trailed off, remembering the conversation he had with Vince long ago. Oh God... was this the Annie who had driven NeeNee nuts? Deanna did say that she knew her, right? Oh Jesus.

"I... I think I'd like to go home now, Gabe. I'm sorry." Annie placed her napkin on the table and picked up her purse.

"Shit," Gabe muttered under his breath. He stifled a sigh and glanced around the room. Sure enough, all eyes were on him and hushed whispers gathered together to create a dull roar of gossip. He should have known better than to bring Annie to such a public place where he was so well-known.

He stood and placed his hand on her elbow, assisting her to her feet. So much for a memorable first date. Well, memorable, but not a good memory.

They said little on the way home. Annie was still too shocked, and Gabe was angry. Mad at himself, mad at Deanna, and even a little upset with Annie, although he wasn't sure why. He walked her to her door with a mumbled half-promise to call her soon, and then went for a long drive before he went home.

Annie went straight to bed. She'd been right after all. It would never work out between them. She was almost grateful to Deanna for reminding them of the fact. Once again, sleep was a long time in coming.

~Part Five~
When Darkness Falls

Chapter Thirty-One

Annie woke to a knocking on her door. Her heart skipped a few beats, wishing- hoping- thinking that it would be Gabe. Chances of that were slim, she hadn't heard from him since he dropped her off at her door after their aborted date three days before.

The knocking came again, louder and more persistent. Whoever it was certainly wanted to see her. She ran a hand through her wild curls, got out of bed, and wrapped herself in a once-fluffy, now-threadbare robe.

"Coming!" she yelled, stepping over her useless watchdog who lay snoring in the doorway. She poked him gently with a toe, out of spite. She stepped back into her bedroom when she heard the front door open. *Oh dear God… Who would…?*

Spike jumped off the bed and shot around her to great their mystery guest. Annie dared a peak around the corner to see a tall figure move into her kitchen.

"Gabe…?" she whispered, hope rising in her once more. She silently moved closer until she was behind him, staring in disbelief.

Gabe arranged the flowers he'd brought in the vase he'd also brought, filling the container with water from the sink. Sure, it was a bold move to just walk into her home like that, and he still wasn't sure why he'd dared. Probably thinking it would be harder for her to not listen to him if he was on the same side of the door. He wouldn't have blamed her if she slammed it in his face had he stayed outside and tried to explain. There was still a chance she'd grab the fire poker and chase him out of the cabin.

He felt her presence behind him and slowly turned around, small smile on his face and a dozen white roses in hand.

"May I have five minutes?" he asked, handing them to her.

"You may have three," she said, ignoring the flowers, and trying desperately not to fall under his spell again. *Losing battle, Annie. Face it. You're still hopelessly in love with the man.*

"Three," Gabe nodded. He set the vase on the table and took her hands in his.

"You… you're at two and a half," Annie whispered, feeling that delicious tingle run up her arms to settle in her chest.

"Then I'd better speak fast. Or not." Gabe couldn't help himself. He pulled her in and kissed her. Kissed her hard and long, his hands on her back to hold her prisoner.

Annie didn't fight him. She was too shocked, too stunned, too darn happy to resist. She even clung to him to keep from falling when he finally stopped kissing her. She really should have slapped his face, the arrogant bastard, but her body wouldn't obey what a tiny part of her mind was trying to tell her.

"Thirty seconds," she gasped, fighting her emotions to focus on what his sorry excuse would be.

A gurgle and a hiss, and then the aroma of brewing coffee interrupted Gabe when he started to speak. *Perfect. Maybe she'd consent to sharing a cup with him...?*

"Ah, you were expecting me," he chuckled, nodding towards the pot.

"Hardly," Annie said, frowning. "It's on a timer. I need to get out and do my chores."

"Mind if I have a cup? I left before I got any this morning."

"Help yourself, Evans. You seem to do as you wish anyway." Annie sat at the table, loving his grand gestures while at the same time slightly annoyed by his grand ego. He honestly thought he could waltz into her home with a cliché bouquet and kiss her into submission? Apparently so. She stifled a smile.

Gabe pulled two cups from the handy hooks over the pot and waited, leaning on the counter, while the coffee finished brewing. No brandishing a fire poker yet... The thought made him smile.

"I'm so sorry about the other night, Annie."

"So am I. We never should have..."

"No, that's not what I meant. Please listen...?"

She nodded for him to continue, wondering what excuse he'd come up with for not speaking to her for so long.

"I'm glad we went out. I had such a good time on our ride, and I loved our time at the restaurant. At least I was until NeeNee reared her ugly head. That woman..." Gabe sighed and filled the mugs. "You take anything in this?"

"Cream, please. On the door in the fridge."

Gabe poured a little into her cup, leaving his black. He set the mugs down before he pulled a chair for himself. Annie said nothing.

"As I was saying, that woman is insane. You um... you know she has a history, right?"

Annie nodded.

"I guess I kind of snapped when she came in to cause trouble. I'm sorry about that, Annie."

Annie nodded again.

"And I was going to call you the next day, but I only had one phone call and it went to Kyle."

Annie blinked. "One phone call? Gabe, what happened?"

"Heh. Seems she wasn't happy with my removing her from the premises. When I got home that night, three cops were waiting for me. I was arrested for assault. Spent the night in jail, and called Kyle to bail me out in the morning."

"Gabe! You're kidding, right? I mean... this is a pretty elaborate excuse for not calling me, but..."

"It's true, love. It's since been straightened out and charges dropped, but it took up all of my time rounding up witnesses to the event. She wasn't hurt, only embarrassed, so the judge threw it out."

"It's rather hard to believe, Gabe."

"It's not something I'd make up! Jesus, Annie! I came over as soon as I could."

"Why?"

"Why?"

"Yes, why. Why are you here, Gabe? Why couldn't you have called, or at least had someone contact me? I've been worried sick about you… Worried that you were hurt, or… or… no longer wanted to see me."

"Aw God… Yeah, you're right. I should have gotten in touch with you somehow. At least had Dee call or something. There's no excuse for that. Can you ever forgive me?"

"I'm not sure yet. Why are you here? I need to know, Gabe. The real reason."

"I'm here because I want to try again with you."

"As in another date?"

"As in that, yes, and more."

"M… more?"

"Much, much more. Annie, I can't get you off of my mind." He took her hand in his, bringing it to his lips to kiss the palm.

She shivered, the tingles nearly overwhelming her senses.

"I… I don't know, Gabe. Say we do go out again. What then? More Deanna or someone else wondering if you're cheating on your wife. I don't know if I could deal with that, to be honest."

Gabe winced, knowing how very right she was.

Annie pulled her hand away and stood. She walked to the window to look out at the lake below. "Gabe, it's not going to work. No matter that Dee wants us together, I can't do this. And I think that deep down, you can't either. You… you're too moral. You wouldn't hurt her or the boys by doing anything to start rumors. I think you know what I mean."

"You're right in that regard. I don't want to hurt her or the twins. I don't want to hurt you, either… So… Well, I guess I have my answer. I um… Thanks for the coffee," Gabe sighed. He stood and walked to the door.

Annie nodded, unable to look at him when what she really wanted was to be in his arms. "Would… would you keep in touch, Gabe? Let me know how the CD is doing?"

"I'll do that, Annie." Gabe pulled his hat from the coat rack and jammed it on his head. When he saw that she'd yet to look at him, he took it back off and replaced it on the peg. He could use it as an excuse to return later, after she'd had time to miss him some more.

"Good bye, Gabe."

"Bye, Annie." He opened the door and stepped outside.

Annie waited for a moment, and then ran to the door. She stopped herself

442

just in time from flinging it open and begging him to come back.

Spike watched the scene from his position in the loft, totally disgusted with the stubborn humans. He snorted twice and went to curl up on the desk.

Gabe never left the porch. He sat down, running his fingers over the soft feathers of McDonald, and thought about what just happened. Sure wasn't what he'd planned! The thought of a fire poker upside his head was preferable to her lack of emotion, the finality of her good bye. Surely it couldn't be over before it even started, right? No, it would never be over for him. Never ever. He stood and knocked on the door again.

Annie considered ignoring him, but could she really? She didn't want him out of her life! Not ever! Maybe there was a way for them to at least be friends. After all, she was letting him use her song. He'd have to talk to her about that, right? He didn't seem in any hurry to leave, either. He wanted her… truly wanted a relationship with her. Oh, how could she have been so stupid? They were meant to be together! Where there is a will, there's a way, her father had said more than once.

She reached for the door. And saw his hat on the peg. Then again, maybe that's what he wanted, his stupid hat. She snatched it down and shoved it through the slightly opened door.

Gabe held his breath when the door opened, only to let it out in a sigh of disappointment when his hat was shoved into his gut. So much for that. He stomped off to his truck, fishtailing out of her driveway in an angry, hurt spray of snow and gravel.

Chapter Thirty-Two

"Dude, just call her! God! So you fucked up and got busted for tossin' that snake outta the Pub. Big deal. No harm done."

"That's not the issue, Kyle. Were you not listening when I told you the real problem?"

"Yep. So you can't go out with her. Call her. Go over there. Hell, have her come over here. If you're gonna be miserable like you have been, do something about it already. It's gettin' old, man."

Gabe glared at his buddy, moron that he was. Couldn't he get it through his thick skull that it was impossible to have a relationship as long as he was married? And what was up with Kyle's about-face regarding Annie? A month ago he was willing to kick Gabe's ass for even looking at her, and now he was as bad as Dee, ragging on him to try again.

"Gabe, do ya love her?"

"You know damn well I do!"

"Does she love you?"

"For a time, yes… or so I thought."

"Bet she does. Call her."

"I can't. I can't do this… Not to her or Dee. Besides, she made it very clear that she wanted nothing more to do with me."

Kyle shrugged. "Okay. Whatever. I'll talk to you later when you're in a better mood, asshole."

"Kyle, wait!" Gabe slumped in his chair when Kyle stomped out of the office. Christ, didn't anyone understand?

The console phone on his desk buzzed. He slammed a finger on the button to connect. "Yeah, what is it, Jen?"

"Call on line three for you, Gabe."

"Thanks, hon." He stared at the phone for a moment, in no mood to talk to anyone. Could be a potential source of income, though, so he answered.

"Evans."

"G… Gabe?"

"Annie? Oh God… Um… how are you?"

"On my way to work in a moment. What can I do for you?" Oh, it was so good to hear his voice again. She wrapped the afghan a little tighter around her and snuggled into her favorite chair. She really didn't have to work, but she didn't dare talk to him for very long, either. She wondered what he wanted after all this time.

"Do for me? I… But you called me!"

"No I didn't! The phone rang here and I was asked to hold for Mr. Evans!" She hoped he wasn't playing tricks on her, and darn near hung up on him.

"Sure you did. Annie, if this is some sick form of revenge…"

"I did not. How dare you think I'd do something…?"

"Just say what you have to say and leave me to my business, Annie."

"Fine." She slammed the phone down, instantly regretting it.

"Annie!" The phone buzzed in his ear, then surprised him by ringing again. He stared, not yet having disconnected on his end. "Hello…?"

"Call her back, you stubborn ass!" was all he heard before the dial tone returned.

Steve. Well go figure.

"Hello?"

"Annie, don't hang up. Please… Just hear me out."

She said nothing, just listened.

"Steve… it was him, hon. He's back to his old ways. I think he called us both, or something like that."

Annie looked at the dried rose in her hand – the one she'd saved from the bouquet he'd brought over a month ago, which was the last time she'd seen him. Her fingers still tingled when she touched it.

"I lied, Gabe. I have the night off."

"Meaning?"

"Meaning… That I'm sorry too." She took a deep breath. Heck, one of them had to give in, right? "Meaning that I want us to at least be friends."

Hey, it was a start. He could do friends, he hoped. At least she'd still be in his life.

"I'd like that, Annie. I'd like that very much."

"Can… can we talk about it over dinner?"

"Are you asking me for a date?"

"Just dinner."

"Over there?"

"I was thinking we could meet somewhere… That's if you don't mind a bit of a drive."

He'd go to the ends of the earth for her.

"Where?"

"There's a place in Richfield. South of here. I took Michael… Steve… We went there once. It's a nice place and well out of the way. I don't think Deanna… or anyone… will bother us there." She swallowed hard, feeling somewhat sordid for the need to hide from the rest of the world, but she was miserable without him.

"I know the place. I've been there a few times. When?"

"Tonight?"

"Tonight. What time?"

"Is six too early?"

It wasn't nearly soon enough, but it would do. Almost. "You'll see me sooner. I'll pick you up at five, Annie, and don't argue."

She smiled. "Five. See you then, Gabe."

He grinned, hung up, and floated out to his truck. Kyle and Jen watched him go, sharing a confused glance.

Dog met him on the porch and licked his hand in greeting. Gabe treated to pooch to a hearty scratch behind the ears. "She invited me back, Dog!" he grinned.

Dog barked once and Annie opened the door, ready to go. She wasn't wearing anything special, just jeans, a sweater, and her heavy winter coat, but she took Gabe's breath away.

Annie took a quick look at her cowboy, seeing he was in the same casual attire, and had to will her heart back down to a normal, reasonable pace.

"It's wonderful to see you again, Annie." He placed his hand on her elbow and escorted her to his truck.

"It's good to see you again, Gabe," she said when he opened the door for her.

They didn't speak again until they were halfway up Hidden Lake Road. She had no idea where to begin; he had too many questions to even think about which would be the first. Might as well go for broke, her answer would set the mood for the rest of the evening.

"Why the change of heart, Annie? And please, be honest."

"No matter my answer? Even if it's not what you want to hear"

That threw him a little. He nodded anyway. "Even if..."

"I missed you. Even if our relationship can never go beyond that of friendship, I missed you and I wanted to see you again." *Understatement of the year...*

"So you were serious? This is friends only and... and not a date?" She wasn't kidding. It was the last thing he wanted to hear. Well, nearly so.

"Just friends, Gabe, just like I was with Michael."

He swallowed back a sigh. The rest of the nearly hour-long drive was silent but for a little discussion on the unpredictable weather.

They settled into a booth in the back, looking at menus while they waited on a pitcher of beer.

"It's been a while since I've eaten here," Gabe said, rather surprised by the diverse offerings of the drab little bar. "Although I've stopped in for a drink now and then."

"It's been a while for me, too, although this is only my second time here. This same table as a matter of fact."

Gabe looked up. It was in the back, perfect view of who came and went in the front door, near the exit... Christ, she wasn't taking any chances on them being seen.

"Oh? I suppose I never pictured you in a place like this. Date with Tyler, was it? He's into sports bars."

Annie didn't much care for the hint of sarcasm in his voice. Or could it be a hint of jealousy? Regardless, there was no call for either.

"No, not with Tyler. He took me to far nicer places than this. Our favorite was The Reef." *Take that, you pig.* She grinned in spite of herself. "Actually, I was here with your brother. I insisted that we go out; he insisted that we choose a place where he wouldn't be seen. In retrospect, I now understand why."

"Is that why you chose this place?"

"Because I was here with Steven?"

"No, so that we wouldn't be seen."

"Would it make a difference, Gabe? We're here, the food is good, and let's leave it at that."

He felt an inexplicable guilt and shame.

They spent the next half hour sharing memories of Steven. Gabe did most of the talking, relating much of his childhood with his beloved brother. Annie had already heard most of it from that brother, yet still enjoyed hearing the twin's take on life in rural Montana. And it was a safe subject for both of them, no matter that it left them a little melancholy and missing the gentle Evans.

During dessert and coffee, Gabe let loose with a little sigh.

"Something wrong, Gabe?" Annie asked. He'd seemed so happy a moment ago.

"Mmhmm. No, not really. Yes. I wish we were at a place with music," he answered, taking her hand in his.

"Looking for new talent?"

"Wishing I had a place to dance with you, Annie." He gave her hand a squeeze.

She pulled her hand away. "This isn't going to work. I have no idea why I thought it would. Gabe, I think we should go."

"Why, Annie? God, we're having a nice time, actually talking for a change, and…"

"I meant the friendship thing. There's no way that I… that I can pretend we're just friends. I'm sorry, Gabe."

"Oh God," he moaned. "Annie, I don't understand. What did I do wrong?"

She took a deep breath, not quite believing she was about to be so bold, so forward. She stood, gathered up her coat and purse, and gave him a smile. "You did nothing wrong, Gabe. As a matter of fact, you did everything right. Too right."

"And I'm to be punished for it?" he asked, rather confused.

"I suppose that depends on how bad of a dancer I am."

"What…?"

"Music, Gabe. I know where we can go, and … not be seen."

"Annie…?"

"Take me home, Cowboy."

Gabe grinned, slapped a few twenties down on the table, and hurried out to the truck, Annie tucked snugly under his arm.

He had to chuckle at her choice of music. God, it was old. His parents listened to it so long ago, yet it brought back pleasant memories of his childhood, watching Al and Marie slow dance in the living room long after he and Stevie were to be asleep. Romance in its prime, it was.

Annie had also lit a few candles and cracked open a bottle of wine, setting the scene for a romance of their own. He could only wonder at where this would lead. Probably not to her bed, but it sure as hell was in the opposite direction of a mere friendship.

Gabe held her in his arms, damn near sighing in bliss with each breath, while Tony Bennett crooned about leaving his heart in San Francisco. She felt so warm and soft against him, and her perfume made his head spin with its intoxicating fragrance. He'd never felt so content or so much at home in his entire life. She was right when she said that they could never be just friends.

Annie's cheek rested just above his heart. She loved the way the steady beat would pick up a little when her arms tightened around him. Yes, this is what she'd been waiting for. This is why she could go no further with Tyler or Steven Michael. Even if they had to hide from the world forever, she could not live another day without Gabe in her life.

"The wine is getting warm, Gabe," she said well into the fourth song and their first continuous dance.

"Mmmhmm. Let it get warm. I'm too happy right where I am." His arms tightened around her and his lips nuzzled her hair.

Oh, she could feel how happy he was and how hard he'd become against her belly. It was time to put a little distance in between them before she broke down completely. She hadn't been with a man that way in fifteen years, and the very thought of it sent her into a near panic. Panic or anticipation? She wasn't quite sure. Very reluctantly, she gently pushed him away and sat on the sofa, almost gulping her wine in her nervousness.

Gabe sat down next to her. He tossed back his glass of wine and quickly poured another, sipping and actually tasting it this time.

"Is this Annie's version of a time out?" he asked, turning to look at her. He was slightly put out at being pushed away.

"We were moving a little too fast, Gabe."

"We were slow dancing for God's sake! Just how fast was that?"

"But you were um…" Annie's eyes involuntarily glanced at his lap. She felt herself blush crimson before she quickly looked away.

"Oh Jesus. Can you blame me for that? I rather thought we were heading that way, Annie. I mean… You invite me over here, the wine, the candles… God, even the music!"

"Then you thought wrong, Gabe Evans. I… No, *that* was not my intention, and if that's the only reason you are here, well, you can leave right now!"

Gabe stared at her for a long moment. He could go either way with her: righteous anger for her implying and then denying, or be honest with a smattering of humor. Since he was still walking a fine line at re-establishing a relationship, he decided to go with his second option. He was also rather amused at her feistiness in defending her honor. He wondered what had changed her from her extreme shyness.

He curled a lock of her hair around his finger, savoring the silkiness. "I apologize for my gender, Annie. We men don't always think with our brains." He gave her a wink and a wicked grin. "Could you possibly find it in your heart to forgive me for my... assumptions?"

She stared back at him, fighting her own wicked grin. Jeez, he had a way of making her forget everything but his smile, his eyes... hearing that teasing note in his voice.

"I might forgive you if you cut the crap, Evans. Thinking with your brain... Unheard of!" She returned his wink and sipped her wine.

Gabe burst out laughing. "Aw God... Annie, you're priceless!" He kissed the tip of her nose and refilled her glass.

They sipped and talked about horses for a while, very safe subject for both of them, until the bottle was drained. Gabe was feeling mighty fine, although not too fine to drive home, and Annie was downright intoxicated.

"Wine's all gone, Annie Rose. Now what do we do?"

"Mmmm... go to bed," she murmured, eyes closed and very much enjoying the buzzing in her brain.

"Oh? Does that mean you want to have sex?" he chuckled.

"No. I've had sex, Gabe, and I really didn't like it!"

"What?!" He wasn't sure which surprised and upset him more; that she wasn't a virgin (then again, why would she be?) or that she didn't like sex!

"Nope. Didn't like it at all. Disgusting!" she exclaimed with a drunken wave of her hand. "But you know," she continued, opening one eye to look at him. "I've never made love."

"Now that you mention it, neither have I."

"Sure you have. You're married!"

"In name only, Annie."

"Gabe, don't lie to me. You have. I know better." Annie sat up and tried to focus on his face.

"I'm not lying. To me, in order to make love you have to be in love. Otherwise it's just sex."

"Interesting theory."

"Never occurred to me until just now."

"Is it really true, Gabe? You're not in love with Deirdre?" Annie did focus then, looking deep into his eyes for the truth.

"I love her, Annie. I really do, but I'm not in love with her. I've never been in love with anyone before... Never knew what it was until now."

"Just now?" she whispered, touching his face.

"Actually, it was in January, on a snowy hill," he smiled.

"I think I knew it then, too."

"Should I stay here tonight?" God, he hoped she'd say yes.

"You'd be taking advantage of me." Oh, how she wanted him to.

"You don't fight fair."

"All's fair in love, Cowboy. Go home before I change my mind and wake up regretting it tomorrow."

"Even if I promise there'd be no regrets?"

"Tell me that when I'm sober. Go. Call me tomorrow."

"Walk me to the door and kiss me goodnight, then."

"I'll stagger to the door and shake your hand," she yawned.

"Good enough." He laughed softly when her eyes closed again and she sank into the sofa, sound asleep. Well, a woman who could hold her wine was not on the top of his 'must have' list.

He carried her to her room and placed her on her bed, settling down next to her and holding her in his arms until he, too, dozed off.

When Annie woke the next morning with just a touch of a headache, he'd already gone. But she knew he'd been there. A white rose lay in the indentation on the pillow next to her, and his woodsy-spicy scent lingered in the room.

Chapter Thirty-Three

Gabe called Annie as promised. Called her every day, even if the conversation was limited to just a few minutes, which it often was. She was busy working overtime and doing volunteer work for the homeless shelter, and he was nearly overwhelmed with his work at the studio and taking care of a moody Deirdre and two boisterous twins.

Once a week Gabe and Annie would meet for dinner in Richfield, and when he could slip away at night, they'd meet on her break in the cafeteria for a cup of coffee.

It wasn't nearly enough for either of them, yet they had no choice. Annie felt that it was probably for the best; ever since he'd spent the night with her, the thought of what could have happened was never very far from her thoughts. Because of that, she wouldn't allow herself to again invite Gabe in for even so much as a glass of wine after their dates. She didn't think she'd be able to say no if he hinted at making love again.

Gabe, too, couldn't purge that memory from his mind. It had been far too long since he'd had that particular basic need met, and it was rapidly making him insane. His only option was to distance himself from Annie, spending a little more time on the phone with her and less time in her presence. He was very afraid that he'd lose control and seduce her before it was time. Oh yes… there had to be a right time for it. She'd have to ask him.

February dragged into March, bringing with it the predictably unpredictable weather. Snow, rain, sleet, more rain, and a final, very heavy blizzard.

Annie drove home from work, fighting drifts and blinding snow. It took her nearly an hour longer than usual. When she wasn't praying that she'd make it home safe and sound, she was grumbling to herself about all the work she'd face in digging her way through the white mess to the barn – not to mention finding a way to clear her long driveway.

Needless to say, she was stunned when she turned in to her drive and found that it had already been cleared. Near the cabin sat a familiar black truck, complete with a shiny, yet used, plow on the front.

Gabe? What the heck was he doing there?

She parked and hurried inside, smiling at the aromas of fresh coffee and woodsy-spicy. Gabe sat on the kitchen counter, long legs swinging back and forth while he sipped from a mug.

"Good morning, Annie," he grinned over his cup.

"Good morning to you, Gabe," she said with a hint of a teasing smirk. "Still breaking and entering, I see?"

He hopped down and poured a coffee for her, remembering to add a dollop of cream. "No, Spike invited me in when I knocked. He saw how cold and tired

I was after plowing your drive and he took pity on me."

"Uh huh. Well, I'll pretend to believe you and not kick you out. After all, you had my best interests at heart." She smiled her sweet smile and kissed him on the cheek. "Thank you so much, Cowboy. I really do appreciate it."

"It comes with a price, Red," he grinned.

"And that would be? You will take a check, won't you...?"

"Hardly. How are you at making pancakes? I'm dying for a tall stack with some sausage and orange juice. It's been ages..." he sighed, thinking of his favorite breakfast.

"I think I can manage, but you'll have to wait until after I feed my critters first."

"Already done, Annie. I even milked the goat. Kind of."

"She stuck her foot in the bucket, didn't she?" Annie grinned.

"Apparently not the first time...?"

"Gabe, thank you. This... What you did for me this morning... Just why did you, anyway?"

"Well, when I heard about the storm coming, Kyle and I thought we'd have some fun with snowplows. He got one for his Jeep; I got a bigger one for my Dodge. It took me all of five minutes to do my driveway and I wanted something a little more challenging. Yours was perfect."

She sipped her coffee, eyeing him over the top of the mug. He was up to something; she just wasn't sure what it could be. Then again, she'd have a few wonderful hours of his company before he had to leave. Which made her wonder, why wasn't he at the studio? It was nearly nine already!

"Ah, I can tell by the look in your eye that you're entertaining a bit of skepticism, Annie. Really though, it's true. I had so much fun that I wasn't quite ready to stop. I would have done the parking lot at the studio, but in light of the wicked weather I just went ahead and shut it down for the day. A snow day!" Gabe laughed.

"Hm. I guess it's a reasonable enough story to earn you pancakes. Because you went above and beyond, I'll even throw in some blueberries."

"Oh God, I love blueberry pancakes! How did you know, Annie?"

She couldn't help but laugh at that one. He'd already pulled a package of the fruit from the freezer and had it thawing in the sink.

"Not only breaking and entering, but raiding my freezer. Gabe, for shame..."

"Aw, Annie, indulge me, please? I haven't had a decent breakfast in weeks!"

She set her cup down, turning serious. "Really? Jeez, Gabe, why?"

"Because Dee hasn't been feeling well enough to manage more than a bowl of cereal for me and the boys, and I'm a disaster in the kitchen. The hired help generally doesn't come in until after I leave for work. God, that sounded pathetic," Gabe said with a small smile.

"Hm." She gave him a long look. "Alright, you pour the juice and I'll make you breakfast, and while I'm doing that, you can tell me the real reason you're so far out this way so early in the morning. Plowing… Breakfast… Indeed!"

"It's true! All of it. I have a new toy and I'm starving for something that isn't shaken out of a box, and the most important reason I'm here is because I miss the hell out of you, Annie. God, it's been over a week since I last saw you!"

"You're the one who's been canceling dinner, Gabe. Oh, and I can't help it if Edith is lurking around, ready to intrude on our coffee time. I swear she's obsessed with you!"

"She's just a whacko fan. Annoying, but harmless. I think… Anyway, I've come all this way and have all but begged you for some time. Can I at least get a hug?"

"Just a hug?" Annie finished gathering breakfast supplies and started making batter before she turned to him. She gave him a sly grin, again surprising herself at her boldness. She wasn't even aware that she was capable of flirting like that.

Gabe loved it. He missed the shy Annie somewhat, but this little tease was much more fun. "A hug and maybe a kiss?"

"I already gave you a kiss. Right here… Remember?" She gave his cheek a light pinch.

"My mother kisses me like that. I was thinking more of… Oh, something like this." He threw caution to the wind and quickly pulled her to him. He kissed her. Kissed her hard and demanding at first, tapering off into something tender and lingering, finishing it off with a soft moan and a gentle brush of lips.

Annie's knees darn near buckled underneath her. Had he not been holding her so tightly, she would have been nothing more than a puddle of Benton all over the floor. He'd never kissed her like that before!

Tingles raced through her body, centering in her most sensitive area. Not only had she never been kissed like that before, she'd never ever felt so aroused, so full of longing to feel a man's touch. Gabe's touch.

Gabe damn near tossed her over his shoulder to carry to her bedroom right then and there. He knew that at that moment she was beyond resisting. If not for the rumbling in his stomach, he would have. But the truth be told, he really was as hungry as a bear in spring; *that* basic need overruled all the rest.

He kissed her forehead and turned her back to the task at hand. "Breakfast, and then we'll continue this… conversation a little later."

"I think I hate you, Gabe Evans," she mock-growled, whipping the pancake batter a little harder than necessary. How dare he kiss her like that and then demand to be fed?! How dare she let him…? *Focus on cooking, Annie, and not on what a narrow escape you just had.*

Gabe poured juice and set the table, updating Annie on Dee and the twins while she flipped pancakes. He told her about everything at the studio while they ate. She laughed at the tales of Kyle's silly pranks while they washed and dried the dishes together, and two hours later they finally noticed just how bad the weather had become when Dog barked to be let out.

"I'll get him, Annie." Gabe opened the door, snow blowing in, coating his body.

Dog peeked out and quickly changed his mind about the urgency of finding a tree.

"Oh shit," Gabe moaned. The snow was piled halfway up to the doorknob. "We've got a little problem, Annie." He shut the door and brushed himself off.

"Figures," she sighed. "Oh well, at least I don't have to go in to work tonight."

"You don't?"

"No. One of the other nurses wanted the weekend off and asked me if I'd switch with her. Since I have no life, why not? I have the next two nights off."

"Seriously?"

"Seriously. It's a good thing, too, because I don't think my poor truck could get through all of that snow! Jeez, Gabe, there's over two feet of it now, and this road is always the last to be plowed in the county. No reason to hurry since mine is the only house out this way."

"Closer to three, I think," Gabe mused, joining her at the window. "I'm not sure my truck would make it, either."

"What about your fancy new plow? If you leave now, I think you'd manage to get home. I'm sorry all of your hard work was in vain. Gosh, you can barely tell where the drive is again!"

"Do you really want me to go, Annie?" he asked, twining a lock of her hair around his finger. He was contemplating twining all of it around his hand to bare her neck, giving his lips complete access. *Mmm...*

"I was hoping you could stay a little longer, but it's coming down so fast! If you don't leave now, you'll be stuck here." Which wasn't such a bad idea. Yes it was! She couldn't resist him for much longer. Then again, did she really want to?

No.

Yes.

No!

Oh God, why did he have to be married?

"I wouldn't mind waiting out the storm with you, Annie."

"What about Deirdre and the boys? They need you there, Gabe. She sounds as if she's not feeling well enough..."

"Taken care of, Annie. The woman I hired to help out was there when I left. She said she wouldn't mind staying if the weather became too bad for her to leave. She's spent the night before, and the boys like her as a babysitter. They might miss me, but they don't need me."

"You always have an answer for everything, don't you?" Annie sighed, admitting a delicious defeat. She felt his hands close on her shoulders and she leaned against his solid bulk. Oh, he felt so good. The idea of having him all to herself for the day felt even better. Also, the thought of him there all night? She shivered, not letting her thoughts go any further.

"I… I suppose you c… could use the um… the guest room," she stammered.

As if. Gabe grinned and kissed the top of her head. "Thank you, Annie. I couldn't ask for a more gracious or more beautiful hostess. Now… About that conversation we had before breakfast…?"

He turned her around and lifted her face to his. Even though he could see the desire in her eyes, it was overshadowed by fatigue. How could he have forgotten that she'd just worked a twelve-hour shift,

her third in a row at that?

"What about it?" She let herself touch her palm to his cheek, and then moved it to cover her mouth when she stifled a yawn.

"We'll continue it later. You get to bed and get some sleep. I'll keep myself occupied. You're low on firewood, and I want to check on your critters, and I might even nap myself."

"Thank you, Gabe." She gave him a long hug; both relieved and disappointed, and took herself off to her room.

Gabe walked her to her door. "Sweet dreams, Annie Rose." His fingers combed through her autumn curls as he gave her a short, tender kiss before gently shoving her into her room. Christ, shoveling the snow from her driveway with a teaspoon would have been far easier than not jumping in to bed with her. And yet he managed. Kyle wasn't far off when he teased Gabe about having nerves of steel.

Annie woke, slightly groggy and disoriented after a very hard, deep sleep. Although she knew she had dreamed, she couldn't remember what it had been about, only that they were pleasant. Probably about Gabe.

She glanced at her clock to see that it was after five, time to get rolling and ready for work. She slipped into her robe and headed for the bathroom, only to find the door shut. *What the…?*

"I'll be right out!" said a very familiar voice.

Gabe…?

Oh jeez, how could she have possibly forgotten that he was there? She grinned and went to start a pot of coffee. He met her in the kitchen, wrapping his arms around her from behind and kissing her shoulder.

"Mmm… I could get very used to this," he sighed, gently swaying with her.

She was thinking the exact same thing.

"…And I thought about making dinner for us, but I'm not about to subject you to that quite yet," he chuckled.

"Give me a minute or so to wake up and I'll save us both from starving." Annie turned in his arms, wrapping hers around his waist. "What would you like?"

"You."

"I meant for dinner! Jeez!" She couldn't help but grin.

"You. And some more of you for dessert."

"And what will I have?" Oh God… Flirting was one thing, but this? She'd never gone that far with her teasing comments before.

"It would only make sense, Annie… Me!"

"Seriously, Gabe…"

"Alright," he said with a mock-sigh, "my absolute favorite dinner is beef stew. With dumplings."

"Perfect, since I have everything I need for that. Did we get much more snow?" she asked, reluctantly pulling away from him to pull a package of stew meat from the freezer.

"About another six inches, but the wind is pretty wicked and blowing up some pretty impressive drifts. Worst storm we've had in years."

Annie popped the beef in the microwave to thaw. "I should say so. I… I'm glad you're here, Gabe."

"Any particular reason?" he said with a grin.

"I'm not sure, really. It just seems right somehow. And yet it's not. This… Well, it's morally wrong…"

"How so?" His grin vanished.

She gave him a pained look. "Do I have to say it?"

"No," he mumbled, understanding completely. On and off throughout the day he'd been having the same pangs of guilt, somewhat, anticipating what the night might bring.

Annie poured two mugs of coffee, handing him one. "How can something so right be so wrong?"

"Dee doesn't think it is wrong. God, Annie, she wants us to be together. She couldn't hustle me out of the house soon enough when I told her I was coming over here this morning."

"I know, Gabe, but maybe she… Oh jeez, how do I say this?" She could feel her face burning in embarrassment.

"Just say it. I'm not all that easily shocked," he answered with a small smile.

Annie swallowed hard, sipped her coffee, and checked the meat in the microwave. "You… here all night. Does she think that I… that we… oo God, Gabe, I'm not that kind of person! It might be different if you weren't… if we were…" She stopped and collected herself. "Gabe, it's not right for you to stay here with a woman who isn't your wife, especially since your wife is home alone."

"You didn't seem to mind the last time, Annie."

"I was drunk! And I thought you were leaving. It's not the same. This seems so… so premeditated."

"Maybe it was… on my part."

"At least you admit it," she snapped.

"Jesus…" Gabe grumbled, and then said, "Annie, I'm not sure what she thinks, and it's not as if I'm… well, betraying her. I told you just how it is with Deirdre and me. It's a marriage of convenience, and it always has been. I'd be taking nothing away from her because it's something she never had in the first place!"

Annie looked at him again. "You're saying that the two of you never… Um, never mind. It's none of my business."

Gabe said nothing. To deny it would be an outright lie, to confirm it would only add to Annie's feelings of guilt. Don't ask, don't tell. A lie by omission. He didn't much care for it, yet it seemed to be the only option he had. His guilt meter went up a few degrees.

Annie remained quiet while she prepared dinner. Gabe wandered off to watch the evening news. Suddenly, the very promising night ahead had turned into a long wait until he could leave.

When the veggies and meat were boiling on the stove, Annie retreated to her room to dress in her warmest clothes, trying like heck to not think about the man in her living room. She forced herself *not* to glance at him when she went for her coat, which was hanging next to his on the rack.

She shoved her feet into her boots, and a second after her hand closed over the doorknob, she felt him behind her. Never heard him approach, just felt his presence.

"Where do you think you're going?" he asked, stepping between Annie and the door.

She bristled, not at all liking to be question – judged even – in her own home.

"I have to see to my animals, not that it's any business of yours."

"They're fine. I made sure they had plenty of food and water, Annie. Or is it that you want to be free of me for a while?"

Annie didn't answer, but merely zipped her coat and waited patiently for him to move his interfering butt out of her way.

Gabe stared hard at her for a long moment and seeing that they were at a stalemate, stepped aside and flung the door open. "Fine. Go. And just see how far you get… stubborn wench."

A gust of icy wind blew in, stealing Annie's breath away and pretty much making that darn cowboy right again. Jeez, the snow on the porch was piled in a drift up to her waist. It would take forever for her to trudge and fight her way the hundred yards to the barn, assuming she even made it that far.

Gabe pulled her back inside and shut the door. "As if I'd even let you attempt it. Annie, I grew up in Montana. Snow like this was common every winter, and it can be damn dangerous. It's true that one can freeze to death mere feet from shelter."

"Right again," she said, her voice edged in sarcasm. She stripped off her outerwear and stomped off to check the woodstove. Figures that he'd already loaded it, and it was burning with a cheery warmth. She stood, staring at nothing, considering her limited options.

Gabe flopped in the favorite chair, annoyed yet amused. "Face it, Red, you're stuck with me. " He gave her a wicked grin when she turned to glare at him.

"I could always lock myself in my room with a good book," she countered.

"You could, I suppose."

"Or go clean the basement…"

"Perhaps…"

"But dinner will be ready pretty soon. I'll think about it while I make the dumplings." She stalked off to the kitchen without giving him another look. Jiffy mix and milk were dumped into a bowl and mixed just enough, and then spooned in big lumps onto the boiling stew. She replaced the lid on the pot and turned around, only to bump into that big, dumb, too-damn-silent-when-he-walked cowboy.

"I wish you wouldn't do that." She growled, attempting to get by him.

"Do what? Come in to offer my assistance?"

"Sneak up on me like that!"

"I never sneak. You're just not as aware of your surroundings as you should be, Annie." He grinned and tweaked her nose. Lord help him, if he didn't retain a sense of humor, it was going to be one long miserable night for both of them.

"Oh, I'm aware," she said, batting at his hand. "There are just some things I'd prefer to ignore!"

"You wound me," he chuckled, helping her set the table.

"Not enough. You're still alive and babbling." It was getting harder every minute to stay mad at him.

"You are one damned difficult woman, Annie Benton. But you know what? I love you anyway. God, I love you…" He didn't care if she protested or got pissed off. Fate had thrown them together tonight, and before the sun rose the next morning, she'd know just how much he loved her.

He pulled her into his arms and kissed her breathless.

Annie's initial cry of protest was muffled by warm, demanding lips. Although her brain protested, her heart and body overruled, melting against her cowboy and kissing him back. Her brain ceded to the inevitable and allowed the thoughts of angry indignation to be swept away, replaced by sensation and desire. Gabe was impossible for her to resist or deny. She needed him, loved him more than she ever thought possible.

Gabe broke the kiss and gently pushed her away. "Annie, I love you. It would be so very easy for me to… to not stop with just a kiss. But I promised myself that the choice… the next move would be up to you. Because I love you." With that, he kissed her gently on the forehead and went to sit in the favorite chair again, giving her some time to think.

Think she did. She stood at the stove, pretending to stir the stew while she considered what had happened. What was happening? What would happen…?

So what if he had conspired to be snowed in with her? Fate, disguised this time as the weather, had conspired with him. The snow outside was much more than had been predicted. He was right about her being stuck with him.

Why was she denying the both of them the chance to fully enjoy what Fate had tossed their way? Her morals, righteous as she thought them to be? Heck, in this day and age it was no big deal to sleep around, married or single. It may not be right, but was it so very wrong if you loved someone? Marti was a prime example of having many sexual relationships, and Annie certainly didn't think any less of her for it, not that Marti slept with married men.

So why not? Who would know besides Gabe and herself? Spike and Dog would never tell.

Annie giggled at that thought and made up her mind. Gabe did love her and had proven it by not taking advantage of her or trying to seduce her – too much, anyway.

Yes, tonight would be the night, although on her terms. He wouldn't know a thing about it until just the right time.

Annie smiled to herself, a romantic little plan forming in her mind. Again, she was a little stunned by her boldness, but why not? She'd waited all her life to find her cowboy and waited far too long to find a love like she knew they shared. She deserved at least one night to revel in it.

"Gabe, dinner is ready." She ladled the steaming stew into a bowl and set it on the table.

Halfway through dinner she broke the strained silence. "How about a game of Monopoly and then an early night?" she said, feigning a yawn.

"Uh… Sure. I suppose. I get the car…" He wondered how she could be so tired. Christ, she slept all day!

"You can have the car. I always take the dog anyway. But I get to be the banker."

"It's your game," Gabe all but mumbled. Jesus, didn't that kiss mean anything to her? He was still shaking with it!

"And after that I think I'll take a nice, long bath and dive into that book I was thinking about earlier. Maybe a glass of wine while I read…" she mused.

Gabe all but groaned, picturing her in the tub, a froth of bubbles covering up just enough of her to make him crazy for what he couldn't see.

"Mmhmm. And then some nice, warm flannel jammies and a big soft bed. Perfection…" Annie sighed.

Gabe did groan then. The thought of her in flannel jammies was just too damned sexy. Well, her wearing only his pajama top and him wearing only the bottoms…

"Oh dear. That reminds me… You don't have anything to sleep in, do you,

Gabe?"

"N...no, but then again, I usually don't wear any... Um... Never mind," he gulped.

"Oh? Interesting." Annie threw him a coy smile and continued. "Michael... Uh, Steve left plenty of clothes in the guest room. I'm sure you can find something if you like." She finished her meal and started the dishes.

Gabe sat there, mouth agape and wondering just what the hell she was up to. It failed to register in his befuddled mind that his brother had stayed in the cabin enough to maintain a wardrobe.

The game of Monopoly was short. Very short. Annie lost on purpose, even cheated a little by tucking some of her colorful play money back into the till when Gabe wasn't looking. It wasn't easy, either, since his eyes rarely left her, be it staring into her eyes, or letting his drift to certain points south. She could barely look at him, not daring to give away her thoughts. The desire she'd sensed from him was overwhelming and overpowering, and the mere sight of him sent her libido to a level she wasn't even aware existed.

"Annie, you are, by far, the worst player in the history of mankind," Gabe chuckled when she sighed in defeat. "I'd even go so far as to say you suck!" He winked and finished off his beer, grinning to himself. Oh yes, she lost on purpose, and rather quickly at that. Just maybe...

"And you're rude, Mr. Evans," she smirked, holding out her empty wine glass for him to refill. "I do not suck."

"Maybe just lick and nibble then?"

"Gabe Evans! Indeed!" She giggled and stood up, swaying slightly. There was nothing like a cold bottle of Reisling to warm the blood and fog the brain just enough to take the edge off her nervousness. Her little buzz was absolutely perfect.

Gabe laughed and got up to fetch another beer.

"Just for that, sir, you'll tidy up this mess and take Dog out to find a tree, although I think a rail on the porch will be sufficient considering the weather. I'll deal with the mess later. I'm going to take a nice, long bath, and then go to bed. Another glass of wine and a good book... yes, that's exactly what I'm in the mood for. The guest room is at your disposal." Annie smirked again and flounced off to her room, leaving her glass of wine on the table and slamming the door behind her.

Gabe could only stare after her.

"What the hell was that about, Dog?" he mumbled, surprised at her actions yet again.

Dog couldn't have cared less. If Geoffrey Alan didn't get him outside soon, it would be the door jamb and not the porch that would be watered all too soon.

Annie wasted no time with her preparations. Half a dozen candles were lit, and her finest, peach-colored silk nightie was place temptingly on the bed, which she then turned down. The nightie was merely a prop; she had no intention of actually wearing it.

As soon as she heard Gabe take Dog outside, Annie grabbed another bottle of wine and one more glass, and shot into the bathroom. She was right back out to grab some roses from the vase on the counter, peeling away the petals on her way back.

More candles were lit in the bathroom, and the tub was soon filling with lavender-scented water. She sprinkled the rose petals on the swirling surface of the water and poured a glass of wine for Gabe, then sank down into her romantic bath.

Gabe stomped in ten minutes later, madder than hell at the persnickety Dog, who insisted on sniffing every porch rail before deciding on, and watering three of them. Why the hell couldn't the critter just pee and get it over with?

Because, Dog was thinking, Annie Rose needed a little time to herself. He stretched, yawned, farted, and fell into a deep sleep, dreaming doggy dreams of getting locked into the Milk Bone factory.

Gabe flopped in the favorite chair with a fresh beer; gazing at the "mess" he was supposed to tidy up. He stared at the full glass of wine, which had been abandoned on the table. His right eyebrow arched and a grin split his lips. The little minx had done it again. Left it on purpose, so that he'd have an excuse to disturb her bath, being the gentleman that he was. She couldn't very well enjoy her bath and book without her wine, could she? He thought not.

He picked up the glass and all but skipped to the bathroom, raising his hand to knock, and then stopped. Nope, it wouldn't be all that gentlemanly on his part. He went into the guest room and stripped; tossing his clothes on the bed, and then went back to the bathroom door, lightly rapping his knuckles on the only barrier between him and his Annie, not counting Annie herself. He took a deep breath, waiting for an answer.

Annie grinned. It must have worked, and he was out there now with her forgotten wine.

"This better be good, Evans. I just got all nice and relaxed, up to my neck in bubbles," she sighed, looking at the clear water swirling around her, with the petals floating and then sticking to her damp breasts.

"Um… your wine, Annie. You… forgot it. Should I leave it outside the door here?"

"Didn't I say I just got into the tub? I'd have to get out again to fetch it, possibly risking a slip and fall on the wet floor. Close your eyes and bring it in, would you? Just leave it on the sink." As if he would.

"But if I close my eyes, wouldn't I risk banging into something and possibly hurting myself? That might result in a law suit, Annie! Not to mention possible death, since it would be impossible to get an ambulance out here tonight."

"You do have a point, Gabe. It seems we have a dilemma here. Okay, come in, but no peeking or I swear I'll blind you with bubble bath."

Gabe stifled a laugh and opened the door, his breath hitching and the romantic ambiance of the room. His breath hitched and Mr. Happy twitched. Twitched and began to swell, and he couldn't do a thing about it, not even apologize for his condition.

He walked to the tub and stood before her, glass in hand, his body displayed in the light of the flickering candles. He dared peek, despite her warning, and nearly groaned. No bubbles hid her nakedness, and he'd never seen anything or anyone more beautiful than Annie in all her wet glory, staring back up at him.

Annie's breath drew in sharply when she gazed at him, standing there, wearing nothing but a dazed smile. In her long career as a nurse, she'd seen countless men in various states of undress, and even more types of body styles, but never one so perfect as the man in front of her, and never in circumstances such as this.

From far away she heard him murmur her name, yet she wasn't quite ready to end her visual feast. Her eyes lingered on his chest for several long moments, taking in the well-defined musculature of his shoulders and pecs. A haze of black hair, neither too much nor too little grew across the broad expanse of upper body, tapering to a thin line that grew into a thick nest at his groin. Her eyes widened, stopping there, seeing what his jeans always covered up. Never ever had she seen manhood that large, and it was still growing, throbbing with every beat of his racing heart.

She watched, mesmerized, until she tore her eyes away and let them roam further down, getting her fill of strong thighs and calves. For the first time since she could remember, she wanted to look her fill at the male body other than in a clinical sense. For her first time ever, she wanted to discover the mysteries and wonders of a man and a woman coming together. True, she was no virgin, but her two times with Richie on the night they married had been dismal and disappointing at best, an experience she was loathe to repeat until now.

"Annie...?" Gabe murmured again, unable to believe the vision in front of him. She was even more incredible than he ever could have imagined. He set the glass down on the ledge of the tub before he dropped it, his eyes drinking in the candle light flickering on her the rosy blush of her otherwise pale skin. Her hair, highlighted by the tiny flames and droplets of moisture rising from the steaming tub, gleamed with red and gold, and the ends of her curly tresses floated down around her shoulders and breasts.

Dear God... her breasts. Gabe couldn't help but stare at the lush curves half submerged, the nipples taut, poking up under a very thin veil of rose petals. He hadn't seen anything like this in a very, very long time. Deirdre, although perfect herself, was very petite and had very little curves at all, especially in that area. Gabe, being the lusty male he was, absolutely loved those curves.

"Annie," he murmured a third time, hoping like hell she'd snap out of the trance, which seemed to hold her prisoner. He prayed she'd ask him to join her.

It worked, and her green gaze met his blue one.

She swallowed hard and moved a bit, making room for him in the tub. He groaned and took a step forward, anticipating that first, wonderful, heated, both-of-them-naked kiss. He braced his hands on the ledge of the tub and leaned down, lowering his head to his Annie's. Their eyes locked again, and he imagined her heart beat the same as his, racing, and her arousal matched his towering level.

Closer and closer they came, eyelids drifting shut, breath mingling, moist lips slightly parted and eager. Nose brushed against nose, and Gabe was so focused on the woman that he failed to hear the door squeak open and the click of toenails on the floor until it was too late. Something cold and wet pressed against the cleft of his buttocks and he screamed, falling right into the tub on top of a shocked Annie. She tried to jump up and escape the unwarranted attack, and then burst into laughter when she saw Dog, looking rather confused, cocking his head at Gabe. Jeez, he'd only wandered in to get a drink from the toilet, and then was compelled to have a sniff of the bare backside between him and his goal. Seriously, he was a dog, after all.

Gabe's reaction was epic. He sat up, sputtering, flinging every curse word he knew or could manufacture at the poor critter, then turned to Annie, ready to let her have it too. He worked up a volley, and then stopped, staring at the woman laughing hysterically at him. No, not at him, but with him. He shoo'd Dog away and sat back on his heels in the water, thinking that it was inevitable for something like this to happen.

Dog snorted, shook splashed water from his head, got his drink, and meandered back to his place on the couch.

Annie got herself under control. As much as she was lost in the moment of potential romance, this was priceless, and did a good job of releasing any tension either of them might have had. She reached a hand out, touching Gabe's face, and politely thanked him for bringing her wine to her.

Gabe's mouth opened and closed a few times, no sound coming out, finding him at a loss for words. He caught the gleam in her eye and smiled, then leaned forward again, finally getting that first, anticipated, no barriers anymore kiss. His arm curled around his Annie, pulling her against him, both of them drowning in renewed passion.

The kiss seemed endless. Gabe was drowning, with his head spinning and his body literally tingling all over. This was definitely a new experience for him, to be so affected by the contact of a woman's lips, and… Dear God, some tongue? He nearly groaned, accepting Annie's invitation to step things up a notch.

Annie had no idea what got into her. Her shyness melted completely away, and the wine she'd consumed had nothing to do with it. This was it. Gabe was the one. She'd always thought so, and now, with this kiss, it was confirmed and soon to be consummated.

Her lips parted more and her tongue darted out tentatively, to be met with equal eagerness on his far more experienced one. Just when she thought she couldn't take much more of such incredible pleasure, she felt him pull away.

"Gabe," she murmured, already missing him, then gasped when his hungry mouth was at her neck, sucking a kiss just under her jaw, and then moving even lower to tease at her nipple.

"Don't drown," she breathed out, looking down to see that his nose barely cleared the water.

He glanced up at her, a grin teasing at his lips. "Good point," he said, and stood up, pulling Annie up with him. He stepped out of the tub, lifted her into his arms, and carried her to her bedroom, kicking the door shut behind him.

Dog wandered over to see what the noise was, and nearly slipped in the trail of bathwater leading from one room to the other. He couldn't help but cock his head and raise an ear in confusion when he heard the strange sounds coming from Annie's room. First time for everything. He wandered off to annoy Spike.

Chapter Thirty-Four

Gabe spent his alone time being giddy in love, his daylight hours working his tail off to get his music going, and mixed in with the two, his unspoken, subconscious fears occasionally rising to the surface. He'd feel a slight shortness of breath or a sharp pain in his chest or head during these times, but blew it off and did his best to ignore it. Still, it scared him when he did choose to think about it.

There was also Deirdre to consider. She had been unusually quiet since the day Steven had made his unexpected and last appearance. He often looked at her when she was lost in thought, wondering where those thoughts were taking her.

Dee was, indeed, lost in thought. She was happy for Geoffrey and Annie, but was fighting pain and depression every waking moment. Only her sons kept her from giving up. She put up a brave front in front of James and Jeremy; she didn't want them to see their Mama suffering. Geoffrey wasn't fully aware of it, either. Deirdre wanted him to concentrate on his relationship with Annie, who might notice her condition, so she avoided seeing her. They still spoke on the phone occasionally, yet Deirdre never invited her over.

Eric and Irene moved from the trailer into an even smaller, cheaper apartment. Irene had developed an infection in the fractured bone and could barely walk, let alone handle the steps of the trailer. At least the apartment was ground level and the rent was more affordable.

The journals lay forgotten in Annie's closet. She had read the first one, telling of Rosalind's childhood, but in her happiness with Gabe, she never even thought about them anymore. Steven Anthony Michael's words were a fading memory. Who needed to know why any of this happened, just as long as it did?

Life for Gabe and Annie was good, great... glorious!

The snow melted and the daffodils opened their bright yellow heads to reflect the springtime sun. The lake was once again the brilliant blue gem in the heart of the woods, and new life was evident everywhere. Gabe's CD was ready to market with eleven new songs and the new version of "The Dream." Annie couldn't believe that she had actually written a song that was now going to be heard by hopefully millions of people.

Eric and his aunt were coping with their situation as well as could be expected, but rejected all of Annie's offers to help them out. They could handle this on their own, thank you very much. Annie was hurt; she had never seen either of them act so cold before, it bordered on hostility! She had tried, and she had to be content with that knowledge.

Deirdre seemed to be perking up a bit. She was still silent, but was more active than she had been. She would take her sons to the museum or the library several times a week. They visited the small art institute and the planetarium. She wanted her children to spend as much time with her as they could, and to learn as much as they could before she was gone.

Yes, life was good for Gabe and Annie. Until disaster struck.

It happened in the first week of April.

SD Productions was broke.

No more money.

Not a single penny.

Checks bounced, creditors called and threatened. Gabe was stunned, Kyle was unusually quiet, and Jerry the accountant was nowhere to be found.

"Kyle! Jenna! My office, now!" Gabe yelled into the lobby the second he heard the couple walk in door. He'd been trying to track down his missing funds for most of the night and had finally succeeded, to a point. Now there were many questions, and those two had damn well better have some answers.

"Gabe, you're here early," Kyle said, bouncing the room.

"I've been here the entire night. Since nine a.m. yesterday if you want to get technical about it. I don't relish spending a Sunday at the office, either. Sit. Both of you." He was still in a state of shock over what he had found, but wanted to give the Davidson's a chance to explain. He patted the stack of ledgers in front of him.

"Care to explain?" he asked Kyle, then looked at Jenna with the same question in his eyes.

She looked at the books. *Oh shit, he knew.* And she had been so close to replacing the money. Now what? Kyle, you better have a back-up plan.

Kyle turned fifty shades of red when he saw the bookkeeping ledgers on the desk. Not only were the ones Gabe actually knew about setting there, but Kyle recognized the other ones - the ones only he and Jen knew about.

"Uh, yeah. No. I mean..." He wasn't sure what to say. At least his buddy didn't look like he was ready to commit murder... yet.

"Don't try to feed me any bullshit, Kyle. Just tell me. Where is our money?" Gabe asked in a very quiet, tired voice.

"Our money? Well, it's... it's... Oh God, Gabe, it's gone?"

"Apparently. Now just where the fuck it go?"

Kyle and Jenna looked at each other. She gave him a nod, encouraging him to tell; it was too late for trying to cover it up any more.

"I... I... It started out... Well, I needed a loan," Kyle began. He took a deep shuddering breath and closed his eyes. It would be easier to confess if he couldn't see the shock and disappointment in his partner's eyes.

"I needed a loan. We were gettin' a little behind at home, you know, on the bills, and I didn't think it would be a problem if I borrowed a few grand from the company. I called Jerry and he said that we were doing okay money-wise, that it shouldn't be a problem taking some out for a little while. Jen cut me a check and things were cool. I paid some of it back, but before I knew it, I was right back to where I started. I took some more... and then some more. I thought maybe I could invest it in some short term stuff, and get it back into the account before... well, before now anyway. Jerry was helping out with the investments." He opened his eyes and saw the look of disbelief on Gabe's face.

"Hey! Call him! He'll back me up on this," Kyle said defensively.

"I tried. It seems he thought that now would be an opportune time for a vacation. I believe he went to the Caymans," Gabe told them. "My God, Kyle, why didn't you come to me if you needed some cash? You know I'd give you anything you needed. We've been through this already, man. God, didn't you learn the first time?"

"I didn't want you to know. You always got it together and me... I can't seem to get it that way. I didn't want you to think I was a total asshole in not bein' able to hold onto a buck."

Gabe didn't say anything. He thought of Kyle's lifestyle, his expensive toys, his big house full of kids, and his taste for gambling. He was surprised that Jen hadn't kept a closer rein on her husband's wallet after the problems they'd had a few years before, but it was a moot point now.

"Just how involved was Jerry in all of this?" he asked.

"At first, he wasn't. He just let me know that he could juggle some figures if he had to. Then about two months ago he offered to do some investin' for me. Since he's the moneyman, I figured why not? He told Jen how to work the numbers here so things would look on the up and up, and then he'd take care of the rest. He'd send an occasional check so I figured that I was makin' some money. Things were cool. I didn't pay much attention, what with the work we been doin' on the CD and all. I didn't think there was any problem. Uh, how bad is it?" Kyle nearly cringed with the last question.

Gabe sighed and slouched into his chair. It was bad. It could not have been worse. They were hundreds of thousands of dollars in debt. Christ, the musicians needed to be paid, the recently hired staff... well, their paychecks were no good with nothing in the bank to cover them. And to top it off, there was a master tape of the best music SD had ever done just sitting there. They had no money to get it rolling.

There was no money coming in, either through private contracts or through anyone who might back the new CD. Gabe could cover most of the debts with his own funds, but SD Productions was still finished. They were back to where they had started eight years ago. At least they had once had a reputation as a large concert draw; maybe they should make a comeback. Too bad it was the last thing he wanted to do.

"Kyle, this is it for the company; there's nowhere to go from here. I can take care of the payroll, but that's it, we're finished," Gabe told him, his voice flat and showing no emotion.

Kyle swallowed hard. This was a disaster. He was about ready to lose his house and Jen's new car, and now they were both unemployed. Christ, how could he have been so fuckin' stupid? Not that it was his entire fault; there was still that prick Jerry to consider. Wonder how hard it would be to track him down and kick him in the ass with the pointy toe of his boot, then proceeded to finish him off with a well-placed heel between the eyes?

Aw God, what were they gonna do? And what about the CD? Kyle knew that it would sell well, if only they could get it out. Then there was always suicide....

"Kyle? Any thoughts on the matter?" Gabe asked.

"I don't know what to say. I'm sorry sure won't fuckin' cover it. Isn't there anything we can do?"

"Not that I can think of. I have already contacted the police regarding Jerry, not that it will do any good. Do you have any idea how much of our money he has? Any idea at all?" Gabe asked.

Kyle and Jenna shook their heads. They did have a vague idea, but after this morning's conversation it was probably more than they could have imagined.

"From what I can figure, over the last several months more three million dollars has vanished. How much of that you two are responsible for, I don't know. I don't want to know. I'm sure the police will want to know, but not me."

The Davidson's were stunned. Three million? They had only taken about ten thousand! Kyle wasn't even aware that SD had that much money! Where had it all come from? Better question, where did it all go?

Gabe picked up one of the ledgers. "Whose idea was it to be so creative with the figures?" he asked them, and then threw the book back to the desk.

They gave each other a guilty look. Actually it had been Jerry's idea, but they had gone along with it.

"Gabe, please let me explain," Jenna pleaded. "I think we were taken in by a master con..."

"Well duh..."

"Kyle and I had no idea this would happen; we just needed a little help. And it was our money too, you know. Jerry had such a good idea with the investment thing it seemed stupid not to do it. He showed me how to 'arrange' the numbers so that you wouldn't notice. I had no idea that he was planning to do the same thing." She was nearly in tears. "Do you have to involve the police?"

"I'm afraid so. I hate to do it, but what choice do I have? This is not a matter of taking a few pencils home from the office, or something trivial like that. We are talking about the livelihoods of two families, not to mention the others involved, depending on us for a paycheck. I won't press charges against you, if that's what you are worried about, but you have to take some of the responsibility for this mess," Gabe told her. He sighed. The same feeling of apathy he had before he met Annie took hold of him again, only this time it was accompanied by disappointment and a hint of depression.... That damn depression that he thought he'd purged when he'd married Dee. He prayed that it wouldn't come back.

This was probably his fault, too. He should have been out hustling up some new talent and looking for backing instead of spending so much time in the studio, or at least hired someone to do it for him. He was so sure that the new CD would be the answer to their money problem that Gabe had dumped quite a bit of his own cash into SD's bank account, just so it would be there when they needed for the production and marketing. Now, it too, was gone. Things would be a little tighter around the Evans' house for a while. Fortunately, Deirdre hadn't been in a spending mood lately. She had hired a full-time housekeeper/part-time nanny to help her out, but she spent nothing else.

Should he even tell her about this? She hadn't been well at all lately and Gabe feared that it was the beginning of the end for his wife. He wished Steve would come back and help her.

Maybe Annie might have an idea. She knew nothing about business, but she was clever. Just thinking about his Annie made Gabe feel a little better. He did a little attitude adjustment, pulling a Mr. Cheerful from his bottomless bag of characters.

"So, what to do, people?" he asked Kyle and Jenna. "We have a fantastic bit of music just waiting to be unleashed on an SD-starved world, but no way to get it to them. We have no money to continue operating here, but I doubt that we could sell the damn place anytime soon. I also have the feeling that you two are still in a tight spot financially, and I would be willing to take care of that if you want me to... if you will let me."

Kyle decided to swallow his pride. Just this once. Actually, he had no choice. He had thirty days to make up two house payments, or it was history. He would have to sell the boat and the motorcycles - he could live without those, and with any luck they could hang on to Jenna's vehicle. She needed it to haul around the kids anyway. Still, it was a grim picture. Why had he been so goddamn stupid?

He'd let Gabe help. Thank God he was even willing to, and not kicking Kyle's ass from there to Cleveland.

"Okay, dude... I really could use a hand but I have no idea where to even begin. I'm good with a guitar, not with money." He gave his best buddy a tentative grin.

"Obviously," Gabe said dryly. "Fine. Then Jenna, I'll pick your brain. Suggestions? Comments?"

"Hey, don't you want to pick my brain too?" Kyle joked.

"I'm afraid that would be akin to picking one's nose; neither is a pleasant thought," Gabe laughed.

Jenna laughed too. Maybe things would work out after all. Gabe had always managed to work miracles before...

The trio sat together and mapped out a plan for the Davidson family. They would lease their house, letting the renters make the house payments with just a bit to spare, and the Davidson tribe would move into Gabe's home. They practically lived there anyway.

Gabe would fire the housekeeper/nanny, and Jenna would help Deirdre. Kyle's toys would be sold and the money used to help pay for Jenna's vehicle. So far, so good. Now, what to do about SD?

Chet had an idea. "Hit the road, Jack!" he squawked.

Gabe and Kyle looked at each other. It might work. Kyle was ready to tour again, having had another small taste of it in Canada, and he had never really wanted to quit in the first place. Jenna started to object, but then thought better of it. This was the price she had to pay for her part in this mess. It wasn't like it would be forever, and she would have Dee around to keep her company and take her mind off Kyle.

Gabe was torn. The idea of touring again made his skin crawl. He liked the performing part of it, he just hated the rest. The worst part would be his separation from Annie. Christ, what was she going to say about this? Nevertheless, if he wanted to keep his career he had no choice.

"I'll start making some calls," he sighed. There was a lot to be done.

Gabe and Annie sat on her porch, enjoying the warm spring evening. She was faintly surprised; this was the quietest he had spent at her home since their ride in January.

"Annie, I need to tell you something." Gabe took her hand; this was going to be very difficult. "Where to start...?" he trailed off.

"What is it, Gabe? Is it Deirdre? The twins?" She was becoming very worried.

"No, they're all fine. It's the company... it's finished. SD Productions is no more."

"Oh, no! What happened? I thought... The CD... Gabe?" She felt as if she had been kicked in the stomach.

"It seems our trusted accountant as absconded with the funds. Every goddamn penny. Not even enough left to buy birdseed for Chet." Gabe let out a humorless laugh. "And we were so close."

"No, I can't believe it! Isn't there anything you can do? I have some money, you can have that. I could even sell off some of this property. Oh Gabe, I..."

"Thank you, love, but that won't be necessary. Kyle and I have come to a decision, one that was probably inevitable anyway, but we have decided to tour again. It will just be for the summer; just long enough to recoup some of our losses and promote the CD. With any luck. I've lined up someone to start booking us, and the guys from the band are all for it." He gave her a quick smile. "We already have a date set up in Canada. They rather liked us up there. After that we'll go wherever we can... go where we have to. There won't be any real money until we pay off those involved, but after that, well, we can only hope..." Gabe went on to explain exactly what happened, glossing over Kyle and Jenna's part in the mess.

Annie took it all in. This was worse than she had expected. Even though he didn't say so, she had the feeling that the Davidson's had a big part in the disaster. If they were so destitute as to have to leave their house and move in with Deirdre, well, something was going on. At least Dee would have someone else there while Gabe was gone.

Gabe, gone. No, this was worse than worse. How would Annie ever survive without him? He had become her best friend, her life even! No, not good at all.

"When will you be leaving?" she managed to choke out.

"Not for a month or so. We have to buy equipment, rent a bus and some trucks, and tie up some loose ends. After Canada, I'm not sure where we'll be. So far it's only three days up there, but you never know. We still have some time together, and I will call you every day that I'm on the road. Maybe you could get some time off and join me?"

"We'll see. Where are you getting money to buy all of this? I thought there was nothing left."

"Dee. Steve had a rather large insurance policy and left it to her. She wasn't even aware of it until recently. Al and Marie sent her a box of books they had found in the apartment over the garage - that's where Steve lived when he wasn't out chasing cows. Anyway, you know how Dee is with old books... Hey, did you ever read those journals?" Gabe asked.

"What? Oh, yes... One or two, but I haven't thought about them in forever. I've had other things on my mind," she teased.

"Hmm... me too. Anyway, Dee pulled out a children's book Stevie had saved for some reason, and the policy was in it. She said I should have it, that he sent it when I needed it most."

"He always told me that he would be there whenever I needed him," Annie said quietly. "It must be the same for you."

"I'm sure it is. Annie, you know I don't want to do this - leave you, I mean. God, we're becoming so close, so..."

"Don't, Gabe. I understand. I don't care for the idea, but I understand. It's only for a little while, and we've lived without each other for this long, a few more months won't matter. Much, anyway..."

He pulled his Annie close and gave her a quick kiss. "Thank you. That means a lot to me. Well, I guess I'd better be going; I have a lot to do tomorrow. Steve left enough money to get some CDs made for the tour. Can't have the fans leaving the show without a little souvenir... at fifteen bucks a shot," Gabe laughed.

"Hey, go all the way and have some tee shirts and posters made up while you're at it. Edith and all her 'sisters' will spend their life savings on that stuff," Annie joked.

"Ew, you had to mention that hag. I was just beginning to feel good!

Actually, that's not a bad idea. I wonder if it's in the budget."

"How much would something like that cost? I have some money just sitting around doing nothing but collecting a couple percent on interest. It should be out there doing some good."

"No, I won't ask you to do that. It's too much..."

"But I want to. Make me a partner or something. In case you forgot, I do have some interest in this venture. You will be doing "Dream Again," won't you?"

"Of course! That's the name of the tour! SD's big comeback... I hope. No, it will be. It has to be. And you, my love, are responsible for it."

"I wouldn't go quite that far," Annie protested, although she was thrilled that he felt that way.

Gabe stood and walked to the steps of the porch. "I should go."

She nodded. Some day he wouldn't have to, but until then...

"I'll see you tomorrow. Let me know how much you need for Edith's tee shirt."

"God! There you go again. I fear I shall suffer from nightmares tonight, as the mere thought of the woman strikes terror in my heart!" Gabe laughed; dodging the doggie chew toy Annie had picked up and thrown at him. "Is that any way to treat Dog's personal belongings?"

"Go. Dream your little dreams of trolls and gremlins, and call me tomorrow!" She blew him a kiss.

Gabe left, feeling like this all just might work out after all.

Chapter Thirty-Five

Annie looked at the calendar. April twenty-ninth. Gabe would be leaving the next day, weeks sooner that he had anticipated. As if by magic, (or Steven) calls came rolling in for bookings. Apparently SD hadn't been forgotten about after all. It was amazing how everything had come together in the last two weeks. The CDs, shirts, and posters were ready, funded by both Steve and Annie. The equipment was purchased, tested and packed away in rental vans. The bus was chartered and hotel reservations made. Montana would be their first destination, then off to Ontario. From there they would hit Michigan again, and then head southwest, heavily promoting the CD. Annie wasn't sure who the mortal miracle worker was who had arranged all of this, but he definitely deserved a medal! Gabe had said that he had never seen arrangements made so quickly, almost to the point of impossibly fast.

She sat in a chair on the porch, waiting. Gabe would be over soon to pick her up and they were joining Kyle and Jenna for dinner. Deirdre was supposed to go as well, but didn't feel well enough. She said she'd just have a quiet night at home with her boys.

Annie and Jenna had become quite good friends, once Jenna knew the truth about Gabe and Dee, and Annie looked forward to spending the evening with the Davidson's. It didn't take long for her to think of them as family, too.

Spike walked over to her and jumped into her lap.

"Well, Bubba, it won't be long and it will be just you and me again," she said to the cat. "I hope the summer flies by, but I have a feeling it will be the longest one of my life."

Spike agreed with Annie Rose, up to a point; it would prove to be the longest year of her life. He glanced up at the approaching vehicle. What an ugly monstrosity it was, this SUV. Such strange names humans had for their possessions. He snorted and retreated to his loft.

The foursome had a fun last night together. Bowling, beer, pizza, and Kyle's tasteless jokes kept them laughing for most of the evening. By eleven, it was obvious to anyone who cared to look that Jenna and Kyle needed to get home. Soon. They were about to lose control of their uncontrollable libidos right there in the bowling alley. Annie was amused - although slightly shocked, and Gabe wondered how they had held out this long. He told Kyle to take them all to the Evans', and Gabe would take Annie home in his truck.

She was home by eleven-thirty. Gabe gave her a most proper kiss at the door and said he would call her in the morning, then left. Annie watched him until his truck was out of sight. She was a little more that disappointed that he hadn't asked to stay even for a minute or two, but maybe he wanted to spend a little time with Deirdre before it was time to go. After all, they were very close friends. She walked into the cabin and shut the door. She still hadn't gotten around to remembering locking it.

What to do now? She was nowhere near tired yet, being on that third-shift schedule, so bed was out of the question. There were no tiresome household chores to be done, and even the green house had been emptied of its plants, which were all happily growing in the yard surrounding the cabin. With the exception of the roses, of course. They were due to be planted next weekend.

Maybe read a book? Annie jogged up the stairs to the loft to peruse her rather extensive collection of literature, but nothing sparked her interest. Well then, maybe a nice relaxing bath and a stiff drink would make her sleepy. It was worth a try.

Gabe drove to the top of Annie's driveway and stopped. What the hell was he doing, leaving her like that? Christ, he kissed her like he would have kissed his sister! He should go back and give her a proper good-bye. No, that's why he left in such a hurry in the first place. He wanted so much to do more than just kiss her. Maybe it was Kyle and Jenna's influence, but he couldn't get his mind off 'it'. Well, not necessarily 'it', but Annie, and making love to her. It had been far too long since they'd been together that way, and he was positively aching for her.

He pulled onto the road, still thinking about his Annie in his arms, telling him how much she loved him. He wanted to hear those words more than anything. He knew she did and she told him enough, but was it ever really enough? Not for him it wasn't. Maybe she needed to hear it from him again, too. He knew damn well that he could never tell her enough. And he couldn't leave without telling her one more time.

Gabe slammed on his brakes and spun the truck around, back to his Annie.

Annie made herself a 'bomber' drink - just a little one, and slipped into her big ol' tub where the scented water enveloped her all the way to her chin. She closed her eyes and leaned back, relaxing as she listened to SD playing on the stereo. At least she could have this much of him.

He pulled up to the darkened cabin. She hadn't gone to bed already, had she? He had to at least check. Spike met him on the porch when Gabe knocked softly on the door. He could hear his music on the other side and smiled. At least she was thinking about him. He tried the door handle, and as expected, it opened. Still no security issues here.

Spike ran in ahead of Geoffrey Alan and stopped near the greenhouse door. He gave a soft meow, attracting the man's attention. The man walked over to Spike, who then led him into the greenhouse.

Gabe looked at the cat. Hey, he helped once before, maybe he had something else up his furry little sleeve. He followed him into the greenhouse and looked around. It was empty except for a few pots of flowers on the bench. White roses. What else?

"Thanks, cat," he whispered to Spike.

The cat snorted and left the room.

Gabe picked the most perfect bud he could find, which was easy enough since they were all nearly perfect. Quietly he made his way towards the back of the cabin. Both bedrooms were empty, so she must be in the bathroom. In the tub? He could smell the lavender scent of the bath salts and see the flicker of candle flames reflecting on the floor, just under the door.

He heard a noise above him and looked up. Spike was watching him from the loft. Damned if that cat didn't just wink at him again! What the hell...? The worst thing she could do is throw him out. Gabe shed his clothes and went to join his Annie.

She heard something plop into the water, just under her nose, and the aroma of rose penetrated the scent of the lavender. What the...? She opened her eyes and looked down. In the dimness of the candlelit room she could make out a white rose bud floating in front of her, just above her breasts.

In the merest of whispers, she said, "Gabe?"

That was his cue. He slipped into the tub with his Annie, taking her into his arms and telling her that he loved her, had always loved her, and would love her forever.

Annie was in heaven. But no... Heaven couldn't be this grand, this glorious, and this magnificent! She returned Gabe's passion with everything she had, and then some.

From the bathroom they moved to the bedroom, totally lost in each other.

Deirdre woke at dawn, vaguely aware that Geoffrey had not made it home from Annie's. She walked down the hall to his room, and seeing his empty, untouched bed, she frowned. As much as Annie and Gabe were meant to be together, it still hurt the current Mrs. Evans that she was in second place.

Chapter Thirty-Six

Annie could barely contain her excitement. Gabe was due to be back any day now, and it would be the first time she had seen him in over a month. He had called her every day as promised, but it still was not enough. After that night when he had dropped in so unexpectedly, a mere phone call would never again be enough. She still got weak in the knees when she thought about that night. Never in her wildest dreams could she have imagined making love to be so incredible. It was better than her first time with Gabe, and the other few times they'd been together as well. She forced herself to stop thinking about it. Not only were her knees weak, but her breath caught in her throat, her heart did a flip-flop in her chest, and her tummy... well, and her tummy had been a bit of a problem lately anyway, so it didn't count.

Chet squawked from his new home in Annie's cabin, and she hoped that he wouldn't launch into yet another naughty limerick about a man from Nantucket. That Kyle was something else, teaching the poor bird all of that filth (even though it was pretty funny at times). No wonder Dee refused to let Chet into her home after the SD offices were shut down and Jenna was taking care of any business regarding the tour out of the Evans' house, specifically Gabe's office.

Annie yawned, wondering why she had been so tired lately. She wasn't working any overtime as of late, and life around the cabin bordered on boring. Maybe she needed to be around Gabe... absorbing his endless amounts of energy to feel anywhere near alive. She only had to wait less than twenty-four hours. Now, to fill the time between now and then...

Jenna decided to jog around the park one more time. She had taken up the activity shortly after Kyle left; it helped relieve the tension that was usually relieved by him. Must be that's why Gabe used to run miles every day when he was in his 'women are vultures' phase of life and totally avoided the female sex. Thank God her husband would be home tomorrow! She didn't think she could take one more day without him. And if she felt this way, she could imagine what he was going through.

Her feet hit the pavement in a steady rhythm as she ran and thought about the last month. It was so strange actually living at Deirdre's. The women had become closer than ever after she told Jenna the truth behind her and Gabe. Who'd have thought? Dee also told her bits and pieces of the scene with Steve appearing to Gabe and Annie. Jenna obviously didn't want to believe it, but Dee wouldn't make something like that up, and her mind was still pretty much unaffected by either drugs or her disease, so Jenna figured that there must be a little something to the story. She had hinted to Annie about it, but Annie didn't say much other than she knew who Gabe's brother was. Then again, she never denied any of it, either.

Annie had been a frequent visitor at the Evans' home lately, ever since Eric moved in. The place was getting to be a regular halfway house for the homeless and destitute! Eric's aunt couldn't kick some infection, and she had to be hospitalized again, which meant they lost their apartment and the kid was on the street. Deirdre found out about it somehow and took him in. He was a nice kid, but very quiet. Dee, Eric, and the twins would spend hours holed up in the twins' bedroom and Jen wondered what they did in there. Deirdre never said a word about it, and Annie didn't have a clue.

Jenna was glad that Annie really wasn't the bitch Kyle had said she was. They had been having a lot of fun together lately; she even taught Jen how to ride a horse. The two of them took long rides through the woods by Annie's place. There was one spot that they went to once that was spectacular. It was a clearing high above the lake. It had a really interesting bench and the view was breathtaking. Jenna wanted to stay there for a while, but Annie seemed really sad while they were there, so she didn't push it.

She stopped at a picnic table for a short break and wondered if Deirdre was finished reading her new book yet. She'd found it when the kids had been playing hide and seek. When Jenna couldn't find them, she decided to check the off-limits attic. Sure enough, there they were the six of them gathered in a far corner of the room. They seemed to by tugging on something, so she went to investigate. She saw a small, leather-bound chest partially protruding from a sliding door in the wall of the attic. Ooh... secret panels now! She waved the kids aside and pulled the box from its confines.

The children gathered around as Jenna opened it. The smell hit them first. A pungent, dusty, herbal aroma assaulted their nostrils. Eww! She slammed the lid down, but not before she saw the contents of the chest. Books, about a half dozen of them. She thought it would be something Dee would be interested in, and might help get her out of that depressing mood she had been in lately.

Jenna took the box to Dee's room and placed it on the bed. Her eyes lit up as she opened it and removed a book. She sat on the bed, opening the diary and waving Jenna away at the same time. Must have done the trick! Jen smiled and left the room.

Jenna resumed her run. As she reached the last half of her turn around the park, she heard the whine of a diesel engine straining up the hill in front of the house. It sounded like a bus... Could it be? She flew to the center of the park where the trees weren't as thick, and sure enough, she could see a dark blue charter bus pulling up in front of the Evans' home.

The air brakes squeaked and hissed as the bus came to a stop, and Jen began running towards it, waving and calling Kyle's name.

Kyle stepped of the bus, thankful that he didn't have to spend one more goddamned minute on it for a whole week. Christ, that part of this business sure sucked. He heard someone call his name. *Jenna?* He looked towards the house but didn't see her. Wait, it was coming from the park. He walked around the front of the bus and saw her there. Oh God, she looked great. She was running towards him, wearing not much more than a pair of sneakers, skimpy shorts and a sports bra.Ooh, and she was all sweaty and....

Kyle took off at a run, meeting his wife halfway into the park. He threw her to the ground in a flying tackle, pinned her arms above her as sat over her, and then proceeded to give her a month's worth of kiss. Minutes later they were heading into the park where the trees were the thickest.

Gabe watched from the window of the bus, chuckling at the Davidson's running towards each other. Thank God those two are finally together again, as Kyle was becoming quite unbearable to be around. He grabbed his backpack, which held presents for Dee and the boys, then exited the bus; he'd get the rest of his luggage later.

Deirdre heard the bus outside. Damn, he was home early, and she would have to get back to this later. She set the dusty book aside and gave a sigh of frustration. This was just as fascinating as Rosalind's journals, but in a much darker way.

When Jenna had brought her that old leather chest full of books, Dee had been excited, just because she loved to read. Then she touched one. She shuddered as she remembered the momentary revulsion she had felt when she had first picked up one of the diaries, but the feeling quickly passed into one of compelling curiosity. She needed to read these, had to find out what they contained. They were dated from the late 1800's, and written the firm hand of an Irish woman named Megheen.

Dee had waved Jenna away and lost herself in Megheen's troubled life.

Annie sat on the marble bench and looked out at the lake. She had no idea why she came up here. She always felt sad whenever she even came near the place and hadn't been up her since her ride with Jenna a few weeks ago, and that was the first time since she had been there since her last talk with Michael.

Steven. What had become of him? Did he go back to where ever now that his job was done? She missed him. Even though she talked to Gabe every day and visited with Jenna and Deirdre, she was still lonely. Other than Gabe, Michael was the only person Annie truly loved, absolutely trusted, and could talk to about anything. Must be she didn't need him anymore, which she supposed was probably a good thing. But still... to lose such a friend forever nearly broke her heart.

Wanda nickered, bringing Annie out of her reverie. She looked around to see what the horse was talking about, but saw nothing. And what was with Adonis today? She had gone out to the barn for her daily ride and Donny would have nothing to do with her. He stood at the far end of the pasture and refused to come up. Wanda was right there, so Annie took her instead. The mare needed the exercise anyway.

Oh God, would this day never end? Annie missed Gabe so much she could hardly stand it. She rose from the bench and went to stand by a tree at the edge of the clearing. She sighed as she looked below her to where the earth dropped away.

Wanda nickered again.

Annie ignored her. A gaggle of Canadian geese flew overhead, honking noisily, the racket making her head ache just a bit.Might as well go home; this place was just getting her down. She turned from the cliff and walked back to her horse. Her head was down as she looked for pebbles and sticks to kick out of her way in a poor attempt to relieve her frustration.

Wanda nickered again.

So did Adonis.

Annie looked up to see her other horse standing next to the bench, his tall rider looking down at her with intense blue eyes.

"Gabe!" She raced over the few yards separating them.

He kicked his foot over the saddle horn and jumped to the ground, and met his Annie halfway across the clearing. He swept her up into his arms and buried his face in her autumn hair.

"God, I missed you," were the only words he said before he laid her down on the soft, grass-covered forest floor and showed her just how much he missed her.

Annie and Gabe rode slowly back to the cabin, letting the horses pick their own way home. The sun had set long ago, and the moon was just now appearing above the trees. A light breeze blew through, bringing a chill to the air. She shivered.

"Cold?" He asked. It was the first word he had said since he told her that he missed her. She still hadn't said a thing. All that needed to be said up there in the clearing had been done with a look, a touch, a caress. Afterwards, Gabe held Annie in his arms as they watched the sunset, and then once again lowered her to the forest floor.

"Just a little," she said, answering his question. "I didn't expect to be out this late, so I didn't bring a jacket." She shivered again as the breeze picked up.

"I have just the solution." Gabe guided Adonis as close to Annie and Wanda as he could, then pulled his Annie from her horse and into the saddle in front of him. He wrapped his arms around her saying, "Better?"

"Much." She snuggled into her cowboy, hardly believing what just happened, any of it: from the moment she had seen him in the clearing, to just being scooped up onto her knight-in-shining-armor's horse.

Gabe kissed the top of her head and held her tighter. *Take your time going home, Donny boy, take your time.*

Neither of them said another word until they reached the barn, then Annie broke the silence. "How did you find me?" she asked.

"I didn't. Your horse did. When I pulled up to the cabin, he was raising all kinds of hell out there in the barn. I thought maybe something was wrong so I ran out there. I saw that Wanda and a saddle were missing and I figured you were out on a ride. So, I tossed a saddle on Adonis and let him have his head. He brought me straight to you."

"Strange… He wanted nothing to do with a ride earlier and that's why I took Wanda."

"Maybe he knew I'd be coming over tonight. Maybe Spike told him," Gabe joked.

"Spike? Don't be silly, he would never come near the barn. That would make him 'common'… associating with mere farm animals," Annie laughed.

"Well then, I just don't know how to explain it!" Gabe said in mock-exasperation.

Annie gave him a sidelong glance and unsaddled Wanda, then grabbed a brush and began grooming the horse.

"Feel free to take care of Donny. After all, it's your fault that he's all sweaty," Annie teased.

"Fine. Just see if I ever keep you warm again," Gabe teased back. He unsaddled Adonis, then grabbed both saddles and carried them to the tack room.

Annie watched him. It was hard to believe this man spent the better part of his working day sitting behind a desk. Or at least he used to. He looked so… so right, there in the barn. He certainly knew his way around a horse, too. She'd have to ask him about that later. In all their time together, and in all of their conversations, he had never really talked about himself, at least the little things. He talked about Steve often enough, but never himself. Annie knew who he was now, but what was he like before? Before Annie? Before Deirdre?

Well, that could wait. He was returning with a bale of hay slung over one strong shoulder. The material of his shirt was pulled tight across his chest, and she could make out every detail of his muscular torso. Oh jeez… She felt herself growing warm all over. Would a third time today be pushing it?

Gabe glanced up at Annie as he dropped the bale of hay to the floor. Aw God… the way she was watching him - he knew that look. Would a third time today be too much? Not for him. He kicked apart the bale, making a fragrant pallet on the barn floor. Lacking a blanket, he peeled off his shirt and tossed it onto the hay. He saw that his Annie never took her eyes from him; her expression never changed. Once again he took her into his arms and kissed her hard.

Annie smiled as she felt herself being lowered to the floor yet again. Three times in one day wasn't too much, and she would never look at a bale of hay the same way again.

✦ ✦ ✦

James and Jeremy sat in their room coloring pictures that Eric had drawn for them

"Will Uncle Gabe be tucking us in tonight?" James asked.

"Prob'ly not. 'Member? He's at Goose-mother's tonight," Jeremy answered.

"Oh yeah, I forgetted. When do we get to live there? Daddy said it would be pretty soon and I want to ride the pony," James sighed.

"I don't know, and call her Annie; Daddy said so. And don't forget to call Uncle Gabe 'Papa'. Daddy said so."

James stuck his tongue out at his brother. "I know, I know. I'm not stupid. But we can say what we want in here, so long as Mamma and Eric aren't here. Or anyone else."

"Well, don't forget. It's not time yet."

"Jer, will you miss Mamma when she's gone?"

"Yeah, but she told us that she would still be here, we just won't see her, 'member? Just like Daddy."

"But we see Daddy, why won't we see her too?"

"Dunno. But that's what she told us, and she always tells the truth," Jeremy told him.

Yeah, but I'll still miss her," sighed James.

"Me too," agreed Jer.

They went back to their coloring in silence.

While Annie fixed dinner for Gabe and her, he told her about his first month on the road. The venues had been small but enthusiastic, and SD was definitely on the comeback trail.

"I wish you could have been there, Annie," he said as he told her about his first performance. "I'll admit, I was kind of scared... well, not exactly scared, I just didn't know what to expect. It has been a very long time.

"The entire stadium was black, not a single light on. I hadn't yet checked out the crowd - you know, to see how many were out there. And when we came out on stage, the crowd didn't know we were there until Wolff started in on the violin... the beginning of "The Dream." That's what we opened with. Anyway, it became very quiet in there; the music has that effect on people... rather haunting. Mick joined in on the drums and the lights came on. God, Annie, it was great! The house was packed. Over five thousand people jumped to their feet and started cheering and applauding... I'd forgotten what that was like. It's such a rush!" He smiled at the memory; he had really enjoyed himself.

She saw the look in his eyes and felt an unaccustomed stab of jealousy.

"They loved us, Annie. We did all the new songs - except yours, and I don't even know how many of the old ones, then came out for three encores. We did "Dream Again" last. It was perfect." Gabe rose from the table and went to the stove where she was making omelets. He wrapped his arms around her and kissed her neck. "Just perfect."

Annie's momentary jealousy vanished. It was hard not to get caught up in

Gabe's enthusiasm, and she turned to face him.

"So they liked my song?"

"They loved it. We nearly sold out of CDs and had to call Jenna to put in another order so we would have some for the next concert. I had to use my own money to do it, but it has since been repaid - and then some. Your shirt and poster idea paid off too, partner. You might have quite a return on your investment. After just one month there is light at the end of the tunnel, financially speaking. We still have a long way to go, though."

"I'm glad it's going so well. Did you happen to see your parents while you were in Montana? I'm not exactly sure how close you were, where you performed at."

"As a matter of fact, I did. Didn't I tell you?"

Annie shook her head.

"Oh. Well then, we were never got closer than a hundred miles to the old homestead, so I rented a car and drove out there on a down day. They were quite surprised to see me. We had a really nice visit, then they showed me where uh, Steve's final resting-place was. It was all I could do not to laugh! God, could you just imagine...? Anyway, they made a nice rock garden and the earthly remains of Steve and Whiz were sprinkled over it. Mom almost started to cry as we stood there looking at it, and I so wanted to tell her that he was fine, but that will be up to Steve."

Annie had turned back around and was dishing up the omelets. She handed Gabe a plate and they returned to the table.

"Have you seen Steve since... since that day?" she asked.

"No. You?"

"No, I haven't. Haven't 'felt' him either. Do you think Deirdre has seen him? She has been so quiet lately, and rather depressed. I'm really worried about her, Gabe. Her health seems stable; she is no worse, no better than she has been, but it's like she is a million miles away. The only time she shows any signs of life is when she is with the twins."

"Probably not. And you're right; she has been distant lately, ever since that day. Do you think we should talk to her, ask her about him?"

"I don't know... I'll see what Jenna thinks. She's around Deirdre much more than I am."

"Good luck. You won't see much of her as long as Kyle is around. God! Can you believe those two?" Gabe laughed and told Annie about the scene in the park.

Spike joined the couple at the table and looked from one to the other. Good. Things were as they should be. Annie Rose flipped him a bit of ham from her omelet. He shot out a paw and tossed the meat into his mouth. He gave his whiskers a quick brush, and then retreated to his loft.

Gabe saw Annie throw some of her food to the cat. He gave her a look that was half question, half frown.

She noticed. "I know, I'm probably breaking some rule about feeding a cat at the table, but it's kind of a game we play. Do you have a problem with that?" she asked, slightly defensive.

"No, I guess not. Look, Chet's jealous."

Annie looked over towards the bird, which was hanging upside down from his perch and making his 'whimpering puppy' noise. Kyle had taught him that one, too.

"Then he can have some of yours. That is, unless you want me to make him one of his own. He's sounding pretty pathetic over there," Annie laughed.

"I'll give him mine," Gabe sighed, and took the bird the small amount of egg that remained on the plate. He finished clearing the table and put the dishes in to soak.

Annie got up to help, but he waved her away. She sat on the sofa and watched him tidy up the kitchen.

"So, Montana was perfect. How was Canada?" she asked.

"Even better, if that were possible. The first town was nearly a sell-out, and the second one was. They had so many requests for tickets that they added a second show. Didn't bother us a bit. We would have done a third, but the town was so small that I think pretty much the entire population made it one or the other of the shows. I'm hoping that in the future it will be bigger cities, bigger venues. More money, less travel. I don't want to be away from you any more than I have to."

"I won't argue with that, but don't you enjoy it? You seem to when you're talking about it. It isn't just for the money any more, is it?"

Gabe thought for a moment. "At first it was, but not so much anymore. I'm sure I'll get sick of it soon enough, just like the last time, but now... now it is like a drug. Standing up there, thousands of people screaming just for you... it grabs you. You want more, and the more you get, the more you want. But like I said, I'll tire of it soon enough. I've got something much more intoxicating right her." He joined Annie on the sofa.

"Whatever. It sounds kind of like you don't know where you will be playing next, do you?"

"Not really. I know which state we'll be in, but some of these towns I've never heard of. I do know that Chicago, Detroit and Nashville are definitely not on the list. Oh well, maybe next year..."

Annie gave him a sharp look. "What do you mean, next year? I thought this was a one-shot deal, only for the summer!" she snapped at him. She hadn't meant to sound so bitchy, but it just popped out before she could stop herself.

"It was just a figure of speech," Gabe said slowly. He had never seen this side of her before; he hoped it was a fluke.

"I'm sorry. I don't know what's wrong with me lately."

"Why, what is it?" he asked, concerned.

"Nothing, just a little more tired-feeling than usual. I want to sleep all of the time... probably just boredom. But no more; you're back, and I want our time together to be perfect. I have an idea... The weather is supposed to be great tomorrow, so let's invite everyone over for a barbecue. The twins can ride Wanda, Eric can help them, and Deirdre can relax by the lake. Have Kyle and Jenna and the kids come too. We'll have a bonfire and roast marshmallows and..."

Gabe interrupted. "I didn't want to have to share you with anyone, but that doesn't sound like a bad idea. Give everyone a chance to unwind. Hey, is the lake warm enough to swim in yet?"

"No, not unless you're a polar bear, but it might be warm enough to wade in. The kids can at least play on the beach. McDonald would love the company."

"Speaking of the odd couple - or at least half of them, where have they been? I haven't seen either of them since I've been here."

"I don't know. They go down to the lake and are gone for hours at a time. I think they go away to bicker so I won't yell at them," Annie told him. "Go call Deirdre and invite everyone over for tomorrow. You don't think that they have plans already, do you?"

Gabe laughed. "No, except for maybe Kyle and Jenna, but I'm sure they could find a quiet place in the woods around here for their 'trysting'. Just as long as it's not 'our place'," he said, referring to the clearing.

"I don't think they'd find it, even if they made it that far. It's a magical place, and I don't think that they'd be, uh... welcome there," Annie said quietly.

"It is magical, isn't it? I'll never forget the first time I saw it; it was like a kaleidoscope with the colors swirling all around. It was incredible! I always thought it was some kind of hallucination until I saw it again. With you, in Canada... Remember?"

"How could I forget? Until recently, it was the best day of my life," Annie said, then added, "And the worst."

"Best and worst?"

"I wouldn't even begin to know how to explain it." She sighed and snuggled a little closer to Gabe. Best, worst... it didn't matter anymore.

"Indulge me. At least try," Gabe said. He really wanted to hear what she had to say about that day.

Annie closed her eyes and thought back to that wonderful, horrible day in January... her woodsy-spicy cowboy, Deirdre's husband, her fantasy, reality rearing its ugly head...

"It started long before Canada. I'm not exactly sure when, but... Gabe, this is going to sound really crazy. I don't know..."

"Annie, after what we have seen, you know, with Steve, do you think anything else could be crazier?" He gave her a quick hug. "Tell me."

She nodded. "I guess you're right. It all started about five years ago. My parents had died... Well anyway, I was at my grandmother's place looking for the gardens. I found a rose bush and I touched it. Here is the crazy part - I had a... a vision. I saw you. Oh jeez... and it was so vivid! And that wasn't the last time either; I saw you many times after that and every night I would have the same dream about you. I almost recognized you in the cafeteria that night. You seemed so familiar, but I didn't know from where. Then I recognized your cologne on the afghan after you little visit and it started coming together. By the time we met in Canada, I was hopelessly, irrevocably in love with you. There was no going back."

Gabe smiled; it was exactly what he wanted to hear.

"And then?"

"Canada." Annie shivered ever so slightly. "Yes, Canada. I was on top of that beginner hill and I heard that voice. I turned around and there you were... Oh God, Gabe, it was just like in the song!" She couldn't speak for a moment, so overcome was she by emotion. "Then I found out for sure that you were Deirdre's husband. That was the 'worst' part. I wanted to die... and I think that's why I got a little drunk that night. It's no excuse, but it happened. And then there was that song you sang. I imagined that you were singing it to me and me alone."

"I was. You were on my mind with every letter I wrote... every word I sang... every note I played." Gabe punctuated each pause with a kiss. "And then?"

"And then... it was over. Us. We. We were over. You were going home to the wife, and I was going home with a hangover," Annie sighed.

"And a few dozen roses," he added.

"Yes, the roses. That darn near killed me."

"Really. I certainly had no murderous intentions when I purchased them," he teased.

"No, it wasn't like... wait. The strangest thing happened when I took one of the roses from the vase. The aroma brought back memories; memories of things I had never done, never experienced... and the next thing I knew I was writing something. A poem, I think. I haven't thought about it since that day... I wonder what I did with it."

"Ask Spike," Gabe laughed.

"What is it with you and that cat?"

"Nothing. He is... he just... oh, never mind. What was the poem about?"

"I don't really remember. Something to do with roses, I think. I wonder where I put it." Annie pondered.

"It will show up, I'm sure," Gabe assured her.

"Gabe, do you realize that this is the first time we've really talked since you left, other than 'how's the weather'?" Annie said as she turned to look at him.

"Yes, I do. And you seem to have lost that refreshing, endearing, yet at times frustrating shyness," he replied, and kissed her on the nose.

"Hmm... There's nothing like a roll in the hay to take the edge off," Annie quipped.

"That was entirely your fault, you randy wench, looking at me like that. God! It was like the grand lady and the stable boy all over again!"

"Don't bore me with your tiresome fantasies, or it's back to the barn with you," she proclaimed in a stuffy British accent.

"Promise?"

Annie threw a doggie chew toy at him.

"When do you have to leave?" she asked, turning serious.

"In six days. We've got..."

"No, I mean tonight. What time tonight?"

"Who says I have to?"

"Shouldn't you be home to tuck in James and Jeremy?"

"I am under the impression that they aren't expecting me. As I was telling them good-bye before I came over here, they told me to have fun and tell goose mother hello, and that they would see me tomorrow. The odd part is that I never told them where I was going; they just knew."

"Goose-Mother. Where did they ever get that name? Jenna told me about it a long time ago, but I... honestly, it kind of creeped me out!"

"I think they are referring to McDonald and the circumstances of his birth... or would it be hatching?"

"But how would they know that?"

"Steve," they answered in unison. That would explain it.

"I wonder what else he told them," Gabe said. "You know, he still might be appearing to them to help with Deirdre's... with Deirdre... Annie, how much time do you think she has left?" His throat tightened. It suddenly dawned on him that Deirdre was, indeed, dying.

"Gabe," she said as she took his hands, "To be honest, I'm surprised that she is still alive. She's stable right now, but her cancer is so advanced that... that she could begin to fail at any time. Have... have you made any arrangements?"

"No, it never crossed my mind. I mean, I didn't know..."

"Why don't you call her, just to check on her? Right now before she goes to bed. I know, invite them all out tomorrow. Let's have some fun!" Annie handed him the phone. It was a new, cordless one, complete with answering machine.

After Gabe's call, he and Annie took a walk by the lake. Halfway around, they ran into the odd couple heading home and still bickering about only they knew what. The four of them stopped and faced each other. Annie and Gabe shared a glance, as did Dog and McDonald, then human looked at animal. The humans burst into laughter and the animals continued on their way; their heads held high in righteous indignation.

Chapter Thirty-Seven

The morning dawned bright and clear. Annie woke with a smile on her face and rolled over to reach for Gabe, but he wasn't there. Her eyes flew open. Oh jeez... where was he? This wasn't that damn dream all over again, was it? She fought to control the panic that threatened to overwhelm her... It was real - it had to be real!

"Gabe?" she said in a choked whisper. She felt dizzy and sick to her stomach, so she rolled onto her back and took a few deep breaths. The nausea went away.

Oh God, where was he? He had been here, hadn't he? Annie took another deep breath and sat up in bed. She looked around the room for evidence - anything that would prove he had been here. She could find nothing. Even the extra pillow on her bed looked untouched.

So, it had been a dream after all. Nothing but a wonderful dream. Well, at least she would see him soon; he was due home today... unless she was truly insane and had imagined everything all the way back to Gramma's rose garden. Maybe she was in a mental hospital somewhere, riding the wild waves of some mad, perpetual hallucination... Now that idea was crazy.

She was here in her own cabin, in her own room, in her own bed, and if she didn't get to her own bathroom soon she would puke on her own floor. Annie slapped a hand over her mouth and made it to the toilet just in time.

After a quick shower she slipped into a pair of shorts and a tee shirt, then made herself a cup of tea and went to the porch to drink it. It was a beautiful morning and promised to be a warm day as well.

Annie was feeling much better now. She kicked her feet up onto the porch rail and leaned back in her chair. She closed her eyes and listened to the birds, the bees, that damn odd couple bickering non-stop, and the sound of a maul splitting wood. What the...?

She jumped from her chair and raced across the porch to the side of the cabin. Oh God... there he was - shirtless, his jeans riding low on his hips, his muscular back glistening in the morning sun... Gabe. She stared in disbelief, having convinced herself that it really had been a dream.

He turned around and waved at her, then went back to the business at hand.

She had to sit down. She was dizzy again, but it was soon replaced by the same warm feeling she had felt last night in the barn. Annie stared at the man working out there in the morning sun. Never had she seen anything as... as beautiful as he was. Maybe 'beautiful' wasn't exactly the right word, he was way to masculine for that, but it was the best she could come up with. Perfection was a good one, too.

Gabe tossed the last of the split logs into the cart; he'd haul them down to the fire pit at the lake later. He used his shirt to wipe the sweat from his face and walked over to where his Annie was sitting on the edge of the porch, the height of which brought her eye-level with him.

"Good morning, Miss Benton, and how are we today?" he asked, then gave her a quick kiss and his lopsided grin. He went back to toweling the sweat from his chest, again using his shirt, while he waited for her answer.

"We are... are uh... f... fine," she managed to say.

He gave her a skeptical look. "Are we sure? We seem to have a strange look... Ah yes, I seem to recall that very same green-eyed gaze. Wait, it's coming to me..." Gabe closed his eyes and placed his fingertips on his forehead, appearing to be deep in thought. "Coming to me... that's it!" He opened his eyes and looked at her.

"You were standing behind your noble steed, watching me as I carried fodder for that very animal. That look; it captured me, held me prisoner, compelled me to..."

He had been slowly moving towards Annie, each word bringing him closer until he was a fraction of an inch away...

She leaned forward in anticipation and wasn't disappointed.

Gabe lifted her from the porch and carried his lady to the barn. Earlier that morning he had taken a blanket from the house and stashed it away in an empty stall... just in case. He was a very considerate stable boy.

Annie batted away the wisp of hay with which Gabe was tickling her nose.

"Stop. You are already doomed to rot in hell for you wicked ways, don't compound the matter by annoying me further," she said in mock-seriousness.

"Am I to understand that you don't enjoy this?" He gave her nose another touch with the hay.

"No, I don't."

"How about this?" Gabe began moving the wispy stem down, down her chin, down her neck, down...

"Stop!" Annie smiled and sat up, then grabbed her shirt and pulled it back on. "We have to get back and start preparing for the big shin-dig. I've got a ton of stuff to do, and thanks to you I'm way behind schedule."

"You don't need to do a thing. Not only do I know my way around a barn," he grinned, "but I also know my way around the yellow pages, and I can use a phone. The caterers will be here around noon, and the guests around one. All you need to do is look pretty and you've got that taken care of already. So as near as I can figure we still have another hour or two to while away in the hay."

"Wow, you have been busy. But I still have to feed..."

"Done and done. Every critter here has been fed, watered, brushed, curried, and even milked where necessary. What do you do with that goat milk, anyway?" Gabe asked.

"Dog and the cats usually get it. I rarely get through a milking without a foot getting dunked in the bucket. I thought she would have dried up by now... Lord, her kid is over a year old, but she keeps on producing, so I keep milking."

"Good, since that is who got this morning's offerings," Gabe laughed.

"Foot in the bucket?"

"You would be correct!"

They laughed and lay back down on the blanket.

After a few minutes of silence, both deep in their own thoughts, Annie said quietly, "Thank you, Gabe."

"For what?"

"Everything... just everything. I... I love you."

"I love you, too."

Annie heard the sound of a diesel engine coming down the drive. The caterers had come and gone, so who could this be? She glanced out the window and was met with the sight of a big blue bus parking next to her truck.

"They're here," Gabe yelled from the porch.

She watched as the Davidson children, all blonde and boisterous as their parents, jumped from the bus and ran to the lake. James and Jeremy followed, with a frazzled-looking Jenna hot on their heels. Eric was next, then Kyle, who helped Deirdre down the steps. Gabe was waiting for her at the bottom, and escorted her to the cabin. Just as Annie was about to leave her room to greet Dee, she saw more bodies moving from the bus. There was Wolff, Mick, Dave... It was SD! This would be a party! She ran to the porch to greet her guests.

How could the day not have been a success? The children played in the lake, watched over by Jenna and Eric, Dog and McDonald. Gabe had the caterers erect an awning near the beach so that Deirdre would have a place to relax out of the sun, yet still be near the action. Wanda was saddled, and all of the children, and even some of the adults, took a turn around the pasture. Kyle designated himself master of the coals and cooked every steak, rib, and burger consumed that day. Gabe attempted to help him, but was slapped away with a greasy spatula. There was no way that Kyle was gonna let his buddy ruin their barbecue; Gabe couldn't handle anything more difficult than boiling water.

Shortly after dinner, as the adults were sipping beers and talking quietly among themselves, Annie noticed that it was unusually quiet. Where were the children? Must be in the barn or the cabin. She decided to check and walked up the hill away from the lake.

She saw Dog sitting on the porch of the cabin, but McDonald was nowhere in sight. Uh-oh... Just what were those kids up to? Annie raced up the steps and into the cabin, and hearing giggles from the bathroom, went there first. She didn't know whether to laugh or cry at the scene before her.

Her big, beautiful tub was filled to overflowing, with McDonald floating peacefully in the middle. Water covered the floor, along with several pots of flowers which had been knocked from the tub's ledge. Seven children fought for position, trying to reach McDonald in the center of his new pond. Not one child had a dry spot on them, and most were covered in flowerpot mud.

Annie must have made a noise, seven heads turned to look at her. She said nothing, just pointed towards the door. One by one, the children passed by her, heads hanging low in anticipation of the upcoming punishment; not necessarily by Annie, but from Jenna, who they had seen waiting for them in the living room.

Annie plucked the goose from the tub and sent him out after the children, then turned back to survey the mess. It was going to take a long time to clean this up. She threw some towels on the floor and started in.

Nearly an hour later she was finished, and just in time to see Gabe light the bonfire. Once the logs were burning nicely, he went to sit with his wife. Annie only minded a little; after all, not everyone knew the truth. Out of respect for Dee, Gabe and Annie had kept their distance, acting only as friends and not as lovers. Still, she would have loved to be sitting with him and watching the fire.

After toasting marshmallows, Kyle, Jenna, and Eric took the children off to the semi-swampy north end of the lake to look for frogs and other cold, slimy creatures. Deirdre had her lounge chair moved closer to the fire, and sat watching the flames dance. The band members gathered around the beer keg, discussing tales of the road. Annie began carrying dishes up to the cabin so that there wouldn't be so much work later. Gabe met her in the kitchen.

"I have been waiting all day, just for a moment alone with you," he said, pinning her against the wall.

"I was by myself for an hour, cleaning up that damn bathroom. Where the hell were you then?" *Ewww... that bitchy note in her voice again. Better watch it, Annie.*

Gabe released his hold on her and took a step back.

In a frosty tone he said, "I apologize for my children making such a mess in your home. I assure you that it won't happen again."

"I'm sorry, Gabe, I didn't mean it like that. It's just so hard to be near you, and not with you. Please, Gabe..."

He took her in his arms and held her close. "I know what you mean. I should have told the guys the truth about us, avoid all this subterfuge, but it's a little late for that now.

She pulled away from him. "Didn't they question when you didn't take the bus over here with them? Or when you called me every day while you were on the road, or why you're here all the time and your wife is at home? Isn't it obvious how you feel about me? Don't you ever talk to them about me, or am I your dirty little secret?" Annie knew that she should shut up; she didn't even know what drove her to say such things! She really didn't feel that angry about the situation, but she was so damn tired lately!

Gabe didn't reach for her again as taken aback as he was by her words, her tone of voice. He tried, but failed to keep the hurt and anger from his voice.

"No, you are not some 'dirty little secret', but I cannot go flaunting a mistress in front of a wife, especially Deirdre. Not that she would care... hell, she loves the idea of us together. However, now that I am once again in the public eye, I have to watch my actions. You never know when one of those goddamn photographers will be there shoving a camera in your face, or some fucking reporter will be twisting your words to suit their needs. I have a family to look out for!"

Now it was Annie's turn to be stunned. She had never seen him so angry! She wanted to apologize, to hold him and have him kiss away the hurt, take her to the barn and...

A mistress? God, what an archaic term! Is that what she was to him now? A mistress? She couldn't even look at him.

He felt terrible. He hadn't meant to say all of that, even if it was all true. He couldn't publicly love Annie without hurting his family, and it was his family if only by default. What was wrong with her anyway? Didn't she know how much he loved her? She had to know! In these last twenty-four hours they had become so close, shared so much... how could she not know? And yet she was turning away from him.

"Annie..." Gabe said as he touched her shoulder.

She shrugged off his hand. She was so near to bursting into tears, that even the sound of his voice could trigger an emotional breakdown.

Maybe he should give her a few minutes to cool off. He'd go talk to Dee; maybe she could give him a woman's point of view on this mess. He didn't want to leave his Annie, though. Maybe he should just carry her to the bedroom, get the whole misunderstanding out of the way and tell her he loved her until she got it through that beautiful red head.

"Annie," he said again.

She flinched at his voice.

Well, he could at least apologize. "I'm sorry," he said, and left the cabin.

Sorry? Sorry for what? Being such a prick? Sorry that she wasn't falling into his arms, apologizing? Sorry for getting involved with her in the first place? Sorry for loving her? Annie was floundering deep in a pool of self-pity and not even trying to climb out. Fine, let him take his sorry ass out of here then. Go back to the wife when you're done with the mistress. She walked over to her favorite chair and threw herself into it. She hugged the woodsy-spicy afghan close to her and let the tears fall.

Geoffrey joined Deirdre on her lounge chair. He sat on the end, long legs astraddle, and facing her.

She pulled herself up, sitting with her legs crossed to give him room. She waited for him to speak; it was obvious that something was on his mind, and it probably had to do with Annie. She suspected that Annie had told him, but wanted Geoffrey to be the one to bring up the most delicate subject.

Gabe looked around to ensure that he and Dee had complete privacy. The guys were still working on emptying the keg of beer, and the mighty explorers were still out trudging through the swamp. He was sure that Annie was still in the cabin. Good. They could talk.

"Dee, what's wrong with Annie? I can't seem to figure her out anymore," he sighed.

She knew exactly what was wrong, but went along with his ignorance. "What do you mean, Geoffrey? What is it?" She leaned forward in a show of concern.

"I don't know. This morning was so great, yesterday too, but tonight... Well, I was just up at the cabin, trying to have a moment alone with her, and she went all... all bitchy on me! I couldn't say anything right. Actually, I said a few wrong things, but she wouldn't listen when I did try to apologize. I don't know..."

"Geoffrey, did she say anything else? Give you a reason for her behavior?" Deirdre asked. Maybe Annie hadn't told him after all.

"No, not really. Wait, she did say that she was tired lately, but God! She was never this way when she was working all of that overtime, why now?"

"Now Geoffrey, you know how women can be. We are an emotional lot; especially if... around that time... you know what I'm trying to say, don't you?"

"Oh! Uh, yes. At least I think so. Whoa, I've never had to deal with this before. You were never like that, were you?"

"I am not given to letting others know of my troubles. If I were 'like that', you would have never known."

"I suppose, but I'm not sure that that's all there is to it."

They sat in silence for several minutes, then Gabe turned away to stare at nothing across the lake.

Deirdre studied his profile, which was highlighted by the firelight. Something dark twisted in her mind, and then spread throughout her body. She began having thoughts about Geoffrey the way she had previously only thoughts about Steven. Steven, who had left her without a single word of good-bye. She was still angry with him. However, Geoffrey was still here; here with her, here for her. He was still her husband.

The darkness in her mind pushed Deirdre out and let something else in.

Gabe thought about Annie as he picked at a splinter on the wooden lounge chair. He really should go try to apologize again, even though she started it. How the hell was he supposed to know the kids trashed the bathroom and she was left alone with the mess? That, and she should have expected him not to be overly friendly with her in front of the children and the guys; their relationship could not become public until his wife… until Dee was gone.

He looked up at his wife. Despite her being so ill, she was still beautiful. Her blonde hair had begun to grow back, and lay in soft, thick curls around her head. Her bone structure, which had always been perfect, was even more sharply defined than ever, and her skin had taken on a translucent quality. Maybe it was a combination of firelight, moonlight, and Gabe's pain of Annie's rejection, but he began to find Deirdre damned attractive. She had never ever caused him any kind of hurt. As a matter of fact, she had always been there for him, ever since Steve had died. She'd sat with him for hours on end, getting him through those nights when the nightmares rocked him from his sleep. She had talked him out of his bouts of depression, preventing him from seeking the mind-numbing effects of the drugs that he had used before he had met her. She cooked for him, cleaned for him, took care of his every need – even that one he tried to deny, and just plain loved him. Why was it they had never actually fallen in love with each other?

"Geoffrey?" Deirdre whispered.

"Hmm."

"You're staring. Something on your mind?"

"What? Ah... no, nothing. I just never realized that your hair was so curly," he said.

Gabe reached out and touched one of the curls in question. It felt like silk against his fingers.

"It never used to be, it grew back in like this. Do you like it?"

"Very much." His finger moved from her hair to her cheek.

She smiled. This might prove to be easier than she thought. Annie could have him back after she was finished with him, if she ever was.

"Do you think she might be ready to talk to me yet?" Gabe asked, returning his hand to pick at the splinter.

"Who? Oh, Annie? Give her a few more minutes. She'll have a good cry, and then be all contrite and putty in your hands."

"Thanks, Dee. Sometimes I don't know what I'd do without you." Gabe cupped her chin in his hand and leaned over to kiss her cheek.

This was her chance. She leaned forward to accept Geoffrey's kiss, and at the last moment turned her head, meeting his lips with hers.

Gabe's reaction was unexpected, especially to him. Deirdre's kiss shot through him like an electric current, followed by a bolt of lightning. He quickly pulled away from her, surprised, excited, and just a little guilty. The dormant passions so recently awakened by his Annie seemed ready to be accessible to the next available female.

Why had Dee done that? She'd never done that before, except on a rare occasion when they both had needs, and not since she had gotten sick. He looked deep into her eyes, hoping to find the answer. What he saw there again both surprised and excited him. Her pale blue eyes had changed to a glittering black. This was not his wife looking back at him.

She smiled at Geoffrey as he jumped back; she had anticipated this move and grabbed the collar of his shirt. The way he was looking at her right now... it sent chills down her spine! She placed her hand on the back of his neck and pulled him towards her.

He hesitated for only a moment, and then kissed her again.

Annie sat at the top of the hill waiting for Gabe to finish his talk with

Deirdre. After he had left her alone in the cabin, she did indeed have a good cry. Five minutes of tears was enough to purge the self-pity, and Annie felt like Annie again. She would find Gabe and apologize, and then make it up to him later tonight. She knew he loved her, and he was right about the negative publicity. She could wait; forever, if she had to.

She had run to the top of the hill, looking for Gabe, and then spotted him sitting with his wife. Annie could only see their silhouettes against the fire, but she could tell that their conversation was serious. She decided to just sit there and wait until they were finished, giving them some privacy.

She felt a little sick again, watching them. Why was he touching her hair like that? Not very brotherly... maybe he was just complementing her, making her feel better.

But she went numb as she witnessed Gabe's next move. He was kissing her! She felt a moment's relief when he pulled quickly away, but when she saw Deirdre's arm reach out and easily pull him back in, Annie felt her world explode. She couldn't watch; she couldn't look away. Oh God, Gabe, why?

Wolff nudged Mick and pointed to the boss and his wife. "See, told ya. Now where's my fifty?"

Mick slipped Wolff a bill and shot back: "Yeah, well he's getting it from the redhead, too. I got a hundred on it."

The men touched their beer glasses and the bet was sealed.

Annie would have given anything not to have overheard them.

Gabe found himself pushing Deirdre back into the chair, or was she pulling him? Not that it mattered, as he seemed powerless to drag himself away. He continued to kiss her, began to caress her, and was nearly lying on top of her before he came to his senses. What the hell had gotten in to her? What the hell had gotten into him, for that matter? He didn't want Dee, he never had. He only wanted his Annie.

He pulled Dee's arms from around his neck and sat back on the end of the chair, looking at her. He didn't much care for the smug, self-satisfied look on her face, either. And her eyes... Who the hell was that looking back at him? Something from far, far away in his memory nagged at him, yet he couldn't place what it was. The only thing that came to mind was of something very disturbing and quite evil. The thought made him shiver.

He rose from the chair and backed away a few steps before a movement on the hill caught his eye. He turned to look, his worst fears coming true. She'd seen him and misinterpreted everything, apparently. Christ, and now she was running towards the cabin. Gabe's heated blood turned to ice. He gave Deirdre a quick, scowling look and went after his Annie.

Mick nudged Wolff and nodded towards Annie, then Gabe. "See? Told ya!" He held his hand out to Wolff and received his fifty back, plus another.

"Annie! Annie, please open up!" Gabe stood outside of her bedroom, resting his forehead and the palms of his hands on the door. It seemed as if all of his energy had drained away with each step he took up the hill to the cabin. Tremors shook his body and he had a horrible ache in the pit of his stomach.

"Annie, please... let me explain. It was just a silly little kiss, that's all." Yeah, right. Thinking about it again, it had been much more, and if he'd been in Annie's place... Oh God, what she must be thinking. He gave the door a weak slap with the palm of his hand, then turned around to lean on that same door, slowly sinking to the floor. He folded his arms on his raised knees and let his forehead drop to his forearms. She had to listen to him, had to understand...

But how could she ever understand when he, himself, did not?

Spike walked from the guest bedroom, stopped to glare at Geoffrey Alan, then trotted up to the loft. Geoffrey Alan had made a big mistake. It wasn't entirely his fault, but he hadn't been strong enough to resist. If he wasn't careful, he would repeat the mistake over and over again.

This new force was a strong one and Spike did not like it a bit. He paced back and forth in the loft, growling to himself, his fur standing on end. A strong force indeed. Pray that Steven Anthony would be allowed to return and assist. Spike could not handle this alone.

Annie sat on the floor in the corner of her bedroom, clutching the woodsy-spicy afghan to her chest just as a child would cling to a security blanket. How dare he come back into her house? She'd be damned if she'd open the door to her bedroom now. Explain? Explain what? She had seen him kiss Deirdre, push her down on the lounger, and begin to touch her just like he had touched Annie this morning. Oh, there was no explanation on earth that could excuse what she had seen. He needed to leave, take his precious family and his damned friends as well, and leave. Now.

She walked to her bedroom door and listened. She could hear him breathing on the other side, it sounded almost as if he were crying. Well boo hoo. Just who had hurt whom here, anyway? She gave the bottom of the door a vicious kick, guessing that he was leaning against it, and was rewarded with a solid thud on the other side. Good! That should get his horny little attention!

"Mr. Evans, please make my apologies to our... the guests, as I won't be able to do it myself. I'm not feeling very well. Thank them for coming for me. Good-bye." She was tempted to kick the door again, but decided against it, she had wasted enough time on him already.

She lay on her bed and waited for the sound of the diesel engine starting, signaling her that it was taking them all away and she could have a normal life again.

Gabe continued to sit outside of his Annie's door. His spine hurt where the door had come in contact with it after her kick. He deserved it. Christ, what was he thinking kissing Dee like that? What the hell had gotten into him? What a mess this all was.

"Gabe?" Kyle called into the cabin. "You in there?" He peeked around the door, not sure what he was expecting to find. "Gabe? We're gettin' ready to leave. Wanted to tell you and Annie thanks." Where was he? Wolff said that he saw him come up here an hour ago, and that should have been plenty of time to... Kyle smiled. So much for the 'never'.

"I'm here, Kyle," Gabe sighed, as he walked slowly from the shadows under the loft. "Everybody on the bus?"

"Every last one of them. Where's Annie?" Kyle asked, looking around.

"She's... not feeling well. Asked me to thank you all for coming, so thanks."

"Gabe? You okay? You seem pretty bummed out. Is Annie alright? She's not really sick, is she?"

He made a non-committal noise, and said, "I'll walk out to the bus with you."

Gabe prayed his acting skills would get him through the next few minutes. He stood in the front of the bus and looked at his friends and family. As much as he loved them all, he would give up each and every one of them forever just to have another minute with his Annie.

"Hi, everyone. Annie apologizes that she can't be out here herself, but she isn't feeling well. She wanted me to thank you for coming, and hopes that you all had a good time." Just for good measure, he added, "She can't wait to do it again."

Unfortunately, his acting skills were not strong enough to cover his grief. He turned and stepped from the bus.

"Goose-Mother is in trouble," whispered the twins to each other.

"Trouble in paradise," sighed Wolff.

"Bet'cha another hundred the redhead wins," Mick muttered.

"I hope Annie feels better soon," Jenna said to Kyle.

"Ha! The bitch doesn't stand a chance," Deirdre said to herself.

Eric glared at Deirdre, wondering what the hell happened to her. She hadn't been herself all afternoon. Actually, she hadn't been herself since yesterday when she started reading those old books.

Gabe decided to walk down to the lake to make sure the fire was out. From the top of the hill he could see the coals glow, as if someone had just stirred them. He continued his walk to the beach and came to a stop next to the man who stood on the shoreline.

"Steve."

"Gabe."

"As happy as I am to see you, it cannot be a good sign, can it?"

"I'm afraid not."

"Christ, Steve, I fucked up big time tonight. What am I going to do?" he moaned.

"I wish I could help you, brother, but I'm not even supposed to be here now. I came only to warn you."

"Warn me?"

"Yep. Dee isn't... herself. As much as I'd like to, I can't elaborate. Beware of her, Gabe, and don't give up on Annie. She needs you now more than ever, and there's also another to consider."

"What the hell are you talking about? Can't you ever just come out right out and say what needs to be said without all the goddamn riddles?" Gabe snarled. This was really beginning to piss him off. He was tired of all the subterfuge, the hidden messages.

"I'll accept your apology for this little outburst; we'll blame it on the events of the evening." Steve smiled, then continued, "Gabe, listen. When I was here before I got a little more involved in your lives than I was supposed to and now we are all paying for it. For that, I apologize to you. I wouldn't be here now, but I was summoned and they were required to let me go. I can only stay long enough to give you a warning, which I did. Please remember what I said."

"What did you say?" Gabe snapped. He watched as Steve shook his head, sorry that he couldn't say more. A faint blue light began to form around him.

"Gabe, one more thing... I think James and Jeremy would like a pet. Why don't you get them a cat?" He winked and vanished.

Gabe was thrown by that last comment. What the hell did a cat have to do with anything? Steve knew that he didn't really like cats, and the boys had never asked for a pet. Now, just what was that warning? Probably just some 'watch your step' bullshit. Well, it was a little late for that now, wasn't it? He dumped a bucket of water on the coals, and the fire was out. He knew exactly how it felt.

Gabe didn't know where to go from there. He couldn't stay with his Annie (was she still his?), and he sure as hell couldn't go home and risk running into Dee again. He couldn't go to Kyle's... obviously. Maybe he could just sleep in the barn tonight. Wouldn't be the first time he'd bedded down in a stall, probably wouldn't be the last. Maybe he should buy himself a horse and take up where Steve left off, traveling the country and chasing cows. No responsibilities, no worries, no Deirdre... but there would also be no Annie.

He opened the door to a stall, the same one in which he had spent such a glorious morning. He kicked a pile of straw into a makeshift bed and wrapped the blanket around himself. It still smelled of his Annie. He sat in the corner, wishing to God he could start this day all over again.

A cat wandered in to join him. It curled onto his lap and stared at him with an amber gaze. Gabe talked to the cat as he stroked its soft orange fur.

"I tell ya, Spike, I really fucked up tonight. Do you think she'll ever forgive me?"

Spike wasn't sure. Their love was strong enough to survive anything, but Geoffrey Alan and Annie Rose had to be aware of that fact, and the new force was determined that they would remain in ignorance - just as it had tried before. He purred softly as the man's hand ran over his back. Steven Anthony had sent him out here, and although the cat wasn't sure why, he was certain that Geoffrey Alan would have the answer. Spike would have to be patient and observe everything.

The man's hand became motionless, he was asleep. Spike lowered his head onto his front paws, and he, too, slept.

Chapter Thirty-Eight

Annie's eyes felt swollen and scratchy; too many tears, too little sleep. She was scheduled to work that night, so she planned on doing her chores early, then going back to bed. She still felt kind of sick; must be the stress of... him. She didn't even want to think his name.

She skipped breakfast and headed for the barn. As she slowly walked across the yard, she formed her little plan for the day: first the barn work, and then finish with the house. Any mess left by the lake could rot for all she cared. She couldn't face going town there again... not to where he and Deirdre had been.

Annie was so engrossed in her own thoughts that she even didn't notice Gabe's truck still parked next to her own.

She forced herself to go into the barn, and the memories of yesterday morning washed over her as soon as she smelled the hay. She choked back tears as she fed the small critters first, and then turned to the horses.

"I don't think I'll be riding today, Donny, I'm just not feeling too well," she said as she brushed the horse. "And it's not just because of Ga... him, either. I really have been feeling sick lately. I should probably go get checked out, but it's not that bad. It kinda comes and goes... Maybe it is just nerves."

She ceased brushing the horse and sat in the straw at his feet. She could feel the tears coming on again, along with another wave of nausea.

Adonis lowered his head until his nose was level with her ear. How he wished he could speak, to tell her to go to the man in the stall just down the aisle. Forget everything that had happened and just love him. However, since an animal cannot speak, he only blew gentle puffs of horsy air onto her bowed head.

Annie reached up and stroked the big, circular cheek of her horse. At least he seemed to understand her misery. Although he never answered her, she could always talk to him.

"Donny, why would he do something like that?" she asked after the sick feeling had passed. "Why would he all of the sudden, out of the blue, be like that with Deirdre? Did he... did they both lie about what their marriage is really like? Is it some sick game they play, getting someone else involved? I can't understand it." She stood up and continued to brush Adonis. "I still love him, though. That is one thing that will never, ever change. All my life, and even before that, I have waited for him... Oh God..." Her head dropped against the horse's neck, her tears overwhelming her.

Gabe listened while Annie talked to her horse. Maybe there was hope after all.

"What do you think, Spike?" he whispered to the cat sitting on his lap.

Spike looked up at Geoffrey Alan; the man could be so incredibly dense at times. He jumped to the floor and walked to the stall door, looking back at Geoffrey Alan every few steps. He twitched his tail twice and walked into the aisle.

Gabe watched the feline stroll across the stall. It almost seemed as if Spike wanted him to follow. Well, around here anything was possible, especially with that cat. He wanted so bad to go to his Annie, to hold her, apologize to her, to beg her forgiveness and kiss away her hurt, but he remained rooted to his bed of straw. What if she rejected him again? Would he be able to live with it? As if he had a choice in the matter. *Come on Gabe, get up. Do it! You can't live with the uncertainty of this miserable situation any longer.*

"Spike!" Annie said, "What the heck are you doing in here? Slumming?" She was truly shocked. It was the very first time the cat had ever come near the barn, let alone soiled his dainty paws on its straw covered floors, and now here he was, sitting on the feed box in Adonis' stall. She reached over to give him a scratch on his head but he jumped away, avoiding her touch. That was strange, not wanting his daily dose of adoration.

"Spike, where'd you go?" Annie stuck her head out of the stall and saw the cat duck into another one. 'The stall'. She swallowed hard and went to follow him. Her hands were shaking, and her legs were so weak that she could barely walk the ten feet that would take her to... to what? There had to be something going on, otherwise Spike would not be down here. She stopped just short of the stall door but could go no further. The memories of yesterday were just too painful.

Spike peeked out of the stall and saw that Annie Rose was just standing there, staring at the floor. Well, he had gotten her this far, now how to get Geoffrey Alan the rest of the way? He sat down on the disgusting floor and twitched the end of his tail... thinking.

Gabe heard his Annie walk down the aisle and stop. Did she know he was here? Maybe if he... Oh God, this was a crazy idea, but maybe if he talked to Spike, told the cat how sorry he was that he hurt his Annie, just maybe she would listen. It was worth a shot. Now if he could only find his voice.

That's it! Good idea, Geoffrey Alan. Spike trotted over to the man and jumped onto his lap. He fixed his deep amber eyes on Geoffrey Alan's intense blue ones. *Go ahead - bare your soul...*

Once again, Gabe was under the power of the cat's gaze. He began to speak, his words coming slow at first, then picking up in a passionate intensity as he confessed to Spike.

Annie heard a voice, the voice... his voice. What that voice did to her caused her already weak legs to buckle underneath her and she slid to the floor, trembling.

"I don't know what happened, Spike," she heard Gabe say. "I was asking Dee what I could do to make up for the things I said to my Annie, and the next thing I knew, well, I most definitely did not plan on what happened! I didn't even want it. It was all very strange... it was like it wasn't Deirdre sitting there. I have no idea who it was, but it seemed... familiar somehow. And Deirdre! God, she certainly wasn't pushing me away... quite the opposite; it was all I could do to get away from her!" Gabe paused for a moment.

My Annie! Gabe had called her 'my Annie'. She was his Annie... It brought fresh tears to her eyes.

"I really don't have any excuses. It happened, it was a mistake, and I would give my life if I could take away the hurt I've caused my Annie. I love her, cat, I always have and I always will."

You are right about giving your life for her, Geoffrey Alan. It has happened before; pray that it doesn't happen again.

She had heard enough. It was time to end this, once and for all. She loved him and he loved her and nothing else in the world mattered. Oh God, but she felt sick again. It took all of her energy to pull herself up to a standing position, and she needed to lean against the wall for support. This was more than just stress making her feel this way.

"Gabe..." she whispered.

He looked up to see his Annie leaning on the stall door. Her face was nearly as white as the shirt she was wearing and beads of sweat stood out on her forehead.

"Annie?" Gabe jumped up and ran to her, catching her just before she hit the floor in a dead faint.

Spike hadn't quite expected this, but at least they were together.

Gabe wasn't sure whether the situation warranted a trip to the ER, so he chose to take her to the cabin. From there he could assess if she were in danger. She moaned as he placed her on the bed. Was that a good sign? Her eyes were beginning to open...

"Annie. Come on, Annie, wake up," he pleaded, giving her hand a gentle squeeze.

She looked around her... she was back in her room. Gabe must have carried her here from the barn, in his arms... and she missed it! Her weak, shaky feeling was nearly gone and she was beginning to feel 'normal' again. She sat up on the edge of the bed, next to Gabe, and tried to regain her equilibrium.

"Are you alright now?" he asked.

She nodded.

"What happened? Or more importantly, has this happened before? You said you haven't been feeling well lately, should I take you to a doctor?" His voice was full of concern.

She shook her head. "No, I've never fainted like that. Usually it's just a little dizziness and a lot of tired. I haven't eaten since yesterday afternoon, and I think that that, and everything that happened last night... well it must have caught up with me, that's all. I'm fine now." At least she would be as soon as they were back together.

"Are you sure? You still don't look all that well," Gabe said, placing his hand on her cheek.

Annie trembled when that familiar tingle shot through her body at his touch. It didn't matter what he did with Deirdre last night, she could never stop loving him, and he needed to know it.

Deirdre sat at her window seat, sipping a cup of tea and once again reading Megheen's diaries, smiling at a memory here, frowning at a memory there. It would be different this time around, she'd see to it! She was surprised when Geoffrey hadn't come home last night; maybe Annie hadn't seen them after all. No, the look on his face when he talked to them on the bus positively screamed misery. She'd seen them all right, and wasn't about to forgive Geoffrey any time soon. So, where was he? Maybe she had better call Annie and check, just in case. He should be here with his family right now anyway. Her blue eyes darkened to a glittering black as she reached for the phone.

"I'm sorry," Gabe said to his Annie at the exact moment she said it to him. He placed a finger on her lips.

"Me first," he told her. "What you saw last night, well, what can I say? I can offer no explanation and certainly no excuse. I won't insult you by even trying. I can promise you that nothing like that will ever, ever happen again. Never doubt my love for you, Annie, no matter what you may see, or what you may hear. Never doubt my love. Understand?"

She nodded, although his last words made her wonder what he meant. She'd better ask him; she wanted no more misunderstandings between them.

"Gabe, what do you?" Her last words were interrupted by the ringing of the phone. She sighed and reached across the bed to answer it.

"Hello?"

Deirdre.

Annie shoved the phone at Gabe, and then rose from the bed. He grabbed at her hand to try to prevent her from leaving, but missed. She quickened her pace and left the room, heading for her favorite chair. It wasn't until she sat down that she noticed the afghan was missing. Probably still in the bedroom, but she wasn't about to get it now.

Spike jumped onto her lap, although not for his daily dose. He stared toward the bedroom, occasionally letting out a low growl. Like Annie Rose, he was listening to Geoffrey Alan's conversation with Deirdre Felicity.

"Hello?" Gabe said.

"What is it?" he sighed.

"Yes, I was here all night. Why?"

"Annie is fine, just tired."

"No, nothing else, just tired."

"I suppose. I'll be there in an hour or so."

"I know they miss me, Christ, I miss them too. Tell them I'll take them to the park or something, maybe even bring them a surprise." Gabe reached over to pet Spike, who had jumped up next to him on the bed.

"Yeah, whatever."

Annie jumped when she heard the phone being slammed onto the receiver. Ooh... not good for Deirdre! The thought almost made her smile.

Gabe stalked out of the bedroom, his face dark with anger. Although Annie felt a moment of fear upon seeing that look, she had to smile. He was carrying Spike as one would a small child. The cat sat upright in his arms, with one paw behind his neck. It looked as though he were holding on.

Annie's smile made Gabe smile. He glanced at the cat he was holding and turned a very subtle shade of red.

"Nice cat," he said, and let Spike jump to the floor.

"He's different!"

"Annie, I have to get going. Dee said that the twins were asking for me, and I really should spend some time with them while I'm home."

"I know. Go and have fun with the boys. You can bring them here if you want, but I have to work tonight and I'll need a nap later. I... I didn't sleep very well last night."

"I'm sorry, Annie, really. What can I do to make it up to you? Just say the word and it shall be done."

"I don't ever want to talk about it, or even think about it ever again. We said a lot of things to each other that shouldn't have been said, and I apologize for that. I have no idea why I've been so moody lately. Anyway, I'd prefer if Deirdre didn't call here for a while, and could you let her know that I won't be visiting for a while, either? I hope you both understand why."

"So, are we friends again?"

She rose from her chair and went to him. Putting her arms around him she said, "That, and more."

As much as he wanted to take her back to the bedroom, or better yet the barn, he was content to hold her close, telling her he loved her.

As for Annie, that was enough for right now.

After a few moments Gabe said, "Guess who I saw last night."

"I'm not sure I want to know," she replied.

"Sure you do. It was Steve. After everyone left, I went back down to check on the fire and there he was, standing next to the lake. God, I was so glad to see him after everything... everything that happened."

"Wish he would have paid me a visit. I really could have use a few minutes of his time myself. What did he say?"

"I don't know. I mean, I can't remember all of it. I do remember yelling at him, though."

"Why?"

"He was talking in riddles again and it pissed me off. He did say something about a cat."

"Gabe, if he came back it may mean that there is something wrong. Think... What did he say?" Annie had a bad feeling about this.

"Just a minute... I remember telling him I screwed up and he agreed, then he said he couldn't help me because he interfered too much the last time he was here. Wait! He said something about Dee... Warned me about her. To tell the truth, I had stopped listening to him by then. Just before he left, he said something about the twins wanting a pet. He suggested a cat."

"Weird. Are you going to get them one?"

"Highly unlikely. We have enough people running around that house without adding another body. Besides, I'm not a cat person," he said.

Annie smiled at that last comment. Spike had jumped to the back of the chair and Gabe was giving him his daily dose of adoration.

Spike purred as Geoffrey Alan scratched that special spot just under the cat's chin. So, Steven Anthony had suggested a cat, eh? Maybe a special cat? One to watch over the Evans' household while Geoffrey Alan was away? Maybe a particular cat to keep as eye on Deirdre Felicity while Geoffrey Alan was home! Spike jumped into the man's arms and volunteered for the job.

Gabe's eyes widened in surprised as the cat leapt from the chair.

Annie's opened even wider.

The couple shared a speculative glance. Was this some type of sign? Omen? Message?

Spike pulled Geoffrey Alan into his amber gaze once again.

"Annie, do you think Spike would like to live in the big city for a while? I think the twins would like a pet, and Spike and I get along quite well."

"That is entirely up to him. I'll miss him, but it seems to be the right thing to do somehow." She reached up to pet her cat.

Gabe looked at the clock. "I'd better be going... I'll call you later. Would you mind if I took the boys for a ride? It's about time they learned what a horse is for. Steve would want that."

Annie agreed. "That's fine with me. Wanda is great with kids; Eric learned to ride on her. Spend as much time as you like, and if you want take them out in the canoe later. I think they'd like that. There's fishing poles in the barn somewhere. Make a day of it!"

"Sounds great. I'll see you again in a few hours." He gave her a quick kiss and headed for his truck, still carrying Spike.

Annie waved as the two of them drove away.

Spike made himself right at home in the Evan's house. Once the introductions were over and he endured petting by all seven of the children, the cat set out to explore. He began in the basement, noting every room, every window, every nook and cranny. He did the same on the first and second floors, and not a square inch of the home had escaped his scrutiny. He chose Geoffrey Alan's leather sofa as a place to relax when he wasn't needed somewhere else. He avoided Deirdre Felicity's room whenever possible.

There was only one place left to examine. Spike's fur bristled as he climbed the steep steps to the attic; the force had been here for a very long time. The cat could also feel the serenity of Steven Anthony. That was a good omen; it meant that he was still around and available to help if needed.

Spike found the space in the wall where the diaries had lain, hidden for nearly a century. He could still feel the hatred, the jealousy, and the thirst for revenge that been expressed in the words written in the books. Perhaps it was time to make friends with Deirdre Felicity and find out exactly what Megheen had been planning so long ago.

"Geoffrey dear, although I'm happy you chose to give the boys a pet, I cannot understand why it had to be a cat, and Annie's cat at that. Couldn't you have got them a puppy?" Deirdre asked.

"I thought they'd like a cat. I like cats," he replied.

"Since when? I was under the impression that you had an aversion to them."

"I can take 'em or leave 'em, but I like Spike. He's a different kind of kitty," Gabe smiled.

"Different? Odd or strange might even be a better word to describe him. He makes me uncomfortable; the way he stares at me is so... unnerving!" she said with a delicate shudder.

"Hmm... that look of his can be compelling, but he is just a cat. He is quiet and well-behaved. Just look at how he took all of that abuse at the hands of the children... not so much as a growl." Gabe was rather proud of Spike's good-natured tolerance of those rowdy kids.

"I suppose... Alright, I don't mind if he stays," Deirdre sighed. She was quiet for a moment, and then asked, "What are your plans for the day? I thought Jenna could take the children to the park for a while, and then you and I could have a chance to... talk. Catch up on the last few weeks. You can tell me all about your remarkable comeback tour."

Gabe gave her a long look; he didn't like where she was going with this. "I was under the impression that I needed to rush home to be with the twins, and now you want to get rid of them for a while? What are you up to, Deirdre? While we're at it, what the hell was that little stunt you pulled last night? Annie just happened to see it and... Christ, do you know what it did to her? It damn near killed her!"

"Geoffrey dear, as I recall, you were a most willing participant in our little moment of tenderness. Don't lay the blame solely on me. Admit it, you didn't find it at all unpleasant now, did you." Deirdre's eyes darkened and glittered.

He had to turn away from her. She was right on all counts, and the memory of what she had felt like under his fingers was beginning to make him want to repeat it all over again. He had to get away from her.

"I will be spending the day with just James and Jeremy, and we will be at Annie's if you need to reach me in case of emergency. Otherwise, I'll see you when I drop the boys off this evening."

"Drop them off? You're not staying here tonight? Geoffrey..."

Deirdre could not let him stay with Annie tonight, yet what could she do to stop him?

"Where will you be spending the night?" she asked.

"Anywhere but here," he informed her.

Deirdre flipped on her television. One of those horrid tell-all Hollywood scandal shows was airing, and it gave her a marvelous idea.

After a day of fun in the sun with his nephews, Gabe and the boys had dinner with Annie. The twins made a most sincere apology to her for messing up her bathroom the day before, and they promised never to be naughty for her again. She gave them each a big hug, telling them no harm done. It was only water and a little dirt, after all.

Before they left - Annie to work and the Evans' to their home, Gabe promised her that he would go to Brighton that night and join her on her lunch break. He also asked if he might use the guest bedroom until he had to go back on the road. She was more than happy to oblige, as long as he stayed out of the guest bedroom and shared hers instead.

A smiling Deirdre met Geoffrey at the door the moment he returned with James and Jeremy. She took his hand and led him to the living room, where she introduced him to the journalist and photographer she had called, who would be doing a story on SD's comeback tour. The tentative title for the article would be 'Three Days Off the Road: At Home with Gabe and Kyle'.

He could feel his blood pressure rise until he thought for sure his head would explode. How dare she? She knew damn well how he felt about this kind of publicity. Granted, it might sell a few more CDs, but to invade his privacy like this?

Gabe dug deep within himself to maintain a civil tone as he listened to Deirdre and the reporter plan out his week. Just what was that bitch trying to do to him now? He'd never be able to see Annie while these two were hanging around. Christ, he had to stop this, and now.

"Excuse me, I don't mean to seem ungrateful regarding your generous offer to cover our tour, but I'm afraid that I have already made plans for the week. I would consent to a short interview and a few pictures, but beyond that I'm not available. I'm sorry. Kyle should be returning soon, and I'm sure he would be most happy to give you what you need," Gabe said, giving them a cold smile.

"Oh Geoffrey, don't be silly. You know perfectly well that you can reschedule your, ah, appointments this week. This is important for you career and it would mean so much to all of us." Deirdre gave him an ominous smile, and her black eyes glittered.

Gabe had to avert his eyes away from her. What was it with that look? Why did it affect him so? There was no way she was going to get away with this. She was deliberately trying to keep him from his Annie.

"Deirdre, you know that Annie expects..."

"Annie?" asked the reporter. She gave a sly glance to her cameraman.

"Yes, Annie. Geoffrey's... assistant and co-writer," Deirdre explained to her guests, then said to her husband, "She'll understand, Geoffrey. You two can have your tiresome little meetings later. Please, indulge us just these few days."

Gabe stood and said, "I'm sorry, but no. I cannot do it. If you want to arrange an interview, you may contact Jenna Davidson and set up a time. Now if you'll excuse me..."

He stalked from the room. Spike met him at the door, and together they retreated to Gabe's office.

He ran his hand down the orange fur of the cat in his lap.

"I don't know, Spike. Something is definitely wrong with her. Steve was right; she's not herself. Even her eyes are different... Darker, almost sinister. I'll ask Annie tonight if Dee's illness could be causing some kind of mental breakdown. In the meantime, let's try to sneak away from that damn journalistic nightmare in the other room. Let Kyle deal with them."

As if on cue, Kyle burst into Gabe's office with the nightmare in tow.

"C'mon Gabe, I told Rocky and Bullwinkle here that we'd take them out for a drink. We can tell them all about our triumphant return to the world of music," he announced.

"You take them. I have plans," Gabe snapped. His blood pressure was beginning to rise again.

"Cancel 'em. This story could really help our career and you should be in on it, don't you think?" Kyle asked, just noticing Spike. "Hey, isn't that Annie's cat? What's it doin' here?"

"Just visiting. I'm not doing this story, and I'm not going out for a drink. I have time for one interview tomorrow and that's it. Take it or leave it." Gabe was past trying to hide the irritation he was feeling, and it was evident in his voice. "Christ, she's back," he moaned, hearing voices in the foyer.

The journalist, Roxanne Rockwell a.k.a. Rocky, wasn't about to let that arrogant bastard off so easy. Mrs. Evans promised a juicy three days with the tasty Gabe, and she was not about to pass that up. Why Deirdre was so free about sharing her husband, Rocky didn't know or care but she was determined to get what was coming to her.

Spike agreed.

506

Rocky put on her sexiest smile and sat on the arm of Gabe's chair. She ran an idle finger down Spike's back, then let it travel back and forth across Gabe's hand and said, "Mr. Evans... Gabe, won't you please just let us have three little days out of your life? You'd hardly even notice that I was around... unless you want to notice, of course." She leaned a little closer to him until her cleavage was just under his nose.

Spike shot out his lightning-fast paw and left a bloody furrow across the seductive hand of Miss Roxanne.

Rocky shrieked and yanked her hand away from the vicious cat. She glared at Spike, and then looked at Gabe to see what he was going to do about this dangerous animal. He was smiling! The bastard was actually smiling! Oh, this was too much. He would pay, and pay dearly. She looked to her photographer for help.

Wes Bullard, a.k.a. Bullwinkle, didn't know what to think. He shrugged a shoulder and hid a smirk.

Gabe continued to grin like a fool. Spike was a different kitty indeed!

Kyle was very unsuccessful in holding back the hysterical laugher about to overtake him. It had begun when Rocky made that pathetic attempt to seduce the unwilling Gabe, and then the cat getting revenge! Oh God! Before he could stop himself, he blurted out, "That's Annie's cat alright! Lookin' out for her man!"

Gabe shot him a look, hoping the idiot would shut up before he said anything else, which did not go unnoticed by the now-furious Rocky. Yes, he would pay dearly!

She grabbed Bull's arm and dragged him to the door. She stopped, turned to Gabe and said, "Mr. Evans, I will get my story. You had your chance to have it told your way, but now it will be done my way. I was promised three days, and you can bet that I will have them!"

She slammed the door on her way out.

Shit! This was all he needed: a fuckin' reporter with a vendetta.

"Did you have to nearly take her hand off, Spike?" Gabe asked the cat, and seeing Spike's slightly offended expression, gratefully thanked him.

Kyle was beginning to realize what was going on.

"Hey, man, I'm sorry. I didn't think you would object to a little free publicity like that, but now I see why you would. You think Rocky was serious?"

"Dead serious. I won't be able to fart without her knowing about it. Don't you know who she is, Kyle?"

"Some reporter, why?"

"Christ, man, do you live in a cave? That woman has written more trash and ruined more lives than anyone in recorded history, and has caused at least one suicide with that excrement she calls journalism. Why Deirdre called her, I'll never know! You remember when Stevie died, and that bitch shoved a microphone in my face and asked me how I felt about his death? Christ, I wasn't even aware of it yet!"

"That was Rocky?"

"Yep."

"Ew. What you gonna do?"

"I know what I'd like to do, but it carries the death penalty in several states." Gabe walked to the window and looked out.

Rocky waved at him from her car.

This wasn't going to be easy.

He sighed and said, "I'd better call Annie and let her know what's going on."

He punched in the numbers for Brighton and asked for the Pediatric ward, then asked for Annie once he had reached her department. As he sat listening to what passed for music meant to entertain one when on hold, he heard a soft click as someone in the house picked up a phone. Gabe glanced back out the window and saw Rocky grinning at him. She was listening in on the cordless phone she had stolen from the living room. The bitch was ruthless! He slammed his phone onto the desk, breaking it to pieces.

"Goddamn it, Kyle!" he roared. "What the hell is going on? Why is it so fucking difficult just to try and have a normal life? All I want to do is live quietly in that cabin by the lake. Just me and Annie and the twins, and hopefully some kids of my own. Is that too much to ask? Is it? Apparently. Instead, I'm stuck with a wife I never, ever wanted, this goddamn museum of a house, a career turned to shit, and a life back on the road."

Gabe spun around and kicked his guitar from its stand, sending it flying across the room to smash on the far wall.

Kyle's arms flew to his face to protect it from the resulting wooden shrapnel. This was by far the angriest he had ever seen his buddy, but instead of fearing him Kyle felt sympathy for him. This was no act, and the poor guy was really hurting.

Gabe leaned heavily on his desk, looking at the floor. His voice was low and hoarse as he said, "And now... and now I've got her to deal with."

"Her? Who, Rocky?"

"What? Rocky? Yeah, her too."

"Who else did you mean?"

Gabe turned around and sat on edge of the desk. "The lovely Deirdre. Have you noticed anything... different about her lately?"

Kyle thought for a moment, then said, "Not that I can put my finger on, but now that you mention it, yeah... just over the last few days. But then again, we've only been home a few days, so who can say for sure?"

Gabe debated on whether or not to tell him what happened, and then decided to fill him in on at least some of the details.

"Kyle, I need to tell you something, and I want you to promise to hear me out and say nothing until I'm finished. Agreed?"

"Sure, buddy, anything you say." He really did want to help his partner; he owed him that much after the way he treated him last January.

"Okay, here goes. I'm sure you are aware that Annie and I have a relationship."

Kyle smiled and nodded.

"It's not just a relationship; I love her. She is the one I have waited for all of my life, and we are meant to be together. You um… You know how I've always been a little subtly obsessed with the green eyes and autumn hair…"

Kyle nodded. "Wasn't always so subtle, Gabers."

"Yeah, well… Anyway, I wish I could tell you what all was involved in bringing us together, but it's far too incredible and too complicated to believe, so we won't go there. Deirdre was the one who made it possible. She and Steve. She was thrilled with the fact that I had finally found Annie, and before the tour she was nearly shoving me out the door every night so that I could go see her.

"We took things very slow and it was all very proper. I never spent more than a few minutes at her place, other than to pick her up and drop her off when we'd go out. When we were out in public there was never any physical display of affection. I couldn't risk any type of scandal hurting the twins or Deirdre. Annie understood."

Kyle just had to ask. "Are you trying to tell me that you never…"

Gabe shrugged and looked away, then looked back at his friend. "I never… we never… at least not until late March. And not often after that, either."

"Nerves of steel, man, nerves of steel," Kyle said, somewhat in awe. "And you've only been home for two days. How the hell could you stand being around her all day yesterday and not… well, you know. Shit! You spent most of the day with Dee. What was that about?"

"Just for appearances. You and Jenna are the only ones who know about Annie, and we want to keep it that way. I don't give a flying fuck about what the rest of the world thinks of me, but Annie is a good person, and I don't want her involved in any negative publicity. I don't want James and Jeremy hurt, either."

"And Deirdre?"

"Yes, Deirdre. You wouldn't believe what she did last night!"

Gabe told Kyle of her strange behavior, of Annie witnessing the scene, and the subsequent rift between them.

"Christ, no wonder you murdered your poor guitar. Wasn't it an anniversary gift from Dee?"

"Was."

Kyle flopped onto the sofa. "Is she still out there?" he asked, referring to Rocky.

Gabe glanced out the window and saw Bullwinkle running towards the car, camera in hand. Aw no… if that son of a bitch had been taking pictures….

He bolted from the room and out of the house in an attempt to catch the unscrupulous photographer.

Bull hit the car as Gabe was hurtling the iron fence, and the dastardly duo escaped in a haze of tire smoke. Gabe did see a bloodied hand stretched above the roof of the car, honoring him with a middle-fingered salute.

This was not good.

Deirdre sat at her window seat and watched the scene unfold outside. This was coming along far better than she could have ever imagined. Geoffrey would be a virtual prisoner in his own home, not daring to expose himself to that Rocky bitch. She knocked back two fingers of the fine Irish whiskey that had been delivered only hours ago, and smiled. One more drink, then she'd go tuck the brats into bed.

"James, Jeremy? Little loves? Let Mama in, please; she wants to read you a bedtime story."

The twins exchanged worried glances, and then turned to their father.

"What should we do, Daddy?" they whispered.

Steve smiled at his sons. "Go ahead and let her in, she can't hurt you. Just remember, she might look like your mama, but she's not. Your mama is safe. As a matter of fact, I think she may be going for a ride on Whizbang right about now, and I won't be very far away. Now, remember what I told you earlier?"

The boys smiled and nodded. The heroic Whizbang would never let anything happen to Mama. They waved good-bye to Daddy as he did the blue light trick again.

Gabe ran to his truck, thinking he would chase down the car racing away, but decided against it. Instead he used the phone in it to call his Annie. The ward clerk told him that she was unavailable to come to the phone; did he want to leave a message? He did. He instructed to have her call him as soon as possible, and then left the number of his cell phone with the clerk. Nothing to do now but wait.

Rocky and Bullwinkle drove once around the block, and then parked their car two houses down from the Evans'. From this vantage point they could see anyone who arrived or left, and were still close enough to pick up his phone calls on the stolen phone - assuming he hadn't yanked that base unit out of the wall yet. That man had quite the temper! Bull got some great shots of the flying guitar, and the rage on Gabe's face that accompanied it. Rocky was in a near frenzy, outlining different captions for the anticipated photos and making notes for her revenge story.

Annie tried desperately to keep up with her workload. It was one of those rare nights straight from hell where nothing was going right. The admissions rolled through the door seemingly non-stop, and two nurses had called in sick. Her patients seemed to be constantly on the call lights for the most annoying reasons - fluff my pillow, bend my straw, hand me a tissue... and not one of her ten kids had a parent staying the night with them.

As she made another hurried pass by the reception desk, the clerk shoved a paper at her. Annie mumbled a thanks and shoved it into her pocket; she'd read it when she had time.

By the time two a.m. had rolled around and she was finally caught up, she realized that she hadn't heard from Gabe. Maybe he was waiting for her to buy him a cup of coffee in the cafeteria.

She went to check. Nothing.

Annie called the cabin. Maybe he was waiting for her to call him there.

No answer. She couldn't very well call his house, not at this hour anyway. Wait, that paper the clerk gave her... maybe that was a message from him. Now, what the hell did she do with it? Annie checked her pockets and found nothing. She went through her charts, thinking maybe it got mixed in with one. Again, nothing.

Think... Edith! Edith needed a piece of paper to make a note regarding a maintenance problem in one of the rooms, and Annie had absently handed her one from the stack of scrap paper she kept in her pocket. Oh God, not the message! She paged Edith to call back right away.

The housekeeper denied seeing any message on the paper Annie had handed her. She was not about to let anyone know she had Gabe Evans' private phone number!

Gabe kissed the twins goodnight once Deirdre had slithered back into her lair. He was quickly developing a deep hatred for his former best friend and confidant, and had to constantly remind himself that her behavior was probably due to her illness just to keep from doing her great bodily harm.

Why hadn't Annie called yet? Gabe was on the phone to Brighton several more times, and was told that she had indeed received his message and would call as soon as she got the chance; it was a very busy night. He wrapped himself in the colorful afghan on the sofa and stared into the darkness of the room, waiting...

Kyle and Jenna retreated to their room, but didn't engage in their usual activities. He filled her in on the ugly situation of Deirdre and the dastardly duo, and begged his wife to keep an eye on Mrs. Evans.

Deirdre sat at her window seat and looked out at the car down the street; they'd keep Geoffrey within her reach. Did she dare go down to his office and talk to him? Perhaps she should wait until he was asleep; he'd be more vulnerable that way. She'd take a short nap until it was time to visit her husband. She'd read a little first though, as the diaries had been bringing the most interesting dreams.

Deirdre slept, and once again the dream came. She was no longer the gentle, petite, blonde Dee, but a wild, voluptuous, raven-haired Megheen.

She stood at the edge of cliff, looking over the edge at the broken body of the man lying on the rocks below. No! It wasn't supposed to happen like this! He wasn't the one who was to die tonight; it was to be the red-haired bitch.

She turned from the gruesome sight of her ex-lover's corpse and slowly made her way back to her cottage. Anne would pay for this. Megheen would track her down. No matter where she had to travel to or how long it took, Anne would pay.

She lit a candle and pulled the leather box from under her cot. She pulled a book from the box and began to write, recording the events of the night, along with her thoughts, feelings, and vows of revenge. She replaced the book and blew out the candle.

She felt refreshed after her short nap. She couldn't remember if she had dreamed, but it didn't matter. Geoffrey should be asleep by now. She looked into his bedroom, not really expecting to find him there, and then quietly made her way to his office.

That damn cat was sitting in front of the door again. One would think he was standing guard! Deirdre kicked at the animal, connected, and caused him to roll a few feet away from the door. She slipped into the office and shut the door before the cat had time to run in after her.

There was just enough moonlight shining into the room for her to see without tripping over anything. She lay on the sofa next to Geoffrey and softly called his name. He made a noise in his sleep (did he say Annie?) and moved over, giving her more room on the couch. She called his name again and he opened his eyes.

Geoffrey looked up at the woman hovering over him. Megheen. He had told her time and time again that they were through; he wanted nothing more to do with her. Years ago they'd had a brief affair, but that was ancient history and she needed to move on. He was engaged to Anne now, and they were to be married at the end of the month. What was she doing here now?

"Just one last time, Geoffrey, one last time before you marry," Megheen whispered.

He made the mistake of letting himself look into the hypnotic gaze of those glittering black eyes.

He should have known better. His mind shut down and his body took over.

He reached up and pulled Megheen to him.

Spike rolled from the force of Deirdre Felicity's kick, frantically trying to regain his footing. He could not let her in there alone with Geoffrey Alan! His forward movement ceased as he hit the wall and he immediately turned and ran for the office, but the door shut in the cat's face. He was too late. He would need help for this one.

Spike raced up the stairs to Kyle and Jenna's room and began yowling loudly outside their door.

"What the hell is that?" Kyle asked, extremely annoyed at having his sleep interrupted.

"Dunno. Sounds kind of like you did a few hours ago," Jenna teased. She gave her husband an intimate squeeze.

"Sounds kind of like a... a cat. It's Spike! What the hell is the matter with him?" Kyle jumped from his bed and pulled on a pair of boxers, then opened the door to the frantic feline.

"What the hell is your problem?" he snapped at Spike.

Spike stayed in the hall, yowling and pacing. He had to find a way to make Kyle David follow him. There, on the floor! It was a crude idea, but it might work. He raced into the room and grabbed the pair of Jenna Leigh's panties that had been tossed aside earlier in the evening, then raced back into the hall. He waited at the top of the stairs until he saw Kyle David run towards him.

From there the chase wound through the house and ended at the office door. Spike dropped the panties at Kyle David's feet.

As Kyle David bent to pick them up, Spike placed a silky paw on the man's cheek. Kyle David looked up in surprise, and was drawn into an amber gaze.

"Oh shit!" he whispered. He stood and looked down at this different kind of kitty. Damn! The cat just nodded to him! Kyle shook off the creepy feeling it gave him and knocked loudly on the office door. He didn't dare just walk in.

Gabe woke to the sound of someone banging on his door. The sound registered an instant before he realized that a female was sprawled across his bare chest, and that female was not his Annie

Aw Christ... He pushed her to the floor, feeling just slightly guilty about the rough handling of the frail woman, but so appalled at the situation that he really didn't care what the hell happened to her. He sat up and glared at her, taking in her half-dressed appearance. At least it didn't get very far, as he was still wearing his jeans… even if they were unzipped. The banging on the door stopped.

"Gabe, you in there?" Kyle whispered.

He cleared his throat and in a very hoarse, disgusted voice said, "Yeah, just a minute."

In a much quieter, angrier whisper, he snarled to Deirdre, "Get dressed and get out. I don't know what the hell has gotten into you lately, but it will stop now! I'll be leaving here in the morning and not coming back. If the boys want to see me, Kyle can bring them to Annie's."

Dee quickly covered the anger in her own voice and sweetly replied, "Will you be taking the reporters with you? They'd be most interested in your 'second home'. I'll bet Annie would love to entertain them in that dreary little cabin; trotting out all of her little animals to pose for pictures..."

Gabe jumped from the sofa and went to the far end of the room. If he didn't put some distance between him and Deirdre, he would literally kill the bitch. She was deliberately trying to keep him away from his Annie.

"Get out. Get out of here now, before I totally lose control and give them goddamn reporters something to write about."

Geoffrey's voice could not have sounded any more lethal and acting had nothing to do with it. Deirdre was genuinely frightened of him for the first time since they'd met, and hurriedly put her robe back on. She backed towards the door and said, "This is not over. You owe me. I have waited far too long for this, and I'm not about to give up now."

She opened the door and ran out, nearly knocking Kyle over in her haste to escape.

Kyle walked into the office, followed by Spike, and Gabe was never so glad to see anyone in his life. On shaky legs, he walked to his desk chair and sat down. He didn't want to ever touch the sofa again.

"Christ, Kyle, you couldn't have come at a better time. Thanks!" he told his friend.

"Uh, sure. What the hell is going on, man?" Kyle was beyond confused.

"It's Dee. She... I... my God! When I think of what almost happened! Again! I have to get out of here. God, I sure wish Steve would come back and help me with this one," Gabe said, more to himself.

"You're talking crazy. Steve?"

Gabe looked up at Kyle. He'd almost forgotten that he was in the room. "Never mind. I need a drink. Would you mind...?"

"Only if I get one too." Kyle wandered over the bookcase, and then returned with two very large glasses of scotch. "This should help." He handed his buddy one of the glasses.

"Thanks. What time is it?"

"Dunno. Around five, I think. Why?"

Gabe shrugged a shoulder. "Annie never called. You don't think she is mad at me again, do you?"

"Why would she be? You two made up, didn't you?"

"Pretty much, but we haven't had any time to be alone together. I have to talk to her... Toss that here, will you?" He pointed to his phone on the floor next to the sofa.

Kyle handed it to him.

Gabe hit the redial button and was connected to Brighton's Children's hospital, but just as Annie answered the battery went dead.

The phone sailed across the room, smashed through the window and came to rest in the roses just outside of the house.

Gabe turned away from Kyle and dropped his head to his arms, which were now folded on the desktop.

Spike jumped to the desk and placed a silky paw on Geoffrey Alan's right shoulder.

Kyle went to his friend and placed his hand on Gabe's left shoulder.

Steve stood in the corner, unseen and helpless. A tear slowly rolled down his troubled face.

Annie's pager went off, indicating that she had a phone call. Maybe it was Gabe. She raced for the nearest phone and picked up the line, only to be met with nothing. She glanced at her watch; it was too late for him to be calling anyway. She called home one more time, just in case he was there. All she heard was her own voice on the answering machine.

Chapter Thirty-Nine

Gabe finished packing his clothes just as the sun was beginning to rise. And he still hadn't come up with a plan to evade Rocky and Bullwinkle, who were still parked down the street.

Kyle stood at the bedroom window, observing the observers.

"You aren't going to believe this," he said to Gabe.

"At this point, nothing would surprise me. What is so fascinating out there?"

"Rockhead and Bullshit just had food delivered. They're serious about this, dude! Are you sure the cops won't do anything?"

"Nope. Unless they are creating a disturbance, it's a public street and they have every right to be there. On the other hand, if I so much as look at them cross-eyed, they'd have my ass thrown in jail faster than you could say prison bitch!

"This sucks."

"Eloquently put."

Kyle was silent for a moment, and then said, "Isn't there any way you can sneak out of here? Through the back yard or something?"

"Not without scaling several fences. My neighbors are uh, very private, security-conscious people. Also, there are a few large canines next door with which I have failed to bond. Any way you look at it; Rocky, jail, or dog, someone wants a piece of my ass!"

Kyle laughed. At least Gabe was getting his sense of humor back.

Spike strolled into the bedroom and jumped to the top of Gabe's dresser.

"Have you ever noticed anything different about him?" Kyle asked, nodding towards the cat.

"Spike? Christ, there is nothing normal about him. He's the most amazing cat. God, if it weren't for him we never would have discovered "Dream Again," and the list goes on." Gabe walked over to give Spike his daily dose.

"Hmm, well then I guess I should tell you that he was responsible for your rescue this morning. Just like Lassie, he was; grabbed Jenna's underwear and took off runnin' so that I'd chase him! Hey, have you ever looked, really looked, into his eyes?"

"That I have, Kyle, that I have."

"Any ideas yet?" he asked, changing the subject.

"No. You?"

"No."

"How about you, Spike? Has that brilliant feline brain found a solution to our little dilemma?" Gabe joked.

Spike snorted; he thought that Geoffrey Alan would never ask! With a twitch of his tail, he jumped from the dresser and walked into the hall. He stopped, looked at Geoffrey Alan and Kyle David, and then trotted to the stairs. Maybe these two would figure it out this time and Spike wouldn't have to resort to dog-like tricks again.

Since anything was possible with this cat, Gabe followed him immediately, and Kyle took only a few seconds longer. The cat led them to the basement stairs and sat, waiting for the door to be opened.

"Maybe this is where he wants us to hide the bodies after Rockhead and Bullshit mysteriously disappear," Kyle laughed.

"Let's find out." Gabe opened the door and the trio descended the steps.

"This place is creepy enough to hide bodies in. Goddamn, Gabe, haven't you ever heard of home improvement?" Kyle asked, carefully making his way across the damp, dirt-covered floor.

"Other than a testosterone-fueled sit-com, no," was his sarcastic answer. "Of course I have, you ass! You remember what this house looked like when I bought it; it was practically falling down around my ears! I simply never found a reason to use the basement, so I never thought about finishing it off. I can't tell you the last time I was down here."

"Or anyone else for that matter. Goddamn place smells like a graveyard. Hey, we should shoot a video down here. It's already full of special effects. Just think of all the money we would save not havin' to buy cobwebs. Are there rats down here? Spiders... snakes? Zombies. We need some zombies..."

Gabe stopped in his tracks, turned around and looked straight at his friend.

"Kyle. Shut.Up."

"Sorr-eeee," Kyle whined in a hurt voice.

Spike came to a stop in front of the door to a small room. He sat and looked at Geoffrey Alan.

What the hell? Gabe opened the door and walked in.

The room was empty.

"Dead end, cat. Any more bright ideas?"

Spike walked to the center of the room and began to dig. Gabe walked closer, mystified by the cat's predictably strange behavior. He tripped over a solid object embedded in the floor.

"Ow! What the hell is this?" He knelt closer to examine the offending object. "Kyle, go to the kitchen and bring back some flashlights. We may have found our answer."

By the time Kyle returned, Gabe had cleared most of the dirt away from the wooden door covering the hole in the floor. Together they lifted the trapdoor, using the iron ring which Gabe had tripped over.

"Cool!" Kyle said as he flipped on a flashlight, which illuminated a ladder leading to a sub-basement. "What do you make of this?"

"I have no idea. Shall we?"

Kyle clapped his hands together. "Ooh, an adventure! Lead on, McDuff!"

Annie slowed her truck down as she approached Gabe's house, and saw that his truck was still in the driveway. So much for sharing her room. As much as she wanted to give him the benefit of the doubt, that icy feeling was forming in her belly again. She might as well go home and try to sleep; last night had been a bitch and she could hardly keep her eyes open. As she drove by the front of the house, she noticed a man on the sidewalk taking pictures. She slowed again and took a closer look at what he was so interested in. The window to Gabe's office was smashed; he must be the insurance company photographer working on the claim, even if it was pretty early for them to be out. Now for another question: how had the window been broken? She slowed even more trying to figure it out.

The photographer turned as Annie rolled past, snapping a picture of her tired face peering from the truck's window. He gave her a sly grin and a wink, and began walking to the car parked a few houses down.

Annie looked in her rear-view mirror and watched as a woman exited the vehicle and gave a thumbs-up sign to the man. Very odd... very odd indeed.

"Bull, that was perfect! If that was that Annie person... God! This will be a great story! I'm glad you had the sense to know what I wanted when I waved to you." Rocky was beside herself with excitement. It was sheer investigative reporting that she had thought to hit redial on Gabe's cell phone, (which she had retrieved from the rose garden and replaced the dead battery with the one from her own phone) and gotten Brighton Hospital. It was sheer luck that she had looked up as Annie was driving by, and Rocky had seen the Brighton parking sticker in the window of the truck driven by a woman in nursing scrubs. Luck continued to smile upon her as she waved to Bull, hoping that he'd catch the nurse on film.

Rocky was dying to follow the red truck, but didn't want to risk losing Gabe.

"I've got to pee. Keep an eye on 'em," she told Bull, then trotted off across the park to the public restrooms. More luck!

"God, this goes on forever..." Kyle mumbled.

The men had been walking for what seemed like miles in a cramped, wet tunnel. Gabe figured that they had traversed the length of the park and were nearing the river, and Heaven only knew where they would end up.

"I notice our cat declined to join us on our expedition," Gabe said. "He's smarter than I thought."

"Remind me to kill him later," Kyle grumbled as he stepped in yet another deep puddle of stagnant water.

"Hear that?"

"What?"

"That sound. I think it's the river... C'mon." Gabe quickened his pace through the tunnel.

They turned a sharp corner and were met with daylight.

"Hey, it's the light..." Kyle started.

"Don't even say it," Gabe shot back.

They had to crawl the last few feet to exit the shaft.

"Where are we?" Kyle asked as he brushed the dirt from his jeans and looked around.

They were halfway up the hill leading to the river, and standing in front of a thick grove of trees which hid the entrance to the cave.

"About two miles from the house. The water treatment plant is just around that bend; I can smell it from here," Gabe told him. "I'm going to head over there and call Annie. You get back and run interference with... Rockhead and Bullshit." He gave his buddy a tired, lop-sided grin.

"You got it. Call me later." Kyle gave Gabe a friendly punch on the arm. "Good luck, man."

"Thanks. Oh, one more thing; watch out for Spike. I don't want anything to happen to that cat. Keep an eye on Deirdre, too. I wouldn't be in a position to be alone with her if I were you," Gabe warned.

"I have Jenna to guard me," Kyle laughed.

Gabe waved and began jogging towards the plant.

Annie threw feed to the critters, and anticipated crawling into a nice, soft bed. She was so extremely tired this morning, even more so than usual, that the horses would have to do without their daily brushing. She gave them each a little extra grain as a treat and an apology, and all but dragged herself back to the cabin. She heard the phone ringing as soon as she hit the top step. Any other time she would have let the machine get it, but Annie was hoping to hear from Gabe. She summoned up her remaining energy and ran into the cabin, answering just in time with a breathless, "Hello?"

"Annie! Oh God, it's good to hear your voice."

"Gabe? Where are you? Why didn't you call me last night?" She was happy to hear from him, yet still just a little ticked off that it had taken so long.

"It's a long story. Can you pick me up?"

"Pick you up?"

"I'll explain later. I'm at the water treatment plant. Do you know where that is?"

"I do, but Gabe..."

"Just hurry, Annie, and... I'm probably being paranoid, but if you see someone you think might be following you, don't come here. Um... drive into town and park at the north end of the mall, by the music store. I'll find some way to contact you from there."

"Gabe, what is going on? You're scaring me!"

"You're in no danger, don't worry about that, but I've got a reporter on my ass and she is out for blood. No one I love is safe from her poison pen. I'll fill you in when you get here. Be careful, Annie... I love you."

"I will. Gabe?"

"Yes?"

"I love you too."

Forty-five minutes later, Annie pulled up to the gate of the chain link fence surrounding the water treatment plant. Her stomach lurched at the odor emanating from the facility and into her truck. She closed her eyes and tried not to breathe too deeply, praying Gabe wouldn't take very long to find her. When she opened them again, she saw Gabe emerge from the guard shack halfway down the driveway. The sight of him made her blink and take a second look.

He was a mess. Black muck clung to his boots, and was spattered up the legs of his torn jeans. His shirt was also torn and covered with dirt and grass stains. Dried blood covered both arms from wrist to elbow, and was also smeared on his face. It scared the hell out of her! She jumped from the truck and ran to meet him.

"Oh my God... Gabe, are you alright?"

"I am now that you're here, Annie. I'm so damn glad to see you!" He wrapped his arms around his Annie and held her close, never wanting to let go again. He did, though, leaving an arm around her waist and hurrying her towards the truck.

"Did you see anyone who may have been following you?" he asked.

"Hardly anyone was on the road out this way, so no, Gabe."

"Good. Let's get home."

"Are you sure you're alright?"

"I'm fine, Annie. I took an unexpected trip down the side of the riverbank is all. I hit a patch of slippery something, and slid headfirst across the rocks. Damn things cut the hell out of me."

"I'll patch you up when we get home, Gabe," Annie said, stifling a yawn. "I'm sorry, but would it be okay if you drove back? I can barely keep my eyes open and..."

"'Nuff said, Annie," Gabe interrupted, opening her door and lifting her in. Poor thing looked dead on her feet, and he felt terrible that he was cutting into her snooze time like this.

Back at the cabin, while she cleaned and bandaged his wounds, he filled her in on the details of Rocky and Bullwinkle, hinted at Deirdre's little escapade, told her of the demise of the guitar and cell phone, and of Spike's discovery. By the time he got to the place in the story where he all but threatened the plant guard for the use of the phone, she was nodding off, nearly falling from her chair. He caught her and carried her to her room, tucked her in, and gave her a soft kiss on her forehead when she mumbled a sleepy "thank you." Gabe wanted to crawl in with her and get some sleep himself, but he was far too filthy to even consider it. He tossed his clothes in the washer and himself in the shower. The stinging spray of the hot water relaxed him, and for the first time since the party he felt good. Really, really good. He smiled to himself as he dried off, then went to join his Annie, all snug under the covers. Just as he was about to climb in with her, his underlying guilt of what happened with Deirdre poked at him. He settled for another kiss to his Annie's forehead, and the bed in the guest room instead. It would be a long time coming before he felt worthy enough to share Annie's bed again.

It took Kyle nearly an hour to get back to the house on Park Street. He was tired, cranky, and extremely pissed off at not being able to wake up next to Jenna. He hoped she wasn't too worried about his absence. He needn't have worried. The house was still silent when he snuck up from the tunnel and the basement, and a quick check on Jenna told him that she hadn't even missed him. He'd take a quick shower and then wake her up in one of their favorite ways.

As he scrubbed shampoo into his hair with his eyes scrunched shut to keep out the soap, he felt a rush of cool air when the shower door opened. A soft hand reached down to grab him and fear shot through him, remembering Gabe's warning about Deirdre.

He swallowed hard and whispered, "Jenna?"

The hand tightened on him and relief flooded through him when he heard her say, "Of course! Just who were you expecting, Lover?"

◆ ◆ ◆

After a refreshing nap, Annie and Gabe shared a late and rather horrible breakfast cooked by the disaster-in-the-kitchen Gabe, and once again he repeated the story of his latest mess.

"So there you have it. You're stuck with me until Thursday, Annie. After that, it's back on the road again," he sighed.

"That's only three days, Gabe. I guess I'll have to live with it," Annie replied, stifling a yawn. Three whole days of only her and her cowboy. It would have to be enough for now.

"I suppose you have to work tonight?"

She said nothing, but rose from the table and walked to the telephone. She called staffing at Brighton and told them that she wasn't feeling well, and wouldn't be in that night. She then unplugged every phone in the house, returned to Gabe, and in a bold move for her, sat on his lap and wrapped her arms around his neck.

"Not anymore," she whispered, brushing her lips against his.

The kiss didn't last as long as either one of them would have liked, but things needed to be done and they had a long night to look forward to. Gabe cleared the table and started the dishes, and Annie went to move the laundry from the washer to the dryer.

"Did you unplug every phone?" Gabe called out.

"Every last one! I want three days of no interruptions," Annie hollered back.

"No phone calls," he grinned.

"No running off to work," she laughed.

"No kids," he sang.

"No Deirdre," she muttered.

"No shit!" he snickered, moving up behind her, wrapping his arms around her waist.

"No clothes?" she said, and held up the rags that were once Gabe's jeans and shirt.

"What happened?" he asked, poking at his shredded jeans.

"This." Annie reached into the washer and pulled out a handful of sharp stones. "I have a funny feeling you didn't check your pockets before you tossed your clothes in."

"Never even thought about it, given that my wallet and cash are still at home on my dresser. My little excursion today was entirely unexpected. Those rocks are from the river bank. I had no idea I'd brought back souvenirs from my fall. Oh God, they didn't hurt your washer, did they?"

"No, but I'm afraid you are now without a thing to wear."

"Hey, I'm wearing a smile! Does that count?"

"Between that, and the towel around your waist, you're decently covered. I certainly don't mind, but eventually you'll have to get dressed sometime," Annie said, turning in his arms. She felt her breath catch yet again at the sight of his broad, hairy chest, right in front of her nose.

"True, but not for three more days. I say we make the best of the situation," Gabe murmured, tangling his fingers in her glorious hair.

"Soon. I have to pick up a few groceries, now that I have an unexpected but very welcome guest. I'll pick up something for you, too, while I'm out."

"Thanks, Annie. I'll pay you back on Thursday."

"Don't worry about it, Gabe. I want to get going, though. Wait… Michael's clothes! Can you wear them?" she asked, nodding towards the guest room.

Gabe found himself frowning a little, rather jealous, realizing his brother had, indeed, lived with Annie.

"Um… no. We haven't been able to share a wardrobe in a very long time. His were too tight for me." He let go of her and went back to the task of washing dishes.

Annie stared after him, rather surprised by his sudden coolness.

"Gabe?"

"Go shopping, Annie," he sighed, trying to get his anger under control. Just how close had they been, anyway – dead or not!? Was this some sort of revenge for the Danni fiasco? No, Stevie wouldn't have done anything like that. He never lied, either. Gabe took a deep breath, pasted a smile on his face, and turned around.

Annie's new fears melted away and she went to him, welcoming his embrace, damp hands and all.

"Go, Annie. The sooner you go and get back, the more time we'll have tonight."

"I'm practically out the door, Gabe," she replied, not making the slightest attempt to move. "I'll be a few hours, though. There's another place I need to go, and I'm not sure… Well, I've never been there before, so I'm not sure how long it will take."

Gabe kissed the top of her head, and then added another lingering kiss to her lips. He pulled away, gave her a smack on the tush, and sent her on her way.

His Annie hadn't been gone for more than fifteen minutes and Gabe found himself extremely bored. There wasn't much to do around the cabin, and he certainly didn't feel like sitting around without his Annie. He couldn't even take Adonis for a ride without risking some embarrassing injury. Oh, for a pair of pants! He went so far as to force himself to try on a pair of Stevie's, but they just didn't fit. So much for a ride, although he could go for a swim and not have to worry about appropriate attire.

Dog and McDonald joined him on his walk down to the water, bickering as usual. Gabe dropped his towel on the beach and dove into the cool water, the chill of it giving him a momentary shock. He swam across the small lake and climbed to the rocks on the opposite shore, almost remembering a night long ago when he'd parked there, indulging in some self-pity. Ironic, the cure to his ills had been so close and yet so far for all this time.

He sat there for a long time, just thinking about his life so far. What a long way he'd come since his wild youth. Who'd have thought he would go from the drug addicted know it all-be it all superstar to the responsible businessman and family man that he was today? Parties, booze, women, drugs of all kinds… Christ, he'd overindulged in it all, nearly dying because of it. Then Steve saved Gabe from himself, time and time again. Yet Steve couldn't save himself and left his family for Gabe to take care of, which kept Gabe grounded and able to stay on the straight and narrow. He had let go of ever finding his green-eyed dream and married Deirdre.

Then he found her, his Annie.

Gabe chucked another rock into the lake and sighed. Yep, he'd found her, and found his true home, too. This is what he wanted, this is where he wanted to live, and his Annie was the woman he wanted to spend the rest of his life with. It was time to cut his old life loose. He'd give Dee her divorce and ask his Annie to marry him. To hell with what the rest of the world might think.

Another rock went sailing through the air to splash into the water. Yeah, right. He was only fooling himself. There was no way he could abandon Deirdre or the boys no matter how much he wanted to stay in the cabin across the lake and never have to leave. His Annie wouldn't let him do that anyway.

His Annie. He thought about her some more as he watched the sun set and the moon rise over the trees. The cabin remained dark. He sat on the rock and shivered, and wondered just where the hell his Annie was now.

Annie drove to the mall and called the Evans' house from a payphone. Hopefully Kyle or Jenna would answer, and Annie breathed a sigh of relief when Kyle picked up. Immediately, he warned her in a roundabout way not to say too much, but would meet her in ten minutes to talk more.

Kyle grabbed Gabe's packed duffle bag and threw it in the back of the Jeep, then covered it with some old newspapers and other assorted trash from his vehicle, just in case someone got a bit nosy. He whistled a happy little tune and drove over to where Rocky and Bullwinkle were parked.

He jumped from his Jeep and bounced over to their car, tapping on the window just above Rocky's head.

Leaning his face into the opening window, he said, "Hey hot mama! I'm headin' to the mall. Wanna come?"

"Fuck you, decoy duck. I'm not leaving here as long as he's still in there," Rocky spat.

"How about you, Bull? Wanna go for a little ride?" Kyle lisped, flipping a limp wrist and tossing the man a wink. "I'll let you take pictures…"

Bull turned fifteen shades of red and looked away. It was an offer he didn't really want to refuse, assuming Davidson had really meant it.

Your loss!" Kyle laughed, and bounced back to the Jeep. That was just too easy.

He found Annie right where she said she'd be, at a shop with which Kyle was very familiar. He had been known to spend too much time and far too much money it that particular store. They spent an hour making just the right purchase, then Kyle tossed Gabe's bag into Annie's truck and gave her a hug.

"Tell him that's from me," he joked, referring to the hug. "Tell him I miss his long, lingering, hot looks, and his bulging muscles, and tell him that…"

Annie raised an eyebrow. "Kyle, really! I had no idea."

"Don't even go there, Red," he said, backing away.

"I get the message, Kyle. Don't worry; I'll harass him for you. We'll see you on Thursday," she laughed, then added, "Kyle thanks. This really means a lot, you helping me with this."

"No problem. I'm glad he finally found you, Annie."

She smiled and drove away.

"That son of a bitch!" screamed Rocky. "Double crossing son of a bitch!" She had just talked to Deirdre, who informed her that Gabe had been missing since early this morning. Mrs. Evans had no idea where he was, only that he was not in the house.

"I'll bet Kyle was going to meet him somewhere," Bull sighed.

Rocky hit him with her powerful little fist. "Of course he did, you ass! And he told us where. C'mon!" She put the car in gear and high-tailed it to the mall.

They cruised the parking lot until they spotted Kyle's Jeep parked next to the red pickup truck that had passed them that morning. Oh yeah… Rocky had hit pay dirt!

They sat a few rows back and took pictures as Kyle and Annie exited the store, transferred bags and embraced. They followed Annie when she left.

Annie looked in her rear-view mirror to see that the car was still back there. She had first noticed it parked in the back of the nearly empty lot when she came out of the market with her groceries. It pulled away soon after she did, and Gabe's earlier warning came back to her.

She slowed the truck so that it would catch the next red light. The car was right behind her now and Annie could see the passengers, recognizing the man as the photographer from this morning. Must be Rocky and Bullwinkle. Now what to do? Gabe had been adamant about not being found, so she could not go back to the cabin as long as they were on her tail. She couldn't hope to evade them by out-driving them, so that left outsmarting them. But how?

She drove aimlessly for nearly an hour, concerned that it was already getting dark and Gabe would be getting worried; she had to do something soon. Annie prayed for a miracle of any kind and headed for Hidden Lake Road. Just as she turned onto it, her prayers were answered.

Up ahead a deer shot across the road. Annie drove by it and looked in her rear view to see the car behind her fell back as the rest of the sizable deer herd meandered across the road, blocking the reporter's way.

She still didn't dare go back to the cabin, but she did know of a place to hide. She raced to Gramma's place and hid the truck behind the thick trees where the house had once stood. Minutes later, she saw the headlights of the dastardly duo's car go by. They slowed as they passed the remnants of the driveway, and then sped up again.

Annie waited, then waited some more. The car returned several more times, as if not able to believe that they had lost her on this straight road. She continued to wait until she was sure that they would not return, and the moon was high in the sky before she dared leave the cover of the trees.

The first thing she noticed when she pulled into her driveway was that the cabin was dark; not a single light on anywhere. Was that a good thing or a bad thing? She didn't want to wait to find out. She slammed the truck into park and ran up the steps, calling Gabe's name. She searched every room but found nothing. *Calm down, Annie, maybe he's in the barn waiting to surprise you like a good little stable boy.* That pleasant thought did nothing to calm her already shredded nerves. On shaky legs, she ran to the barn; again, finding nothing. She was two quick seconds away from panic when she heard Dog bark from the lake. Gabe must be there; he had to be!

The clouds had rolled in, obscuring what little bit of light the moon had offered, and Annie had to carefully pick her way down the hill to the beach. Dog and McDonald were there to greet her, but no Gabe; only the towel he had been wearing much earlier indicated that he had been there. She picked it up and felt the damp from the humid night, which had absorbed into the cloth; it had been out here for a very long time.

She was losing it. She dropped to her knees in the wet sand, hugging her arms about her and began slowly rocking back and forth. She squeezed her eyes shut in a futile attempt to hold back the tears as once again, Gabe was taken from her.

The moment he saw the headlights of the truck turn down the drive, he dove into the frigid water. Thank God; his Annie was finally home. It took him longer than expected to swim to the opposite shore, as all of his landmarks disappeared once the clouds covered the moon, throwing his world into inky darkness. Only the occasional soft honk of McDonald was heard to help guide his way back.

She moved from her knees and sat on the beach, clutching the towel to her. She stared out at the lake, searching, but not finding any sign of Gabe. The black water blended into black rock, which blended into black trees, and then to a black sky. The only sounds to be heard were the gentle lapping of the water on the sand and the occasional splash of some aquatic creature. Her head lowered in despair.

McDonald let out a soft honk and Annie looked up to see a break in the clouds. Silver moonlight reflected off the lake, highlighting the trees, the rocks, and the man rising from the water.

"Gabe?" she whispered.

"My Annie," he whispered back, and took her into his arms.

Rocky and Bullwinkle drove back to Gabe's house after losing the red truck. Rocky could not for the life of her figure out where it had gone. The road was straight, and except for a few hills, you could see forever. Goddamn deer anyway, she should have driven right into Bambi and his buddies. Well, there was always Kyle to try to get some dirt on. The dastardly duo resumed their surveillance of the Evans' home.

Kyle and Jenna sat talking on a secluded picnic table in the park, not far from where Rocky parked the car. Kyle had filled his wife in on everything that Gabe had told him, and told her of the adventure through the tunnel. She had been shocked when she heard about Deirdre, and promised to keep an eye on her.

"Look who's back," Kyle said, pointing to Rocky and Bull.

"Oh happy day," Jen replied sarcastically. "Isn't there anything we can do to get rid of them?"

"I dunno. I wonder where they went off. I hope they didn't figure out that Gabe left, or worse, where he went."

"I'll bet they did find out, why else would they have left? And, you can bet they didn't find him, or they would not have come back."

"My wife, the voice of reason. So, why are they back?"

"Most likely revenge on you. What did you say to them before you left?"

"Just asked them if they wanted to come with me, why?"

"About two minutes after you left, they tore out of here like a bat out of hell. I was all the way in the back yard, and I could hear Rocky screeching something about being double-crossed. God! That woman is something else. Kyle, I think that they think that you tricked them or something."

"Well, better to have them after me than after Gabe. We have nothin' to hide."

"Are you sure?"

He gave her a confused look.

"Just who were you expecting in the shower this morning?" Jenna grinned.

"Ha ha," Kyle said flatly, and then in an excited voice asked, "Hey, are you up for an adventure?"

"Oooh! A quickie in the tunnel?"

"Later. No, I think Rockhead and Bullshit need to be taught a lesson about screwin' with people's lives. This is probably illegal; are you game?"

"Sure! That is... if we can't have a quickie in the tunnel..."

"Tramp."

"Pig."

"Bitch."

"Bastard."

"Stop! We can't start this now," Kyle grinned. "Okay, here's the plan..."

Kyle strolled over to the dastardly duo's car and knocked on the windshield. Rocky glared out at him, daring him to say anything.

"Rocky! Missed you at the mall. You too, Bull. Hey, since you two plan on spendin' some time with us, why don't you come on in and have a drink. Can't have you out here loiterin' in the street and draggin' down the property values now, can we?" Kyle gave them his 'best friend' smile.

"Kiss my ass, you bastard," Rocky sneered.

"Now, that's gratitude for ya," he snickered. "Really, I'm sorry about last night; I shouldn't have laughed. C'mon, I still owe you one anyway." Kyle stepped away from the car so that Rocky could exit.

She was suspicious. Her reporter's instinct told her that something was up, but she couldn't quite put her finger on it. Well, what could he possibly do to her, and she would be getting back into the house...

"Okay, one drink, but I still think you are up to something."

"*Moi?*" Kyle said in a hurt tone. "The only thing I am up to is to get some publicity rollin' for this tour. I want to make some serious money so that we can finish remodelin' our house and get the hell out of Gabe's. So, how 'bout it? Friends again?"

"I'll see. I won't be too hard on you, but Gabe is still on my shit list." Rocky grabbed her briefcase and climbed out of the car.

While Kyle distracted Rocky and Bullwinkle, Jenna snuck back into the Evans' house. She had a quick conversation with a surprisingly normal Deirdre, and then made a few phone calls. A package was discretely delivered fifteen minutes later, as Kyle, Jenna, Deirdre, Rocky, and Bullwinkle sat in the living room, enjoying their first drink and some idle conversation.

"Roxanne, Mr. Bullard, I'm so glad that you decided to join us for a drink," said a gracious Deirdre. "I apologize for my husband not being here; business, you know."

"Will he be here later?" asked Rocky.

"He said he would, and Gabe's usually pretty reliable," answered Kyle.

"Just where is he, anyway? We... I didn't see him leave." Rocky was still a bit suspicious of this whole 'drink' thing, especially with Mrs. Evans acting like she was oblivious to the story of 'what happened to Gabe'. Nevertheless, she was in the house again and just might uncover some tasty little tidbit of scandal.

"Who's to say," said Deirdre with a wave of her hand. "He's always flitting about here and there. I never could keep track of him."

"Well, do you expect him back soon?" Rocky asked. She wanted to rub it in Gabe's smirking face that she was once again a guest in his home.

"When I talked to Gabe earlier, he mentioned something about meeting with his... assistant," Jenna told them. "He said he'd try to make it before ten, if possible, but not to worry if he was a little bit late."

Rocky glanced at her watch: nine-thirty. Shit. Well, at least the drink was tasty. She'd never had one of these before and asked Kyle what it was.

"Just a little concoction Jen whips up in the kitchen sink. What is it that you call it, my dear?"

"Marti's magic. Got the recipe from a friend," Jenna answered, giving Kyle a sly wink.

"Hmm... What's in it?" Rocky asked.

"Sorry, sworn to secrecy," Jenna apologized. If the woman only knew...

"His assistant... I thought that was your job, Jenna," Rocky smirked, smelling a story again.

"Oh, I am in the office, but Annie is when they are on the road. Kind of a second job for her," she explained.

"Annie on the road..." murmured Kyle in a dreamy voice, talking more to himself. He wanted to get Rockhead very interested, get her distracted, and then drop the bomb. "You know, she should probably be in this story, too. She's very important in Gabe's life."

"Really." Rocky discretely hit the record button on the tape player that was a permanent resident in her pocket. "Maybe I should interview her. Do you have her number?"

"I'll get it for you later," Kyle said. "It's the least I can do for you after all the trouble we've been; you know, with the cat thing and all."

"I remember. That and a few other things made me think that you were no longer willing to do the story. Why the sudden change of heart?"

"Like I said, publicity. Plain and simple. Gabe is too stubborn sometimes, so we let him have his little tantrums and then we do what we want anyway. Eventually he sees that we're right, not that he'd ever admit it."

"I see. Well then, tell me about... about everything!" Rocky said in a cheerful tone. "I seem to have left my tape recorder in the car, so this isn't like a formal interview or anything, but I'd love to hear anyway." She gave Kyle her sexiest smile.

Kyle smiled back at Rockhead. Christ, she was practically drooling at the thought of him letting something juicy slip out. Maybe he should do just that, get her mind so mired in her own muck that she won't know what hit her. He just hoped Annie would forgive him for what he was about to say.

"As I told you, Annie is Gabe's... assistant. She also wrote one of our new songs. Says Gabe 'inspired' it. Likewise, he wrote a song for her. In Canada. That's where we got the idea to make a comeback."

"Was Annie in Canada as well?" Rocky asked. So... 'assistant', was it? Was she Kyle's assistant too? They were getting pretty close out there in that parking lot.

"Sure was! Spent the weekend with Gabe and me... skiing. God, what a good time we had!" Kyle looked around to make sure the wives weren't looking and gave Rocky a conspiratory wink.

"Oh! Interesting..." Rocky was practically salivating; this sounded like the beginnings of a three-some story; wonder what the wives had to say about that?

"Jenna, how did you like Canada? Did you ski, too?"

"Oh, I didn't go. Deirdre and I thought the guys needed a break from us, so we sent them away. They met Annie up there," Jenna answered with wicked grin.

"You weren't there either, Deirdre?" Rocky was right, this was a gold mine!

Deirdre smiled. She was feeling very good today; nothing like she had been, with that dark feeling coursing through her and taking over her mind. Today, Deirdre was in control, and having a wonderful time setting up this horrid woman for a big fall.

"No, I'm afraid I don't care for skiing. Besides, how can a husband have any real fun with a dreary old wife tagging along?" she sighed.

Rocky had to restrain herself from squirming in her seat. Holy Christ, a ménage-a-trois! With the wives' blessing! This was cover-story quality and she wouldn't even have to embellish on the facts! Now, to find out more about that slut, Annie.

"Jen, this drink you made isn't very good," Kyle whined.

"Of course it is. What's the problem?" she snapped back.

"It evaporates way too fast. Mine's gone already. Anyone need another, besides me?" Kyle asked.

Four glasses were held into the air and Kyle went for more of the brew.

Rocky stifled another yawn. She couldn't figure out why she felt so tired during all of this most stimulating conversation. Although no one came right out and said it, Kyle, Jenna, and Deirdre alluded to the fact that Annie was having an affair with both Kyle and Gabe. Tonight was Gabe's turn for a toss in the sack. *God, not another yawn!* She covered her mouth with her hand, and fought to keep her eyes open.

Kyle, Jenna, and Deirdre exchanged glances; it wouldn't be long now. Minutes later, Rocky and Bullwinkle were snoring where they sat. The three left awake high-fived each other and went to work.

An hour after Gabe swam to shore and to his Annie, the couple slowly walked back to the cabin. Neither one had said a word; tonight, no words were needed. They could always talk tomorrow. Annie's bedroom door shut behind them with a soft click. Had Spike been present in his loft, he would have smiled his feline smile.

"Kyle, you are going straight to hell for this one!" Jenna laughed.

"Yeah, well if you die before me, save me a good spot," Kyle retorted.

"Quiet, you two; we must hurry. I have no idea how long this drug will last, especially on Mr. Bullard," Deirdre said to them.

The trio went to work, stripping the dastardly duo down to their underthings, and proceeded to place them into rather compromising positions.

Kyle seriously thought about taking up photography as a profession for a moment or two as he used Bull's camera and all the film he could find. The film he had found in the camera was destroyed on the spot. Deirdre found Rocky's hidden tape player and taped over the evening's conversations with nursery rhymes from a tape belonging to James and Jeremy. The irony of 'Humpty Dumpty' and... 'The little dog laughed to see such sport, and the dish ran away with the spoon', was not lost on her.

Spike took the opportunity to relieve himself in Rocky's expensive leather briefcase. He shrugged a kitty shoulder; after all, it wouldn't be the first time it had contained excrement, although of a different nature.

Once the deed was done, Jenna pulled the car up into the driveway and tossed in the now-empty camera, the tape player and the befouled briefcase. She added half a bottle of vodka for good measure. Rocky and Bullwinkle were dumped into the backseat, still not decently dressed, and then Kyle drove them to the park... and added a few little illegal items of his own. It was easy enough to find drugs in this town even if he didn't use them.

He ran back to house to call the police, reporting lewd and lascivious acts in the very park where his innocent children played. Minutes later, flashing red and blue lights could be seen across the road as the half-naked drunks in the car were arrested. Kyle placed one more phone call using Gabe's recovered cell phone - complete with Rocky's fresh battery, and the local television and newspaper crews were waiting at the police station when Rocky and Bullwinkle arrived.

A good time was had by all.

Chapter Forty

Gabe sat on the sofa, playing his new guitar and working on a special song for his Annie who was napping in the hammock on the porch. She wasn't kidding when she said she had been tired lately. Whenever they were not engaged in some physical activity, be it riding, canoeing, or 'it', Annie was fighting to stay awake. She insisted that other than feeling sleepy, she was otherwise fine. Great, even! Gabe had no choice but to believe her; she looked great. In her happiness at having him back, she had taken on an inner-glow, a soft radiance. The shadows that had darkened her green eyes had disappeared, and she wore a perpetual smile. Although he had thought it impossible to love her any more than he already did, he found himself discovering that it was indeed possible; especially after the gift she had given him on their first morning together.

He had gone out to see if any of the groceries Annie had purchased survived, and was surprised to see his luggage in the truck. How she had managed this, well, he couldn't wait until she woke up so that he could ask her. He quickly dressed in his own clothes and returned to the truck. Once the cab was unloaded, he checked the truck's bed to see if anything had been missed. All that was back there was a long, rectangular box with a card attached. He saw his name on that card and carried the box into the cabin, then patiently - well, somewhat patiently - waited until his Annie was awake.

She made him suffer in his anticipation of seeing what was in the container. After a leisurely breakfast and recounting the meeting with Kyle, then telling him of the great escape from Rocky and Bullwinkle, she noticed the box.

"Oh yeah, I almost forgot. This is for you," she said, handing it to him.

Gabe felt like a kid at Christmas. He had recognized the store's sticker on that box, and had a very good feeling that he knew what was inside. He was not disappointed. He couldn't count the number of times he had picked up that very guitar in the store, telling Kyle how much he wanted it but didn't want to hurt Deirdre by bringing another one into the house. He had several at the studio, of course, but this one was always special. Why he never bought for the studio, he didn't know. Maybe because it was that one instrument that would be your friend, the one you pick up and play when pondering the mysteries of the universe. The one that entertains a few close friends sitting around the fireplace as the snow falls outside. The one you sit with and write that very special song just as he was doing now, and his Annie had brought it to him. He would treasure that guitar, just as he would always treasure his Annie.

Gabe put down the guitar and went to check on her. She was still snoozing, so he walked up the long driveway to check for the mail and the newspaper. What he found made his day. It would be worth waking Annie up for this! He raced down the hill and jumped to the porch, not even using steps.

"Annie! You're not going to believe this!" he cried, handing her the newspaper.

"Hmm?" She opened one eye, taking in the man standing in front of her who was clad only in a pair of faded jeans. Jeez! Who cared about a stupid newspaper with this standing in front of her? She got that special smile on her face and opened the other eye, but her delicious view was blocked by the dingy gray of the newsprint paper. Her eyes opened even wider. She sat up in the hammock a little too fast and nearly fell out.

"Oh my God!" she laughed. "This is too funny!"

The entire top half of the front page was filled with a drunken and partially-dressed Rocky and Bullwinkle, in handcuffs and being led across the parking lot of the police station.

The headline read: "The Dastardly Duo Spice up a Slow News Day."

"Gabe, I think it's time to plug in the phone and call Kyle. I want to find out what's going on!"

"If I know Kyle, he will know exactly what happened," Gabe laughed. The master prankster strikes again.

Gabe consented to call Kyle, but if Deirdre answered he would just hang up; he didn't even want to hear the sound of her voice, let alone talk to her. Jenna answered and put Kyle on the line.

"Gabe buddy! Miss me?"

"Only about as much as being caught with my pants down on the national news. How you doing?"

"Just ducky, and you?"

"Couldn't be better. Working on a new song."

"How's Annie?"

"Where do I begin? God, Kyle, I am so happy right now! How have I survived so long without her?"

"I'm happy for ya; she's good people. Hey, this is probably a seriously stupid question, but have you two been keepin' up on current events... say like watchin' the TV or readin' the newspaper?"

"Exactly the reason I called. I just happened to see where our crack journalistic team was busted in the park across from my house. You wouldn't happen to know anything about that now, would you Kyle?"

"Oh, sure... blame me!" he laughed. "Christ, Gabe, that bitch used her one phone call to call me instead of her lawyer."

"She wanted you to bail her out?" asked a surprised Gabe.

"Hell no! She called to threaten me. At least that's what I think she was doin'. Ya know, I wasn't aware of just how many ways there was to say 'screw you' to a person, but Rockhead sure educated me. She really is a potty mouth! Anyway, I very politely told her that should we ever hear from her - other than a formal letter of apology of course, or if she were so much as to ever mention our names or refer to us in any way, shape or form, I will be developin' the many rolls of film we took durin' a little photo session she and Bullshit attended. She wouldn't remember it, of course, bein' unconscious at the time, but I assured her that it did happen! I'll send her a roll just to convince her to keep her mouth shut."

"Good God, Kyle, you didn't! Gabe exclaimed.

"Did. With a little help from Jenna and Deirdre."

"Deirdre? She was the one that started this whole goddamn mess in the first place."

"I know, but she was back to her old self yesterday. I think it's safe for you to come home now," Kyle told him.

"I am home, Kyle. I don't ever want to leave here again."

"Hmm... Then I probably shouldn't remind you that we have to leave tomorrow."

"You are a prick, sir. Thanks," Gabe said dryly. "Since you were so kind as to remind me of that fact, I shall now hang up on you and make the most of my time remaining!"

"That's me... always spreadin' sunshine," Kyle laughed. "I'll see ya tomorrow, Gabe."

"Yeah. Hey Kyle?"

"Yeah?"

"Thanks, man. Thanks for everything."

"*De nada.* See ya."

Annie and Gabe rode up to the clearing above the lake. He had packed a light dinner for the two of them in the saddlebags, along with a bottle of wine. He planned to watch the sunset with her, and then ask her to marry him. Just before they left, he snipped a bud from the rose bush next to the cabin and wrapped it carefully in damp paper towel to keep it fresh. He wanted everything to be perfect.

The sun disappeared over the distant hills, leaving the sky a most wonderful shade of lavender, rose, and gold. Gabe and Annie stood at the edge of the clearing and watched as a flock of Canadian geese landed on the lake far below.

It was time. Unfortunately, Gabe was, for the fourth time in his life, at a loss for words. Christ... he knew exactly what he wanted to tell her, he just didn't know how to say it! This was a whole new experience for him; his asking Deirdre to marry him was more like a business proposal. Well, he could always go for the traditional, down-on-bended-knee approach, or how about the kiss her breathless and whisper 'marry me' scenario. Or, he could hang from a tree branch by his knees and sing 'Annie would you marry me' to the tune of Pop Goes the Weasel'. Gawd... now he was just being silly. He'd just have to wing it and hope for the best.

As he walked over to Adonis' saddle to retrieve the flower he had brought, Annie began telling him the story of the clearing and the marble bench.

"This place has always been special," she began. "My grandparents used to come up here all of the time. They'd sit on the bench and watch the sunset. There used to be a table and another bench up here, but Grampa had it brought down to the house when they got too old to make the trip."

Gabe walked up behind her and put his arms around her.

"It is a very special place, very special," he said.

"Every year on their anniversary, my Grampa would bring Gramma up here. He'd give her a bouquet of white roses that he grew - he was a magnificent gardener, and they'd watch the sunset. It was a tradition that began when he..."

"Proposed to her?" Gabe interrupted in a low, meaningful voice.

Annie turned around and looked up at him. "Yes," she whispered.

He pulled the white rose from his pocket and said, "Should we continue the tradition?"

She stared up into intense blue eyes.

He stared back into sparkling green ones. Gently, he ran the soft petals of the rose bud along the line of her jaw.

She reached up and took the flower, never taking her eyes from Gabe's as he asked, "Annie, will you marry me?"

"I... I..." She couldn't speak. This was so entirely unexpected! Oh, she wanted to marry him all right, more than anything in the world, but there was still one little problem: Deirdre.

"I'm going to take that as a yes, because I will not take no for an answer," Gabe murmured.

Annie began to protest, then thought better of it. They only had one night left together and she didn't want anything to happen that could ruin it, and speaking of Deirdre would surely do it. She moved into Gabe's arms and held him close.

"Let's go home," she whispered.

Home.

Home to the cabin to share one last night with his Annie. After his tour was done, he would return to the cabin and never leave again. If there was anything left of SD Productions, Kyle could have it. Gabe no longer had any interest in it and he had enough money in his account to support Deirdre and the boys. Once she was gone, he'd sell that monstrosity of a house and bring the twins to live with himself and his Annie. He would discuss it with her later and then work out the details; tonight it would just be the two of them.

Much later that evening, they lay together in the hammock on the porch, listening to the chirp of the crickets and enjoying the warm June night.

"Gabe, this has been on my mind all night. What inspired you to bring that rose up to the clearing tonight? Have you been talking to Steve again?" Annie asked.

"I'm not sure why I did it; it just seemed like the thing to do. What would Steve have to do with it?"

"I just wondered. Years ago, when I first met him - as Michael, he told me the story of my grandparents and the white roses. I thought that perhaps he told you too."

"No, this is the first I've heard of it. Rather a romantic tale, wouldn't you say?"

"Hmm... Gramma was full of romantic tales. I wish she were still around; I loved listening to her," Annie sighed.

"Well, my dearest, she is."

"What? How do you figure?"

"Her journals. You still have them, don't you?"

"Yes, I do! I'd forgotten all about them. Deirdre said that we should read them together, and since you've been gone, well, I just plain forgot about them."

"We're together now; are you up for a little light reading?" Gabe asked.

"As a matter of fact, I'm very curious about what Gramma wrote. Come on; they're in my room," Annie said, jumping from the hammock.

"Now there is an invitation I won't turn down!" Gabe laughed. He picked his Annie up, carried her into the cabin and deposited her on the bed.

"I thought you wanted to read," Annie said.

"I do. You. I thought I'd brush up on my Braille," Gabe grinned.

"You are going straight to hell!" Annie laughed. She rolled from the bed just as he dove onto it; he missed her by inches.

"Damn! So be it. If you feel we must read, then read we shall. Whip 'em out, baby," Gabe sighed.

They read far into the night and early into the next morning. Gabe read aloud as Annie followed along. His wonderful, marvelous voice had a hypnotic quality to it, and she was transfixed. With Rosalind's ability to write a story and Gabe's gift as an actor reading a story, it didn't take much imagination to see in one's mind, history played out.

Chapter Forty-One

Annie sat in her favorite chair, writing in her new journal. She had been so touched and inspired by Rosalind's documentation of her own life, that she thought she'd give it a try. Besides, she needed to let her feelings about missing Gabe out instead of keeping them all bottled up. No wonder she was teary-eyed half the time. From now on, there would be no more of that. If she felt bad she would just write it out, and the next day read it and realize how silly she had been in the first place. She prayed that it would work.

Annie's Journal, June 18, 1996
Gabe left today. I'm not sure when I will see him again. He did promise to call every day, so at least I have that much. It was so hard to let him go. I've only known him since January, and during that time we haven't really had all that much time together. Still, it seems like I've known him forever. He asked me to go with him to see him off, but I couldn't - not with Deirdre there. I don't know if I'll ever be able to talk to her again. But enough about her. We finally read Gramma's journals. My God, I couldn't believe what was in there! Hundreds of stories about my ancestors; who, what, where, and when... even a few why's. I found it most interesting that I had a relative named Anne who was engaged to marry a Geoffrey. How's that for irony? He met with an unexplained, tragic death. A local 'witch' was suspected, but nothing could ever be proven. Apparently, she and Geoffrey were lovers at one time and G. rejected her. Sounds like the makings of some historical romance novel. The witch - Megheen, vowed revenge on Anne for the death of Geoffrey. Like it was Anne's fault; she was hundreds of miles away at the time. She was to meet G. but missed her coach. M swore that no matter how long it took, Anne would pay. Anne ended up marrying someone named Michael - more irony! I don't know where Gramma got this story, but it made for a good read. Gabe got a kick out of it saying that we were the re-incarnation of A and G. Said that it was meant to be, and I should never argue about it again. (I did make the mistake of mentioning Deirdre, and that we can't be married because he still is. Bad Annie! I should have known better.) Maybe we were together in a past life, and that's why he seems so familiar. Weird. So, until he is back with me, I will go to work, ride, WRITE, and sleep. I'm still tired! Maybe I will go get checked out.

Gabe sat in the back of the bus trying to write, but it was a daunting task, as the roads were nothing but shit - full of potholes and idiot drivers. The bus was either swerving or bouncing non-stop.

He wasn't working on a song, or even a story; he had begun to keep a journal, inspired by the master of journal keeping, Rosalind.

Gabe's Journal, June 18, 1996

Today was one of the worst days of my life. Once again, I had to say good-bye to my Annie. I asked her to take me to my house and see me off, but she declined. In retrospect, it was rather insensitive of me to ask her to come to Deirdre's home. I called Kyle and he picked me up. My Annie was very brave about the whole affair; she kissed me good-bye and waved until we were out of sight. I miss her so much already. We did have a most interesting night last night. We finally read through her grandmother's journals. Fascinating! It seems the tradition of the white roses being given to loved ones did not begin with my little offering last night; it has been going on for well over one hundred years, beginning with a -get this - a Geoffrey and Anne. She was a gentlewoman of the Delaney clan, and he a rogue from some well-to-do Irish or English family whom Anne had tamed and then claimed. Claimed, much to the dismay of the wicked Megheen, who was the woman spurned by Geoffrey several years earlier. Hell hath no fury.... She vowed revenge on Anne, swearing that she would pay no matter how long it took. She would travel through time if necessary. Maybe she is what got into Deirdre, if one believed in that nonsense. Deirdre. I just cannot figure that woman out. When I arrived home (so to speak) she was the Deirdre I knew and loved. I was still very cool to her, as my trust in her met its demise on Sunday. Still, it was hard to believe it was the same woman who did what she did in my office the other day. After several hours of the old Deirdre, I let my guard down. She came to my room on the premise of helping me pack, and the next thing I knew she was in my arms. I looked into her eyes - big, huge mistake. I felt the same as I did on the beach and again in my office. I will never, to my dying day, know what it is about that look that does that to me! Once again, that wonderful Spike intervened. I managed to push Deirdre out and lock my door until it was time to go. And now, here I sit on this fucking bus with every mile taking me further away from my Annie. If it weren't so important to keep SD Productions alive, I'd dive out the window this very second and run the entire way back to the cabin. But since it is not to be, I shall throw myself into this mad venture 100%, give it my all, and make America fall in love with SD all over again. If Annie were here it would be a whole different story. I'd travel forever if she were by my side. Of course we would have to bring Spike; someone needs to keep an eye out for us!

Annie's Journal, June 25, 1996

I just have to write this down! Jeez... I was watching the music television station yesterday and Gabe was on it doing an interview! He never told me that was going to happen! Oh, and he looked so handsome on camera... no wonder he has a huge female following. And funny! The interviewer was trying her darndest not to crack up over his smart-ass remarks... Kyle sure wasn't helping, either. If those two ever decide to quit the music biz, they could do comedy. I always knew they were best friends - they have been since college, but I could really see it when they were together like that. It was almost like they could read each other's minds or something. Jen said that they tend to get into too much trouble when they're on the road with no one to 'chaperone' (meaning her?) but I think they just have a good time when they can. And why not? As long as they're not chasing other women...

Gabe's Journal, June 26, 1996
I actually agreed to do an interview for one of those inane music television shows. I detest the media for many reasons, but Kyle argued a good point - that we need some publicity, so I found myself in front of the camera. You know, I actually enjoyed it! Or perhaps I enjoyed harassing the not-to-bright woman who held the microphone. Regardless, it went well. Kyle was full of his usual bullshit and we had fun bouncing one-liners off of one another. Gotta love that man. And to think we used to hate one another so bad that we actually attempted to fight to the death in our first week of college! I'll never forget that day, but that memory is for another time. I miss my Annie terribly and cannot wait until the day when I can take her in my arms and never ever let her go. Well, perhaps I'll let her go long enough to hold a child of ours should we ever have one. God, that would be great! I'd love to have a little girl of my own. I wouldn't turn away a boy, but a girl... my most precious little daughter. Perhaps I should discuss children with my Annie before I get my hopes up, though. Odd, but in all of our short time together, the subject of a family has never come up. Maybe the thought of taking on my 'readymade' one has put a bit of fear into her heart. I sure hope not.

Annie's Journal, July 1, 1996
I can't believe it! This is just too incredible. I finally broke down and went to the doctor to find out why I am so tired all of the time. I, oh God, I can barely write the words! It would make it real if I do, but it is real anyway, so here goes - I'm pregnant. It must have happened the night before Gabe left - the first time. How could I not have known, or even suspected? Jeez, I'm a nurse! I should know these things! Gabe needs to know. I can't tell him. He never mentioned having children before. I know he likes them; he is wonderful with James and Jeremy, but becoming a father at his age? Not that he is that old, but he is not that young, either. I don't know. Then there is the little matter of having a child out of wedlock. I know that in this day and age it is no big deal to society; but it still is to me. I managed to talk Gabe out of divorcing Deirdre - she doesn't have much time left anyway, and now I almost regret it. I wish I had someone to talk to about this. Hello!!! Michael, are you listening?? When Gabe calls me tonight I'll kind of hint at it and see what his thoughts are. I'll decide what to tell him then. He'll have to find out eventually, because it's not something I can hide! Won't the girls at work have a field day with this one! Annie the nun is PG. At least Marti will sympathize with me. But I'm still not telling anyone

until I absolutely have to. And how do I feel on the matter? Scared. Scared to death, and thrilled beyond belief! A baby! It would be so much easier if Gabe were here to share this with me, but until I know how he feels... He loves me though. He couldn't possibly love me because of this, could he?

Gabe's Journal, July 1, 1996

Somebody should just shoot me through the goddamned head. I did it again. I hurt my Annie. When I called her tonight, she was so happy, and I was a prick. I had a hell of a day and took it out on her. The bus broke down again, and Wolff and Mick got into a fight. I broke it up and got a black eye for my trouble, and then Kyle took off for parts unknown while the bus was being repaired. I ended up having to bail him out of jail for illegal gambling. Son of a bitch was hustling pool with an undercover cop or something stupid like that. I should have let him rot. If that weren't enough, when I called to check on things at home, Deirdre started whining about the kids. I really didn't need to hear about that - Christ! What can I do about it? I'm five hundred miles away! I told my Annie about that, (along with everything else) said what a pain in the ass kids can be. She was very quiet after that. Hope she isn't going through that 'time of the month' moody crap again. I sure as hell don't need it right now. Still, I should have apologized instead of just hanging up on her. Maybe I'll find myself a gun and just fucking end it all now.

Annie's Journal, July 4, 1996

I haven't heard from Gabe in three days. I'm not sure what to think. I called Jenna to see if there was a problem and she said no, everything is just fine. They were doing a huge Fourth of July celebration with four other bands in Oklahoma and having a great time. So why doesn't he call? Is he mad because I started talking about kids, and how great they were? I can't believe what he said about the twins. Maybe he doesn't want a child after all. I really need to talk to someone about this, before I go insane. Damn Marti for taking another job with that traveling nurse agency. She won't be back in town for three months. Maybe I could talk to Jenna. She has always been a good friend. I just hope she can keep a secret.

Gabe's Journal, July 5, 1996

I tried calling Annie all day today. Her machine isn't even picking up. I hope I can reach her at work tonight. I need to tell her how sorry I am for treating her the way I did. I sent her flowers - roses of course, but I need to talk to her. Hell, I need to do more than that. I need to hold her, tell her how much I love her and cannot wait until we are married. I want to start a family with her. I wonder if she wants kids. God, I wish we would have talked about that before. I swear that Deirdre is fucking possessed! She has been calling me far too much lately, talking nonsense about me coming home for a day or two to renew our relationship.

What relationship? I talked to Jenna about her, and J. says that D. is just fine - no changes other than the usual tired, weak, sick woman. That certainly isn't what I hear when I talk to her! That does give me an idea though. I think I'll fly home for a day to be with my Annie. We have a few days between shows coming up; it would be the perfect opportunity. Give me a chance to get away from Mick and Wolff for a while. Those two are worse than the odd couple. I'm beginning to suspect it's a lover's spat. Go figure!

Annie's Journal, July 6, 1996

Gabe sent me some flowers - white roses. There was no message; just a card that said 'Gabe' and it wasn't even his handwriting. I had to buy a new phone today. The one I just bought with the answering machine was junk. It wouldn't ring in and the machine wouldn't pick up, and it even interfered with the rest of the phones in the house. Maybe Gabe did try to call - I just didn't know it. He could have left a message at work for me though. Speaking of work, that Edith is driving me nuts! She is constantly badgering me for information about Gabe and the tour, and what he is doing and blah blah blah. I'd like to tell her to f**k off, but I don't want to hurt her feelings. I kind of feel sorry for her. I had to laugh at this - I found out she is married to Richie. What a loser! I didn't tell her that I was married to him eons ago, and then she'd be bugging me about him, too. And I DON'T CARE!!! My pants are starting to get a little tight. I should talk to Jenna - soon.

Annie's Journal, July 7, 1996

I talked to Jenna today. Made her swear that she wouldn't tell a soul. She was thrilled! Wanted to do the baby shower thing and all that. I told her to slow down... it would be quite a while before we got into all that. I told her that Gabe didn't know yet, and that I was rather hesitant to tell him because of the situation - everything, really. She said that she understood, and my secret was safe with her. I do feel a little better sharing this with someone. If only Gabe would call. He did leave a message on my NEW machine, but his phone wasn't very clear and I couldn't understand what he said.

Gabe's Journal, July 7, 1996

As much as I miss my Annie, I must admit that I am having a wonderful time on this tour. I had completely forgotten what it is like to be on stage and entertaining the masses... I loved it before, but I got caught in that goddamn death-grip of coke and speed (and the heroin, but NO ONE knows about that other than Stevie)... not to mention the nightly drinking binges and the parties. And the women. Christ, I can't even believe I used to be like that. Kyle and the guys are hovering over me as if I'll fall back into that decadent lifestyle but they needn't worry - never again will I touch any of that shit... well, maybe the drinking, although not nearly as much as before. A beer or a shot every now and won't hurt. But no drugs - not even a joint. Nope... I have my Annie and my family to look forward to now and the day can't come soon enough when I will have them back. But until then I'm going to make the best of my time on the road. And in one more day I'll have a brief taste of it when I fly home to be with her. It can't come soon enough.

Gabe's Journal, July 9, 1996

I flew home to be with my Annie last night. It figures that she would be working. I didn't make it there in time to catch her before she went in - actually, I didn't know she was going to work. Damn overtime! I did buy her a cup of coffee, though. We had a wonderful half-hour together in that stinking cafeteria, and then an even more wonderful three hours after she got home. We didn't talk much, but then, actions speak louder than words! And there was a whole lot of action going on. Christ, now I'm beginning to sound like Kyle! I really do need a break from that man. Annie has something on her mind but she wouldn't say what it was, not that I gave her much time to chat. I guess if it was that important she would have said something. She is starting to put on a little weight, but she still looks great. I don't care. She could be the size of Adonis and walk like McDonald, and I would still love her. Love her forever and ever and ever. Amen.

Annie's Journal, July 9, 1996

Gabe just left, and I'm feeling much better about our relationship. For a while there, I was beginning to wonder! I still haven't told him about the baby. I tried to several times, but was distracted each time. Ah, but what a distraction! I just have to write down what happened last night - it was so... Anyway, I picked up an overtime night (big surprise) and took my little quiet time break on the bench in the service hall down by Ptomaine on a Tray (my pet name for that hole they call a cafeteria). I was relaxing - eyes shut again, and I caught a whiff of woodsy-spicy. The imagination must have been working overtime again - or so I thought. I opened up my eyes and there was my cowboy, asking if he could buy me a cup of coffee. I practically threw myself at him, I was that glad to see him. We didn't have much time together; he only had a few hours until he had to catch his plane back to some dusty little town in the mid-west. (He said it probably wasn't even on the map.) Still, he flew home just to see me! I wish we could have had more time though - I really need to tell him, and I just can't bring myself to do it over the phone. I have some vacation time coming; maybe I'll take it and be with him for a while. Sure! Why not? I've always wanted to be a groupie. Tee hee.

Gabe's Journal, July 15, 1996

Kyle just informed me that I am to become a father. I wasn't aware that he and I have been having sex! There, that was the only levity I'll bring into this subject. It seems that my Annie is with child, and has thus far neglected to inform me. Kyle only knew because Jenna told him after my Annie told her, swearing her to secrecy. Neither Kyle nor Jenna could ever keep their mouths shut. Now, when will I hear it from the mother? What reason could she possibly have NOT to tell me? I couldn't be happier with the news (assuming that it is indeed true) but with the dark cloud of my Annie not telling me hanging over, well; I'm just a bit hurt. Doesn't she trust me? How could she not know that this is the most wonderful news ever? I should have been the first to know, not Jenna. Now I'm sounding childish, but at this point I do not even care. I still haven't been able to reach Annie - it's been two days since we have been able to talk; playing telephone tag is not my idea of a fun time. I would love to set down a specific time for our conversations, but that is nearly impossible with all that is going on now. God! I'm going to be a father! I hope it's a girl.

Annie's Journal, July 17, 1996

Finally! I thought I would never hear from Gabe again, but he just called. He only had a few minutes before the show, so the conversation wasn't very long. Damn! He sounded very distracted, and when I asked him if there was something wrong, he snapped at me and said that he should be asking me that very question! This separation is becoming very difficult. I don't know how much more of it I can take. I managed to talk my way into getting two weeks of vacation in August, but that is still two weeks away. I need to find out where Gabe will be during that time so that I can be with him. Jenna thinks it is a great idea and would join me if Deirdre was better. I guess she has been really weird lately, talking very strange and staying holed up in her room for hours at a time. I feel terrible for the twins to have to see their mother going through that. Jenna says that they are handling it just fine, and understand that it really isn't 'their' mother. I wonder if Steve is still with them. Maybe I'll make a trip over there, just for a quick visit. I think I'm able to handle seeing Deirdre now, and I really do miss Spike. That settles it. I'm going.

Gabe's Journal, July 17, 1996

I called Annie tonight, just before the show. I gave her every opportunity to tell me the big news, but she never uttered a word about it. Maybe Kyle was misinformed - and I was so hoping that it were true. I can't let myself think about it; it makes me too depressed and that is not a quality that I relish in myself. I spent far too much time in my earlier years fighting that horrid condition, and I'll be goddamned if I let it ever get to me again! I will keep my mind off of it by concentrating on the show - which, by the way, is more successful than I would ever have imagined. We are still getting calls to be opening acts for some of the major talent doing the county fairs. I have no idea why this is happening; I have never heard of something like this happening before. The bands are usually booked far in advance and some of this 'major talent' has never had anyone open for them. I have decided to add some special effects: new lighting, smoke, lasers and such to make it more of a visual show along with our fantastic sound. We'll have someone opening for us before too long. I have resigned myself to this traveling - even made my peace with the fucking bus (although it still isn't very reliable). If only my Annie were with me.

Annie's Journal, July 20, 1996

Great news! SD will be coming back to Michigan to do some big show sponsored by a local radio station. It is an all-day affair, with eight different bands taking the stage. It just so happens that it will be on the first day of my vacation, so guess where I will be! I hope that he will go along with my idea to travel with him for a week or two. I'll tell him about the baby then. We have been fortunate in the fact that for the last three days, we have been able to talk, but we really need to see each other. He sounds so depressed when he talks to me about not being able to be with me, but when he talks about the show and the changes he is making in it, he perks right up. I'm glad that he has something to take his mind off of us not being together. I wish that I did. I can't even ride any more - I don't want to do anything to put my baby in danger. My baby - I still can't get over the fact that I am going to be a mother! The guestroom will have to be changed into a nursery. Hey, that's what I can do; get my own project going. I'll start re-doing the room - just as soon as I get back from my vacation. I wonder if it will be a boy or a girl.

Gabe's Journal, July 20, 1996

I just informed my Annie that we will be in town in a little over a week, doing some gig for a radio station's big country weekend. We were scheduled to be an add-on, but were moved up to be one of the headliners. This is all so incredible! Our show will be on after dark, so the new special effects will be even more dramatic. I can't wait until we can try them out. I was going to use them in the next show we do (in one of those crappy little towns with a population smaller than my tour bus) but why waste it on them? We'll introduce it in Michigan. I heard that there will be over half a million people in the audience! SD in your face, America! I cannot stop thinking about the baby that almost was. Kyle still swears that it's true, that Annie did tell Jenna about it. So why haven't I been told? Christ! What if it isn't mine? No, that's impossible. Annie would never, ever... would she? I never thought I would either, and yet it damn near happened with Deirdre the horrible! She has been calling my cell phone lately and hanging up shortly after I answer. I figure it has to be her, since only a few people know the number and she is the only one unhinged enough to do something like that.

Annie's Journal, August 1, 1996

Today is the big day! My bags are packed and loaded into the truck, Jill is here to critter sit for me, and my Gabe will be in my arms before the night is out! They were supposed to roll into town yesterday, but that stupid bus broke down again, and they had to spend the night in some icky no-tell motel. From Gabe's description, it had all the qualities of a third-rate porn movie, right down to the (ick!) stains.... Gross! He is so funny sometimes. Most of the time, actually. I miss him so much. I went to see the twins yesterday (planning my visit to coincide with Gabe's arrival) and they seem fine. Eric, the boys, and I spent an interesting afternoon in their room. Steve has been talking to them. They know that Gabe is their uncle and not their father, and they also hinted that Deirdre is no longer their mother. I wasn't quite sure what to make of that until they told me that she was Megheen. I was totally creeped out. I guess she must have told them the story of the witch (she did read the journals too) and this is their way of coping with her bizarre behavior. I only saw Deirdre for a moment, and she was very strange. Her eyes were very dark and she hissed-yes, hissed at me that I will pay. My brat and I will both pay. I wonder if Jenna told her about the baby. She denied it when I asked her, but how else would Deirdre know? Ow! There's that stupid cramp again. Must be the excitement of knowing that my wait is over. Only a few more hours...

Gabe's Journal, August 1, 1996

We have to go on in about an hour, so I thought I'd write for a minute. Annie was supposed to meet me here a while ago, but there are so many people out there that it will take her a week just to wade through them all! I left word with security to bring her back as soon as she shows up. Jenna and Kyle have been missing for three hours now - I sure hope he makes it back in time. I'm about ready to blow up this fucking bus. Goddamn thing broke down again, causing me to miss an entire night with my Annie. I think I'll do just that. The second this nightmare tour is over, we'll have a big party and the bus will provide the entertainment as it blows heavenward in great ball of flame. We'll tape it, too; should we decide to do another video we'll have some good footage. Christ... Deirdre just walked in. This is all I need.

Annie's Journal, August 1, 1996

Gabe's concert just ended. My God! He is so incredible! It will be a while before I can get back to his bus, so I thought I'd describe the show. He finally got around to using all that new special effects stuff he spent so much money on. When the show started, there was no one on stage - everything was black. Then a mist started swirling all around and Wolff began playing the intro to 'The Dream' on his violin. It was really cool. That music is so haunting. Gabe and Kyle rose from the middle of the stage, standing on a rock, just like on the CD cover and began to play. The audience went crazy. They loved all of the new lighting and the lasers were pretty good, too. They played about ten songs, and then finished with 'Dream Again'. This is the most incredible part. Gabe actually found me in that huge crowd! I was about ten rows back (having had to literally fight my way that close) and he saw me. He never took his eyes from me during the entire song. After it was done, he gave me that special smile and waved for me to come back stage. Everyone around me was staring at me - rather embarrassing, but I don't care! The crowd is really thick around the security door, so I'll just wait until it thins out a bit; a few more minutes won't matter now. Besides, being jammed in with all of those people has made me feel kind of woozy. And that cramp has been nagging me all night. Damn nerves!

Gabe's Journal, August 1, 1996
Goddamn fucking bitch! I will kill her! I will wrap my hands around her skinny little neck and kill her if I ever see her again! She is lucky that security is so thick around here and took her away before I actually did it. I was waiting for my Annie to come back to the bus and instead of her, Deirdre walked in. I asked everyone to leave - yet another huge mistake - so that I could have it out with her. I was going to tell her that I wanted a divorce - immediately- and that I would never be setting foot in her house again. All ties would be cut except for a weekly check to keep them in necessities. The second the last person was out of the bus, she was all over me. I avoided looking into her eyes (yes, even I can learn from previous mistakes) but it did no good. She threw me down onto a seat and proceeded to... I can't even write it. I found it amazing the strength she had though. Is she really as ill as she appears to be? Regardless, she was on top of me and kissing me (she was doing a lot more than that too but it sickens me to even think about it) when who should pop onto the bus but my Annie. She was devastated. She never said a word, just turned pale as a ghost and ran from the bus. I tried to catch her, but Deirdre tripped me and I fell, nearly knocking myself unconscious when my head hit the floor. Deirdre laughed. I stood up and turned to kill her then, but security was on the bus about then - probably wondering what sent Annie out of here in such a state. It was all I could do to shove the bitch towards the guards to get her away from me. I never thought I was capable of such hate. I spent the next three hours searching for my Annie, but it would be literally impossible to find her in this mass of humanity. I even went to the cabin, but she wasn't there. I left her a note on her door, telling her that what she saw was by no means what she thought it was - it wasn't anything like the beach incident, and for her to call me back right away. I'll go back over there later tonight and explain. Maybe she can get a few days off of work and come with me on the tour. We are heading for Kentucky, and I think she would love it down there.

Annie's Journal, August 2, 1996
I lost the baby. I lost the baby and Gabe, and I can't even cry about it; I'm

just too numb. I will never forget - as long as I live- what I saw on that bus last night. Having that happen once - well, it was difficult, but I overlooked it. Shit happens. But again? Maybe it was entirely Deirdre's doing, but the look in Gabe's eyes- I know that look, and I should be the ONLY one to know that look. The bastard. Fuck him. Yes, I actually said it. And I mean it. After I left the bus, the cramp became cramps, and I started bleeding. I don't know if it was going to happen anyway, but it certainly progressed quickly once I saw what I saw. I started to go home, but halfway there I realized that it was serious and brought myself to the closest hospital - which fortunately wasn't Brighton. At least no one there will find out about this. The baby was too young to survive anyway. It was a girl.

Gabe's Journal, August 6, 1996

I still haven't been able to find Annie. I went back to the cabin, and Jill, the girl taking care of her animals said that Annie was supposed to be with me - that she had taken two weeks of vacation and had planned on spending it with me. She hadn't heard a word otherwise, so... God, what a mess this all is. I even checked the hospital to see if - God forbid, she had been in an accident. No one there has heard from her either. I have been running up quite a phone bill trying to locate her. I'm thinking about hiring someone to look for her since I'm stuck in Kentucky for the next two weeks. From here it is Nashville - I still can't believe that, either! Back to my Annie... I talked to Jenna about the alleged pregnancy, and she insisted that it was true. Annie even showed her an ultra sound picture of it. They think it's a girl, although it's still too early to tell. Why hasn't she told me? I just cannot understand it. I'm going to be a father! Now, I just need to locate the mother.

Annie's Journal, August 8, 1996

I decided to check myself into the hospital for a little mental health R & R. Everyone thinks I'm on vacation anyway, so what the hell. It is very pleasant here, and the staff is very supportive. I still haven't been able to grieve over either the baby or Gabe. I'm hoping that I can soon, so that I can get my life back on track. This has to come out or it could be very devastating to me mentally. I wish Michael were here. I was going to call Jill, just to check on my critters, but decided not to. I found that I really don't give a shit about anything anymore. Not one damn thing. That's not good and the tiny part of reason still left alive in me understands that, hence my voluntary hospitalization. Physically, I'm still tired from the miscarriage. It was a very long, very difficult delivery.

Gabe's Journal, August 10, 1996

I still haven't been able to reach my Annie. I will admit that I'm terrified. No one has heard from her. She has dropped off the face of the earth and it's my fault. I will take that guilt to my grave. Deirdre said absolutely not to a divorce but I will get one anyway. I could still murder her, although I fear that would be counter-productive. I don't think Steve would let it happen anyway. I sure could use his help about now, the son of a bitch. I'm going to be a father! I cannot stop thinking about it! I can't wait to hold my daughter in my arms, kiss that little brow, and change those smelly little diapers. I have this perpetual picture in my head of my Annie, our baby and me, all snuggled together on the sofa in the cabin, the wood stove keeping us warm as the snow falls in great, fat flakes outside. That is what keeps me going through all of this. That and the skyrocketing success of SD. We are no longer just an opener. We will be headlining in Nashville after all. True, we are filling for a cancellation, but still... We are bigger now than we ever were before.

Annie's Journal, August 14, 1996
Well, I'm home again. The 'vacation' was restful, but hardly helpful. I am still numb, empty and filled with hate. I will function and that's that. Jill said that Gabe has called every single day looking for me. Good. Let the bastard suffer. Now he will know what it is like to have something more precious than life itself ripped from him without warning. Fuck him. I'm going for a ride.

Gabe's Journal, August 15, 1996
Annie is home. She still isn't speaking to me, but thank God she is home, and safe. I only know this because when I called, she answered. As soon as she heard my voice, she told me to fuck off and slammed the phone down, but at least I know she is safe. If it weren't for the tragedy of this entire misunderstanding, I would have laughed. Imagine her saying the 'F' word! I never would have thought it possible. Kentucky is a beautiful state. I think I'll bring my Annie and the baby down her for a vacation next year. We can rent a houseboat and float around for a whole week of nothing but sun, water, and long nights under the stars.

Annie's Journal, August 20, 1996
I found a handy little device to put on my phone to block unwanted calls. I won't have to deal with his annoying shit any more. Adonis and I have been spending a lot of time together. I bought a new saddle. It's made for cross-country racing, and we have a new hobby. God, can that horse ever move! I never realized how fast he was, and he can jump anything! I was always scared to try jumping before, but now I don't care. Not about one damn thing.The only time I really feel anything is when we are racing through the woods at breakneck speeds, jumping anything in our path. Danger is a rush. Fuck Gabe. Fuck the world. And I'm going to shoot that goddamn Edith if she says one more word to me about that man.

Gabe's Journal, August 21, 1996

Annie still isn't speaking to me. The tour is beginning to wind down now; only two more weeks to go, then it's home to the cabin. She will have to have forgiven me by then, right? She isn't even answering my calls anymore. Must have discovered caller ID. Jenna talked to her yesterday, but only for a minute. She asked how the baby was doing, and Annie said 'what baby?' and hung up on her. I felt chills when I heard that. I have recently re-discovered prayer. I am constantly praying that nothing bad has happened, but I can't shake the feeling that something else is wrong with Annie other that her anger at seeing Deirdre and me. Steve, if you're out there, I could really use some help now!

Annie's Journal, August 28, 1996

I heard that he is supposed to be home next week. I'll have to start remembering to lock my doors. Jenna is becoming just as annoying as he is. She calls nearly every day to check up on me, asking how I am doing, and if she can help in anyway. She can't take a fucking hint, either. Her number is now on my call blocker. Eric called. I did try to be civil to him, but it wasn't easy. They all have this conspiracy going on over there to make me forgive the little demigod who brightens up their dreary little world. Gabe this, and Gabe that, blah blah fucking blah. I don't care if I ever hear is name again. I'm going for a ride.

Gabe's Journal, September 4, 1996

At long last, this miserable tour is over! We made a ton of money, and have been on the charts for most of the summer, and everybody wants a piece of SD. I don't care. None of it means a thing without my Annie. I went to the cabin today to see her. Her door was locked and she wasn't there. I think she must have been on Adonis, as he wasn't there either. Brilliant deduction, Sherlock! I was going to take Wanda out to look for her, but the mare appeared to be favoring a leg and I didn't want to take any chances. I waited for three full hours, but she never showed, so I went back to Deirdre's, only to see the twins. They really are great kids, and I did miss them. I'll just hide in my room whenever I'm here. The lock seems sturdy enough to keep that bitch out.

Annie's Journal, September 4, 1996

How dare that son of a bitch come here! I can't believe he had the nerve to show his cheating face anywhere near me. Thank God I was on a ride at the time. It's all I do anymore, since I quit working. Well, not actually quit, but took an unpaid leave of absence for unspecified reasons. I guess all of that goody-two-shoes behavior over the last decade paid off. My supervisor didn't even question my reasons for wanting to leave, just told me my job would be there when I was ready to come back. Back to him. I saw his truck from the top of the hill, and then went into the cover of the woods until he left. Shit! It took him forever to leave. Doesn't that man get it? He blew it. I had a dream about the baby last night. I think I may have cried in my sleep. If only I could when I'm awake, maybe I could get rid of some of this hate. I suppose that if I cared, I would care. But I don't.

Gabe's Journal, September 10, 1996

I'm afraid that Annie and I are truly finished. She has yet to say a word to me other than the famous 'fuck you' and she is never home when I go over there. She is always out on that horse of hers. I think she knows that I am there, and stays away on purpose. I did catch a glimpse of her yesterday. I was driving by where I went off the road last winter, and I saw them racing across the field. That horse is damn fast and she was riding like a mad woman, jumping anything in their path. God, it was a beautiful, although frightening sight. I laid on the horn and waved and she pulled her horse up. She looked over towards me, and then disappeared into the woods. I ran as fast as I could, trying to catch her, but to no avail. There was just too much area to cover. I cannot believe that it's over. After all that happened to get us together, and the depth of our love, it just seems impossible. Another thought just occurred to me; why in hell is she riding like that if she is pregnant? Is she trying to lose it? I find it difficult to believe that she could be so hard-hearted about something like that. She is the gentlest, most loving person on earth. She could not deliberately destroy another life like that - or could she? Does she hate me that much that she would destroy our child? Steve, if you are out there, I really need you now!

Annie's Journal, September 10, 1996

I saw him yesterday. He was in his truck on Hidden Lake road. My cowboy. Adonis saw him too and tried to run over to him, but I turned him into the woods to prevent it. I'm not sure exactly who I was preventing from going over to him. I felt such loathing at the sight of him, yet something deep inside me tried to fight its way to the surface, something I haven't felt for a long time - ever since that day. I must be able to feel something and the numbness isn't as deep as I thought. I can still feel pain, and I don't ever want to be hurt like that again. I had another dream about the baby last night. She looked just like her father. I need a drink.

Gabe's Journal, September 15, 1996

The private investigator I hired last month finally gave me his full report, even though Annie is home. No wonder she is suffering so. It seems that on that night, that fateful night when my life ended, Annie drove herself to the hospital where she was admitted to labor and delivery. She lost the baby. Our baby. My God, if I am feeling this bad, I can only imagine what she went through- is still going through. I have tried to contact her by any means possible, but I can't even catch her at work - it seems that she quit. She needs help desperately, and there is nothing I can do for her. At least I have Deirdre to talk to. She has been her old self lately, although I still see a flash of those glittering black eyes once in a while. I think she is up to something, but I am beyond caring anymore. Beyond caring so much that I did something I swore I'd never do again. But only to help me get through this... and just a little dope won't hurt, will it?

Annie's Journal, September 17, 1996

I received a letter from him today. I tossed it in the trash, but as I went about my day I could not forget about it. It took nearly half a bottle of scotch before I could bring myself to read it. I had to read it, if for no other reason than to free myself from thinking what it may have said. Speaking of scotch, I rather enjoy it. It's bitter, which matches me, and it can quickly rekindle the numbness should it begin to wear off. Now, back to the letter. He wants to meet with me - hopefully to reconcile, but if that is not possible, he wants to apologize for not being there when I needed him the most. And just what part of my life would that pertain to? I needed him twenty-four hours a day, seven days a week. Needed him most. Bullshit. I sure could have used him to support me the night she died, but no - he was in the arms of his wife. The wife he claimed to hate so much. The wife who was never really a wife at all, just a pity marriage. Maybe I will meet with him after all, just so I can see the look in his eyes when I tell him that his daughter is dead. How's that for pain, cowboy? But then again, maybe he would be thankful for that fact. I don't know. I don't know anything anymore. Even the death rides on Adonis are beginning to wear a little thin. A long swim in the lake is sounding better all the time. A very long swim, carrying a very heavy object. I need another drink.

Gabe's Journal, September 21, 1996

I still haven't heard from her. I was hoping that she would at least respond to my letter, but so far, nothing. Deirdre said that Annie was hurting, and it may take a very long time to get over it; the loss of a child is devastating no matter when you lose it. I just wish that she would let me in so that I could help her. I'm beginning to get one of those headaches again. I was smoking a little weed to relieve them and Dee caught me. Said she had a better way without the dope. 'What the hell,' I said; I didn't want the boys to find out their papa was pothead anyway. She then proceeded to make me a cup of foul-smelling tea and give me a neck rub that worked wonders. I still find it difficult to believe the strength she has. She looks to be at death's door, and then she pulls one of these numbers. I fell asleep during the massage, and woke feeling much better. Since then, my daily headaches are quickly relieved by her ministrations, followed by a refreshing nap. I am still a bit suspicious of her, but it seems that it doesn't really matter anymore. I've lost everything that means anything to me. SD Productions has opened its offices and studio again. The Davidson's will be moving back into their house as soon as the lease is up with their tenants; mid-October, I believe. I hired a competent office manager to keep an eye on Kyle and Jenna, and leave most of the paper work to him. I go in and write and do a little recording with Kyle and the guys, but otherwise I spend most of my time in my room with the guitar she bought for me. It is even too painful to say her name any more. My head is pounding; I think I'll find Deirdre.

Annie's Journal, September 22, 1996
None of my clothes fit anymore. I have to use bailing twine just to keep my pants up, cuz even my belt is too big. I really wasn't aware of this until Michael pointed it out to me. Yes, Michael. He saved my life. I was deep into another bottle of scotch and contemplating that long swim, and decided to go for it. I was going to take one last ride on my beloved Adonis, then end it all. I wrote a letter to Jenna, telling her to take care of my animals - especially Spike (how I miss that cat) and to remind her that her bird is still here singing his naughty little songs. Everyone was given a few days' worth of food and water, and then I went for my final ride. I rode to the other side of the lake where the water is the deepest, and there is a 100-foot drop straight down - no trees to get in my way. There is also a small waterfall there; in other circumstances it would be a very beautiful spot. I was ten seconds away from taking that final step, when I heard the sound of a horse rapidly approaching. I turned around, and there he was. All thoughts of suicide were driven from me at the sight of him. For the first time in months, I cried. He held me for hours as the dam holding back my buried emotions burst and Annie was reborn. I told him everything. He already knew of course, but still. It felt so good to unburden myself with the one person who truly loves me, no matter what. He never offered me any advice or told me to forgive his brother; he was just there for me when I needed him the most. We went back to the cabin and dumped my stash of booze down the sink. He handed me back my letter to Jenna, saying that she really didn't need to read it now, did she? We burned it in the woodstove. He spent the entire night with me, just being there. He did point out the fact that I needed a new wardrobe, or had to start eating again. One or the other. He also said that I should get my ass back to work! And you know - I think that's a good idea. I'm still not ready to see 'him' yet, but I want my life back. It wasn't all that bad, after all. Just before Michael left, we had a small memorial service for Gabriella Michaela - that's what I named my daughter. Michael placed a small square of white marble in the center of the rose garden, and then sang 'Amazing Grace'. He sings almost as well as his brother. We each placed a white rose bud on the stone and said good-bye. I now have some closure with the loss of her. I start work next week. It will be good to get back to the exciting world of pediatrics.

Gabe's Journal, September 25. 1996
At last I have come to the conclusion that it is truly finished with Annie.

This will be the last time that I will even think of her name; the pain is just too unbearable. I'll turn my energy into making Deirdre's last days comfortable and raising my nephews to make their father proud. SD Productions has never been busier, and I have been spending much more time there, wheeling and dealing, making music and making money. I miss that damn Chet, but he is one last connection to her. And Spike. He is no longer the cat he once was. He seems depressed too. Maybe I'm just transferring my feelings onto him. He lurks about the halls, watching every move Deirdre makes when she is around me. She hasn't tried the seduction thing since I've been home, but I can't help get the feeling that she is still not satisfied with our platonic relationship. Not that it matters any more. At times I would almost welcome her 'attention' if for no other reason than to forget my... her, and just feel loved.

Chapter Forty-Two

Eric, James and Jeremy sat in the twin's room discussing Deirdre, or at least discussing the person in Deirdre's body.

"I want mama back. I don't like the lady in there very much," said James.

"Me neither," said Jeremy.

"I agree," said Eric. "Did your dad say what we should do about it?"

"No, he just told us that she can't hurt us. He hasn't been around in a while anyway. He said it is hard for him to come back whenever he wants to," Jeremy told him.

"Well, we have to do something. She's the reason Annie and Gabe broke up, and they need to get back together. What does Deirdre do in her room all day anyway? I know she lets you guys in there once in a while; do you ever see anything?" asked Eric.

"Not really. She reads a lot," said James.

"Yeah, she reads those stinky books we found in the attic," added Jeremy.

Spike jumped into Eric Thomas' lap for his daily dose of adoration, and listened as the boys discussed the evil Megheen. They were right; something had to be done so that Annie Rose and Geoffrey Alan could reunite. This was a tragic, tragic situation. Spike would have given anything to be with Annie Rose during her time of need, but he was merely a cat and could do nothing. She was recovering, though; Steven Anthony had told him so.

"I think that maybe we should find out what's in those books. Maybe there's a clue as to why she's so damn strange lately," Eric said.

"You swore," giggled James.

"You said 'damn'," giggled Jeremy.

"So I'll go straight to hell for it. Big deal. Besides, I'm old enough to swear if I want to. You guys aren't, so don't do it again. Where is she right now?"

"She's in Uncle Gabe's room. He has another headache and she made that smelly tea for him. He says it helps him sleep, otherwise he'd chuck it out the window."

"Good. That gives us at least a half-hour. C'mon." Eric rose to leave, followed by the twins.

Spike stayed behind in the twin's room. Once they had left, he walked over to where Steven Anthony had appeared and jumped into his companion's lap. His purr sounded distressed as Steven Anthony stroked his orange fur.

"Cat, things are not good in this house. Megheen has already gotten to Gabe, even if he doesn't know it. If she isn't destroyed soon it will be too late for Gabe and Annie, even after Deirdre dies. He'll be so filled with her poison that he'll completely forget about his Annie. God, it was bad enough that she lost the baby, she shouldn't have to lose him too." Steve ran a quick hand over his eyes, wiping away the hint of a tear.

Spike ran a silky paw over his own face; his tears were beyond a hint.

The boys listened at Gabe's door and could hear him talking to Deirdre. Good... and they continued on down the hall until they reached the rose-colored room. It was not hard to find the diaries; the pungent odor of the box containing them gave away their location almost immediately. The boys sat down to read.

"Drink you tea, Geoffrey dear, then I'll get rid of that headache for you. Have you heard from Anne... Annie yet?" Deirdre asked, handing him a cup of steaming liquid. It was hard for her to not smile. She had won! Anne was out of his life and she, Megheen, was back into it. She wished that Deirdre's body was a healthier one, but after all, she was a witch and could keep it going for quite a while longer. And there was always Jenna's...

"No I have not, and I'd thank you not to bring up the subject again." Gabe took a sip of his tea. "Christ! What the hell is in this swill, anyway? If it didn't work so well I'd chuck it out the goddamn window!"

"So you've told me time and time again. Either drink it or don't; it matters not to me. I am not the one suffering here." Megheen smiled her glittering, black-eyed smile at Geoffrey.

"Fine." He finished off the foul brew in two big swallows. He would have much rather have smoked a joint to help his pain, but promised Dee that he'd not touch it again.

He peeled off his shirt and walked over to the bed, then chucked his pants onto the floor as well. At first he had remained fully clothed, but since he trusted Deirdre now and he napped any way, he could see no point in leaving all of them on. He lay on his stomach, using his forearms for a pillow and sighed as her surprisingly strong hands kneaded away the knots in the muscles of his neck. The familiar fog caused by the tea settled over him and he slept.

"Geoffrey," Megheen whispered. She gave him a little shake. He moaned but did not wake up. Good. As usual, her little potion worked its magic - just as the one she use to cause the headaches had never failed her. She rolled him over onto his back and had her way with him.

"Uh, guys?" Eric said to the twins as he read through a diary.

"Yeah?" they answered in unison.

"This stuff in here is a little deep for kids your age, so I'll read it myself and let you know the highlights, okay?"

"Deep?"

"Yeah, you know, too much for you to comprehend. It's almost too much for me to comprehend! I think Jenna needs to see this. She may not believe it, but she may be willing to help."

"Okay. She wants Annie to be with Uncle Gabe too, so I'm sure she'll help."

Eric gathered up the rest of the books and shoved the empty box back into its hiding place under the window seat. He hoped that Deirdre wouldn't want to read them for a while.

"James, Jeremy, when Deirdre comes out I need you to distract her for a while so that we can read these. Can you do that?"

"Sure! She already says that we are too much of a distraction sometimes," James said.

"That's not what I... never mind. Insist that she take you to the library or something. Whine, cry, and throw a tantrum... just do something. I need her gone for about another hour or so. Can you do that?"

"Sure. No problem. She is always in a good mood after Uncle Gabe is taking a nap. She'll be nutty in our hands," James giggled.

"That is putty, you dolt," Jeremy corrected, punching his brother on the arm.

"Nutty, putty, who the hell cares? Just get her out of here!"

"Done and done!" assured the twins. They went back to their room to conspire.

Eric found Jenna in the kitchen, preparing an army-sized dinner for the Evans-Davidson household.

"Jenna, could I talk to you for a minute? It's important."

"Sure, Eric. Are you feeling all right? You aren't sick again, are you?" she asked, placing a hand on his forehead.

"No, nothing like that. Can we go into Gabe's office for this? It's kind of secret, too."

She gave him a long look. This boy was seriously frightened! "Let's go," she said, taking his arm.

They locked the door to the office and sat on the leather sofa together.

"Take a look at these," Eric said, and pulled the diaries from the inside of his shirt.

"Oh God, those stinky things? Ewww! What are you doing with those?" she asked, wrinkling up her nose.

"Read. Start with this one and just read. This is why Deirdre has been so weird lately, and why Gabe and Annie aren't together. I haven't read all of them; just this one and part of this one. I'm really scared, Jenna. This is so creepy."

She read three pages then ran to the kitchen to turn off the stove. Dinner could damn well wait.

Gabe rolled over and stretched; once again, his headache was gone. He'd had that disturbing dream again though, the one of the dark-haired woman. It made him feel disgusted and dirty; as if he needed to shower and scrub the filth she exuded from his body. He looked at the clock; damn, he'd slept right through dinner. Oh well, it's not like he was hungry; he only ate to keep from dying, which was beginning to sound like an option he might consider. He reached for his pants and pulled them on, followed by his shirt. He didn't bother with his boots; by now everyone would be gathered around the TV watching some inane game show or shit-com. Maybe he'd go for a walk in the park and get rid of some of the cobwebs in his head that were left over from that disgusting brew Deirdre was always foisting on him.

As he passed his office, he heard the low mutter of voices coming from within. This irritated him, as it was off limits to each and every member of the house. He grabbed the door handle, only to find it locked.

"Who the hell is in there?" he yelled, and slammed the door with the flat of his hand.

The door opened immediately and Jenna pulled him into the room with such force that both of them lost their balance and ended up on the sofa.

Gabe jumped up as soon as he landed; he still felt extremely repulsed by what had happened on it with Deirdre. He walked to his desk and sat on its surface.

"Would you two care to explain what the hell you are doing in here?" he asked.

Jenna and Eric exchange looks. Would Gabe even begin to believe this? Eric figured he would because of Steve, but Jenna wasn't so sure. He was always so logical, so down to earth, and this... this was straight out of a horror story!

"Gabe, I... we found something; something that might explain Deirdre's behavior, and why Annie is no longer, uh, why you two... uh... Here. Read." She shoved a diary into his surprised hands.

"Christ, what is that stench? Smells like that damn tea Dee brews up..."

Gabe looked at the book in his hand. Aw God, not more old journals. Hadn't he suffered enough because of someone's idea of what should be? "I really don't care to get into this," he said and shoved the book back at Jenna.

"You have to. If you ever hope to have a chance with Annie then you have got to read this! You're the only one who can undo what's been done!" Jenna was near tears in her fear and frustration.

"Please, Gabe, you have to," Eric pleaded.

He looked at the two of them. He could see fear in both of their eyes, and Jenna was trembling. Perhaps he should at least see what had upset them so.

He opened the diary and began to read. Halfway through the second page he had Jen fetch him a very large drink. *Megheen*. He had read that name in Rosalind's journals, and now here he was reading the witch's diaries. He was filled with disgust and revulsion as he read of her obsession with the first Geoffrey and her hatred for Anne. He was horrified as he read about how the woman had plotted and planned to kidnap and do away with Anne so that Geoffrey would return to Megheen. Gabe was on his third drink as he read how Geoffrey uncovered the plot to kill his Anne and sacrificed his own life, falling to his death while Megheen watched. Megheen cursed Anne, vowing to have her revenge on the woman. She swore to do it no matter how long it took. Anne moved from the area soon after Geoffrey's death and married another, and Megheen lost track of her.

She spent her few remaining years nurturing her hatred and broadening her skills in the dark arts. She wrote her spells and potions on the pages of the diaries, making notes in the margins as to what she would use them for when the time came. Gabe nearly vomited when he came to a spell that would cause the death of the unborn. He felt a deep anger and betrayal when he read of a potion to cause pain in the head, and of a tea that would bring sleep. His revulsion hit its acme when he read of how Megheen planned to seduce him should she meet him again in another life, and he felt murderous rage when he read again of how the witch planned to exact her revenge on Anne.

Jenna had to physically restrain him to keep him from killing Deirdre.

"Gabe, you can't go after her! It is not her fault that she's acting this way. We have to find a way to drive out this... this thing that is in her. Gabe! Look at me!" Jenna was holding him back, and it was becoming a losing battle. "Gabe!" she screamed.

He turned to look at her.

"So what do you fucking suggest?" he sneered, shrugging off her hands.

"I don't know, but you can't kill her. There has to be some way... Let's catch our breath and think about this for a minute." She flopped on the sofa once Gabe had returned to the desk.

"I wonder if there is a spell or something in there," Eric said, and pointed to the diaries.

"No, I read them all cover to cover, and I didn't see anything," Jenna sighed.

"Why the hell would the bitch write something that would bring about her own undoing?" Gabe asked. He still felt that a slow, lingering death would be the answer. At least it would make him feel better.

The momentary silence following was interrupted by a soft scratching on the other side of the office door.

Spike.

Gabe jumped up to let him in. Christ, if anyone could help him it would be this cat!

Spike strolled over to the desk and jumped up next to Geoffrey Alan. He sniffed at the books, sneezing at their pungent smell. One by one he examined the diaries, knocking them to the floor as he rejected one after the other. This! This was the one. He placed his paw on it and looked up at Geoffrey Alan. This was the one that didn't have the foul odor to it. It had something in it to overpower the evil aroma which would have otherwise exuded from its ancient pages.

"This one? Is this the answer, Spike?" Gabe asked the cat.

Jenna thought he was nucking futs until she saw the cat nod slightly at him.

Gabe opened the book and began to scan the pages.

Nothing.

556

He looked closer, trying to see if perhaps he missed something in his haste. Still nothing.

Frustrated beyond words, he resorted to his old habit of flinging offending objects across the room. The book hit the wall and exploded in a flurry of age-yellowed papers. He tossed back the rest of his drink and glared at the mess of the floor. The glass followed the path of the diary, smashing on the same wall as the book.

"Gabe..." Jenna said softly, and bent to pick up the broken glass.

He just glared at the floor.

The papers on the floor.

The papers under the glass on the floor.

The paper that was a different color than the rest under the broken glass on the floor. Very slowly, he went and picked it up. He was right; it was different from the rest. It was folded into quarters, and looked as if it had been compressed for a very long time; perhaps hidden in the cover of the now ruined leather diary? Gabe held it under the desk lamp and began to unfold it. Spike sniffed at it and gave a quick meow. This had to be it!

Deirdre-Megheen returned from the park with the brats. Why they had insisted on staying past dinner hour, she would never know. The only reason she had allowed it was because she was reliving her previous 'visit' with Geoffrey and the memories were just too delicious to give up too soon. As her hand touched the door handle of the house, she felt as if someone had punched her in the midsection. Someone had her diaries! She could feel it, and what was worse, one of them had been nearly destroyed! She raced up the stairs to her rose-colored room and retrieved the leather chest. It was empty! Who could have taken them?

She stalked to the twins' room, and then realized that they had been with her so they could not possibly have them. Eric! He had been very distant lately; it could very well be him. She threw open the door to his room, ready to confront him; it was empty. That left who? Jenna? Geoffrey? Kyle? That was laughable, Kyle was the biggest buffoon ever spawned from modern man; he was oblivious to everything swirling about him.

Where was every one, anyway? She went to the living room and saw that the brats had joined the Davidson brats and their moronic father around the television set. Where were the rest of them? Geoffrey's office?

Megheen listened outside the door; they were in there all right, but she couldn't hear what they were saying. Her diaries were in there also - she could just feel it. This was not good, not good at all. What if they found the secret spell? She should have destroyed it long ago but never did; one just doesn't know when something like that might come in handy - for another witch, of course.

She felt ill. She had to get into that room and get her property back before it was too late. She pounded on the door, demanding to be let in.

"Just in time," Gabe laughed. There was no humor in it. He opened the door and let her in.

"Looking for this, Megheen?" he asked, waving the paper over his head.

She took a few staggering steps towards him and stopped.

"Give it to me. It will do you no good now; the damage has been done. She lost and I won, and you will never see you precious Anne again," Megheen sneered.

"You think not? I beg to differ. There is no force on this earth, no force in the universe that will stop me from loving her." Gabe told her.

"But you are forgetting she no longer loves you! Has she not proven that? Tell me, Geoffrey, when was the last time you talked to her? And what was the last thing she said to you? Hmm? Should I refresh your memory? And also, you might recall how hard you tried to win her back with your numerous phone calls, visits, and letters... not to mention the pathetic 'send her flowers' bit. She doesn't love you, she never really did! Why else didn't she tell you that she was carrying your brat? I've known it since the day of her dismal little party. No, she never loved you. I am the only one who could ever love you as you should be loved. Now, give me that paper..."

"She loves me. She always has, and she always will. She was devastated by your actions, and then by the loss of our child, which I hold you solely responsible for. You will get this paper over my dead body." Gabe snarled.

"Ha! You are a pathetic man, holding on to a dream that will never be. Give it to me!" Megheen lunged for Geoffrey, only to be stopped by Spike as he jumped at the woman.

Megheen's reference to a dream shot through Gabe as her other words never could. The Dream... Dream again. Annie did still love him, of that he was sure. He began to read the words on the paper just loud enough for Megheen to hear.

She laughed. "You are a fool! In order to get rid of me, you need to have your true love in the room with you, or at least one of her possessions. Have you either? I'm afraid not. Forget it Geoffrey, you have lost." Megheen walked to the door of the office then turned, saying: "I'll see you tomorrow, I'm going to bed."

"Wait. I do have one of her possessions, the cat. And I have a feeling that my Annie will be here soon - if not in person, then at least by her voice." Gabe placed his hand on the telephone seconds before it rang. He smiled at his brother who was standing in the corner, unseen by the others in the room. Steve had whispered to him just seconds before that his Annie would be calling.

"Hello?"

"Gabe? It's Annie. I, uh, Michael... Steve was just here, and said that you needed to talk to me, that it was a very important matter. Is Eric alright?"

"Annie! God, it's good to hear your voice. Eric is fine. Steve was there?"

Gabe stared at Megheen as he talked to his Annie.

"Annie, this is very important; I need you to recite... no, don't say anything yet, please. This is very important. I need you to recite these words after me. I'll explain later. Would you do that, for me?"

She was confused but said that she would. Michael had practically begged her to call Gabe, so it must be important. Even though she was done with the man she at least owed his brother this much.

Gabe read the words on the paper aloud, and then held the phone out to Megheen so that she could hear as Annie repeated them. With each phrase, Megheen's, - no, Deirdre's - body began to wither. The glittering black eyes faded to a dull blue as the supernatural life force drained from them.

Gabe spoke the last words.

Annie repeated them.

Deirdre slid to the floor in a dead faint.

And Megheen was gone.

Jenna ran over to her friend and placed her hand on Deirdre's throat, feeling for a pulse.

"Oh God, Gabe, what just happened here? Thank heaven she is still alive."

"Annie?" he said into the phone.

The line was dead.

"Gabe, we have to get her upstairs to her room. Please help me," Jenna said, in tears.

He just stared down at Deirdre. He knew that it was all over, but was still loath to touch the woman.

"I'll take her up."

Jenna looked up and saw Steve standing in front of her. So it was true. She would never really believe it, but there he was. He helped her to her feet, then picked up his ladylove and disappeared into the hall. Jenna stared at the hand Steve had touched; it felt very strange... all warm and kind of tingly.

Gabe burned the diaries in the fireplace after everyone else had gone to bed; after he had tucked in his nephews and thanked Eric for his help, after he had kissed the Davidson children good-night, and had a last drink with Kyle and a still-stunned Jenna - who was attempting to explain to her husband what had just happened.

This part of his life was over. He left the house and walked, cutting through the park and crossing the bridge over the river. He passed the city limits and continued on, with no purpose, no destination. For hours he walked, trying to sort out in his mind why his life had ended up this way.

He found no answers.

Chapter Forty-Three

As dawn broke, he found himself sitting on the marble bench watching the lake change from black, to rose and then to gold as the sun climbed high in the sky. The water was a vivid blue before he moved from his seat. He began to walk around the rim of earth overlooking the lake until he came to a bit of rock hanging over the trees. It was a beautiful spot; the small creek poured into the deep blue water below with a light trickle that tried, but failed to bring a feeling of peace to his troubled heart. He could sense a deep grief in this place that had been replaced by a great joy; someone's life had been saved on this very spot. It would be wrong to take his life here.

Gabe moved on, somewhat saddened that he hadn't been strong enough to continue to fight the depression he'd battled forever. But maybe it was time to give up. He'd held on this long only in the hopes that he would finally find his dream, and now that was forever lost to him. So why go on existing?

He walked deeper and deeper into the woods, thinking of the easiest way to exit this earth. He just couldn't decide, so he sat to rest underneath a large oak tree and looked above him. The branches were sturdy and would support his weight. Now, if his belt were long enough it would be over in minutes.

It was such a wonderful day; the leaves were just beginning to turn color and the sky was an intense shade of blue. At least his last glimpse of life would be that of something beautiful.

Annie saddled Wanda and mounted up. Adonis was gone and she needed to find him as soon as possible. She let the mare have her head, hoping she would lead her to the missing horse.

Wanda trotted up the hill and to the clearing, but Annie saw no sign of his having been there. The horse picked her way through the trees along the edge of the lake, and still Annie saw no clue that Adonis had been there. The mare brought her to the waterfall; still nothing.

Wanda then turned into the woods. She stopped at a large oak tree and Annie dismounted, thinking this would be a good place to rest. She leaned against the tree and closed her eyes. Thoughts of him filled her mind. Just what was that phone call all about yesterday, anyway? It had been so good to hear his voice again, even though she wanted nothing more to do with him. But still... Did she still love him? She did. When all was said and done, she did. She could never go back to the uncertainty of their relationship, not as long as Deirdre was around, but what about after that? Would he still want her? He had stopped calling her quite a while ago and had made no other attempt to contact her. But jeez, the way he had sounded on the phone yesterday... Annie had to hang up to keep from losing it. At first she thought she was still angry with him, but now she could admit that she wanted to tell him that she loved him; always had, always would. Dream and Dream again. She sighed and remounted her horse. Back to her search. Had she looked up into the giant oak, she would have been stunned at what she saw.

"C'mon, Wanda, let's head for home. He'll come back when he is damn good and ready," Annie sighed. After searching for another hour, she was tired and frustrated, and kept thinking about 'him'. She'd go home and see if anyone needed someone for overtime. Nothing like work to keep your mind occupied.

Gabe brushed at the thing tickling his face and his hand met with the solid face of a large horse. He opened his eyes. Adonis? What the hell was he doing way out there? The horse nudged him in the chest. Gabe stroked his face, then grabbed the horse's forelock and was pulled to his feet. He gave Donny a quick look and noted that he was without saddle or bridle. That must mean that Annie hadn't been out riding and gotten tossed. So just why was this beast out here? Was he once again being saved by her benevolent animals? He looked up at his belt tied to a branch about eight feet overhead. God, had he really been that serious? He grabbed a handful of the horse's mane and swung himself onto the horse's back.

"Take me home, Donny boy."

Adonis turned and cantered into the woods, heading back to the cabin.

She led the mare into the barn and was stunned to see her missing horse quietly munching hay in his locked stall. Who...? She did a quick check of the barn to see if someone was still lurking about, but found nothing. She even peeked into 'the' stall, half-hoping...

She took care of Wanda's needs and walked back to the cabin. One mystery after the other. Maybe Steve brought the horse back; he had been hanging around lately.

Annie caught a flash of movement in her rose garden. There was someone in there, just below the level of the remaining flowers. Her throat turned to dust as she neared the garden and saw the top of a head of crisp, black hair. Oh, God no! Not him, please not him. Quietly, she walked up and observed him. He was tracing his finger along the named etched in the small piece of white marble in the center of the white roses, and his shoulders shook as he fought to keep in his grief.

Annie could watch no more. She turned and ran to the cabin, locking the door behind her. She threw herself onto her bed and refused to answer the frantic knocking that came from the outside of her home.

Gabe had to admit defeat. She was not about to answer the door. He wanted so much to take her in his arms and apologize for everything, and to share their grief over the death of their daughter. Gabriella Michaela. He liked that name. He wondered who she would have looked like, Mommy or Daddy?

He jumped from the porch and walked up the long drive, stopping first at the rose garden to pick one of the remaining buds; this might be the only tie he would ever have with his little Gabriella.

He walked nearly five miles before he was able to thumb a ride back into town. Once he made it home, he took the rose and his beloved guitar and placed them both in a far corner of his closet. Another chapter closed.

Chapter Forty-Four

Annie's life returned to its pre-Gabe days. She worked, she rode, and she still wrote occasionally, but never again wrote in a journal after the last entry about talking with Michael. She was nearly content as long as she didn't think about 'him'. She avoided the clearing above the lake, and instead would ride to the waterfall, thanking Michael each and every time she went there for saving her life.

Occasionally she would see 'him' at the hospital visiting Eric on his ever-increasing admissions. With the exception of one incident, Annie usually spotted him first and avoided being out in the hall until she was sure that he left. The one time when he was the first to see her, well, it was anything but pleasant.

She had arrived almost late for work and was hurrying to the time clock to punch in. She ran into him as he rounded a corner, nearly knocking them both off balance. He grabbed her shoulders to steady her, and then looked down at Annie. She still hadn't looked up to see who she had hit, but then she didn't need to; his woodsy-spicy scent washed over her like a bad dream. She felt the pressure of his hands increase on her shoulders and tried to pull away.

"Annie," he choked in a hoarse whisper.

"Excuse me," she said, managing to extricate herself from his grip.

Gabe's hands dropped to his sides and he took a step back.

She glanced up and met his intense blue gaze; she had felt that familiar tingle again at his touch and could not stop herself. She saw emotions flicker across his face before he donned his actor's mask and cut them off, leaving nothing but a cold glare that froze her to the bone.

"My apologies," he said, and then turned and walked to the elevators.

Gabe's life also returned to its pre-Annie days, but he was far from content; he merely functioned. Eric had become a permanent resident in the Evans' home; his aunt having never fully recovered from her injury and was residing an assisted-living facility. The Davidsons moved back into their home, but were still frequent visitors. The twins were still a bit strange, although wonderful children. Deirdre was Deirdre again, and after a few weeks she and Gabe recaptured their previous relationship of very dear, very close friends. She talked him out of deep depression more than once, and her heart broke to see her Geoffrey dear suffering so. Her health declined steadily after the Megheen incident, and she spent most of her time in her room sleeping.

Steven never returned.

SD Productions had never been better and Gabe had to add an even bigger staff to handle the increasing workload. Kyle found his creative niche and was churning out songs, one after the other. The partners recorded another CD but

Gabe's heart was never really into it, and the sales were nowhere near what "Dream Again" had been.

Gabe bought himself a horse. The stallion had neither the intelligence nor personality of Adonis, but he was big and fast and fearless; he was exactly what Gabe needed. He stabled it just outside of town and rode every day after work, sometimes leaving early just to feel the powerful animal pounding underneath him as the wind whipped in his face. He began to understand why Annie had ridden like she did on her Adonis.

For one brief, shining moment in his otherwise bleak life, Gabe held Annie in his arms. He had been to visit Eric, when she had rounded a corner and smacked right into him. It took all of his self-control to hide what he was feeling, especially after she looked at him with those sparkling green eyes; eyes that said she wanted nothing more to do with him. There was nothing he could do but turn and walk away.

Annie answered her phone and was pleasantly surprised to hear who was on the other end.

"Jenna! How have you been?" she asked.

"Fine and you?"

"Can't complain. I've been working a lot, getting ready for Thanksgiving, although I don't know why; it will just be Dog and me at the dinner table," Annie sighed.

"Annie, the reason I called was to see if I could come and pick up Chet. I don't know if you were aware, but we opened up the studio again and it just isn't quite the same without that damn bird." She gave a weak laugh.

Annie was disappointed; she had been hoping that Jenna would have something quite different to tell her. Maybe some news about him...

"Uh, sure. He doesn't seem very happy here anyway. I think it's too quiet for him... no stimulation. He hasn't recited a dirty limerick in weeks. When did you want to get him?"

"Would today be too soon? I can run out there while the kids are in school. The twins started first grade you know."

"No, I didn't. I've kind of been out of touch since... well, for a while. Today would be fine. Jenna, how is Spike doing?"

Now it was Jenna's turn to be disappointed. Chet was the only excuse she could think of to talk to Annie. Her real agenda was to find out how she still felt about Gabe.

"He's okay. He spends his days sleeping on Gabe's sofa, and his evenings sleeping on Gabe's lap. Do cats ever really do anything but sleep?"

"Only when they think no one is looking. Uh, how is Ga... how is he doing?"

Finally! Jenna smiled; Annie was still interested.

"He's... he's doing as well as can be expected. He works, he rides, and he hides in his office. God only knows what he does in there; it's as silent as a tomb when he's in there. He doesn't even play his guitar like he used to. Annie, quite frankly I'm worried about him."

"I'm sorry; I don't know what to say. Maybe he needs to talk to a therapist or something."

"Annie, would you mind if when I came to pick up Chet, well, could we talk for a while? There are some things that you should know. You may not want to hear it, but you have to be told."

"I don't know... I really don't want to go dredging up the past. I went through hell and I don't care to relive it."

"Annie, please. This is very important, and just maybe it will help you to understand why things happened the way they did."

Annie was becoming just a bit irritated.

"Do you really think it matters anymore? I've put that all behind me; I don't want to even think about it!"

"Annie, please. I'm now officially begging. Just give me an hour of your time, and then you will never hear from me again if you don't want to. Please!"

Her irritation was not sufficient enough to ignore Jenna's heart-felt plea. Against her better judgment she said, "Okay, I guess so. When will you be here?"

"Is an hour too soon?"

"No, that will be fine. The sooner this is over, the better. Jenna, could you bring Spike when you come?"

"Sure. Gabe will miss him, but I think Spike is homesick. I'll see you pretty soon."

"Fine. Bye then."

"Bye."

After giving Spike a welcoming hug and sending him off to the loft, Annie sat with Jenna at the kitchen table. She poured them each a cup of coffee and waited for Jen to speak.

She looked at Annie and said, "I know I asked you earlier, but after seeing you I have to ask again; how are you?"

"Fine, why?"

"Forgive me for saying so, but you look like hell! How much weight have you lost, anyway?"

Annie looked down at herself. "I don't know, I haven't really been keeping track. Is this what you came over to say?" she mumbled.

"I'm sorry. It's just that... God, Annie, what happened?"

"What happened? Jeez, where do I start with that?" she cried in exasperation.

"Again... sorry." Jenna paused, then said, "Annie, you're miserable, Gabe's miserable - why can't you two work things out? You still love him, don't you?"

Annie looked away and said nothing.

"I thought so. Now I want you to listen to me. Don't say a word, just listen. I have a little story to tell you. Several stories, actually, but they all tie in together. The main point in all of them is that Gabe still loves you."

Annie still said nothing, but flinched when she heard his name. And that he still loved her.

"It was the hardest thing he ever had to do, leaving you to go on tour. He never wanted to do that, but thanks to my idiot husband and me he was forced into it. Kyle told me that when they weren't performing or rehearsing, Gabe would take long walks, sometimes alone, sometimes with Kyle. When he was with Kyle, he talked of nothing but you. This went on right up until the tour ended. He also kept a journal. I... I found it and read it. Annie, I shouldn't tell you this, but he knew about the... the baby. I told Kyle and he probably told him. Gabe wondered why you never told him about it. It hurt him that you kept it from him."

Annie's eyes welled with tears. "I didn't think he wanted a child. I tried to tell him several times, but I never got any indication that he would be happy about it."

"Oh, Annie, he was thrilled! Every day he would write something about her, he was hoping for a girl. And then he found out what happened... you losing it. He felt terrible. He wanted so much to be there for you, for both of you. Why did you shut him out?"

"That was his doing. Him and Deirdre. I just happened to catch them going at it on the bus after that concert in August. It wasn't the first time, either."

"Not the first time?"

"No. I just happened to see them the night of my party, too. Do you have any idea what that did to me? Any idea at all? My God! Just thinking about makes me want to puke. I can't talk about it anymore. I'm sorry. Thanks for bringing Spike back." Annie rose from her chair and started for her bedroom.

Jenna grabbed her hand. "Sit. This brings up another little part of the story. Gabe was not responsible for any of that. Neither was Deirdre..."

"You expect me to believe that?" Annie shouted. "I saw them! I saw the look in his eyes, I saw hers, too. Not responsible? Oh, you've got to come up with something better than that. Good God! Not responsible... Jenna, they were all but fucking, and it was rapidly heading that way!"

Jen was a bit shocked at Annie's language, but it was understandable under the circumstances. "It's true. I wish I had the proof to show you, but Gabe destroyed it. I saw it, though. I read them... it was horrible."

"What on earth are you babbling about now?"

"Megheen's diaries. She was responsible. She described everything, how she was going to get her revenge, how she was going to seduce Geoffrey, everything!"

"Who the hell is Meg...? Did you say Megheen?"

"Yeah. She lived hundreds of years ago and came back through time to break up you and Gabe."

"Oh, now there's a story I'll believe," Annie said sarcastically. "I read about her in my Gramma's journals. The wicked witch. Sure, she may have existed, but tracking me down over the years? Did Gabe tell you this? Is this his pitiful excuse... the devil made him do it?" She laughed a bitter laugh. "God, that is just too much."

"I saw her, Annie. She was no less real than Steve."

She snapped out of her hateful mood. "Steve? You saw Steve?"

"I did. He helped me up from the floor, and then he carried Deirdre to her room."

"Oh God. You'd better start at the beginning, Jenna. Tell me everything."

Jenna did. She started with the discovery of the diaries in the attic, and of Deirdre's delight at receiving them. She described every detail of Deirdre's odd behavior, sparing Annie from the sordid facts of Megheen and the headache relief. She told her of what the diaries contained, and of the potions and spells. She ended by telling Annie of the final showdown in Gabe's office, and of Spike's involvement in the whole affair.

."..So you see, it was not their fault. She was just as powerless as he was," Jenna finished.

"My God!" Annie slumped in her chair. She felt as if every bit of energy had been drained from her. Gabe had suffered nearly as much as she had, although his was more guilt-related. Nevertheless, he had suffered. Her heart turned over at the thought, and she was very near to calling him and begging him to forgive her for not trusting him, when Jenna spoke again.

"This took its toll on Deirdre, too. I know that she probably wasn't supposed to have lived this long, I do know how sick she was... is, but I saw her shrink right before my eyes. She must have aged ten years when Megheen was driven out. She needs help with everything now. Gabe hired a part-time nurse for when he is at work, and he takes care of her at night.

"Annie, there was a time when I thought Gabe was going to kill himself. It was the day after all this happened. He disappeared. He just took off after telling everyone good-bye, and walked away. He was gone for nearly a whole day; we were all scared to death. When he did come home, he never said a word to anyone. He stood in the hall staring at some flower he was holding, and then disappeared into his room. He didn't come out again until late the next morning. He was still pretty quiet, but at least he started back on his normal routine. He spends a lot of time holed up in his office, too. He's usually silent, but one night I heard him talking to the cat; he was talking about Gabriella someone. I think he was crying."

Annie's throat closed. She didn't know how much more of this she could take.

Jenna continued, "He still has a lot of bad days. Deirdre can usually cheer him up a bit, but I think it is more to please her than what he actually feels. The only time he really shows any signs of life is after he rides that great big horse of his."

"He... he has a horse?" It was safe territory for Annie, talking about horses.

"Sure does. Great big thing. Huge, even. It's coal black and kind of reminds me of that horse Steve used to have..."

"Whizbang."

"Yeah, Whizbang. You know about him?"

"Yes, but I'll tell you about that later. What is Ga...? his horse's name?"

"Brute. Fits him, too. We dropped Gabe off at the stable one day while his truck was being fixed. He rides every single day, no matter what. Anyway, when we went to pick him up he wasn't back yet so we went up to the loft... never mind about that. We were looking out the window, watching for him to come back, and we saw him tearing across the field. Scared me to death! I didn't know horses could move that fast! And jump! There are a bunch of downed trees and crap out there, and they were jumping everything. It was like he had a death wish or something."

Annie could understand that perfectly.

"But I didn't come over here to talk about horses. You and Gabe need to get together and talk this out. You have both suffered far too much and far too long to let it continue. Don't you agree?"

Annie did agree, but was still hesitant. "I don't know, Jenna. So much has happened; I don't think it could ever be the same for us again."

"Why the hell not? God! Do you love him or don't you?" Jenna nearly yelled, but toned it down to an almost normal voice.

"I do. I never stopped. There was a time when I hated him for what he did to me and our baby, but I've worked through that. I don't know that I really hated him; I just hated everything in general. I'm scared of ever having to going through that again..."

"Annie, if this is too painful for you just let me know... but what happened with the baby?"

"It will always be painful, but I'll tell you anyway. The day of the concert I had been feeling a cramp off and on, and then when I saw Ga... them in the bus, it was all over. I had to drive myself to the hospital, and I lost her. I don't know if the shock induced it or if it would have happened anyway, but I did blame him for the longest time."

"Oh, Annie, I'm so sorry," Jenna said and put her hand on Annie's. "No wonder you wouldn't talk to him."

Annie nodded and tried to fight the tears. She stood and walked to the window overlooking the rose garden where the small square of white marble shone in the autumn sun.

"I named her Gabriella Michaela," she whispered.

Jenna said nothing, but went to her friend and held her close. The two of them stood there for the longest time, staring out at the flowerless garden.

"Gabe. Gabe!" Kyle yelled. Damn! He was at it again; he was so lost in his own thoughts that Kyle thought his buddy would never find his way out.

"GABE!"

He snapped out of his daydream.

"What is it, Kyle?" he said in a tired voice.

"I finished that last piece. Wanna hear it?"

"Not now. I think I'm heading out early today; I'll see you tomorrow."

"Heading for the barn again?" Kyle asked, annoyed.

"Yes, I am. Do you have a problem with that?"

"No. Well yeah, I do. What happened to you, man? All you ever do is mope around here or ride that damn horse. Christ, your music even sucks! It took us forever to finish up yesterday; we finally just eliminated you altogether and I had to carry the vocals. It still sounds like shit, but it's all we got."

Gabe shrugged a shoulder and pushed his chair away from his desk, then rose to leave.

"Oh no you don't!" Kyle walked to the door and kicked it shut. He was pissed and Gabe was going to hear about it.

He sighed and sat back down; he'd stay until Kyle was done ranting. It was easy enough to shut out the sound of his voice and crawl back into Gabe's dismal dream world. It was dark and quiet there, and he could just float away into oblivion.

Kyle stalked back over to Gabe's desk and leaned over it, getting right into his partner's face. Hey, it had worked on him when Gabe did it, who says it wouldn't work on Gabe?

"Look at me. Don't shut me out like that, you bastard, look at me!" Kyle yelled. He slammed his fist on the desk for emphasis.

He saw Gabe give him a bored look, but at least he was looking.

Kyle continued. "I want you to tell me just what the hell your problem is. You haven't been the same since... God! Since August! I know it probably has something to do with Annie, but Christ! You're nothing but a fucking zombie anymore! I'm sick to death of watchin' you walk around here like your brain took a leave of absence. I can't remember the last time you told a joke, or even smiled. Shit! You haven't even harassed me! Do you even know what's goin' outside of Gabe's world? It's almost Thanksgiving, were you aware of that?"

"Am I supposed to care? Well then, I care... and thank you for the update. Are you quite finished now, as I would like to go for my ride," was Gabe's almost-sarcastic reply.

"Christ, Gabe, you have got to do something about this. Just 'cuz you're miserable doesn't mean you have to make everyone else that way too, and that's what you're doin'. You are, were, the lifeblood of SD; I was just along for the ride. We were doin' so good for a while and now it's turnin' to shit again, and it's not my fault this time. And if it's Annie, either forget her or go get her. You still love her, don't you?"

"Kyle, sometimes you are so incredibly fucking dense. Of course I still love her! I always have and I always will. For the longest time I was sure that she felt the same way about me. Now... well, I don't. I've lost the two things in my life that meant the most to me, and I just don't care anymore."

That was the longest speech Kyle had heard out of Gabe since this whole mess began. Maybe he should tell him what Jenna was doing; the worst that could happen was that he would kill Kyle, and that was highly unlikely. Wait... two things?

"Two things?" he asked.

Gabe glared at him. "I stand on my earlier conviction - you are so incredibly fucking dense! Yes, two things: Annie and my daughter."

Good. There was still some emotion left in him. Kyle hated to do it, but he pushed his friend further. The man needed to open that wound and let the poison out. It was the hardest thing he had ever done in his life.

"Yeah, right... the baby. A girl, huh? Did Annie finally tell you she was preggers?" he asked in a bored voice. He was totally unprepared for what happened next.

Gabe shot over the top of the desk and grabbed Kyle by the throat, exerting just enough pressure to scare the hell out of him.

"You bastard! You fucking, insensitive bastard! Christ! How can you speak like that knowing...? Christ!"

Gabe pushed his pal away from him and fell back into his chair. He spun around and stared at the wall in front of him, and he could feel all the grief that he had tried so long to repress begin to spew forth.

"Let it out, man, just let it out," Kyle said softly.

And Gabe did.

For nearly an hour, Kyle sat in silence as his friend purged the poison that had eaten at him for months. Gabe told him everything, beginning with Deirdre and the beach, ending with finding Gabriella's memorial in the garden, and everything in between.

."... I knew for sure it was over when I saw her at the hospital. We literally bumped into each other and I grabbed her shoulders to keep her from falling. The look she gave me... there was nothing there Kyle, nothing. No love, no hate, nothing. She pulled away from me as if I were some loathsome disease too horrible to touch. I let her go and left. I haven't seen her since."

"I had no idea. I'm sorry, man. God, if I had only known, maybe I could have done something to help. Damn, this sucks."

"Again, eloquently put," Gabe said, and gave him a weak smile.

Kyle looked at his watch; quitting time and beyond. SD's offices should be empty by now.

"C'mon, let's go listen to that piece I finished," he said.

Gabe sighed. "If you insist. I don't feel much like riding anyway."

"Gabe, if Annie wants to, would you take her back?"

"Kyle, if you were any more intelligent, you could qualify as a single-celled organism. Of course! But I wouldn't be 'taking her back'; I never left her."

"Gabe, Jen went over there today, to Annie's. She said that she was goin' over to get Chet back, to bring him back here, but she really went over there to find out how Annie feels about you." Kyle cringed as he said the last sentence, expecting some type of repercussion from Gabe.

"Did she now? And what were the results of this little misadventure?" he asked quietly.

"I don't know... I haven't heard from her. I thought she'd be back before now."

"Perhaps Annie shot the messenger," Gabe said, more to himself.

"Huh?"

"Never mind," he sighed. He no longer wanted to listen to Kyle or his music. He just wanted to go home and play his guitar, the one hidden in the back of his closet.

Thanksgiving at the Evans' home was less than festive. Gabe managed to nearly burn a turkey with 'fixins', and fed it to the boys. James and Jeremy wolfed theirs down, Eric picked at his, and Gabe shoved his plate aside untouched. He had been feeling better lately and even food was beginning to have some flavor again, but he just wasn't into it today.

He had talked to Jenna the day before and she informed him that even though Annie had been deeply hurt, she did indeed still love him. Gabe wanted to believe it, but the memory of his last look from Annie rekindled his doubt. Maybe Deirdre would have some advice.

He knocked softly on her door and entered her room.

"Deirdre?"

"Geoffrey dear, come sit," she answered in a dry, hoarse whisper.

He sat on the edge of the bed and looked at his wife. She was nothing but skin and bones, and looked ten years older than she had six months ago. And he had never loved her more.

"How are you feeling?" he asked, giving her a kiss on the forehead.

"About the same, tired and achy all over. How was your dinner?"

"Hardly worth calling dinner," Gabe laughed. "I'm not much of a cook."

"I'm surprised that you even attempted it, given your history in the kitchen. You should have accepted Kyle's invitation; Jenna knows her way around a kitchen."

"I know, but I couldn't leave you here alone, not on Thanksgiving."

"Oh, bother! I don't mind. Now tell me what is on your mind... as if I didn't know."

"You could always tell, couldn't you? Jenna talked to her the other day."

"And?"

"Apparently Annie still has feelings for me."

"This surprises you? I have always known that she loves you, Geoffrey dear. She always has, and always will."

"Then why the hell don't I know it? Why am I here and she's there?"

"So go to her. Tell her that you love her; make her listen!"

"You make it sound so easy," Gabe replied sarcastically. "She figured out how to lock her doors, remember?"

"Geoffrey dear, think. What would Annie be doing today? Who would she be spending her holiday with? After she has eaten her solitary dinner, what would be her next move?"

Gabe gave Deirdre a confused look.

"I have no idea. Enlighten me, please!"

Geoffrey dear, saddle up that Brute of yours and go for a ride. You meet some of the nicest people on horseback!" she told him with a gleam in her eye.

A very real smile spread across Gabe's face; the first genuine one he'd had in months.

"You're right; a ride does sound good about now. Thank you Deirdre."

"You are most welcome, Geoffrey. Have a lovely time."

Gabe changed into an old pair of jeans, threw on his boots and ran to his truck. He still had four hours of daylight left and he didn't want to waste a second.

He parked the truck and borrowed horse trailer halfway down Hidden Lake road, then unloaded Brute. In seconds the horse was saddled and Gabe was on his way as the powerful animal thundered over the frozen fields. Now, where would Annie be?

He heard Adonis whinny in the distance, and it sounded too close to still be at the barn. Gabe smiled and turned Brute towards Annie's horse.

They saw each other at the same time. Gabe had slowed Brute to a stop on top of a large hill, and Annie was atop Adonis at the bottom. As one, they raced for each other.

Annie waved, excited to see him again.

Gabe's heart beat harder, faster than the pounding hooves of his galloping horse.

"Michael!" Annie yelled, still waving.

Gabe's heart nearly quit. He pulled Brute to a sliding stop when she once again called him Michael.

Annie was nearly on top of him before she became aware of whom she was looking at. The smile on her face disappeared and was replaced by an emotionless mask.

"Gabe? I... I thought..." she stammered.

"That I was my brother? Sorry to disappoint you." His short-lived joy at seeing his Annie racing towards him quickly turned into that gut-wrenching pain with which he had been all too familiar. God! What a stupid idea this had been. Why did he even imagine that it could work? He turned Brute around and cantered up the hill. Stupid, stupid, stupid!

"Gabe! Wait!" Annie yelled. She gave Adonis a solid kick, sending him flying after the black.

Gabe couldn't face any more rejection today; not now, not ever. He had only run from one other thing in his life before, but he was doing so again now. He dug his heels into Brute, forcing the horse to greater speed. He heard Annie call him again. If she wanted him that damn bad, she would just have to prove it and try to catch him.

He slapped his horse with the ends of the reins and Brute began running full out.

Annie thought for sure that Gabe would stop and let her talk to him; didn't Jenna say that he still loved her? So, why was he running away? Jen must have been mistaken.

Annie gave up. She pulled back on the reins, attempting to stop Adonis.

The horse had other ideas. The second he felt the pressure of the bit in his mouth, he threw his head forward, yanking the reins out of his rider's hands. Adonis was now in control.

Annie grabbed two handfuls of mane and prayed that her horse had not gone insane.

Adonis tore up the hill, gaining on the black horse ahead of him. He flattened out into a dead gallop; the blood of his Arab and Thoroughbred ancestors pushing him to a speed he had never reached before.

The horses crested the hill together, and Adonis moved ahead, nipping at Brute as he passed.

Christ, Annie must be crazy riding a horse up a hill like that! Gabe gave a quick glance behind him. Sure enough, she was leaning forward in the saddle as Adonis thundered closer, but something wasn't right. He looked again as Adonis drew near, nipping at Brute. The reins! Annie had lost her reins and was mounted on a runaway. Adonis could trip over the flying leather strips at any moment, causing them both to crash to the ground.

Gabe said a quick prayer and yelled to this horse.

The stallion had an agenda of his own. He was not at all impressed with this smaller, cockier gelding passing him, and biting him in the process! He gave Gabe one last burst of speed and pulled level with Adonis.

As soon as Gabe was within reach, he snatched his Annie from the back of the crazed horse and pulled her onto the saddle with him.

Brute slowed to a stop.

So did Adonis.

Gabe held his Annie close, thanking God that she was safe and in his arms again.

Annie clung to her cowboy, fighting the delicious, familiar tingle and staring at Adonis. She could have sworn the damn horse just winked at her.

Gabe turned Brute towards the cabin. Adonis followed quietly a few paces behind, carefully avoiding the reins dragging along the frozen ground.

"My God, Annie! Are you alright?" Gabe asked as soon as he was able to talk. Sheer terror had driven his voice from him.

"Hmm... Fine. I, uh, I can probably ride Donny back; he seems to have calmed down now."

"I think not. He's damn lucky if I don't decide to shoot him through the goddamn head, putting you in danger like that."

"Really, Gabe, he's fine; look."

Gabe turned around and looked at Adonis. The horse was walking calmly behind them, tame as a baby bunny. He watched as Donny gave his head a shake and fixed a large brown eye on Gabe's intense blue ones. Good God, the horse just winked at him! He should have known better. He smiled to himself and pulled his Annie closer.

She was about to protest again, but it just felt too damn good right where she was. She let herself relax against Gabe and rode the rest of the home way in silence.

He dropped his Annie off at the cabin then rode to the barn to take care of the horses. He brushed both of them down, giving Adonis an extra portion of grain instead of a bullet to the brain.

Annie was waiting for Gabe on the top step of the porch. She still didn't feel comfortable about letting him into her cabin, or her life. She wanted to apologize to him earlier, but hadn't thought any farther ahead than that.

Gabe sat down next to her and played with a piece of straw he had brought back with him from the barn. He wished he had a cigarette, but lacking one, the straw would have to do. He tapped it on his knee, sliding it through his fingers until it reached the end, then turned it over and repeated the process, again and again and again.

Annie watched, wishing that she had something to relieve her nervousness.

After several moments of silence, Gabe asked, "Are you sure that you're alright?"

"I'm fine. I've ridden that fast before, but usually with reins."

"I don't mind telling you, it scared the hell out of me," he said. His hands still shook slightly as an after effect of his recent fright; that, and sitting so close to his Annie.

"Me too. I don't know what got into him; maybe it was having a strange horse around."

"Perhaps..."

They sat in silence for a few more minutes, and then Gabe said in a quiet voice, "I missed you, Annie."

"Gabe, I... I wanted to apologize for treating you the way I did. Had

I understood exactly what was going on, well, things would probably be different right now. Jenna told me what happened, and I'm sorry."

"Not any more than I am. God! When I think of what you must have gone through, all alone... I am so very, very sorry, Annie. I'm not even worthy to ask your forgiveness."

She decided that Gabe had to know how she was feeling if she were ever to live in peace again, be it with or without him.

"It was bad. It was worse than bad, it was hell. Your brother saved my life, Gabe. If it wasn't for him, we would not be having this conversation right now."

"He saved me too - the first time. Adonis saved me the second time, and then Kyle saved me for a third time. I don't know if I have been spared to do great things on this earth, or if I am living out my hell right now."

Annie nodded. She knew what that hell was all about and she never wanted to return; she felt as if she were teetering on the brink right now. She couldn't let him back in, at least not yet, and she had to tell him before things went too far; she just couldn't bring herself to speak.

Dog and McDonald could be heard returning from the lake, bickering as usual.

Gabe gave a short laugh. "Some things never change, do they?"

Annie remained silent.

"Annie, I have to know... what's next for us? This... this uncertainty is killing me. I love you. I have never stopped loving..."

She interrupted. Her voice shook as she said, "There is no us, Gabe. I never want to go through that kind of pain again, and if there is no us, there will be no pain."

He was devastated.

"Aw, Annie, please don't say that. We can't end this, can't end us! It was meant to be. God! Just look at everything that happened to bring us together! You can't ignore that... And I know that you still love me; I dare you to deny it." He grabbed her shoulders and turned her around, forcing her to look at him.

"Look me in the eye and deny it!"

She could not.

"You're right, Gabe, I do still love you and that's why I can't let you back into my life, not now anyway. I'm not willing to share you with... with Deirdre anymore. Although I was told the reason for what happened, the trust is gone. Besides, she needs you right now and I won't force you to choose. I... I'm sorry. I think you'd better go now." She couldn't take another second of sitting next to him. Her strong desire to be his Annie again was at war with the memory of the hell she had endured, spurred on by the thought of him living in Deirdre's home. The total effect was just too overwhelming. She stood on the step and turned towards the door.

"Annie…" he murmured, and grabbed her hand.

"I can't, Gabe, I just can't." She gave his hand a small squeeze then gently pulled it away.

She walked into the cabin, locking the door behind her.

So… that was it. She just walked away and locked him out of her life. Gabe leaned back on his elbows and stretched his long legs out in front of him as he sat on Annie's porch. He stared out over the lake watching the iron-grey clouds roll in, not having a clue as to his next move. Maybe he'd just sit here and freeze to death.

Christ! How could she say she loves him one minute and then say she never wants to see him again? Damn Deirdre and her bright ideas. He should have followed her advice though and made Annie listen; he had so much to tell her, and he desperately needed to know why she had never told him about Gabriella. He was tempted to take the Neanderthal approach and kick her goddamn door down, demanding answers, but he just couldn't find the energy to move from the porch.

It began to snow; great, fat flakes fell from the leaden sky. The wind momentarily changed directions, bringing the smell of wood-smoke to Gabe's nostrils. The picture he had carried in his head all summer of his little family flashed through his mind. He glanced at the bare rose garden and its square of marble. Yes, there was such a thing as hell on earth. He walked to the barn, saddled his horse and slowly rode back to the truck.

Chapter Forty-Five

Eric sat at the foot of Deirdre's bed listening as she talked about her remaining days - and his.

"Don't be frightened of death, Eric. I was nearly there once, and it wasn't all that horrible," she told him.

"I was there too, and it sucked. But ya know, I'm ready. I'm so damn tired of all this crap. I've been in and out of the hospital six times since Thanksgiving. I can barely breathe, and I'm just tired," Eric wheezed.

"I know, dear. It has been a difficult time for us all. Nothing has been the same since... well, since Geoffrey and Annie went their separate ways. I was so hoping that they would be married by now. How is Annie doing; you are the only one who sees her anymore."

"Terrible. She's really skinny and her hair is... is all dull looking, and she looks like someone punched her in the eyes. She still acts like Annie, but I don't know... she's different."

"Hmm... Geoffrey too. I simply cannot understand why they couldn't get back together. It's obvious that they still love each other; why else would they be so suffering so? They are supposed to be together; it was destined. May we will have a Christmas miracle and they will find each other again."

"I don't know if I'll be around that long," Eric sighed.

"Nor do I. I'm surprised I've held on this long, and that has only been in the hope that I'll see Geoffrey happy again," Deirdre said.

"Deirdre, will we see Michael, uh, Steven when we die?"

"I'm sure that he will be right there waiting for us, Eric, waiting to take us home."

Gabe looked at the calendar; only one week until Christmas. He'd be glad when it was all over. The cheerfulness of the holiday season grated on his nerves as nothing ever had before.

Christ, where the hell was Kyle? He was supposed to be here an hour ago so that they could drive to Chicago because his idiot of a partner had stupidly set up a business meeting there instead of insisting that the clients come to them. Oh well, Kyle planned on doing a little shopping while he was there anyway. He wanted to find just the right present for Jenna and the mall in town didn't have much to offer. Gabe figured that he'd better do some shopping as well; otherwise Santa would be skipping the Evans' home this year. The twins needed something to brighten up their lives, as Christmas promised to be even more dismal than Thanksgiving had been. Both Eric and Deirdre had been admitted to the hospital the past week, and the prognosis for both was poor.

Since that dismal Thanksgiving, Gabe had been busier than ever. It seemed as if he never had a moment for himself any more, which was a good thing; it

576

kept thoughts of her away. His time was divided between trips to the hospital with Eric, either to have him admitted or visit him once he was there, the ever-increasing success of SD Productions, taking care of the twins, and seeing that Deirdre lacked for nothing. He also developed an interest in real estate and was in the process of purchasing some properties in the area. The fact that he no longer had time to ride somewhat lessened the deep regret over having sold Brute.

The day after Annie had locked him out of her life, Gabe had called the stable and instructed the manager to sell his horse; he could never look at Brute again without thinking of holding his Annie close to him in the saddle. It nearly broke what was left of his already shattered heart to part with the horse, as he had gotten quite attached to the stallion. The manager called him back a week later saying that the horse had been sold, and Gabe would find the payment deposited in his account. He never asked where or to whom Brute had been sold.

Gabe turned around in his chair and sighed, then pulled a peanut from his desk drawer and tossed it to Chet. The bird caught it in his sharp beak, dropped it and said, "Thanks, prison bitch, now bend over and pick it up." That goddamn Kyle had been at it again.

As if on cue, Kyle burst into Gabe's office.

"Hey, buddy, ya ready to go?" he asked as he bounced up to Gabe's desk.

"Only for the last hour. Where have you been?"

"Uh, talking," Kyle answered, looking about the room.

Gabe raised an eyebrow.

"To whom?"

"Uh, Jen."

"On the phone?"

"No, she stopped by. Why?"

"Well, while you were talking the shirt that you have on inside-out has attempted to escape through the fly of your pants. There is also a pair of panties hanging out of your pocket," Gabe grinned.

Kyle's face turned a festive shade of Christmas red as he shoved the silky underwear deep into the pocket of his jeans.

"Well, we did talk... a little," he said sheepishly.

The trip west on I-94 was predictably boring; Kyle talked non-stop and Gabe pretended to listen. The business meeting was productive and contracts were signed, and Kyle was now free to roam Chicago with an apathetic Gabe tagging along. He did much of his shopping in the lingerie department of the various stores that they visited, and while Kyle was busy selecting gifts for Jenna and flirting with the salesgirls, Gabe stood off to the side, leaning against the wall. With his thumbs hooked in the front pockets of his jeans, he daydreamed... totally oblivious to all the female attention being directed his way, attracted by the lopsided half-smile on his face.

Gabe was having one of his very, very rare good days when his thoughts of

Annie were fond memories and the thankfulness of having had the opportunity to have loved her, if only for a little while. The dying ember of hope was fanned, and flickered a little on days like today.

Impulsively, he left the shop where Kyle was up to his blond head in females and frilly underwear. He walked along the street thinking of Annie and glancing into store windows. As he walked by a shop stuffed to the rafters with antiques and nick-knacks, his attention was caught by a child looking at him through the glass. He stopped to get a better look. She appeared to be around four years old, with long, coal black hair and bright green eyes. She reminded Gabe very much of James and Jeremy, and her eyes - they looked just like Annie's. He smiled and waved at the little girl.

She smiled back and held an object out to him with both her hands. He moved closer to see what it was, but a glare on the window prevented him from seeing it clearly.

He opened the door and went into the shop.

The little girl was gone. There was no one in the store except him and the bored clerk behind the counter. Weird... Gabe was certain that he had seen... Christ, not more of this twilight zone shit. He stalked back to the door and stopped in his tracks when he saw it. The tiny sparkles were still swirling inside of the glass dome of the snow globe. He walked over and picked it up, and knew that he just had to have it. He gave the clerk the ten bucks more than was asked and went to find Kyle, eager to get home.

Gabe unlocked the passenger side door of the truck for Kyle, and then walked the front around to let himself in.

"Finish your shopping?" Kyle asked as he got in, knowing full well that Gabe hadn't even started.

"Hmm? No, only bought one thing."

"Really. Not bad, considering you were staring off into space the entire time we were out."

"While you were immersed in the delights of the lingerie department, I stepped out for a moment. I bought something for Annie."

"Annie? The same Annie who won't have anything whatsoever to do with you? I thought you two were all done."

"I never said that I'd have the opportunity to give it to her, but I had to buy it for her," Gabe explained. "And you need not remind me of how she feels about me; I'm fully aware."

"So, what did you get her?"

"This." Gabe pulled the globe from his jacket pocket and handed it to Kyle. "Check out the details."

"Shit, there's enough of them in there! What kind of loser sits around all day putting this crap together?" he muttered as he examined the glass-enclosed landscape.

"No appreciation for craftsmanship. Look at it Kyle, really look at it."

"Hey, that looks like Annie's cabin. It's pretty small, but it looks just like it! And there's the lake, and those killer hills... What's that on top, in the clearing? Looks like a rock or something." He held it closer to his eyes, straining to make out the tiny object. "Wait... it looks like a bench or something. Hey, this is kind of cool." He shook the globe and watched as the glittering snow swirled around, catching the remaining sunlight.

"Kyle, you wouldn't know this, but there is a clearing exactly like that, right down to the tiny bench, in the hills above her cabin. This..." Gabe tapped the globe, "This is Annie's place. Read the bottom."

He flipped it over and read the caption etched in the e bottom. "A little slice of heaven? Yeah, I guess if you're goddamn Grizzly Adams or something."

"Fuck you, Kyle," Gabe said with a good-natured laugh, then grabbed the globe back.

The trip home was as predictably boring as the trip there.

With only a week to go before Christmas, Annie finally broke down and bought a tree. She had very little of the Christmas spirit, but it seemed wrong somehow not to have one. She decorated it using tiny white lights and an assortment of things from nature. She made most of the ornaments and the angel tree-topper, and was very pleased with the results; so pleased, that she thought she'd ride out to the woods and cut some pine boughs for more decorations in the cabin.

She walked into the barn and greeted her critters. The usual noise ensued until she hollered for them to be quiet, and all was peaceful once more. Annie gave Wanda a quick grooming, followed by Adonis, then turned to her latest acquisition.

As she entered his stall, 'the stall', Brute turned and nickered to her. Annie tapped him on the rump to move him over, giving her more room to work. She spent a little more time than usual brushing Gabe's horse.

Why she had bought him, she would never know, but as soon as Eric told her that Gabe was selling him, she knew that she could never let him go. Him... Gabe or the horse? She wasn't sure.

Annie saddled the stallion and made straight for the pine grove; it was bitterly cold and she was looking forward to getting back to the warmth of the cabin and a cup of hot chocolate.

Usually she avoided riding by the trail leading to the clearing, but today she felt the urge to up there. It was the first time she had been there since the day Adonis had disappeared.

Annie sat on the bench as the snow swirled and sparkled around her. She thought of Gabe, and of Gabriella, and for the first time the memories brought no pain. She smiled as she remembered the dream she had had about her daughter so long ago.

She and Gabe had been sitting on this very bench, watching the little girl play with Dog. Gabrielle turned around to smile at her mommy and daddy, her little four-year old face and her hair very much resembling her father's, and her sparkling green eyes identical to her mother's. The dream had been short, that being the only scene, but Annie never forgot that face. Maybe someday she could put all of her pain behind her and she and Gabe could start over; just maybe there would be another child.

Both Annie and Gabe's 'good' day was short-lived. Deirdre and Eric were both failing rapidly. Gabe spent his every waking moment with Deirdre, talking to her about the fun they had had over the years, the twins, Steve, and Annie.

Deirdre hadn't much strength left in her, and she was more often unconscious than awake, but with what energy she had left she use to encourage Gabe not to give up on his Annie.

He listened only to please her; he knew how Annie felt, whereas Deirdre had never given up hope.

Early on the morning of Christmas Eve, James and Jeremy said good-bye to their mamma for the last time. They knew that it was coming; Daddy had told them. Steve promised his sons that their mother would be going to a beautiful place to live, just like at Grampa Al's house. She would be young and pretty again, and she would ride Whizbang in the mountains every day. James and Jeremy were happy for Mamma and knew that she would always be around for them, even if they couldn't see her.

Gabe was very proud of his nephews for the way they handled themselves regarding Deirdre's impending death. He was also certain that his brother had prepared them for the tragic news.

Jenna and Kyle said their good-byes to their dear friend and took the twins home with them. Kyle spent an entire day without smiling once.

Gabe went to sit with his wife, refusing to leave until it was all over.

Deirdre felt her Geoffrey dear take her hand. He was such a good man, and she did love him so. She tried to squeeze his hand every once in a while just to let him know that she was still with him, but the effort was just too great. She listened as he apologized for the events of the summer, and of the horrible things he had thought and said about her. She only had a vague memory of Megheen, which had come from what she had read in the diaries, and had no memory of her actions.

Geoffrey continued to talk, thanking her for being his friend for the last seven years, for giving him two fine nephews, and for bringing Annie into his life. Although their time together had been brief and had caused unbearable pain, Geoffrey told her that he would do it all over again a thousand times, no, a million times, just to feel that incredible love of his Annie once again. Deirdre smiled; he had been truly happy after all. She hoped and prayed with her last breath that he would find it again.

Deirdre looked up to see a blue light filling the room; her Steven was

580

coming for her. She gave Geoffrey's hand one final squeeze and let go to reach for her cowboy.

Steve looked down at his ladylove. She was just as beautiful as the first time he had seen her as Juliet at the rodeo so long ago. He smiled and offered her his arm.

"My lady," he said.

Deirdre rose from the bed, free of pain and full of youthful energy. Her long, pale blonde hair swirled about her as she walked to her Romeo and took his arm. The blue light vanished, taking the two of them with it.

Gabe felt Deirdre squeeze his hand and looked down at her; it was the first movement he had felt from her in hours. A barely perceptible blue light formed around her and she took one last breath. Her hand fell away from his and lay lifeless on the bed.

"Take good care of her, Steve," Gabe whispered. He gently kissed Deirdre's bony forehead and left the room, glancing at the clock on his way out.

Midnight.

Merry fucking Christmas.

He needed a quiet place to be alone for a while, and headed for the usually deserted hole of a cafeteria. The one person, who truly loved him, no matter what, was gone, and he was totally unprepared for how much that thought staggered him. He made his way to a back table and fought unsuccessfully to control his grief.

The ward had been exceptionally quiet over the last several days, with only the most critically ill children there; Christmas was not the time to be away from home. Annie scanned the patient list as she set her bouquet on the reception desk, and then went to the locker room to hang up her coat. When she returned, several of her co-workers had gathered and were admiring the roses.

"Hi, Annie," Maggie said. "Would you happen to know where these came from?"

"I grew them," she replied.

Gayle, the ward clerk, picked them up and held them to her nose. "How on earth did you grow roses at this time of the year?" she asked, inhaling deeply.

"A few years ago I had a small greenhouse built onto my cabin," Annie answered. "It's so much nicer to grow my own flowers than to have to buy them. Even better, it's like having summer all year 'round."

"What, you don't like winter and all that beautiful snow?" laughed Marti.

"Marti, you of all people know how I feel about winter... But wouldn't you like having flowers all year long?"

"Got me there, Annie-bananie."

The bouquet was passed off to Kathy, who gently touched a white bud. "These are so pretty," she sighed. "Who are they for?"

"Eric. I don't think he has much time left… just too tired to fight any longer."

"I know, poor kid. The sooner he goes, the better for him," Maggie said sadly.

"He's already been through hell," Kathy agreed. "It's time for him to know some peace."

Tears welled in Annie's eyes and the other nurses noticed before she could turn away.

"Oh God, Annie, I'm so sorry!" Maggie apologized, giving her a quick hug.

"That's all right; I feel the same way. I just pray he doesn't have to suffer much longer."

The day shift nurses shared a glance, aware of Eric's rapidly deteriorating condition. It was not going to be a pleasant night.

"So why white roses?" asked Julie, a day RN. "What good will they do now? Eric won't even look at us when we're in his room."

"Oh, it's a long story," Annie briefly explained. "Just something special my grandmother used to do."

"Well, no time to tell the tale right now," Marti said with a sly smile to the group at the desk. "It's time for report and I don't dare to be late! That day shift has absolutely no sense of humor…"

The nurses mentioned began to good-naturedly moan about the lazy slugs taking over for them, and the entire group walked to the break room.

Annie filled out her report sheet and checked her charts. Her assignment for the night was small, being only two babies with respiratory infections, and Eric. The infants had their parents spending the night with them, a fact in which Annie was very grateful, for now she would be able to devote as much time to the older boy as was needed.

She spent a half hour with each of the babies and their parents, explaining the plan of care for the night and doing her assessments. She took vitals, dispensed medication, and then instructed the parents to let her know if they needed anything. Someone would peek in every hour or so to check IV lines and make sure all was well, but other than that the families wouldn't be disturbed.

Annie retrieved the roses from the desk and went to see Eric.

She wasn't prepared for what met her when she entered the room. Eric did not look at all like the same kid she had left only twelve hours ago. The oxygen being forced into his diseased lungs was no longer helping, and he was sitting with the head of his bed as high as it would go in order to aid in his breathing. His wasted body appeared to be only a shadow as he slumped across the over-bed table, fighting for every breath.

"Eric?"

He glanced at his nurse, barely moving his head.

"Eric, I'm going to turn the light on while I check you over, and then I'll leave it off for the rest of the night."

A small nod of his head was his only response.

She began her assessment.

His skin was very dry and he had no extra flesh anywhere, and even though he was thirteen years old his body was the size of a ten-year old child's. He was being fed via a tube inserted through his abdominal wall and into his stomach, and his fingers were rounded and thickened at the tips, a condition known as "clubbing" due to prolonged oxygen deprivation.

She continued her assessment.

Eric had a bluish tinge around his lips – again, not enough O2, and his lungs sounded worse than Annie had ever heard. She knew he wouldn't last much longer and really should be in the ICU, but given his prognosis, prolonging his life would be crueler than letting him die. He had an order for no resuscitation, so any measures taken would be against his wishes anyway.

Annie didn't bother to finish with the rest of the exam. She could see no point in it, as this child wouldn't last the night. She would probably go to "nurse hell" for not completing the job, but it was a chance she was willing to take.

"Eric, I brought you a little Christmas present. It's not much, but they are nice to look at. They're from the plants we started last summer."

He didn't look up, just shrugged a thin shoulder.

"I'll put them on the shelf next to the sink. If you want to look at them you need only move your eyes."

Another shrug.

"Well, I can see how popular I am in this room tonight," Annie joked, "so I'll take my act elsewhere. I'll leave you alone for now and be back in an hour or so. You know how to reach me if you need be sooner than that."

A final shrug of an emaciated shoulder.

Annie gave him a tender kiss on his bony forehead, turned out the lights, and left the room. She would have given anything to remain and hold him and tell him everything would be all right.

She glanced in one last time before moving on. The light from the street lamp outside was shining directly on the roses, causing them to give off a pale glow. Kinda eerie.

With a sigh, she sat down at the computer and entered her data, and then signed off the meds in the charts. She made herself a cup of tea and waited for Eric to call.

She didn't have long to wait.

A terrible, racking cough could be heard from down the hall and the call light above Eric's door lit up; Annie was in his room in seconds.

"What is it, Eric?"

He continued to cough, but waved her over with a pathetically deformed hand.

Annie pulled a chair close to the bed and sat next to him. This was the beginning of the end, and she would be there for a while. When his coughing subsided a few moments later she gave him a sip of water.

Maggie stuck her head in the door.

"Can I get anything for you? Annie... Eric?"

"Maybe you can see if someone can take my patients for the rest of the night? I'd like to stay in here for a while."

"Sure, Annie, no problem."

Maggie smiled at Eric and gave Annie the "I'm glad I'm not in your shoes" look, and shut the door on her way out.

Eric leaned back into the pillows on his bed, even though breathing was easier for him in his former position over the table.

"Annie... Annie, I'm scared." Each word he spoke was released in a tortured whisper.

"I know, Eric. I won't leave you alone tonight."

"Michael won't either," he murmured, closing his eyes and reaching for her hand.

Annie felt herself grow cold as she took it.

Michael... He always seemed to be just around the corner even though she hadn't seen him in months.

Michael... He had filled their lives with magic and love during those summers, which now seemed so long ago.

Michael... He had promised to always be there for them when they needed him most, so where was he now?

They needed him tonight.

"Annie? The flowers... Want them," Eric whispered.

She brought the bouquet to him. His hand groped blindly about, searching, until she placed it in his fingers.

He brought the flowers to his nose.

"Can't smell anymore," he gasped, beginning to cough again.

"Eric, don't try. Just relax."

"Talk to me, Annie. Tell me about the summer... That's what I want to remember when I go."

She knew which summer he was referring to. She didn't want to remember, and yet the memories were so wonderful that she was loathe to forget them.

As she quietly reminisced, Eric's breathing grew easier and a hint of a smile formed on his lips. She heard him murmur, "Remember, Michael?" or "That was great, wasn't it, Michael?" She wondered if he was hallucinating.

Annie talked on and on, reliving every moment of that summer. Yet instead of the overwhelming sadness she had expected to feel, she felt... not quite happy, but light. At peace. Michael's memories induced a presence that was almost palpable, and Annie thought that she could almost smell his special scent: a combination of leather, horse, and the fresh pine air of a mountain forest.

"Annie," Eric whispered with great effort.

She leaned forward in order to hear him better.

"Take this," he said, and handed her a single rose. "Keep it with you tonight… all the time."

"Thank you, Eric, I will."

"I'm going now. Michael says it's time," Eric whispered, his last words.

His eyes closed, and his breathing became fainter and more erratic.

Annie recited the poem she had written for him. Through her tears she said, "At times I think you've forgotten me, Lord, when my troubles are too much to bear. My prayers go unanswered for so long and I wonder if you're really there. Then you send a message that I'm not alone. Your Holy Spirit will guide my way home. My empty soul is soon filled with love, sent on the wings of a snow-white dove.

"When darkness surrounds me – pulls me within, and I no longer know wrong from right, you don't abandon me to my despair. Shadows are banished in Your Holy light. Your words console me; their message is clear. I let go and let you end my fear. For he who believes in you will never die. I let my faith rise with the white dove, and fly."

Annie felt an almost perceptible squeeze from Eric's hand, and finished the poem.

"My soul's at ease. My mind's at rest. I trust in God, for He knows best. Peace in my heart as I close my eyes. I go to where the white dove flies."

Eric took his last breath, and Annie let her tears fall.

It was over.

She cried for several minutes, and then activated the call light to bring Maggie into the room.

"I'm so sorry, Annie," Maggie murmured, hugging her. "You go take a few minutes and I'll call the attending. We'll take care of everything else."

Annie didn't argue. She would have done the post-mortem care on Eric if she had to, but was extremely grateful that it wasn't necessary; she was just too close to the boy.

The women took one last look at Eric and walked out.

A faint blue light filled the room, and the man who had been waiting unseen in a shadowy corner walked up to the bed. Gently, he touched Eric's forehead and then bent to kiss it. He took a rose from the bouquet, and quietly vanished.

Annie went to the bathroom in the nurses' lounge and splashed some cold water on her tear-stained face, and looked at herself in the mirror. God, she was a mess. Her usually sparkling emerald-green eyes were now a darker, smoky green, and her red-gold hair was dull and limp, nothing close to the shining beauty it had commanded last summer.

She grabbed a stray tendril and smoothed it back onto her head as she turned away from the glass. If she still cared about the way she looked, she would have been dismayed at the dark smudges under her eyes and in the hollows of her cheeks, and the way her scrubs hung from her too-thin body. She sighed again and went to find a place to be alone for a while.

Gabe felt something soft brush his arm and looked up to see a white rose on the table before him. He didn't even have to guess who had placed it there; it could only be Annie. He raised his eyes to hers and saw that she too had been crying. Oh God, not Eric... not tonight.

"Buy you a cup of coffee?" she asked him through a sad smile.

He looked down at the rose, and then picked it up, slowly twirling the stem in his fingers; he didn't dare hope that Annie's coffee comment could mean anything.

Maybe it was a mistake coming over here; Gabe was ignoring her. Well, she tried, and she needed to get back to work. Annie turned to leave, and then stopped. She did want to let him know about Eric, and that if indeed Deirdre had died, she wanted to offer him her condolences; she'd try one more time. She sat across from him and placed her hand on his.

"Gabe, is it Deirdre?"

He jerked his hand away from hers and nodded, continuing to watch the rose as it spun in his fingertips.

"I'm sorry; I know close the two of you were," Annie said softly.

Gabe nodded again. "She was my best friend. She was always there for me, Annie, especially after you...we... well, she wouldn't give up on me; wouldn't let me give up on myself."

He sighed and tossed the rose to the side of the table.

"And now she's gone too," he said to himself. "Christ, I don't know how much more of this I can take."

Oh jeez, how was she going to tell him about Eric? He had to know; the two of them had become quite close over the summer.

"Gabe, I'm afraid that I have some more bad news; Eric passed away, too... just a little while ago."

"I thought as much." His grief quickly turned to anger. "Goddamn it, it just never ends, does it? You let someone into your life, you love them, and the next thing you know they're gone. Steve, Dee, Eric... you." Gabe laughed bitterly and said, "Even Spike and my horse are gone. I'm just sick of the whole goddamn mess. Excuse me, I need some air." He jumped up from his seat and stalked from the cafeteria.

Annie would have given anything to go after him, but she really needed to get back to the floor. She prayed that he wouldn't do anything drastic.

Gabe drove through the heavily falling snow to his house on Park Street.

He walked from room to room in the cold, dark building, looking at the objects and art Deirdre had collected over the years. Other than a few family photographs and the contents of his office, there was nothing of Gabe in this house. This was Deirdre's home, never his; he had merely resided here. Didn't matter that he had practically built it with his own hands, pouring his time and sweat into it, it had always been her home. Never his.

He went to his office and sat on the floor in the corner, resting his arms on his raised knees. He felt lost; lost and adrift with nothing to anchor him to anything anymore. Only his responsibility to the twins kept him from seeking death once again.

A flash of blue caught his attention and Gabe glanced out the window behind his desk. It had stopped snowing and the sky was beginning to clear. Moonlight slowly flooded the room, illuminating the glass dome of Annie's present, which he had placed on an overflowing bookshelf. He stared as the artificial snow inside of the globe glittered and swirled around the small cabin, the miniature lake, and the tiny marble bench in the clearing.

Aw God... he had found his anchor. He snatched the globe from the shelf and ran to the truck. Twenty minutes later he drove down the long driveway to his Annie's cabin.

Gabe stood on the porch, took a deep breath, and tried the door handle; it opened easily with a flick of his wrist. He smiled and went inside. The instant he walked into the cabin, he knew he was home. The faint smell of wood-smoke and cinnamon wrapped around him, comforting him the way the afghan on his favorite chair soon would.

He placed Annie's Christmas gift under the tree then stood back to admire the festive sight. He loved what she had done with the cabin. Fresh pine boughs tied with red and green ribbon lined the windowsills, and the tree... He had never seen a tree decorated without shiny balls, different colored lights and all that tacky silver tinsel hiding the natural beauty of the evergreen.

Annie's tree warmed his heart and flooded him with the Christmas spirit which had up 'til now evaded him. He reached out and touched a red bow illuminated by the tiny white lights scattered about. His hand moved to a sprig of baby's breath tucked into the needles, and then to a pinecone. Dried flowers of all kinds were sprinkled throughout the tree and an angel made of straw graced the top.

Gabe found a white rose bud and placed it in his shirt pocket, right over his heart, and continued to study the tree. The only other ornaments were bits of white birch bark tied with a golden thread and bearing the names of Annie's loved ones. He saw one for Spike, Dog, McDonald, Wanda, Adonis and Brute. Each of the goats had one, as did the rabbit, the barn cats, and the chickens.

As he looked higher in the tree, Gabe saw one for each of the Davidson's, Eric, James, Jeremy, Steven-Michael, and Deirdre. At the very top were three more, tied with golden cord and accented with tiny white rose buds... one for Annie, one for Gabe, and one for baby Gabriella.

He felt his knees give way and he staggered back, falling into the chair. She did still love him! He had been right to come back here tonight.

He wrapped the afghan around him and kicked his feet up onto the ottoman. Spike strolled over and jumped into his lap.

Peace settled over Gabe and he slept.

That was how Annie found him the next morning.

Chapter Forty-Six

Gabe's nostrils twitched as the aroma of coffee being brewed penetrated his sleep; it had been a long time since he had woken up to that smell. A silky paw reached up to bat at the moving nose. His eyes popped open and he found himself staring into a familiar amber gaze.

"Spike!" he said, "How the hell are ya?"

Spike twitched his tail and jumped from Geoffrey Alan's lap; it was about time the man came home. The cat glanced at Annie Rose on his way to the loft and saw that she was smiling.

Annie handed Gabe a cup of coffee and then sat on the sofa. Her surprise and delight at seeing his truck in the driveway when she pulled up still hadn't worn off. From the moment he had left the cafeteria last night, she had been worried sick that something bad would happen to him and she would never see him again. She would be forever grateful that she hadn't locked the cabin door before she had left for work.

His Annie was smiling at him. She hadn't gone to hide in her bedroom and she hadn't kicked him out of her home. No, instead she was smiling at him and handing him a cup of coffee.

"Thanks," he said, raising the steaming mug slightly.

"You're welcome," she answered.

Gabe took a sip then set the cup on the floor next to the chair. He sat up, turning to look directly at her.

"Annie, considering what happened last night, you know... Deirdre and Eric, would it be inappropriate for me to wish you a Merry Christmas?"

"No, Gabe, I don't think it would be."

He thought for a moment and then smiled.

"Well then, Annie, would it be inappropriate for me to give you a Christmas gift?"

"No, Gabe, but only if I can give you one too."

He raised an eyebrow in surprise at her then walked to the tree. He reached under it and brought out the snow globe.

"Here," he said as he handed it to her. "Merry Christmas."

Annie took the globe and gave it a quick shake. Her eyes lit up as she studied it, recognizing the lake, the cabin, and the tiny white bench.

"Oh my God, Gabe! Where did you get this?" she asked in a voice full of astonishment. "Did you have this made?"

"I wish. No, I found it in Chicago. Look at the bottom; the inscription."

"A little slice of heaven," she read. "That is what I used to call this place! How did you know?"

"I didn't; it was already there when I bought it. Do you like it?"

"It's perfect! Look, it even has the clearing and the bench!"

She shook it again; the snow glittered and swirled.

"This is amazing! Oh, Gabe, thank you!" Impulsively, Annie threw her arms around her cowboy and gave him a quick kiss.

He wanted to take it further, but didn't; at least this was a start.

She realized the position she was in and quickly let go; it was still too soon. She walked over to the window so that the morning sun would reflect off the snow in the globe.

"I still can't believe that you found this. How did you do it?"

Gabe joined her at the window and watched the miniature blizzard in the globe.

"It was the strangest thing; Kyle and I were in Chicago, he was shopping for Jenna and I was bored to tears, so I went for a walk. As I went by one of those pseudo-antique-real junk shops, I saw a little girl looking at me from the window. She reminded me so much of James and Jeremy that I stopped for a closer look.

She was holding something out to me in her hand but I couldn't quite make out what it was, so I walked into the shop, and she was gone! As I was leaving I happened to see this. The snow was still swirling around as if someone had just shaken it. Once I saw exactly what it was, I just knew that you would have to have it."

Gabe took a big chance and placed and arm around his Annie's shoulders. "I'm glad that you like it; if it hadn't been for that little girl..."

"Little girl? The one that reminded you of the twins?" Annie felt the hair rise on the back of her neck. In her dream of Gabriella, her daughter had reminded her of Gabe's nephews; they looked just like their father, who looked nearly identical to his brother.

"Mmhmm. She looked enough like them to be a third twin - a triplet! She was about their age, maybe a year or two younger, and she had beautiful, long black hair and..."

"Green eyes?" Annie interrupted, as her own eyes welled with tears.

"Uh, yeah. How did you know?"

She held the snow globe close to her heart and turned to face him. "There is still one thing we have never talked about, Gabe. I'm not sure if I can get through this, but here goes... The baby... Gabriella. I... I don't even know where to start." The threatened tears now spilled over as Annie thought of her little girl.

"Annie," Gabe murmured as he held her close. "Oh, God."

"I was so happy when I found out that I was carrying your child, Gabe. I wanted so much to tell you, but there never seemed to be a good time; something always came up, and I couldn't just tell you over the phone. I was going to tell you the night... the night of the concert. I'd even picked out names and I wanted to see of you liked them. And then... oh God... I lost her, Gabe. I left the concert and it started. I barely made it to the hospital.

"I never got to see her, but I know what she would have looked like; she came to me in a dream. She had long black hair, and looked just like her father, but she had my eyes. I'll never forget that face as long as I live."

Gabe couldn't speak; he could only hold his Annie closer as they wept for their child.

When he was once again capable of speech, he told his Annie that he had known about the baby almost from the beginning. He had waited, hoped and prayed that with the next phone call she would tell him the news, but it never came. He wasn't aware she had lost it until mid-September when he received the news via a report from a private investigator he had hired to find her. Gabe had been devastated. The loss of his child, his Annie, and the incident with Megheen had nearly driven him to suicide. He let down all of his defenses and told his Annie of his trip into the woods, and of his belt still hanging in the big oak tree.

A new bond formed between them; a bond stronger and deeper than either one could have possibly imagined. They had completely opened up to one other, leaving no lingering questions or doubts.

Gabe wiped a tear from his Annie's cheek and kissed her nose.

"Did I hear you mention that you had a gift for me too?" he said, giving her that lop-sided grin.

She reached up and touched his cheek, placing her thumb in the almost-dimple under his lower lip. "I did say that, didn't I? It's somewhere out in the barn; it's kind of big," she answered, grinning.

"In the barn; now that is rather vague... are you coming out to show me?"

"No, I think I'll make us breakfast. Suddenly, I'm starving! Besides, you'll know it as soon as you see it."

"Starving... so am I! Make extra, and fix Spike a plate, too. I'll be right back."

Gabe grabbed his coat and ran down to the barn, eager as a kid at Christmas.

She would have given just about anything to see the look on his face when he saw Brute standing there. Oh, what the hell! Breakfast could wait. She grabbed her coat and went out to the porch.

Moments later, man and horse exploded form the barn and raced to the cabin, sliding to a stop only feet from where Annie was standing on the steps.

"God, Annie, I don't believe this! How did you... God!" Gabe's smile could not have possibly been any wider. He reached across and pulled his Annie onto the horse with him, holding her tight against him.

"Gabe, you could at least have thrown a saddle on him; now we are going to smell just as horsey as he does!" She snuggled a little closer to her cowboy.

"Then we'll just have to jump in that big ol' tub of yours and get 'un-horsey', won't we?" He laughed. "Come on, let's go for a ride."

The stallion carried them up the hill, through the woods and straight to the clearing. As they sat atop the big horse, looking over the frozen lake, the snow glittered and swirled around them. Gabe suddenly remembered the flower in his pocket; it must be an omen.

He pulled it out and said, "Annie, the last time we were here I asked you a question. You never gave me an answer, so I'm asking again..."

She turned to look at him.

He tucked the white rose bud behind her ear, smoothing her autumn hair away from her face.

She reached up to cover his hand with her own.

"Annie, will you marry me?"

This time she gave him an answer; she said yes.

They chose April thirtieth for their wedding day, just because.

The twins, Al and Marie, the Davidson clan, Marti and Jill, and the staff and musicians of SD Productions all witnessed the ceremony near the rose garden at Annie's cabin. After a reception at the cabin, everyone took their leave, the Davidson's taking the twins with them. Mr. Geoffrey Alan Benjamin Evans carried his bride across the threshold of their home.

From the loft, an amber gaze observed the scene and then retreated to a dark corner to run a silky paw over a very self-satisfied face.

From the pasture, the horses grazed contentedly knowing that it would be days before they were called upon for their services.

From the clearing, man, woman and adolescent stood looking out over the lake.

"My lady," Steve said, "I do believe that it is time for us to go home."

"I believe that it is, Steven. Come, Eric," Deirdre said, holding her hand out to the boy.

Steve grabbed Whiz's reins and placed his arm around Deirdre's waist. The four of them walked into the shadows of the woods and disappeared into a vivid blue light.

From the marble bench, two white roses turned a pale red-gold in the setting sun.

Author's Note

With a few exceptions, none of the characters in this book are actual people, nor do they closely resemble anyone I've ever met. However, a few of the animals are real, as are their stories. Spike is a real kitty, now fourteen years old, and although he's not a mind-reader like Annie's cat, he's quite perceptive and too smart for his own good.

Adonis was inspired by a colt I knew from his birth. He was perfection the moment he was foaled, and quite likely the most handsome horse I'd ever seen.

The story of McDonald is true. My dog, Nick, and I actually saved the last egg from a nest of homicidal (goose-icidal?) geese. The gosling, Pooder, was a pampered pet who really did live on my porch, and Nick was his best buddy. I swear they had frequent conversations and debates with each other.

The character of Eric was inspired by an actual young man, with whom I spent quite a few hours, and shed more than a few tears. Enough said about that out of respect for him and his memory.

Thank you for reading, and I do hope you look forward to more stories from Gabe's world.

Read an excerpt of

A Novel Idea

the sequel to White Roses

Saturday, May 22nd

"You were right, Annie. Today is a perfect day for a picnic," Gabe said as he turned Brute, his horse, into the woods.

"Uncle Gabe is right, his Annie," echoed James, who was sitting in the saddle in front of his uncle.

"No, his Annie was right," corrected Jeremy. "She said it first; he just 'peated it."

Annie gave Jeremy a quick hug. They were both riding her horse, Adonis, on the trek to the clearing. She loved the twins as if they were her own, and Jeremy was her favorite - if she had a favorite. He was so much like his Uncle Gabe, where as his brother seemed to take after Kyle... strange. Regardless, her heart melted each and every time they referred to her as 'his Annie'.

She had been looking forward to today ever since she had suggested it earlier in the week, and she had a special surprise for her family. Annie would tell them as they watched the sun set over the lake.

Dog ran ahead of the horses; he had detected a very familiar scent, and it was growing stronger as he neared the clearing. He was the only one to witness the flash of blue that illuminated the trees as the riders came up behind him.

"Oh, his Annie! Look!" Jeremy whispered in awe.

"Uncle Gabe, you didn't tell us this was a magical place," said a shocked James.

Annie and Gabe shared a knowing glance; had they expected anything else?

The sunlight filtered down through the trees and hit the white marble at the edge of the clearing, causing sparks of color to shoot from the water droplets clinging to the white roses in the center of the table. A light breeze whispered through, bringing with it the fluff of the cottonwood trees; it was almost as if it were snowing. Once again, the clearing had been transformed into a fairy-land. Once again, Steve had been there.

"Gabe, the table... did you?" Annie asked.

"Wasn't me. Man, that Steve is just too much! Maybe this is his wedding present to us; what do you think?"

"Well, if it is, it's perfect! Let's get unpacked."

The four of them ate, snoozed in the sun, and told stories. Annie told them the tale of her grandparents, and of the white roses. Gabe regaled them with the saga of his becoming lost in these very woods, and how the odd couple saved his life. James and Jeremy had a fine time playing fetch with Dog, then collected rocks to see who could chuck one all the way to the lake. Gabe was the only one who even came close, having had the most experience at chucking things.

As the sun turned from gold, to rosy-red, and then to a deep lavender, the Evans family sat on a blanket at the edge of the clearing where the earth dropped away. Gabe looked at Annie and his nephews, and felt total peace in his heart. Life had indeed been kind to him, and if all he really had to put up with was that slime-ball Paul, well then, so be it; he could handle that. He pulled his Annie a little closer to him and whispered that he loved her; had loved her forever and would always love her forever.

Annie smiled; now was the time to tell him. She took his hand and placed it on her belly, saying: "Gabe, you are going to be..."

The rest of her words were drowned out when an explosion rocked the clearing.

Paul sat on the highest hill of Hidden Lake road and laughed as the ball of flame and debris shot high into the twilight sky. So much for the quaint little cabin by the lake! It had been too easy, actually, taking care of this small problem. A casually mentioned outing by Geoffrey to Kyle, and the day and time of the home's demise was set. Add to that a phone call to the bank, reporting stolen credit cards and checks by a Mr. Geoffrey Evans... Now, to make like the concerned brother-in-law, and offer his place of residence to the homeless Evans family.

Spike's nose twitched as the smell of propane wafted its way into the loft where the cat was sleeping. *Oh Lord, no!* The feline was instantly awake and raced down the stairs, his silky paws barely touching the steps. He ran to the window overlooking the rose garden and saw a tall man running up the drive. Paul Ian... he should have known.

Spike's sharp ears picked up the crackle and pop of a fire just below the window where he was observing the retreat of the arsonist. *Steven Anthony, this cat needs you now!* Spike raced for the doggie door, and was nearly out safely when he felt himself being hurtled through the air by the force of the explosion. He could smell his own fur burning as a black void descended upon him.

McDonald was enjoying a solitary swim while he waited for Dog's return, and they could continue their bi-lingual debates about life in general; they never seemed to agree on anything, especially which one of them was Annie's favorite.

The goose had just dunked his head to grab at a bit of seaweed when the lake imploded around him. His ears rang and his equilibrium was momentarily lost, and he darn near drowned when he tried to breathe before fully removing his head from the water. He turned a pale blue eye to the hill and watched the flaming bits of log sail heavenward.

For the first time in his life, McDonald took to the air and flew up the hill. He knew the Evans family was out, but what of Spike? Every animal on the place knew of the cat's lofty status, bestowed upon him by a power even higher than Annie could ever hope to attain; even higher that Steven-Michael could ever reach.

McDonald circled the yard once, then twice before he found the cat. It was a grim picture. Spike lay still as death, and curls of smoke rose from the singed, orange hair on his body. McDonald landed close to the most revered feline and gently placed his body over Spike, releasing the water that had been trapped in the downy feathers of the goose's breast.

Spike stirred slightly when he felt the coolness of the water ease his burns, and then almost smiled a kitty smile as McDonald gently nibbled at a silky paw.

Annie screamed when Gabe threw her to the ground and covered her body with his own, protecting her.

The twins hit the dirt like they had seen on TV, and had practiced when they played army with the Davidson children.

Brute and Adonis broke their tethers and vanished into the woods. They ran for nearly half a mile before they overcame their fear and returned to their people.

The twins looked at each other and whispered, "Paul."

Gabe held his Annie close to him and thanked God that she wasn't hurt.

Annie nearly went insane as an all-too-familiar cramp ripped through her abdomen; she prayed that she wouldn't lose this baby too.

Dog was nowhere to be found.

Oh God, Annie, are you alright?" Gabe asked once he had recovered from the shock of the whole situation.

She nodded. Aside from that single pain, she was fine.

"The twins... where are they?" she asked, looking around.

Oh, Christ! Where were they? Gabe jumped to his feet and scanned the clearing.

"James! Jeremy!" he yelled, but received no answer. This cannot be happening... must be a dream, no, a nightmare. He'd wake up soon and his Annie would be right there next to him and... A voice from the lake broke into his thoughts.

"Uncle Gabe, down here!" shouted Jeremy.

Gabe looked below him and saw the twins wave, and then take off running around the endless corner of the crescent-shaped lake. He didn't want to leave his Annie, but he couldn't let young boys go running off in the dark like that, either.

"Go after them, Gabe, I'll be fine. I'll bring the horses back with me," Annie said, rising to her feet.

Gabe nodded and made his way down the steep hill, crashing through the brush and losing his footing more than once in his haste to catch up to his nephews. Once at the lake, he began to run along the shoreline. He passed the rock where he had nearly frozen to death, and knew the cabin would be in sight shortly. Too bad it wasn't.

Gabe staggered and fell to his knees as he saw the flames leaping high into the sky, feeding off the remaining logs that had been his home. Oh, God... no...